LOVEJOY

LOVEJOY

An omnibus

featuring

FIREFLY GADROON
THE SLEEPERS OF ERIN
THE GONDOLA SCAM

Jonathan Gash

CRESSET PRESS

This is a Cresset Press Book
20 Vauxhall Bridge Road, London SW1V 2SA

An imprint of the Random Century Group

London Melbourne Sydney Auckland
Johannesburg and agencies throughout
the world

This edition published 1991

1 3 5 7 9 10 8 6 4 2

The right of Jonathan Gash to be identified as the
author of this work has been asserted by him in
accordance with the Copyright, Designs and Patents
Act, 1988

Printed and bound in Great Britain by
Cox & Wyman Ltd, Reading, Berkshire

ISBN: 0 09 177101 3

Contents

FIREFLY GADROON   9

THE SLEEPERS OF ERIN   211

THE GONDOLA SCAM   433

For

A story for Susan and Germoline, Erica and Betty, with thanks to Paul for the rock bit.

FIREFLY GADROON

CHAPTER 1

This story begins where I did something illegal, had two rows with women, one pub fight, and got a police warning, all before mid-afternoon. After that it got worse, but that's the antiques game for you. Trouble.

I was up on the auctioneer's rostrum. But all I could think was, if that luscious woman crosses her beautiful legs once more I'll climb down through the crowd and give her a good hiding. She was driving me out of my skull.

As soon as I clapped eyes on her I knew she'd be trouble. We'd turned up for the auction that morning to find Harry the deputy auctioneer was ill. That caused a flap. Gimbert's auction rooms had three hundred assorted antiques—some even genuine—to auction off before the pubs opened. Old Cuthbertson caught me as I arrived and quaveringly asked me to stand in for his sick assistant. It's not exactly legal to do this but, we antique dealers often ask ourselves, what is?

'Why me, Cuthie?' I asked sourly. It was one of those mornings. I felt unshaven, though I'd tried.

'You're honest, Lovejoy,' he'd said earnestly, the cunning old devil. It's a hell of an accusation. That's my name, incidentally. Lovejoy. Crummy, but noticeable.

The trouble is I'm too soft. Anyhow Cuthbertson's too senile to lift a gavel these days, and he offered me a few quid knowing I'd be broke as usual. So, amid the jeers and catcalls of my fellow dealers, I took the rostrum and got the proceedings under way.

Gimbert's is a typical auction, such as you'll find in any sleepy old English market town. That means corrupt, savage and even murderous. Beneath the kindly exterior of contentment and plaster-and-pantile Tudor homeliness there beats the scarlet emotion of pure greed. Oh, I'm not saying our churches hereabouts aren't pretty and the coastline invigorating and all that jazz. But I've always found that when antiques come in at the door morality goes out of the window. You can't blame people for it. It's just the way we're made.

It was a blustery September market day with plenty of people in town, refugees from the stunning boredom of our unending countryside. Gimbert's was crowded. Naturally the lads were all at it, shouting false bids and indulging in a general hilarity as soon as I'd got going. I soon stopped that by taking a bid or two 'off the wall' (dealers' slang: imagining an extra bid or two to force the prices higher and faster). I got a few million glares of hate from my comrades but at least it brought orderliness, if not exactly harmony. Old Cuthbertson was at the back silently perforating his many ulcers.

'Here, Lovejoy,' Devlin called out angrily. 'You on their side?'

'Shut your teeth, Devvo,' I gave back politely, and cruised on through the lots. The girl crossed her legs again. Devlin's one of those florid, vehement blokes, all front teeth and stubble. You know instantly from his dazzling waistcoat and military fawns that he's a white slaver, but even his eleven motor-cars can't prove he's not thick as a brick. He's supposed to be Midland porcelains and early silver, which is a laugh. Like most antique dealers, he couldn't tell a mediæval chalice from a chip pan. I once sold him a Woolworth's plate as a vintage Spode (you just choose carefully and sandblast the marks off). Pathetic. Devlin's been desperate to get even with me for two years. Thick, but unforgiving.

By Lot Twenty-Nine we'd settled down to a grumbling concern with the business of the day. Between bids I had

time to suss out who had turned up and let my eyes rove
casually over the crowded warehouse while the next lot
was displayed by the miffs (dealers' slang, to mean the
boozy layabouts who indicate to bidders which heap of
rubbish comes next). There was the usual leavening of
genuine customers among the hard core of dealers, but
most were housewives. The lovely bird with the legs didn't
seem a dealer, yet . . . She crossed her legs. Everybody
noticed.

'Next lot,' I intoned. 'Regency corner shelves, veneered
in walnut.'

'Showing here, sir!' The miff's traditional cry turned a
few heads.

'Who'll bid, who'll bid?'

They were quite a good forgery. Most of us there knew
that Sammy Treadwell makes about one set a month in
his shed down on the waterfront. A grocer from East Hill
started the bidding, thank God, or we'd be there yet. He
got them for a few quid, cheap even for a fake. A minute
later there was the usual bit of drama. An American chap
in a fine grey overcoat was bidding for a manuscript letter
which some rogue had catalogued as being from Nelson's
father, the Reverend Edmund, the year before Trafalgar.
Even from my perch I could see it had all the hallmarks of
a forgery. From politeness I took a bid or two but the
Yank seemed such a pleasantly anxious bloke I decided
on a whim to protect him and knocked it down to a loud
antique dealer in from the Smoke. I didn't know it then,
but I'd just given myself a lifeline. The Yank looked
peeved because I stared absently past his waving arm, but
I'd done him a favour. By Lot Fifty the bird was worrying
me sick.

I kept wondering what the hell she was up to. She was
neither bored housewife nor dealer, which leaves very
little else for a good-looking bird in a sleazy auction to be.
She'd obviously sat down merely to flash her legs more

effectively, which is only natural. She'd dressed to kill, with that kind of aloof defiance women show when it's a specially risky occasion. Throw of the dice and all that. And her gaze kept flicking back to the same place in her catalogue, something on the seventh page. Items in the high hundreds at Gimbert's are usually portabilia, small decorative household objects or personal pieces, snuff-boxes, scissors, needle-cases, scent bottles and visiting-card cases, suchlike. There's always a display case full.

I started looking about at Lot One Sixty to give Tinker Dill my signal. He's my barker and 'runs' for me. A barker's a dishevelled alcoholic of no fixed abode whose job is to sniff out antiques wherever they may lurk. Tinker has a real snout for antiques. I pay him for every 'tickle', as we dealers say, though most other barkers only get paid when a purchase is completed. As Tinker can't afford to get sloshed twice a day without money, you realize how strong the stimulus actually is.

I needn't have worried. At Lot One Sixty-Two in he shambled, filthy and bleary-eyed as ever. He has this sixth sense, helped no doubt by a few pints in the Ship tavern next door. I suppressed a grin as dealers near the door edged away from him. Tinker pongs a bit. Outside it was coming on to rain, which made his woollen balaclava and his old greatcoat steam gently. Still, if you're the best barker in the business you've talents Valentino never dreamed of. He gave a gappy grin, seeing me on the rostrum. I signalled in the way we'd arranged for him to bid on Lot One Eighty. To my relief I saw him nod slightly. He was still fairly sober. It would go all right.

We plodded on up the lot numbers. Helen was in, being amused at the way I was struggling to keep my eyes off the flashy bird's legs. Helen's too exquisite and stylish to worry about competition. She gave me one of her famous looks, a brilliant smile carefully hidden in a blank stare. Helen's good on porcelain and ethnological art.

We'd be together yet but for a blazing row over a William IV davenport desk about which she was decidedly wrong. I was in the right, but women are always unreasonable, not like us. Anyway, we split after a terrible fight over it.

Big Frank from Suffolk was lusting away between bids, and the Brighton lads were in doing their share. Our local dealers formed a crowd of sour faces in the corner. We were all mad about the Birmingham crowd turning up. They were here because of a small collection of Georgian commemorative medals, mostly mint. I knocked the collection down to them for a good price. Nothing else I could do but take the bids chucked at me, was there? The whole place was in a silent rage, except for the Brummie circus. A group of early Victorian garnet and gold pendants went cheap after that, though I sweated blood to get the bids going. A glittering piece of late Victorian church silver went to Devlin for five of our devalued paper pounds. I thought, what a bloody trade. If I knew Devvo he'd advertise it as an Edwardian ashtray. It hurts, especially when nerks like him are the ones with the groats, and deserving souls like me stay penniless.

So, in a cheery mood of good fellowship, while pedestrians hurried past outside in the rain and visitors sloshed up to the Castle Park to feed the ducks, in happy innocence I gave Tinker his signal to bid for the next item. My heart was thumping with pleasurable anticipation. It'd be mine soon, for maybe a quid.

'Item One Eighty,' I called. 'Small portable Japanese box. Maybe bamboo. Offers?'

'Showing here, sir!' Bedwell, the head miff, called from one of the cabinets.

I beamed around the place as the mob shuffled and coughed and muttered. There was very little interest. It'd go cheap.

'Anybody start me off?' I called brightly, gavelling

merrily like the over-confident idiot I am. 'A few pence to start?'

Tinker was drawing breath when the bird cheeped into action. 'Ten pounds,' she said to my horror, and we were off.

That's how the frightening trouble began. There was no way I could have stopped the evil that started then. And none of it was my fault. Honestly. Hand on my heart.

I'd be completely harmless if only people would leave me alone.

The crowd of bidders usually divides as soon as it's all over. Some throng the tea bar at the back of the dank warehouse and slurp Gimbert's horrible liquid, moaning about the prices of antiques. The rest surge into the Ship and sob in their beer, full of tales about missing a genuine Stradivarius (going for a couple of quid, of course) by a whisker last week. As I feared the big Yank collared me as I climbed down from the rostrum.

'Excuse me, sir.'

'Eh?'

The rotund weatherbeaten face of an outdoor man gazed reproachfully down at me. He was the size of a bus.

'You missed seeing my bid, sir. For Lord Nelson's father's letter. I've come a long way—'

I glanced about. Most of the mob had drifted—well, sprinted—pubwards so it was safe to speak. 'Look, mate. Nothing personal. But Nelson's dad snuffed it two years before that letter's date. And it began, "Dear Horatio". Wrong. He was called "Horace" by his own family.'

'You mean . . . ?'

'Forged? Aye. Go to the Rectory in Burnham Thorpe and have a butcher's—I mean a look—at his dad's handwriting. He got little Horace to witness the various wedding certificates sometimes. Always look at originals.'

His gaze cleared. 'I'm indebted—'

I had to be off. 'No charge, mate.'

He was eyeing me thoughtfully. 'If I may—'

But I shot out. The girl had vanished in the scrum. I was blazing. I collared Bedwell, miserable as sin among the tea-drinkers. He's a long thin nicotine-stained bloke. Funny shape, really. Miffs are usually sort of George III-shaped and sleek as a butcher's dog. Good living.

'Where is she, Welly?' I tapped his arm.

He grinned and nudged me suggestively. 'Always after skirt,' he cackled. Then he saw my face and went uneasy. 'Gawd knows, Lovejoy. Took that little basket and went.'

I groaned and bulleted into the yard. There's a side door into the tavern, but nobody's allowed to use it. Dolly intercepted me. Luckily she had her umbrella up against the drizzle or she'd have clouted me with it.

'Lovejoy! I knew you'd try to sneak off—'

'Oh, er, there you are, love,' I tried, grinning weakly.

'Don't give me that!' She stood there in a rage, shapely and expensively suited. Blonde hair in that costly new scruffy style. I glanced nervously about in case other dealers were witnessing my discomfiture. 'You've made me wait hours in this filthy hole!'

'Er, look, angel—'

'No. You look, Lovejoy.' She blocked my way. I danced with exasperation. I had to reach Tinker, get him to find the bird who'd got my beautiful antique bamboo cage. 'I'm thoroughly sick of your high-handed—'

'See you later, love.' I tried to shift her gently but she struggled and stayed put.

'That's just the point, Lovejoy! You won't see me at all. Do you seriously put me second to a cartload of junk?'

I stared, flabbergasted. Sometimes I just don't understand women. She actually meant antiques.

' 'Course,' I told her, puzzled.

Her aghast eyes opened wider. She gasped. 'Why, you

utter *swine*—' I saw her matching handbag swing but deflected it and she staggered. I held her up while her legs steadied.

'Listen, chuckie,' I said carefully. You have to be patient. 'Antiques are everything. Cheap or priceless, they're all that matters on earth. Do you follow?' Her horrified eyes unglazed but she was still stunned at all this. 'And *everybody* comes second. Not just you. Even me.' I straightened her up, gave her a quick peck to show I almost forgave her.

She recovered enough to start fuming again. 'Of all the . . .'

'Meet you tomorrow, love.' I let go and darted past.

This door leads to the back of the saloon bar. A chorus of insults rose from the solid wall of barflies as I emerged.

'Here he is, lads! Our auctioneer!'

Tinker was already half way into his first pint. I honestly don't know how he does it. He never stops from noon to midnight. I gave him the bent eye while Lily the barmaid scolded me for coming in the wrong way.

'Typical, Lovejoy.' She pushed me under the bar flap into the smoky bar to get me out of her way.

'Don't serve him, love,' the dealers shouted.

I'd nicked a bottle of brown ale on my way through so I didn't mind whether she did or not. Tinker's horrible aroma magically thinned the throng about us.

'Who was she, Tinker?' I breathed the words so the hubbub covered my interest.

'The bird with the big knockers?' He shook his head. 'She's new round here, Lovejoy. I didn't know whether to keep bidding or not—'

'Shut it,' I growled. She'd been so determined I'd knocked the precious One Eighty down to her, amid almost total silence. Dealers love a dedicated collector, especially a luscious bird intent on spending a fortune for a worthless wickerwork box. I was furious because it wasn't worthless at all. I'd hoped to get it for a song and make a month's profit. Instead I was broke again and the girl had vanished.

'Pint, Lil.' Tinker hardly muttered the words but Lily slammed a pint over. Tinker's ability to get served is legendary. I paid, this being my role in our partnership.

'Then why the hell aren't you out finding her, you idle burke?' I spat the insult at him, but kept smiling. Disagreements mustn't be obvious in our way of life, especially among friends.

'I am.' Tinker grinned a gummy grin. 'Lemuel's following her.'

I subsided at that and swilled my ale while he chuckled at my discomfiture. Lemuel's an old derelict who still wears his soldier's medals on his filthy old coat. He sleeps in our parks and church doorways and looks and pongs even worse than Tinker, which is going it somewhat. He has a nifty line in conning our wide-eyed and innocent social services ladies for every shekel they possess. Luckily for the nation's balance of payments, Lemuel recycles this colossal drain on sterling through the merry brewers of East Anglia and the sordid portals of our betting shops. He hasn't picked a winner since he was eight.

'Taking it up regular, Lovejoy?' Devlin's beloved voice boomed in my ear, getting a few laughs at my expense. Nobody hates auctioneers like a dealer.

'Maybe.' I gave the world my sunniest beam. 'You got a job yet, Devvo?' A laugh or two my side this time.

'I've a bone to pick with you, Lovejoy.' He loomed closer. He's a big bloke and never has less than two tame goons hovering behind his elbows. They follow his Rolls everywhere in a family saloon. They were there now, I saw with delight. It's at times like this that I'm fond of idiocy. It gives you something to hate. 'That Russian niello silver pendant. You didn't see my bid.'

'You bid late,' I said evenly. 'I'd already gavelled.'

'You bastard. You nelsonned it.' He meant I'd looked away deliberately — after Nelson's trick at Copenhagen — another illegal trick auctioneers sometimes use. The place had gone quiet suddenly. People started spacing out round us. Devlin became poisonously hearty. It's the way every burke of his sort gets. He prodded my chest.

'Don't do that, please,' I asked patiently.

'Gentlemen . . .' Lily pleaded into the sudden silence.

'I came especially for that pendant, Lovejoy.' Another prod. Thicker silence.

I sighed and put my bottle down regretfully. I've never really seen that whisky-in-the-face thing they do in cowboy pictures. Maybe one day. Helen moved, white-faced, as if to stand by me but Tinker drifted absently across to block her way, thank God. I didn't want her getting hurt.

'Ooooh! There's going to be *blood* everywhere!' That squeal could only be Patrick, our quaint — not to say decidedly odd — colleague in from the Arcade. He had his latest widow in tow to buy him pink gins from now till closing time. I saw one of Devlin's goons turn ominously to face the main saloon. The other neanderthal was grinning, standing beside his master with a hand fumbling in his pocket for his brass knuckles. You can't help smiling. Imagine chucking your weight about for a living. I despair of us sometimes. Where I come from, nerks like him would starve.

Good old Devlin dug my sternum again. 'I reckon you owe me a few quid, Lovejoy.'

'Don't do that, please,' I said again. 'Last warning, lads.'

The neanderthal mimicked me in a falsetto. 'Don't do that, please.' He laughed. 'Shivering, Jimmie?' A Glaswegian, if I wasn't mistaken. He reached out to prod me so I kneed him and broke his nose with my forehead as he doubled with a shrill gasp. He rocked blindly back, clutching himself, blood spattered across his cheeks and mouth. You can't blame him. It doesn't half hurt.

'You were saying, Devvo?' I said, but he'd backed away. His other goon glanced doubtfully from Devlin to me and then to his groaning mate. 'Look, girls,' I said, still pleasant. 'No fuss, eh? The auction's over with. And everybody knows you're too stupid to handle antique Russian silver, Devvo.'

I was honestly trying to cool it but for some reason he went berserk and took a swing at me. A table went over and some glasses nearby smashed. I snapped his left middle finger to stop him. It's easily done, but you must make sure to bend it rapidly back and upwards away from the palm—keep the finger in line with the forearm or it won't break, and you'll be left just holding the enemy's hand politely and feeling a fool. Devvo's face drained and he froze with the sudden pain.

'Well, comrade?' I was saying affably to the third nerk when the crowd abruptly lost interest and filtered away back to the booze. Sure enough, there he stood in the doorway, shrewdly sussing the scene out, the Old Bill we all know and love. Neat, polite, smoking a respectable pipe, thoroughly detestable.

'You again, Lovejoy?'

'Thank heaven you've come, Inspector!' I cried with relief, hoping I wasn't overacting because Maslow's a suspicious old sod. 'I've just separated these two.'

'Oh?' Sarcasm with it, I observed, and a uniformed constable in the doorway behind him.

'Some disagreement over an antique, Inspector, I believe,' I said smoothly, staring right into his piggy eyes with my clear innocent gaze. 'This man set upon Mr Devlin—'

Maslow asked, 'True, Lily?' She reddened and frantically started to polish a glass.

'Aye, Mr Maslow,' Tinker croaked. 'I seed it all, just

like Lovejoy says.' With his record that took courage.

Maslow swung on Tinker and pointed his pipe. 'Silence from you, Dill.'

'Perhaps I can help, Inspector.' Helen lit a cigarette, head back and casual. 'Lovejoy merely went to try to help Mr Devlin.'

'Are you positive, miss?' He sounded disappointed but kept his eyes on me. I blinked, all innocence.

She shrugged eloquently. 'Difficult to see clearly. It's so crowded.'

'Very well.' He jerked a thumb at Devvo's goons. 'Outside, you two.'

'Here, boss,' the uninjured nerk complained to Devlin in a panic. 'He's taking us in.'

'Be quiet.' Devlin was still clutching his swelling hand, pale as Belleek porcelain. 'I'll follow you down.'

Maslow turned to give me a long low stare as the heavies went out. He leant closer. 'One day, Lovejoy,' he breathed. 'One day.'

I went all offended. 'Surely, Inspector, you don't think—'

Maslow slammed out. Patrick shrilled, 'Ooooh! That *Lovejoy!* Isn't he absolutely *awful?*'

A relieved babble began. Devlin left for hospital a moment later, the constable delightedly piloting the Rolls. From the pub window I watched them go.

'Hear that, Tinker?' I demanded indignantly. 'Maslow didn't believe me.'

'Yon grouser's a swine,' Tinker agreed. Grouser's slang for an aggressive CID man.

'All clear, Lovejoy?' Lemuel ferreted between us and clawed my bottle out of my hand. His eyes swivelled nervously as he downed it in one.

'One day I'll get a bloody drink in here,' I grumbled, ordering replacements.

Lemuel wiped his mouth on his tattered sleeve.

'That's an omen,' he croaked excitedly. 'Blood Drinker, tomorrow's two o'clock race at—' It was becoming one of those days. I put my fist under Lemuel's nose. 'Ah,' he said, hastily remembering. 'That bint. I found her, Tinker.'

I glanced about, making sure we weren't being overheard, and met Helen's eyes along the bar. She raised her eyebrows in mute interrogation. Don Musgrave and his two barkers were with her. Don's antique pewter and English glass, and does a beano among tourists on North Hill. He's been after Helen for four years, but he's the kind of bumbling bear type of bloke that only makes women smile. Anyway, he hates cigarettes and Helen even smokes in bed. I gave her a brief nod of thanks and turned back towards the yeasty pong of my two sleuths. Owing women makes me edgy. They tend to cash in.

'Any chance of a bleedin' drink?' Lemuel croaked. 'I had to run like a frigging two-year-old.'

Irritably I shoved my latest pint at the old rogue. He absorbed it like an amoeba.

'She's a souper,' he said at last, wheezing and coughing froth at me. I tried not to inhale but being anaerobic's hard.

'Eh?' That couldn't be right.

'Straight up.' Lemuel nudged Tinker for support. 'I was right, Tinker.'

'Souper?' I couldn't believe it. Anybody less like your actual starry-eyed social worker was hard to imagine than that luscious leg-crosser. She'd seemed hard as nails.

'I got money from her for my auntie's bad back.'

'Which auntie?' I demanded suspiciously, knowing him. He grinned through anaemic gums.

'Got none.' He and Tinker fell about cackling at this evidence that the Chancellor too can be conned with the best of them. I banged Lemuel's back to stop the old lunatic from choking. All this hilarity was getting me down. Tinker spotted my exasperation as Lemuel's cyanosis faded into his normal puce.

'The Soup's down Headgate, Lovejoy.'

'Here.' I slipped Tinker three quid. That left me just enough for two pasties, my nosh for the day. 'Tell Helen I'll see her in the White Hart, tennish tonight.'

'Good luck, Lovejoy.' Tinker made his filthy mittens into suggestive bulbs. This witticism set the two old scroungers falling about some more. I slammed angrily out into the wet.

CHAPTER 2

The rain had stopped but town had filled up with people. I cut past the ruined abbey and across the Hole-in-the-Wall pub yard. Our town has a gruesome history which practically every street name reminds you of. Like I mean Head Gate isn't so called because it was our chief gateway in ancient days. I'd better not explain further because the spikes are still there, embedded in the ancient cement. The heads are missing nowadays. You get the message.

I hurried through St Peter's graveyard, envying the exquisite clock as it chimed the hour. These big church clocks you see on towers are almost invariably 'London-made' early nineteenth century, which actually means Lancashire made and London assembled. You can't help thinking what valuable antiques these venerable church timepieces are, so casually unprotected on our old buildings. The thought honestly never crossed my mind, but don't blame me if one dark night some hungry antique dealer comes stealing through the graveyard with climbing boots and a crowbar . . . I trotted guiltily on, out into the main street among the shoppers towards the social security dump.

You may think I was going to a lot of trouble over a modern bamboo box, and you'd be right. I wouldn't cross the road for a hundred as a gift. But for a genuine eighteenth-century Japanese bamboo firefly cage I'll go to a great deal of bother indeed.

A question burned in my brain: if scores of grasping citizens and greedy antique dealers can't recognize an *oiran*'s—star courtesan—firefly cage, then how come this bird can? And she had bid for it with a single-minded determination a dealer like me loves and admires—except when I want the item too. Of course I was mad as hell with the sexy woman, but puzzled as much as anything. I don't like odd things happening in the world of antiques. You can't blame me. It's the only world I have, and I'm entitled to stability.

You can't miss the Soup. Our civil servants have naturally commandeered the finest old house in Cross Wyre Street, a beautiful fifteenth-century shouldered house where real people should be living. I eyed it with displeasure as I crossed the road. The maniacs had probably knocked out a trillion walls inside there, true to the destructive instincts of their kind. The smoke-filled waiting-room held a dozen dishevelled occupants. I went to the desk that somebody had tried to label 'Enquiries' but spelled it wrong. This plump blonde was doing her nails.

'Yes?' She deigned to look up—not to say down—at me. I peered through a footage of sequinned spectacle trying to spot her eyes. I'm a great believer in contact.

'A young lady, one of your soupers—er, dole workers—'

She swelled angrily. 'Not *dole*! Elitist terminologies are utterly defunct. Sociology *does* advance, you know.'

First I'd heard of it. Elitist only means greedy and everybody's that. I'd more sense than to argue, and beamed, 'You're so right. I actually called because one of your, er . . .'

'Workers for the socially disadvantaged,' she prompted. One of the layabouts on the benches snickered, turned it into a cough.

I went all earnest. 'Er, quite. She dropped her purse at the auction an hour ago.'

'How kind.' The blonde smiled. 'Shall I take it?'

'Well, I feel responsible,' I said soulfully.

'I quite understand.' She went all misty at this proof that humanity was good deep down. 'I think I know who you mean. Maud Endacott.'

The bird hadn't looked at all like a Maud. The receptionist started phoning so I went to wait with the rest. George Clegg had just got in from the auction, and offered me a socially disadvantaged cigar. I accepted because I can't afford to smoke them often and tucked it away for after. He's a vannie, mover of furniture for us dealers. He labours—not too strong a term—for Jill who has a place in the antiques arcade in town. Jill too is a great believer in contact. She's mainly early mechanical toys, manuscripts, dress-items and men. Any order. George leant confidentially towards me, chuckling.

'That tart frogged you, eh, Lovejoy?'

I shrugged. He meant that she'd got what I wanted, which is one way of putting it. 'Don't know who you mean.' George was shrewder than I'd always supposed.

The phone dinged. 'Maud will see you now,' the receptionist announced, still Lady Bountiful. First names to prove nobody was patronizing anyone.

I gave her one of my looks in passing. She gave me one of hers. I leant on her counter.

'I wish I was socially disadvantaged,' I told her softly. She did the woman's trick of carefully not smiling. I waved to George and climbed the narrow stairs looking for the name on the door.

Sure enough the bird's room was crammed with radiators. I sat to wait, smouldering. The bloody fools had drilled the lovely ancient panelling full of holes for phone cables. Mind you, it was probably only oversight that had stopped our cack-handed town council flattening the lot into a carpark. I rose humbly as the bird entered. I noticed her stylish feminine clothes were now replaced by gungey tattered jeans and a dirty tee shirt. Back to the uniform, I supposed. She too was being humble—until she spotted who I was. Her concern dropped like a cloak.

'Oh. It's you.' She turned and slammed the door. 'I bought that box quite legally, so—'

'I know.' I thought, box? You don't call a precious antique firefly cage a *box*. Unless, that is, you don't know what the hell it is. Odderer and odderer.

'Then what are you here for?' She sat, legs and all. I watched her do her stuff with a gold lighter and cancer sticks. No offer of a cigarette, but she blew the carcinogens about for both of us to share.

Meekly I began, 'Er, I wondered about the box . . .' Her eyes were unrelenting stone, but it's always worth a go. I smiled desperately like the creep I am. 'I'm trying to make up a set,' I lied bravely. 'An auctioneer isn't allowed to bid for himself, you see.'

'And you want to buy it off me?' She shook her head even as I nodded. 'No, Lovejoy.'

'Perhaps a small profit . . .'

She crossed to pose by the window, cool as ice. 'I've heard about you, Lovejoy. The dealers were talking.'

'They were?' I said uneasily, feeling my brightness dwindle.

'If *you* want something it must be valuable.' She sounded surprised. '*Is* it?'

'I'm not sure.' Another lie. I gave as casual a shrug as I could manage, but my mind was demanding: *Then why the hell has she paid so much?* You can't do much with an antique firefly cage except keep fireflies in it.

'They say you're a . . . a divvie.' Oho. My heart sank. Here we go, I sighed to myself. She inhaled a trickle of smoke from her lips. Everything this bird did began to look like a sexy trick.

No use pretending now. 'That's my business.' I got up and headed for the door.

'Is it true, that you can tell genuine antiques just by feeling, intuition?'

I paused. Failure made me irritable. 'Why not? Women are supposed to do it all the time.'

She stared me up and down. I felt for sale.

'Then why are you in such a state?' she asked with calm insolence. 'Just look at you, Lovejoy. A skill like that should make you a fortune. But you're threadbare. You look as if you've not eaten for a week. You're shabbier than the layabouts we get here.'

I swallowed hard but kept control. Never let the sociologists grind you down, I always say. 'It's taxes to pay your wage, Maudie,' I cracked back and left, closing the door gently to prolong its life.

I was half way down the stairs when this harridan slammed out and yelled angrily after me from the landing. '*Lovejoy*!'

'What now?'

'You've turned the central heating off, Lovejoy! It's freezing.'

You have to be patient with these lunatics. 'Your door's the only one on the staircase that's original eighteenth-century English oak,' I said tiredly. 'Heat'll warp it. The others are Japanese or American oak copies and don't matter. Think of it,' I added nastily, 'as socially disadvantaged.'

'You're insane,' she fumed down at me.

For a moment I was tempted to explain about the rare and precious beauty in which she worked so blindly each day. About the brilliant madrigalist who once lived here,

and of his passionate lifelong love-affair with the Lady of
the Sealands. Of the delectable ancient Collyweston
stone-slated roof, unique in these part, which covered the
place. Of the fact that the cellar was still floored by the
genuine Roman mosaic and tiles of the oyster shop nearly
twenty centuries old. Then I gave up. There's no telling
some folks.

'Cheers, Maudie,' I said, and left it at that.

Downstairs George Clegg was whining at the grille for
his handout as I passed the main room. If he'd got a move
on I could have cadged a lift home in his new Lotus.

Pausing only to see if the Regency wrought-iron door
plates were still securely screwed in—regrettably they
were—I stepped boldly out on to the crowded pavement
and saw Devlin and his two burkes getting into their Rolls
outside the police station at the end of the street. Devvo's
hand was all strapped up. He saw me and paused,
glaring. He ignored my wave.

Oh, well. Anyway, it was time for my lesson.

CHAPTER 3

Buses to my village run about every hour, if there's not
much on telly in their drivers' hut at the bus station. I
waited uselessly by the post office over an hour, finally
getting a lift in Jacko's rackety old coal van. There's no
passenger seat. You just rattle about like a pea in a drum
and slither nastily forwards every time he zooms to a stop.
Jacko's an ancient reformed alcoholic who fancies himself
as a singer so you have to listen to gravelly renderings
from light opera while he drives. He can't drive too well,
just swings the wheel in the vague hope of guessing the
van's direction. He dropped me off on the main road.
The van stank to high heaven of bad cabbage.

There's a narrow footpath down the brook. It cuts off a good half-mile because the road has to run round the valley's north shoulder. I set off along the overgrown path, Lovejoy among the birds and flowers. Some people actually leave civilization to tramp our forests and fields, the poor loons. One couple I know do it every Saturday, when they could be among lovely smoky houses and deep in the beautiful grime of a town's antiques. No accounting for taste.

As I trudged I remembered Maud Endacott's face and got the oddest feeling. She'd been so determined, sure of herself. She'd paid over the true market value for a little cage—yet she didn't know what it was for, where it was from, its age or its value. And from the way she'd behaved she'd been prepared to pay every shekel she possessed to get her undeserving hands on it. None of it made sense.

For the last furlong I kept thinking about the exquisite Japanese masterpieces of the Utamaro school. His lovely woodblock prints don't look much at first, but with familiarity their dazzling eroticism blinds you. The truth is, Utamaro loved women. Women are everywhere, even—or maybe especially—in his *The Fantastic Print-Shop* series. You can't help chuckling to yourself. Of course he tried his hand at prostitutes, star courtesans and all as well. The point is that the brilliant lecher made lovely erotic art out of everything he saw. There's nobody else in the Ukiyoe School quite like him.

The reason the famous old Japanese prints kept haunting me as I walked was the fantastic lively detail they crammed in among all that sexy eroticism. One famous picture came into my mind's eye as I entered my long weed-crammed garden. Eishosai Choki's lovely silvered night painting, say 1785, give or take an hour. In it, a luscious courtesan holds a small cage on a cord. It's a firefly cage. And, straight out of that desirable print two centuries old, had come the little bamboo cage I'd auctioned off to Maud Endacott this morning.

My thoughts had gone full circle. I fumbled for my key, and found I wasn't smiling any more.

After swilling some coffee and chucking the birds a ton of diced cheese I felt a lot better. Rose the post-girl had called and pulled my leg about fancying Jeannie Henson who now runs old Mrs Weddell's grocer's shop, our village's one emporium. 'Make an honest woman of her,' Rose cracked merrily, shovelling a cascade of bills on to my porch. 'I would,' I gave back, sidefooting them aside for the dustbin, 'but her husband's a big bloke.' She mounted her bike and bounced suggestively on the saddle. 'That's never put you off before,' she said sweetly. 'Get on with you or I'll tan your bum,' was the best I could manage to that. 'Oooh, Lovejoy. When?' She pushed off down my gravel path to the non-existent gate. I waved as she pedalled up the lane, grinning. Funny how women have this knack of always getting the last word. Something they're born with. Usually it's irritating as hell. Today, though, it cheered me up and I went back in smiling.

I fried tomatoes for dinner, dipping them up with brown bread and margarine. They're all right but the actual eating's not a pretty sight. I had tried to make a jelly for pudding, only the bloody things never set for me. It's supposed to be easy, just pour water on these cubes and hang about for a few hours, but I've never had one set yet. I always finish up drinking them and they're not so good like that. By the time I'd washed up it was nearly time for Drummer. I'm always nervous at this stage, so I whiled away the time phoning a false advert to our local paper.

This is the commonest of all secondary tricks in the antiques game, and my favourite. I'm always at it. It creates a demand for something you want to sell, like this

Bible box .I had. I had to cash it in urgently, my one remaining asset.

I dialled, putting my poshest voice on because I knew Elsie was today's newspaper adverts girl and she'd rumble my trick unless I was careful. I used to know her once.

'An advert for the Antiques column, miss,' I bleated in falsetto. 'Wanted urgently, English Bible box, oak preferred. Nineteenth century or older.'

'Address to send the bill, please?' Elsie put her poshest voice on too. Cheat. She's even commoner than me.

'Ah. Hang on, love.' I fumbled quickly through the phone book at random. Riffling the pages a name caught my eye. Oho. That posh address which kept getting burgled of its antiques, the careless burkes. Hall Lodge Manor in Lesser Cornard. Who deserved conning more? I read it out in full to Elsie, pleased at the idea of giving that snooty village something to talk about. 'And please include the name,' I added, still falsetto. 'Mrs Hepplestone. Send me the bill.' Damn the cost.

Happily I settled down with Hayward's book on antique fakery, pleased at having 'done a breader', as we dealers say. By tomorrow evening enough dealers would have read the advert, and my Bible box would be in great demand once I flashed it. Tough on poor old Mrs Hepplestone, though. Still, I thought indignantly, what was the cost of a grotty newspaper advert, for heaven's sake? And serve her right for being careless with her antiques. If I remembered right she'd been in the local papers at least three times for having her place done over. Paintings, ornaments and medallions had all gone in a steady stream. You'd think they'd learn.

The knocker clouted three times, bringing me back to earth. Drummer, I thought nervously. I got up to answer the door, my palms sticky like a kid at school meeting his teacher, and me the best antiques divvie in the business. I ask you.

*

'How do, son.' There he stood, looking like nothing on earth. Old tartan beret, scarf at the trail, battered clogs, shabby overcoat and enough stubble to thatch a roof. He lives down on the estuary with this donkey since he retired, giving rides to children. What a bloody waste of the world's last surviving handsilversmith. You'd think he'd live better in his old age, but he likes drunken idleness.

'Er, wotcher, Drummer.'

'Nice day.' Nervously I started to lead the way round the side of the cottage. 'How did it go, Lovejoy?'

'Er, not so good, Drummer,' I confessed nervously.

He smiled and paused to thumb a bushel of tarry tobacco into his pipe. 'Improving?'

'Well . . .' My throat had gone dry. I waited with nervous politeness while he did the fire magic.

The old man is gnome-sized, a mobile bookend. He's one of these blue-eyed Pennine men who are gnarled and grey-haired from birth. They seem a special breed, somehow, weirdly gifted and imaginative beyond the ordinary. They tend to speak in odd sentences which have most of the meaning in the breaths between. He looks dead average—until you see him at a benchful of raw silver. Then his rheumy old eyes spark and clear and his arthritic hands instantly become as tough as a wrestler's and graceful as a temple dancer's.

In a puff of grey tobacco smoke we walked into the back garden, Drummer's smile twinkling brighter at the unkempt state of it all. I ignored his silent criticism. Plants have enough troubles without me making their lives a misery.

My forge is actually a garage with a couple of brick structures—furnace and hot-sand table—erected near one wall. There's an end window opposite the up-and-over door. That's about it, except for a bench made out of old packing cases for tools and any stray pieces of wood I can cadge.

I offered Drummer the only stool. He sat and reached across the bench for my gadroon. I stared. The instant transformation in him gets me every time. It's remarkable. From an old codger in clogs he becomes slick, certain, completely in command. He hefted the heavy steel plate about with casual ease. It cripples me just to hold it upright.

'This it, Lovejoy?' he said at last, squinting along the rim.

My heart sank. He actually meant: and you've brought me here to see this travesty, Lovejoy, you useless burke?

'Er, yes, Drummer. That's it.'

He laid it down and smoked a bit. I looked dismally at my gadroon and waited for the verdict while Drummer gazed out on the bushes. It was honestly the best I could do. My arms and elbows still creaked.

I'd better explain here about the Reverse Gadroon because it's important.

I'd been lucky to find Drummer, lucky beyond belief. He's the last of the real hammermen, a genuine 'flatworker'.

In days of yore silversmithing was silversmithing, every task done by eye and hand. The polishers, modelmen, finishers, all *did* their work. They actually *created*. And of all these master craftsmen the greatest was the hammerman, because he had the terrifying responsibility of beating plain silver into a thing of miraculous beauty. Without skill and love the final form would be piteous, sterile. But with these two utterly human qualities the luscious virgin silver catches fire. The design draws life and love from its hammerman, finally glowing and throbbing with a pulsating beauty of its own. This explains why some silversmiths were superb, while some silver—even good antique—is only moderately good. There's a million designs, almost as many patterns as silversmiths. But of them all, none is so difficult, risky and beautiful as the Reverse Gadroon.

Drummer used to be an apprentice silversmith at Gurrard's in the Haymarket. Now he's the last of the line. I first realized who this old duffer was in a pub about a year ago, and just couldn't believe my luck. I might have missed it if I'd been casually gazing the other way. Through the bar-room fug I saw this pair of crooked old hands take a bent halfpenny from the Shove-Ha'penny board and straighten it against the brass pub-rail with a flick of a metal ashtray. Mesmerized, before I knew what I was doing I'd pushed through the mob in a second and collared the old scruff, and demanded, 'Can you do that trick again?' Everybody laughed, thinking me sloshed.

'Aye, son,' he'd smiled. We were in people's way trying to reach the bar. He took the coin and tapped once, bending it literally like paper. Then straightened it perfectly flat again with another tap on the rail. And all the time he looked at me, smiling.

I'd cleared my throat, daring the question. 'Have you ever heard of a Reverse Gadroon?'

His amusement lit with interest at the reverence in my voice. 'I've done it, son. Now and then,' he said, by which he meant for half a century.

And that was it. There and then I'd started learning from him, twice a week in my homemade forge. I even began exercises trying to strengthen my arms and shoulders, with dismal results.

It sounds easy. You take a tray of solid silver and hold it by the bottom edge over a patterned tool held in a vice. The idea is to hammer the silver's perfect upper surface over the die, thereby impressing the die's design. Then you move the tray a fraction, and hammer again. Do this all the way round, using even blows every time. If you've held it right, judged every single blow to perfection, struck with the massive hammer at exactly the right spot and with the same force, if you've turned the silver exactly the same distance for every blow and never stopped until the whole piece is finished, and if you are possessed of Olympian strength, endless stamina and unerring judgement, then you've done a Reverse Gadroon. But make a fractional error, pause a split second or weaken, and you've ruined the whole solid chunk of precious silver. Nowadays machines do it all, without the slightest risk of a human error—or human love—creeping in. It's called progress.

Drummer's the last living original silversmith. I don't mind his eccentricities, that he's been made redundant by the onward rush of mechanization. I don't mind that for the past twenty years he's lived in a shack down on the estuary giving donkey-rides for a living. To me Drummer's a great man, a genius. But when he's gone, God forbid, I'm determined there'll still be somebody to pass on his priceless skill of the Reverse Gadroon.

Me.

Only at this particular moment I'd made another balls-up. Drummer gazed at me, puffing.

'Not so good, son, is it?'

'No,' I said miserably. The last time he told me off like this I felt suicidal, except living's hard enough as it is. I practise on thin steel sheet, cut in ovals. To take the weight I'd rigged up a wooden grip on a counterpoised cord. Old Drummer screwed his eyes at it.

'Look, son,' he said at last. 'Pretty soon you'll have the strength. After that it'll just be practice, direction and power.'

That sounded hopeful. 'And then I'll do a proper silver pattern?'

'No, son.' He rummaged for more tobacco. 'You're a

divvie, son. Stick to your trade.'

'Sooner or later I'll do a Reverse Gadroon,' I said doggedly.

'You're too immersed in antiques, lad. A new hammered silver's not antique. That's why you'll never do it, never in a million years.'

I ticked off on my fingers, narked at the old duckegg. 'Strength, Drummer. Practice. Direction. Level power,' I snapped. 'You said yourself I'll soon—'

'Give it up, son. Germoline could do better.'

Germoline is his donkey. I watched his match flare between puffs. 'Then what's missing?' I honestly couldn't see.

'Fire, son. In you.' He rose sadly and gave me the stool. 'Listen, Lovejoy. There's no such thing as weakness, getting tired, making a mistake. It does itself.' He opened the door. 'When you've got the fire in you, the Reverse Gadroon does itself.' He gave a slow grin. I was so mad I didn't smile back.

'But—'

'You've got it for antiques, son. Not for new things.' His gaze saddened me. 'Got a motif?'

I spoke without thinking. 'A firefly,' I said. Why I said that I'll never know.

'Fireflies? Never heard of a firefly gadroon, but why not?' He nodded and made to go. 'Might as well ruin a firefly pattern as any other, mate.'

We parted after that, still friends but me in low spirits.

'Look, Drummer,' I began at the gate. 'Er, I'm a bit strapped . . .'

He chuckled. 'The money? Forget it, Lovejoy.' I give him a quid every lesson when I can. I said I'd owe it. 'I don't need any fare. Joe's picking me up at the chapel.'

'Cheers, Drummer.'

He gets a lift from a chap called Joe Poges, our coastguard on Drummer's bit of coast, who comes into the village to see his sister. Her husband's one of these characters mad on racing pigeons. Drummer sets them free on the river and they fly home again. Have you ever heard of such wasted effort?

I stood until Drummer's small figure had vanished up the lane. Then I went back into the garage and tried and tried on a new sheet of iron. All I did was make it look like a clinker. After an hour I sagged to a stop, sweating and exhausted.

It had been a hell of a day. First losing the firefly cage like that. Then crossing Devlin and antagonizing Inspector Maslow. Then losing out with Maud. And last but not least getting the elbow from Drummer. Well, I thought in my cretinous innocence, it couldn't get much worse, could it?

I gave the day up and went back to reading Hayward on fakes.

CHAPTER 4

I'm not one of these constant blokes, urbane from cockshout to midnight. By the time the pubs opened I'd cheered up. Life is variation, after all, and I'm up and down with the best of them. Late that afternoon Tinker rang in with word of an inlaid early Victorian knifebox going cheap at Susan Palmer's antique shop on the wharf. And he'd sent Lemuel after a set of Shibayama knife-handles in Dedham but didn't sound very optimistic. Neither was I, to put it bluntly, because Lemuel knows more about astrophysics than antiques. Anyway, the horse-racing at York never finishes till five and I knew he'd lose the bus fare on some nag because he always does. The good sets are real ivory with inlays, the rare Shibayama being a composite of bronze and iridescent stones. (Always check that it is ivory and not synthetic ivorine; and the more varied the inlays—insects, birds, butterflies—the more pricey.)

'I'll bet,' I told him sardonically over the blower.

'Straight up, Lovejoy,' he croaked. 'Brad's going over tomorrow.'

Oho, I thought. Brad's mostly flintlock weapons and lately Japanese militaria, but he never goes anywhere without good reason.

I decided after a quick think. 'Okay, Tinker. Suss it.'

He caught me before I could hang up. 'Lovejoy, she come after you today.'

'She?'

'That sexy souper, the one with the big bristols.' He cackled evilly. 'You'll be all right with her, Lovejoy—'

'Shut it,' I told him. He did, but I could still feel his gappy grin down the wire. 'What did you tell her?'

'White Hart, eightish. That all right?'

I let him go, feeling much chirpier. Maybe she'd seen sense and wanted to sell me the firefly cage after all. Perhaps it wasn't what she'd expected. People commonly make this sort of mistake, assume some trinket box has secret compartments crammed with jewellery. You have to learn that the antiques game is one of dashed hopes.

Served her bloody well right.

Dusk was falling as I plodded up the lane. I have a lump of corrosion shaped like an old Austin Ruby somewhere in the long grass but its road licence ran out at an inconvenient moment of poverty. So until I strike a Rembrandt or two it waits, patiently oxidizing in the evening mists, and I walk everywhere. We have no street lights owing to the simple fact that we have no streets. Our three pubs are the only nightlife, except for a maniacal crowd of sweaty badminton players straining ligaments in the village hall, and a church choir murdering Palestrina twice weekly to the utter despair of our new choir mistress. The desirable Hepzibah Smith is a pneumatic young graduate from the Royal College of Music. She was attracted to our village not so much by an impressive musical tradition as the job we wangled for her bloke, a gigantic pear-shaped blacksmithing hulk called Claude who farriers horses on a local farm. Nobody laughs at his name, unlike mine. I could hear our choir from the path through the graveyard as they lumbered through the *Agnus Dei*. It came on to rain about then, heavenly retribution I suppose.

Most folk shun the Tile and the Queen's Head but the White Hart's always heaving like noodle soup by seven-thirty. It's here that local antique dealers congregate for nocturnal boasting about deals they haven't actually made, in order to make sure everybody else is misinformed about deals they actually did pull off. Naturally our eternal wail is one of having sold the Crown Jewels too cheaply, of missing a cheap John Constable by a split second. The game is never to question the tales too deeply. They're all false. You'd only embarrass everybody by making some antique dealer admit that he couldn't have just snapped up Holman Hunt's *Light of the World* from a bloke in the flea-market. Just go along nodding and tut-tutting with sympathy. You can even make up a few tales of your own. The sober truth is that deep down in all the smoke and crap of the taproom every single dealer has had his hands on at least a few precious glowing beautiful antiques in the past few hours. Except me, that is, I thought, standing dripping in the doorway. And even I have a Bible box.

After the silence of the dark hedgerows outside the cacophony from the crowd dinned my ears. I'm always blinded for a minute while the light and the smoke tear at my eyes. Then my lungs adjust to the taproom smog and I push in, aiming for the bar.

'Hello, Lovejoy,' came from all sides.

'Watch your women, lads,' from some wit. 'It's our favourite auctioneer.'

'Make much profit, Lovejoy?' That was Joe Lampton, antique musical instruments and books.

I grinned. 'I charged Cuthbertson commission, Joe.' I got a few approving laughs.

Tinker was among the boozy crowd. I slid into the space his noxious vapours kept clear. Lemuel was over by the fireplace unerringly selecting cripples from tomorrow's Newmarket line-ups. Joe Lampton followed, pulling a first edition of Anne Cobbett's housekeeping handbook from his pocket. My chest clanged from lust, but I kept a calm face.

'This any good, Lovejoy?'

While Ted the barman got round to me I felt the book gently. In her day Anne Cobbett was as famous as Mrs Beeton. Be careful, though, because good modern photo-lithographic productions exist of many old books including *The English Housekeeper*—the paper and binding give them away. Any genuine old item, though, will scream its genuine character as soon as you get in reach. Joe's book was genuine all right. I told him so and valued it for him, loving the touch of the pages and the thick spine.

'Thanks, Lovejoy.'

I carefully wiped my hands down my trousers a few times as he merged happily with the mob. As I'd opened the book a fine chalky powder had fallen out. Doubtless some diligent housemaid had wished to protect an important household asset against bookworm by powdering the flyleaves with mortared white lead in a muslin bag. It's poisonous to *Homo sapiens* as well as to bookworms. Don't forget this when bookshop browsing.

Tinker was complaining. 'Here, Lovejoy. You could have charged Joe for pricing that bloody book. You always do it bleedin' free.' He was only worried where the next pint was coming from.

I shrugged and paid my pasty money over for a pint for him. I got the half. Mercifully Lemuel was still absorbed with the horses.

'Shut it,' I said. 'Run round.' Dealers' slang: summarize the main antique business of anyone knocking about. He slurped a gill and wiped his mouth on his oily sleeve before beginning. Sometimes I wish he wasn't so horrible. People are always on at me at the state he's in, as if it's my fault.

Helen wasn't in yet, I observed, but through the mirrors I could see Olive and Bill Tatum deep in an alcove, probably plotting their new stall in the town Arcade. That's the glass-roofed monstrosity which ruins the High Street. Bill hasn't much go in him, but Olive's fierce determination to out-Sotheby the rest of us spurs him on to a greater glory than his handbarrow of disintegrating trinkets in the Castle Yard.

'Olive and Bill mortgaged again,' Tinker croaked in a whisper seeing my glance. 'They bought that Staffordshire collection Jill got from Colchester.'

I nodded to show I'd heard him and swallowed my sudden hard anger. We were leaning on the bar, apparently chatting affably. In reality we were reckoning the chances of leaching anything we could out. That was important news about the Tatums. They'd now be desperate to sell rather than buy for the next month or two. Jill on the other hand would be a keen buyer—always assuming she could spare a few minutes from her latest young seaman. I could see her snappy poodle in the grip of a bewildered youth at the other end of the bar while Jill saw to her lipstick. She has one sailor after the other. Never the same twice. Tinker says they get danger money for just putting in to East Anglia.

I prompted Tinker, spotting a familiar cropped head

against the far wall. 'Jason?'

'You saw him buy, Lovejoy.'

Jason, once a regular army officer, now goes straight as an antique dealer in silver and furniture. A surprising success in the Arcade. He'd successfully bid high for a satinwood commode today, to the annoyance of the Birmingham crowd.

'And Tom Haslam's started ferrying.' Tinker's beer had gone. He gazed forlornly into the glass while I tried not to notice.

'A lot?' Tom's one of the wealthier dealers so this was important too.

'Almost every stick. And running it.'

Roughly translated, Tinker was reporting that Tom had decided to start exporting antiques wholesale to Continental buyers, and illegally at that. It's really smuggling in reverse. Hereabouts it's simple enough. We have too many small inlets for the coastguards' peace of mind. Ferrying gives a profit that's fast but 'flat', as we say—you tend to get as much profit this month as the next. If you think about it, this implies you're being underpaid for the better quality antiques. Curiously, dealers who ferry are regarded with a mild sympathy by the rest of us. They should worry.

I asked about Patrick, now busy shrieking at Deirdre—his latest widow I told you about—for doing his pink gin wrong. Tinker eyed the battle with distaste.

'But, darling . . .' Deirdre was expostulating. She inherited a fruit farm down on the estuary and is bent on reforming Patrick with the proceeds, which is a laugh. A sad one.

'And your *hat*!' Patrick screeched viciously. I honestly don't know why she puts up with him.

Tinker snorted. 'He bought three finger jades today—'

'Japanese or Chinese?'

'Dunno, Lovejoy. Does it matter?'

Today's accent certainly was eastern. I thought a bit as the far door swung open and Maud Endacott stepped inside. I decided it did matter. 'Yes. Find out who he sells to.'

Lemuel saw us just then and weaved foggily towards the bar. To my relief Maud Endacott advanced, through a shoal of ribald remarks. Oddly enough Big Frank from Suffolk was with her. Big Frank says he has wives like other folk have 'flu, time after time and every virus different. He paused to chat with Olive and Bill. Maud came on like the Light Brigade.

'Lovejoy.' She stood facing me, trouble all over. Tinker began to edge away. So did Lemuel, and so did I. I'd lost both rounds so far. There seemed no point in a third.

'Sorry, love,' I said. 'Just going.'

'Three pints, please,' she said over my shoulder. Tinker and Lemuel reappeared like magic, trapping me against the bar but avoiding my eye. Loyalty, I thought bitterly. She got a complicated vodka thing for herself and paid up with a flash of notes that momentarily quietened the pub into reverence. I hadn't known sociologists got a percentage.

'And again, please,' she told Ted. He was hovering handily, ogling. Tinker and Lemuel cackled and slurped frantically, ready for another.

I made sure I spoke softly. 'What's the game, Maud?'

'Want a job, Lovejoy?' She gazed at me over the rim of her glass. 'Antiques.'

'For . . . ?'

'For me.' She squeezed my arm but I've had tea-ladies before. A tea-lady's our slang for a bird who teases a knowledgeable bloke on until she's learned all he knows in his own particular field—say, Georgian manuscripts. Then she'll ditch him and take up somebody else and repeat the process. Lucrative, but definitely one-way.

I shook my head. 'No, love.' Tinker nudged me

desperately. I gave him the bent eye, implying that barkers do as they're told or get a thick ear. He ducked back into his beer.

She smiled sweetly. 'I understand there's a fee, Lovejoy.' And the world shivered to a quivering halt right there in the pub's unbreathable air. Money's nothing in itself, not really. But it's the golden ladder you climb to reach antiques. My resolution faded. Maybe I could eat again, something except fried tomatoes.

'Er, well . . .'

'See you outside in a minute.'

'Er . . .' But she'd already crossed over to Big Frank. They seemed very, very friendly.

'For Christ's sake charge her, Lovejoy,' Tinker croaked urgently in my ear. 'Sod that little box.'

'Lemuel,' I asked. 'That Shibayama set?'

'Oh.' He got into his whining crouch. 'Sorry, Lovejoy. Never reached Dedham. Lost the bus fare. My pocket. Must be a hole . . .'

Typical. I told the two of them to be in the Arcade tomorrow noon. Helen would be narked that I'd missed her, but Tinker was right. I'd have to get a groat from somewhere or I'd starve. But why me? Big Frank's as good a dealer as they come, which admittedly is really pretty mediocre. Maybe he'd failed her in some way, I thought unpleasantly.

Anyway, wisely or not I pushed my way to the pub door and out in a mood of total hope, which only goes to show how really thick I can be. My judgement in antiques is great. In everything else it's just the opposite.

Outside was pitch black and drizzling. A car swished by, all lights and aggro. A few people slammed in and out of the public bar. I waited under a tree in the bitter cold like a duckegg. The way Maud spoke back there it looked like she wasn't going to let the firefly cage go. I wondered idly about Maud and Big Frank. Headlights turned in to the forecourt and blinded me.

'Lovejoy?'

'Hello, Dolly.'

The motor's lights dowsed. Only the shrouded pub lanterns showed her standing gleaming in the darkness. Maybe men like blondes because they're easier to find in the dark. I'd never thought of that before. We dithered before I lost as usual and had to speak first.

'Look, love,' I got out after clearing my throat a million times. 'I've a job on just now. And, er, sorry about today—'

'You're an outrage, Lovejoy.' Her voice was quiet, flat. She stepped closer and slowly lit a cigarette. 'I don't know what's got into me, Lovejoy.'

What can you say to this sort of stuff? 'Er, well, love—'

'Don't invent excuses.' She seemed without emotion. 'I must be insane.'

Women make me nervous when they're in these odd moods. I wish they'd stay fair-minded and reasonable like me. Life would be a hell of a sight easier.

'I'm not a . . . slag, Lovejoy.' Her voice was unchanged. 'Is that the word?'

'I know you're not.'

'Don't bother even saying it.' She sounded tired, resigned. Her eyes lit in a passing motor's beam. We waited politely until the distant noise faded, as if the countryside's belly had rumbled. 'You always were . . . eccentric.' I drew breath but she went on in the same level voice, 'I have a busy husband, nice home, good furniture. Funny that I never rated you till we met again. Are you broke?'

'No.' I lied defiantly. 'I've this job on . . .'

A voice called. 'This way, Lovejoy.' Good old Maud, goose-stepping out right on time. 'Where the hell are you?'

'Mmmmh,' Dolly said. '*That's* the job, I suppose?'

'Yes,' I said eagerly. 'She's got this antique . . .'

Dolly put her hand on my face. 'Shhh. See you tomorrow.'

Then she'd gone, clipping off among the cars. She never even glanced towards Maud's voice. Maud was working on her mouth with lipstick by pencil light when I finally found her midget car. How did Big Frank get in, I wondered. I made it, finding joints I never knew I had. She watched another motor's headlights sweep the trees.

'I suppose that cow's your fat blonde?' Dolly's not fat, but women hate each other on sight. No telling why. A man's stupid to join in, so I ignored the crack.

'Where are we going?'

'Yours,' she said curtly. 'Direct me.'

So I did.

'Jesus Christ. What a *dump*.'

I said nothing, but was secretly pretty narked. I think my cottage looks really quite good, thatched roof and all that. It's just a bit dog-eared because I don't get much time to tidy it. I heard her derisive snort at the faded wooden sign against one of the apple trees: 'Lovejoy Antiques, Inc.'

'Leave it further up the drive, please,' I asked.

'Drive? This is a frigging swamp with gravel, Lovejoy.' She drove in anyway.

Charming. I got out and felt for the keys. If I forget to switch the alarm off before opening the front door our village's vigilant bobby infarcts. He's always moaning about it.

'Cut the lights, please,' I asked. 'Er, the hedgehogs don't like them . . .' She ignored that and drummed her foot impatiently. 'Come in.' I held the door. She waited while I put some lights on, then pushed through the little hall.

'You actually *live* here? I wouldn't have come if I'd known.'

I shrugged and made a feeble pass at clearing some books for her to sit on the divan. It unfolds into my bed. There's quite a lot of space in the living-room, really, but it never seems to be as available as it might be. Maud walked past the space I'd prepared and moved about the room, flicking aside the curtain to inspect the kitchen alcove with distaste. I noticed the grime on the windows.

'It's a shithouse, Lovejoy.'

I was red-faced, shovelling things aside on the low table for her handbag. She sat at last. I know I don't create much of an impression as a high-powered antique dealer but she needn't be quite so blunt.

'Can't you get anything better?' she demanded. 'We ought to condemn it.'

'It keeps me in antiques,' I explained. The trouble is that when I'm embarrassed I go defensive, as if everything's my fault.

'You're really into this antiques crap, aren't you?' For the first time some gleam of curiosity showed. 'Here. Open this.' And she pulled out the bamboo firefly cage.

You have to smile at some antiques. This little cage stood jauntily on my table, cockily aware of its undoubted elegance. Its side and top netting had frayed, of course, but the little half-door at the bottom was intact and the side and bottom struts of bamboo were perfect. It was no taller than a few matchboxes.

'What's so funny, Lovejoy?' Maud gazed from me to the cage and back.

Still smiling, I took the lovely intricate cage. Light as a feather. The ancient maker would have searched for days to find the right bamboo. Then he would have seasoned it, exposing it to sun, laid it in the right direction, talked to it, encouraging the pieces to become accustomed to a new life. Then slicing, and balancing on his outstretched finger to ensure an even lightness. At last, the incredible detailed jigsaw assembling, and the delicate net windows to retain the fireflies. Then the *oirans*, those lovely women, the star courtesans so dedicated to feminine elegance, would take it, wandering in the gardens of the Green Houses. Among the night-blooming flowers they would catch fireflies until the little cage would glow with a soft nebulous splendour. And at the Hour of the Rat, about midnight, the first-rank lady courtesan would finally lie reclining in love with her ardent suitor by the seductive glow of its gentle but brilliant emanation, perhaps watched through the screens by her *shinzo*, invariably so eager to learn the breathlessly inventive techniques with which the *oiran's* erotic skills lifted her soul to her lover's as they soared —

'You're a fucking nut, Lovejoy.' Maud was still looking at my face. 'Get on with it.'

Crump. I breathed a deep breath and opened its door carefully.

Maud watched, puzzled. 'Is that it?'

'Yes.'

'Nothing inside? No other places?'

I sighed. She had the secret-compartment syndrome I told you about. I examined it carefully. 'No.'

'What the hell *is* it?'

I looked at her sitting there. Aggressive. Trendy. Impatient, full of certainty. Clueless as the rest of them. Everything that everybody is nowadays. And a sociologist to boot. I thought, what's the use?

'Just a box.' I said a mental apology to it. 'Was that the job you mentioned? You could have opened it yourself.'

'No. I just wanted to see you do it. *This* is the problem.' And she pulled out another.

I stared. Another firefly cage? Exactly the same, a small rectangular tower on four round stumpy legs. A front part-door. Side and top netting. But all black as

Newgate's knocker and glittering with an extraordinary
dark lustre I'd never seen before. I reached over and
picked it up. Heavy and cold. I looked at one top corner
of the little door where it had been chipped by some
lunatic trying to lever it open. Good old Big Frank. It's a
wonder he hadn't used a hammer. I inspected it with a
hand lens a long while before the penny dropped. *It was
made of coal.* And I mean real coal, the sort you burn in a
grate. The netting over the windows, the door and its
handle, even the minuscule hinges. The entire thing was
coal. Somebody, perhaps the maker, had covered it with
black lacquer, presumably to keep it from smudging
things, maybe to strengthen it. Coal carvings are
occasionally still done, but this small fragile cage was
superb, far higher quality than most. Yet it felt modern.

I readjusted my face. A gaping expert's unconvincing
to a customer.

'Who made it?'

'Just open it, Lovejoy.' That cold determination again.
'And give me a cigarette.'

I glanced at her as I felt at the exquisite little cage of
living coal. She sat there almost quivering, her eyes fixed
on the object with an eagerness that could only be called
lust. I realized she'd bought the bamboo firefly cage
hoping it would reveal the way this copy opened. And it
hadn't.

She snapped her fingers at me impatiently. 'I said
cigarette.'

If I was putting up with her for the price of a pasty I
sure as hell had no fags. 'I'll tell your mother you smoke.'

'Sod it.' She rose and paced among the clutter. 'This
place is bleeding perishing, Lovejoy. Light the fire.'

I ignored her and attended to the cage. The coal
version had something the bamboo antique had not. If
you ran your fingers down its length there was a faint step
just palpable halfway. Squinting sideways you couldn't

see it. Another use for the coat of lacquer, to conceal a carved line round the cage? I took a pin from a drawer and slit the lacquer along the line, feeling my way in fractions. So the carver had copied the bamboo cage exactly the same but different, so to speak. It could easily be lacquered again.

'Is there likely to be anything inside?' I asked.

'How the hell should I know?' She was sulking furiously now. Our relationship was going downhill. I wouldn't have minded except she was the one with the money.

It seemed worth looking at the cage from all angles. The box was slightly smaller at the top than the bottom, like to bits of a telescope. I pressed the top down gently. After a faint pause it slid easily into the bottom half a little way and the door swung open. The whole thing was its own key. Clever.

That stopped the sulks. Her lust came back, force nine. 'Give it here, Lovejoy!'

'Hang on.' I deflected her hand and peered in at the little space. Empty. I'd guessed that.

Now, I thought. If a box was meticulously designed to conceal its own hollow emptiness, whatever needed hiding had to be in the walls, right? And since there was no other key . . . I held the little door ajar and pressed the box's top half down again. I was wrong. Not the walls. It was in the legs. One was hollow.

The corner of the box floor tilted leaving a triangular hole. Keeping the cage firm I switched the lights off and got my pencil torch to peer down inside the hollow stumpy leg. Nothing except faint spiralling down the wall of the hollow. For a moment I caught a brief flash of mauve, or thought I did. I looked again but only saw the black interior of the hollow cut deep into the leg. I showed Maud.

Just my luck. 'Whatever was in there's gone.'

'Shit.' She snatched the cage before I could move. She

peered into the minuscule hollow leg of the coal cage and glared at me in disgust. 'Useless.' She put the lights on and halted, staring at me. 'What's up, Lovejoy?'

'Nowt.' But I was clammy and cold for no reason. You feel stupid when that happens.

'You're white.' Maud pulled her coat round her. 'No wonder, living in this gunge. It's freezing in here.'

It had been the shadow. Maud's firefly cage had cast a shadow in the dark room. The pencil torch had thrown a curious blunt dark patch on my wall, very fleeting. I'd only caught it with the corner of my eye for an instant before it vanished as Maud bent to look in the cage. I was shaking like a frightened colt.

I'm honestly not the imaginative sort. No, honestly. After all what's more stupid than letting yourself get scared of nothing? And a shadow's nothing. I mean to say, a grown man, for God's sake. I mopped my face with my sleeve, cold and hot all at once.

A motor-horn sounded twice outside. I started towards the window but Maud snorted.

'Keep calm. It's only my gig.' She was still mad at not finding anything, but what had she expected? She'd still got two glorious works of art, one a genuine antique, the other a brilliant modern copy in a unique material.

'Gig?' I nodded wisely thinking, what's a gig? Must be some sort of motor car.

She rammed both firefly cages into her handbag and snapped it shut. My stomach turned at the risk the two beautiful little objects were running, living with good old Maud. I suppose my face changed because she was suddenly amused.

'These things really turn you on, don't they?' She paused suddenly in the hall on the way to the door. 'Do you want them?'

'Eh?' There must be a catch in it. Birds like Maud don't become instant Sweet Charity for nothing. 'Well, yes. But

I'm a bit short . . .'

'Your pay for opening the cage,' she said. There was a pause full of significance. The hall's only narrow. She came even closer and slowly put her hand round me under my shirt and squeezed with steady insistence.

'Er, well,' I said hoarsely. 'I, er, usually charge, er—'

She lifted my hand on to her breast. Tinker had been right about her. She really was luscious. 'Which is it, Lovejoy?' Her voice went into a husky whisper. 'You can have the cages. Or you can be tonight's gig. Which?'

Well, I'd already got a motor. A motionless one, but definitely a horseless carriage. 'The cages.'

She yelped and pushed me back. 'You *bastard*!' I fell over the carpet.

By the time I'd got up she'd stormed off, taking the cages with her. I went to the door and saw Big Frank's car. It was rolling backwards out of my garden, being followed by Maud's bubble car, and the penny finally dropped. So that's a gig, I thought. A gig's a bloke or a bird, or any combination of the two. Well, well. That seemed the end of Maud and me, and the end of my — well, her — lovely firefly cages. A woman scorned and all that. I shut the door as the phone rang.

'Lovejoy! Where have you been?' Helen.

'Hello, love. Look. Can you come round urgently, please?'

'I thought you'd never ask.' My voice must have sounded odd because she said, 'What's the matter?'

'Something for you. Be quick.'

'What is it?'

'A gig,' I said, casually as I could. 'Oh, love. Can you bring a pasty?'

CHAPTER 5

You must admit, sometimes women deserve gratitude.
Like I mean even with Helen staying I woke sweating and
shivering now and then throughout the night.

Next morning she brewed up in the alcove and fetched
the cups across. I could feel her looking interrogatively at
me, but pretended to be reading Kelly on restoring oil
paintings.

'Lovejoy.'

'Mmmm?' I turned a page carelessly but she took the
book away to see my face.

'You spent a terrible night.' She said it like an
accusation, but who the hell has nightmares deliberately?
No wonder women peeve you.

I said tut-tut. 'Did I?'

'Muttering and threshing all night long.'

I lowered my eyes innocently. 'I'm not used to having
company in bed. Makes me restless.'

She choked laughing and nearly drenched herself in
instant coffee. 'Lovejoy! You're preposterous!'

I watched her fall about. Women are lovely in the
morning, faintly dishevelled but warm and soft. Morning
women aren't half so vicious as the night sort. I always
find they're more fond of me. You can get away with
more after a night's closeness. Odd, but true. Helen's no
exception. She always wears my threadbare dressing-
gown to slop about in. It makes no difference to the allure
you feel, just seeing her sit on the edge of the bed lost
inside the tattered garment. After rolling in the aisles
some more she sobered and asked me about shadows.

'The one you got up to draw on the wall.'

'Eh? I did no such thing.'

She pointed to the wall near the mantelpiece. I'd thought she was asleep when I did it. And there was me tiptoeing about like a fool with my torch half the night, which shows how treacherous women are, deep down. She'd been watching all the time.

'You should have been kipping,' I said coldly.

Helen was at the pencilled outline, head tilted. 'What's it a shadow of, Lovejoy? A leaning castle? A window? A book, end on?'

'Dunno.'

If she hadn't been an antique dealer I might have told her what was on my mind. The lines showed the firefly cage's silhouette almost exactly as I'd cast the shadow last night when Maud called. There's this old iron grate in my living-room with a cornish above and a brass rail about head high. A painting I did years ago of the Roman road at Bradwell hangs nearby. Then there's a space where I used to have my Wellington chest before I flogged it for bread six months back. Then there's a tatty reddish curtain busily festering in whatever feeble sunlight totters through the window's grime, and that's about it. The shadow had stretched obliquely up from the black grate's mantelpiece almost as far as the corner. Climbing up there to mark it in the darkness had been really difficult. I'd nearly broken my bloody neck. I had the odd feeling I wouldn't have been so frightened of the odd lopsided shape if it had stayed exactly like the firefly cage. It was the skewed slanting weirdness of it on the wall that was so petrifying. But why? I closed my eyes. Maybe I was going off my nut. I'd gone clammy again.

Helen came back and put her arms round me. 'Don't be scared, love.'

That really got me. I broke away, annoyed. 'Who's scared?' Some women really nark me, always jumping to stupid conclusions with no reason. 'It's a . . . a scientific problem, you daft burke.'

' 'Course it is, love,' she said, not turning a hair. 'You're right. Sorry, sweetheart. I meant . . . preoccupied.'

That mollified me a bit. 'Well, all right then.' But my eyes kept getting dragged to the grotesque quadrilateral on the wall. I'd used crayon and charcoal to thicken the outline here and there. I've been scared of some real things before, but never a bloody shadow.

'What do you want for breakfast, love?'

'Er, I'm not hungry . . .'

Her eyes narrowed. She went searching.

'Ferreting in people's cupboards is very rude,' I reprimanded.

She started to slam about, flinging some clothes on. 'There's *nothing* here, Lovejoy! Not a single thing to eat.'

'Isn't there? Good heavens! I forgot to call in —'

She had wet eyes when she finally stood over me, arms akimbo. 'What am I to do with you, Lovejoy?'

You feel such a twerp lying down starkers when everybody else is up. Socially disadvantaged. 'Look, love,' I said uncomfortably, but she swept her coat and handbag up and slammed into the hall. The outside door shook the cottage to its foundations. I sighed. Unless you count Tinker, that meant I'd alienated practically all mankind, and even Tinker was narked because I hadn't charged Joe Lampton over divvying his book. Anyway, what is grub to do with Helen? She only eats yoghurt. I lay there listening and thinking, aren't people a lot of trouble. Helen's car started and scuffed away.

The shape scared me. All right, I admit it. Somehow it made my scalp moisten and my palms run. Somewhere it had scared me even worse than now, not as a mere scraped outline done in a wobbly hand during the dark hours, but in a solid terrifying reality, with the great oblique rectangle . . . *I'd seen it before.*

I was in the garden in my pyjamas when Helen

returned. There's this unfinished decorative wall I keep meaning to brick to an end when I get a minute. It's a sitting and thinking wall. She drew the car up. You could tell she was still mad from the way it slithered.

'What are you doing out here, Lovejoy? You'll catch your death.'

'Oh, just watching the birds.' They walk about on my grass being boring. What a life. Nearly as successful as mine. Helen's eyes left me and observed the open cottage door behind me. I was frigging freezing. It was an airy fresh morning and the grass wet through.

'Come back in with me.' She got out, her arms full of brown bags. 'Let's feed you up before we do anything else. I'll go in first.'

'Caviare and chips, please,' I joked, following her. My bum was frozen from the wall. Helen didn't smile. I always think that's the trouble with women. No sense of humour.

About Helen: she is reserved, in charge of herself and usually boss of everybody in arm's reach. She isn't like Angela, say, or Jill or Patrick, who couldn't have made it as antique dealers without considerable fortunes from interested donors. She's a careful blue-eyed cigarette-smoker you don't take for granted. And there's no doubt about her dealing skills, so precisely focused on oriental art, fairings and African ethnology. Helen's not an instant warm like Dolly. More of a slow burn.

While she made breakfast and I shaved I couldn't help thinking about her. Antique oriental art. We'd been close when she first hove in from one of the coastal fishing villages. Eventually she bought a little terraced house in the ancient Dutch quarter near the antiques Arcade, and she'd arrived. Now, I thought, politely passing the marmalade, why are we suddenly so friendly again? It haunted me all the way into town, because antique oriental art includes Japanese firefly cages of the Edo period, right?

Sadly, I'm afraid this next chunk is about that terrible stuff called money and those precious delectables we call antiques. You've probably got cartloads of both. But if you are penniless please read on and save yourself a bob or two.

Helen dropped me in the Arcade. This is a long glass-covered pavement walk with minute alcoves leading off. Each is no more than a single room-sized shop with a recess at the back. It doesn't sound a lot but costs the earth in rates. That's why we dealers regard possession of a drum in the Arcade as a sign that you're one of the elite. Woody's Bar perfumes the place with an aroma of charred grease. We all meet there for nosh because it's the cheapest known source of cholesterol-riddled pasties and we can all watch Lisa undulate between tables. She's a tall willowy PhD archæologist temporarily forced into useful employment by the research cutbacks—the only known benefit of any postwar government. Woody keeps messages for barkers like Tinker while serving up grilled typhoid. I always pop in to Woody's for a cup of outfall first, to suss out the day's scene.

'Wotcher, Woody!' I called breezily. 'Tea and an archæologist, please.'

'It's arrived, lads,' Woody croaked. He's a corpulent moustache in a greasy apron. 'Chain it down.'

'Here, Lovejoy.' That was Brad beckoning through the acrid fumes. He'd only want to moan about the scandalous prices flintlocks were bringing. He couldn't be more upset about it than me, so I pretended not to see him for the smoke.

A few mutters of greeting and glances from bloodshot eyeballs acknowledged my arrival. My public. Pilsen was in, a half-crazy religious kite collector who lives down on

the Lexton fields somewhere. Devlin was absent, which
mercifully postponed the next war. Harry Bateman was
in the far corner still trying to buy a complete early
Worcester dining set for a dud shilling, and Jason our ex-
army man was still shaking his head. What puzzles me is
that Harry—a typical antique dealer, never paid a good
price for anything in his life—thinks other people are
unreasonable. Liz Sandwell waved, smiling. She's high
class, a youngish bird with her own shop in Dragonsdale
village. Her own bloke's a rugby player, but I'd never seen
the geezer she had with her now. She had three pieces of
Russian niello jewellery pendants on the table between
them—think of silver delicately ingrained with black.
One was the pendant Devlin had complained to me
about. I crossed ever so casually near her but Liz stopped
talking so I couldn't hear the prices. Wise lass. That way I
landed Pilsen.

'Wotcher, Pilsen. Get rid of your scroll?'

'A blessing from the Lord upon thy morning,' Pilsen
intoned, hand raised.

'Er, ta, Pilsen.' I sat gingerly opposite while his head
bowed in prayer.

'May heaven bring its grace upon Lovejoy and our holy
meeting.'

'Tea, Lovejoy.' Lisa plonked a cup down. She always
ruffles my thatch. 'Money, please. Woody says no credit
for the likes of you.'

'Ruined any good antiques lately?' We're always
arguing. I've not forgiven Lisa for what the professional
archæologists did to the Roman graves at Stanway,
bloody grave-robbers.

'Don't start.' She edged away. 'And keep your hands off
my leg.'

'Oh God. Forgive thy erring servant Lovejoy his
wickedness . . .'

'Shut up praying, Pilsen.' Religion's bad for the soul.

'That Ethiopian amulet scroll. What's your price?'

'A Cantonese ceremonial dragon kite,' he said instantly. 'Or no sale.'

I sighed. I'd been trying to get that Ethiopian scroll for months. There are literally thousands knocking about, but Pilsen's was special. They are passed down in families which festoon their donkeys, sometimes as many as three dozen dripping from a single beast's neck to protect them on the road. Richer people had silver filigree containers as long as your finger to hold one. Others put them in horn cylinders or leather boxes. At the time of that appalling drought, dealers went over and shipped them on to the antiques markets of the world literally by the hundredweight. St Michael's a popular figure, usually the main one of five pictures separated longitudinally by calligraphed passages from Gospels. The eyes will prove them genuine. Nobody can paint those eyes with only a stick like the old Copts. Those and the delectable glowing brick-orange of the dyes. Pilsen's was the oldest and best-preserved scroll I'd ever seen, and he wanted the impossible.

'A Bible box?' I offered resignedly.

'Get knotted,' said this holy paragon. He gave me a quick blessing and shot out of the door, having been waved at through Woody's window by Maud. Now there's a thing, I thought. Pilsen and Maud. Well, well. Maud took his arm and they strolled off down the Arcade. She was being her beautiful best, suited and high-heeled. The slop of her social worker set was gone. She looked straight off a fashion page. Odderer still. I decided to follow. Lily tried flagging me down from her table but I hurtled past.

'See you in the White Hart, love.'

'But Tinker said . . .'

I dithered frantically, then resigned myself and screeched to a stop. Just as I'm Tinker's only source of income, so Tinker's messages are my only lifeline. Lily hopefully pushed the tissue paper bundles across the table as I plumped down.

'. . . you'll have these.'

That sounded a bit high-handed for Tinker. Lily was risking a bowl of Woody's opaque gelatinous soup. She used to be with Patrick until the Widow Deirdre homed in on him. Now she miserably endures her pleasant husband and all the comforts of home and affluence. Looking across at her I despaired of women. Some just seem to need to carry a heavy crucifix, and I'll bet crucifixes don't come any heavier than Patrick. Yet since losing him she'd been at a low ebb. The trouble is I'm too soft.

'Right, love.' I slipped them into my pocket, nodding. Pilsen and Maud would be in the High Street by now. 'Settle up later tonight?'

Lily was relieved. 'Thanks, Lovejoy. They're not perfect.'

'Who is, love?' I cracked, bussed her and shot out into Arcade, managing to ignore Woody's howl for his tea money, impudent burke. Gelt, for that swill. I ask you.

And Pilsen and Maud had gone. Great. I darted frantically among the shoppers for a few minutes hoping to see them but kept falling over pushchairs and dogs. Margaret was at the door of her shop. She'd seen me streak past.

She curtsied. 'Can I help you, sir?'

I went in resignedly. 'Wotcher, Margaret. Still got the Norfolk lanterns?'

'Special price for you, Lovejoy.'

Gazing about the interior of her enclosure depressed me more. Practically all of her stuff was priced and labelled by me because we're, er, close. Margaret's one of those older women who are clever dressers, interesting and bonny; she has a slight limp from some marriage campaign. Nobody asks about her bloke, whoever he was.

His dressing-gown fits me, though.

'Put them to one side for me, love.'

You'll see a thousand reproduction Norfolk lamps for every genuine antique one, and a real antique pair is so rare that . . . well, it's no good going on. Imagine you took an ordinary earthenware drinking mug, complete with handle, then bored assorted holes in the side. You'd have made a Norfolk lantern. They were used with oil and a perforating wick or, more usually, a candle stump. The holes are often arranged in cruciform patterns. Margaret got them from an old farmhouse. Well, I thought, I owe everybody else. Why not admit Margaret to my famous payment-by-deficit scheme?

'Did Lily catch you with her coal carvings?'

Coal carvings? 'Eh?'

'What's the matter?'

I sat on a reed-bottomed Suffolk chair and fumbled the tissue paper bundles out. There were three. It's difficult not having a lap so I unwrapped them one by one. A little cart, crudely done, an even more imperfect donkey, and a little hut of some sort. All very poor quality, each chipped and frayed. But definitely coal. Miners everywhere have tried a hand at carving the 'black diamond', but there was a world of difference between the lovely firefly cage and these. These were crude rubbish, the most inept carvings I'd ever seen. Modern crap. I wrapped them, thinking hard.

'Are you in trouble?'

'Not yet.'

I had to catch Lily and find where she'd got them, though this isn't the sort of thing one antique dealer ever dares ask another. Oddly, they reminded me of something or somebody . . . I looked up. The alcove had suddenly darkened and there was this chauffeur, resplendent in uniform. I stared. He looked as though he'd left a thoroughbred nag tethered to the traffic lights.

'You Lovejoy?' he snapped, all crisp.

'Yes.'

'Come on.' Clearly not a man to be trifled with.

'Clear off.' I stayed on the Suffolk chair.

'You've to come with me,' he said, amazed. 'Mrs Hepplestone instructs.'

Oho. So my newspaper advert had gone full circle. I'd throttle Elsie for turning me in, especially to a serf like this.

'Sorry, mate.'

He reached over and hauled me to my feet. 'Don't muck me about,' he was saying threateningly when his voice cut off owing to me taking reprisals. I had to be careful because Margaret always has a lovely display of porcelain in, and never enough reliable shelves to show the pieces off properly. He gasped for air while I leant him against the door jamb.

Margaret hastily put the 'Closed' notice up. 'Lovejoy! Stop it this instant!'

'He started it!' Honestly, I thought, narked. It's no good. Even trying to stay innocent I get the blame. There's no justice.

'I saw you!' she accused. 'You fisted him in the abdomen.'

A couple of potential browsers peered in, smiling, then reeled hurriedly away at the scene in the shop. Time I went. No way of winning here for the moment.

'See you, love.'

'But this poor man . . .'

'Chance of a quick sale.' I grinned and left him wheezing.

Lily had gone when I reached Woody's again. I asked Lisa where to but nobody knew. It was one of those days. Thinking hard about the three crummy coal carvings, I wandered disconsolately along the Arcade, exchanging the odd word here and there with the lads and lassies. A kid could have carved better. Yet they were a clue, if I could only think.

Jane Felsham saw me shambling past and hauled me in — well, beckoned imperiously. I've a soft spot for Jane. She's thirtyish and shapely, mainly English watercolours and Georgian silver. She sports a mile-long fag-holder to keep us riff-raff at bay.

'Your big moment to help, Lovejoy,' she told me airily. 'To work.'

Remembering Tinker's admonition to fix a price for my services first, I drew breath. Then Jane showed me the plate. It was wriggle-work, genuine wriggle-work. My mind went blank and I was into her place like a flash. All was suddenly peace and light. Pewter's the most notoriously difficult collecting field, but some pieces just leap at you. This was a William III plate, with a crowned portrait bust of the King centred in a rim decorated by engraved wriggles. It screamed originality. Many don't care for pewter, but its value should ease any artistic qualms you have. Weight for weight it can be more precious than silver. It had the right pewter sheen, like reflection from a low sun on our sea marshes. Modern copies don't have it, though heaven knows some are great. Jane was poking me.

'Lovejoy. I asked is it original?'

'Luscious,' I confessed brokenly. 'Just feel its beat.'

She was delighted. While I priced and labelled it correctly my eyes lit upon a genuine old Sphairistike racquet. I couldn't block my involuntary exclamation. Jane looked puzzled.

'That? I thought it was just an old tennis racket —'

I sighed. People really hurt my feelings sometimes. 'Once upon a time, love, a retired major invented a game for playing on the croquet lawn. He invented a name, too. Sphairistike. It's called tennis now.'

That pewter sheen lured my eyes back but it would cost

my cottage. I asked her if she had any coal carvings. She said no without emitting a single bleep.

I left and did a bit more divvying for the goons in the Arcade, seeing I was unemployed and had passed up the only chance I had of improving matters. Anyhow, I reasoned, Josiah Wedgwood's famous 'Fourteenth Commandment' was 'Thou shalt not be idle,' so who am I to quibble? I asked everywhere about coal carvings. Harry Bateman caught my interest with an old countryman's dove-feeder, genuine eighteenth-century. They make reproductions in country potteries now, but the shape's the same—a big stoneware bottle siamesed to a smaller one, with half of the side scooped from the titch to let the bird drink. Jenny thought she had a priceless item—a King Alfred hammered silver penny.

'It's been mounted, love.' I showed her the plug where somebody had sealed the pendant attachment. Mounts or holes in a coin don't quite make it worthless but my advice is to simply move on.

'Does it matter?' she asked, poor soul. 'That only proves it's real, though, doesn't it?'

'It would have been worth a year's takings. Now . . .' I saw her eyes fill at the disappointment and scarpered. I had enough problems without taking on psychotherapy. And neither Harry nor Jenny had seen a coal carving in months.

Dig Mason was waiting for me and dragged me across the Arcade. He's the wealthiest dealer in the Arcade. I quite like Dig, though he has more money than sense. Like now.

'You didn't buy *that*, Dig?'

'Sure.'

Fairings are so-called 'amusing' pottery figures you used to win at fairs for roll-a-penny or chucking balls into buckets. They were made in Germany between 1860 and 1890, and were given away as worthless in junk shops when I was a kid. Now, things being the way they are, they cost the earth—well, at least a full week's wages for one.

'Hong Kong, Dig,' I said sadly. 'Made this month. That dirt's soot from an open oil-wick.'

'You're kidding—'

It was a ceramic of a man washing himself and stopping a lady from entering. This 'Modesty' figure is one of the rarest, but the commonest (a couple getting into bed, in the form of a candleholder) is also forged.

'I've no time even for the originals either, Dig,' I told him, but he was mortified.

'You must be wrong, Lovejoy—'

He too hadn't seen any coal carvings lately, so I pushed on. All fairings are ugly to me. Hong Kong will make you a gross of the wretched things, properly decorated and meticulously copied, for two quid or even less. A couple of dozen of these forgeries will keep you in idle affluence a year or so—if you're unscrupulous, that is.

As poor as I arrived, I borrowed a coin from Lisa and telephoned the White Hart. By a strange stroke of luck Tinker was in there getting kaylied. He didn't know where Lily had got the three carvings from, either. I slammed the phone down in a temper. A harassed woman was waiting for the phone. She had this little girl with eyes like blue saucers.

'I'm so sorry to ask you,' she said to me. 'But could you watch Bernice while I phone? I'll only be a second—'

Feeling a right nerk, I sat on the pedestrian railing holding this little girl's hand outside the phone-box. Brad happened by on his way to viewing day at the auction. Seeing me there looking daft he drew breath to guffaw but I raised a warning finger and he soberly crossed over looking everywhere but at me. Bernice was about three, and obviously a real traffic lover. She kept trying to crawl under everybody's feet into the motor-car maelstrom. She told me about her toy, a wooden donkey pulling a cart. And the cart was full of seashells. I thought about it a lot. Pewter sheen, like sun on an estuary. Donkey. Cart. Seashells. And a little hut. I showed her my coal carvings, trying to keep my legs out of everybody's way.

Bernice's mother came out, breathlessly dropping parcels like they do. 'Thank you so much. Was she good? It's the traffic I'm worried about . . .'

'My pleasure,' I said. And I meant it.

If I'd had time I might have chatted the bird up. As it was, the baby's toy donkey-cart full of seashells had reminded me that down in the estuary Drummer and Germoline, pride of the seaside sands, make an honest if precarious living. I tore up the streets looking for a lift and saw Dolly's car by the war memorial.

CHAPTER 6

Dolly ran me down to the estuary going on for three o'clock. Our whole coast hereabouts is indented by creeks, inlets, tidal mudflats and marshes. As you approach the sealands you notice that the trees become less enthusiastic, stunted and leaning away from gales on the low skyline. They have a buttoned-up look about them even on the mildest day. Then the sea marshes show between the long runs of banks and dykes. You see the masts foresting thinly among the dunes' tufted undulations. Anglers abound, sitting gawping at their strings in all weathers. A few blokes can be seen digging in the marsh flats among the weeds. Well, whatever turns you on, but it's a hell of a hobby in a rainstorm. A lot of visitors come to lurk among the reeds with binoculars when they could be holidaying in a lovely smokey town among the antique shops, which only goes to show what a rum lot people are.

'Head for the staithe, Dolly.'

'I must be *mad* in this weather, Lovejoy.'

The birds are different, too, sort of runners and shovellers instead of the bouncy peckers that raise Cain in my patch if you're slow with their morning cheese.

There seemed a lot of fresh air about. The wind was whipping up as Dolly's motor lurched us down the gravel path between the sea dykes, blowing in gusts and hurtling white clouds low over the water. A staithe is a wharf alongside a creek where boats can come and lie tilted on sands at low water. You tie them to buoys or these iron rings and leave them just to hang about. Tides come and go, and the boats float or sag as the case may be. The main river's estuary's littered with the wretched things.

'There's *nobody* here, Lovejoy.' Accusations again.

'Drummer's bound to be.'

'I should have brought an extra cardigan.'

We got out. The wind whipped my hair across to blind me and roared in my ears. The force of it was literally staggering. For a moment I wondered what the terrible racket was. It sounded like a thousand crystal chandeliers tinkling in weird cacophony. Then I realized. The masts. They're not wood any more. They're some tin stuff, hollow all the way down. And the wind was jerking the ropes and wires, thrashing every one against its mast. There's never less than a hundred boats at least, either drawn up or slumped on the flats at low water. Say three taps a second, that's three hundred musical chimes every pulse beat, which in one hour makes—

'Lovejoy. For heaven's *sake*!'

Dolly had gathered her camelhair coat tight about her, clutching the collar at her chin. Her hair was lashing about her face. I'd never consciously noticed before, but women in high heels bend one leg and lean the foot outwards when they're standing still. In a rising wind they exaggerate the posture. Odd, that. She was on the seaward side of me, caught against the pale scudding sky. She looked perished and had to shout over the racket of the gale and the musical masts.

'What's the matter?' she shrieked. 'Lovejoy. Stop daydreaming. We could be home, with a fire . . .'

'You're beautiful, Dolly.'

Her face changed. She can't have heard but saw my lips move. She stepped to me, letting go of her coat which snapped open and almost tugged her off her feet. We reached for each other, all misty, and this bloody donkey came between us. Its wet nose ploshed horribly into my palm.

'*Christ!*' I leapt a mile. We'd found Germoline.

' 'Morning, Lovejoy. Miss.'

My heart was thumping while I wiped my hand on my sleeve. It had frightened me to death. Dolly was livid. Normally she'd have scurried about for some bread, or whatever you give donkeys, but just now I could tell she could have cheerfully crippled it. She muttered under her breath and concentrated on not getting blown out to sea.

'Wotcher, Drummer.' He had his estuary gear on, the tartan beret with its bedraggled tuft. Still the battered sand-stained clogs and the scarf trailing across the mud, the frayed cuffs and battledress khaki turn-ups. His donkey looked smaller if anything. I wondered vaguely if they shrank.

'Say hello to Germoline, then.' He grinned at Dolly. 'She loves Lovejoy.'

Dolly managed a distant pat. Germoline stepped closer and leant on me. This sounds graceful but isn't. She wears a collar made from an old tyre with spherical jingle-bells, the sort that adorn reindeer so elegantly. Usually you can hear her for miles. The din of the boats had submerged her approach. Add to that the problem of her two-wheeled cart—it holds four children on little side benches — and even the friendliest lean becomes a threat. Anyhow I leant back feeling a right pillock.

'Want a ride?' Every time Drummer grins his false teeth fall together with a clash. Whatever folk say about our estuary, I'll bet it's the noisiest estuary in the business.

'A word,' I bawled.

'My house, then.'

I scanned the estuary without ecstasy. Over the reedbanks stands Drummer's shed, looking impossible to reach across dunes and snaking rivulets that join the sea a couple of furlongs off. A row of proper houses stands back behind the wharf where the pathway joins the main road, aloof from the seaside rabble. The tallest of them is a coastguard station. It's not much to look at but it has those masts and a proper flagpole and everything. Joe Poges was on his white-railed balcony with binoculars. He waved. Joe's one of life's merry jokers, but all the same I quite like him. His missus gives Drummer dinner now and then. Knowing how much I would be hating all this horrible fresh air, Joe did a quick knees-bend exercise and beat his chest like Tarzan. It was too far to see his grin but I knew he'd fall about for days at his witticism and tell everybody they should have seen my face. I waved and the distant figure saluted.

'That's Joe, Miss,' Drummer explained, his teeth crashing punctuation. 'Home, Germoline.'

Dolly tried clinging to my arm on the way over but I shook her off. I was in enough trouble. There was no real path, just patches of vaguely darker weeds showing where the mud would hold. Twice I heard Dolly yelp and a quick splash. Life's tough and I didn't wait. I was too anxious to put my feet where Germoline put hers. Half way across the sea marsh Germoline turned of her own accord facing me and waited while Drummer unhitched the cart. I swear she was grinning as we set off again. Her hooves were covered in the sticky mud. Drummer always ties blue and white ribbons to her tail, his football team's colours.

We made it. He's laid a small tiled area near the shed door. Germoline jongled her way to a lean-to and started eating from a manger inside. Dolly arrived gasping and wind-tousled.

'Lovejoy,' she wheezed. 'You horrid—'

'Keep Germoline company a minute, please, love,' I said. Drummer went in to brew up.

It took a second for her to realize. Then she exploded. 'Stay out *here*?' She tried to push me aside. 'In *this*? Of all the—'

I shoved her out and slammed the door. It has to be first things first. She banged and squawked but I dropped the bolt. 'Sorry, Drummer.'

Drummer was grinning through crashes of pottery teeth. 'Still the same old Lovejoy. Here, son. Wash them cups.'

I pumped the ancient handle while Drummer lit an oil lamp. There are scores of freshwater springs hereabouts, and some even emerge in the sea. Old sailors still fill up with fresh water miles off the North Sea coast where the freshwater 'pipes', as they're called, ascend to the ocean's surface. They say you can tell where a pipe is from the sort of fish that knock around. Drummer chucked some driftwood into his iron stove. There's not a lot of space, just a camp bed, a table and a chair or two, shelves and a picture of Lord Kitchener and a blue glass vase with dried flowers. A few clothes hung behind the door with Germoline's spare harness.

'Coal carvings, Drummer.' I'd checked Dolly couldn't hear. 'Know anything?'

'Ar,' he answered, nodding when I looked round enquiringly from the sink because locally the same word can mean no as well as yes. 'It's getting the right sort of tar coal nowadays.'

'Much call for them?'

'Ar,' with a headshake. 'I sold three this week.'

I sat at his rickety old table and pulled out the three carvings. 'Drummer,' I said sadly, 'they're horrible.'

'What d'you expect, Lovejoy?' he demanded indignantly. 'Anyway, people needn't buy them. And they aren't bad as all that.'

True. But if these three monstrosities were Drummer's idea of art, then sure as God sends Sunday he'd never carved the lovely firefly cage.

'Just suppose a bloke saw a coal carving,' I got in when his teeth plummeted and shut him up, 'so intricate and clever it blew his mind. Where would he look for whoever did it? Think, Drummer.'

'I already know. My mate Bill.' Drummer inhaled a ton of snuff from a tea-caddy and voomed like a landmine. The shed misted with his contaminating droplets. 'That's better—'

'Who?'

'Bill Hepplestone. Me and him was mates—till he married up this rich young tart. Farm and all. Not far from here.' He pointed to show me the kettle was boiling. 'Stopped coming over at the finish. Too posh. Always trouble, posh women are. Never take up with posh, Lovejoy.'

'*Hepplestone?*' The name's not all that common. I filled the kettle. 'Any idea where he lives?'

'Dead, son. Poor old Bill. Used to be inland, place called Lesser Cornard in a bleeding great manor house.'

'Right, Drummer. Ta.' I rose to open the door, finger to my lips. 'Not a word. I owe you a quid, right?'

Dolly fell in, blue from the wind. Germoline gave me the bent eye as I shut the door again. It didn't look as if they'd exactly got on. I beamed at Dolly but all I could think was, great. That's what I need, to go spitting in the face of fortune. Some uniformed burke of a chauffeur wants to take me right to the bloody place I'm searching for, and I thump him senseless. Really great. Sometimes I'm just thick. Mrs Hepplestone of Hall Lodge Manor. Widow of Bill the coal carver.

Meanwhile Dolly was tottering towards the glowing stove, whining miserably.

'Ah! You're *there*, Dolly!' I tried to beam but she stayed mad.

'I'll kill you, Lovejoy.'

'Now, Dolly . . .'

'We're done, Lovejoy.' She swung at me, blazing hatred. 'Finished! Do you hear? I've taken my last insult from you. I've put up with you long enough—'

I shrugged at Drummer who was enjoying it all, chuckling as he poured the tea out. Women are an unreasonable lot. Now I'd have to find the bloody chauffeur and say I'd made a terrible mistake. What a life.

The next half-hour was the longest I'd ever spent. Dolly sat there in front of the stove with her back speaking volumes of annoyance. She ignored the tea I took her even though I'd given her Drummer's only saucer.

We left when Dolly had warmed enough to move. Drummer came out with us to lead us over the salt marshes.

'Tide's turning,' he remarked brightly, pointing. It looked the same to me, just a few scattered folk among the boats slanting on the mud, though I noticed one or two boats were floating now.

Looking seaward, I saw two vaguely familiar figures. I paused to focus better with my streaming eyes peering into the cold north wind. A man and a girl. They were over among the oyster-beds and seemed to be buying some. A fisher lad was hauling on a rope while the man pointed and the girl crouched to peer down into the water. Neither turned to look our way, not even when

Germoline brayed and tried to catch Dolly's heel with her
hoof. Odd, that, I thought. The fisher lad heard our
donkey, though, and turned to wave, laughing. He takes
care of them, the very same oyster beds that the Romans
established twenty centuries ago. I waved and we moved
on.

We splashed our way across the precarious muddy
shore. It was riskier than before. Puddles were now
ponds, and small rivulets had become streams flowing
swiftly inland. Once-placid dinghies now tugged irritably
at mooring ropes. The almost imperceptible path was
untraceable. In several places Germoline's hoofprints
were immersed in the mud and Drummer led us in a
detour. We were almost back on the foreshore before I
realized. Maud. Only Maud, our beloved social worker,
could be that scruffy, hair uncombed and patched jeans
frayed, quite at home among a straggle of estuary people
hooked on boating. And the neatly dressed bloke,
yachting cap, blazer and white flannels, giving orders to
an oyster lad as if to the manner born — who else but good
old Devlin, doubtless calling for a few dozen oysters to
have with his champers at the hunt ball. I could even spot
his bandaged hand from here. I prayed he hadn't seen us,
and hurried on after Germoline and the others.

Drummer fastened Germoline's cart on and Dolly was
given a free ride. By the time we reached the small
crumbling wharf the estuary was filling with unnerving
speed and the tangle of wrinkled sea marsh was ironed
out into a single choppy flood. Joe waved from his
coastguard balcony and mimed frantic applause at our
feet reaching land, the burke. Drummer handed Dolly
down to the firm ground.

As we left the staithe I couldn't help glancing down
towards the oyster beds. The oyster lad was still working
there but Maud and Devvo had disappeared, a hell of a
trick on a series of exposed mudflats and marshes. You

can see for miles, all the way out to the old World War gun platforms standing miles offshore. Unless they'd gone for a swim, and they hadn't looked ready for that, especially in this cold.

'Lovejoy. For heaven's *sake!*' Dolly was tugging me up the path.

I winked at Germoline and said goodbye to Drummer. He clogged off chuckling with a clash of teeth. Three children were waiting by Drummer's flag for a last ride in Germoline's cart, so somebody was in luck even if I wasn't.

Dolly didn't speak all the way back to my cottage. There she dumped me unceremoniously and did an angry Grand Prix start, though I asked if she'd see me tomorrow at the Castle pond. Half my gravel went whizzing across the grass from the spinning tyres, I saw with annoyance. It would take me hours shovelling that lot back, if I got round to it.

I went in thinking of the estuary, and Devvo and Maud's disappearing trick. She seemed to be going through us antique dealers at a rate of knots. One thing was sure, though. I'd not be included.

CHAPTER 7

Next morning was a red-letter morning, notable for the start of cerebral activity at Lovejoy Antiques, Inc. Not all that brilliant, but a few definite synapses. My threadbare carpet conceals a flagstone inset with an iron ring. Lift it, and you can descend the eight wooden steps into a flag-floor cellar by the light of a candle. It was constructed by loving hands four centuries before this age of jerry-built tat, doubtless serving as some sort of storage place for herbs and harvested stuff. Now it's ideal for antiques—should any ever happen my way by some freak accident. Down there I have boxes of newspaper cuttings and notes to keep track of deals and auction sales.

Hall Lodge Manor had had a rough time. From my cuttings our local papers seemed to give it reverential sympathy whenever antique thieves struck—which happened once every few months. Despite 'elaborate safety precautions' windows were forced, locks picked, alarm circuits were blistered and guard dogs distracted with almost monotonous regularity. And every time a few choice items were nicked. Not a lot, just a few. A Norwich School harbour scene attributed to Cotman went missing in its frame the same night a nineteenth-century tribal figure of Guinea ivory vanished from among a display of similar carvings in a bureau. Nothing else seems to have gone on that occasion. Then a matching pair of Gouthière firehearth bronzes went, and with them a diminutive wood carving described as 'Adoration of the Magi'. Four months later a gang struck again . . .

I poison myself with one of those little Dutch cigars on occasions like this. I went back upstairs and sat in the open air for a think. How strange. Nothing has boomed in value like Norwich School paintings, those reflective dark lustrous oils that find a ready market any- where—and which are very, very hard to identify with precision when you have only a description to go by. And the ivory piece was strange too, because the one type of ivory which all collectors love is the hard best-quality ivory from Guinea, whereas much Ivory Coast, Senegal and Sudanese ivory is semi-soft greyish rubbish. And Gouthière's bronzes may not look much, but they won their way into Marie-Antoinette's boudoir. The wood carving sounded suspiciously like a South German piece, from the novice reporter's bumbling narrative. Pictorial woodwork has never surpassed the brilliant German Renaissance craftsmen like Tilman Riemenschneider.

Round the stalls I'd heard rumours about such a piece for a year or more.

It was the same throughout the whole list. Everything pinched fell into the same category—highly prized, collectable and valuable. *And quite small.* Still, an antiques thief naturally goes for what's valuable and what he can carry, doesn't he?

Hall Lodge Manor had been burgled six times, the last a couple of months before Bill Hepplestone had died. Since then, nothing. I'm not a suspicious-minded bloke but you can't help thinking.

I became worried in case this old bird had me pinned for the robberies from her place. Maslow would believe the worst, suspicion being his thing. I'd have to go and calm her down, make her see reason.

I caught Jacko's van at the chapel and emerged in town two arias later with shellshock and a pong of decaying fish about my person from his latest cargo.

On a hunch I walked down to the pond in Castle Park. Dolly was there, watching children boating, and feeding ducks.

I came chattily up. 'Hello, love. I'm glad you—'

'Shut up, Lovejoy.' She took a deep sobering breath and linked my arm. 'I must be off my head. Come on.'

She stood us both nosh at the bandstand café, asking questions which I did my best to evade. Her odd mood began to evaporate and at the finish she was prattling happily. Eventually I got her to agree to giving me a lift to Mrs Hepplestone's at Lesser Cornard, lucky lass. Needless to say this got her mad again. She kept up a tirade of abuse and reproach all the blinking way.

'And the risks I take for you, Lovejoy.' This was because her husband had been in a few days before when I phoned in my posh voice pretending to explain she'd forgotten her library book at the hairdresser's. She said I didn't sound like a hairdresser's assistant. I tried saying that's not my fault but got nowhere.

We took an hour driving the eleven miles, owing to pulling into a lay-by to—er—lay by for a minute or two. Maybe it was our dishevelled mental state which made us so unprepared for the splendour of Mrs Hepplestone's cranny when we finally drove in to Lesser Cornard. It was palatial, straight Inigo Jones set in a Capability Brown landscape. Dolly was overawed at the trees, the curving rose-beds and the score of minions beavering among the yews.

'I'd better not stay, Lovejoy,' she said nervously as we came in sight of the mansion.

'How will I get home?'

'Er, a taxi, dear? They might let you phone.'

I knew what it was—she was worried her skirt and twin set weren't exactly right for meeting the landed gentry. I caught her patting her hair and fingering her artificial pearl necklace as she drove. She normally saves one hand for stopping me mauling her thighs while her eyes are on the traffic. Mind you, the scene which greeted us was daunting. The house was glorious, a long frontage and vintage doorways. All authentic, every brick. I gave Mrs Hepplestone top marks for defying the lemming rush of demented modern architects and leaving well alone.

Dolly didn't even cut the engine. With a quick wave of her hand she was gone, a flash of red lights showing as she turned past the rhodedendrons. I was alone in an acre of gravel in front of Hall Lodge Manor. I looked quickly about for the chauffeur because I've read my Chandler, but no. None of the gardeners bothered even to look up.

The hall door was open. I dithered like any respectful serf, trying to find nerve. You can feel antiques, actually sense the pulses beating out of a place so strongly it becomes hard to breathe. My chest was bonging like a firebell. And inside the hall there was this suit of armour.

I swear it was original sixteenth-century. Never mind anything else—just look at the fall-away part of the 'sparrow-beak' visor from the side. If it's *concave* and the whole suit feels genuine rush out and sell your house, send your missus down the mines and get your idle infants out doing hard labour. Then buy it. Even if you finish up out in the streets and destitute you'll be one of the few owners of a Greenwich suit of sixteenth-century armour.

So there I was in the porchway being mesmerized and broken-hearted when I suddenly felt watched.

'Lovejoy?'

A lady was sitting under this tree about thirty yards away. Slightly greying but smiling and being amused at a shabby intruder. She was knitting, cleverly not checking what the needles were up to.

I plodded over. 'Mrs Hepplestone?'

'You're younger than I thought,' she commented. 'I expected an old reprobate.'

'How did you find out?'

'The advertisement?' She laughed and made me a space on the tree seat. 'I had a word with the proprietors.'

Funny, but you don't normally think of dailies having proprietors. I'd always thought of them like churches, vaguely existing without belonging. I'd have to watch out—and make my displeasure known to Elsie, gabby cow. She'd no business divulging truth just to save her own crummy neck.

There seemed no way out of this. 'Er, an unfortunate slip,' I stammered uneasily. I suppose it would be fraud or something. Breach of the peace at the very least.

'Nonsense,' she said firmly. Odd, but she was still smiling. My spirits bottomed out. 'It was quite deliberate, Lovejoy. Admit it. Now, before we go any further, sherry?'

Dolly had guessed right, with a woman's sixth sense for social encounters. This was no Woody's Bar. A man dressed like the Prime Minister came out with a lovely gadrooned tray, only Edwardian and therefore not properly antique but it brought tears to my eyes.

'Is he a butler?' I whispered as the bloke receded. He'd left the tray for us on a wrought-iron garden table.

'Yes,' she whispered, amused.

I was impressed. I'd never seen one before. I'd felt like kneeling. The sherry was in a sherry decanter, too. I'd never seen that before, either. And a silver tray really used, not just salted away for investment. No wonder Dolly had scarpered. Maybe I should have stayed with her and had another snog in a lay-by.

Forces seemed suddenly too large to handle. Out of control, I asked dejectedly, 'Will you turn me in?'

'Certainly not.' She invited me to pour while I thought, thank God for that. The glasses were modern, but the silver-mounted decanter screamed London and genuine. Typical work of the Lias family, now prohibitively priced. They're easy to spot because there seem so many letter 'L's in the hallmark. John and Henry Lias were right characters . . . Mrs Hepplestone caught me smiling and joined in.

'Er, nice decanter,' I said feebly.

'Thank you.' She was doing the woman's trick of seeming cool while secretly screaming with laughter. I could tell.

A gardener had lit a bonfire nearby. You can smell wood smoke even upwind. Odd, that. I glanced covertly at the bird while the fire crackled. Stylish, forty-five give or take an hour. Still knitting. Maybe I was expected to make conversation.

'Er, sorry about your, er, chauffeur, missus,' I tried.

'Think nothing of it, Lovejoy. I quite understand.'

Then what was I here for? 'You going to tell me off?'

'No.' Knitting down now, loins girded for the crunch.

'You'll have to forgive me, Lovejoy. I'm unused to . . . your circle.'

Well, I was unused to hers. I forgave.

'The fact is that I was extremely discountenanced when I learned of your—*deception*—over the advertisement. As discountenanced as you probably felt on being exposed.' She smiled to take the sting out of her remark. I'd felt discountenanced all right, whatever that meant. 'But you are very clearly a professional at your trade.'

'Well . . .' I shrugged.

'Everybody seems to know you, Lovejoy.'

'They do?' This conversation was getting out of hand, like the gardener's fire over among the bushes. Too dry. Not enough rain.

'I made enquiries, Lovejoy.' She invited me to pour more sherry for myself. 'So I shall forgive you the chauffeur and the advertisement, and you shall do a simple task for me.'

Typical of a woman, that bit. I gazed about. Beyond the gardens a pair of huge lumbering horses were trotting, trailing an iron thing while two blokes marked the ground with white-painted pegs. Tractors clattered in the background. Maybe she wanted me to drive a tractor a day or two.

She laughed and shook her head. 'No. Nothing to do with my driving teams, Lovejoy.' She made a face. Something rankled with her, and out it came. 'Mind you, you couldn't possibly do worse than my own men. We lose the competition every year to the Wainwrights—ever since that new blacksmith joined them, wretched man.' Probably Claude, from our village.

'Then how simple?' I asked shrewdly, not wanting to get involved in the county set's social wars.

'For an antiques divvie—is that the word?— elementary.'

I brightened. Antiques. 'A valuation?'

'No. I want you to open a little cage for me, please.' She saw my expression go a bit odd because she cut in hastily, 'Not a true antique, I must confess. My husband made it. Rather curious, really. It's a little cage carved in coal.' She took my silence for puzzlement, which it almost was. 'A rather strange hobby, but I understand not altogether unique. I don't want the cage damaged.'

I cleared my throat nervously. This was where I came in, being asked to undo a coal carving. 'Where is it, love?' Maybe there were hundreds of the damned things.

A voice said, 'It's here, Aunt Maisie.'

And it was—held by good old Maud, together with its antique bamboo partner. Today's outfit was a subdued bottle green with sensible shoes, swagger bag, hair neat and chiffon scarf just right. Crisp little modern brooch and all. Just right to go visiting a rich auntie. Maud was beginning to seem like a chameleon. I glanced around, and sure enough there was another antique dealer in the background—also different, as usual. It was Don Musgrave this time, all tweed and hornrims. I began to suspect Maud chose her blokes like an accessory. From the doting grin on Don's face he apparently had other, less decorative, tasks to perform. Maud was using us all up at a rate of knots.

'Good heavens, Maud!' Mrs Hepplestone gestured for more chairs and the Prime Minister strode gravely forth to do his stuff. 'How ever did you—?'

'I borrowed it.' Maud's tone was quite cool and detached.

'But why, dear?' Mrs Hepplestone was in command but Maud was not going to be put under. 'You knew I was seeking an expert to open it—'

'I see you've found one.'

I went red. Bitterness from women always makes me do that. I wish I knew how to get myself cured. 'I opened it for you,' I said defiantly.

Maud's eyes glinted. 'So you did, Lovejoy. But the question is, did you detect some compartment that you are keeping quiet about?'

'Don't be daft.' I rose, reaching for the cages, intending to show Mrs Hepplestone. 'It's too small—'

'Then you won't mind if I do this, will you, Lovejoy?' Maud stepped the few paces to the fire and threw the cages on, watching my face. The crime took a split second. Don reached out for her, sensing quicker than me what she intended, but the cages were among the flames.

'You stupid . . .' I was scrabbling dementedly in the fire but Don and the gardener dragged me back. I ran round to windward, eyes streaming smoke and coughing like a veteran. The serf ran with me and rummaged with a rake but the heat pushed us off. The fire was one of those steady garden fires, hot centre and lopsided flames. Two gardeners were holding me still after a minute. I think I could just see the outline of the coal cage beginning to lick with flames and glowing. There was a curious sparking flash of colour, one single brilliant flash from it. Then it sank into the red hot core. Gone. The antique bamboo firefly cage must have burned instantly.

'Well,' Maud was saying sullenly to Mrs Hepplestone when I came to. 'If Uncle's box had nothing inside . . .'

'It was a keepsake, Maud,' her auntie was reprimanding frostily. 'You had no right—'

'Some keepsake! A piece of *coal*!' with scorn.

'That's not the point, Maud, dear. And look how you've upset Lovejoy. He's white as a sheet.' Mrs Hepplestone's hand took my elbow. 'Do sit down. You're quite shocked—'

I pulled away. No good staring at a bonfire all day, is it? Maud and Don were standing there so I stared at them instead. Don knows I can get nasty. He stepped back uncertainly. 'That was none of my doing, Lovejoy.'

'What's all the fuss?' The crazy bitch was actually

sneering at Don. I admit he's not much of a dealer but he'd never have done what she had. 'You're scared of him! Of *Lovejoy*!' She pealed laughter.

'You burned a genuine antique,' I managed to croak at last.

'It was mine,' she said, ice. 'None of your business.'

'Oh, but it is.' I try not to let my voice shake but it always does when white rage takes hold. I never sound convincing. 'Antiques are everybody's business.'

She laughed again. How I didn't chuck her on the bloody fire I'll never know, iron willpower I suppose. 'Then I'll hire you to buy Aunt Maisie a replacement, seeing you're practically penniless. On commission, of course.'

I gazed at her, appalled. Some people just have no idea.

'Maudie,' I said into her eyes, 'I wouldn't piss on you in hell.' And I turned away. Now that both cages were gone, literally in a flash, they could all get on with it.

I was plodding a mile on the road out of Lesser Cornard village when the familiar black Rolls came alongside. The chauffeur said nothing. I climbed in and got carried home silently but in style, to find the electricity and telephone were cut off for non-payment of bills. That's our bloody government for you, selfish swines. But in my mind was wonder at a mob of antique thieves who hit Mrs Hepplestone's manor house time and time again, but who missed a precious glittering suit of armour—worth a fortune—in the hallway.

I spent the last hours of daylight furiously trying to do the Reverse Gadroon on sheets of tin and finished up in a blind mania hammering the whole bloody lot into an unrecognizable mass, finally slinging the hammer against the wall in a temper. Then I went in and read by candlelight till so many shadows loomed on the walls that I snuffed it out and went to bed fast.

End of a perfect day.

And it really was — compared to the blood-soaked days that came after, though I didn't know it then.

CHAPTER 8

Remember where I said I'm resilient, never miserable for very long? Well, I take it back. I'd never felt so down. Maybe I sensed it was going to be one of the worst days of my life.

I deliver morning newspapers for Jeannie Henson when I'm broke. Not far, only round the village and pedalling like a lunatic to get round before my back tyre goes flat again. It isn't as boring as it sounds. You'd be surprised how many people are up before cockshout. Farm men off to the fields, lads driving cows, women clustering for our first dozy bus, a gasping jogger or two. And, I thought jealously, people in well-lit warm-looking cottage kitchens making lovely meals for each other, seeing they could afford those luxuries.

Doing a paper lad's job is embarrassing but it helps to keep me in the antiques game. I called on my way back for some bread and a tin of beans with my wages. The luscious Jeannie Henson was adding it up when our post-girl Rose came in for a packet of tea.

'Fancy meeting you, Lovejoy!' Rose said, mischievously glancing from Jeannie to me and back. She's a pest.

' 'Morning, Rose.'

'I mean, *rising* so early to *serve* Jeannie!' I went red and mumbled something while Rose fell about at her sparkling wit. She put the money on Jeannie's counter.

'That'll do, Rose.' Jeannie was a bit red, too. 'Time you finished your letters.'

'I like your skirt, Jeannie. New, isn't it?'

'Get on with you!'

Rose slung up her postbag and went, grinning. 'Make sure Jeannie pays you *in full*, Lovejoy. Andy'll be back soon.'

I loaded my stuff while the doorbell clanked to silence. Jeannie smiled apologetically. 'That Rose. Your change, Lovejoy.'

I gazed at the money thinking, one paper round isn't worth all that. 'Er . . .'

'No.' She pushed the money in my pocket. 'Lovejoy. Andy's been on about an extra hand in the shop lately. Don't misunderstand.'

'Oh, I don't.' We assured each other of this for a minute or two. 'Thanks, Jeannie. But it's antiques, you see.'

'I know.' She pushed a wisp of hair off her forehead. 'Well, look. They're firing Wainwright's fields today. It's good money. Andy and Claude are helping. You'd get there in time.'

I thanked her, promising to do a free paper round.

'When you get round to it,' she added with a crooked smile that puzzled me. That explains how dawn found me pedalling along the river dykes between the fens while a blustery wind tried to blow me into the surrounding marshes. It's not my scene, but a few hours' work would keep me for a week, at my high rate of living.

I got to Wainwright's fields and found where the straw lines lay. A small cluster of folk were already huddling on the farm's rise, ready for firing the fields before the ploughing. Everybody helps out in some way hereabouts, harvest in East Anglia being no time for differences. Even penniless antique dealers have been known to lend a hand, I thought bitterly. Andy and Claude the blacksmith were putting people's names down and allocating us bits of the fields.

' 'Morning, Lovejoy.'

'Wotcher, Claude, Andy.' I slung my bike under the hedge and joined them. The lovely Hepzibah Smith our choir mistress was there in her headscarf and gardening gloves, with three or four choristers in tow. They looked as glum as I felt. Wainwright was in the distance on an enthusiastic horse, ready to signal. Wainwright's our local lord of the manor, a cheery, beery bloke I'm rather fond of. He's famous for doing the exact opposite of what the government says. 'Can't go far wrong doing what they tell you not to,' he often remarks in the pub when people ask what he's playing at. Like when the Minister advised all East Anglia to automate and share combine harvesters, Wainwright sold all his that week. Now he uses these huge horses like in the olden days. 'Saved my neck in the energy crisis,' he told me, laughing. I wish there were more like him. A couple of stragglers arrived while we stamped and tried to keep from freezing to death. A whistle sounded somewhere signalling the start of the day's jollity.

'Glad you could come, Lovejoy.' Claude grinned. He knows what I think of the countryside.

'Men on the high fields,' Andy called. 'Women on the low. Places everybody. Get ready.'

Hepzibah gave me a long smile at my hatred of it all and we thinned out, one of us at two-stetch intervals across the harvested fields. I watched with some reluctance as the women went while Claude saw we lined up right and the distant mounted figure of Wainwright checked us in a slow wave. I made the traditional corn dolly, folding the straws into a nice thick handle and sheaving its head up lovely and loose. There was a lad next in line to me, new to field work but vaguely familiar. I made his dolly and showed him the trick of coiling the bottom of the handle so you don't get your hands burnt to blazes. People collect them as endearing knick-knacks but they have a grim history best not gone into. Antique examples are very costly—and unbelievably rare.

I asked the lad, 'You're Joe Poges' youngest, aren't you?'

'Yes, mister. Alan.' He waved the torch experimentally. 'You're Lovejoy. Saw you with Drummer. Dad said I could come as long as I did what the blacksmith says.' I grinned. Catch any of us disobeying Claude, I thought.

'Shouldn't you be helping your brother Eddie with the oysters?'

'Yes,' he said, quite unabashed. 'He has a big order today for the party on Mr Devlin's boat.' To go with the caviare and champagne, no doubt. That explained Devvo's disappearing trick with Maud. They hadn't vanished into thin air, just got on to a boat. I was about to enlarge on Devvo's many charms when a horn blew and Andy came haring along with his torch flaring.

'See you don't go slow like last time, Lovejoy,' Andy panted as I took fire from his torch.

'Okay, okay.' I'd deliberately let my lines of stubble take their time burning last year to give the rabbits and voles an extra escape route. So Wainwright had noticed after all, the shrewd old sod. You have to scuffle your feet about to make sure your straw lines don't ignite before the rest from your torch's drips or your name's mud with the other burners.

Two blasts of the horn came now, and the whole line of us bent on the run touching torches to the straw lines. Smoke rose in an ugly cloud, greyish white. It's a desperate business because the flames take hold and sprint ahead of you. Joe's lad got into difficulties and I had to run across and help him now and then. The great thing is to keep an eye across the other fields and see the wind's not done the dirty by veering. The village women wear showy coloured headscarves easily seen but we've not the sense. The great trick is to look for bobbing torches where the other men are. Women keep in better lines, calling if one of them gets behind.

I don't know if you've ever helped with field burning, but it's a filthy game. It's supposed to clean the fields for ploughing. A real laugh. You start clean at one end of lovely golden parallel piles of straw stretching over domed fields, and finish up kippered in acres of charred ash.

The odd thing was I wasn't excited by it all even though it's an exciting happening. Maybe I was in an odd mood. I don't know. But the running fires caught my attention then as never before. They are erratic, sometimes pausing and seeming likely never to move, the next minute flinging flames along your rows until everybody's yelling you are out of line. I kept looking at the flames, bright reds and golds against black soot. When Maud had chucked that marvellous little cage of carved coal into her aunt's bonfire I had caught a flash of bright green so brilliant it had stayed on my retina a whole minute afterwards. But coal burns red and gold or smoky. Whoever heard of a piece of burning coal flashing green? Yet when I'd opened the cage and shone the pencil torch into the aperture there had been a distinct bluish *mauve* gleam at the bottom. No green. I caught Alan laughing at me.

'Chucking earth won't put it out, Lovejoy,' he shouted.

'Shut up, you cheeky little sod.'

He'd seen me dropping handfuls of pebbles into my burning rows. I tried twigs, a couple of buttons which had strayed on to my jacket, saliva, soil, various stones, a hankie, half a shoelace and anything else I could rip off me and stay respectable. No greens. Assorted colours, but no greens. No mauve. Odd.

All that day we scurried on among the flaming rows of stubble. By the end of the afternoon I was knackered. A great pall of smoke was swirling seawards from the fields. I'd run miles up and down my rows, leaping the rushing fires which splattered and crackled. We did well. The women had been slow for once and came in for a good deal of ribbing when we assembled for teatime nosh. Wainwright fetches grub on a farm wagon. The women bring baskets and add to it. Andy and Claude take over while us burners rest. By a sheer accident I found myself sharing Hepzibah's pie. I'm happy to report that Claude was half a mile off.

'I hear you've been at Mrs Hepplestone's, Lovejoy,' she said innocently.

'Me?' I asked, wide-eyed. I can be innocent as her any day of the week.

'With Maud, wasn't it?' she pressed.

'Signed on for her ploughing team?' Wainwright put in, to general hilarity.

I joined the chuckles though they were at my expense, assuming Wainwright meant that time I'd overturned one of his tractors years ago.

'Claude will win again,' Wainwright continued confidently, taking a chunk of cheese flan. 'Best in East Anglia.' He smiled at Hepzibah.

One of the sooty men spoke up with a headshake. 'Ar; but only since Gulliver left the farms.'

'Aye. Gulliver was a great champion ploughman.' Wainwright rose to tap the cider barrel. 'Word is he's gone to the dogs.'

I listened to the idle country banter. These casual gossip sessions are fascinating if you've time, but I was beginning to feel decidedly odd, and it wasn't Hepzibah's pie. The smoke was ascending seawards. I turned to watch it. It would be hazing the estuary. Maybe it was the unaccustomed effort of the morning but I was uneasy. Or maybe it was the terrible night's dreaming of shadows. Or being so close to Hepzibah's lovely shape yet daunted by thoughts of being beaten senseless by her giant blacksmith. Maybe it was the pall of smoke. Fire. Perhaps

the little firefly cage and its coal copy which Maud
chucked on the bonfire seemed some sort of omen. I
found I was on my feet heading for my bike.

'Where you off to, Lovejoy?' somebody called.

I shouted back, 'Take my fire lines, Alan.'

They shouted after me but I was running between the
charred streaks towards the hedge where I'd left my bike.
I just didn't think, merely tore away in a blind panic. We
were three miles from my village. Then, say four miles to
the estuary.

Oh Jesus, I panted desperately as I dashed, sick to my
soul. Please let Drummer be alive. Please. Or at least let
me be in time to help.

CHAPTER 9

Looking back now, I could have saved Drummer.

If only I'd confessed my fears to Wainwright he would
have done something. I'm sure of it. He's a decent old
stick. Or if I'd explained to Hepzibah; she might have got
Claude to leave the field-burning. And Claude is a good
ally—nobody gets in his way when he's moving. Or if only
I'd just had the sense to ask for a lift, or gone to telephone
Dolly or Helen to run me down to the staithe . . . If only.
Some epitaph.

I pedalled off like a maniac leaving Wainwright's farm
and shot like a bullet on to the Bercolta road. Not even
the wit to save my strength in the early stages. I went like
the wind, cranking my old bike dementedly up and down
the low folding roads until I was knackered. Soon I was
waggling my arms frantically at overtaking motorists
begging a lift but they only hooted angrily back thinking I
was abusing them for bad driving. I collapsed in the first
phone-box I saw after realizing I was reduced to a snail's

pace. I could hardly stand, let alone dial. Unsuspected muscles throbbed feebly as I tried to move me about.

'Get Inspector Maslow,' I gasped, coming to my senses.

'Fire-police-ambulance?' the girl's voice chimed.

'Police, you stupid bitch!' I screamed. 'Police.'

It took a full minute for Inspector Maslow to come on, me shaking and dripping sweat and fuming at the bloody phone.

'Thank God.' I tried to swallow and be plausible. 'Inspector. Look, this'll sound unusual—'

'Who is it, please?'

'Lovejoy. You know, the—'

'Antique dealer.' His voice went funny. 'Yes, I know.'

'Listen, Maslow. Get help to Drummer. Please. Now. You've got radios in your cars, haven't you? A squad car or something—'

'Take it easy.'

'No, for Christ's sake!' I screeched, almost weeping. If he'd been here I'd have strangled the thick bastard. 'Help Drummer.' I began to babble. 'Please, Maslow. Just send one copper. Now.'

'What *is* this, Lovejoy? Are you pissed?'

'No. Honestly.' I struggled for control. 'Please, Inspector. A squad car.'

'Drummer's that old donkeyman, isn't he? Where are you?'

I told him. 'I'm still three miles off. I've only got my bike. Hurry, for God's—'

'Hold it.' The terrifying tones of smug incompetence oozed over the wire. 'On what evidence are you asking me to send a squad car out?'

'Because I'm sure they're doing Drummer!' I yelled, dancing with rage.

'Who?'

'I don't know!'

'Has somebody asked you to pass this message on?'

'No.'

'Then where is Drummer now?' ·

'Where he always is.' It was too much. 'On the sands.' I said again brokenly, 'Please, Maslow. I'll do anything—'

'Let's get this straight, Lovejoy.' He was enjoying himself, I realized with horror. Actually enjoying playing with me like a cat with a mouse. 'You are miles away. Yet suddenly you take it in your head to summon police assistance, alleging that a senile sand pedlar is being assaulted by persons unknown, on no evidence at all?' The seconds ticked away while the burke gave me all this crap.

'Please, Inspector.' I even tried to smile. Pathetic. 'Please. It'll only take you a couple of seconds—'

'Not for wildgoose chases, Lovejoy—'

'I'll pay for the fucking petrol!' I yelled.

'Look, Lovejoy,' the creep said. I recognized the boot in his tone. 'Why not pedal over there and have a chat with old Drummer? Then phone in and—'

I gave up. 'Maslow,' I said brokenly. 'Remember this call, that's all. Write it down. Time, place, date.'

I dropped the receiver and hurtled off again. My chest was sore and my legs felt cased in tin but I made fair speed. The trouble was I felt late, late, too late by days.

Autumn had really come to the estuary. Boats were laid up all along the hard and there was hardly a soul on the staithe, a young couple strolling home and a lounger or two. Joe's other lad was nowhere to be seen near his oyster beds. Just my luck. The tide was on the turn from low. A couple of boats were already stirring on the mudflats. The sailing club's light was still not on, so their bar was still shut. Not yet five. And only four cars on the club forecourt, nobody about. No help there.

'Seen Drummer?' I called out to one old bloke sitting with his dog on a bench.

'Eh?'

I ignored the gormless old fool and pedalled on, down the gravel as long as I could keep going, then jumped off when it turned to sticky mud and stumbled across the sea-marsh towards Drummer's hut. It hadn't seemed so far off the other day. I took no notice of the wet but kept going in a straight line as near as possible, occasionally floundering on my knees and having to push myself up with my hands. Once I glanced over to Joe Poges's look-out point but the idle sod wasn't there when he was needed.

I reached Drummer's hut like a monster from the deep, breathlessly slithering up the slight bank to Germoline's shelter. No sign of either of them. The hut inside was the same as the other day except for a pile of green samphire on the rickety table. It's a sea-marsh plant East Anglians nosh as a vegetable. Maybe Drummer had gone collecting samphire. I knew he sometimes took sacks of the stuff to market.

'Drummer!' I bawled, like a fool. I could see for miles, much further than I can shout.

Outside, the marshes looked dead. Wainwright's smoke was smudging the whole sky to the north, looming out to sea. Looking inland towards the main staithe you could see tracks where I'd chased across. I leaned against the hut, sweating and panting, wondering if Maslow was right but knowing he wasn't. Tracks. If I'd left tracks maybe Drummer and Germoline did too. A donkey can't tiptoe, that's for sure. But the sea was coming in and sea covers footprints in mud.

I clambered up the side of Germoline's lean-to shelter and, shuddering in every shagged muscle, pulled myself on the shed roof. Like an idiot, I grasped the iron chimney for steadiness and burnt my hand on the hot metal. It made me squawk. Wobbling, I rose flat-footed and gazed over the sea marshes. The roof creaked. If I so much as moved I would go through into the hut below.

It's surprising the difference a few feet in height makes to what you can see. Facing me was the staithe, several small inlets now running with the rising tide and the boats foresting the main estuary. The whole of the foreshore was now empty of people, only a couple of birds shovelling in the mud. The most seaward of the oyster beds was now almost under water. Breathlessly I wobbled flat-footed through ninety degrees and balanced feebly, arms out, while I took in that quarter. I was now looking south along the coast. A trio of distant sails showed where the last of the yachts raced on the incoming tide for the Blackwater's swollen inlet a few miles off. A tanker's flat line lay on the sea horizon. And that was all, apart from two small lads digging for sand worms a mile away where some bungalow gardens came down to the shallows.

Another dithering shuffle round on the frail roof in a quarter turn to face directly out to sea. A spready wobble and I straightened up slowly—and saw Drummer on the dunes maybe a quarter of a mile away.

'Drummer,' I bawled.

He was huddled in a mound. If I hadn't caught sight of Germoline standing forlornly with her painted cart I might have missed him even then. From the hut, the bare muddy promontory, laced by scores of small tidal rivulets, extends into the elbow of one of the sea's curved reaches beyond which is this muddy dune. It stands quite off-shore, and is only slightly domed. Most tides cover it. Germoline was over the low hump. Somebody had left her on the seaward side, sure that Drummer wouldn't get up and come home. An ugly thought. I yelled again.

'Help! Joe Poges!' I almost bawled my lungs up. What the hell was that panicky message they always shout on the pictures? 'Mayday! Mayday!' I howled. A seagull rose and hung, swirling gently in the air above me. It didn't even glance my way, the rotten pig. Surely to God, I

prayed desperately, those drunken slobs in the yacht club
would have their bloody bar open by now. It must be
already gone five o'clock. Who the hell ever heard of a
sailors' bar opening late?

I slid down the sloping roof and tumbled on the flat bit
of ground. Now I was practically at sea level I could no
longer see Drummer or Germoline. The clever bastards, I
thought as I started running towards the water's edge.
Cleverer than me, because I'd forgotten to take some
mark to guide me exactly towards Drummer. I glanced
despairingly round, then waded into the cold sea now
flooding into the creek, and hoping I was going to land up
reasonably near where Drummer lay. I waded with arms
out like a scarecrow's for balance and going a bit sideways
on against the force of the running sea.

It was probably only a few minutes but I seemed to be
wading for hours. I kept shouting, 'Drummer, Drummer!
it's Lovejoy. I'm coming,' but in the finish I gave up
and concentrated on making landfall—well, dunefall.
Eventually I managed to pull myself on to a dune heaped
with thin spiky grass and gasped a bit before compelling
my legs to move again. There wasn't much time. At high
tide there would be only a tuft or two of grass above the
water. All the rest would be horribly immersed, deep
below the North frigging Sea, with me and Drummer and
Germoline swirling deep underneath if I didn't watch it.
Moaning with terror, I scrabbled to the central mound
and almost tumbled over Drummer, right on him.
Germoline gave a brief bray, maybe of alarm at the sight
of this dishevelled hulk looming from the sea. I'm never
very presentable at the best of times. At the moment I
could have put the fear of God into anyone.

'Drummer.' I flopped down and tried to turn him over.
'It's me. Lovejoy.'

Somebody had knocked him about, rough and dirty.
There was dirty blood, brownish, on the sand. His tatty

garb was covered in blotches of blood to which sand clung. He still clutched a handful of samphire. Germoline's cart was half full of the stuff. I heard him exhale.

'Lovejoy? It were Dev . . .'

'Oh Christ, Drummer.'

I rose and yelled for help again towards the shore. Nobody stirred. The yacht club's bar was lit now — it bloody well would be now it was out of reach. And Joe's beacon lamp was blinking, but I couldn't recall if it always did that anyway. 'Mayday,' I bawled, incoherent with impotent rage.

I asked stupidly, 'Drummer. Can you walk?' He lay motionless, unconscious. What first aid do you do for a going-over? I'd learned the drowning bit at school, but what's the use? The sea reach was spreading. When I'd started out the biggest dune had been all of a couple of hundred yards long, and maybe half that wide. Now it had shrunk ominously to about thirty wide and eighty long. 'Oh Jesus,' I moaned. 'We're goners.' I'd have to swim for it. The channel between us and the promontory looked too deep to wade now. Germoline would drown before we'd got half way. For a second I stood helplessly watching the spreading black-green rising waters. Its speed was incredible. From a quiet calm reach it had swelled into a fast-flowing mass pouring inland. Within minutes the whole chain of sandbanks lying along the coast would be engulfed. If only I had a torch to signal. Maybe the old geezer with the dog was alerting helicopters and frogmen. I glared wildly out to sea. Maybe the Royal Navy was already proudly mobilizing its one remaining coracle . . .

It would have to be on my own. Even the yachts from the Blackwater were gone now and the sky was fading swiftly into dusk. Great. Why hadn't one yacht at least kept a proper lookout . . . ?

A yacht. A boat. A *boat*! *That's* how you cross an estuary full of grotty sea! And the place was heaving with the bloody things. I rushed to the top of my dune and looked across the estuary. The nearest craft was one of those sea-going power boats with a plasticky roof and silver knobs. It was facing the open sea but rocking sideways on to me. A hundred and fifty yards, maybe more. Certainly not less. It had a chain thing and kept tugging almost as if it were alive and raring to go.

'Look, Germoline,' I said, hauling off my shoes and starting to chuck my clothes into a heap near Drummer. 'Hold the fort, eh? I'll be back. Somehow I'll be back. Promise.'

I went over and patted her head. I'm not much good at it but maybe she got the idea. Down to my underpants, I waded in, gasping and jumping at the water's chill. It was frigging freezing. Panting in small spurts, I flailed into the water, as much to stop perishing as to get anywhere. The sea race pulled me to the left. I floundered right, doing an uncoordinated mixture of crawl and sidestroke. At last I steadied and began to take markers on the darkening shore. The trouble was I kept losing them. I would belt along like a drunk for as long as I could, then tread water, checking if I'd made any progress. It was more trial and error, and a lot of the latter. Proper swimmers count their strokes but I was so panic-stricken that I finally swam slap into the hull with a sickening thump that dazed me before I even saw it. A minute or two clinging on the anchor chain for breath and I edged up it towards the deck.

They are always bigger when you are on board. No time to go exploring. I clambered on to the transparent roof and checked Germoline and Drummer were still there. The sandbank had shrunk, a bare forty yards long now. How daft — I'd not thought to shift Drummer and Germoline to the highest bit. Cursing and blinding, I blundered to the pointed end. The chain looked thin and promised no trouble, but I had a hell of a time pulling it up. Some kind of a small winch stood on the deck for whoever knew how to work it. The anchor came free and the boat began to move. I staggered back into the cockpit carrying the anchor and, bracing a leg against the driver's seat, smashed the slimy anchor against the glossy wood panel of the dashboard. While the boat drifted in the tide race I chewed the wires through, twined the exposed flex and thankfully heard the roar of an engine.

Now it was dusk all along the estuary. I'd zoom aground if I wasn't careful. Lights were showing, greens, reds and yellows. What the hell did they all mean? Red for going forwards, something like that. I flicked switches experimentally. No light, nothing except the engine beating comfortably under my feet. Well, what the hell. I moved the steering-wheel and fiddled with the controls. It seemed simple enough. A throttle but no brakes. How do you stop a boat? Still, you can't look a gift horse in the mouth. I got her front end pointed seawards and took her forward motion off gradually so she gradually drifted backwards towards the dune.

Looking over my shoulder I spotted Germoline, now braying anxiously trying to encourage the motionless Drummer to get them to safety. I shouted I was coming but stopped that when Germoline took a few eager paces towards me. If she wandered off or panicked now it was hopeless. Handling the boat was difficult. The best way I found after several false goes was to keep the engine slow ahead and putting the wheel over inch by inch so the square end moved closer to the dune. I lodged aground with a horrible grinding noise and fell over. I had the wit to shove the gear into neutral as soon as I got vertical again. No good drifting with the propellers broken into smithereens.

'Okay, Germoline,' I said, shivering with cold yet

delighted at one success. Now I only had to work out how you get a donkey to climb aboard a boat from a sand dune. And the dune was now low down. The donkey cart was wheel deep and Germoline was stamping in alarm as the waves climbed her legs. Drummer was still dry.

The trouble is, everything on a boat takes time. I clambered to the front with the anchor and slung it over, then rushed about searching. No planks or boardwalks. Nothing for it. I found this harpoon thing under the side of the cockpit and used it to stove in the cabin door. As long as it was insured. More vandalism, and two planks from the bunks. I slung the rear anchor over the side, hurling it as far as my knackered condition allowed. It was the best I could do.

I flopped the planks between the gunwale and the dune's top. It would be a steep climb, and my improvised bridge wobbled like hell. Germoline would just have to be a good balancer.

Drummer was easier than I expected though I had to drag him all the way. Then there was nowhere to lay him down except the cabin floor, so I dragged him in there with Germoline braying and screaming like a demented thing. I scrabbled back to her, just undid the straps under her belly and left the bloody cart there. By then the sea was over the wheels and the cart was tilting with every wave. The samphire was floating off, and most of my clothes were gone. I got my jacket which had lodged on a dune tuft.

Getting Germoline on the boat was a real shambles. Twice the planks tipped us off. I only got her to trust me by lugging Drummer up and showing her he was already aboard. Then she streaked up the planks on her own and stood, drenched and shivering, half in and half out of the cockpit and coughing like an old sweat.

Drummer seemed to be breathing but I couldn't be sure. The cabin interior was dark. Dusk had practically fallen. I found a length of rope and tied Germoline up to the struts of the cockpit. The trouble was I kept retching, probably reaction from fright, practically getting myself drowned and having to exert my atheromatous frame in an unwonted manner. And I'd swallowed half the bloody North Sea.

I covered Drummer with one of the blankets just as he was because I was scared of trying to straighten him, and bundled a pillow under his head. Then I ripped a hole in another blanket and stuck my head through like a poncho. That left a sheet for Germoline. She didn't like it very much but I wasn't having any backchat from a temperamental donkey at this bloody stage and bullied her into being draped with it. Then I cast off, if that's the phrase, moving us cautiously into the main estuary with the throttle a bit forward. I still couldn't find any light switches. Maybe I'd stoved them in.

The boat must have moved about half a mile when Joe's tower started flashing us. He drove me out of my mind, beaming a light right into my eyes so I could hardly see where I was going. 'You're too sodding late, you useless burke!' I bawled at the light. I cut the throttle so there was hardly any movement, which was just as well because Joe's barmy light made me run into a sankbank. Putting into neutral—I couldn't get reverse—and trusting to the sea's velocity rocked us off and we recovered the midchannel after some time. At least there was a red and a green light up ahead and the yacht club bar's glowing windows. Everywhere else was in gloom now except for the lone red lights topping the old gun platforms miles out to sea.

I made the middle of the staithe by a miracle of brilliant navigation, though to be honest the tide was slower there and only one channel heads that way. The reflections from Joe's daft searchlight even helped me a bit. If I knew how to semaphore I would have signalled what I thought of him, stupid sod.

I don't know how long it took us to get anywhere near the stone wharf but it put years on me. Rocking boats moored in the main reach kept looming out of the darkness and they all seemed to be pointed angrily at us, but by now I didn't care if I sank a few here and there. I was past worrying about details. If the flaming owners couldn't be bothered to get up off their fat arses when I'm shouting that Mayday thing and floundering stark bollock naked in the briny they didn't deserve to own bloody boats in the first place. It was the yacht club lights that saved me from driving straight at the stone wharf. When I saw them nearly in line I put the engine into neutral, left the cockpit controls and dashed forward to chuck the anchor over. Then I did the same at the back end and cut the engine. As I did my elbow caught on a protruding button. A klaxon horn blared for an instant from the front of the cockpit. Now I find it, I thought bitterly. No lights, but a horn at last. Enough to wake the dead, or so I told myself then. I leaned my head wearily on the control panel.

'Help's coming,' I said to Drummer. 'We made it. Hold on, Germoline.'

I reached for the button and kept my hand there for what seemed hours. The horn blared and blared and blared.

CHAPTER 10

They got a quack whose surgery stood across from the staithe proper. I can still see Drummer's body on the yacht club's new carpet. In the dreadful glare of the strip lights you could see what the bastards had done to him. He was in an appalling mess. His face was practically unrecognizable. His arms were deformed, bent the way no arms were ever meant to. Blood caked his nostrils and his stubbly chin. He must have tried to fend the blows off. It was too painful even to think about, the old bloke vainly attempting to evade the maniacal battering on the dunes . . . Somebody gave me a brandy which I fetched up, then some gin thinned out with minty stuff which I kept down.

I've never had much time for club people, especially golfers and these yohoho boat characters. You can never tell what they're saying, for a start. They have private languages. But this crowd was really kind. They'd come out at a rush to our boat and ferried us off, calling their nautical terms in the night with gusto. They carried Drummer on a makeshift stretcher and cleared their posh bar for him, ignoring the muddy filth which trailed from Drummer and me. I asked somebody to please look after Germoline and was told she was safe. ashore — the first time I've been called 'Old Sport' and not got mad.

The doctor gave Drummer a good cautious exami- nation in total silence while the amateur sailors sipped rums and glanced ominously at each other. I wouldn't go and lie down. I'd never seen so many polo neck sweaters in my life. Everybody was very friendly in an awkward embarrassed way. One or two patted my shoulder in sympathy before the doctor rose, folded her tube thing and told us Drummer was dead. 'I'm sorry,' was how she put it. In better times I'd have chatted her up because she was a cracker, especially for a quack, but now all I could think of was Maslow's maddening voice. Joe was seeing to the boat I'd nicked.

They lent me some clobber, trousers, socks, oddly a pair of running shoes and the inevitable woolly sweater. I even got a crested yachting cap. People said things but I could manage nothing back. I think I got out a few words about sandbanks.

An hour or so afterwards they took me to Joe's house. His wife Alice was still up and his two lads, Alan back from Wainwright's and Eddie from the oyster beds, the three of them pale and quiet. I couldn't eat the hot soupy stuff Alice gave me and just went to lie on the couch in their living-room.

All night long I lay there listening to the sound of the sea. It seemed the shortest night on record, though I was sure I never slept.

Joe never rested that night. He worked like a dog, and looked worse than me at breakfast. He and two helpers had gone around all the households on the wharves knocking folk up and asking what they had seen that evening. The local school teacher hit on the bright idea of taking small portable cassette tape-recorders along. They gave the completed tapes to the bobby about six, but people had seen nothing significant, or so they said. Everybody was eager to please. Nothing like Drummer's death had ever happened before in Barncaster Staithe, and Drummer was a favourite among the colourful characters living locally.

I was summoned to Dr Meakin's surgery after breakfast to make a formal indentification of Drummer. I felt stupid because there wasn't anybody for miles around who could mistake Drummer. Anyhow I stood there, muttered my piece, and signed the policeman's paper. Doc Meakin said how sorry she was and thanks for having tried to save him anyway. Drummer was cleaned and brushed down. He lay on a roller stretcher covered with a sheet. A few of the yachtsmen were there signing statements.

The police car brought Inspector Maslow after we'd finished the formalities. By then Drummer had been something over twelve hours dead. In Maslow came, bossy and thick. I watched him arrive with complete detachment, almost as if he were a celluloid image straight off a screen. He had a quick chat with the Staithe policeman, then asked us to clear off, all except one. Guess who. Dr Meakin went with the others after glancing at me. She was worried. I wasn't, not any more.

Maslow crooked a finger at me, chancing his luck. 'A word with you, Lovejoy.' We stood like two bookends in the surgery with Drummer lying to one side. 'Lovejoy,' said the burke. 'What do you know about all this?'

'Only what I told you.' My voice was somebody else's. 'Before it happened, you will recall.'

'Never mind that,' he snapped, puffing up. 'The implications are you know plenty. Are you concealing evidence?'

'No,' I said. I was mild as a duck pond. 'But you did.' My head felt hot and light.

'*Me?*'

'Yes. I notified you of a crime in good time to prevent it. And you suppressed my notification.'

He decided on attack. His sort honestly get to me worse even than traffic wardens. 'You stole an ocean-going motorized luxury launch, Lovejoy.'

That shut me up. Well, I had. Then this big familiar-looking bloke cut in. He'd thoughtfully dallied in the hallway while the rest shuffled outside to stand around the garden lighting pipes. I recognized him as the Yank I'd saved from buying that crummy forgery of Nelson's letter at the auction. It seemed æons ago. He looked all nautical, which was why I'd not recognized him earlier.

'Excuse me, Inspector,' he said. 'Not steal exactly. It's my boat. Name of Naismith.'

'And you gave him permission, sir?' I could see Maslow was going to be stubborn.

The bloke hesitated. 'Not exactly. But I would have, if I'd been here.'

We all thought hard. There was some New World logic

in there somewhere. To me it seemed preferable to that relentless Old World stuff you can never argue with.

'Thanks, mate,' I told him.

'You're welcome.' He ducked out again. A big bloke, he kept having to mind the low oaken beams. I noticed he again idled in the hallway, gazing absently at a seascape hanging by the stairs. Don't say I've an ally at last, I hoped in disbelief. Unless he turned out yet another friend of Maud's. They'd been near each other at that same auction . . . Maslow was apoplectic but trying to stay calm.

'All right, Lovejoy,' he said at last. 'You can go. But watch it, that's all. I'll want you down at the station later—'

'Maslow,' I said, grinning like I'd never done before. 'Piss off.' There was only one witness, though I like now to think Drummer was watching too.

Maslow rounded on me, finger raised in warning. We were as pale as each other. 'Look here, Lovejoy—'

I hit him then, sweet as a nut. He folded with a whoosh and crumpled to the floor. Lovely. I decided to save some of Maslow's punishment for later. The big Yank hadn't even turned round, though he must have heard.

'So long, Drummer,' I said to the sheet. 'I'll do you the gadroon. You see.'

Maslow, trying to stand, crumpled in agony again and fell between me and the door. I kneed him ever so gently on his back, still folded and grasping his belly. 'Out of the way, Maslow. There's justice to be done.' The law has no sense of what's right.

I passed the big bloke in the hall. He was still frowning at the seascape.

'Be careful, Mr Naismith,' I said. 'That's a reproduction.'

'Is that right!' he said affably to the seascape. 'Well, thanks.'

I went out by the back door to avoid Doc Meakin and the others. There was a feeling I'd see more of the big Yank called Naismith.

Before I left the Staithe I went over to Joe's house at the end of the staithe. I asked Joe if I could look at the sea reach between the promontory and the big sandbar where I'd found Drummer and Germoline.

'Can we look from your coastguard place?'

'If you like.' He tried grinning and failed. 'It's only the same sea, Lovejoy.'

Joe's lad Alan ran ahead of us and started explaining about his dad's telescope and instruments. The lookout space was recessed back from a balcony, with walls covered by charts of isobars and whatnot.

'Don't fool me, Joe,' I said, trying my best. 'You never get the weather right.'

'That's the Meteorological Office,' he cracked back fast. 'We're coastguards.'

I looked out. And it *was* the same sea, same estuary. The reach looked narrower, hardly a stone's throw, but then the tide was lowish. And the same dunes. And Drummer's pathetic ramshackle hut, just the same. And the distant old gun platforms low down and miles off. The ocean-going ships on the horizon. The same gaggle of tiny yachts already racing from the Blackwater. Yet . . .

'Something's missing, Joe.'

'Eh?' He scanned the outside world, puzzled. 'No. Same as always.'

'No, Joe. Something's odd.'

I kept looking at one place. Wherever I tried to look, my eyes kept coming back to it. It was the dune, the big mounded dune where I'd found Drummer. Its top just touched the horizon for what seemed an inch or two when seen from here. But so what? And they'd done Drummer on the far side *where they wouldn't be seen from Joe's place*. If I hadn't stood on Drummer's hut roof I'd never have seen him and Germoline, from that different angle.

Joe tried kindness again. 'Go home and have a rest, Lovejoy. Do as Doc says—'

'Lovejoy's right, Dad.'

Joe looked at me, then at Alan. 'Show me what you mean, son.'

Alan pulled at us both, jubilant. We followed him in silence out on to the balcony, as far left as the railing let him. 'Lean out, Dad.' Alan was proud as Punch. '*Now* look at the sea.'

And suddenly I knew. Even before looking I *knew*, knew it all—or most of it.

'Good lad,' I told Alan. I was downstairs and walking off when Joe and Alan came running after me.

'Lovejoy. You didn't even look.' Joe didn't know whether to be annoyed at himself or pleased with Alan's observation. 'It's—'

'I know,' I said. 'The gun platforms.'

'That's right.' Alan was grinning as we walked out, chuffed at being one up over everybody. 'From almost everywhere else you can see three gun platforms. From Dad's lookout you can only see two, because—'

'That big dune obscures it.' I stopped and waved to Alice at her window. 'I'll get the clothes back when I can get a minute.'

'You're welcome, Lovejoy. Here. What's so special about the old gunfort?'

'Nothing, Joe. Forget it. Thanks for everything.' We stood about being embarrassed. I decided to thumb a lift back from the road.

'Cheers,' Joe said. Alan said the same, a bit self-consciously. 'Er, Lovejoy,' Joe called. 'Don't forget Germoline.'

Germoline and her cart were tied at the railing of the

yacht club. A few members were having coffee in the bay of their verandah, clearing throats and studiously reading papers.

'We got the cart and did it up,' Joe added. 'She's been fed, only . . . well, she'll be a bit lost . . . and she likes you . . .'

The cart was spotless. Somebody had laboured most of the night on it. I bet it was the yacht club people now so preoccupied. Germoline's harness was gleaming and her coat was brushed to a fine dark sheen. Even her hooves shone. She looked really posh. Broken-hearted, but posh.

I managed to say after a bit, 'Tell them thanks, Joe.'

'Get in. It won't hurt her.'

I did as I was told. The shafts rocked a bit but Germoline shuffled expertly and we balanced up.

'It's a long way to my cottage,' I said anxiously. Now I had a bloody donkey to worry about.

'She likes work,' Joe informed me. Alice was smiling and nodding from her steps. 'It's Germoline's trade, like antiques are yours.'

I sat there like a lemon holding these straps while everybody avoided looking.

'Er . . . ?' I got out at last, quite lost.

'You say, Gee up, Germoline,' Alan prompted.

'Gee up, Germoline,' I commanded apologetically. 'Please.'

And I rolled home at a slow stroll to the sound of Germoline's harness bells.

One donkeypower. Well, I thought helplessly, it's more than I'm accustomed to.

CHAPTER 11

Countryside never stops being astonishing. When you think of it, it's only a collection of villages dotted thinly among trees and estuaries and other boring pastoral crud. So you'd think news has a difficult time getting itself spread about. Nothing is further from the truth. An hour after I reached the cottage a silent pale Dolly arrived with a hot meal, sat me down to eat and moved about tidying up. Several times she bravely answered the door but didn't let anybody in.

I don't know much about donkeys but I'm sure Germoline knew what was up. After her terrifying experience she'd be daft if she didn't. I was scared the journey home was too much for her but Dolly said she was probably glad of a job, take her mind off things. We went out to her about fiveish just as Tinker arrived stinking of fish meal, Jacko's flavour of the month, and carrying a dirty sack. Dolly linked her arm with mine defensively and recoiled as Tinker came plodding up the gravel.

'Had to walk bleeding miles, Lovejoy,' he whined indignantly.

'Get it?' I'd phoned him from the box by the chapel to bring Germoline some grub.

'Aye. You owe Lemuel for it.' Tinker slung the bag on the grass disgustedly. 'He says it's enough for two days.' He hawked deep and spat messily on the gravel.

'Show us how to feed her, Tinker.'

Germoline was standing forlornly in the garden. She had a half-hearted go at chewing a bit of grass, then sobbed a few heart-breaking donkey sobs. Naturally Tinker grumbled but did it, threading a rope through the sack some way and hanging it over Germoline's face. It looked a dicey business to me, though Germoline got the hang of it smartish. And it stopped her crying, thank God.

'You really need Lemuel for this,' Tinker groused. 'He's a natural with nags.'

'I've heard—from the bookies,' I said sardonically. 'There's a beer indoors, Tinker.'

'Should I fetch it out?' Dolly suggested brightly, thinking of her cleaning, but Tinker had streaked off.

A car screeched to a stop in the lane.

'Lovejoy! You poor, poor *creature*!' Patrick descended, grand with grief in his orange suit and blue wedge heels.

I'd put a couple of planks across the gap in the hedge to show Germoline her territory. Patrick momentarily shed his unmitigated sorrow to curse this arrangement while he stepped gingerly over. Lily followed lovingly. Oho, I thought, where are the widows of yesteryear? Lily's husband was in a cold bed again.

'Wotcher, Patrick, Lily.'

Patrick posed on the gravel, orange trilby tilted and hands clasped to show the depths of his emotion. 'Lovejoy! We've all heard and we're positively *distrait*!' He was going to enlarge further but got bored and decided to notice Dolly. 'Ooooh!' he squealed. '*Love* your pearls, dear! False, though, aren't they?'

You have to take Patrick with a pinch of salt. He's not as daft as he looks. On average he pulls a high-priced deal in minor master paintings once a year, which shuts his critics up for quite a while.

I introduced them all, Dolly as an old school friend.

'No *need* to apologize, Lovejoy.' Patrick fluttered his eyes at Dolly roguishly. 'We won't say a single *mot* about you and Lovejoy rutting the way you do.'

This was getting out of hand. I cut in. 'Patrick, do me a favour. Ask Brad about a boat.' Brad's brother Terry has a boatshed.

'How old, dear? There's only those old sailing barges—'

'Not antique. One that goes.'

If he was surprised at this non-antiques enquiry he concealed it well. 'For you, *anything*! But why, Lovejoy?'

Anxious not to reveal too much, I turned the chat to antiques for a minute or two. Clearly Patrick was disappointed at not finding me moribund. His enthusiasm for the visit weakened visibly when Tinker reappeared from the cottage swigging ale from a bottle.

'We'll go. In case we get *covered* in *fleas*,' he hissed. 'One thing, Lovejoy.' He pulled me aside and whispered, '*Do* tell that sweet Dolly there's a *limit* to how much tan a bottle-green twinset can *bear*. Promise?'

They departed, Patrick abusing Lily for bad driving as she made eight noisy attempts to turn their car. 'You're giving me a headache!' he was screeching. Neither remembered to wave.

'Frigging queer,' Tinker growled after them. 'What's this about a boat, Lovejoy?'

'We need one for a couple of days.'

'That'll cost us,' he grumbled.

Dolly took my arm gently. 'Come in, love. I'm chilly now the nights are drawing in.' I was glad to call it a day.

That day all I could think of was where to get some money. Dolly has a car and her husband has a good job, but could I tap her for a boat's hire, deposit and all? Probably not. And how much is a boat anyway? While she was running Tinker back to town, Helen dropped by to ask if it was all true about Drummer. It was a curiously stilted visit, her standing in the doorway saying, no thanks she wouldn't come in just now. I told Helen thanks for visiting and I was fine but Drummer was killed. She said politely how she quite understood and turned on her heel and zoomed off in her red saloon. I think she sensed Dolly. I went and sat on the grass near Germoline to think.

Devlin, of course, killed poor old Drummer — the only pair of eyes looking seaward at a precise spot on the ocean, from the dune. And I knew roughly why. It was the gun platform, one of the sea forts, as people call them here. Thanks to young Alan, I knew which one.

They stand some miles offshore. Our people built them during the war as flak batteries against enemy raiders. Soldiers were posted there for only limited periods because of the constant risk. It was no rest cure. Between bomber raiders there was the constant fear that every warship was an enemy until proved otherwise. Apart from that there were only the terrifying storms which tried to shove the gun tower over into the deep ocean. And the blizzards. And the fogs, when you began to wonder if the rest of the world had simply vanished . . .

Drummer was dead. It would be me next. I forced myself to think of shadows. A few years ago I unintentionally went sailing, with a bloke who lived on a cabin cruiser. Still does. He had some nautical gadgets for sale, a sextant, two old ship logbooks and a navigator's table from sailing days. I wouldn't even have gone on board but it was one of those fine calm summers when our estuaries are crowded with holidaymakers. It seemed safe as houses. Doug, an old mate of mine, laughed at my fears.

We had a drink or three while we haggled. It was only early Victorian, none the less desirable. I knew I had plenty of keen customers for his stuff. We were both fairly well pickled when I noticed I couldn't see the shore any longer through the cabin window. While we'd been fixing the deal a dense fog had fallen. In fact we couldn't see a damned thing, not even another boat.

Doug laughed again, but this time less convincingly because it seemed we were drifting. Doug's bloody carelessness with his anchor had put us in the most dangerous position you can ever be on water — drifting in a fog.

Naturally by then Doug was too sloshed to think straight. Terror sobered me, but I know nothing about boats. Naturally the nerk's engine wouldn't go, and to cap it all his famous electronic gear failed to bleep. He kept saying, 'We're fine, great,' the lunatic.

About half an hour later foghorns began booming. The most mournful sound in the world except for a sobbing donkey. The trouble is you can't really tell which direction they are coming from. Fog does weird things to sounds. I was sure they were trying to tell us something, but of course Doug was singing nautical gibberish and unable to do anything even if he knew what was going on. We had another drink or two. Not much else we could do for the moment.

Scared as I was, I must have nodded off. I'd been swigging Doug's filthy homebrew since clambering aboard. Anyhow the next thing I remember of this holiday cruise was coming to, still befuddled and grinning with Doug snoring loudly in the cockpit. I sat in the well area peering blindly around at the grey fog. The sea heaved its unpleasant oily surface against the boat. No need to worry, though. Doug, that experienced sailor, said so—sloshed out of his mind but undoubtedly experienced. He'd told me we'd just float in the estuary till the fog lifted.

'Hey, Doug,' I remember bawling from my reclining posture. 'I can see a roof.'

'Eh?' He came to and yawned extravagantly. 'Impossible. You're drunk, Lovejoy.'

But I could, a tilted dark mass exactly like a pointed roof. And there was a noise, an intermittent sucking and slurping. Doug came staggering up from the cabin, stretching and scratching. I pointed. The mass seemed to be hardening and growing fast.

Doug froze. '*Jesus!*' It wasn't even a shout. It was a moan. 'The *gun fort!*' he screamed.

At that moment a faint gust thinned the fog. I gaped at the appalling sight, nearly peeing in sheer terror. We were floating fifty yards off the most colossal thing I'd ever seen. An immense looming black concrete rectangle filled the sky hundreds of feet above us. Vast cylindrical pillars plunged from its flat belly into the sea. They were horribly stained by weed and begrimed by rims of discharged oil. The sea sloshed on them with that gruesome sickening slurp I now realized I'd been hearing for some time. With the erratic sloshing of the greeny-black oily sea around its legs the horrible bloody thing seemed to be wading towards us like a huge uncoordinated giant bent on our destruction.

'Get us away from it!' I screeched. 'Get the fucking boat—'

'We're drifting for it!' Doug yelled. He attacked the stupid engine controls on the dashboard, kicking and blaspheming, while I subsided into an aghast silence as the great malevolent mass seemed to plod its mad way nearer and nearer. To my shame I hid my head between my hands in the cabin, too terrified to do anything, though Doug was screaming for me to come out and help. He called me all the abusive names he knew but I didn't budge. The one glance I gave nearly made me faint. We'd drifted between the tower's obese legs, about forty feet off to either side, and above, the grotesque soiled dripping underbelly of the gun fort filled the whole world, a mass of slanting shadow.

Doug did well from then on, all on his own. I stayed in the cabin mute with terror even when the engine mercifully roared into action. I couldn't bear to look out until Doug yelled that we were clear. Doug became quite chirpy as we puttered home through the lessening fog. I recognized the anecdote syndrome. This would be the basis of one of his famous nautical tales in the pubs along the coast. How I Escaped The Sea Drift In The Worst

Fog . . . He could have the glory any time, I thought fervently. All I wanted was to stand on solid ground and never get off.

Doug assumed I'd been too seasick to help him near the sea fort. I didn't disillusion him. I said, what the hell could you expect from that homebrewed plonk he kept offering me, which gave him a good laugh. I joined in — once we stepped ashore.

That was my shadow. Until now I'd made myself forget. Now I made myself remember.

And I'd done something even more stupid. I'd forgotten to look at a map. I went in and got out my one-inch-scale Ordnance Survey.

Immediately I found another missing link. Mrs Hepplestone's fields ran down to the sea marshes at the estuary's northern shore. Exactly opposite, a small crossed square was printed on the map's blue ocean. 'Platform (dis)', it said.

It fitted into an unpleasant scheme. Old Hepplestone had copied a firefly cage, carving it beautifully in coal. But he had made the legs and base exactly like those of the gun platform — no harm in that, surely? After all, he'd seen it often enough from his wife's lovely estate. Yet there was this irksome little secret hollow leg with the shiny bottom. Empty, but undoubtedly a hell of a lot of time and trouble to make. How odd, to work so cleverly merely to draw attention to an empty hole. *Unless he was drawing attention to something on the sea fort itself?*

A steady stream of nicked antiques had vanished and never been recovered. Now the point is, that the gun platforms aren't just planks on a trestle. Each was a compact fortress garrisoned by a whole artillery company, and capable of resisting assault and blockade. Plenty of room out there for stolen antiques to wait in solitude for eventual collection by night boats.

Dolly came back as I folded the map away. I was glad

to see her. The beautiful woman had brought a portable battery television set and a bottle of wine. I gave her a real heroine's welcome. She might not know it, I swore fervently, but she's going to stay here tonight if I have to rope her to the sink. She seemed delighted at her reception.

CHAPTER 12

I needed a boat.

For a whole thirty-six hours I worked like, well, a donkey. My old Bible box got the full treatment.

If money was needed — seeing wealthy Mrs Hepplestone had scotched my phoney advert — I had to sacrifice a lifetime of principles and make it look the best preserved antique in the kingdom.

Oak fades with age to a displeasing dry pallor, so it's a unique problem. Normally I hate tricks with antiques. I've had more fights and spilled more pints over this evil than any other kind of sin, but it's so common nowadays that antique dealers — and even real people — think it's perfectly proper. And 'restoring' the surface patina invariably ups the value — to the unknowing. Some burkes in our trade have so little sense they'll sandblast and varnish anything that stops still long enough.

A Bible box is anything up to three feet long, usually oak, with a simple plain desk-type lid. If it had been teak the wood's own natural oils would have preserved it. So a gentle rub with a little trichlorethylene (open the windows or your liver rots), then a little teak oil and it comes up lovely. 'Cheap and easy,' we dealers say of teak. I'm really fond of anything that looks after itself like that. Oak can't. In fact it evolves different acids which spoil bronzes, medallions and even some pewter so you have to be careful what you use oak furniture for.

While Dolly went home to win her badges back, I set to. Germoline came to listen while I explained. Some Victorian swinger eager for a bit more gloom had painted it a filthy brown. I began scraping the paint off with broken glass. Some French restorers even use corrosive chemicals and a hose-pipe. I once saw a bloke in a filthy Rouen garage, hosing down a long-suffering bureau as if it was modern gunge. Scraping with a piece of broken glass sounds worse but it's the kindest method. I never use gloves. If my fingers start bleeding it serves me right for pressing too hard. After all, doctors still use plate glass fragments for cutting the thinnest possible sections for electron microscopes, which only goes to show something or other.

The trouble is that 'restoring' isn't restoring at all. It's pretence, a sort of underhand trick. That's why I hate it. You remove all traces of that lovely human warmth, that precious care lavished on a piece of furniture for centuries, that priceless chance of contact with your ancestors. Then you replace it with a splash from a tin. It's a disgusting process.

You need to wash furniture that has 'slid', as we say. I use a little gentle detergent in warm water and a soft shoebrush, with a painter's Rowney S240 nylon brush for the crannies. A careful wipe with some old underpants, then air it on a towel in the open.

I had something to tell Germoline and this was the right moment. 'Coffee break, Germoline.' She plodded round the back after me.

I got her a bucket of water and brewed up for myself. Donkeys drinking are really quite interesting. Germoline's nostrils seemed to go under the surface but not so she spluttered. We rested on the grass beside the Bible box.

'Look, pal,' I said after a few hesitations. 'Devlin did Drummer over, and left you both on the dunes, right? It's something to do with that old gun fort, the one you can see from your dune but not from Joe's lookout. You and Drummer saw Devlin's boat up to something.'

Nobody in their right mind would bury anything on the dunes, because our dunes shift and erode. So it had to be the old sea fort.

'But whereabouts in it?' I asked Germoline softly, giving her a handful of grass. 'It'd take a month to search a place that huge. It'd be like searching a whole ship. Useless . . .'

Germoline stopped noshing and looked at me. I looked back.

'Unless that cage told us exactly *where* and *how*.'

We went back to work, thinking of all those break-ins at Mrs Hepplestone's.

The next bit's unpleasant. You use potassium hydroxide—caustic potash—and all the care in the world because it's dangerous to eyes, skin and everything else you've got. It is necessary to wash the caustic solution off, and this has to be done fast. You need the caustic to alter the oak's colour. Don't wait to see it darken—the oak knows what to do. A swift (five to ten seconds) application and then wash it *all* off, or crystals of the horrible stuff will 'flower' out in ugly little encrustations just when you think you've finished a marvellous job and you'll have to start all over again. Remember all woods are different. Spanish chestnut, for example, goes a rich red under this treatment.

Germoline gave me a nudge just as I'd ended this phase. Eight or nine children were carrying books up the lane to meet the library van. Germoline was doubtless wanting to get down to some hard slog carrying them about like she normally did on the sands.

'Bloody pest,' I reprimanded angrily, but downed tools.

'We aren't to fetch you any more books, Lovejoy.' That

was Ginny, a prim seven-year-old, getting her spanner in first as I came out. 'Miss Smith says you don't return them on time.'

'Miss Smith can get knotted,' I said. I wasn't going to be lectured to by a bossy infant. 'Come and see my donkey.'

They were disbelieving at first but crowded excitedly in. Germoline was a fantastic success.

'A saddle!'

'And a *cart*!'

I took the opportunity of exercising authority, my first and only time, and said sternly, 'Germoline is a specially trained sand-donkey. She's an expert, so do exactly as she lets you. Proper turns.'

'Please, Lovejoy. How do we strap her in?' Trust Ginny.

'Er—'

'You don't know, Lovejoy.' That was Dobber, her scornful little cousin, a two-catapult psychopath of considerable local fame.

I rammed my fist under his nose and threatened to knock his emerging teeth back into his gums. 'I'm not telling you how. It's a test, see? The one who fastens the straps right gets first go.'

They fell about laughing, to my annoyance, while I skulked back to my restoration and let them get on with it.

If you wax antique oak furniture immediately after stripping, something grotty happens. The oak becomes utterly dull, finishing up a miserable grey colour that will never polish up for the rest of its gloomy life. You have to 'lift' it, as we say. Hydrogen peroxide lifts quickly, but the necessary strength (120 volumes is about right) will bleach you as well as every stitch you wear, so watch out. Oxalates are fast too, but need a ghastly pantomime with kettles of hot water. I advise dilute hydrochloric acid and copious washing. It's moderately safe as long as you mind your eyes. My rule is to know where every drop goes, and to wash a million times afterwards.

I locked the workshop door. Actually the oak looked little different even after its acid and water washes when I took it out for its second dry.

Germoline was happily trundling her cartload of children round the garden. Ginny had decided a rider in addition was too much, so a queue had formed. Two at a time rode inside, or one on the saddle.

'We're careful about your pram, Lovejoy,' Gwen called. She meant my ancient little Ruby, overgrown in the long grass. 'Ginny stopped Dobber from lighting its candles.'

'Great.' I wrung a promise out of the mob not to chop my box into firewood while I went in the kitchen for a spirit burner.

With the children's excited racket as background I put a small pan of water over the burner and stood a pot in it. Five ounces of beeswax to a pint of turpentine and stir every three minutes. When I did this first, everything caught fire. Now I have an old dustbin lid and some sacks on hand in case. Make sure the oak is absolutely dry, then brush the wax on with a one-inch decorator's brush, missing no part out, and dry it again. The next bit is really murder unless you know how. I keep a fantail burner blowlamp to get a good spread of flame on the solid beeswax. A local beekeeper gives me that. One pass of the waxblock through the flame, and then you rub it hard on the oak. Every so often you whisk the flame over where you've rubbed. Don't for heaven's sake plonk a block on and just melt it or it'll take ages to clean the great molten mass of crud off. Patiently ease the beeswax in, using the flame as a gentle nudge, remembering that a hell of a lot of bees have a vested interest in your progress. Once done, a stiff carpenter's flatbrush removes the excess wax. The edges are shined up by a small mahogany burnisher. (Just cut the edge of a piece of mahogany at a 50-degree angle, then give the edge two or three soft rubs using grade 100 glass paper. The world's best burnisher. It will last you years and gives a shine nothing else can impart.) Then out into fresh air.

Done.

I sat back on my heels looking at the box. 'Sorry, mate,' I said apologetically. 'But it had to be. I need some money to murder someone.'

'*What* did you say, Lovejoy?'

Oho. Hepzibah Smith, sexy blonde choirmistress and volunteer librarian for the travelling van which brings culture to our midst. I cursed myself for carelessness, rising sheepishly to say hello. 'Hello, you flaxen Saxon.' I grinned with false heartiness.

'Please, miss. Lovejoy was only talking to his box,' Dobber explained.

'I hurt it,' I said, feeling the embarrassment of having restored it.

'Aw,' the children chorused sympathetically.

'It's beautiful, Lovejoy,' little Ginny said.

And it was. We were in a circle, the box on its towel in the centre. It emitted a lustrous honey-gold iridescence. With the natural brilliance any antique acquires from its centuries of love and life, it dazzled us all. I swear even the flinty Miss Smith caught her breath in the momentary silence. Hepzibah broke the spell.

'Yes, well,' she said critically. 'Anybody who talks to a box is silly.'

'Lovejoy has a donkey,' little Dobber pointed out, eyes narrowed for argument.

'And you haven't,' I told Hepzibah maddeningly.

She broke through the rising chorus of explanations. 'That doesn't explain why you children failed to bring your books to the library van. You've made us late for Dragonsdale. Come along, all of you, this instant.'

'Dragonsdale?' We all trooped down to the lane. I had a brainwave. 'If you see Mrs Hepplestone there, tell her I'll drive for her in the ploughing match.'

She laughed, giving me an odd look. 'Are you serious, Lovejoy? I didn't know you could.'

'Saturday, isn't it?' I said airily, blowing on my fingernails to show I moved in high society. 'Been driving for years.'

I was waving them off as Dolly's car swung in.

She climbed out with a bag of shopping. 'What on earth's been happening here, Lovejoy?'

'Oh, nothing. Giving some children donkey rides.'

She fell about at that. 'How very pastoral, Lovejoy.'

I let her go on laughing as we went in. Well, I couldn't tell her I'd spent the peaceful hours working out how to kill Devlin, could I?

He now stood accused, tried and convicted. Being a law-abiding sort of bloke, I would first let Maslow know the result of my mental trial.

Then the execution.

CHAPTER 13

There was no question where I'd sell my precious Bible box to some undeserving swine. Once a week there's a gathering of antique dealers called Ye Olde Antiques Fayre in the Red Lion. The only antique you can be sure of, though, is the Red Lion itself, this being well documented since the Romans first brewed up on the site. I was sad to be harnessing Germoline up that morning, but I had other reasons for going.

I had to create a disturbance, to draw Devvo out, now Devlin and I both knew the game. And I was eager to see which dealer Maud had in tow, as she worked her way through us, so to speak, in her blundering attempts to unravel the mystery her old uncle had left. My Bible box went easily into an old pillowcase. No sign of rain. I asked Germoline to gee up please and we hit the road. At the chapel crossroads our bobbie George Jilks was nodding off, vigilant as ever on the chapel bench. I woke him after asking Germoline politely to hold it a second.

'Sorry, George.' I gave him a moment to splutter awake. 'But supposing I knew who killed somebody?'

'Eh?' His eyes cleared, focused. 'What the hell you up to, Lovejoy?'

I gave up. No use explaining to a nerk like George. 'Tell Maslow from me that Devlin killed Drummer. Cheers.'

I invited Germoline to proceed, George trotting after us frantically trying to scribble in his notebook. As if he can write.

'Maslow knows where, when and how, George,' was all I would say. 'Just tell him.'

He dashed in to phone as we passed his house. I was glad. I felt conspicuous enough driving a donkey cart without having the Keystone Kops making matters worse.

I whistled all the way to town. My personal disturbance was nicely under way.

Town was agog, or what passes for agog in dozy East Anglia. Lots of cars and folk, a small autumn fair in the park and a shirt-sleeved band parping away. The flea-market was in the coaching yard. Margaret blew a kiss, looking unhappily frozen in about six coats as I arrived to a chorus of catcalls. Helen gave me a distant nod. Wrong again. Oh, well. Patrick yoohooed. Lily had forked out for the best patch in the yard for him, facing the main gateway. Lucky old Patrick.

'Don't bring that *beast* in here, Lovejoy,' he screamed, doing a theatrical swoon.

'Get stuffed. Whoa, please.'

Eddie Trasker came over sheepishly as I climbed down. 'Stall money, mate.'

'Don't want one, Eddie. This cart's my stall.'

'Er . . .' Eddie's quite good on late Georgian furniture but weak on donkey parking law. He's a jaunty chequer-suited extrovert everybody likes, so he gets all the rotten jobs like collecting dues.

I turned Germoline round but secretly I was worried about the cart. How do you keep it still? Germoline has no brakes. 'Stay!' I ordered. 'Please.' A good fifty customers were in among the twenty or so antique stalls. Don Musgrave and Margaret were already wrapping stuff for happy customers and Jason had sold a good walnut Canterbury to a bloke who was wreaking havoc backing his car to load up.

Tinker hove in, tattered and bloodshot, instantly all over the Bible box.

'Restored it, Lovejoy? How much we asking?'

'Don't breathe on it,' I cracked. 'You'll strip it again with that breath.' Tinker received the price I quoted for him without surprise and drifted off to put the whisper round.

Within ten minutes I'd sold the box to Jason for a really good mark-up, though not without a pang of genuine grief. He took it off reverently in its protective pillow-case. I gave Tinker his back commission, which made him thirsty and reminded him it was opening time. I could see the nondescript figure of Lemuel feverishly beckoning this news from the pub window.

I shrugged. 'All right, you can go. But find me a set of personal cruets, Tinker. Eighteen-thirties.' This always happens, money burning my pocket when it's earmarked for other purposes.

'Eh? What's a personal cruet?'

'Noshing wasn't always sharing the same sauce bottle

like in Woody's,' I told him caustically. Once upon a time, elegance dictated that guests should be given individual silver pepper and salt-cellars at dinner. I've always wanted a cased set.

He grinned farewell and was off like a ferret. By nightfall the job would be done, deserving a tipsy celebration in the White Hart. A hand tapped my shoulder. Honestly, I was actually smiling as I turned. Here we go, I thought cheerfully. Personal disturbance Part Two. I'm always at my best when hate shows the way.

' 'Morning, Inspector,' I beamed. 'Isn't shopping hell?'

'In there, Lovejoy.' He hadn't brought an army, which was a pity. I wanted spectators, mayhem, blood all round the frigging town. The mob of dealers and customers thronged to a standstill.

'No,' I said, being poisonously cheerful. When you're being pushed about by the Old Bill happiness is big medicine.

'You passed on a message—'

'Pigeon reached you, did it?' At least three customers were still focused on Margaret's early Stonebridge ware. I yelled, 'Pay attention, everybody.'

Maslow started sweating, conscious that the good old public was all ears and him not exactly bobby-dazzling. He went for pomp, silly fool. 'Conduct liable to cause a breach of the peace—'

I boomed heartily, 'Devlin killed Drummer. That's k-i-double-l-e-d. I warned you before it happened. Where and when. So like I mean, sod off.'

Nearby the band played erratically on. Cars and noise filled the High Street. But inside the coachyard you could have sliced the appalled silence with a blunt shovel. I leant forward to him confidentially. The crowd leaned with me, breathless to catch the next bit.

'I could sell you a lovely Georgian pendant, a bargain—'

He went then, pushed through the frozen mob.

I bawled after him, 'I'll not let you forget, Maslow. I've posted the details to the Chief Constable—' No good. He vanished among the shoppers across the street. Margaret came by me apprehensively but I was grinning like a fiend.

'What on *earth*, Lovejoy?'

'It's my new image.' I felt on top of the world—money in my pocket, antiques nearby and vengeance at hand.

'You'll get yourself arrested, Lovejoy,' Jason prophesied. Jenny Bateman ruefully shook a warning finger. All this made me notice the silver eggcase Jason was busily overpricing on his stall. Staring intently at it with my Bible box money corroding my jacket made me notice the early seventeenth-century stumpwork box next to it. Which made me spot a dazzling Queen Anne baby-walker—basically a walnut wood ring, just big enough for a toddler's waist, held between four finialled wooden balls separated by brilliantly turned 'stretchers' or rods. Which made me notice, sweating with excitement, a pile of old theatrical playbills. These currently average no more than half a day's wages, and they're rocketing. Feeling great, I paused for a fatal second. It'd do no harm just to look . . .

Of course I should have first collared Brad about hiring a boat, or phoned Joe Poges at Barncaster Staithe, or maybe the glamorous Doc Meakin—she had a million nautical patients and was bound to have some idea. Instead I finished up an hour later with the stumpwork box—it's a kind of embroidery in which ornamented scenes are fetched out in relief. You get religious scenes, pastoral motifs or moral exhortations on jewellery boxes or vanity purses. Sequins, pearls and occasionally coloured glass beads are worked into the design which, I warn you, isn't to everybody's taste. But the value of stumpwork has soared because three centuries ago women couldn't resist showing little scenes of domestic and other worthwhile labour.

I'm making excuses. All right. I bought it from Jason for about half its value. And the collection of old theatre playbills. And gave Jenny Bateman a deposit on a carved beechwood chair of the Great Civil War period, the first time cane-bottomed chairs made sitting almost comfortable. I got it for half its true value. (A tip, learned the hard way: never forget that the 'true' value is what you can sell something for *the same day you buy it*.)

But it wasn't all self-indulgence. During those two hours I collected gossip about thirty-one antiques nicked in the past three months, about half from my mates. Naturally only the honest dealers had reported the thefts, which meant Margaret—no antique dealer welcomes investigations round his doorstep. Taxmen have long ears. I was impressed by Devvo's industry. No wonder he was our most regular attender at local auctions. How else could he gather reliable information about who had what? It was then I had my one stroke of luck.

A raucous shout made me turn with interest. Mannie, large as life. He is a youth who showed up two years ago as a tourist—a real one—off a coach. He took one look at our antiques arcade and bade a delighted farewell to his astonished coach party. Tell Mum not to cry and everything. He stayed and became one of us. I pushed my way through to where he lounged with this long-case clock.

'For you, Lovejoy,' he greeted me straight off, 'ten per cent discount.'

Mannie has two styles of dress—the new straggly filth look, or a multicoloured caftan thing with bells and a striped pointed cap. Never anything on his feet. It looked like the Dalai Llama had hit town.

'You'll catch your death, Mannie.'

'I've not mucked about with the white face, Lovejoy,' Mannie said earnestly. 'Notice it?'

'Good heavens!' My pretence was a bit theatrical because nobody in their right mind can miss a genuine white-faced long-caser. Especially Mannie. He was half asleep. 'Go back to bed, Mannie. You're knackered.'

He gave a rueful grin. 'Daren't. Left this bird there. I had to fight my way to the door.' He plucked me closer while I examined his clock. 'Here. Know anything about Japanese boxes?' He fumbled in his clothes to a jingle of prayer bells, smoothed the crumbled paper he somehow managed to find. A crude outline sketch of a firefly cage on ordinary notepaper. So Maud had found time for something else during the night besides romping with Mannie.

'Search me.' I hardly glanced at it, ducking the mystery for the moment. The clock was dazzling me anyway.

Nowadays 'grandfather' (properly called long-case) clocks have become something rather special. Twenty years ago they were a space problem, a polishing problem, a servicing difficulty and a plague to keep looking just right. You couldn't give them away. I remember as a lad seeing our auctioneer begging anybody to take two pianos and a derelict long-caser for half a crown. Nowadays everybody's crazy for them, and they cost you the earth.

'No good, Mannie,' I lied. 'No gold tracery decoration.'

'Doesn't matter, does it?'

Long-case clocks are a whole new area of ignorance. If you see a dial embellished with gold tracery you're on to a rare pre-1800 model, such as Thomas Crawshaw made in Rotherham about 1792. The actual dials were sub-contracted out, mostly to Birmingham craftsmen of the calibre of Osbourne or Byrne. Mannie's antique was brilliant, a genuine Samuel Deacon masterpiece. Sam was a merry soul from Barton in Leicestershire who bought his dials from James Wilson, again a Birmingham dialler and who was Osbourne's partner until they had words in

1777. Wilson became a front runner in the fashion of japanning. Remember that the name you see displayed on the dial is the clockmaker's, not the dialler's. It's important—a dial from a prominent dialler makes a wrecked long-case clock worth twice as much as even the best superbly preserved specimen. Always look behind for the iron 'falseplate' on the dial's back. The dialler's name is often engraved there.

'Sorry, Mannie. I need a brassfacer.'

'Never seen one, Lovejoy.'

The first long-case clocks before 1770 had brass faces. Some modern fakers even get the silvered engraving right, so watch out. The white dial fashion is what people want nowadays, though. Don't make the mistake Margaret did. She once turned down a 'porcelain china' dial clock because the dial was neither porcelain nor china. Those terms were only descriptive—the process is a kind of so-called 'japanning', stove-hardening of repeated layers of paint (usually white) applied to iron sheeting. Word is that Osbourne and Wilson were the first-ever dial makers to do it. I have my doubts, though they claimed this to their dying day.

Mannie had dozed off in all this excitement, people all round grinning at him. I kicked him awake and we fixed a price. With the long-case loaded on Germoline's cart, I gave him what I had left for deposit and promised the rest of the money by weekend, may heaven forgive honest liars. Helen found me an old car blanket.

I had a sudden thought. 'Here, Mannie. That Japanese box . . .'

He grinned sheepishly. 'Just a bird who wants to see one. I don't suppose there'd be much in it. Anyway,' he dismissed the matter, 'she said it has to be before Sunday.'

I was hitching Germoline when Brad drifted over and showed me the price of hiring a boat. His relative Terry had written it down. 'Eh?' I'd never seen so many noughts. 'For a bloody battleship maybe—'

He got narked. 'Look, Lovejoy. I passed Patrick's message to my brother. He's quoted a reasonable price . . .'

I reeled off, broken, realizing my stupidity. I now hadn't enough money left for an hour's hire, let alone the three days I'd need to search the sea fort. I'd finished up with antiques but no money. Therefore no boat and no chance of one.

And Mannie had said *before* Sunday.

I felt ill but kept my air of bright friendliness up almost to the bottom of North Hill. There I had to stop and have a shaky half pint in the Sun yard. I'd have had a whole one but Germoline scraped her hoof, so I had to stand like a fool while she slurped the rest.

Sometimes I despise myself. Germoline's stony stare tipped me off why she was mad at me. 'I couldn't help it.' I muttered it under my breath so people wouldn't think I'd gone loony talking to a donkey. 'I didn't know how much a neffie boat costs, did I?'

She said nothing back but I felt the reproachful vibes.

'I'll get a boat,' I said in her ear. 'Just you see.'

Secretly, though, I was glad. No boat meant no terrifying gun platform out on lonely sea. All right, so it meant Devlin would get away with murdering Drummer. All *right*. But why has it always to be good old Lovejoy doing the risky necessary? What the hell's the bloody Old Bill for? They cost enough. Let Maslow do it. I beamed all this psychic logic into Germoline's head but only got accusations of cowardice psyched back.

It was in this happy situation that Maud joined us, arriving in a pink sports Lotus. A mile of engine soldered to a hutch.

'Lift, Lovejoy?'

'Not you again, Maudie.'

She smiled up from her reclining position, looking

ready for blast-off. Earrings, cleavage, I got the whole treatment. I'd never seen so much thigh, and she'd made no move to get out. Why are fast cars only knee-high?

'It's you and me, Lovejoy,' she said calmly. 'We both know it. Don't bugger about.'

The engine went thrum, thrum. I knew how it felt.

'And your pal Devvo?'

'He's playing it too close.' She was delighted at the obvious effect her presence was having on me. 'I *know* Uncle Bill's cage was some sort of clue. To a fortune. I think you know how it links with Devlin's deal. The point is, we've not much time left.'

I didn't let on I'd learned about the deadline from Mannie. 'I do?' All innocent.

'You're the only one, Lovejoy!' Her tongue raked her mouth, wet her lips. Trying to look away didn't help. 'You're crazy for me, Lovejoy, and I want you. Admit it. Between us we'd clean up.' Her face was lovely in that instant, a revelation. 'Not a one-night stand, Lovejoy. I want you for good. Ten minutes of me and you'll never look at another woman.'

'First things first, Maudie.'

If she'd been anyone else I'd have thought her look full of compassion. 'What *is* first with you, Lovejoy? That fat geriatric mare Dolly?'

'Antiques, as always.'

'You're wrong, honey.' She revved her engine. 'It's hate. You'll not rest till you've killed somebody.' Her car slid into a slow reverse and her pretty head tilted. 'My offer refused?'

'What else?' What did she expect? It had felt like a tax demand.

She smiled brilliantly. 'We'll see.'

I climbed angrily into the cart, nodding to Harry Bateman who was just pulling in for a feebly earned whisky. It was Harry's chance remark that put me back in

Germoline's favour—and back on the warpath, through no fault of my own.

'You ploughed that profit quick enough, Lovejoy,' he called.

Ploughed? I asked Germoline to cool it a second. A pause. I gazed about and saw Liz Sandwell arrive, chatting Mel Young up about his watercolours. He's English watercolours, and currently had one by Edward Dayes, who taught the immortal Girtin. She was doing what we are all doing these days: going after the early lesser-known watercolourists. While they're still seriously underpriced you can still make a killing—I mean a fortune, of course.

Harry and Mel zoomed past into the tap room when I collared Liz. 'Your village show this Saturday. Going?'

'Hello, Lovejoy. Yes, all of us turn up.' She gauged me coolly. 'Thinking of setting up a stall?'

'The ploughing competition. A friend,' I lied brightly. 'He wants to enter. Is there a prize?'

She laughed. 'Tell him not to bother. A handsome blacksmith wins them all.'

'What's the prize?' I asked casually.

'A new car,' Liz said. 'Wish your friend luck.'

I nearly fell off the cart but clung on as Germoline trundled us out into the stream of traffic.

A whole motor-car, I marvelled. For driving a grotty tractor up and down a field a few times? A gift. A new car. I ask you. Well, I can drive a tractor. Drive it straight and you've won. Get your furrows parallel—bingo!

'Hear that?' I chirped at Germoline as we went. 'I'll win the valuable new motor Saturday morning—boat hire Saturday afternoon. Wealth and justice Saturday evening!'

We clopped merrily home. I stopped in our village post office and phoned Mrs Hepplestone to tell her that by Saturday she would be the ecstatic possessor of the ploughing championship trophy that had long evaded her. I'd drive her estate to victory.

She was doubtful. 'Are you quite sure, Lovejoy?' she asked uncertainly. 'They're very difficult. When Miss Smith gave me your offer to plough for me at the contest I naturally assumed it was some kind of joke.'

So had I, then. I chuckled lightly. 'Never fear— Lovejoy's here,' I cracked. 'As long as there's no rule against antique dealers . . . ?'

She assured me there was none.

'See you Saturday,' I promised.

We paused at the White Hart, Germoline's unerring intuition at work. I decided to say nothing about my forthcoming triumph to my mates in the saloon bar. I've driven tanks in deserts, halftracks in swamps, once a hovercraft on an ocean, and sundry tractors in the apple harvest. Claude might be a tough blacksmith but I was sure to be odds on.

That night I was the last of the big spenders and got sloshed. Germoline had a forgiving pint too. We reeled drunkenly home at one in the morning, me singing 'Farmer's Boy' and Germoline's hooves scuffing happily in time all the way down the lane.

CHAPTER 14

It was a fighting day. Thankfully I was fresh and wide awake. Germoline snickered as I fed her; she too was raring to go. We were on the Dragonsdale road by nine.

I don't know if you've been to these fairs in East Anglia. They're a real yawn. You do nothing except hang about and try the odd shilling on catchpenny stalls like rolling wooden balls at hoops and such enthralling pastimes. The money goes to some dubious charity, though all charity's dubious. There's sometimes racing, occasionally a few tipsy knights jousting each other off tubby nags and women selling hot grub. If the weather's fine everybody tends to dress up. What with the green grass and the flower show and the bands it's really average, especially if nothing else happens for the rest of the East Anglian year, which it doesn't.

By the time Germoline pulled us in I was unpleasantly aware of the disadvantages of donkey travel. Most of my mates had overtaken us, honking hooters noisily as they burned past. You know the kindly way friends do. I told Germoline what a drag she was but I could tell from her ears she wasn't taking a blind bit of notice. I tethered her to a handy tree in the car park, just a field with cars in it.

'Watch her, mate,' I told the attendant, a shapely bird in wellingtons. 'I'll reward you afterwards.'

'How sweet!' she cried, promising to feed Germoline at halftime. I left the bag of oats in the cart with a plastic raincoat in case it rained. She was about to say more when Liz Sandwell hove in to leave her motor near the gate.

' 'Morning, Lovejoy,' she interrupted sweetly. 'And Viv. Working hard, Viv?'

' 'Morning, Liz,' Viv said, moving off with a glance that meant I had rotten friends.

Liz slammed her door and we set off across to the marquees. 'She's engaged to the vicar, Lovejoy,' Liz said with relish. 'Incidentally, is it true you're going in for the furrow match?'

'*Win*, Liz,' I corrected. 'I need the money.'

'You don't stand a chance. You're a million to one.'

I shook my head disbelievingly. I can never understand these country bumpkins. Anybody can drive a blinking tractor, after all.

The crowds were gathering. It was something past ten and the judges were already writing those rude remarks on the flower exhibitors' cards. Two bands were practising the same melody, their fine uniforms laid across their knees. As they played their eyes flicked across to the opposition, sussing out the strengths of the enemy. Later in the day the adjudicators would come and be imprisoned blindfolded in the small caravan, so as not to be able to bias their scores in favour of their own village band. Like most good theories, this has never worked because people balls it up. I suppose that's why they stay theories.

'Your friend, Lovejoy,' Liz warned me. Across the open car park a great square-looking Rolls had drifted silently into a spare acre, dwarfing the rest of the motors. Devvo. I checked Viv's whereabouts. Fortunately a small throng of infants had materialized and were crowding round Germoline. She would be safe. Oddly, I saw her looking across at the Rolls. Funny if donkeys had good memories.

'Did you get in trouble saying those things about Devlin?' Liz couldn't avoid asking.

'Just because he murdered Drummer?' I shot back. 'Where's the harm in a little gossip?'

She gave me a peck on the cheek. 'I like you, Lovejoy,' she said. 'You're a big softie, but I'm afraid you're going to make a fool of yourself today.'

'Stick around, baby,' I growled, doing my Bogart.

We had stopped by an open roped circle in the centre of the show grounds. A notice announced 'Drivers this way' with arrows. The circle was crammed with monster horses, great things the size of a bungalow. The tractors were probably in the other field. I for one was walking round, not elbowing my way through that lot.

'I'll stroll round, love.' I backed away as one great beast ambled closer. Horses and things always come up to me. 'I know they're supposed only to eat grass, but—'

Liz looked at me, stricken. 'But, Lovejoy. *They're* the teams. For ploughing.'

'Eh?' I almost fainted. 'I'm driving a frigging tractor, you stupid cow,' I bleated.

'No, love. You plough with horses.'

'I'm here to drive a tractor,' I insisted.

'But *anybody* can drive a tractor, Lovejoy. Horses are the test.' I flopped on the ground, broken. Liz sat beside me. 'Does it matter so much to you?'

Claude the blacksmith and a few gnarled farmers were strolling among the giant beasts, patting and prodding and lifting hooves. No wonder people had thought my entering the competition was a joke, especially when I'd gone bragging I'd win hands down. I couldn't even drive Germoline, let alone these beasts. I put my head in my hands. I could have wept.

'I can hook Devlin for killing Drummer if I get the prize. I need the money.'

'How?' she asked, but one glance at my face told her it was no sale. 'Look, Lovejoy. Can't you borrow the prize from Claude? Or money from somebody?'

'Look at me, Liz.' I held my hands out to make the point. 'Who'd lend Lovejoy Antiques a bent penny? Would you?' A bit cruel, but it drove it home. After yelling blue murder in the middle of town everybody must think I was off my head anyway.

'Haven't you anything to . . . ?' Liz tried to help.

I had the antiques, at least, even if they were not paid for. But getting round the dealers on a Saturday would be hopeless. Still, I had to try. Tonight was some sort of deadline out on the old sea fort.

'And there's your little donkey,' Liz was saying.

'I couldn't sell her.'

'No,' Liz exclaimed impatiently. 'Donkey rides. The children love her. Drummer used to bring her to village shows.'

It was true. One thing Germoline knew about was giving donkey rides. I grabbed Liz and hurried her back through the growing crowds as they began to pour from the car field.

'How do I do it? How much do I charge?'

'You remember, as a kid, for heaven's sake,' Liz said, exasperated. 'You mark a place out with those little coloured flags and Germoline takes people round.'

I glimpsed Viv's blonde hair in the distance and whistled urgently. 'Will you help, Liz?' I asked feverishly. 'I'll nick some flags if you'll shout—'

'Honestly, Lovejoy. You're hopeless.'

In about half an hour I was doing brisk business among the marquees. I'd pinched several small pieces of bunting. With string I got from a woman in the grub tent and a few sticks off the hedges I manufactured quite passable marker flags. Germoline was brilliant. She knew the game all right and enjoyed it except when a crowd of yobbos came scurrying through the mob once. Apart from that I did a roaring trade for over an hour, and started doing great.

Helen came and had a cart ride, tipping Germoline a quid which was decent of her. I saw her deep in conversation with Liz and caught her glancing my way. Maybe she thought I'd gone bonkers too. But I forged on, working the crowd and trying to look all paternal the way Drummer did, a sort of cut-price Santa Claus. I got the children rolling in by letting my own supporters, those who'd backed me up when confronted by Hepzibah Smith in my garden that time, have free rides. Germoline occasionally gave extra distances, moving to the band music in and out among my stolen flags. She was great value, Germoline, that morning. I have to give her that. Probably knew it was in a good cause.

A few of the lads hove in to give the bric-à-brac stall the glad eye. This is practically routine among even the most expensive antique dealers. Don't laugh. The only genuine Elizabethan gold and garnet ring in our museum was bought on such a stall last year—for fifty pence. And I once picked up enough profit for a new thatch on my cottage from a set of four Mayer plates which I got for less than a pound. Antique dealers underrated them because *Hausmaler* work is thought to be beneath posh dealers (though nobody turns a nose up at the vast profit they bring these days). A *Hausmaler* is a home painter of white porcelain, usually bought from factories as 'seconds'—ie: faulty. The home painter flourished in the eighteenth century. Franz Mayer was the best of the Bohemians. He bought rejects from Meissen to decorate. He was mad on flowers. People say his enamels aren't up to much but I like them. One tip: if you see a painted insect (beetle, fly, butterfly) on a decorated plate, with nothing at all to do with the theme of the plate's painting, have a quick shufti to see if the insect is painted over a small defect. If it is, you probably have in your hands a *Hausmaler* work. For some reason they're particularly common in East Anglia. They're the first thing I look for at these village fairs. You never need pay more than a tenth of their value. Dead easy profit.

I'd quite forgotten the ploughing by twelve. I was made to remember it in a particularly unpleasant way. Germoline had just taken off with a cartload of four children and one infant, with Liz laughing exasperatedly in close attendance and myself keeping a queue of kids under a semblance of control. Then the sun went out of the sky.

' 'Morning, Lovejoy.' Maslow again. 'Step this way.'

'Don't jump the queue, please,' I said, quick as a flash. 'Make him, Constable.'

George Jilks, my own treacherous village nerk, took my arm. I stepped aside from the children. Maslow had a second constable rocking on his heels nearby, thoughtful lad.

'Licence?'

'Eh?'

'You need a licence for trading, Lovejoy.' He grinned without humour. 'Don't tell me you've forgotten another point of law. And can I see your declaration of income tax—?'

'Cut it, Maslow.' I shook George's arm off and shoved my face at Maslow's. 'I'm doing this for a good cause.' Then I paused. Ho hum.

'What good cause?' He peered at me. 'I'm waiting. Would it be anything to do with Mr Devlin?'

'Er . . .'

'And while we're at it, Lovejoy,' he added smoothly, 'I want to know by what authority you maintain a commercial animal for hire.'

'Don't tell me I need a licence for that too?' The creep. 'Liz,' I shouted. 'Over here.' Liz put an older girl in charge and came back, sobering as she saw my visitor and the uniforms. A small crowd was gathering and was listening curiously. 'Liz will vouch for me, won't you?'

'Er . . . for what, exactly?'

'For . . . well, giving a safe, er, desirable service to the, er, community . . .' I halted lamely. Maslow was grinning now.

'Book them both, Constable.'

'I'm nothing to do with this,' Liz cut in, backing off. 'I was just, er, helping . . .' She merged with the crowd, giving me a mute glance of apology.

'Thank you, miss.'

I saw Helen and waved urgently but she avoided my eyes. You couldn't blame them.

'All right, Maslow,' I said softly. 'Do what you want. But I'll kill Devlin if it's the last frigging thing I do.'

'I'm going to have you certified, Lovejoy,' he said, just as softly. 'And I'll see they stuff you away for a thousand years.'

'There you are!' a voice cooed, and Dolly, beautiful

loyal Dolly, all dressed up with a flowered hat, slipped between me and the Old Bill. She took my arm. 'Now it's really time we moved on, Lovejoy—' She broke off, noticing the bobby. 'Oh *dear*! There hasn't been an accident, has there?'

'Er, no,' I said, bewildered, wondering what the hell she was up to.

'Thank heavens!' Dolly said. 'Is this your friend?' She reached out a gloved hand which Maslow shook mechanically.

'I'm police, lady,' he managed. 'Lovejoy's under arrest.'

'What?' Dolly went all aghast. 'But . . . not for giving donkey rides, surely? In that case, you'll have to arrest me. I own the donkey and the cart, and it was at my instigation that Lovejoy kindly agreed—' I listened, stunned.

'You can only do this for a registered charity,' Maslow snapped.

'Here's our charity number,' she said sweetly, pulling a card from her handbag. 'Lady's Guild for Church Maintenance and Structure. Would you like to contribute?'

'Is there any trouble?' The vicar showed, bless him. And his fiancée Viv with him. My allies had pluralled.

'None, Reverend,' Dolly gushed. 'Lovejoy here has done a perfectly delightful thing, collecting for our church funds. Isn't that marvellous?'

'I'm deeply moved,' the padre said. I entered into the spirit of the thing and hauled out my ill-gotten gains. I even felt all choked up as I passed it over.

'That's that, then,' I told Maslow, smiling to nark him. 'Look, pals,' I said to the children. 'Look after Germoline. One ride every time the church clock strikes a quarter hour, in turn. And feed her in thirty minutes, all right?'

Having successfully swindled the shrieking mob of volunteers into serving Germoline's interests, I took Dolly's arm, leaving Maslow and his soldiery.

Dolly was really great, keeping up a meaningless chatter all the way. We flopped down exhausted as soon as we were in the shade of the tea tent.

'What was all that, Lovejoy?' she asked faintly. 'Did I do right?'

'Thanks, love. You were superb.' I kissed her feebly. At least I wasn't arrested. 'I was trying to get some money to get a boat.'

'How soon?'

'Tonight.' I saw from her face it would be hopeless. To make matters worse the tannoy croaked my name. 'Plough teams please check in,' it squawked. There was nothing for it. 'Come on,' I said. 'I've a field to plough.' I was shaking.

The improvised paddock was crowded with men and shire horses. They looked bigger than ever, and one or two seemed decidedly bad-tempered. A lot of good-natured ribbing was going on from the onlookers as I pushed my nervous way through to the ropes. Mrs Hepplestone was sitting with Squire Wainwright. Both gave me a wave. I waved back with an arm that suddenly felt rubber. Dolly was pushing my arm.

'You can't, darling,' she was saying, aghast. 'They're like in *Gulliver's Travels*.'

'Don't remind me,' I said, shaking her off. 'I've got to try.' Then I stopped, gazing quizzically back at Dolly.

'What is it, dear?'

'Gulliver.' That name. 'Wait, wait!' Wainwright's men had said there was this old bloke called Gulliver, the best ploughman in the business . . . who used to win all the competitions. I struggled to remember. That day in the burning fields. Claude was best *except for Gulliver*, who was now a drunken bum round town, a useless gambler, decrepit. It couldn't be. *Lemuel* Gulliver in Swift's famous tale. And who else knew to an ounce what a donkey ate? *Old Lemuel was the ploughing champion!*

I grabbed Dolly. 'Love, for Christ's sake,' I babbled. 'Get on the phone. Do anything—you understand, *anything*—to phone the White Hart and find Tinker. Tell him to get Lemuel here *now*. Got it?'

Her eyes were wide and alarmed. 'What if I can't?'

'Do it. Tell them to pinch a car, anything.'

She ran off towards the marquees while I swallowed hard and climbed the rope. There seemed to be a lot of chains and iron things about on the ground. People cheered raggedly as the horses were walked about in front of the stand. A group of some five men were there, Claude among them. We shook hands like wrestlers do.

'All right, Lovejoy?' he asked kindly.

'Fine, thanks.'

I was to go third. I got in the way, risking life and limb. I talked incessantly. I mislaid people's harness and lost my entry papers twice and finished up waiting while the judge irritably wrote my entry out longhand. I was frantic, struggling to spin the minutes out. You take turns, I was pleased to hear, one team going at a time.

The game consists in driving these monsters into a field and ploughing a stetch — that's a strip a few yards wide, all furrows parallel. Judges sit and watch your skills. The trouble is you have only the old-fashioned plough to do it with, one furrow every trip. For God's *sake*.

Claude had drawn first. I refused to go into the paddock to be with my team of horses, though the other drivers did. I sat with the crowd glumly watching Claude do his stuff on the sloping field. Even Jethro Tull, the great ploughing modernist of two centuries back, would have been proud of him. Half an hour and he came off his stetch sweating like a bull and sank near me like a small earthquake. I passed him my brown ale which he drained.

'You're next after this, Lovejoy,' he gasped. 'Watch the field. There's a dip midway over.'

'Thanks, Claude.' I rose miserably as the tannoy called. If I didn't go now I'd be disqualified. I had to have my team strapped together, God knows how, by the time the second team came off.

I went over to the paddock sick to my soul. The shire horses looked at me with disbelief as if asking if this was the goon they were landed with. 'I know how you feel,' I told them bitterly. I swear they almost laughed.

'Second team, now entering,' the tannoy squawked, 'is the Ashwood-Pentney team driven by Harris. Spectators please make way.'

I was stepping over the rope when a miraculous croaking cough froze me in mid-straddle. Tinker and Lemuel were pushing through the crowd beind me. Lemuel could hardly stand and Tinker looked knackered. Dolly was with them, sickly pale but pleased.

'Tinker!' I rushed at them, babbling. 'Lemuel! Is your last name Gulliver? Are you the Gulliver who—?'

'Give us a drink, Lovejoy,' he whispered, trying hard to open his eyes.

'With sugar?' Dolly asked. I love her, but Jesus.

'A drink!' I screamed. '*Beer!* Listen, Lemuel.' I grabbed him and pulled him to one side. 'Can you do this? We've got to enter and win it.'

'Fall down,' he wheezed blearily.

'Eh?' I thought I hadn't heard right.

'Fall down, you thick burke,' Tinker rasped.

I fell spectacularly, groaning. Tinker was quicker than me for all his hangover. He was already waving to the judges. They started impatiently across the paddock. I groaned, holding my belly.

'Here, sir,' Tinker was calling when Dolly trotted back

with two bottles of brown ale and a cup of tea, the innocent. 'Lovejoy's got his appendix again. He's entering a substitute.'

'This is a nuisance,' the head judge said coldly, a testy old colonel who'd hanged men for less. Charming, I thought indignantly, doing my stricken act. I really could have been dying. 'Lovejoy's done nothing but procrastinate. Who's the sub?'

'Him.' Tinker pointed to Lemuel who was busily soaking the ale back while Dolly, ever the optimist, held the cup and saucer.

'Gulliver?'

Even in mid-act I couldn't help hearing how the judge's tone changed. His impatience became respect. I let myself recover enough to see Tinker push the tottering Lemuel under the rope into the paddock. Please God, I prayed fervently. Let Lemuel get among the prizes. so I can hire a boat to kill Devlin tonight. I admit it wasn't much of a prayer.

There's a saying, isn't there, horses for courses. It applied to Lemuel like nobody else I'd ever seen before. Three parts sloshed as he was and probably never having handled a nag for some years, what he did was quite uncanny. He sort of shook himself and just walked— swaying unevenly a bit, but definitely casual—into this massive shifting mass of horses and said, 'Come here, you buggers. Let's have a gander at the lot of you.' And the horses looked round and simply did as they were told. I swear they nudged each other, pleased at having swapped a nerk like me for an acknowledged master. The crowd stilled reverently and silently paid attention to the shapeless heap called Lemuel.

He must have been some champion in his time because word shot round. Farmers poured from the beer marquee to the ploughing field. A murmur of approval rolled round the crowd as Lemuel did the oddest things, like

squeezing the shire horses' knees and smacking their
chests, really giving them a clout. Whereas I'd kept out of
their way when they showed the slightest hint of
friendliness, Lemuel just mauled them about. Like
gigantic infants, they tolerated him happily as he
prodded and thumped and strapped them. I noticed the
judges didn't shout at him like they had at me when I'd
taken my time. That's discrimination, I thought irritably.

'Ready, sir,' Lemuel called at last. He took up some
straps and flicked, and the whole ponderous team
thundered slowly from the ring towards the field, hooves
thudding in time and great heads nodding together. It
was a magnificent sight, almost beautiful. Before that I'd
always thought horses really mediocre but Lemuel,
shuffling along behind and swearing abuse, made them
almost dance. I had a lump in my throat as the spectators
rippled applause.

'See that, one-handed out of the paddock, first time?' a
farm man exclaimed near me.

'Better, Lovejoy?' Claude was by me, all eighteen stone
of him smiling in a hurt kind of way.

I was in no fit state for a scrap so I instantly showed I
was still unwell by doubling up again and groaning. Dolly
believed the act and helped me off to sit on an exposed
mound where we could see Lemuel in the distance.

'Go for some more ale, love,' I told her, making sure
Claude could see my face screwed up in pain.

'I don't think you should. They may want to operate,
dear.'

I looked at her. She was serious, actually believing my
act. 'It's for Lemuel,' I explained, making sure Claude
had gone to see our champ. 'I'm only pretending, love.'

'Thank heavens for that, Lovejoy!'

I watched her go, marvelling. Well, it had taken me
some years to link the drunken figure of Lemuel with the
mighty champion ploughman of the Eastern Hundreds,

so who was I to criticize. Smiling, I lay back peacefully, the roar of the distant crowd music in my ears.

At two o'clock the delighted Mrs Hepplestone was presented with the rose bowl for her team's success at the ploughing championships. Lemuel got the keys of his new car. I made Tinker tell him of a certain important matter of murder which I had in mind, and that his prize was required as deposit. We drove grandly down to the estuary and hired a motor launch from Terry's boatyard. Terry showed me the controls and I signed the papers with a flourish. Lemuel's new car went as security and deposit combined. Dolly drove us back to town, and then took me home to the cottage for a quiet rest before tonight's action. I promised I'd make a meal for us both when I got a minute.

CHAPTER 15

Dolly promised to stay at home all evening and all the following day in case I had to phone urgently for anything. She was white and worried, but I was beginning to think that was par for her course. We had a long snogging farewell at my gate before she drove off and I invited Germoline to crack on.

I boxed clever choosing my route. I had more sense than go along the main roads, and selected one of the old cart tracks between the farmlands. Only three miles out of our village there's a turning through the woods where the American War Cemetery stands, which saved me and Germoline miles. The wind was fairly whistling across as Germoline plodded between the rows and rows of sad heroic crucifixes. We made fair speed and reached the estuary a few furlongs below the Staithe about dusk. The big Yank's posh boat was there again, I saw in the lessening light. Mended.

The place looked as peaceful as any holiday cove, with a few noisy families packing up for the day into cars ready for home. Two yachts were riding in, just starting to show lights. An inverted cone was hoisted from Joe's station, meaning I supposed some sort of weather. The radio's always on about them, onshore winds near Dogger Bank and all that.

We went to Drummer's old hut. Germoline's ears pricked and she stared around at me as if asking what the hell. I explained as I undid her cart and stuffed her manger full of some granular material Lemuel had got her.

'It's this way, Germoline,' I told her. 'I'm going to the old fort. There's a load of nicked antiques out there, in the fort's lowest concealed room. I happen to know that because Mrs Hepplestone's old man made a model as a clue. Maybe he was in on it too; I don't know. You saw them doing the ferrying bit, didn't you, cock?' I went on. 'It's reprisal time, Germoline.' She snickered approvingly at this. She was bright for a donkey—just how bright I was yet to find out, and in the most horrible way possible, but at the time I was so full of myself I thought I was in command. 'See?' I said, patting her neck. 'Devvo will come to ship his stuff out to the continental buyers tonight, the deadline. I learned that from Mannie. And *I'll* have pinched it all!' She snickered again, over the moon at my plan. In my innocence I scratched her shoulder and added, 'Of course, he'll come for me, but I'll ram the bastard in the dark. It'll be an accident. I'm not sure if Devvo can swim, but let's hope, eh?'

This was all right, because I can swim like a fish. Anyway, I'd hoped by then to have unloaded all the recovered antiques.

'And when I come sailing back,' I chuckled, 'guess

which clever little donkey will be waiting here to cart the goodies into hiding, here in the hut?' I winked. 'I'll rescue Devvo if he confesses, by which time there'll be enough rescue boats on the scene to witness . . .'

It seemed foolproof to me then. No wonder I was grinning all over my face. I went inside and lit the lantern in Drummer's window to guide me home, and splodged my way back to the Staithe. Terry had said the boat would be all stocked up and full of petrol. I had the keys.

It was a grand thing, long and white. These modern fast craft always seem taller than necessary but I suppose our boat-builders know what they're doing. They charge enough. It had radar, and a mast with a great bulbous thing at the top and a lot of wires. 'Radar's hazy inshore, but invaluable,' Terry had said, showing me how it worked. The idiot had wanted to show me its insides. The point was that none of it seemed missing. I'd got more maps than the Navy. Anyway, I knew where I was going.

I got the engine going by simply pressing a knob by the key. The last family carful was leaving the Staithe as I moved the boat into the channel, carefully keeping my lights off though some white riding lights were showing in the lower creeks. As I turned my craft into the sea lane I could see the single flash of the lightship miles down the coast where the treacherous sands steadily ingest coastal freighters year after year.

I put her at low speed between the promontory of the clubhouse and the shipyard. Somebody flashed one handlamp at me. I ignored them. In the dusk a wind was rising steadily. That tinselly tinkling was beginning to sound again, the wires tapping on the metal masts of the yachts pulled up on the hard. Somehow comforted by the din, I smiled and glanced round at the little harbour. Plenty of lights, street neons reflecting well on the darkening sky. I was reassured. There would be plenty of help there should I need it. Surprisingly how easily lights are seen over a black sea.

'Devvo,' I bleated joyously, 'here I come.'

As I left the shelter of the harbour and the wind's force began tugging for the first time I admitted that I didn't really intend to kill Devvo or his two goons. I'd only be troublesome if they started anything. Otherwise I'd bring them tamely to justice, which was after all what it's about, isn't it? Germoline would be narked because I'd this funny feeling she wanted blood, but women are like that. Even if it did mean helping Maslow to get promotion . . .

The boat started rocking up and down on the choppy sea. Watching the waves rising against my hull made me giddy as I started out between the long dunes into the open sea. I began to discover one thing after another, all vaguely worrying. You'd point the boat at some distant light, and after a minute you'd find your bows sideways on even if you'd kept the illuminated compass perfectly still along one of the lines marked on its glass. Presumably all sorts of nasty currents moving about under the water. I had a chart telling you which way they went but hadn't time to study it seeing I'd spent the afternoon resting, so to speak, with Dolly at the cottage after my exertions of the morning's ploughing.

I must have gone zigzag for more than a mile, correcting every furlong or so on the lightship as the sky darkened. The speedo said I was going about six knots, whatever they are. I tried to make this reading sensible by spitting over the side and watching it float past but got into difficulties by not steering straight so gave it up. The cockpit had an interior lamp which I switched off. If Devvo's boat overtook mine in the darkness I didn't want him spotting me.

The motion of the boat was making me feel vaguely queasy. And I suppose the knowledge that I was drawing near to that enormous great concrete monster out there in the ocean wasn't doing me any good. Anyway, I had a knife with me, a modern piece of Scandinavian metal ten inches long which I'd nicked from one of the tacklers' harness racks that afternoon. I'm like that, a real planner. No doubt Devvo's goons would be knuckled up and maybe armed with a pistol or three. Devvo naturally would be clean as a whistle. My boat chugged on.

My face was wet from spray. The wind was cutting across me now, making my eyes water with the cold, but I could make out the red light on the old sea fort's mast. Was there some gnarled old salt left on the fort to tend the light? Nowadays they were automatic, I supposed, though you can never tell. My spirits rose. Some poor sod stationed on the wretched thing meant at least one guaranteed witness.

I decided to curve right round the fort and come at it from seaward. That would give me less of an edge by reducing the time I'd have. Devvo's merry crew would probably come direct from landward. I cracked another couple of knots on the speedo and turned south-east or thereabouts.

Coming up to a big solid mass sticking menacingly out of the sea in the dark's a frightening experience. It's also very sudden, which sounds odd unless you've done it. I'd kept my eyes on the red beacon that meant the sea fort, which had climbed slowly up the black sky the further out I got. Then it started disappearing and only coming back again when the boat rose on the swell. I tumbled that I must be getting very near and that the lip of the fort's main platform was cutting the beacon off from view. I wished now I'd had the sense to take some daylight measurements.

It was then I heard the rushing, sucking sound of those vast legs of the fort, sloshing in the water. For a moment I almost gave up and turned back. God knows what made me soldier on. It might have been lust for the antiques I hoped were concealed there, or maybe love of Dolly, to show what a hell of a bloke I was. The funny thing is that it might actually have been hatred of Devlin, as Maud alleged, a curious concept. Anyhow I kept going, cutting my speed. I felt stalled but the instruments showed otherwise. The wind had crossed me again and was now whipping at the other side, stinging my eyes with spray and making my face feel cut to ribbons. I was shivering. No wonder these yachting types dress like astronauts. Dolly had brought me a woollen hat and muffler and I have this thick short coat for long drives from the days when I had something to drive.

When the sounds got unpleasantly close I put the beam lights on, and almost swooned. I'd thought I was being careful, but now, with the yellow lamps illuminating the huge fort, I knew it had been cowardice, my typical trick of postponing anything unpleasant. I was about fifty yards off, the boat already being tugged and shoved with the crushing spread of waves round the nearest of the vast legs. There were four, of enormous girth, draped with green weeds and discoloured from corrosion. Metal stanchions had trickled their oxides like blood down the slimy legs, creating an impression of straddled limbs impaled by some giant stapler causing dirty hæmorrhages towards the fast sea. I switched into reverse and for a horrible instant thought she wasn't going to pull away. Then I was standing off about a hundred yards, pushed by the currents in a way I hadn't expected. I wasn't really frightened, but what with the cold and the rising wind and the frigging noise, not to mention that fearsome monster looming above, I felt like staying away at any price.

I was still to seaward. The noise from here was somehow magnified, caught up in the hollow under the belly and funnelled out in a succession of squelches and sucks.

I managed it without much difficulty, except that my

hands were freezing and unbearably sluggish. Once one end was tethered I only had to rush back to the cockpit and throw the gears into neutral then pull her round on the rope the way I wanted. Doug had explained about the rocks between the seaward pair of legs. Modern oil rigs mostly float. These old sea forts are actually built on the ocean's bedrock, with a protecting line of concrete or dredged rock on the side away from the land. In wartime this served both as a breakwater and as a mooring line. Rough, but effective. If I'd worked it out right, the breakwater would hide my boat from direct view from anyone tying up to one of the landward pillars — and the right-hand pillar was the special pillar Hepplestone's model had indicated. I switched off and pocketed the keys, gave one last despairing upwards shine of my torch to fix the layout in my mind and put the boat's lights off.

There were projecting iron handholds from the pillar. Not the easiest climb, but I suppose that was the intention. The first step was about chest height. I'd brought a clothes line and some old gardening gloves, but how the hell you lowered a score of antiques down from a thing like this fort into a bobbing boat on your own without help . . . I climbed. They say don't look down when you're up high, but nobody tells you the other most important climbing lesson, which is: never look up, especially if you're climbing the underbelly of an old sea tower.

The handholds were rusted and slimed. I stopped and shone my torch every three or four just to make sure there was something to grab and that my hand wouldn't be left waving in the air when I needed support. I ought to have kept an eye out for approaching lights at this stage but I was frightened enough. There was this moaning, faint and fairly quiet, as if the wind was hurt at not being allowed in. Give me land any time.

At the top, flat surfaces stretched away into the

distance. I shone the torch only once, clinging on like a tick on a bull. Above me the handholds led up into a rectangular hole like a loft ladder does into an attic. I beamed upwards. The light hit nothing but space, which gave me hope there might be a respectable floor for me to stand on. I climbed in, shaky and trying not to look down. It stank of must and seaweed. Holding on with my left hand I shone the torch on a level with my face and almost shouted from relief. There was a rectangular room about forty feet by forty, almost as if I'd simply climbed into a barn loft. I hauled myself in, scrambling away from that horrible edge and the sea's noise beneath. For a minute I wheezed on my hands and knees, partly relief. Behind me, what had been a hole promising safety had now become the start of a bloody great drop and I didn't want any part of that. I got away from it fast and tried to control my shaking limbs. No wonder Lemuel had looked decidedly grey with fatigue after the ploughing. Until now I'd regarded myself as fit as a flea.

I started first on the flooring, treading carefully, then pushing the walls to make certain I was in something really solid. The feeling of emptiness was all about, as if I'd come to a deserted city. I tried to sense if anyone was here or not, and got no vibes. The fact should have reassured me and didn't.

I walked round and round coughing on the dust. A big empty room with a hole at one corner and a metal door at the other. No windows, no footmarks in the dust except mine. I reasoned that, if Drummer had been killed for seeing them load the stuff in, their route would have to be up one of the landward side legs. Logical. The walls were covered with graffiti, testifying to some intrepid holidaymakers getting their money's worth out of the hired powerboats from Clacton or somewhere. A few faded scrawls from soldiers fervently marking the days off to demob, and that was that. I crossed to the door and pulled it back on its crossbar.

It led up five steps to the start of two corridors. The left one. My torch flickered ahead. It looked about two hundred feet long and was littered with debris, though God knows where that came from. Pieces of planking, some glass and a bottle or two, even a brick. The ceiling seemed to be made of crossbeamed concrete and the walls were the same endless fawn coloured tiers. I trod cautiously along it, realizing that the sound of the sea was getting fainter with each step.

About halfway along, a double entrance led into what must have been some sort of briefing room. It was low but wide, with a central spiral of stairs upward round a thick circular pillar. I vaguely remember the silhouettes of these forts. They all have a flat tier, then a somewhat bulbous turret structure like the highest bit of a lighthouse. There were footmarks in the dust round the stairs, showing that Devvo's happy band had been here. I climbed slowly, holding on to the rail. A metal door blocked the way about the level of the operations room ceiling but it answered to a hefty shove, and I was through into the top of the fort. The lookout room was no more than thirty feet in diameter. Slit windows showed the distant shore lights directly opposite, the lightship's signals from the Sands, and I caught a glimpse of the sea lights shining where the oil ships steamed north-south from the fields and refineries along the coast. I could even have picked out Joe's station and the harbour lights of Barncaster Staithe, but I felt too vulnerable in this derelict place. It was beginning to give me the willies. Perhaps Devvo had heard of my renting a power yacht from Barncaster and was coming without lights, same as me. The slimy creep, I thought indignantly. Just the sort of rotten filthy trick he would get up to. The trouble was I had no real plan, which was what was making me mad. I'd assumed that if I'd got here first I'd somehow be in control, able to dictate terms to Devvo. Now I wasn't sure I'd done right.

I could threaten him with the police, of course, though Maslow was about as useless a threat as you could imagine, and Devvo had already got away with murdering Drummer. After a few times I decided to change my original non-plan to a new non-plan. The thing was to try to find the antiques first, maybe shift them to some place in the fort where I could keep them under lock and key, for use as a bargaining counter.

Time was passing. Nervously, I hurried down from the turret into the big operations room and began an urgent search of the rooms leading off it. It was a huge place, bigger even than I had imagined. Like a ship, always so much more space than you dream of. I raced from one place to the next, shoving metal doors open and spluttering on the dust that hit me every time. A third of the way around, I was soaked in sweat, and realized I'd never get round the place in just a few hours. I had to think. Of course I'd known it would be a big task but assumed that my luck would carry me through. Maybe, I began to think, I'd trusted luck instead of brain.

There was only one thing I hoped I had that Devvo and his goons hadn't, and that was a knowledge of the deep chamber waiting for me in that special pillar. Maybe it was where the antiques were waiting . . . ? There was only one way to find out, though I hated the idea. Logically, any search had to commence there.

I entered the rectangular room shining my torch every inch of the way. I didn't want to touch anything until I was sure I wouldn't go hurtling down into any abyss I couldn't get out of. Despite my fear I felt a twinge of excitement. Plenty of signs of activity here. It was an isomer of the room I'd climbed into at the other corner of the fort. The same rubbish, same design—but here the dust was trodden and most of the debris had been shoved aside into one corner. There was the same dark rectangle, with ugly sea sounds loudly echoing up through it. This must be Devvo's regular way in. I followed the treads easily, back into the corridor and along to a trio of steel doors. The adjacent enclosures were marked 'Latrines' and 'Ablutions'. Most of the piping had gone and the doors hung askew on rusted hinges. I shivered. The idea of soldiery long gone was too spooky for me. I turned my attention back to the three rooms. The doors were solid metal, curiously new. My heart sank, though I'd have done the same thing. If I'd been Devvo and my mob were robbing all the country houses in East Anglia and wanted to stash the loot away, I too would have found which rooms were situated near to one of the pillar climbs. Then I'd have built my own new steel doors in, just as he obviously had, and simply used the place as a castiron cran, a drop. Safe as houses—in fact safer.

I shone my torch obliquely under the door and peered through the keyhole. It didn't give much light but enough. By waggling my head I could spot the stuff. A load of small cases, wooden crates, even a few ordinary suitcases. Of course. Everything had to be small. You couldn't winch up a suit of armour. Half of it would drop off or it would swing and be damaged. The room was some fifteen feet from door to wall, perhaps a former store room. The second too was packed, every sort of packing case, crudely nailed tea chests, brief cases, shopping bags taped up into ball shapes. And the third. Dog tired, I sat on the floor. This was Devvo's cran all right. Now the enormity of the task came home to me. I'd found Aladdin's cave but no trick to get the solid steel doors open. And it would take a handful of men some time to drop that much down into my waiting boat. Ludicrous even to imagine one bloke trying it on his own, even if I could get inside. There was no way to snaffle his loot. And simply watching and reporting back to Maslow would be pointless. All evidence would be gone.

My tired mind told me, with the heat on over Drummer, all traces of Devvo's connection with the fort would need to be removed. And it had to go tonight, fast. It's well known that antiques robberies are a summer pastime, ready for the relatively high prices of autumn auctions. It's also the season when new deals brings money flowing in from the 'nick trade', as we call it.

I'd lost my edge. Now I was waiting here with no advantage. Devvo would clear off laughing and leave me to trail home with my tail between my legs. Not even having to lift a finger, the bastard. I'd assumed I would pose a serious threat. Now I was no threat, not even a faintest irritation. Yet . . .

I got up wearily and went back to examine Devvo's route in again. This was the way he'd come, where his goons would drop the crated antiques into his boat. Easy with a net. The place was cold as ever, but there was something, something different. I shone round and walked every inch. Then I cursed myself for not having spotted the obvious. A notice in faded paint, letters two feet high no less. I'd walked past it for a quarter of an hour without reading the thing. 'Ammunition winches not to be used for the carapace retraction.' I had to think about that. There was a winch support projecting from the wall, its chains rusted and old but looking pretty serviceable. I tested it, swinging on it cautiously and trying to dislodge the projecting girder before searching for the iron rings. If they'd gone to the trouble of telling soldiers not to use this winch for shifting the piece of flooring, then it was proof that it could be used just for that purpose. I wound them round the wheels and pulled them through the iron rings in the carapace. Easier if I'd brought some oil. There were three rings set in the floor. A fourth was rusted to blazes.

Good old Archimedes. I practically flayed my gloves

pulling the link down so the concrete paving rose to lean on the wall beneath the winch. A space was left about four feet square, exposing quite respectable steps, suggesting that nothing here was meant to be hidden so much as preserved. Perhaps in the event of enemy forces attacking, and the defenders having to retreat like Douglas Fairbanks doing his sword bit on the staircase? I descended slowly, my torch pointing ahead. They were ammunition vaults, a core of chambers placed vertically alongside stairs and a lifting well as if for a regular elevator. Warning signs were everywhere. As soon as I'd realized what the chambers were I dashed back to the winch and dismantled its chain. I was in a nasty sweat. If Devvo turned up while I was down there I didn't want him gently nudging the slab in place and leaving me entombed. That precaution gave me confidence as I decided to go further down. In any case, if Devvo's loot was in the sealed rooms up top, what was in old Hepplestone's concealed chamber down below at the bottom of this pillar's steps?

I went down scared in spite of all my precautions. The place looked untouched for years. No footprints in the dust, no graffiti, and no rubbish. Therefore Devvo had not been down here, either. And the winch up top had been practically unserviceable. At every level I checked in the ammunition rooms, one to every landing on the stairwell. Empty, just faded War Department instructions stencil-painted on the walls and doors.

It was then that I realized I must be about the level of the sea outside. It felt horrible. Above the water you feel there'd be something of a chance. I stopped and pressed my ear to the concrete wall but jerked it away the same instant. It sounded frigging awful, as if the sea were trying to get in, the swine. I shone down and realized I was near the bottom of the pillar. Another couple of floors and I'd be on bedrock. But if anything valuable was hidden down here, surely decades of scrounging idle soldiers would have found it?

The stairs came to a dead end at a door, metal and reinforced. A notice read: 'C.O. or authorized Acting C.O. only.' I felt something, steadily but gradually begin warming me. There was something down here, something worth coming for. I cleared my throat and shoved but the door wouldn't give. I returned to the ammunition room on the landing above and set to on the door hinges with my tacklers' knife. They are the usual military projecting pin type. I got the door off but clobbered my knife. Well, easy come. Gasping, I dragged the heavy door down the concrete stairwell, getting my arms practically dislocated at each bump and making a hell of a din.

The door would do as a battering ram, seeing I had nothing else. About six feet from the lowest stair to the block room, just too much. I'd probably rupture myself but what the hell. With the torch lodged on one of the stairs I took some deep breaths and dragged the door up three steps. Holding it against the wall I undid my belt and got it round one edge. Not much of a sling, but it might give me a bit of extra leverage. I inhaled, heaved on my belt in an ungainly lift and staggered down the three remaining stairs, the strap cutting my hand. The full slanting weight of the bloody door was on my shoulder as I swung it forward. It took me about ten minutes and seven more goes before the obstructing door yawed inwards and I could clamber through. I'd nearly creased my back.

Light reflected from the whitewashed interior. It was a small chamber, the first room of circular design I'd seen in the fort, with the single word 'Counterbalanced' painted on the wall. A red arrow indicated the flooring. Not concrete in regular rectangles, I observed, but evenly laid around a central void about three feet wide. Something was so important that only the commanding officer was allowed in — or somebody he'd appointed to do a special job. And *here*, not anywhere else. I felt suddenly uneasy. A sealed room, restricted access, deep down where any intruder would hardly bother to look . . . And situated underneath a tier of rooms which in wartime would have been packed with ammunition. It had all the hallmarks of a place you retreat from, where the departing officer could create an explosive exit. I swallowed, dry as a plank, thinking how carelessly I'd slammed the door in with my improvised battering ram. I could have been blown to blazes.

A ladder projected from a central hole. A mournful wail sounded outside, a ship of some kind. Whatever it was up to I fervently hoped it steered clear of the fort. I didn't want it careering into this particular pillar while I was in its base. Other horns were sounding now. Stiff with goose-pimples I shone into the hole and saw the ladder end about twelve feet down on the bedrock. I almost yelped from fright. It was horrible, gazing down on to solid rock. Actual rock's not bad in itself, but this bit signified the bottom of an ocean and I was down there, at the end of a great concrete tube.

The sickening realization froze me. *Sea bed*. I moaned and backed off. No antiques, no valuables. Time for me to be off, I was thinking, when something flashed in the darkness, from a stray torch beam. I found I'd shot off to the doorway in a panic, one foot on the first upward step on the way out of the wretched place. Like the fool I am I dithered, my torchlight wavering shakily on the wall. A quick listen. Nothing except the distant muffled hoots of boats, more and more of them now. That gleam. Now I'd come so far, what's another few feet? I flashed my torch up the concrete steps. Still alone. There was still time.

Practically creaking from the frigidity fear always brings, I lay on the floor with my head hanging over the edge and waggled the torch round. A concrete slab projected into the cellar from its wall, probably a support, but what for? I decided I was wasting time. Better to be frightened quick and get it over with. I got up and tried the ladder. It felt firm. I went down, prickling all over, and stood petrified on the living ocean bed. You could only call it a cellar with a knobbly floor, the remaining space where the hollow pillar had been constructed to stand on the sea bed. Quite empty.

Nothing. Just a circular room, concrete walls, that one projecting slab. But a gleam *had* shone back at me. And it had come from down here. Faint, yet rich and lustrous and . . . *and mauve*! Like when I'd opened the little hollow leg of Hepplestone's coal cage. I stepped about on the uneven floor, shining my light at the rock. It was so raw and irregular it appeared quite randomly cobbled, yet all of a piece. The engineers must have simply decided to build where they found a solid upthrust on the sea bed. No good doing it on sand. Even I could see that. They'd probably just blasted it to solid rock and built like mad. The North Sea in 1939 had been no place to dawdle. And one or two of the areas seemed faintly goldish, faintly green, shiny. I knelt to look. And suddenly knew. Goldish *and* green. Greek. Chrysos and beryl. *Chrysoberyl*. 'Ooooh,' I moaned, frightening myself by the chamber's resonance.

I'd been a fool. Chrysoberyl, the natural metamorphic rock which mothers alexandrite. One of the first things you learn in the antiques game is a list of old tricks and legends. I'd stupidly forgotten one of the commonest sayings, remember alexandrite is *emerald by day, amethyst by night*. I could almost hear Blind Benny's voice, drumming his teachings into me night after night in Petticoat Lane as a lad. Take an alexandrite ring into daylight and it glows a perfect emerald. But dance in the glittering artificial lights of a ballroom and it transforms into a luscious deep amethyst. Old Man Hepplestone, one of the workers building this fort in the wartime rush, had put a flake of it in the bottom of the copied cage's hollow limb to show not only *where*, but *what*. I'd seen it flash green in the cold sunlight when Maudie had chucked it on the fire. And by artificial torchlight in my cottage I'd seen its mauve gleam.

I sank back on my heels, kneeling on a fortune. Weakly, realization began to come. I had everything. At last I had money, power, wealth to set up in London. Dear God, I could practically buy out Christie's. I was rich as Croesus. Made for life. My hands were shaking as I fondled the craggy protuberances of the floor. The whole floor was chrysoberyl, one of the most valuable minerals on earth, worth every antique I'd ever handled—

'Found anything, Lovejoy?' a voice boomed suddenly from above me.

I jumped a mile and found myself babbling at the shock. 'Who's that?' I knew perfectly well.

'Me. Devvo.' The ladder twisted suddenly and crashed down, clouting my shoulder and knocking the torch away.

Blackness enveloped the cellar. I scrabbled helplessly for the ladder. Just as I felt it a dreadful slithering sound shook the cellar. The faint rectangle above where a torchlight was suddenly wiped out. The darkness became total. For a second I could not understand what had happened. Then even when I realized Devvo or somebody had shoved the enormous iron door over the manhole it took me a full minute to realize I was sealed in. More slithering sounded. I could hear two voices.

'What are you doing, you bastard?' I bellowed, deafening myself.

Devvo chuckled. 'Fixing your tombstone, Lovejoy.' A feeble line of light showed and was gone.

'Let me out,' I yelled, disgusted at my fear. The vicious pig had sealed me in, maybe wedged the metal door some way.

'No, Lovejoy.' Devvo sounded breathless from his exertions. 'Serves you right, nosey sod. Going to hide down here and bubble me, were you? You can frigging well stay down there for good. Snide bastard.'

'I'll get you, Devvo,' I screamed. I flung the heavy ladder upwards, nearly braining myself as it clanged on the door and crashed back. It caught my leg a chance swipe. Cloth and skin tore.

'Keep trying, Lovejoy.' Breathless but calm.

'I'll help you nick antiques, Devvo,' I babbled, ashamed at myself. I'm pathetic.

'Not now, you won't.'

'Please, Devvo. I'll take back what I said about you killing Drummer.'

'That old fool had to go, Lovejoy,' Devvo called back. 'Like you, mate. I've too much to lose.'

'You're not going to leave me, Devvo?' Crawler.

'I am that.' His voice was receding.

'I know where there's stuff worth millions, Devvo.' My screech echoed within the cellar. 'Please, Devvo. It's here. There's a ton of chrysoberyl—'

Aghast, I heard them talking about fog outside as their footsteps sounded above. I even heard Jimmie the goon ask Devvo for a match and Devvo's reply, 'No smoking till we're outside. We don't want Old Bill finding clues all over the place.' He didn't believe me, the moron, the sadistic killer.

The steps sounded fainter. I thought, this can't be happening to me. Not to *me*. It can't happen. People will come. Devvo will turn back. Maudie will arrive. Dolly will bring the police. The Navy'll see the boat . . .

Then they had gone and I was where I'd always feared. Finished.

CHAPTER 16

Darkness is the worst. Well, second worst. Second to being entombed.

I'm not scared of dark places. No, honestly I'm not. No more than anyone else. And solitude's a precious commodity, if you like that sort of thing. But being at the bottom of the sea bed sent me demented. I sweated and shivered, shouting and pleading though Devvo and his goon were no longer in earshot. I yelled incoherent explanations of the chrysoberyl, promises, bribes, anything.

Sobbing in fear, I hurled myself repeatedly at the ceiling, foolishly hoping to reach the rectangular opening's margin. Once I even thought I touched it but nearly broke my bloody ankle falling on the rock. I battered upwards with the ladder. I begged and pleaded, wept and screeched abuse. In those few minutes I regressed from *Homo sapiens* through a few million years, finishing up a shambling whining hulk whimpering and scratching in a cave. I became again a feeble thing of reflex, *Homo neanderthalis*, an animal with less brain than Germoline. Utterly disgusting. Fright made me pee repeatedly, hardly a drop every time. I almost knocked myself senseless against the projecting slab. I cursed it soundly, regaining my old anger. Stupid bloody army engineers, leaving one great slab like that sticking out. You could brain yourself on it if you weren't careful. And what for? Typical, just typical. You'd think they'd have just built this lunatic place and got the hell out.

Then gradually I was brought back to my senses. Perhaps it was rage at the fort's builders. Or at Devvo. Or at the plight I was in. Or just me. Or at everybody in good

old East Anglia beering up and snogging and going about
their lawful business, selfish swine, with me left to die
miles offshore out there — *here* — under the ocean.

'Oooh,' I moaned, terrified.

Whatever else, I had to keep that horrible thought
from my mind. Ignore the reality of cold, of silence and
darkness. Think. *Think*.

Think of Germoline, waiting out there by Drummer's
shed, trusting in me to come back loaded with antiques.
Think of the engineers under the impetus of war, slogging
night and day in the cold and mud out here. I sat on the
fallen ladder and slowly and ever so slightly began to
cerebrate.

My head was still ringing from catching it on the
projecting slab. What was it I'd just said to myself? . . .
You'd have thought they'd just have built this lunatic
place and got the hell out? But they hadn't. They *hadn't*.
They'd most carefully made, deep down at the bottom
of one supporting pillar, a single projecting slab.
Apparently for nothing. Nothing could lean on it. A
winch bar, then? No. Nothing could be winched up to
it — you build winches at the top of places, not in cellars.
Some architectural necessity, then . . . but what? I know
nothing about architecture, especially of sea forts, but no
amount of thinking could explain the projection. The fort
itself was huge. Its four supporting pillars were huge as
well. This projecting slab, big as it seemed, was relatively
small compared to the fort.

A strange unease settled in my belly. Whereas I'd been
scared out of my skull a few minutes before, a coldness
came in me now, fear of a totally different kind. Something horrid underlay all this. Something old man
Hepplestone possibly knew about and which was
gradually starting to dawn on me. My white-hot panic
vanished. My mind plodded on to a clear frosty logic.

A construction team, labouring hard out in a

dangerous ocean, struggling to erect this sea fort in the hectic rush to war, doesn't pause to build something useless a million fathoms down. Local legend says they lost a man a day from drowning or injury on every single fort. Add to that the bombing, the worry about enemy ships . . . I was suddenly too scared to move. Counterbalanced. Exactly what was counterbalanced?

'Keep calm.' My voice echoed funereally, scaring me worse. Hepplestone's cage. You pressed it down, and a bit of the floor had pivoted aside. *Counterbalanced?*

The way down had been carefully locked so that I'd had to improvise a battering ram to get in. And only the C.O. or his aide were allowed down, even though it led nowhere. Cellars *never* go anywhere. Everybody knows that. The glamorous image of a retreating swordsman came back to me again, retreating stair by stair. Suppose the fort was stormed. A brave C.O. might want to sacrifice everything to save a fortress falling into an enemy's hands so close to shore. Or he might have *orders* to . . . to . . . Jesus. I swallowed, my throat dry. No wonder it was locked, the doors solid metal. Something was mined, or self-destructive. And I was in it. And I knew now what was counterbalanced. It was the slab. Somehow it pivoted. And it could be done by one person, 'The C.O. or authorized Acting C.O.', the notice had said. *Or.* Therefore not both. Therefore even a knackered Lovejoy could unbalance it on his own, after which . . .

I went 'Oooh', sitting still, frightened to move a muscle. Supposing I did manage to turn it. What the hell happened then? Maybe it would prove a way out — into the frigging sea. Who needed that, for gawd's sake? I'd seen enough films to know that the bloody sea's crammed with sharks and tentacled monsters. A pivoting slab in a wall would let the whole frigging North Sea into my black prison — definitely bad news. Worse, supposing it *did* let me out? *What else did it do?* That ghastly feeling of being in a mine recurred. How long did mines take to blow up once you set them ticking? Or do mines only tick in comics?

I tried to talk myself out of it. 'It's all make believe,' I said aloud. Sweating clammily, I brought up perfectly sound reasons for the War Department being too careful to leave sinister explosives in our trusty old sea forts.

Aren't they?

One thing I could do, meanwhile. If I was going anywhere I'd at least take a piece of the chrysoberyl with me. The ladder would help to bash a piece of the scaggy rock floor free. Careful, though, to stay away from the projecting slab in case I unbalanced something in the darkness.

I got down on my knees and began feeling the rock. My torch was broken. I'd have given anything for my pencil torch. I laid the ladder pointing at where I remembered the projecting slab to be and took bearings from that, using feel. Then I quartered the cellar in my mind and set to, my fingers fumbling across the rock inch by inch.

Chrysoberyl looks like nothing on earth, just rock with faint greens and yellows and the odd brownish creamy material. You feel for smooth areas the size of your fingernail, especially where they end in crazed bits as if somebody had criss-crossed the rock with a file. There were several excrescences feeling like this. I finally chose one about a yard from where I guessed the room's centre was.

A small fissure extended to a depth of about my hand to one side of the rock piece I'd chosen. It was as wide as a fist at the top, just big enough to ram my broken torch in and leave it sticking upright. The ladder was easy to lift but difficult to keep on its side edge. I held one end as high as I could, over the torch. I stepped aside and let go. One would be the hammer, the other the nail. It took me a dozen or so goes before the ladder's plunging metal side hit the torch with a dull clack and I heard the chrysoberyl splinter. A few chips spattered about my cell but I could ignore those. The biggest piece was about a couple of pounds, an unimaginable quantity. I got it into my lap, gloating like a delirious miser, though God knows what I had to be pleased about.

It was a winner. Irregular as hell, the lump had nine facets with smooth silky flat surfaces. Three of them led into gritty crazed patches. I could feel the delectable richness of the beryllium salt and its violet lustre. Supposed to be unlucky for sailors, it is none the less sought after, and the clearer transparent stones are very valuable. Most come from the Urals, Ceylon and parts of Africa, with a few from Colorado. A single 10 carat natural would buy a family house. Not antique, but I was in no position to argue against free wealth.

The question was whether to wait and rest or to waggle that slab and hope for the best. But wait for what? Death in this cellar? Devvo would return my boat, simply make sure it was found tied up at Terry's when dawn broke. Everybody would reach the same conclusion as Maslow—that Lovejoy had scarpered with a load of nicked antiques. Devvo would be thoughtful enough to leave a giveaway antique in the boat. I was done for in any case. Nobody would come after me. That was the truth.

I put the chrysoberyl piece in my pocket and, hands reaching out in front, stumbled carefully across the uneven floor towards the wall where the slab was.

I knew that you breathe *out* when rising in deep water. How many steps had I descended? Maybe about ten flights or so, say, a dozen steps to each flight. Say about eight inches a step. That's ten times twelve times eight over twelve, in feet. I worked it out as best my incoherent mind would allow. Eighty feet. Christ, it seemed a hell of a lot of water. I resolutely avoided working it out in fathoms. I'd learned too many grim fathomy poems in school to do that. Fathoms always sound to me distances you sink, not distances you float — and I badly wanted to float.

My heart was banging almost audibly and my palms were hot and dry. The cellar was freezing. I'd been a fool not to bring Tinker. He'd have been useless because he's always even more scared than I am but at least he could have kept watch. I'd been thick, as usual. I peed against the wall. There was enough water out there without carrying some with me. I undid my shoes, took them and my socks off and stripped to my underpants, replacing only my jacket. The lump of chrysoberyl stayed with me. At least human beings float. I hesitated. One more worry. Is there such a thing as a non-floating man? If so, I was bound to be it. Oh God.

I felt the projecting slab. The floor beneath it seemed solid rock, like the rest. Supposing it didn't move? Supposing it wasn't the slab which was counterbalanced but some other thing elsewhere? Fear made me reach out and pull the slab the instant the thought came. And I was engulfed in water, roaring, howling water.

I was buffeted and knocked, pulled and swirled. Water forced into my nostrils. I hadn't got a decent breath in. I tried to open my eyes but saw nothing. I didn't even know if they were open. I was spinning. Something seemed to have hold of my right arm. I screamed into rushing bubbles, threshing and kicking in the vortex, perhaps some instinct not to die from nitrogen bubbles in your blood, diver's disease. I didn't know which way was up. All I could hear was the terrible rushing noise, hissing like a steam train. Things seemed to keep on pulling at me, my arms and legs and shoulders. I kept trying to kick clear, as though at clutching enemies but the water tugged a million ways at once. A minute was too much. I needed to breathe but to do so would mean drowning. I kicked madly, flailing arms and legs and doubling my body in agony. My head wanted to burst.

Something belted my neck and scraped my shoulder. I clouted it back, not feeling the pain. I felt a hard smooth surface and me sliding along it curving upwards. How did I know it was upwards? Breath came into me, pressing me out and setting me choking. I choked and retched and choked.

And floated.

It was odd, that first breath. The air was curiously warm. I wasn't able to believe it actually was air. For a moment I wondered if this was drowning, that this stuff I was sucking in and gushing out was actually water. The fact that I was floundering dizzily beside one of the great pillars and on the sea surface, being lifted and lurched tantalizingly near to the metal stanchions, seemed somehow irrelevant for an instant. I realized I was delirious for a few seconds. Reflexes kept me surfaced. Not drowning but floundering. Great bubbles heaved and popped about me. The trouble was I couldn't see far.

'What the hell was that?' a voice shouted. Devvo. I couldn't judge the direction.

My choking stopped but I was splashing like a flounder.

'Some boat, maybe.' That was Devvo's goon, breathless from lumbering the antiques.

'What d'you expect me to do, in this frigging fog?'

'Can it or I'll can you.' Devvo.

Fog? A wave slammed me against the pillar. I was lucky not to be brained. Fog. That explained the horns from passing ships. It also explained why the sea was not running murderously high. Thick fog, low waves, they say on the coast. Noises sounded close to, thumps and a creaking, presumably Devvo's boat loading up. I peered stupidly about, lifted and sloshed down by the swell. As if anybody could check position from distant lightships in a fog with a ten-yard visibility. My mind was too stupefied. Simply to strike out might be suicidal because I could be swimming away from the fort. Above and around a great greyness. No lights. Merely me heaving near a vast pillar in the endless bloody ocean. Distant foghorns wailed again making me shiver more.

Driven by fear, I told myself angrily, cerebrate, you idle sod. *Which way*? I turned my head. Foghorns. Where else but further out to sea? You don't get ships on shore. So left was land, right was east. I listened, tugged and shoved by the heaving sucking sea. An intermittent shushing sound came from the right. Rocks, the ridge protruding from the sea between the seaward pillars. I drew breath and let go, flailing towards the shushing. It was less than a length and took me years.

I don't even remember reaching the rocks or finding the rope. Maybe I blacked out or, knowing me, fainted from relief. Blokes shouting brought me to, a shout of directions and an insult.

'Last case, Devvo.'

'Thank Christ. I'm frigging frozen.'

'Slowly, you stupid get.'

My boat. I couldn't see it but there was a rope in my hands, and I was sprawled on sea-washed rock. Only a terror-stricken idiot like me ties eleven knots in a single rope to moor a boat. I grasped it one-handed and tugged. Something out in the grey darkness nudged my leg. I just kept from screaming and leaping away. Surely to God after all this it had to be my boat and not a shark.

I stuck my foot out at the sea and hit something solid but which moved as a body, undulating with the sea. Benign but definitely there. Like an ape, I swung one-handed, pulling like mad.

It made me remember sharks again. I splashed like a

drowning rat, finally getting one leg over the brass rail and feeling my way back until I reached the glass windows. I was safe. Nearly frozen to death, but in my own boat. I should have danced with delighted relief. Instead I retched up the other half of the sea.

It can only have been a few minutes. I'd cut the ropes first with the ship's knife and pushed away from the fort's pillars before scrambling into some clothes. The sea drift seemed to be swirling past me away from the sound of Devvo's men. I judged it would take me away from the fort pretty quickly without the engine. I was useless, unable to stop sicking up water and shivering.

I counted to five hundred before finding a handlamp and looking round the cabin. That was probably far enough. The engine caught first go. I don't know why that's always more astonishing than it would be in cars but it is. I found myself grinning in a kind of astonished ecstasy. I could simply go home if I wanted. I was free. Out and free. There was a quarter-bottle of brandy in a cupboard but I didn't feel like celebrating that much. I let the engine idle while I did exercises to thaw out, and sussed out the radar. Fog means radar. The fort stands a good three miles from the coastal sea lanes, and about five from the Sands lightship, so there was time despite the speed of the sea.

You switch on and a greenish radius appears, belting round and round this little telly screen. The whole cabin becomes ghostly, something out of a horror film. It leaves a faint green outline, the shape of the coast. You can alter the scale with a few knobs but I didn't touch those after one hesitant go, scared to damage it and finish up blind in the fog. There were several extra dots about that weren't on the map. I felt terrific, really proud of being in charge of my own destiny. I could head for the estuary, there on the screen, any time I wanted. But I didn't.

I did a few turns, using minimal throttle for quietness and watching the small screen. It was quite simple. Turn one way and the screen stayed conscientiously drawing the coast always in one direction. By this time I'd identified one green mark as the fort. If I watched it carefully it would show Devvo's boat too as it pulled away. I hadn't a clue what I'd do then.

The centre of the radius on the greenish screen practically joined to the fort's dot before I heard it, that terrible swooshing and slurping noise of the sea against the fort's pillars. Cutting the engine down, so as to just about keep me stationary as far as I could tell, I settled down to wait. Warmer now, and thinking at last. Thinking and listening. Devvo couldn't have left yet. I heard a couple of shouts from up ahead.

I honestly swear I intended no harm. Cross my heart. Honestly, I mean it. I was so thankful to have got out of that great monster I'd have been daft to go risking myself again, just for vengeance. Vengeance is a motive to be avoided. Too costly. Probably I was waiting to see what would happen to the antiques.

I found a score of plastic-wrapped pork pies in the diminutive fridge, Terry's boatyard's idea of nautical cuisine. It was also mine. I wolfed six and polluted the North Sea with wrappers.

Sailors trust radar. I'd heard them talk about it often enough. So when I saw a small green dot leave the solitary larger dot I decided I'd have to follow across the oily sea. It could only be Devvo's boat, loaded with its crated cargo. It stopped for a full five minutes, then moved a few hundred yards and stopped again. I followed it but cleverly kept at the same distance. The screen helped me to judge, and finally the dot began to move steadily. I couldn't hear an engine, so they couldn't hear mine. I followed, honestly still intending no harm. I'd be the perfect bystander.

I straightened up at last and settled on the same course towards the estuary. Say ten minutes and I would be in the mouth of the Barncaster creeks.

And so would Devvo, which would be his tough luck.

CHAPTER 17

Time often has a will of its own. Some hours go like a bomb. Others trail past like clapped-out snails, like now. My boat was static. I'd been stuck in one position for hours, about a mile offshore as far as I could estimate.

Devvo's boat had slowed down, then stopped. Naturally I'd stopped too, reversing to kill the speed, then holding her in neutral. A few times she needed a touch of the propeller to keep station but not often. Once I heard Devvo's boat throttle up loudly and saw the radar dot move to stand offshore a furlong further or so. I instantly pulled out a similar distance. Maybe he was afraid of being swept in by that sinister rush of the dawn tide when it came.

To still the engine would leave me dawdling if Devvo shot off fast. Even then I wouldn't lose him altogether but I wasn't sure how our boats compared for speed. I'd risked too much to let him get away now. I remember thinking this quite clearly despite not knowing why I simply wasn't trotting home to a hot meal.

Through the hours we had drifted steadily southwards along the coast in the thick fog. Now I was completely safe and a winner I couldn't help gloating, believing Devvo was now in my hands, virtually my prisoner. Perhaps lulled by the reassuring sense of security I began to nod off. Every now and then I caught myself snoring and frightened myself to death by jerking suddenly awake. When that happened I scanned the radar screen feverishly to make sure Devvo's boat hadn't given me the slip. I invented games to keep awake, and very exciting they were. Counting foghorns, a real gripper. And seeing how many different tones I could detect—high, low, gravelly. Every now and then I gave the throttle a nudge just to keep the engine on its toes. Everything had to be ready for it, though what 'it' was I couldn't imagine. Once I was pulled from a personal twilight by a deep muffled *crump* from seawards. I listened hard and peered blindly about but the sound didn't recur. A single swollen wave lifted the boat a minute later, then was gone. Sleepily I put it down to an extra-super supertanker passing and went back to waiting.

I'd hoped for the fog to clear as the night wore on, but if anything it grew thicker. Maybe the after-affects of my immersion and the fright I'd had were greater than I thought. Anyway I grew so cold towards dawn I went to sit inside the cabin for a few minutes. There was a kettle and one of those gas-burners, with clean water from plastic pipes. It took some time but I made hot water. Teeth chattering, I took it and a couple more pies back to the cockpit. Maybe I'd caught malaria from the sea, or was that polio? By then I'd ripped a blanket into an improvised poncho. I felt like nothing on earth. A sartorial mess, but drowsily confident. I nodded off a little, fell awake, checked the screen. Devvo was still there.

'And, Devvo,' I said quietly, 'so am I.'

A seagull perching on the cabin roof gave me a momentary thrombus about an hour later.

'Watch it,' I told it laconically. 'Stuffed case-mounted seabirds have gone up thirty-seven per cent.' It eyed me hungrily and I chucked it some pie. Watching it go made me realize I could see it. The elementary fact forced itself into my sleepy brain. *See?* Seagulls don't fly much in fog. Therefore as I'd dozed the fog had started lifting. And dawn was coming.

I wearily rubbed my face to alert myself. My engine's deep mutter sounded strong and quiet as ever. A few exercises standing up in the cockpit did nothing to help my stiffness so I stopped that and got some more hot water, hurrying back to watch the screen.

Gradually the darkness lessened. I knew that the boats tend to move about the estuary even in the early hours. Our few fishing vessels would be easy to spot on radar. They usually headed straight out, Indian file, and I knew from Joe there were only four in harbour.

As dawn came, today merely a sulphurous yellow version of darkness I realized the boat was now rocking more than it had, perhaps some sign that the tide was on the turn. I was too tired to start looking tide tables up at this stage. I just wanted to get the whole thing over and done with, but exactly how I did not know.

At exactly six-thirty by the cockpit chronometer Devvo's boat started up with a roar. It was too near for my comfort. Maybe my vigilance was going. I heard it quite clearly and moved sloppily into pursuit. Of course they didn't know they were being followed so it wouldn't seem to matter much. The screen showed them heading southwards, not steering into the estuary but going parallel to the coast. Maybe they were looking for their rendezvous. A freighter from Holland, perhaps? Or that big grey coaster which people rumoured made pick-ups for the Hamburg antiques trade? Port Felixstowe is rumoured to be cast-iron so it would have to be in one of the creeks. Probably Devvo had waited because he was early. Why, I wondered idly as I steered a following course south, was the stuff not transferred out at sea? Easy enough when it was calm like this, and much less likely to be sussed out by the coastguards, fog or no fog. Two knots, I observed. They must have time to spare.

At this funeral speed keeping Devvo's dot tracked was

easy. By guesswork I was some three furlongs from him, hardly more than a stone's throw. We seemed to be a half-mile off the estuary now. As the choppy water began to rock me unpleasantly side to side the sound of a bell came clearly across the harbour mouth. That would be one of the buoys which lined Barncaster's lower reaches. Once I heard an engine start and the sound of a car's horn. I even glimpsed a tall mast's riding light. The screen wasn't much use now. It had blurred into a haze of green. I didn't much care, because any company meant safety.

The sky was lightening with every second. Dense fog everywhere still, but things were definitely looking up. Land and daylight. Those plus my—well, somebody's—precious load of antiques equalled success. And my precious chunk of chrysoberyl, with private knowledge of a King Solomon's mineful in my own private spot on the seabed. With the loot I could easily hire a couple of professional divers . . .

I was gloating like this when I noticed a green blip moving quickly out from the green haze which indicated the crowded estuary. A shrill engine was audible, and getting nearer. Well, I thought resignedly, it's about time Joe Poges showed up. I'd done nothing wrong so far, or so I thought. If anybody was in the clear it was me. Devvo would get ten years, richly deserved. The engine sounded closer. And the police would prevent anybody doing anybody else any GBH, right? Maybe it was all for the best.

Suddenly uneasy, I noticed Devvo's boat had slowed. I cut speed, if you can call a slow drift speed. From the rate at which he was now going it looked as if he'd slipped the engine altogether. After a hesitation I too went into neutral. The green blip from behind was coming on faster. My boat was between the two. And now Devvo's boat was moving again—*northwards*? Towards me.

Slowly, but definitely with deliberate intent. I could hear both, and see sod all. Worried, I looked up and swung my head to listen. Maybe I should try the radio now, raise Joe Poges and say what was going on but I didn't know how, and wavelengths are Greek to me. I'd actually bent to fiddle with it when a boat hurtled at me out of the fog roaring with bows raised like it was taking off. I had a single second to shove the gear lever forward. The boat crumped against my boat's side, flinging me off my feet with a numbing shock. I wobbled upright into a world abruptly gone mad and grabbed the throttle, bellowing in alarm.

The bloody boat was the same one I'd used to rescue Germoline, the big Yank's estuary yacht, flying its commodore's flag. I'd seen it all in a millisec as it loomed out of the fog. I yelled frantic insults and slammed some way into my boat. The quicker I was out of this the better. I glared around into the thinning fog but saw nothing. The boat had vanished. In my sudden fright it seemed to me that engines sounded from every direction. I was just taking off landwards when I saw on the screen that Devvo's blip had gone. But between the estuary and me a steady blip was slowly circling, probably Devvo, waiting over there in case I ran for land. And another was closing swiftly at me. I shoved the throttle and headed for Devvo's blip, cursing myself at the chances I'd now have to take.

How thick I'd been. It was so obvious. If my hired boat possessed one of these radar gadgets, it stood to reason Devvo's would. Of course he'd have seen me on his radar and simply led me on. Then he'd waited until one of his goons could row ashore—maybe on an inflatable dinghy of the sort my boat carried—and nick a boat, by merest chance the Yank's again. Unless the Yank too was in on it?

The following blip was closing fast, now in earshot. I

glared around into the fog like a cornered animal. Nothing. The sea was increasingly choppy now and I was finding standing difficult. The tide must have started. And Devvo's blip was starting at me. There seemed no way home. Whichever way I steered I'd get trapped between the two of them, a bobbing walnut in the jaws of a seaborne nutcrackers. My only advantage was that my boat was as big as the commodore's. I risked a glance at the radar screen. My own engine's sound dulled theirs, and I'd lost all sense of direction. Nobody would see us from the shore. Worse, the nearer we were to land the more blurred the screen. There'd be a real risk of running aground on one of those frigging sandbanks. I'd be a sitting duck. After all this.

In a sudden rage I burst the throttle into life and felt the deck lift as the boat accelerated into the estuary mouth. In for a penny in for a pound. No use looking at the hazed radar screen now. The rocking and shuddering practically flung me out. I realized in fright that I hadn't even donned a life-jacket, and the boat carried six. Going so fast, the bows lifting and juddering nastily, I could do nothing else except gasp at the speed and hang on to the wheel to keep her straight. I gaped at the fog ahead, hoping I'd guessed the distance right. The fog rushed past me, parting and flinging past my face. Fear of what I wanted to do was draining me of willpower. Any strength I'd possessed had been left in the fort back there. Another glance at the screen. The swine following was as fast as me — and so close. Devvo's blip was rapidly closing from ahead. I cut the speed back with a jerk.

They came at me simultaneously. Jesus, but Devvo's boat looked big, a destroyer compared to mine. It came suddenly cutting the water into great level spouts through the fog, its engine deep with intent and power. In that second I glanced from front to back, judged the relative speed. The commodore's boat was in line, coming at me, about twenty feet to go. I cracked the throttle ahead, curving to the right in the start of as narrow a circle as I could go, screaming abuse at the engine to move us.

'You idle bastard,' I bawled at it, terrified. The commodore's boat tried following, hurtling round into a great banking curve and spraying a wall of sea up on to Devvo's advancing bows and lifting its pale side. The crash wasn't so much a crash as a clang with a muffled clatter. I was too busy wrestling with my steering-wheel to see much of what happened behind. I could again see nothing when I'd recovered and got my own boat slowed and straightened up in the choppy water, now surging unpleasantly high. The fog was light yellow now, pale, quiet. And empty. Engines muttered nearby. Somebody shouted.

While I was checking the screen a sudden whoosh sounded. I swear I even felt the heat. A reddish glow penetrated the fog for just an instant and was gone. A swift turbulence rippled across the sea, the blast tapped against my face, and that was that. Somebody's boat had exploded, maybe the commodore's again. Dear God. That's all I needed. I headed out to sea again, with the blip I guessed to be Devvo somewhere among the green haze that was the estuary's banks. Which one was he? This close inshore the radar seemed sod-all use. I cut the engine and peered at the screen. Twenty, there must be twenty discrete blips there, if not more, and a haze that could mean anything. A bell was clanging. Somebody must have heard the explosion and be calling the men out to help, though exactly where was difficult to tell. They'd see as little as me in this fog, I thought, though the more boats put out from shore the merrier, as far as I was concerned. All I needed was one friend. The trouble was I'd got none. My belly was cramped and my chest still thumping from the realization that the explosion might have been me.

At this point I seriously considered standing some miles offshore till the fog cleared. It didn't take much to make me realize what an error that would be. Devvo's boat was bigger and faster. Nothing would please him more than having me out there with no witnesses and no chance of assistance. This fog was a blessing for him. For me it was yet another danger. So it had to be inshore, and soon.

I swung round, slow but steady. The radar swept the coast in a great blur. I decided to ignore it. The tide would be running, filling the inlets and creeks and bringing up the boats as distinct radar points. But which of the fleet of static boats would turn out to be Devvo's?

Then I had a brainwave. Drummer's creek, where the commodore's boat was normally moored, where I'd struggled across to that sandbank. It filled at the tide. Only a short distance over the mudflats to Drummer's hut and Germoline. I could make it safely to land, moor there, dart across the mudflats past Drummer's shed to tell Joe Poges and simply have him arrest Devvo! Once I reached land there'd be no problem. I could of course cruise boldly up the estuary, but I knew Devvo well enough by now not to do the obvious thing. He would get me for sure, probably ram me, claiming that stupid Lovejoy—that clumsy, dangerously unskilled sailor—had made some mistake and caused some calamity. His boat would cut mine in two like it had the commodore's, and I'd go for a burton. And the fog, thinning all too slowly, would hide all.

I guessed I was almost about the spot where I'd escaped from between the two boats, and flicked out of gear to search for debris. Maybe the explosion had been both of them after all, not just the commodore's boat alone. My spirits rose. I might be free this very moment. A loss of a lot of antiques, but I would survive.

Something floated close by, wood maybe. A clue to who had suffered the destruction. I leant down to peer at the water and an oily hand rose from the sea and grabbed at my arm. '*Ooooh!*' I flailed back, screaming and gasping and beating at the horrible thing. It was coated in black slime, blistered almost beyond recognition. I screeched in terror, lashed out at it with my feet as it kept coming, lifting out of the heaving sea in a mad benediction and finally clinging to the brass rail. I kept kicking and screaming from fright until it slipped away leaving a ghastly bloodstained oily mark on the gunwale. I flung the gear in and roared away fast as I could go. My teeth were chattering and my hands uncontrollable.

The boat had bucked a good half-mile with me whining and shivering at the wheel before I got my mind back again and cut speed. Thank God no innocent boat was in the way or I'd have bisected it without a chance. While she slowed to idling I struggled to regain control of myself. My hands were jellies and I was cursing and blinding about being out on the bloody ocean in the first place. It took me ten minutes to steady up and stop shaking all over. I couldn't even look at the smears on the gunwale. The terrible fact was I'd just killed a man. Killed. Whoever it was had been a shipwrecked mariner, and I'd just killed him. He'd reached for help and I'd . . . and I'd . . . I heard myself moaning and tried to stop. All right, I'd panicked, been terrified. But my instincts to help had been submerged—I swallowed at the word— well, overcome by horror. And what was worse I'd felt the propeller chop, pause, jerk before pushing the boat on, as if it had . . . almost as if something in the water had fouled the propeller and been cut . . . been cut . . .

Naturally I made excuses. I told myself it had probably been Devvo's goon, and he'd been armed. I told myself it was a boarding attempt and not a plea for rescue, but I knew I was lying. How much of my savagery had been Lovejoy the buffoonish antique dealer, and how much sheer hate? It might even have been envy of Devvo's wealth, his birds, his power. I had a splitting headache. I'd have given anything just to reach land and go to sleep. But a living man, badly burned from the explosion, had been reaching from the sea for help, and I'd killed him. Being scared's no excuse. Vengeance isn't, either.

An unutterable weariness settled on me. Maybe it was the cumulative exhaustion, maybe the permeating cold. But maybe it was the wretched suspicion of myself. As I said, I've always believed that there's nothing wrong with greed. Nowadays it's one of the few remaining honest motives. But I'd always thought myself a pretty kindish bloke, even if some characters get on my nerves. Well, whatever I thought, being depressed was only stupid. I had to go through with it. No escape out to sea. Staying here meant that sooner or later I'd run out of petrol, wreck myself or do something just as hopeless in the fog. Nothing for it. I'd turn south, aim for Drummer's creek fast as I could go, and get the hell off this ocean to turn Devvo in.

As I spun the wheel I somehow felt I was cutting my losses.

I took bearings from the radar screen. Its haze had diminished and I was able to spot the seaward bulge, south of which Drummer's creek started. Despite this, heading inshore in fog's hair-raising. East Anglian sea fogs are famed for density and patchiness. Several times I let the way fall off until my confidence returned. Tiredness and cold were taking it out of me and concentrating on the screen was proving difficult, though I hadn't been scrapping Devvo on the ocean as long as all that. Collingwood in his wooden sailing ship had waited for the French fleet three years without a break.

My instincts were dulled, practically non-existent, but something made me uneasy. By rights, the nearer I got to Drummer's creek the more relieved I should have been.

Instead I grew increasingly edgy and fidgety. Once I even started whistling, nervous as a cat, stopping myself as a precaution. The screen was now only guessing where the long sandbanks lay, though I wasn't unduly worried. From the time I'd pulled Drummer off I remembered that the sea flooded swiftly in from the south until the sandbank was cut off. I could easily find my way by letting the ocean do it for me. On impulse I cut the engine. A gentle waft of air cooled my cheek. Maybe that would lift the fog, another worry. Another ten minutes and I'd be opposite the southern arm of Drummer's creek. I felt the erratic seas swirling me on, pulling jerkily as the dangerous undercurrents competed for the boat. The only benefit was I knew which way the tide was going.

It was then I heard that familiar tinkling of the wires on masts. The faint breeze was helping. I could use the sound as a crude direction-finder. I began to hear the sea's sounds, until now suppressed by the engine. I stood upright at the wheel, stupidly wrinkling my face as if that would let me see through the fog better. Telling if you are actually drifting in a fog's one of the hardest things on earth. The sea doesn't help because it moves like you do. Instinctively I found myself keeping quiet and just listening to that magic tinselly sound, my only guide.

Despite my caution the sense of unease persisted. Something was wrong, horribly evil. I took off my plimsolls and padded carefully around the boat, peering nervously over the side to make sure no oily hands were planning to crawl up like blistered crabs and come scrabbling at me . . . I became so apprehensive I switched everything else off, too: radar, lights, cockpit light, cabin bulbs and chronometer light. The boat drifted on. Once I panicked, feeling sand or something scrape the keel. Another silent creep around the boat to peer over the side at the water to make sure . . . but of what? I returned to the cockpit and sat nervously by the controls. Ignoring the cold, I stripped completely except for my jacket with its weighty chrysoberyl lump in the pocket. I could easily chuck it off if anything happened.

The boat began swirling. Even though I could see damn all I was sure she was swinging round as well as being pulled forward into Drummer's creek on the tide's flood. If I lodged on a sandbank now it would be no real hardship. I'd have to splash over the side as soon as I grounded, and wade inland for Joe, just walk across the mudflats, home and dry. A bell clonked once, mournful over a considerable distance. No use. I considered going forward to sit on the front but decided against it, seeing I didn't know which was front any more. I might be drifting into the creek backwards.

Feeling sick's natural when you're scared, and nausea was welling up in me. I felt I'd kept quiet so long I must have forgotten how to speak or whistle. The fog was no lighter, and the sea gave nothing away, just floating about looking enigmatic. I was almost in despair. There seemed no end to my frigging messes, one after the other. Fright's a ridiculous thing. I told myself this so often I became fed up and stupidly reached for the starter, rather do something than nothing.

Then almost within reach somebody went, '*Shhh . . .*'

CHAPTER 18

I froze, hand outstretched. The sound had come from behind me, obliquely left . . . about sixty feet off, maybe? But sounds in fog . . . The cold blank air was moving against my face but was opaque as ever. I swung around, heart bumping, desperately trying to see and sickened at my ineptitude. All I could remember of my entire life seemed fright, far back as I could go. A grown man terrified of shadows, of fog, of sea, of oily hands and now speechless with terror at a whisper. Anybody's whisper.

'Let's go out and find the bastard,' a voice growled. From the *right*.

'Wait.' Devvo, definitely Devvo. Quiet, assured. 'Lovejoy'll come. I know him.'

'We could do him easy out there.' A complaint, the burke's voice louder, closer, and this time from over my bows. I must be going round and round on the water like a top.

'We wait here. And he knows it. That's why he'll come this way. He's trying for us as much as we are for him.'

Another grumble. 'Let's get it over with.'

'Shtum it. Sounds carry in this.'

It was here, and now. No escape, no chance of quietly escaping in Drummer's creek. I felt clammy. How odd that Devvo believed I was the hunter and not hunted. Maud had said something similar. Yet I'd been like a rabbit in a barrel of ferrets since last night.

I was done for. To wait would be useless. To run for the open sea was equally hopeless. I'd known that all along. To drift meant sooner or later our boats would come together by chance in this creek. It wasn't as wide as all that after all, and when all the sandbanks and flats are submerged a quick sweep of the radar would reveal me, a precise dot on a spread of an otherwise empty screen. To shout for help would simply tell Devvo where I was. I contemplated swimming for it, but in what direction? I might head blindly out to sea in this fog. How stupid to think of missing East Anglia by miles. I'd drown, and I'd done enough drowning for today. I closed my eyes wearily. Finished after all. And in the most pathetic, hopeless way possible. To go out whimpering and useless. Maybe that was me through and through.

'Give uz a light,' I heard somebody say in a low voice,

closer, the burke just wanting a fag, casual and sure. The sheer frigging effrontery of his calm certainty was suddenly galling. I felt heat rise in my throat. My cold vanished in a sudden burst of hatred. If I was going to get done I'd take one of these bastards with me, maybe both. I thought in a blistering blaze of white-hot fury, all *right* — let's frigging go. I slipped the clothes from round my shoulders and slithered down into the cabin, tiptoeing feverishly about, opening drawers and cupboards and stupidly almost clunking myself unconscious with a great flat board thing which fell outwards from the cabin wall. I caught it in time and hoped I'd concealed the sound. A few pieces of cutlery, a series of plates and a stove with that gas thing. Gas? I ducked back to it, getting down to look at it under the sink. Gas is liquid, in a flatish metal bottle with brass screw top. Compressed. You release it by turning the valve. I screwed the brass nut closed and waggled it free of its tube and restraining clamps. It was unbelievably heavy. So I had a metal bottle of compressed gas. I felt the boat swing suddenly and scrape, a creak from somewhere. The boat was slowly being pulled over the flooding mudflats.

I swallowed hard to get my mind moving. Flame-throwers. They were only big cylinders of gas, weren't they, with some kind of lighter at the front end, and a valve with a trigger. I'd seen them in the army. Nobody liked using them because of what they did and the risks you took. People were always getting burned in training. But I didn't even want to be on the cold end. I wanted to be nowhere near it. Everybody knows that these characters that make homemade bombs are always the first to get themselves crisped. What a rotten thought. I was shaking still, but rage had taken over. I wasn't thinking so much as doing.

I reached up and shut the water off at the cock. That left a long plastic tube, transparently full of water itching to run into the sink. I opened the tap and it glugged noisily out, air bubbles blubbering upwards.

'Hear that?' somebody said nearby.

'Shhh.'

They'd heard the waste water fall into the sea. I'd not had the sense to plug the sink as I'd run the water tap. The boat swung suddenly again, sending me off balance. My knee caught on the bloody bunk. It wasn't much of a noise, but in the state I was in it seemed like the clap of doom.

They'd know by now. I tore the plastic tube away from its fixture and bit savagely through. The end went on the gas bottle's nozzle. No time to fix it there for good with wire, even if I had any wire. A light. I needed a light. I searched frantically, throwing caution aside and scrabbling in the supplies for matches, a cigarette-lighter. The bent plastic tube was about six feet long. I needed a pole, a boathook, anything. Surely there'd be a boathook on a stupid boat? I found an unused mop and tied the tube along its length with a feverish series of twists, using the orange-coloured strings from a life-jacket to keep it there. I emptied the quarter bottle of brandy over the mophead. Brandy burns. But I still needed some means of igniting the thing, preferably when I was some distance away. I found matches, the sort you have to strike and keep hold of when you're setting fire to something. Sodding hell. I really was a goner.

Lugging the mop and the gas bottle I crept out into the cockpit. I couldn't let it slip at this stage, not now. Then I had a brainwave. Collingwood, Nelson, the fireship tricks. If I was going to go I could go as a fireship. The least I could do for Drummer. And up here there were plenty of ropes, wires and a railing I could tie my weapon to.

Fog all around still, but thinning. I peered about and wobbled precariously forwards, never thinking that they might come at me from the side or behind. I'd have to get the engine started up again if I was going to do any good—or any bad, whichever way you saw it. Silently as I could, I lashed the mop pole to form a kind of bowsprit, sticking out at the front. Once tied, it projected somewhat sideways, but that would have to be. That made it easier to strap the gas bottle through its brass screw top and round its neck to the low railing that ran round the boat's entire edge. Great. I was almost pleased.

'Over there!' The shout came from behind. 'I saw something!'

'Where? Where?'

They hadn't started their engine, which meant they weren't certain yet. I crouched by the gas bottle with my matches, wishing I could be at the controls as well as up front. Then I might have stood some chance.

The fog swirled, waved across my tired eyes in great clouds. A definite wind was coming up. People often say the tides change our weather. I peered about, but only saw that terrible daunting opacity. The sea was gurgling now, and the waves had decreased into millions of rapid ripples. The tide race was starting, washing into the creeks and obliterating the coastlines again with its sinister swift onslaught.

Another shout from one side but I was too exhausted and bewildered to make sense of it. My mind had one scheme and this was it. Any further planning was beyond me. I clung miserably to the railing while the boat scraped and rocked its way helplessly into the reach, whisked in on the speeding tide.

'Got him!' They'd seen me. I looked frantically about. An engine roared so close it sounded on board with me.

For a second of panic I almost left my matches and leapt over the side. If I hadn't been so weary I probably would have, but my mind was programmed to its single plan. As it was, I saw Devvo's boat loom out of the fog

some forty feet off, going past at slow speed. It looked
enormous. The wave at its front showed they were moving
against the tide. I saw a dim dark blob of grey in the
cockpit cabin. Another was holding on at the front. I
struck a match, let it fall and swore. I turned the brass
screw on the gas bottle and heard the hissing sound of the
escaping gas at the front of the projecting mop. And I
couldn't reach the frigging thing. It was sticking so far out
from the bows that I couldn't reach where the gas was
escaping. Flame-thrower, match and fireship, all
together, and I couldn't use any of them. I moaned at my
stupidity.

'I see the bastard!'

'*Take him!*'

Devvo's boat suddenly sounded different. The engine
roared, settled into a deep thrum as its screws churned
the sea. I swore and clawed at the mop, pulling it back
through its lashings. I'd light the bloody thing if I had to
hold it in my teeth. I cursed and swore. I'd done it in a
hurry but the bloody thing wouldn't come back in. I
struck another match and held it out, clinging with one
hand to the brass railing and trying to reach from the
front. And I did it. But I'd never checked to make sure
the gas being released was a reasonable jet. The whoosh
of the igniting gas flung at me. I let go at the shock, away
from the roaring heat, and fell with a splash. I was in the
sea, done for differently but just as surely finished.
They'd get me now.

I came up spluttering near the boat. It wasn't moving
and I could see it clearly by the furiously roaring spray of
fire in the bows. Something was dripping from the mop
head, maybe the plastic tube melting under the flame. I
felt the heat and flailed clumsily away. Devvo's engine
shook the water. The vibes trembled through me as his
boat neared mine. Somebody shouted again. I struck out
for the opposite side away from the sound of the engine,

using breast stroke because it's what I'm best at and it shows least when you are in the water. The flame's sheen on the sea gave me some guidance but only relative to the boat. Something bumped.

'Pull her in. He'll be in there—'

Metal clanged on metal. Boats rubbed. A bump of fibreglass on solid wood or something. Another few clangs and scrapes and the engine muted to a mutter. It was exactly then that the explosion came. I was lifted by some enormous force, the sea squeezing me before I heard anything at all and the blast thumping on the back of my head. The sea sank almost the same instant, plunging me under and setting me fighting for the surface and air. Suddenly things were spattering about me. And behind a sustained roar and heat and noise, a screaming and somebody splashing in that roaring. I thought I heard somebody scream a name but wasn't sure. The ochre-coloured blaze made the sea visible underneath the fog for some distance. I was too bewildered to reason what might have happened. I knew that somebody else was in trouble out here in the fog-filled creek besides me. For once I wasn't dying on my own. From the horrible sounds behind me somebody else was at it too.

I struck feebly away from the fire, never mind where. Another, less intense whoosh sounded. The sea sucked, dipped, swelled but less severely this time. I couldn't keep swimming for long. The cold and my tiredness were making it difficult enough to float, let alone move. For a second I trod water, peering underneath the fog with the gilded sea surface reflecting the fires. I had to look. The boats seemed gigantic, piled almost in one heap. Both were blazing. Even as I looked some glass shattered with a crack, perhaps the heat. I don't know what had caused the explosion, whether it was my gas thing or the boats colliding and the petrol . . . *Petrol*. Terror-stricken, I saw it on the surface, a pure yellow heat spreading towards me. I gave a squeal of alarm, tried to turn feebly . . . and then I heard it. A donkey's coarse braying, up and down, over and over, to my right. It sounded near, very near. Germoline's voice.

I tried to shout again, excitedly drawing in a breathful of sea in my anxiety to get Germoline braying again, and almost sank. I splashed up again coughing and vomiting water, weakened further. I tried using my hands merely to keep me level, drew a long breath and yelled at the top of my voice: '*Germoline*!' Almost instantly a succession of donkey brays came, but I was on my back and couldn't place the direction. Stupid. I struggled wearily vertical, treading water again, but she'd shut up again, probably listening as hard as I was.

I tried shouting from this position but was too breathless to get up steam. I flopped exhausted on to my back again, to draw breath, let out her name in one despairing bellow and pushed myself vertical again, treading water.

'Keep shouting,' I yelled, turning towards the bray. 'Germoline!'

She gave three steady brays almost as though she knew what to do. I homed on them, finding after each one I was successfully pinpointing the next.

'Germoline!' I gasped. 'Germoline.'

I couldn't shout any more. I floundered blindly on, flopping my arms over and splashing like hell. I kept trying to shout but managed finally nothing more than a sort of weak talking, gasping out her name as I went. Several times I thought I saw something up ahead but no longer had the strength to hold my head out to see. I felt I'd been going for days before I realized I could not hear her braying any more. Gone. I must have lost her. I gave up, stopped swimming, lying on the water and trying to concentrate all my energies in keeping my face up to breathe. The current was pulling me now, probably running round at the full of the tide inside the creek and starting me out to sea. I swear I'd practically nodded off, when I was swept against these four hairy legs. I was so frightened I let out an almighty yell, but it was Germoline, standing in the tidal shallows. I clung gasping to Germoline's lovely legs and flung an arm over her neck, standing rocklike on the mud-covered flats.

'Darlin',' I gasped. She stood there, bracing breast deep against the flood. 'Up, love,' I wheezed. She was just turning, her tethering rope trailing where she'd pulled it away from her stall, when I heard a cry from seawards.

'Lovejoy!' Devvo's voice.

'Devvo?' My shout back was a mere wheeze. I tried taking a few waded paces but fell and had to sprawl against Germoline for support. My legs were rubber. I couldn't move without Germoline.

'Lovejoy.' The voice was feeble but real and solid. He always did sound in charge, Devvo. Always so bloody sure of himself. 'Lovejoy! Help, for Christ's sake . . .'

'Keep shouting!' I yelled, finding some strength from somewhere. 'Keep shouting! I'll get a rope.'

'My leg's gone, Lovejoy,' Devvo shouted in a hoarse gurgle. 'I'm burned . . .'

'Hang on, hang on!'

I turned Germoline and urged her out of the sea and up on to the flats, geeing her more decisively than I'd ever done. She splashed across the muddy shallows with me clinging to her neck. We came to the hut before I had time to focus. I staggered inside, grabbed a couple of rope hanks, and drove Germoline down the way we had come, following our trailing marks back towards the water. I could still hear the crackling of the blazing boats but could see nothing. I rasped a bit but got out a respectable shout.

'Devvo! Where are you?'

Nothing.

'Devvo!' I screeched. '*Devvo!*'

A feeble shout came, sounding some thirty yards off. 'I'm here, Lovejoy. The water . . . I'm burned . . .'

'Which way are you going, Devvo?' I shouted. 'Looking towards me, which way are you going?'

'It's pulling me . . . left, left.'

'I'll wade out, Devvo!' I got hold of Germoline's mane and urged her to our right, tying the rope round her neck as I splashed along the sea's edge. I got her maybe a hundred yards, shouting all the while, before taking hold of the free end. I reeled out into the water, all but knackered. It was surprisingly shallow, coming slowly up to my chest as I flopped and waded out. And I found Devvo, or rather Devvo found the rope.

I felt a weight behind me on the rope, simply turned and there Devvo was. He'd drifted against the lifeline which linked me to Germoline. At least, I thought it was Devvo. He was a ghoulish mess of blisters and burned skin, blackened around his face and all his shoulder, floating on the surface about ten feet off and just keeping his mouth up. His hair had gone.

'My legs, Lovejoy,' he groaned. 'I can't move.'

'Here. It'll hurt.'

I slid along the rope and tied it round his waist, lifting it to settle under his arms the way seemed best. He cried out in agony a few times as the rope bit. The sea was just too deep for me to stand. With each attempt I became weaker. I hooked my arm under the rope and let it come on to my shoulder. My arms wouldn't work any more. Germoline brayed again, worried for me.

'One more second, Devvo,' I gasped, craning my neck up for air. 'I'll go and we'll pull you in, mate.' I called him mate. Him, that had murdered Drummer.

'I can't hold on . . .'

'We'll get you in.'

'I can't see, Lovejoy. You won't leave me, eh?'

' 'Course not.'

I dragged myself weakly along the rope until I touched the bottom and crept forward, utterly done, pulling myself weakly back to the fogged shore. Germoline was waiting patiently as I crawled on to the mud beside her. I honestly thought I was dying from exhaustion. I lay there, unable to move a muscle. I couldn't even support my own weight, but I'd done it. I'd saved Devvo, atoned for killing the owner of those oily hands out there on the black sea. All it needed now was for Germoline to pull him in. And thank God Germoline was there, bracing solidly against the rope as the tide tried to drown Devvo. She was just waiting for my command, bless her loyal little donkey heart.

'Right, love,' I gasped up at Germoline's dependable form above me. 'Pull.'

Nothing happened. Not a muscle.

'Germoline,' I wheezed. 'Please, cockie. I can't do it.' I was looking up at her.

'Lovejoy!' came weakly from the sea. '*Lovejoy*. For Christ's sake.'

Something spluttered out there in the creek.

'Germoline,' I bleated. 'Pull, lovey. Pull. Please.' Didn't she understand? I tried to get up but my muscles weren't moving. I felt indiarubber, like those elastic toy things you put into different shapes for children. Maybe she didn't know what to do.

I struggled up her forelegs and sagged over her neck, too done even to straddle her. She felt so warm and Strong. All that power.

'Fucking gee up, Germoline,' I gasped in her earhole. 'Please, lovey.'

Not a twitch. Her head was turned seaward, almost as if she were listening to that awful burbling.

'*Lovejoy*!' came again offshore. 'Please . . .' A gagging sound. I knew it well. I'd been making the same sound for what seemed hours.

I found tears running down my face. I wobbled off Germoline's neck and tried pulling on the rope, the seaward side. It barely lifted out of the water.

'Please, Germoline,' I said. 'Sweetheart . . .'

I was helpless. The rope sagged, tugged a few times, drifted, sagged. Once I looked into Germoline's eyes. She gazed back with that calm with which an infant watches another who's crying, almost dispassionate and without the slightest sympathy. I suppose cold's the word I'm looking for, something like that. Once or twice I shouted for help, that Mayday thing, without any real hope. In any case Drummer's creek was nothing but a waste of mudflats at the best of times. Flooded at high tide, it was even more desolate.

Numbed, I found myself sprawled on the mud, leaning against tough little Germoline with tears streaming down my face and those horrible sounds growing fainter out on the waters of the streaming creak.

There came a time when the rope stopped tugging, but it must have been an hour before I could move. Every muscle I had was screaming. Even breathing was painful. As soon as I could I left Germoline there, tethered to something unspeakable floating out in the creek, and followed the marks back to Drummer's hut by crawling, stopping every few yards to recover.

It must have been a good two hours later that I returned, clumping across the receding tidal lip to where Germoline waited. She said nothing. I was still falling a bit and my muscles weren't coordinating too well, but at least I was clothed and in some of Drummer's old garb and had got warm. I'd even brewed up and tried a slice of bread with some cold samphire on it but fetched that up.

I unlooped the rope from Germoline's neck, and pulled her round to face the land again. I simply let her end of the rope fall and left it as it had been, trailing into the ebbing tide.

I didn't get her straps right on the cart, which is something that normally makes her irritable. This time, though, she was as good as gold and tolerated my clumsy fastening while I got her roughly hitched. I had to sit in the cart then and just let her get on with it. I couldn't have gone to report to Joe Poges at the Staithe for a gold clock. The straps made it hard for Germoline but she seemed to know the problem and struggled gamely across the mudflats on to the hard with me in the cart. We came upon a man from the lobster fishery chipping and bending away over some of his pots. He looked up as Germoline clopped on to the stone staithing.

'Good heavens,' he called pleasantly. 'Bit odd weather for donkey rides, eh?'

'It is that,' I said. He straightened up and watched us go past.

That was all that was said until we reached home. I took the same way I'd come, through the American War Cemetery and back into our village through the woods. The cemetery looked more heroic than ever in the changed light, but I'd rather have the people any day.

When we reached the cottage I was too far gone to unhitch the straps. My joints seemed to have stiffened all everywhere. I fell out of the cart whimpering with aches and hurts.

I looked at Germoline. She gazed steadily back with that cold look. I noticed her eyes were a brownish grey.

'You're as bad as me,' I croaked, and went inside.

CHAPTER 19

I woke into sunset, disorientated as hell and aching all over. Little Ginny was shaking me with the self-righteous face of a child aware that somebody was neglecting their duty.

'You have to get up, Lovejoy,' she was saying.

I growled, 'Sod off.'

'Ooooh,' from little Dobber, eyes wide.

I creaked upright and tottered out after them into the garish sunlight. I was surprised. The world was still there, Germoline was plodding round the garden and three children taking turns to walk her. The trees were still hanging around. Everything really average as ever, almost as though it was only to be expected. I sagged on to my unfinished wall, feeling about eight hundred. An evening breeze whistled round my limbs.

'What did you get me up for, you pest?' I demanded, avoiding Germoline's eye—as Germoline was avoiding mine.

'Tinker sent Harry to say get out of town, Lovejoy.'

'Eh?'

I was shivering. Surely to God things weren't going bad even further? I felt I'd done enough. Harry's our famous flower-pincher, a six-year old liberator of floral tributes from their churchyard pots. He escapes them back into the forests and woods, a one-child anti-liturgical plague which has struck as far as three whole villages away. It was his turn with Germoline. I shouted—well, croaked—him over.

'Tinker says they're coming to arrest you, Lovejoy.' He was quite calm about it.

'You've to hit the road and get out of town,' Ginny

confirmed. Telly Westerns.

'It sounds like it,' I said.

The children were looking doubtfully from me to Germoline and back again.

'Don't worry,' I said reassuringly. 'I'll get a bigger one. For speed.'

I heard Ginny's mother calling them back for their grub.

'We hope you make it to Utah, Lovejoy,' Ginny told me gravely. 'And that the Red Indians don't get you.'

'Can we have Germoline if they do?' little Dobber asked.

'I'll talk to her about it,' I told them, and saw them off up the lane.

I wished getting away from Maslow was so easy. I went in to make some grub, wondering where the hell's Utah.

Maslow came about five o'clock. He didn't come in, just stood grandly at my door. He informed me that certain investigations were proceeding concerning certain events related to certain deaths concerning certain antique dealers. While insufficient evidence was available on which to base an arrest, he wanted me down at the police station to help him and others with their enquiries. I said to get stuffed. He smiled at that, and said I was not to leave the cottage under any circumstances without notifying him or his duly authorized deputy. I watched him go, knowing that Constable Jilks, our flying peeler, would be hovering in the lane.

I stayed at home, resting some more, and then strolled up the lane at a geriatric limp for a pint at the White Hart. Word had got round about my escapades. I was treated like a mild explosive. Tinker was there. Ignoring his air of despondency, I got him into an alcove.

'This rock piece, Tinker.' I passed the chrysoberyl over. He turned it in his mittens. 'To Silver Joe.'

'What the bleeding hell is it?'

'Never mind. Ask Silver Joe to price it. Then pass word to me. I'll be in prison. If the price is right I'll let you know, and you can have the commission on the sale. Joe can chop it for me.' I meant to divide the proceeds, not the rock. I'd give half to Terry for his rotten old boat and half to Lemuel for his car. The value of the rock should cover it, with luck. I didn't tell Tinker the value because prices tend to show in his face more than mine at times like this.

Silver Joe's a reliable old rogue given to homemade jewellery. His brother works in London, though, and I knew he'd dance with delight at the sight of the precious mineral. If Maslow had left me alone I'd have loved a crack at the piece myself, but it was better this way. At least I'd go to gaol not owing everybody on the outside. Tinker went a bit white about the gills when I said that about the car and the boat, fearing the worst. He didn't ask after Devvo.

The pub was quiet that evening. The dealers left me alone, only Tinker and Lemuel bravely coming to cadge a drink or several. Helen and Brad looked in for a minute but left after a bit of whispering together in the somnolence. It was a real mortuary. I explained to Lemuel that his car was a goner owing to an accident with Terry's boat. Seeing that his car was the deposit . . . Lemuel took it better than Tinker, funnily enough.

Finally I told Tinker to get me two hundred ounces of pure silver from Silver Joe and to leave it in my converted garage. It's the sort of thing you can still do in our village without any risk of theft. Keeping alive and trying not to commit murder are a lot more difficult. I've found that.

I did the work three days later. Dolly was with me and I felt fresh and in reasonable health. Dolly respected my long silences, seeming to understand what was about to happen. The police had called several times asking me to make statements. I'd refused, even when they brought Maslow. I wasn't having any, and they were still in the lane, nodding to Dolly and eyeing her legs every time she went out. Once she came back from town looking fraught, but that was maybe her husband creating hell. Constable Jilks tried to come in once when it was raining, and several times I'd caught Dolly brewing up, feeling sorry for him stuck down in the lane while everybody else was in their warm house, but I put a stop to that. He wouldn't bring me one when I was in the nick, that was sure. Let him do without.

The silver was oval, done on an improvised sandtray, heated by my foot bellows of leather and hollowed ash. I'd have liked to use elder, like some of the northern men, but you can't get that too easily in the south, not of the quality. I'd got Ian, Andy's lad, to bring me all the dense logs he could find from the tithe cuttings, when all the extra wood in the village is given to the church. God could spare it. I had a pile as high as the garage when the time came.

The die was the easiest part, as with most dies that aren't too recessed. I used hard steel on account of the wear it was going to have to take. A piece as thick as a finger, made convex at one end, the sides filed flat to allow a good grip in the vice, and then cutting and filing the dome into a firefly pattern. I wanted it very stylized. After much thought I chose one of the patterns from traditional Chinese fireflies, more symbols than actual drawings. The mood was on me, and I knew it. I was in a trance, hardly eating, dreaming hours at a time between filing the metal tip into a firefly.

That took the first day and half the next. I tried to rouse myself then, for the coming ordeal. I paced myself because of the state I was in, took decent rests and had good meals in between.

Dolly was great, bringing grub and never asking what I was doing. Several times she fended people off and had one nasty fight with a pretty young reporter called Liz. I wasn't too sure I wanted her to win that one, but thought maybe later, if . . . The rest of the second day I saw to the silver, making certain the edges were stencilled, the base clean and the casting of the dish impeccable. Casting's fairly easy. I had to sand one small nick in the oval's centre, but didn't have time to repeat the whole thing. Maslow would be along for me any day once he'd gathered enough lawyers against me. I was for it, just as he'd said. I'd be lucky to come out at the other end.

I slept late that third day. Dolly didn't put the radio on, just let me go out after breakfast into the watery sunshine and start. I walked about nervously to keep from distractions, idly kicking sticks and grass, going round and round the garden as the mood came into me. Now and then I returned to the garage and bellowed the fire up. I always use the old charcoal-burner's trick of banking the furnace up with clods, forcing the heat to stay alive yet closed during the nights. I'd uncovered it and got the fire drawing easily within an hour of getting up.

The silver was in my hands before I'd made any conscious decision to start the Reverse Gadroon. It was heavy and ponderous, hellish difficult to control. On any normal day that would have put me off, but today I was above everything and simply went on, fixing the firefly die into my vice and getting the angle right. I began practice with a quick tap, using the sheet metal to get my arm going and make sure the die would hold nice and tight. The fact the marks showed neat and precise through the metal was no surprise to me, not on that magic day. Oddly, it was like watching Drummer.

I hitched the huge silver dish to the hanging pegs and

got the homemade pulleys running free. It took the heavy silver oval beautifully. One rapid dash to the furnace for maximum heat, and I laid the hammers out on the improvised benching. I have this great iron stool and perched myself on its edge. My throat was dry as hell and my eyes gritty from the sand table, which smoked and flickered behind. I spun the great silver oval, flat as a pancake, on its suspending clothes pegs. All ready. One more hitch at the stool to centre me against the die's position, and I was off. I was in a dream, floating. I even wondered if it was me there.

I simply watched the firefly gadroon come through the silver. One hammer blow, almost as if done by somebody else with me looking, fetched the indentation through the silver, impressing the firefly design. A smooth movement to one side a fraction of an inch and the hammer fell again, a loving stroke, not a blow. And again the impression came, meticulously in position against its neighbour. And another blow and another. Another. Another.

The hammer's sound drugged me. It was true love, the silver assimilating into itself the heavy loving strokes. And somehow, with every stroke of the hammer, the great silver oval spun itself that fraction of a turn into position to receive the next loving penetration of the rigid die. Round it spun, flashing reflections of the golden-red furnace colours. The hammer lifted and fell. The great dish spun. I heard somebody singing and only dimly realized after some minutes that it was me. My arms that had been arthritic and hopeless for the past three days were doing the silversmith's work of their own accord. It was as if I were simply watching Drummer's gnarled hands as, time after time in this same spot, he'd shown me the wondrous gift of the gadroon. I slammed on in the smoke, oblivious of aches and weariness, sometimes shaking sweat from my eyes and hefting the hammer down again and again as my hands flicked the ponderous dish in the air before me. It was beautiful, this spinning for the act of love, the silver seeming to quiver and move of its own volition as the hammer bore down and down again upon its gleaming surface. The last stroke brought the patterns into one circumferential oval, precise and ideal. Without a second's pause I saw my right hand flick the heavy hammer aside with a crash and bring the lighter hammer into position, starting off round thesilver's edge again with the same loving actions, spinning and beating.

It must have been less than half an hour but when finally the sounds ceased I couldn't believe that my private blissful eternity had come to an end. The silver had spun the last time, and now hung there. I dropped the last hammer and sat there looking. The furnace flickered and darted colour off the silver surface. Its margin was indented now, the firefly design meeting exactly in its brilliant dance round the edge. The distances were right. The small markings where the design had to be fetched into precise line were there. It was magical, as beautiful as any gadroon design I had ever seen. And it was a reverse design, the most difficult of all. Done blind, guessing exactly for every one of the several hundred glittering impressions.

I had done it. I found I was drooping over the bench, wheezing like my old leather bellows. The exaltation left me gradually. I got all my creaks back. I straightened and turned to place the dish on the sand tray, ready for its three silver ball-and-claw feet.

Tinker was at the pub when I phoned and told him to bring the big Yank urgently, tell him I'd done the Reverse Gadroon. Dolly and me sat waiting on the divan.

She knew there was something wrong. I suppose I'd led

her on a bit, for the sake of peace. I decided now was the time.

'They'll come for me soon, love,' I told her. 'There's an order out for me. I'll have to go with them.'

'But for how long, darling?' Dolly was instantly worried about socks and things for me to take. She's great. I had to grin.

'Some time,' I said. I told her about the silver dish in the garage. 'Tell Tinker to take it to Silver Joe and see its claw feet are put on, properly finished.'

'Silver Joe,' she repeated for memory's sake.

Somebody was at the door then. It was the big Yank, the commodore whose boat I kept wrecking. He came in smiling, refusing Dolly's coffee as he sat. I didn't blame him because Americans are used to the proper stuff.

I said, 'It's too much of a coincidence that your boat was around so much, Mr Naismith. Am I right?'

'That's right, sir.'

I sighed. That's all I needed, I thought wearily. This New World politeness when my world was crumbling. Despite all, he was watchful as a cat.

'Tell me one thing. Drummer's death.'

'None of my doing. I'm nothing to do with that side.'

'You're the broker for the nicked stuff, right?'

'That's so, sir. Only the business side.'

I kept gamely on. 'And your position at the yacht club's a front for popping the nicked antiques to the Continent. Right?'

'Correct.'

'I'll tell nothing of it. But on your way out step into the garage. You'll see a Reverse Gadroon, silver, two hundred ounces, on the hot sand table. I've not time to fix its feet, but it's handmade. By me.'

I saw his eyes widen in astonishment and he made to speak. I cut him short. He'd have to suss the rest. This wasn't the sort of conversation that could be finished with

Maslow in the room. 'I can do it,' I said. 'Again and again. Drummer taught me. And they allow arts and crafts in clink, where I'm going. *You* could provide the blank cast silver bowls, dishes, anything. If there's any difficulty tell them it's only plated, or maybe pewter. They won't know.'

'I see.' His brain was on the go. I knew he was thinking of the laws in the USA, where possession of a genuine antique silversmith's personal marking die is quite legal. Here it's a criminal offence. 'I see,' he said again.

I drew breath. 'Er, about your boat. It wasn't intentional. I didn't mean to sink it. They came at me.'

'I accept that. I'll prefer no charges.' He leant forward. 'The idea is that . . . er . . .' he glanced at Dolly, pausing. Dolly was already packing some clothes up for me but she was in earshot. 'Er, you might consider making some items for shipping abroad, by any means I chose?'

'Maybe,' I said.

'A handmade Reverse Gadroon's unbelievable.'

'Check on it,' I told him. Drummer would have been proud.

'Can I take it with me?' he asked.

I thought on this. Maybe he'd better, seeing I expected Maslow to put me in a cage. I nodded. 'But I want Tinker there, until we agree a price. Silver Joe as referee?'

'Done.' His grin came back and we shook hands. 'Maybe I'd better wait outside,' he added, getting the feeling between Dolly and me.

I let him go, a nice bloke full of politeness still. I accepted his version. Nothing was further from his behaviour than aggro. He was the antiques broker for the nick trade all right. And I was sure he'd had nothing to do with the killing of Drummer, especially seeing how well he had behaved when I'd rescued Germoline that time.

Tinker came shuffling in while Dolly and I talked on

the divan. She was crying and saying I could get a lawyer. I didn't know any so I'd have to leave that side to trust. Tinker was jubilant.

'I seed it, Lovejoy!' He meant the gadroon. 'Drummer'll be smiling all over his face, Gawd rest him. And that Yank's dancing wiv delight, mate.'

Mate. I let him prattle on for a while but I had called Devvo mate while he'd begged me for help. And I'd let Devvo drown, me and Germoline. Maybe I deserved gaol, or maybe I was just tired.

Something was on Tinker's mind. 'Here, Lovejoy. Did you really do for Devvo and his burkes? I'll say you was with Lemuel and me.'

I gazed back at him. The loss of his principal source of income for booze—namely, me—was practically the end of his normal everyday life, but he was still in there sticking up for me, the stupid old get. I went to look out of the window at the garden for a minute.

'Leave it, Tinker,' I said when I could speak the words. 'Look after yourself while I'm in the nick. The Yank will see you get your lolly.'

'I could tell the Old Bill we wuz at Sotheby's.' He was all eager, but I shook my head. Just as well I did for Tinker's sake because just then Maslow walked in. No knock, notice.

'Get your coat, lad,' he said to me. 'You're under arrest. Among other things, for destroying a sea fortress, property of our Sovereign Monarch—'

'Eh?' It had damned near destroyed me, never mind the other way round. Then I remembered that ominous *crump* out to sea, and the single great swelling wave that lifted my boat . . . Oh hell. The 'counterbalanced' exit from the chamber must have been a destruction device. If I'd half the sense I was born with I could have worked that out.

Maslow was deliriously happy watching my face. 'And,'

he said, grinning some more, 'complicity in the murder of —'

'Don't bother,' I said evenly. 'I'll come quietly.' I've always wanted to say that.

I had quite a send off. Germoline looked at me as I went towards the police car. Our worthy Constable Jilks was there, important but embarrassed at all this. I told him it was all right, George, and not to worry. Maslow ordered me to get in, but I went across to say so-long to Germoline. She was grave, thinking whatever were things coming to, but aware there wasn't much of a way out for either of us.

I told her, 'Germoline, I've made arrangements with Lemuel to take you to Mrs Hepplestone's.' I scratched her neck and left her there, kissed Dolly and got in between these two constables. There seemed nothing else. Dolly was weeping. Well, I wasn't too happy either. I wound the window down.

'Oh, love,' I called to Dolly. 'Count the teaspoons after these coppers have gone. Okay?'

She nodded, sniffing into a hankie. I sighed. It had been a joke. The trouble was Dolly *would* count them all, and keep a list at that. Germoline watched us go.

We rolled down the lane. I noticed the big Yank had vanished and that his car was nowhere in sight, a shrewd nut if ever I saw one. You can't teach the Yanks anything about running a business.

'What the hell?' Maslow muttered.

As our car turned towards the chapel there were two grotty figures waiting by the side of the hedge. There was hardly room for our big police motor to squeeze past. I saw the pair of them, tatty as ever, come to attention as the car cruised slowly past. Lemuel had his medals on still, and Tinker was looking his worst. The silly old fool presented arms with a stick.

Maslow had reached out furiously and wound his window down, when I leaned forward and tapped his shoulder. Hard.

'You dare, Maslow,' I said softly, my hand resting casually near his neck. 'You fucking dare.'

He paused. The two old fools were standing there at the salute, the wind flapping their tattered coats. A few of the villagers were watching in astonishment by the bus stop. Maslow looked angrily across at his apprehensive driver. 'What are you waiting for?' he snarled. 'The Guards' band? Get on, get on.'

I didn't look at the ridiculous pair. It was hard to swallow. The car edged past and we drove off, but Maslow had the last word. They always do. By the main town road he'd recovered and was smiling at some secret success. He unleashed it as we settled down towards town.

'One thing, Lovejoy,' he said. 'It'll be hundred to one, you getting off.'

'Them's bad odds.'

'Either way we'll have you,' he said pleasantly. 'Oh, incidentally. One of the court's advisers has asked personally to take your case. Social worker with a special interest.'

'They're all the same to me,' I told him.

'Really?' he said cheerfully. 'Tell you one thing. The last thing I'd want is five years' court probation in Maud's tender loving care.'

Maud? That cannibal? I croaked, 'Maslow, you wouldn't . . .'

'Wouldn't I, Lovejoy?'

'Look, Maslow. Please . . . *please* . . .'

The swine said nothing. He just laughed and laughed and laughed, and we drove on to town.

THE SLEEPERS OF ERIN

A story for Freda and hers, for Susan, Glen, Babs, and
Yvonne who wanted such a start.

This book is dedicated as a humble offering to the memory of the ancient Chinese god T'ai Sui, who afflicts with poverty and pestilence all those who do not dedicate humble offerings to his memory.

Lovejoy

CHAPTER 1

Everybody wants them.

You want them. I want them. Everybody. The poor in the gutter, famous actresses, millionaires on yachts, robbers clinging to drainpipes, dreamers, hookers, killers. Everybody.

And what are they, these things?

They are exquisite. Beautiful. Breathtaking, crammed with soul and love. They also happen to be inflation-proof. They resist monetary devaluation and wars, plagues, famines, holocausts and the Great Crash.

They're antiques.

The trouble is, there's blood on most. I should know, because I'm an antique dealer. Yes, your actual quiet, friendly, placid bloke who sells you old pots and paintings and things in perfect tranquillity.

This story starts where I'm bleeding to death.

Hospitals always stink of ether, though they say it's not used much now. Like in most places, nothing ever really changes. The ceilings whizzing past overhead looked cracked and unpainted, the bulbs and fluorescents grubby, not a lampshade in sight. All those big lagged pipes still there. The swing doors in Emergency had been replaced by flexible flaps since last time, but they came together with an appalling crash just the same. Hospitals kill me. The nurses had the same massive watches pinned to their bosoms, to put your eye out when they lean over you. I tried telling the prettiest one it was only an accident, honest, and not to call the police.

'You shut up,' she said crossly. 'I've had quite enough from you in the ambulance. There's blood everywhere.

It'll take hours clearing up.'

A detached voice said, 'Is this the injured tramp?'

'Bloody cheek,' I croaked.

'You shut up,' the nurse said again.

'How did it happen?' that detached voice demanded.

I said, 'I fell.'

'You shut up,' the nurse said.

A house doctor looking like a knackered teenager said bitterly, 'The bastard's O rhesus negative.'

Five faces glared hate down at me, as if blood groups are anybody's fault. An older voice, just as tired, said anyway it would have to be operating theatre and to call out the anaesthetist. 'Take him into Number Three. Another plasma, and do a rapid crossmatch.'

It sounded horrible. 'Look,' I said upwards, trying to be helpful. 'Don't go to a lot of trouble—'

They all said together, 'You shut up.' Manners no different, either.

I woke up some time during the night feeling sick. Somebody had a tin thing under my chin. A fob watch donged my eyeball. Skilled hands mangled my damaged arm so I almost screamed with the pain. A light seared into my skull. Torture's gentler.

'Yes, he's conscious,' a bird's voice said.

A pleasant-looking bloke was standing patiently by when finally I came to. He tiptoed solicitously forward.

'Lovejoy?' The kindest voice I'd heard yet.

'Mmmmh?'

He smiled, full of compassion. 'You're under arrest,' he said. That brought a wash of memory. It made me groan.

'You shut up,' the nurse said.

Fingringhoe Church is out on the sea-marshes. Miles from anywhere. In fact, it's even miles from Fingringhoe, which only goes to prove something or other.

I'd been in this lonely church, kipping on one of the

rear pews after Sal had gone home, and thinking myself alone. A voice woke me, echoing.

'It's okay!' it said. 'All clear.'

Clarkie's voice was instantly recognizable. Sensibly, I kept still so I made no noise. Clarkie always was stupid, hadn't the sense to suss the church casually as if he were just admiring the stained glass windows. I lay on the pew, tired out after Sal but amused at listening to Clarkie's ponderous footfalls in the aisle. He's subtle as a salvo.

'Fasten that bleeding door, Sam.'

The church door boomed to, sending echoes round the interior. He must have his partner Sam Veston with him, a no-hope knife man if ever there was one. Talk about antique dealers. They say they're experts on pre-Victorian domestic furniture, which is hilarious. They're thick.

'What we do first, Clarkie?' Sam sounded nervous.

'Silver. There'll be a safe in here somewhere.'

They were somewhere down the church now. I sat up quietly to watch Clarkie and Sam set to work on the vestry door.

Sam asked, 'Whose was that frigging great Bentley?'

'Dunno. Some bird doing the church flowers.'

'She took long enough,' Sam grumbled.

I smiled. That would have been Sal, leaving for home. Clarkie and Sam must have waited in the hedgerows while Sal and I made love on the back pew. I'd come earlier on foot so they'd assumed Sal was alone. Incidentally, don't go thinking that loving in church is the height of blasphemy. It's God's full-time occupation. Anyway, Sal has an influential husband who would see me off if we were rumbled.

This infamous pair were interesting. I'd never seen anybody (else, that is) carrying out a robbery in person before. Clarkie had tried the vestry door and was standing to one side while Sam rummaged in the lock with a spider — that's an improvised key made of bent wires. You shape it as you go. Very much trial-and-error, but that's all you can expect from antique dealers these days. Now, if Sam had taken the trouble to learn how a splendid three-centuries-old lock was constructed, or had the slightest inkling of the beautiful workmanship which had gone into it when the ancient locksmith crafted it . . . I sighed. Antique dealers haven't a clue. Pathetic. God knows why, but dealers always want to prove that ignorance really is bliss. It honestly beats me. I could have turned that lock without breaking my stride. Clarkie is a minor antique dealer who 'specializes' in everything. He hangs hopefully on the coat-tails of any dealer rumoured to have a cerebral cortex, and picks up the odd trade swap now and then. Thick as a plank, the biggest deal he'd ever done was a quarter share in a piece of Derby, that costly John Milton figure holding a scroll. (You'll still occasionally come across Derby pieces in junk shops, but not as often as you used to.) I saw it, a luscious gold-touched white about 1776 or so. It was genuine, but that was entirely miscalculation on Clarkie's part. He is your actual average antique dealer, which is to say an incompetent, acerebral buffoon whose idea of research is somewhere to the left of guesswork. That deal was a year ago and I knew Clarkie was now on his uppers, though I had never known him do a church over before. It was an interesting sidelight on my colleagues, and I observed their progress with delighted fascination.

'What about a hammer and chisel, Clarkie?' Sam asked.

'Right. Smash the bloody thing.'

I wasn't having that. 'You dare,' I said.

They yelped. Clarkie dropped his bag of tools with a crash. Sam had sprinted half way to the door before they realized it was only me and screeched to a stop.

'It's Lovejoy,' Clarkie gasped.

'Christ.' Sam was grey-faced from fright. 'I thought it was the Old Bill.'

'You silly sod, Lovejoy.' Clarkie mopped his face. 'Made me come over queer. What you doing here?'

I scoffed, 'I wouldn't pay you in marbles, Clarkie.'

'We're just . . . just doing a lift,' Clarkie said apologetically. Sam looked from Clarkie to me and began to edge towards the church door. That was in case I ran out yelling for the peelers.

'And you're not going to stop us,' Sam added. He pulled out his knife and held it loosely at waist height, a really sinister threat calculated to strike terror into the most savage nun. You have to laugh. No wonder antique dealers have a bad name.

'Piss off, Sam,' I said, getting up and walking past him to join Clarkie, my footsteps echoing from the stone-flagged flooring. I noticed the church was not as bright now. The daylight was seeping from the sky and the hard sun shadows were ashed into a sad grey.

Clarkie backed off as I approached. 'Now, Lovejoy, mate,' he began nervously. 'This scam's nothing to do with you.'

'You're right.' I toed his bag of tools. It clanked like a shunting yard. They must have brought every tool they owned. 'And it's nothing to do with you, either.'

'What do you mean?'

'I mean get lost, Clarkie.' I grinned. 'I'll count to ten and you hide, eh?'

Sam spoke up. 'It's only a cloth job, for Chrissakes.' I should have listened to the despair in his voice and saved myself an operation, but maybe I was too clapped out. Anyway, I didn't. 'Cloth job' means robbing a church, an enterprise with a very respectable history if you think about it. Nowadays it's so common it's almost routine. There's hardly an antique dealer in England who bothers to ask any more where you got that old chalice or ciborium. Auctioneers are twice as bad, having no reputation to lose.

'Not today, Sam,' I told him. Honestly, to this day I don't know why I was taking this attitude, especially over a run-of-the-mill cloth job. Even priests are hard at it, flogging their own church silver on the side. Maybe it was the lingering sense of Sal's loving, whatever. Anyway, right or wrong I decided not to let them do it.

'You know we've *got* to, Clarkie,' Sam wailed. Which should have alerted me even more.

'You've got *not* to, Clarkie,' I corrected. 'Because I say so.'

'Erm . . .' He swallowed, eyed me.

I was honestly surprised, yet another warning bleep. Clarkie had seen me angry once, and I know for a fact he was very, very glad to be neutral on that occasion.

'Clarkie,' I warned gently, and he nodded. The bag clonked against his thigh as he picked it up and walked towards the door.

'For Christ's *sake*!' Sam squawked, but he trotted obediently after Clarkie. Smiling, I shut the door gently behind us and crossed the gravel with them to where their old van was parked. They must have left it in a lay-by up the lane towards the village until Sal left.

'Now, lads,' I said as the engine coughed into action. 'You two nellies leave this place alone, right?' I shook a warning finger at them as the van began to roll. 'I'll count the teaspoons. Cheers, Clarkie.'

'Cheers,' Clarkie muttered, but I could see he was dismayed. I wouldn't have thought a mere interruption would have him terrified as all that, but then I wasn't thinking.

I'd actually turned away when I heard Sam yell, 'You bastard, Lovejoy!' Like a nerk I paused affably, and felt a searing pain swipe through my left arm above the elbow. Sam bawled, 'Off, Clarkie!' The van scattered gravel. Its wheels spun and the engine roared, and there I was, left standing in a country churchyard fifty million miles from anywhere, staring stupidly at my arm with my brilliant scarlet blood spurting out into the air in front of me going *shish-shish-shish*.

For one instant I was quite unconcerned, wondering mildly what had happened and casually touching my arm where the blood was spouting. There was no further pain. Then, in a horrid cold terror, I realized. Sam had flung his knife. My artery was cut — *my* fucking *artery* was *cut* and I was frigging *dying*.

I tore off my jacket, blood going everywhere, ripped off my shirt sleeve and wrapped it round in a clumsy knot and got the blood stopped. I went back inside and used a candlestick to wind the tourniquet tighter, then ran.

About three minutes later, I reeled into the church organist's cottage in a worse state than China but alive. The old geezer had a certificate in first aid. He had a high old time, and nearly killed me enjoying himself doing complicated splints and knots until the ambulance came and took me prisoner and nurses were saying you just shut up.

CHAPTER 2

The police gave me two days before I was officially charged. It was quite a ceremony. My arm was sutured, the artery repaired, thank God. The nurses were behaving abominably, as if I'd done myself an injury on purpose just to annoy them. They'd hardly said a word to me, slamming about the ward and heaving me about like a sack of nuisance.

The chap in the next bed was a misanthrope, a real prophet of doom called Smith, accused of osteoarthritis.

A worse temper, and he could have slipped on to the
hospital staff unnoticed. Opposite me was a cheerful little
bloke with a gastric ulcer. It was old Smith told me I
would be charged that morning.

'You're for the high jump, old son,' he said with relish.
'Nicking stuff from churches.'

'That can't be right.' I was so confident. I was a hero.
(I'd prevented a crime, right?)

'You wait.'

'Tell 'em the tale, Lovejoy,' the gastric ulcer called
across. 'I'll alibi you for fifty quid.' He fell about at this
witticism.

Sister Morrison, our ward sister, came in then to tell us
to shut up. I liked her, really, a quiet if bossy Irish lass,
mid-thirties, in dark blue. She brought two coppers in
and stood formally aside while they did their thing.

'Lovejoy?'

'Yes.'

'We're police officers,' the older one said. 'I'm
Detective-Sergeant Ledger.'

'Congratulations. What's this arrest bit?'

'Theft of church property.'

'Please can you be a little more specific?' I asked
politely.

He smiled a wintry smile over a notebook. 'More
specifically, two chalices, two patens, one ciborium and
one monstrance. All precious metals. And,' he added
with relish, 'one brass candlestick.'

There was a protracted silence, enjoyed by some more
than others. I cleared my throat.

'Erm, wasn't the vestry door locked?'

'Opened by a skilled hand,' Ledger said. 'Yours.'

I thought, well, well. Odderer and odderer. And I
thought I'd been a hero.

'You're a long shot, Lovejoy,' he continued. 'What with

your record, and that paten being found in your cottage.'

'Lovejoy,' Gastric Ulcer cracked, 'our alibi deal's off.'

'You've had it, son,' Smith prophesied. A nurse hissed at him to shut up.

Sister Morrison was looking at me. 'Are you all right, Lovejoy?'

'Mmmmh?' I'd been thinking. 'Oh, yes, ta.'

The Old Bill was in his element. 'You will be brought to trial—'

'Sure, sure. Look,' I said, because you can't help worrying about small things. 'Don't mind my asking, but *what* paten in my cottage?'

'The one in your cistern.'

'We had a search warrant,' the assistant peeler said with pride.

'Well done,' I said absently. 'And the rest of the stuff?'

'Only you know the answer to that, Lovejoy.'

'It's disgraceful!' Sister Morrison snapped. 'A grown man robbing an unprotected church!'

I ignored her and spoke directly to the Old Bill. 'What's your theory, Ledger? That I sliced my arm, ran home in daylight carrying a load of church silver, buried the loot, carefully put one piece in the cistern—the first place you lot would look—then caught the bus back to get a candlestick for a tourniquet? Something like that?'

'Accomplice,' Ledger said.

'I trust antiques, not people.'

'True, Lovejoy.' He was really enjoying himself, better than a birthday. 'The trouble is, what were you doing in a lonely church if you weren't robbing it?'

Smiling, I drew breath to answer, then said nothing. I'd been there to make surreptitious love with Sal. Sister Morrison was looking again. 'There is that, Ledger,' I said at last.

They went about eleven o'clock. I'd no idea there was

so much paperwork to getting arrested. Nothing but forms. Last time they'd only had handcuffs.

'See you in court, Lovejoy,' Ledger said from the door.

'It's a date,' I called cheerily back, trying to be pleasant. At least they hadn't told me to shut up.

Sister Morrison was oddly terse, silencing my two companions and drawing my bed screens when I said I was tired. She sent some atrocious nosh along at noon but otherwise saw to it that I was left alone apart from one frantic episode in the early afternoon when a gang of nurses invaded my sanctuary, hoovered me and reemed me out, then flung me back gasping like a flounder while they went to punish old Smith in the same way.

All that day I thought hard. My mind was still a bit soggy from the anæsthetic but it began firing on the odd cylinder at last. What had seemed an innocent—well, nearly innocent—dust-up with Clarkie and his tame knife-throwing goon Sam was now disturbingly complicated. Worse, it had become two separate problems. First, I was under arrest for theft. That bit I could understand. But the second bit was crammed full of evil vibes I hated even more.

To start with, Clarkie normally wouldn't get in my way at any price. And Sam Veston for all his bravado with his pet knife usually walked very carefully round me, after a slight disagreement he and I had had in an auction room two years ago when I'd cracked a few of his ribs. Yet Clarkie had actually hesitated, foolhardy youth, when I'd told him to scarper. And Sam had dared to do me untold harm. The point is that normally neither of them would have dared anything of the kind. I remembered that look of despair on Sam's face, and his plaintive cry, 'We've *got* to, Clarkie!' Why? Antique dealers don't *have* to do anything, except survive.

Of course I'd have to crease Clarkie and Sam when I

got sprung from hospital, human nature being what it is. An antique dealer of zero resources just can't afford to be knocked about without at least grumbling a little. Weakness is all very admirable — in others. Nothing teaches you this like the antiques trade. But somebody — somebody 'skilled', Ledger had told me — had opened the vestry door and presumably cracked the safe in there, ferried off the church plate, entered my cottage, popped a patten in the cistern, then bubbled me to the Old Bill. Again, why? But most of all, what was *I* doing in all this mess?

At four o'clock I thought, right. When the rest of the ward were watching the match on telly I got Sister Morrison to let me use the trolley phone in the anteroom. She sent a nurse to wheel me down. I knew the number well enough. Naturally with my luck it was good old Geoffrey who picked up the receiver.

'Horsham Furniture here,' I said briskly. 'Could I speak to Mrs Dayson, please?'

'I'll get her.'

A door closed, then Sal came on, puzzled but guarded.

'It's me,' I said. 'Listen, love — '

'Don't you "love" me!' she blazed. Obviously good old Geoffrey was now elsewhere. 'Where have you been, Lovejoy? If you've been with that bitch again, I'll — '

'That bitch' was Helen, an antique dealer I'm, er, friendly with — or any other woman Sal cares to think of in the same context. There wasn't time for one of Sal's special one-way discussions so I broke in and told her I was in hospital. The beeps went twice until she came down through the superstrata.

'Listen, love,' I said urgently when she was coherent. 'This is important. Did anybody see you leaving the church?'

'No, darling. Oh God. What have they been doing to you?'

'What about Geoffrey? Did he . . . ?'

'No. He was in court,' she said impatiently. 'Oh, darling—'

'Eh?'

'He sits on the bench. Stay there. I'm on my way.' I thought, now she tells me. That was all I needed, Sal's old man the local magistrate. I'd be lucky not to get shot.

I rang round three pubs before I got Tinker at the Queen's Head.

'That you, Lovejoy?' he croaked blearily into the phone against the taproom noise. 'Where the bleedin' hell you bin? Everybody's goin' daft lookin' for you. I've got one of them carved wooden geezers carrying two ducks waitin' up Sudbury way—'

'Jesus.' The moan came out involuntarily. There had been rumours for months about a German limewood figure. They're worth a fortune, if you can lay hands on them. Tinker's my barker, the best sniffer-out of antiques in the business. Now he finds it.

'I can't hold her for ever, Lovejoy,' Tinker gravelled out. I heard somebody shout across the bar if that was Lovejoy on the blower. 'Yes,' Tinker bawled back. 'Here, Lovejoy. I've found a Yankee Windsor chair, I reckon, but funny wood—'

'Shut it, Tinker. Listen. Get over to the County Hospital, Charrington Ward—*no!*' I almost shouted the command to stop his repeating the instruction all over the pub. 'Say nothing. Just drink up and get over here. But one thing. Find out where Clarkie and Sam Veston have disappeared to. I'm going to dust them over on the quiet.'

'Right, Lovejoy.' He gave a gulp. 'Where'll you be?'

'Waiting,' I said sourly and rang off.

It was when I was reaching up to ring the bell to be wheeled back to bed when I noticed there was an open wall hatch ajar nearby. Through the gap I could see Sister Morrison's head bent over the day's reports in the ward office. Quickly I wondered if she could hear. Not touching the bell, I said carefully, almost in an undertone. 'Sister, please.'

'Yes?' She didn't look up.

'I'm ready to go back now.'

'I'll take you.' She got up and walked round to come for me. She must have heard every word.

Her face was ice. Great, I thought bitterly. Now I was not only a church plunderer, but a self-confessed adulterer and a murderous revenge-seeker as well. Win friends the easy way, I always say.

The rest of that day was not too good so I won't dwell on it. Sal came in, lovely and perfumed and dressed to the nines, frantic with worry and demanding to know every detail. She wept a bit like they do, and told the staff nurse that no expense was to be spared. 'Thank you,' Sal got frostily back, 'but Lovejoy is being paid for out of our taxes.' Surreptitiously she gave me a handful of notes in case I needed to send out for anything. The trouble was she became distinctly cool when I said what had happened.

'Police?' she gasped faintly. 'You mean, really? In actual court?'

'Yes, love. Somebody must have planted a piece at my cottage to bubble me.'

Sal said, 'Oh, darling,' but it wasn't her usual voice, full of possessiveness and humour. It sounded ominously like the sailor's elbow. 'Not . . . not in the *news*papers?'

'It's okay,' I reassured her cheerfully. 'I'll sort it out —'

She fingered her red amber beads, Chinese nineteenth-century. I'd got them for her fairly cheap in a local antiques auction before Sac Freres dragged them off to their Bond Street lair.

Sal is beautiful, really stylish. I was so proud of her there in the ward with the nurses enviously eyeing her gear and Sister Morrison going thin-lipped at the sight of such glamour. I mean, after all Sal was *my* visitor. The only good thing to have happened to me for ages. To my dismay Sal suddenly discovered she had to be going. She kissed me, full of courage about it but clearly taking to the hills. She said she would phone morning and evening, that final psychotherapy of a departing lover putting the boot in. I watched her go, saw her pause and wave from the door before the flaps swung to. Over and out.

In contrast Tinker's appearance can only be called earthy. He stood there, peering hesitantly into the ward. Imagine an unshaven, clog-shod old stick of a bloke approximately attired in an old army greatcoat, holed mittens and a soiled cloth cap, looking every inch a right scruff. Now double it, add an evil stench and you have Tinker Dill. Sister Morrison was instantly hovering on guard against mobile filth. I could tell that plagues and other epidemics had sprung to mind. I admit he's no oil painting but I still wasn't having anybody taking the mickey, so when Gastric Ulcer opposite exclaimed, 'Gawd almighty!' I smiled one of my specials and clicked an imaginary pistol gently at him, which perforated his next witticism. He looked away.

Antique dealers have barkers like armies have skirmishers—to nip around and suss out the scene. Boozy and shabby Tinker may be, but I wouldn't swap him for a gold clock. He sat beside my bed, ponging to high heaven and toothily agog at the ward bustle and the nurses, but mostly at the spectacle of me with my limb trussed up.

'Gawd, Lovejoy,' he croaked out. 'What the bleedin' hell you done? I thought we were doin' a deal.'

'Wotcher, Tinker. Sam and Clarkie.'

'Eh? Oh, aye. Gone to King's Lynn.'

'Wise lads,' I said. 'You tell me the minute they're back, right?'

'What if they don't come?'

I grinned. 'Then I'll go and get them.'

'Like that, is it?' He lowered his head confidentially for his favourite phrase. 'Here, Lovejoy. We in trouble?'

I told him the glad tidings step by step, him groaning and muttering every inch of the tale. When I came to the bit about Sam slinging the knife at me he stared.

'Sam? Him? Gawd, I thought he knew better than try you, Lovejoy.'

'You've spotted it, Tinker.' I listed the mysteries one after the other. 'Neither Sam Veston nor Clarkie would push their luck that far. Then there's the question who actually *did* do the cloth job. And why they bubbled me for it.'

Tinker ahemed at that and glanced about. We were speaking softly because we always do in the antiques game. Old Smith in the next bed was apparently dozing and the bloke to my left had been gruesomely cocooned in a crinkly transparent tent full of tubes ever since I'd arrived, but Tinker was right to be careful.

'Here, Lovejoy,' Tinker muttered. 'You didn't do it, right?'

'Right.'

He thought a minute. 'Then who did?'

'Whoever's got the rest of the church silver, you thick burke,' I explained wearily, getting out the notes Sal had left. 'Look. Here's some gelt. You'll have to manage till I'm out. See Helen, and Margaret Dainty. And Jason in the Arcade. You're looking for *any* church silver, okay?'

'Somebody new, or somebody old?'

That was a point. 'I reckon it's a newcomer. A clever antique collector.'

'How do you work that out?'

I asked, 'What's the least expensive church silver, Tinker? Chalice, ciborium, monstrance, patten?'

'Patten,' he said straight away. 'Only weighs a twentieth of a chalice at most.'

'So he drops the cheapest on me, and keeps the rest,

Tinker. See? Couldn't bear to part with it.'

I sent him off after telling him to check my cottage now and again till they let me go. Not that there's anything valuable in it. Things had been bad lately in the antiques game. It was one of those times when everything seems to be owned by everyone else.

One funny thing happened as he rose to say so-long. Sister Morrison came up and said there was a cup of tea and some cake in the ward office for Tinker if he wanted. Now, this really was odd because women usually want to get rid of him as fast as possible. He went all queer at the invitation because non-alcoholic fluids send him giddy but I gave him the bent eye and he accepted.

'See you, Lovejoy, mate,' he croaked and shuffled off after her.

'Cheers, Tinker.'

Sister Morrison kept Tinker in the office, pouring for him and talking. I could see them through the ward glass. She didn't even make him take his mittens off when passing him the biscuits, an all-time first. I saw him wipe his mitts on his cuffs the way he always does and she didn't even wince. They took a hell of a time over one measly cup of tea, so long in fact that I began to get edgy. I've never known Tinker miss the pubs opening and time was getting on. Maybe she was giving him a talk on hygiene or something. Irritated, I buzzed my buzzer but only got the staff nurse who came and gave me an injection with a syringe like a howitzer. When my bum had been rubbed sore and I was allowed to sit up Tinker was not there any more and Sister Morrison had gone off duty.

Next morning the newspapers were full of it. I was a celebrity.

Not a hero, but definitely a celebrity.

CHAPTER 3

Being stuck in hospital is grim enough. Being the baddie in the black hat as well is terrible. For some days they gave me the full treatment. Even Gastric Ulcer opposite sent me to Coventry, while old Smith read out loud ever-worsening reports about me in the local rag.

It was a real gas. Nurses belligerent, physiotherapists sadistic. The X-ray people who did my arteriogram were obviously disgruntled at having to handle so repellent a specimen of degraded humanity. The surgeons were unchanged, though, merely concentrating when they came round on my repaired artery and telling me to shut up. It was a hell of a life, relieved only by Tinker's somewhat erratic appearances when he called to report the problems in the normal antiques world outside. Curiously, in all this only Sister Morrison showed any sort of balance about me. Her attitude came to light in a way I found embarrassing but it brought her into the problem on my side so I'd better tell it as it happened.

It was on a Tuesday morning when the library lady came round. By then I was desperate for anything on antiques. Tinker had failed at the town library because they'd slung him out for being filthy and having no fixed abode, and I was re-reading a bundle of old issues of the *Antique Collector*. These glossy magazines give me heartburn at some of the careless things people say about antiques. They speak of them almost as if antiques have no soul, which only goes to show.

The promised visit of the library trolley finally came, to my delight, with a splendidly plump matronly bird, all tweeds and blue rinse, parading grandly down the ward dispensing books right and left. I was in ecstasy, because

I'd asked for a text on Ming underglaze blue of the Wan-Li period and the new monograph on the London Clockmakers' Company in Queen Anne's reign. You can guess the state I was in, excitedly watching the elegant lady trundle nearer and nearer between the rows of beds. She came, smiling and chatting, handing out the books and writing her little green cards which said who wanted what for next time. A real Lady Bountiful. She gave Gastric Ulcer his, a thing on greyhounds, and left old Smith his book about pigeon breeding. Then she turned away and went on.

I'd been left.

Apprehensive, I called, 'Erm, excuse me, please.'

'Yes?' she managed, preoccupied with the books and her list. She didn't look up.

'Erm, have you any for me?'

'Subject?' she said absently, still not a glance.

I felt my face redden but got out, 'Antiques, please.'

'I'll check,' she said smoothly, still so very busy. Then she went on to the next bed. Not a word.

Great. Umpteen days trapped in a rotten bed, no antiques anywhere and me suffering withdrawal symptoms worse than any addict. I turned my face away. Bloody hospitals. The difference was that heroin addicts and alcoholics would be kneedeep in intense young sociologists, empathizing like mad, but I was a pariah.

Then a gentle Irish voice uttered my name. 'Have you Lovejoy's books, Mrs Williams?'

'I must have forgotten them, Sister.' Determinedly casual.

'Really, Mrs Williams?' The voice was still soft and enquiring. 'And will you have time to bring them?'

The ward's customary din went quiet. The nurses froze. A couple of old blokes woke up in alarm at the unexpected silence.

'I'll have to see, Sister.' The reply was offhand, but with

that familiar flint-hard core of self-righteous sadism only the pure at heart can manage.

The gentle voice became a bandsaw. '*Nurse!*'

Feet pattered. 'Yes, Sister?' dimply little Nurse Swainson bleated.

'Collect *all* the patients' books this *instant*, and escort that person from the ward — *now!*'

'Yes, Sister!'

Nervously I sat up again. Already the centre of World War Three, the last thing I wanted was the fourth to happen along so quickly. Sister Morrison was calmly dialling at the central phone.

'Excuse me, Sister,' I called nervously. 'Can't we leave it, erm — ?'

'Shut up, Lovejoy.'

Her pleasant voice returned. 'Hello? Sister Morrison here, Charrington Ward. Why have my patients been ignored by the library services, please?'

'*Sister!*' Mrs Williams exclaimed, scandalized.

'Erm, Sister,' I pleaded in a quaver, thinking, Oh Christ. Little Swainson and another junior nurse were scampering about the ward snatching everybody's books and flinging them back on the trolley. It was pandemonium. The two old geezers, relieved the ward's usual cacophony was back, nodded off happily again.

'My charges,' Sister Morrison continued, 'are no better and no worse than any others in this hospital. If you are not able to provide . . .' It went savagely on for a full minute, about ten lifetimes. Finally she slammed the receiver down and turned.

'Nurse Swainson, Nurse Barton, Nurse French,' that alarming voice rasped. 'I thought I told you to escort that *person* out forthwith!'

'Yes, Sister!' voices chorused. A trolley rumbled. Books flew and thumped. We cowered in abject terror. Old Smith grumbled to a fraught Nurse Swainson and practically got castrated for his pains as his pigeon book was ripped out of his hands.

Mrs Williams, as she was being bundled unceremoniously out of the place by a gaggle of nurses, tried a last desperate rearguard action. 'I'll complain to the highest authorities about your conduct, Sister!' But she lost that one as well.

'The best possible thing you can do, Mrs Williams! Lies are not the sole prerogative of the hospital library! Kindly *go*!'

I heard Mrs Williams being scandalized all the way to the lift which ran down through the hospital to the Voluntary Services division two floors below.

'Lovejoy!' I looked up as the bandsaw rasped out my name. 'Lovejoy.' The lilting voice was back again, gentle as ever. 'Please accept our hospital's apologies.'

I must have been a bit down, because I couldn't raise much of an answer to that.

The book trolley came creeping back an hour later. An apprehensive young Red Cross volunteer shakily dished books out in total silence. From fright, we'd all forgotten what we'd asked for and took anything she gave us, but my books were among them. Through the whole episode Sister Morrison was calmly writing out the ward report in her office, ever so innocent. The volunteer finally wheeled her trolley past the ward office when leaving, hugging the corridor wall in a wide curve as if the office was radioactive.

She leapt a mile when Sister Morrison quietly called her name. 'Yes, Sister?' she yelped, white-faced.

Sister Morrison smiled. 'Thank you,' she said sweetly, and let her go.

And hospitals are supposed to be there for your peace of mind. They're not there for your health, that's for sure.

You get 'discharged' from bankruptcies, armies and

hospitals. It was two weeks to the day when I got clearance from the consultant surgeon. I'd displeased him by calling him 'doctor'.

'Surgeons are addressed as Mister,' he told me testily, scribbling my clearance. 'Physicians are addressed as Doctor.'

'Sorry, er, sir.'

'Never been the same since that Yank hospital series on telly in the 'sixties,' he grumbled. He tore off a paper and handed it to Sister Morrison. 'Surgical Outpatients next week, Sister.'

He left the office, leaving me to be documented out. I watched her as she slipped my instructions into an envelope and ticked items off on the file. She was an attractive bird, if only she didn't hate me quite so much. This was the first time I had been in the office, though Tinker had been so favoured almost every visit. Galling. I suspected the old devil of trying to con her into lending him a few quid for beer, this being his great trick. When I asked him what the hell they talked about he only gave his horrible gappy grin and said to mind my own business, even though I threatened to thump him. Once he even joked about it, asked if I was jealous, the cheeky old sod.

As she wrote, a wisp of her pale hair curled round her nape on to her collar. She looked exquisite in spite of that crummy uniform, especially so preoccupied sitting that way with her legs twisted round each other like women can. Good enough to eat. And as for that delectable glass on her desk, it really put her in a breathtaking setting. The loveliest thing on earth, to me it was like an oasis.

There are millions of differently shaped glasses, but this was a marvel. 'Plain Straight-stem' drinking glasses are often anything but that. Antique dealers call them 'Cylindrical', which is a laugh, because they are nothing of the kind. This was Irish, too, a pedestal-type glass with a thick base, having collars top and bottom, but pristinely simple and unadorned. You usually find them — if at all — engraved with names, monograms, or personalized florets rather than plain.

I gazed at the rare little gem enraptured. Sister Morrison or somebody had stuck a single rose in it, a stark reminder of all the boring countryside we have hereabouts in East Anglia. It says a lot for its quality that the glass's beauty was quite undimmed by a grotty rosebud.

She clipped the papers and passed them over.

'Ta. That it, Sister?'

'Outpatients at two o'clock. You're not to be late, Lovejoy.'

I looked at the office floor. 'What if I can't make it? The police . . .' Ledger had told the hospital to phone Culver Street police station about my progress. She coloured slightly, which showed me she had already done the deed. A man's cough sounded from somewhere above my head.

'They will see you make the clinic,' she said, looking away.

'Thank you.' I meant it but she flared.

'Lovejoy. Isn't it time you mended your ways, went straight?'

'I am straight.'

Her face was suddenly pink with vehemence. 'You are hooked on vengence. I know what you'll do — go after Sam Veston and . . . and this Clarkie person. And I know why. You'll get into still more trouble over this church silver. And all because of that horrid woman. There's simply no *point*. It's all so stupid. Can't you see?'

I stared. How the hell did she know so much? Admittedly, she must have heard a little when I'd made that first phone call, but . . . I thought of Tinker's cosy little teatimes with her in this very office and my good hand flexed in anticipation. I'd cripple the gabby old sod.

Again that rasping cough from over my head. I glanced up. There was a small row of receivers on the wall. One was lit by a small red pilot bulb. Light dawned in my thick skull. I leaned forward and peered through her window down the rows of beds. The bloke in that transparent tent moved slightly with a cough. It sounded over my head. My heart sank.

'You heard everything?'

She nodded, correcting me. '*Over*heard.'

That explained her taking my part like she had. And she'd heard the Sal bit, for God's sake. And the true story of the cloth job. And my threats. And on top of that, she was clever enough to have got all the rest of my sordid history out of Tinker. What she hadn't overheard she'd wheedled. That's women for you.

'Are you going to tell?'

'No — as long as you promise not to fight these two people.'

The age-old dilemma of falsehood or truth confronted me. As always, perfidy won. I looked straight into her grey-blue eyes, and swore I'd not lay a finger on Sam and Clarkie.

'I promise, Sister,' I told her. 'Thanks for trusting me.'

'I'm aware,' she went on, 'from my conversations with Mr Dill of the everyday violence of your business, but there's no reason for you to be so shabby morally or physically.' Mentally I promised Tinker hell. I'd teach the silly burke to blab about our sordid game to a do-gooding cherub like her.

I grovelled uncomfortably and nodded, pulled my forelock and swore I'd be honest and true. Anything to get away from those earnest eyes and that high moral tone. As it happened, Ledger saved me just as I was feeling suicidally holy.

He came in smiling. 'On your feet, lad. G'day, Sister.'

A uniformed constable hovered outside, partly to catch

me if I made a run for it and partly to ogle the nurses' legs. Ledger was full of beans. Sister Morrison abruptly became her old frosty self while they signed me over like parcel post.

'You won't handcuff him or anything, will you?' she asked, a last brave try to lessen my burden. Ledger said no and boomed a hearty laugh. I rose to go.

As it happened it was the last laugh he probably had for years, because at that moment the most gorgeous creature I had ever seen in my life stepped into the office. Lustrous dark hair, overwhelming perfume, attired in furs and material that obviously cost a fortune, she wore so much gold and jewellery every step she took made her chime like a Buddhist temple in a gale. For an instant she stood there while we all gaped, then she stepped forward with a little cry and enveloped me in a suffocating embrace while I tried to keep my swathed arm from being crushed.

'Lovejoy, darling!' she cried softly. 'I've come at last! To stand by you! To . . . *own up!*'

There were tears in her dark amber eyes. I swear I'd never seen such remorse.

'Eh?' I nearly asked who the hell she was but her eyes said *not yet, not yet*. I shut up.

'It's no good, darling,' she sniffed. 'I tried to stay away, but I couldn't bear to read what they were doing to you. Day after day of absolute agony!'

'Lovejoy's been well cared for!' Sister Morrison said in her bandsaw voice.

The bird ignored her and sailed straight on into the big scene. 'And now, *arrest!* Oh, dearest darling! I'll tell the truth, reveal all to protect you!'

I'd never been in a Victorian melodrama before so I was stuck there, dumbfounded, under this exotic creature's armpit. The gimlet-eyed Ledger was quicker-thinking.

'Truth?' he ground out ominously. 'Own up to what?'

She dropped me and swung theatrically in obvious torment. I nearly fell over. Sister Morrison saved me as the woman rounded on Ledger, her bosom heaving, all Lilian Gish in dazzling colour.

'Own up to what, Corporal?' she said soulfully, gloved hands clasped together and eyes welling with tears.

'Detective-Sergeant.'

She ignored him too and appealed to the heavens. 'Own up to what? To what happened the night of the crime! Proving poor Lovejoy's complete innocence! Own up to his nobility in sacrificing his own reputation to save mine!'

There was a lot of hate around. Ledger turned puce, and Sister Morrison, having enjoyed herself preaching sweetness and light at me a moment ago, now looked as peaceful as a panther. I was lapping it up, sensing rescue.

'Don't, darling,' I said brokenly, right on cue but guessing a script quicker even than Ingrid Bergman ever did.

Tearfully she wrung her hands, though the size of her superb Edwardian double garnet rings (once so fashionable worn on ladies' gloved fingers) caused her some difficulty. With a clang of precious metal she turned to me, a sob in her voice.

'It's no good, darling! How could I go on?'

'Madam. What is your connection with this man?'

She blotted her eyes with a lace handkerchief so beautiful it dried my throat. You just don't get lace more exquisite than the lace the Sisters made at the Youghal Presentation Convent in County Cork before 1913. It's flat-point lace, and some find it too indiscrete on edgings, but to me it's perfection. When I came to she was raising her eyes adoringly.

'Lovejoy was in the church with me, Lieutenant—'

'Detective-Sergeant.'

She was terribly brave, Mary Queen of Scots on the scaffold. She reeled slightly. I thought that was a bit much, but I steadied her manfully. 'I'm—I'm married, you see. Lovejoy knew that, didn't you, darling?'

'Please, love,' I muttered, all heroic.

'We met in the church. Yes.' She raised her head so the light from the window stencilled her profile really well. 'Yes! I admit it! We were . . .' her voice sank to a piteous whisper . . . '*lovers*!' She said klov-erz.

'I deny it!' I cried, clearly heartbroken. Sister Morrison's eyes lasered into me. She didn't believe a word of it, the suspicious bitch. Women are like that. No trust. I often wonder why that is.

'My card, Major.' The woman passed him a card and a bulky envelope.

'Detective-Sergeant.'

'My statement is inside, witnessed by a notary public. You'll recognize his signature, Constable.' She fluttered her eyelashes. 'Lovejoy and I were . . . being klov-erz in the church when we saw these four men trying the inner door. Lovejoy sent me away while he tried to stop them.' She sobbed quite effectively for a quick incidental moment. 'I saw him run out, holding his arm. The candlestick, that terrible journey to the organist's cottage . . .'

'And where were you?'

'Too terrified,' she swept on. 'Too *selfish* to help! I was in my car down the lane.'

Ledger's gaze locked on mine. 'Is this true, Lovejoy?'

I faced him nobly. 'I cannot compromise a lady.'

Pure hate shone from him. 'And you, lady. How do I know *your* story's true?'

'Oh. Didn't I tell you? My chauffeur was with us all the time. Keeping watch. He saw the men, too. His statement's in the envelope as well.' She eyed Ledger shyly. 'Properly witnessed, of course, Colonel.'

'Darling,' I reproached her, thinking it was Christmas.

'You'd do this for me?'

She took my arm briskly, now quite matter-of-fact. 'Are you ready, darling?'

'Lovejoy.' Ledger had ripped the envelope and was scanning the four typewritten pages. He looked up quickly. 'What's this lady's name?'

I said, 'Erm . . .' but she was too quick for us both, simpering, 'Lena Heindrick. But Lovejoy always calls me Cherub, don't you, darling?'

'Yes, Cherub.'

Ledger was now an unhealthy purple and his breathing was funny. Still, if he infarcted now he was in the right place. He'd have ten doctors competing for his remains in a trice. He gave a despairing flap of his arms.

'All right,' he growled. 'But one day, Lovejoy. One day . . .'

'Thank you, Corporal,' I said innocently and drew Lena close. 'Let's go, er, Cherub.'

Had I known it all then, I'd have gone with Ledger like a lamb, and counted myself lucky. Instead I went proud and smiling, like the nerk I am.

Going down to the car park I asked in a whisper who she was, but she only kept up that determinedly fond smile and whispered, 'Not yet, Lovejoy. Not yet.'

CHAPTER 4

'What's the game, missus?'

We were in the back of this Rolls the size of a tram. She just smiled and lit a cigarette with a cube of bullion shaped like a lighter.

'Game, Lovejoy? No game. I'm deadly serious.'

'Drop me here, please.' We were passing the antiques Arcade. 'Ta for the rescue.'

'You're going to your home with us, Lovejoy.'

'Who sez?'

'Kurak says.' She pointed with her fag at the chauffeur. He had a neck like a tree-trunk. 'And Kurak is a good obedient man.'

'Yooorr serffint fur life, modom,' the bloke said. He didn't even turn.

'Get him from Goldfinger?' I joked, but was thinking, funny accent. Keats had once written 'sea-spry' for spray, but Keats was sort of Cockney. Funny name too, but us Lovejoys of this world don't joke about names. She too had a slightly foreign accent. Lovely bird, but older than I'd thought at first. Luscious, though. Edible.

'My husband Kurt is waiting in your cottage, Lovejoy.'

I started to ask how he'd managed to get in without a key, but remembered the silver patten in my cistern and shut up.

My cottage stands on the side of a little wooded vale on the outskirts of a village a few miles out of town. It is truly rural, as house agents say, meaning cheap and gungey, but I was glad to see the old heap in its tangle of weeds. The village council told me off last autumn for having a garden that always looks back-combed. I'd lost us the Best-Kept-Village-in-East-Anglia Competition by my display of 'horticultural negligence', and unreasonable hatreds had smouldered against me ever since because that cardboard cut-out toytown near Melford won again. They polish the pavement.

I stepped out, grinning like an ape and taking a deep breath. Your own smog's always best for breathing, isn't it? A giant Bentley on the gravel path dwarfed my thatched dwelling.

'Lovejoy, I presume.' This elegant stoutish man was in my porch (get the point? *My* bloody porch). He was smoking a cigar, his waistcoat chained in with baubled gold. Maybe ten years older than Lena, he wore that sleek

air of affluence you only see on politicians and butchers'
dogs. I'd never seen a cleaner bloke. His teeth looked dry-
cleaned, his shirt a façade of polished marble. You could
tell my grubbiness unnerved him. To preserve the sterility
of his podgy-bacon hands, he carefully avoided shaking.
'I'm Mr Heindrick.''

Good old Kurt waved me in, bloody cheek. I heard him
say to his bird, 'Lena, my dear. The interior is rather . . .
unappealing. Perhaps you would care to wait in the
Rolls?'

'I'm curious, Kurt,' her bored voice cut in as she swept
past.

'As you wish, my dear.'

The Heindricks were making me feel like a specimen in
a jar. I admit the place is always a bit untidy and they had
got me off Ledger's hook, but I can get very nasty when
I'm narked, and they were narking me at a worrying
speed.

The cavalcade followed me into the main room, Kurak
with them.

'Sit down, please, Lovejoy.'

Kurt seemed to change as I looked around the familiar
interior. The police must have done a thorough search, in
their own inimitable style. Like customs men, by law the
Old Bill don't have to tidy up after shambling your
things. My kitchen alcove was strewn with crockery and
pans. I only have one set of curtains and they were in a
heap. The place was a wreck.

Mrs Heindrick stood gazing round in awe. I swept some
old newspapers off a chair for her. She sank gracefully on
to it, not losing poise.

'Why do you cut them up, Lovejoy?' She meant the
papers.

'Important bits about antiques.'

'So this is where it all happens!'

'All what?'

Kurt posed before my cold fireplace like a Victorian father about to pronounce. 'Mrs Heindrick means your nefarious dealings, Lovejoy.'

Being up so long was taking it out of me, but I wasn't having that. 'Look, mate,' I said tiredly. 'Nobody calls me neffie and gets off without a limp. I'm no better and no worse than the rest. Okay, so you sprung me. I appreciate it. But I don't take kindly to being sneered at.'

Good old Kurt looked interested. He smiled and apologized with grace. 'You will forgive, I hope. An older man sometimes finds difficulty recognizing the values of a . . . a person so much younger than himself.'

He nearly said 'scruff'. I'd have scruffed *him*. Instead I nodded. 'Accepted. Well, folks. Thanks for the rescue and all that. Now I suppose you'll be going.'

Nobody moved. Kurt said, 'You're wrong, Lovejoy.' I looked round. Kurak stood by the door. The woman was half-smiling, observing me with her head tilted. Nobody was going anywhere yet.

'Wrong?' I guessed.

'Your description of yourself is completely false.'

'What are you on about?'

'Saying you're no better and no worse than the rest.' He smiled quizzically round at me. 'You are exactly both, Lovejoy. There's no need to pretend. Not with us. We're your friends.'

'Explain, Kurt,' Mrs Heindrick said.

'Explain what?' I asked innocently, thinking: These bastards know about me.

Heindrick deliberately dropped ash on my threadbare carpet. 'You are a financial wreck, Lovejoy. Your antiques business, *Lovejoy Antiques, Inc.*, is a deplorable front for this derelict hole. You have no fewer than eleven sets of impressive calling cards claiming—quite fraudulently—you belong respectively to Sotheby's,

Christie's or Glendinning's of London. Your liaisons with women—'

'Now look,' I said weakly.

Mrs Heindrick leaned over and pressed my arm. 'Shhh. You're interesting.'

Kurt sailed glibly on. 'Your liaisons with women cross all known marital boundaries. Currently you consort with Mrs Sally E. Dayson, a magistrate's wife of Dragonsdale village.' He twinkled a mischievous smile, the swine. 'And with Mrs Margaret Dainty, antique dealer of the town Arcade. And with Miss Lydia—'

'Look,' I snapped. 'Where's this leading?'

'And sundry others,' he cruised on, 'as far as your perennial poverty permits. You own one jacket and two frayed shirts. You live and look like a filthy tramp on the bread line. Apart from the . . . shall we say *donations* given you by these undoubtedly generous women, you shun affluence. Your one associate is Tinker Dill, a senile drunkard who sleeps in the town doss-house, on the rare occasions he is not destitute, and cinema doorways and pub yards when he is.'

I said defensively, 'That's not my fault. I give him what I can.'

'Curiously true,' Heindrick said. 'You are the only antique dealer who we could find who pays his barker fairly. Yet you live in squalor. And it gets worse. Your police record covers dozens of shady—'

'The police are biased.'

'Of course,' he said politely. 'But your record includes an alarming number of fights, thefts, disturbances, wholesale robberies, and several deaths.'

'Those were accidental.'

'Naturally. We know that most sincerely. Don't we, my dear?'

'Most sincerely, Kurt.'

You couldn't help looking from him to her. Sincerity

was very, very lacking.

Heindrick's voice hardened as he continued. 'It all adds up to a shady, penniless antique dealer scrounging a meagre living off any woman who wants ravishing by an unshaven shabby down-and-out crook.' He nodded with sadness. 'Oh yes, Lovejoy. You're worse than the rest of us. Much, much worse.'

The silence lasted a fortnight while I mopped my forehead with the sleeve of my good hand. The bare bones of Heindrick's tale were true, but I'm not as bad as that. And none of anything's really been my fault, not when you look at things honestly. Events get distorted in the telling. Everybody knows that.

Mrs Heindrick pressed my knee. 'It's a matter of record, Lovejoy.' The hypocritical bitch had the gall to sound sympathetic—most sincerely, of course. Irritably I pushed her hand away.

Kurt crossed to stand before me, a curiously threatening picture of affluence. 'On the other hand, Lovejoy, you're better than the rest of us.'

I cleared my throat. 'Better how? You've just proved the opposite.'

'Because you're a divvie, Lovejoy.'

I should have guessed. They knew all the bloody time.

'Divvie' or 'div' means different things to different people. To teenagers the word divvie means a numbskull, a stupid nerk. To a housewife it's a shopper's discounted dividend. But to antique dealers a divvie is somebody almost magical. I can't even explain it myself.

The nearest I can get is saying that something happens inside you when you come into the presence of a real antique. Maybe its love reaches out to touch you, that secret recognition each of us carries inside.

You ought to know first that most antique dealers, in addition to supreme and unadulterated ignorance, possess a blind spot for antiques. The tale of Sid Greenshaw will help to explain:

Sid is our local faker. He paints 'priceless' early English watercolour paintings. One day he was commissioned by a Paris gallery for ten copies of an eighteenth-century painting by an artist called Cozens. This sad genius isn't heard much of nowadays, but the mighty Constable, the immortal Turner and that bobby-dazzler Tom Girtin thought him the greatest genius 'that ever touched landscape'. And he very nearly was that good. Check for yourself—his stuff's in the galleries.

Anyhow, so far so good for Sid Greenshaw. Faithfully he set to work copying from an actual original which the Paris gallery thoughtfully sent over. Sid is painfully slow doing Cozens fakes because, right up to the moment that John Robert Cozens died insane, he used a strange monochrome underpainting technique as if painting in oils. It takes an inordinate length of time to fake a Cozens, not like a Samuel Palmer or a Constable, which have to be done at speed.

So Sid contentedly worked on between other jobs in his attic, leaving partially completed 'Cozens' for the monochrome underpaint to 'fix', as we say, and doing a cracking job on the phoney frames. He's a real craftsman is Sid, one we're really proud of along the estuaries of East Anglia. Anybody will tell you where he lives—and usually how he's getting along with his latest creation. He's no secret except to the poor buyers.

Well, the time came when, after months of skilled labour, Sid began to send off his fakes to Paris. (We ship them crated up as unsigned 'Reproductions', the signatures usually being done by specialist forgers on arrival.) Now this French lot decided to get Sid to do them because of his famed ability, which was a mistake because naturally, while the money was coming in, Sid did what every other forger does: he made a 'foreigner'—one fake just for himself. In time he dutifully sent off the ten fakes, plus the Cozens original, and sold his extra fake to a pal in Lavenham for a few quid. There was one slight snag: the stupid goon *had sold the original Cozens painting to his pal by mistake*. He'd sent eleven fakes to Paris.

It was a real laugh, especially for Sid's pal in Lavenham who made a fortune once the truth dawned. You can imagine. The Montmartre gallery did its nut because they now had eleven fakes instead of ten plus their priceless original. Sid's name was mud. He eventually bought off their heavy mob by giving them three years' free hard labour making fakes—under close supervision. That way, he kept his hands and feet. Which for such a daft mistake was a bonus.

I tell you this amusing story to explain what a divvie is. A divvie could never make a mistake like Sid had, because a genuine Cozens—a genuine *anything*—shrieks and clangs and hums like a chime of cathedral bells. A fake just hangs there, a splatter of paint on paper rimmed by strips of wood. A zero. A dud. No sound, no magic melodious clamour. The odd thing is that a divvie like me quivers with these mystic emanations just by being in the same room as a genuine antique. You hardly need bother to look. God knows how it works. Just as a water-diviner doesn't need actually to see the water before his twig writhes with the magic vibes of the subterranean river, so it is with me. Had Sid called me in, the siren song of the genuine Cozens would have been unmistakable. Needless to say, a divvie is worth his weight in gold—to anybody with enough money to buy genuine antiques, that is.

Like, it seemed, the Heindricks.

'Yes. I'm a divvie.'

They exhaled simultaneously, exchanging a glance. Kurak stirred. Quite honestly, that was the first time I felt queasy in their presence, and was not pleased. Others call it worry, but to me it's fear. Lena Heindrick was looking at me with undisguised interest now. Kurt's attitude was one of curious relief. I tried to suss out Kurak but by the time my eyes swivelled he had arranged his expression accordingly and revealed nothing. Where had I seen him before?

'Then you are the one we . . . desire, Lovejoy.'

That ambiguous line from Lena. I said, 'Me? What for?'

'A little trip. To find something old and valuable in the ground.'

'Lena, my dear,' Kurt warned.

'Trip? Where to?'

'You will be told as soon as you are fit.' She smiled. 'Foreign, but you need no passport.'

'I'm going nowhere, luv.'

That smile moved its wet mouth and I heard, 'Then I'll phone Detective-Sergeant Ledger and tell him you blackmailed me into providing your alibi.'

'Blackmailed how?'

'I'll think of something, Lovejoy. A woman's always believed when she makes an accusation concerning sex or money.' We all paused, considering. Hardly a proposition from Wittgenstein, but still food for thought.

She collected her gloves, saying, 'That will be all so far, I think. Kurt?'

There was something curiously displeasing in the way she had taken over. Kurt stood there exhaling smoke and smiling most sincerely. She rose to go and we all moved obediently. I knew from the way we were avoiding each other's eyes that she knew my sudden hunger. The trouble is, women always end up the boss. She pressed my arm, smiling into the middle distance.

'Do get better soon, Lovejoy. We have *so* much to do.' Kurt patted my good shoulder as he passed.

It was just then that the phone rang and everybody else froze. I jumped a mile. Kurt gave me the nod. I went to answer it, Kurak balefully letting me pass by twisting his gigantic torso.

'Wotcher, Lovejoy!' Tinker, phoning in the hubbub from some pub orgy, clearly delighted with himself and three parts sloshed as usual. 'I found Clarkie and Sam! They're in the A12 caff.'

'Good evening,' I said politely. 'Thank you for your enquiry.'

'Eh?'

'I'll try to arrange matters accordingly,' I said smoothly. Kurak loomed at my elbow to listen.

Tinker got all peeved at my apparent disinterest. 'You told me to find the bleeders, Lovejoy!'

'Excellent, sir,' I warbled. 'I'll attend to it.' Quickly I replaced the receiver. Kurt was behind me, suspicion creasing his brow.

'Who was that, Lovejoy?'

'Tinker Dill, ringing from the boozer.' I pushed past him back into my room. 'He's found an antique I was looking for.'

'Business as normal, then?' Kurt said pleasantly.

'Almost.'

Lena Heindrick gave a woman's careful riotous non-smile at my bitter reply, and cruised calmly past out of the cottage. Kurak smouldered his way to the Rolls, vibing pure hate in my direction. The end of a riotous party. Kurt strolled behind the wheel of the Bentley.

As the Rolls crunched away Lena Heindrick's window wound down.

'Make it soon, Lovejoy,' she said, still not looking directly at me. 'We're in a hurry.' Kurt just smiled.

I said nothing, watched them off and did not wave.

Then I tore back to the phone. Ted, the White Hart

barman, fished Tinker from the maelstrom of the taproom.

'Tinker? Lovejoy. Get me a lift, sharpish.'

'Here, Lovejoy,' he croaked tipsily, peeved. 'What were all that?'

'Never mind. Hurry. Try Helen or Maud or Margaret. Anybody but Patrick.' He would scream the house down at the first sign of aggro. 'I'm going to bend Clarkie and Sam.'

'Oh Gawd—'

I said, 'You heard,' and went to brew up while waiting, but my tea bags had been nicked. Bloody police. Nobody thieves like them. If it wasn't for them there wouldn't be all this crime about.

CHAPTER 5

It was getting dark by the time we reached the nosh bar on the A12 road. Clarkie's motor was among the cars and lorries, so we settled down in the car park for a long wait. Rain tapped on the roof and fugged the windows.

'Can't I go in for a pint, Lovejoy?' Tinker asked hopefully. He'd gone almost an hour without.

'No.'

'The boozers will be closed soon,' he grumbled.

'For heaven's sake, what are we *doing* here, Lovejoy? It's *pouring*.'

Janet Erskine had been the only lift Tinker could get me. Approaching her forties, she was even more scatterbrained than the rest of us antique dealers. She says she specializes in 'All kinds of antiques and things', which reveals all you need to know about her brain power. Be careful with Janet, though. Her ignorance of antiques is mindbending. Oddly enough, her good humour and her luck were a legend. I had often wondered if, beneath that frilly gear and blowsy exterior there didn't beat the soul of a secret divvie, but finally decided statistics were against that theory. She is always highly scented, very flouncy and feminine. I like her. We could have done worse. Her husband works in an ambulance depot somewhere in town, playing billiards and swilling tea.

'Waiting.'

'Frigging Clarkie's in there getting sloshed with Sam —'

'Tinker,' I said over my shoulder, 'give me your boot.'

'Eh?'

'Your boot.'

Mumbling indignantly, Tinker passed his old army boot over. I tilted to examine it in the light from the caff. It ponged to high heaven.

'What on *earth*!' Janet exclaimed.

I stopped her switching on the interior bulb to help, and chucked the boot behind me to Tinker. 'Cut the tongue out. And give me both your laces.'

Tinker knew better than ask daft questions like what for. 'I've only got one. But you can have me belt, Lovejoy.'

'What's going *on*, please!' Janet cried.

'I said laces, you stupid burke.'

'It's string.'

I nicked Janet's manicure set and made Tinker pierce four holes in the leather tongue with her nail scissors. Under my instruction he threaded the lace and the string through.

'You should be in bed, Lovejoy,' Janet accused, with the self-righteous anger of a woman fetched out in bad weather. 'You've only just left hospital.'

'Tie them in loops, Tinker.'

Cars and lorries came and went. We waited another sulky half-hour before the door flashed a slice of yellow light into the wet night and Clarkie and Sam showed. A third bloke with them turned to our right and went towards a big articulated lorry. It looked like Dickie Dirt, least reliable of our vannies, but in the darkness you couldn't be sure. Knowing Dickie, he would have some woman waiting snoozing in his cab. He never goes far without one.

'You want me wiv yer, Lovejoy?' Tinker's unconvincing quaver gave me a free grin.

'No. Stay here.'

Janet started up indignantly, 'But he has no *coat* . . . !' so I put the door gently to and floated through the rain among the saloons and road haulage wagons. The night air felt fresh after the boutique-riddled smog of Janet's car. I reached Clarkie's motor before they did, and stood in the shadow of a goods vehicle as the chatting villains approached.

The one good thing about East Anglia's countryside is its flint stone. Over the ages these decorative little round stones have provided temples for Rome, roads for the Early English, castles for the Normans, dazzlingly beautiful spired churches for the post-Conquest Christians, and sparks for the Brown Bess gunlocks of civilization's biggest — and last — empire. They are attractive and smooth, and come in sizes from giant cobbles to small pebbles. Best of all, they lie everywhere, in fields and lanes. Waiting for Tinker and Janet to arrive, I had collected a dozen walnut-sized flints. If there had been enough time, a couple of practice throws with my improvised sling would not have come amiss. A bit lopsided with only one good arm, I had to let them get almost too close before letting fly with my first shot. The stone caught Sam in the throat and he fell against a small Ford, choking.

Clarkie said, 'What the hell . . . ?'

I spat my next stone into the sling and held it against

my chest. The remaining ten stones were in my pocket on my good side.

'Only me, Clarkie.'

'Who's that?'

The poor goon was in oblique light from the caff while I was still in shadow. Sam looked in a hell of a state. For a minute I wondered if I'd done him some serious damage—after all, Goliath got done the same way—then suppressed the twinge. The sod had nearly killed me.

'Lovejoy!'

He yelped and backed away, leaving Sam to rot and trying to shield his eyes against the light. I whirled the sling and gave him the next stone in his midriff. He folded with a whoof and fell to his knees on the tarmac, groaning.

'Don't move, Clarkie.'

Loading the biggest stone I had, I stepped up to Sam and kicked him as insurance before carefully toeing his knife away under the Ford. He couldn't have been all that badly injured because he had been surreptitiously easing it into action, the pig.

'For Christ's *sake*, Lovejoy . . .'

I punted Sam again in his groin.

'Hands and knees,' I said into his scream. 'Both of you. Side by side.'

Most of the bigger trunk road cafés have a footbridge over the road, joining the two sections. I herded Sam and Clarkie through the teeming rain on their all fours on to the footbridge. Nobody could see us through the gloom—I hoped. They shuffled on all fours over the bridge. Occasional cars swept by underneath, putting a gruesome wash of light across the scene. I kicked them both hard occasionally to make sure they would be handicapped at least as much as me. Well, they had four arms to my one. Fair's fair.

'Whoa, lads,' I commanded, whirling my sling in what I hoped was a threatening manner. It went *whum-whum*. The world was beginning to oscillate unsteadily. I began to realize I hadn't eaten for some time. All this aggro was draining me, so I was pleased when Clarkie vomited from pain. I needn't worry so much if we were all ailing. Sam just lay there wheezing, clutching his groin.

'What do you want, Lovejoy?' Clarkie whispered. 'Honest, we meant no harm.'

'Clarkie.' I stepped closer, whirring my sling. 'You and this pillock nearly did for me. See this sling? If I let it go, it'll go through you like a dose of salts.'

They whimpered, scrabbling away from me along the footwalk while the cars swished wetly underneath. I edged after, still whumming my sling.

'I want you to do something, Clarkie.'

'Yes, yes, Lovejoy,' he babbled. 'Anything.'

'Throw Sam off the bridge. Now.'

'Christ!' Sam screeched. I punted him and he whooshed into silence.

'You can't . . .' Clarkie whispered.

'Or,' I said affably, 'he throws you off. When he recovers consciousness, that is. Be sharp.'

'Please, Lovejoy. For Christ's sake, it was all a mistake. I swear it.'

Whirring the sling was tiring me fast. 'Who made you rob the Fingringhoe church?'

'I don't . . . I can't . . .'

'Right.' I made a sinister show of being about to unleash the sling and Clarkie yelled up, 'I'll tell! I'll tell!'

'Who?'

'Joxer paid me. He set it up. He was there, signalled when we were to leave the Colchester road lay-by and pull the job.'

'Joxer? You telling the truth?' I didn't believe him.

'Honest, Lovejoy. Forty quid and he'd keep watch. He

had muscle, Lovejoy. A scarey great bleeder with him who said nowt. We didn't mean it, Lovejoy. Please.'

So there I was, torn between mercy and revenge. Sooner or later somebody has to chuck in the sponge on vengeance. Otherwise we're all at war for ever and ever, and life's nothing but one long holocaust. I thought angrily, why should that somebody be me?

'Right, Clarkie,' I said, and turned as if to go.

Next morning Janet woke me by rolling on to my sore arm. I shot into consciousness with a scream of pain and cursed, full of self-pity, while she rose blearily and brewed up.

I was still grousing when she came back with a tray, eggs and toast and bowls of those flaky bits with nuts for adding milk. The phone had rung while she was up but I refused to go and fiddled with my dud radio instead. She answered it.

I asked, 'Where did you get all this grub, love?'

'Called in at home taking Tinker back to town. Remember?'

'No.' I'd slept all the way, dozy as an angler's cat. 'I remember some stupid bird giving me a blanket bath before she let me rest. And feeding me some rotten broth.' With Janet's broth knocking about no wonder there's all this malnutrition.

'Broth's good for invalids.' We started breakfast in a peeved silence.

It was quite ten minutes before she told me it had been Ledger on the phone.

'Mmmh?' I asked innocently. 'How is he?'

'He wanted to know where you were last night.'

'Nosey sod.'

'I said you were resting here. Tinker and I were with you.'

'Great,' I said. 'I'll see your honesty is duly rewarded.'

Janet was slightly pale about the gills as she told me Ledger's bad news. Poor Clarkie and his partner Sam Veston appeared to have fallen from a footbridge on to the A12 near the Washbrook turn-off. Both were in hospital, with severe internal injuries. Poor Sam was very dicey. And, would you believe it, in the very same ward I'd just left, Sister Morrison's ward in the male surgical block.

'What a coincidence!' I exclaimed, meeting her stare with all the frankness and innocence of which I am capable, which is virtually unlimited. 'Fancy—'

'Lovejoy.' She gazed at me. 'When you went to talk to Clarkie and Sam, nothing happened, did it? I mean to say—'

I chuckled. At least I tried to, never knowing quite what chuckling sounds like. 'You mean, did I beat them up and throw them off the bridge?'

'Well, yes.'

'With one arm? Just out of hospital? And them two big tough men, armed with knives?' I went all noble and quiet. 'I see, Janet. So you believe like the rest, that anything bad around here is my fault, even when I'm obviously still weak—' If I'd been upright I would have put on a convincing limp.

She put her arms round me, nearly tipping the tray. 'No, darling. I'm sorry. It's my stupid imagination.'

'That's all right,' I said brokenly, being all forgiving. 'Is there any more egg?'

'Yes, darling.' She scrambled out of bed. 'Half a minute.'

I shouted after her, 'Love. Throw my robin some cheese, if there is any. It's tapping on the window. And when Tinker rings ask him to suss out Joxer Casey for me, sharpish.'

Janet's patch was warmer than mine so I edged across the divan to pinch it. My nineteenth-century walnut carriage clock showed a disgraceful ten o'clock. Another hour and the pubs would open, bringing Tinker staggering into the world again. One hour after that and I'd have Joxer by the throat.

Remembering Lena Heindrick's words, Ireland's the only place that could be described as 'foreign, but you don't need a passport'. And Irish Joxer's a boisterous Dun Laoghaire man who works in a shed near Priory Street in town. I felt quite perky. It was the first link I had.

The only trouble with confidence is that it never lasts. I was to learn this elementary lesson the hard way.

CHAPTER 6

Janet had to go at eleven-thirty. She made yet another breathless phone call home to explain her absence, drenched herself in gallons of scent from an array of misshapen bottles out of her handbag, and we hit the road just as the rain stopped. She dropped me near the old priory ruins in the town centre and gave me a couple of quid to be going on with.

'Eat, darling,' she commanded. 'See you tonight.' Smiling, I watched her go. She'd told me, 'I'll *have* to call in. We have this Ming celery vase on offer.' She meant celadon, not celery. Knowing Janet, it could be anything from the Portland Vase to a plant pot, though with her fantastic luck . . . She shares a stall with Sandra Mesham, a lovely girl. Sandra's pretty good at early Islamic ceramics and calligraphy, and did Arabic, Sanskrit and art at college. She has a lovely figure. Janet hates her.

Saturday morning turns any town centre into hell. With the crowds and the traffic I was too preoccupied to give Helen more than a passing wave. She's the only really breathtaker we've got among the dealers, and was beckoning me from Jason's window. Probably she wanted my say-so on that terracotta portrait bust of the Florentine Benivieni, supposedly a genuine article made about 1530 when the great philosopher was getting on for eighty. Tinker had told me the tale during one of his hospital visits, now Helen was keen to buy but uncertain. I knew what was worrying her — the world's greatest-ever terracotta faker, Giovanni Bastianini, had done brilliant fakes which went for fortunes in the 1860s. I'd sent a message to Helen through Tinker to buy the damn thing outright because, like the famous Billie and Charlie medallion forgeries, Bastianini fakes are now more famous than the originals. And, by that incomprehensible quirk of the public, often more pricey. Helen had obviously got cold feet and wanted me to divvie it for her.

Full of the comradeship for which antique dealers are famed, I quickly looked away from Helen's alluring beckon — not easy, this — and ducked into the alley between the music shop and the grocer's. In a dozen strides you leave the heaving street behind and enter a different world.

This is the amazing thing about these East Anglian market towns. Their main streets could be mistaken for part of the busiest city in the world. Step a few paces to one side, and you recede centuries.

The tranquil ruins of St Botolph's Priory are fairly immense as ruins go. They stand between the huge nineteenth-century brick reconstructed priory and the old churchyard. Several figures were standing among the gravestones talking. Others moved carefully about on the trimmed wet grass. I recognized most of the local dramatic society, including Marcia. Their next open-air production was due soon. They looked perished.

' 'Morning, Lovejoy.'

'Wotcher.'

'Want a part, handsome?'

There was a roar at Marcia's crack. I smiled weakly and edged past the rehearsal. She meant the time when I stood in to read three announcer lines to start a Melville skit and nearly fainted from fright. I'd been going out with Marcia at the time.

'Never again,' I said fervently.

'We stop in an hour, Lovejoy. Free lunch?'

'Don't trust you actresses. You'll give me a part again.' I tried to keep it light and made the path safely. Marcia was smiling far too brightly. A few of the others shuffled and looked at the grass as Jimmy Day the producer quickly took it up.

'Go again, people. Page thirty of your Fourth Folios . . .'

A relieved laugh broke the embarrassment and they went easily back into Big Bill's *The Winter's Tale*, saving Marcia from her brief lapse so I didn't mind Jimmy's dig at me.

Joxer's shed is a converted chicken coop, and is situated among the nettles and brambles which overgrow tall fencing rimming the churchyard. Some lone heroine was busy scraping lichens from a nearby headstone to record the inscription as I opened the creaky door.

'Top of the morning, Joxer.'

'Hello, Lovejoy.' He looked up from his workbench. 'Watch that bleeding draught.' He is our plate man, and was busy French-plating across a damaged Sheffield plate. He had the silver leaves still in block, thank God, or they would have gone everywhere at a breath, and his agate-stone burnisher all ready with the plastic comb and toothpicks handy on the shelf. He's a good workman, is Joxer, so it was all the more upsetting for him when I reached across and took hold of his bunsen fan-burner and ran it gently up his arm.

'Be careful, you frigging lunatic? You burned me! What—'

He dropped everything and tumbled off his stool.

I leaned on his workbench. 'You never *do* get these seams right, Joxer,' I lectured sadly. 'Genuine Sheffield plate has seams. Electroplated stuff is uniformly coated pure silver. How many times do I have to tell you to follow the seams when you do *cuivre argenté*?'

'What's up, Lovejoy?' He was scared, which was fine by me, because I was in a temper.

'People say French plating's only good enough to repair Sheffield plate worn down to the copper, Joxer.' I snuffed the bunsen and slung a hammer into the plank wall beside his head. He yelped and jumped. 'About a certain church at Fingringhoe, Joxer.'

He licked his lips, looking at the door. 'What about it, Lovejoy?'

'Poor Clarkie and poor Sam. Make sure you send flowers.'

His shoulders sagged in surrender. He's not daft. 'I knowed it was you did them over, Lovejoy. Only you could be that cruel.'

'*Me?*' I'm honestly astonished by this kind of accusation. No other antique dealer contributes to the Lifeboats Appeal like I do. And it's always other people force me into violence. If only everybody would leave me alone I'd be an angel.

'Yes, you.' He righted the stool and lit a rolled fag. 'I told them to look for somebody else, only they were hooked on this Kilfinney thing.' He gave a wry wink at me. 'A Dun Laoghaire man helping those Limerick people's a terrible thing, Lovejoy.'

'Really?' I said politely. For me these places might as well be on Saturn.

'It was a woman and a man. Rich, Rolls motor, the lot. She's boss, I think. Called him Kurt, talked like Froggies

in some language to each other. Hardly any accent.' He
blew smoke. 'It had to be Fingringhoe, that church, that
day, that hour. They wouldn't say why. I'm no cloth-job
man. You know that, Lovejoy. Clarkie jumped at it for
forty quid.'

Which sounded like the Heindricks all right. The top
silver leaf lifted gently on the bench beside me, which
meant that somebody with the strength to lift the creaky
door into silence as it opened was coming in behind me. I
saw Joxer hide a smile in his glance at me, and smiled
openly back, which meant he knew I knew he knew about
that somebody.

'Wotcher, Kurak,' I said without turning round. 'You
touch me and so help me I'll do the opposite of what you
want. Otherwise, I'll come quietly.'

'He means it, sor,' Joxer said quietly towards the door.

The door groaned as the giant bloke let it go. 'Then
come,' he growled.

'Say please,' I said, still not looking. My spine felt
crinkled.

After a silence, 'Please,' landed across my shoulder like
a cross.

'Certainly,' I said. 'Cheers, Joxer.'

I was to remember what happened next for a long, long
time.

Suddenly Joxer said, 'Lovejoy. Can't you watch a
minute with me?' He'd gone quite pale, as if realizing
something horrible.

'No,' I told him. I was in enough trouble, and he'd
done me no favours. His expression was abruptly that of a
man looking at the end of the world.

'Cheers, boyo,' Joxer said. His voice was fatalistic but
quite level.

If I were not so thick I'd have expected trouble of the
very worst kind. But I *am* so thick. So cheerfully I walked
with Kurak up to the street, waved to Marcia among

Jimmy Day's acting crowd, and was driven off in grand style.

That's how wars begin, by not thinking. My kind, that is.

CHAPTER 7

The Heindricks' house was even more imposing than their motors. It stood overlooking the Blackwater estuary. The gardens had that scrubbed look which only a battalion of dedicated gardeners can give, and the drawing-room where we sat had that radiance which unlimited wealth imparts.

'You travel in four days, Lovejoy.' Kurt could have been one of his own antiques, he was that polished. He was clearly monarch of all he surveyed, and possibly of everything else as well. Standing before his log fire and issuing directives, he caused a weary sinking feeling in my belly. All my life these bloody people have been giving me orders with complete disregard of the consequences—for me.

'Will I?' I said sourly.

'You will.' He smiled with benevolence. 'Mrs Heindrick will meet you at the destination.'

His missus clapped her hands—and I do mean actually clapped them, as they once did for slaves. Instantly a rather surly bird appeared with a tray of those small cakes. She had already done one circuit but I'd had all the savouries. I was still famished and tried to be casual reaching for the fresh plate. God knows who invented manners. Whoever it was had never felt hunger, that's for sure. It's desperately hard taking less than you want in other people's posh mansion houses—and everybody, honest and dishonest, knows that's the truth.

'The terms will be excellent, Lovejoy,' Lena said. She had spotted my glance at the retreating bird's shape, which is typical of women's sly behaviour, but I was only interested because I'd never seen another slave before. Mrs Heindrick's lips thinned with displeasure. She must have detected the same kind of lust when I glanced at the oil painting, but she wasn't as narked at that. 'Beautiful, isn't it?' she said. 'It's—'

'A copy.' I wasn't really glad, but it was one in their eye. The pair of them exchanged significant looks.

'But laboratory tests show it to be an original early eighteenth-century oil of a seafarer, Lovejoy.' That from connoisseur Kurt, whose untold wealth had always gained perfect grovelling agreement to any banal utterance he chose to make. Until now.

'Oh, John Tradescant was a seafarer all right.' I rose, touched the oil's surface reverently and found myself smiling as the warmth vibrated in my fingers. 'And it's old. But a famous building off Trafalgar Square'll be very cross if you go about telling fibs, mate. *They've* got the original.'

'John who?'

I was enjoying myself. 'Tradescant only sailed about to nick seeds, bulbs, plants, anything that grew. His dad was as bad. He even raided the Mediterranean pirates to get a bush or two. Between them they introduced a load of stuff—apricots, Persian lilac, Michaelmas daisies, the larch. They did Russia, the American colonies, North Africa. Tradescant's collection became the Ashmolean at Oxford.' The old copyist had got Tradescant's wryly wicked smile just right, but the date of 1612 was a shade earlyish.

'A *copy*?' Lena Heindrick spat out a vulgar curse, which made me blink.

'Don't knock copyists. Turner himself started out as one.' It's a daft joke we play on ourselves, really. Find a genuine flower painting by Palice and it's not worth a fiftieth of the price of a Turner copy. 'Copy and original are linked by greed, Mrs Heindrick.'

'Don't be so bitter, Lovejoy.' She was smiling again and the thought crossed my mind that she had only been goading me. 'Let's get back to that subject, then, shall we? Money.'

'A good daily rate, all expenses paid, and a share of the profits.'

I weakened at the thought of money—which meant antiques and food, in that order. 'Four days? Why so soon? You said I could get better first.'

'Because if you stay here you will be in even more trouble.' Kurt exposed his pearly teeth. I just couldn't imagine him ever growing stubble. The hair follicles just wouldn't dare.

'I'm not in any trouble.'

'Oh, but you are. Detective-Sergeant Ledger's phone call to your . . . consort Janet this morning was quite explicit.'

The mansion was plushily furnished with a skilled admix of antiques old and new. I couldn't help feeling sad, having been at the original auction some years ago. The old East Anglian manorial family had sat there in pained dignity while us dealers and auctioneers had robbed and fiddled them blind. Here's a free lesson: promise me you'll never, never, *never* sell up by means of an in-house on-site auction. This or any other doorstep selling is ruinously wrong. You might as well just throw the stuff outside to the rag-and-bone man. At least he'll give you an honest donkey stone for it. A shoal of antique dealers and auctioneers won't.

'More blackmail?'

'Yes.' He smiled and decanted sherry—the Kurts of this world do not simply pour—while Lena pressed the cakes on me. She was watching me nosh with a kind of appalled awe, but it was all right for her. Women don't get hungry, only peckish. 'It has become a matter of urgency. If you will go about throwing people off footbridges and talking to the careless Joxer . . .'

'Have you had me followed?' There was even a peacock on the lawn, radiantly displaying its fan. Lena Heindrick saw me looking and smiled.

'Of course.'

'Okay. Where do I go?'

'You'll find out when you arrive.'

'Why can't whatever's there be fetched here for me to suss out?'

'Why do you suppose it's only *one* thing, Lovejoy?'

'Mrs Heindrick hinted,' I said, wondering if that was true.

'Very lax of us all, my dear,' Kurt said without admonition. 'But especially Joxer.'

Lena shrugged, an attractive business. She had dressed for the interview in a neat black dress with only a late Georgian alexandrite brooch for ornamentation. Plain matching belts go in and out of fashion, but she wore one, the right touch of disdain towards those birds who need to conform to prevailing styles. I could have eaten her. Kurt was as clinical as ever, stencilled in a Savile Row jacket and city trousers. It was as Joxer said. Clearly she was in control, Kurt the mere business end of the team.

'You will be given your ticket and an allowance on the journey, Lovejoy.' Kurt came near to cracking a joke by adding, 'Performing our task will keep you out of mischief, no?'

'Only possibly, Kurt,' Lena smiled.

Kurt chuckled at that, his flabby jowl undulating. I watched, fascinated. Why didn't his starched collar sever his jugular? But I got the joke. 'Only possibly' meant a rip, a scam, a lift, something illegal anyway. *And I knew it was in Kilfinney*, wherever that was. My one concealed trump card.

Then Lena shook me by catching my hand as I reached the nth time for the proffered plate. It had one cake left, but that was Lena's fault. Posh cakes are only little and don't fill you.

She said, 'One thing, Lovejoy. Sister Morrison?'

'You mean outpatients?' It was a good thought. That sombre-eyed lass would go berserk if I failed to make the appointment.

'No. Your relationship with her.'

'Nothing I can do about that. It wasn't my fault she ballocked me most of the time. Why?'

She smiled then and let me reach the grub. 'Only that she has called twice at your cottage.'

'She did?' I said blankly. 'Probably to confirm my clinic appointment, something like that.'

Kurt interposed, on cue. 'The fewer encumbrances the better, Lovejoy, while you're working for us.'

I stood then but kept my temper out of respect for the delectable antiques all around. Nobody tells me who can call at my cottage and who not.

'Who says I'm working for you?'

Kurt chuckled. Lena looked me up and down with amused insolence. 'Me,' she said softly. 'Kurak will call for you at midnight, four days from now.'

'Not me, mate,' I told her, and left.

They saw me crunch down the avenued drive. Kurt must have given some signal because Kurak stayed leaning against the Rolls and watched me go.

I got a lift from a school football bus, coming back from a match. They'd lost six-nil. If I'd half the sense I was born with I'd have recognized the omen, but not this numbskull. Within seconds of being dropped on North Hill I was in the Marquis of Granby pub phoning the hospital to bleep Sister Morrison and claiming it was an emergency.

CHAPTER 8

Sister Morrison was not keen on coming off duty straight into a pub so we met by the post office. She came driving up in grand style, and I darted across the pavement once I was sure she was the woman at the wheel. The town's traffic always builds up a little in the early evening but she coped calmly. All that surgical training, I supposed. She didn't even tut as the rain started again before we made the road out to my village.

'Did I get you in trouble, Sister?'

'I was just coming off duty anyway.'

It had been an awkward phone conversation nevertheless, with me stuttering that I was only phoning to check my next appointment and her saying it was all right and she would explain the details while giving me a lift. I looked at her as she drove, profile in repose and coat collar turned up to catch the tendrils of hair as they came beneath her knitted hat.

'Sorry I wasn't in, erm, when you called.'

'That's all right. I only called on the offchance.'

That couldn't be true. She must have got my address from the records and actually asked the way to my cottage once she reached the village. We have no real road signs, and numbers are unknown. Some offchance.

She was making me nervous. I'm not used to serenity, never having experienced that condition myself.

'Which part of Ireland are you from, Sister?'

'Sinead.' Only she almost pronounced it Shin-neighed.

'Where's that?'

She fell about laughing, with momentary difficulty controlling the wheel. 'Stupid man. It's my name. I mean stop calling me Sister. You're not in hospital any more.'

'Gaelic?'

'Ten out of ten.'

'I've always wanted to visit Dublin. A bookseller-printer there owes me.'

'Don't go scrapping till your arm's mended.'

There's nothing you can do when a woman's got the upper hand, especially when that woman has washed your bum twice a day lately. I fell silent. Sisters clearly had more ways of shutting you up than mere nurses. She must have felt concerned because she resumed, 'In the west of Ireland we have traditional names. It's only recently easterners have moved into the market.'

She shot a glance at me and changed up for the long pull on the hill above the brook which marks our town boundary. Beam lights of an oncoming car lit her face and brought my reflection into the windscreen. Our reflected gazes met.

'Erm, we'll go to the White Hart, if that's okay.'

'Me in my old coat?'

Nursing staff aren't allowed in public houses wearing uniform. I knew that. Sinead had on a navy blue topcoat. I can't see these things matter much, but women find disadvantage in practically anything.

'Bear right at the fork.' My cottage had been abused enough lately by visitors. Anyway, as we ran together through the rain into the tavern porch I thought she looked bonny.

The pub crowd naturally gave her a cautious scan, when we pushed in, all except Patrick who let out a shrill whoop and trilled a roguish yoohoo. The usual weird mixture of dealers and barkers were busily slurping booze, pretending the antiques game was going just perfect. Tinker saw us and reeled across, ponging to high heaven and filthy as ever, greeting Sister Morrison with such familiarity everybody stared. He showed every sign of joining us till I gave him the bent eye and a quid.

'I thought we wuz broke, Lovejoy,' the stupid old soak croaked.

'Er, my reserve.'

'Mr Dill.' Sinead had her handbag open as we crammed into the nook furthest from the fire. 'Lovejoy can't carry the glasses. His arm. Would you please oblige?'

Tinker scarpered to the bar with her money while I tried to recover my poise, and still I went red. The hubbub battered our ears. Sister Morrison saw me sussing out the crowded, smoke-filled bar and leaned forward, her eyes glowing with interest.

'Who are they all? Everybody knows you.'

A faint scent wafted the smoke aside for an instant. 'Well. Yon, er, eccentric bloke with the silver gloves and red bolero's Patrick. He's a dealer, not as daft as he pretends.'

'And his lady-friend?'

'Lily. She's married, but loves Patrick. She deals in William IV furniture, when Patrick leaves her the odd farthing for herself.'

That set me off chatting about them all. The elegant Helen, raising her eyebrows at the sight of me bringing in a class bird. Old bowler-hatted Alfred, the Regency prints and mezzotint man, battling with his moustache to get to his pint ('His wife's too fierce for him ever to go home,' I explained). Brad the cheerful extrovert flintlock weapon specialist. Big Frank from Suffolk, currently half way through his second pint, his fifth wife and the latest Sotheby's silver catalogue. Poor Denny Havershall, desperately trying to sell a Cotman forgery to the morose Wilkie from Witham—hard going, because Wilkie had faked it in the first place. And Denny's wife Beth had just produced her second little girl last week. Then there was the blonde Marion (mostly Roman pottery and early Islam ware) suggesting to the wealthier

Jason from East Hill that they make a go of a partnership. Tarantulas make similar arrangements.

'He's a cold fish,' Sinead observed.

Which surprised me, so I had another look. Marion was working her eyes and cleavage overtime, ignoring the table's beer puddles despite her splendid Aran woollie. Jason's ex-army, and our one inherently wealthy dealer. He has a big place overlooking the Blackwater estuary. Telling Sinead that reminded me of the Heindricks, which reminded me of the spot that I was in, which reminded me I needed to know why Sinead had been seeking me.

Tinker came with the drinks, all agog with urgency. The goon had brought Sinead a pint as well, but in a handle-mug, this being his idea of gentility.

'Here, Lovejoy. The Old Bill's out for you.'

'George?' He's our village bobby. Whatever it was, I'd manage him.

'No. Ledger. But no paper.'

Thankfully, I nodded relief at this news that Ledger held no arrest warrant. 'Ta, Tinker.'

'And Harry's bought that collection of pot tennis balls from Dragonsdale.'

'Hell fire,' I cursed. Harry has a stall in the town antiques Arcade. I'd been hoping for them, a genuine mahogany-cased set of four.

'Pottery? But that's impossible.'

'He means carpet bowls,' I explained as Tinker dived back towards the bar. 'Queen Victoria's favourite indoor game. They fetch about fifteen quid apiece, but a cased set's damned hard to find. A full set is three lots of four, with a little white "jack" the size of a golf ball. You play like lawn bowls.'

'You're upset,' she interrupted in wonderment. 'Over a pottery ball?'

'They're very rare now, especially in mint condition.

These had a luscious blue circle-and-petal design.'

'You should buy things when you see them,' she was preaching, when my red face beaconed through to her and she dried. 'Sorry, Lovejoy. Are you really broke?'

'It's being in your lousy hospital,' I groused. 'I missed all sorts of chances.' Discomfiture gave me the courage to ask outright what was burning in my mind. 'Look. Why did you come to the cottage?'

'Not here,' she said quickly.

I drew breath to say why the hell not when our little party ended.

Marcia ruined everything by coming to aghast us all. She rushed in excited and dishevelled, choking on the news that there had been a fire. Joxer's work shed in the Priory ruins had burned down after a small explosion had occurred. People were saying it was one of Joxer's gas bottles, that kind of thing. Some of the amateur dramatics men in the Priory parish hall, painting new sets in a desperate race to meet their dress-rehearsal deadline, heard the sound and rushed out to investigate. They made heroic attempts to beat the flames down, but without much hope. Then the fire brigade had arrived and had a go. The Priory ruins were, well, ruined anyway and the new church hall was safe, so what? Marcia had looked everywhere for Joxer to tell him, but he was nowhere around.

Nobody seemed to have been hurt. Sinead relaxed at that. It was probably her nursing instinct which made her so tense at Marcia's babbled news. Talk resumed. We all made clucking noises and some kind soul gave her a port-and-lemon. Then we all forgot it. Except me.

I sat for a long time looking at the table as the taproom babble went on and on, over and over Marcia's account. Patrick dramatically fainted, with Lily, his accolyte, frantically trying to bring him round with smelling-salts from his mauve handbag. After a long time I realized

Sinead had taken my hand. I wasn't scared, not really scared, but a hint is a hint is a hint. All Heindrick had said was, 'Very lax of us all,' and poor Joxer gets his old shed blammed. I could only think of my grotty little cottage. It looked like the Heindricks had a divvie after all.

Sinead shook me gently.

'Are you all right, Lovejoy?' she was asking, and I came to. Her grey-blue eyes were anxious. I looked into them, thinking, well, all living is risk, isn't it?

'Yes, fine, thanks,' I said. 'Look, Shinny. About Ireland . . .'

CHAPTER 9

Things went from bad to evil that night. It seemed to end on an increasingly worse note every few minutes. First, Sister Morrison dropped me off outside my cottage about an hour afterwards. We talked in her car, mainly about Mrs Heindrick, even though I was dog-tired.

'That's what I wanted to tell you, Lovejoy. She's up to no good. She's been on the phone asking about your condition.'

That narked me. 'She could have asked me.'

'Don't worry. I disclosed nothing, and the doctors won't.'

One thing struck me. 'Why were you reluctant to tell me this in the tavern?'

'That cold fish.'

'Jason?'

'Yes. Mrs Heindrick's friend.'

Again that disturbing chill touched my neck. 'Friend? Are you sure?'

'I saw them both leaving my cousin's place together the

day after you were discharged from my ward.'

'Cousin? Er . . .'

'Joe. Joe Casey. He's like you, an antique dealer.'

Odd, that. I'd always thought I knew everybody in East Anglia. Now there were all these unexpected cousins and friends of friends. Worse, friends of enemies.

Sinead went on, 'Joe doesn't trust her, that's for sure. He did a few small jobs for the Heindricks. They were so bitchy about his work, checked every little detail.'

Well, if they were paying a workman they would naturally want good value. But I was thinking, Casey? Joe Casey? The name sounded oddly familiar.

'Recently?'

'Yes. Now. He even had to start work for them twice when it was dark. I ask you. He told me about it and we had a good laugh.'

And *still* it seemed unimportant, though I was to learn different before the night was through. I said thanks for the warning, and we made our rather stilted goodnights. Puzzled, I watched the red tail-lights flicker as she drove off along the hedged lane. Too many problems and too knackered a brain to cope for the minute, so I went in thinking it was time I had a quiet night. Things would seem clearer in the dawn.

He came for me about two, keeping on knocking even though I was yelling I was coming, for heaven's sake. There were headlights outside from a car reversing to face the lane slope.

'Who is it?' I called, pulling the bolt.

'Police.'

'Come off it, George.' I peered blearily into the gloom. Our village bobby stood there, at least as embarrassed as I was. 'You're not proper police.'

He drew himself up at that insult. 'You're to help us with our enquiries, Lovejoy. Get dressed.'

'I've just come out of dock, George. How the hell could I have pinched, forged or stolen any antiques? And you've Mrs Heindrick's alibi for that cloth job.'

'Murder investigation,' he said.

That shook me. 'Eh?'

'Get him out here,' another copper called wearily from the car, stationary now. 'Ledger'll be going, berserk.'

George wouldn't say any more so I dressed awkwardly and was whisked in town by a dozily irritable constable in a posh police saloon. So many things about the whole business had bewildered me that it was only one more mind-duller when the motor cruised the wrong way down Priory Street and pulled up at the narrow iron gate leading to the ruins. The bobby parked illegally and led me through the old graveyard with the aid of his torch. Ever been in that state of mind where you can fully understand everything that's going on, yet you know you're not really taking any of it in or even believing what you see with your very eyes? Well, that was me when up ahead through the spectral yew trees we heard voices and caught sight of the great ruined arches washed by shifting torchlights. I *knew*, but didn't gather quite what everybody was on about.

'This way, sir. Mind your head.'

The lights blended into a brilliant glow as we came into the main flooring opposite the sanctuary area. A generator whirred, steadied, and floodlights hit from three directions. I'd never seen so many of the Old Bill not in a procession. Ledger was talking with two other plainclothes blokes and jerked his chin at me to follow among the mounds and gravestones.

'You took your time, Smethurst,' he grumbled to the constable.

'My fault,' I said, more to nark Ledger than from pleasantry.

'Know what, Derby? Every bloody thing's Lovejoy's

fault. Torch.' One of his tame nerks snickered, and beamed his flash. Ledger led us through the nettles towards another island of floodlight where Joxer's shed had once stood. Now the scene was a shambles of charred bricks and stench. An angry uniformed copper approached. He was covered in ash. Sweat glistened on his stained face.

'Sir. These fire-johnnies are buggering us about.'

'Stop them, Lynley.'

A yellow-helmeted fireman came up, sweatier and even angrier. The six others at the scene wore white helmets. Presumably he was the gaffer.

'Sergeant Ledger! My duty is to excavate and neutralize all fire—'

Ledger spat on an innocent floodlit nettle. 'Your duty is to make it safe here for my men.'

'Then that means—'

'Standing by until we tell you.'

The furious fireman tried to overbear but Ledger wouldn't give way, and stepped down to where Joxer's floor once was. I had difficulty seeing even where the bench had been. Ledger scuffed the debris and balanced on a piece of corrugated metal, part of Joxer's fallen roofing. Ash clouded in the beams up to our knees. The white glare and the abruptly stencilled shadows made it a mad lunar picture.

'Tell him, Derby.'

Derby intoned, 'Antique dealer and fabricator known locally as Joxer, height—'

'Yeah, yeah.'

Derby shrugged, skipped some. 'Found dead in his burning workshop. Cause of death yet to be reported, but—'

'Skull fracture,' Ledger cut in. 'Our quack says it *might* have been falling brick.'

Joxer was dead. So somebody had been hurt in the fire

after all. I remembered Sinead's sudden tension at Marcia's news.

'Might means might not, Ledger.'

'True, Lovejoy.' He kept balancing on the debris, hands in his pockets, looking at me. 'You accuse Clarke and Sam, and they inexplicably leap off a motorway bridge. You visit Joxer, and he gets stove in and stoved.'

'And you're arresting me for coincidences?'

'Don't be silly, Lovejoy. Last time that rich tart unhooked you. Same thing'd happen.'

'Would it?'

'Lovejoy.' He came and stood by me. If I didn't know better I'd have said he was feeling sad. 'You're in something deep with that pair of crooks—'

'Which pair, exactly?' Things were stupifying me.

'The Heindricks. And I want you to know something.' Derby was standing close by. 'This old town of ours saw the Roman Empire out, saw the back of the Saxons, Normans, and withstood the Black Death. It's going to survive the Heindricks. Understood?'

'Yes.'

'Even if the Heindricks team up with a wriggler like you, Lovejoy.'

'Okay. But what do you think happened to Joxer?'

'I believe the Heindricks—or you on their orders—foully murdered Joxer and tried to burn his corpse.'

'What makes you think—?'

Ledger lost patience. 'Piss off, Lovejoy. Sign him out, Derby.'

Derby produced a clipboard and asked me to sign a form stating I had been interviewed at the site of a crime or accident. He gave me a pen. I started to sign, then tilted the board to catch that garish light and read it several times till Ledger asked what was up.

'Ledger, who's Joseph Xavier Casey?'

'Joxer. His real name.'

A piece of gnarled twisted iron the size of a small horseshoe lifted from the ash as I moved my foot. Burning anything gives off a terrible stink. My breath was slow coming, but the sound it made caused Ledger to look harder. I signed his stupid form quickly, thinking of Sinead's cousin Joe Casey who did clever special nocturnal work for the Heindricks. I'd been so wrapped up in my own plight I hadn't even thought. Sinead had told me about her cousin Joe Casey soon after we heard Marcia's news in the pub. She must have thought I'd realized they were one and the same person.

'May I have a lift home now?'

His hesitation made me mad, but I maintained my sorrowful visage. He's a cyncial sod. Not one ounce of trust.

'Lovejoy. If I once find you—'

'I don't feel so good.'

He agreed, with yet more mistrust, which was how I thankfully found myself in Constable Smethurst's car bombing back to my cottage. Near the brewery I conned a coin from the lad to ring my doctor urgently, or so I told him. Anyway he could afford it. The Old Bill pay themselves enough. I tried the hospital, saying it was an urgent message for Sister Morrison. The beleaguered Night Sister frostily told me that personal calls were forbidden on internal lines, and anyway Sister Morrison didn't live in the nurses' home. That was the end of my day. About three-thirty I waved so-long to the copper and went indoors, not even a respectable failure.

The rest of that night was a bad one for me. The trouble is, when you are so utterly tired it sometimes works the opposite way and you can't drop off no matter how hard you try. I'm one of these people who never cares whether I sleep or not, which is okay as long as you aren't grieving. And I was.

My divan bed unfolds in my cottage living-room. I've

no upstairs, except for a crummy bat-riddled space under
the thatch, which you climb into like Tarzan of the Apes.
I hate those ceiling lights which always dangle glare in
your eyes, so my two electrics are controllable table
things. Tonight, though, I was in a familiar morose mood
and fetched out my old brass oil lamp to shed a more
human glow on the interior. Then I drew the curtains
and lay in bed, thinking of Joxer and the state I was in.

Folk come and go in your mind at the best of times,
always in and out of your life. Because of all this
movement, it's a sad mistake to try to keep things just as
they are, though God knows enough people desperately
keep on struggling to. Okay. That's life, and I have sense
to accept it. But Joxer had been killed, and I wasn't going
to accept that one little bit.

The Heindricks wanted a divvie—me. They'd given me
four days to recover. Then they were sending me
somewhere, a place overseas where I wouldn't need a
passport. Lena Heindrick had said that. And Joxer had
said Kilfinney. As a warning, as a tip-off? I'd never know
now he was dead, but you don't need a passport to Eire
and Joxer was Irish and Kilfinney sounded vaguely that
way on . . .

To my astonishment I woke with my robin tapping like
hell on the window, greedy little swine. I'd slept into
daylight, which was just as well. I was in a hurry.

Four days' start on the Heindricks.

Just a word here about antiques, because nowadays
there's more villainy over antiques than oil, sex, and
foreign currency put together. And antiques are my only
skill.

There's the legit kind—honestly made way back in
history (or 50-plus years ago, if you choose to believe the
recent British Customs and Excise ruling) and honestly
bought and sold, with dated receipts and all. Then there's

the phoney, usually a forgery made with ignorance and clumsiness and instantly detectable at a range of miles in a London peasouper. Then there's the 'tom', which once meant newly nicked jewellery of any kind but now means anything precious but stolen. Naturally, we lowlifes use the term to include antiques because antiques are the most common items of burglary nowadays. Which brings me round to the subject of *your* own valuables, and the noble art of stealing. If you own anything old, learn this next bit by heart.

Once upon a time, valuables were stolen by stealth. Skilled burglars did Murph-the-Surf scams à la Topkapi. You know the scene: teams of ex-service SAS types dangled from ropes or did the hang-glider bit between skyscrapers. You remember the screaming newspaper headlines and the Hollywood films that followed. Well, all that excitement was great while it lasted—thrills, spills, and the sequelæ of the Great Train Robbery meant good news copy, became a real industry in fact. Not any more. Things are different now. Times are modern. Above all, times are *new*. And the newest thing of all nowadays isn't bad manners, idle teenagers, or hysterical marching on Parliament. The newest thing now is theft, plain old simple stealing, by sleight-of-hand. And you don't use a team or a league or a twilight army. You do it on your tod, on your little own. And usually you get away scot free.

Think back over the latest rips. Notice anything special? They were casual and quiet. No, the main feature of modern robbery is it's a walk-in. In other words, the thief is legit and law-abiding *until the rip's pulled*. Don't believe me? Then you just keep an eye on the papers for a month or so (preferably July or August, peak months for nicking antiques). The famous Van Dyck portrait of Queen Henrietta Maria wasn't ripped from Nostell Priory by helicopter squads with flame-throwers and gasbombs. Somebody paid a quid admission fee, cool as you please, and sussed the place out first. And he had time to nick nine other paintings and four precious miniatures as well.

You'll notice something else while you're thinking about it. Antiques aren't merely ripped from private mansions. I mean, I sometimes think I'm the only bloke on earth who hasn't nicked Rembrandt's 1632 portrait of Jacob de Gheyn III from the Dulwich Picture Gallery in London. (It's small and painted on wood rather than canvas, so that helps.) It gets lifted regular as clockwork, and the last two times were walk-ins through the guarded entrance in broad daylight. One bloke simply popped the Rembrandt in a plastic shopping bag and pedalled off on his bloody bicycle. I ask you.

See what I mean? No banzai-parachute-grenade-Jaguar-jet-to-Morocco jobs nowadays. Museums and art galleries expect those. It's the 'oncer', as antique dealers call it, the legitimate art-lover who strolls in, and strolls out. And anybody can stroll, right? The big question stuck in my mind. Now that it's easy as all that, what the hell did they need a divvie for? And Kurak crisped old Joxer for being too chatty about their little enterprise, so it wasn't a simple walk-in. And it wasn't going to be any easy cloth job, either.

CHAPTER 10

Sunshine slammed into the cottage as soon as I pulled the curtain back. I'm not keen on a lot of fine weather, though birds seem to brighten up in it. Needless to say, my horde of garden scroungers were glaring in at me. Shakily I diced a grotty piece of cheddar and went outside to sprinkle it on the decorative little half-completed wall near by backdoor. I'll finish it when I get a minute. The blue tits have to manage with nuts in a net string on the apple tree but the robin's daft on cheese. Ten minutes later I had made myself more or less presentable and was entering Lyn's little garden down the lane carrying my egg wheel. The back door was open.

'Am I allowed?'

'Lovejoy!' She was at the table with her twins. They let out a shriek and hurrayed me into the kitchen. They were having breakfast, so I'd guessed right. 'Come and sit *down*! Just *look* at you, with your arm all *bandaged*! We heard such *awful* things about you, in the paper and *every*thing!' Lyn gave me a quick buss, and the girls sploshed milky lips on my cheek. Lyn and me had been quite close before she went and married a decent, reliable wage-earner. Which only goes to show you can't really depend on women. It was honestly coincidence which brought Lyn and her family into the same lane as me. Honestly.

She bustled about to get coffee, all pretty and pastel colours and yapping platitudes like they do. It was quite a hero's welcome. I was quite moved. It could easily have been the sailor's elbow even though I sometimes baby-sat for Lyn and David.

Little Rebecca asked, 'Did you have your dinner in prison, Lovejoy?'

'Shush, Becky!' Lyn reddened and said could I stay for breakfast because it was only eight o'clock and she was just going to do some for herself.

'Er, thanks, love.'

Alison, Rebecca's twin, was painstakingly dipping egg soldiers. She confided to me in a whisper, 'We haven't to say you're in prison, Lovejoy. Not to *anyone*.'

'Shush, Lally!'

'It's true!' Alison retorted. 'Daddy said!'

Rebecca joined in. 'We've to tell everybody you're

staying at your Auntie Lydia's.'

'Just listen to the pair of you little sillies!' Lyn's face was scarlet with embarrassment. She skated toast on to a plate for me but avoided my eye. I hadn't realized everybody down our lane knew about Lydia, my one-time learner assistant. She was not quite my auntie. Which accounted for Lyn's moods lately. Hey ho.

Alison had five egged soldiers now. With the deliberate actions of a child deciding to feed someone else, she directed one into my mouth, frowning with concentration. Rebecca was undeterred.

'Daddy said—'

'Becky! Eat your breakfast!'

'Daddy said you didn't really steal the church's kettle,' Becky explained.

Allies in unexpected quarters always warm your heart. I smiled at the kettle bit. 'Tell him ta.'

'Daddy said *you'd* not have got caught, Lovejoy.'

'Becky! One more word out of you!' Lyn cracked an egg on the edge of the pan. Women do that great. I've tried it but the shell always clings tight at the rim and the egg slides on to the floor.

Alison took up the refrain. 'Mummy said—'

'Both of you! Not another word!' Lyn dithered furiously between the stove and the table, threatening with a spoon. 'Absolute silence until you get down, or no playschool! Do you hear?'

The twins' faces turned mutinous but it must have been some threat because they went quiet. On my last babysitting visit they hadn't been speaking, some ferocious dispute over who had the right to move Lally's pot pig from its place on the windowsill. Lally had on her hooped red hairband, only plastic or something. I resolved to try to find her an antique one of woven glass—blue and white plaited, soft and pliable as silk. They are expensive, but one might turn up as a 'balancer', as we call the small antiques thrown in to make up a price. The shape of Lally's hairband made me think of something vitally important, but it escaped my consciousness as Lyn asked, not looking, how I was managing.

While she got the grub I told her all about my arrest, but omitted the Heindricks' part in my release. I made it out to have been a mistake. Naturally I said nothing about Sal, or Joxer for that matter.

'Lyn, love. Selling houses.' Her husband David is a chartered surveyor.

'Lovejoy! You're not thinking of—?'

' 'Course not. It's, er, this house somebody's selling in Sudbury. A dealer I'm friendly with might put a deposit down.'

Lyn smiled and tipped the fat over the edges of the eggs. She'd stir it all into a mess soon, knowing I can't stand looking into those reproachful orange egg eyes on the plate. 'And we thought Lovejoy came to see us, didn't we?' she said almost playfully to the twins.

'I did, love. If somebody puts a deposit down on a house, but doesn't sign anything, is it a legal sale?'

She looked doubtful and began to stir the yolks in. 'I don't believe it is. Not till the written contract is exchanged. I'll ask David.'

I thought for a minute. 'Could you?'

'He won't mind. He'll phone me about ten o'clock.'

'Lyn, love, I'll be away a day or two. Can you do my wheel?' I'd put it on the kitchen floor.

'That old thing? What is it?'

I explained. It is only a wooden wheel suspended on a crank. You lodge fresh eggs in holes in the rim. 'Give it a quarter turn dawn and dusk, and the eggs don't go bad. Victorian.'

'Oh, Victorian,' she said, voicing an age's criticism.

'You're jealous. Just because the Victorians invented everything and conquered the world on foot—'

'You need a fridge to store eggs.

'Whatever you say.' Women are like this.

'We'll turn your wheel, Lovejoy.' Lally and Rebecca chorused. They were so keen to get started I knew my eggs would be spin-dried as soon as my back was turned.

'I'll do it, Lovejoy,' Lyn corrected, glaring them down. 'Where are you going? Somewhere nice?'

'Maybe,' I said, swallowing a sudden twinge of apprehension.

Then Becky said in her penetrating whisper, 'Don't be frightened, Lovejoy.'

'Frightened? Of what? Who's frightened?' I demanded coldly, but that shook me. Kids say some bloody wrong things at odd times when they should shut up.

'I told you to be quiet, miss,' Lyn said, placing my food and looking at me carefully now.

'Yes. Eat your breakfast,' I added sternly.

The twins said together, watching, 'You eat yours.' So I did.

Then I went to sell my cottage shakily and a bit scared, because I wasn't sure if they'd try to kill me here first or wait till I reached Ireland.

Patrick had only just risen when I arrived on East Hill. By a curious blunder, our village bus had arrived on time so I was in town by nine-thirty and waiting for Lily to come to the door. The antiques shop had started out as Lily's, but it is Patrick's now, for obvious reasons. I often wonder if Lily's husband will ever ask for his deeds. Lily came to the door and let me in. She looks an absolute wreck in daylight. I closed the door and followed her down the narrow hallway into her living-room. Someone screamed. It was Patrick, all dramatic on the couch with his eyes padded.

' 'Morning, Patrick.'

'Lovejoy,' he moaned. 'I might have known. You

thundering great *clumsy*, you. You deliberately *slammed* that door.'

Lily tugged anxiously at my arm. 'Shhh, Lovejoy. He's got one of his heads.'

But I was in too much of a hurry for suchlike gunge and said, 'That's a rotten dressing-gown, Patrick. Can't you afford better?'

He sat bolt upright, glaring and spitting venom. 'Vermilion and sepia are natural *partners*, you cretin!'

'It's the scarlet belt, Patrick. Doesn't go.'

He rose and rushed apprehensively to a full-length wall mirror and paraded a minute, tying and untying his belt. 'Oh, Lovejoy, don't you think so? Are you sure?'

He looked ridiculous, but you daren't tell him so outright. 'It's a problem,' I murmured, my stock phrase when I haven't a clue.

Patrick rounded on Lily. 'Why didn't you say, silly cow!' he shrilled.

'Well, dear, you were so certain . . .'

I cut in. 'You want my cottage, Patrick?'

'*What?*'

He'd been after buying it for years. 'You want to make an offer? I'm trying to raise some gelt to build up my stock.'

'You're going to sell, Lovejoy?' Lily breathed. 'Oh, Patrick, darling—'

'Shut up, silly cow,' he commanded. 'How much, Lovejoy?'

'Well, I'm having it valued today. Naturally I'd want at least the market value . . .'

His eyes narrowed for business. 'You'll give me an option?'

Innocently I shrugged, smiling. 'I don't mind much. Just thought I'd drop round and let you know because—'

'*Please*, Lovejoy,' Lily exclaimed. 'Patrick's always loved that spot.'

'Well . . .' I dithered, really quite convincing.

'*Please*. We'll put down a deposit, to be first.'

'Look, Lily, it's not even been listed for sale—'

'Then we'll be at the head of the queue, decide terms later.' She rummaged in her handbag and fetched out a lovely thick virgin cheque-book. It was beautiful. 'It need only be a token sum.' That sounded horrible. I needed more than token sums.

'I'm not sure . . .'

'Let's see,' she mused, finding a pen. 'The usual deposit's, say, ten per cent of the purchase price, so let's say half of that?'

'No.' Patrick was gauging me warily. As I said before, he's a shrewder nut than he makes out, the pest. 'Point five per cent's ample.'

'All right.' I put the best face on it I could manage and five minutes later was down their steps carrying a crossed cheque, not for as much as I had hoped, but stealers can't be choosers.

My luck was in that morning—or so I thought in my ignorance. The phone kiosk opposite the Ship tavern had not been vandalized, by some strange oversight. After listening to a brisk altercation between Rebecca and the operator, Lyn breathlessly managed to wrestle the receiver away from her offspring and accept reversed charges for the call. I asked if David had phoned in.

'Yes, Lovejoy. I asked him, like you said.'

'Were you right?' I meant about the house purchase law.

'Yes. David says the legal point of sale is the formal exchange of contracts. He says if you want to call in tonight he can explain in more detail—'

'Thanks, love. That's great. You've really helped me. So long.'

'Lovejoy?' That was Rebecca, penetrating the conversation by some bedroom extension. 'Are you in prison again?'

'Becky! Put that down at *once*!' Lyn's voice receded as she ran to the next room, her receiver clattering my earhole.

'Shhh, love,' I said furtively, doing my sinister act. 'I'm going to Ireland, but it's a secret, right?'

'Right,' Becky whispered.

Emerging from the kiosk I felt good about the information, but something was niggling. It was the kind of odd discomfort which comes when you remember passing a face in a crowd and only realize hours later it was a long-lost friend. Something was wrong, and I couldn't put my finger on it.

When I'm in one of these uncertain moods I gravitate towards antiques, but first I solved the innocent little Kilfinney mystery. The town library had opened by then. It consists of a modern hexagonal brown brick monstrosity with metal-and-glass doors which function like a nutcracker. I strongly believe they are a Malthusian solution for the population problem of our cripples and geriatrics, but no analyses have yet been done to count corpses. By a whisker I made it to the safety of the foyer, dishevelled and bruised.

'Hello, Marlene!'

The girl on the desk was frantically dialling on the emergency phone. 'Mr Scotchman! Mr Scotchman! Lovejoy's in! He's on the escalator!'

I gave a royal wave down to her as I was lifted among a throng of grannies and housewives up the moving staircase. More people than just myself have hated the new library, and not only because our lunatic town council demolished thirty sixteenth-century dwelling houses and Mr Wesley's chapel to erect it.

'Guard me, Auntie!' I said piteously to an old grey-haired lady as we cruised heavenward. 'They'll want to chuck me out.'

'The very idea!' she quavered. 'Stay close to me, young man!'

'And I only want to look up my grandad's birthday.'

'They're too bossy by far!' her mate warbled, grasping her umbrella with grim intent.

'Thank you, thank you.'

At the top the thin, belligerent form of our town librarian, Scotchman, was standing. He stepped forward, a fierce smile stencilling his lips. 'Out, Lovejoy. *Out!*'

Sad and humble, I murmured, 'I knew it. Poor old grandad . . .'

'Fiend!' my older protectress cried, prodding the librarian aside.

'Fascist!' Her mate buffeted him against the wall with her basket and I was past, trotting into the reference section. People lifted heads and tut-tutted, but I was at the famous 1837 Lewis *Topographical Ireland* in a flash and looking up K in Volume II.

There was a Kilfenny, a Kilfeighny, a Kilfinnane and Kilfinney in Limerick in 1837, so I supposed there still was. Keeping a wary eye on the main glass door, where Scotchman cruised in impotent fury and glared at me, I waved cheerfully once, then read, absorbed.

The ashes had cooled among the ruins.

Places look so different in daylight, don't they, quieter and more controllable. Standing there among the weeds and tombstones I felt my old discontent return. Here, at this precise spot in the Universe, poor Joxer had died. The silent malevolence of the Heindricks' Slav chauffeur, the almost jovial calm of Kurt's admonition, the sexy allure of the feline Lena—on the face of it they didn't add up to much, yet look here. Ash and charcoal. Restless, I scuffed the ashes and walked slowly along the wire mesh fence. Some white police marker tapes were still there. Lazy sods. The weeds in the corner of the Priory's ruins stood tall, but those in the vicinity of the crime were trampled down, presumably by the firemen and the Old Bill.

Over towards the church hall which the dramatic society uses there is a minuscule cobbled road leading to the town's main street. They used to fetch the horse-drawn hearses there at funerals. No car-tyre tracks traceable that way, and the street road that ran along the churchyard's top slope was free to anybody.

I walked back to Joxer's ashed workshed. The little redbrick factory on the other side of the tall wire mesh was functioning busily. Its nearside wall was smudged with black. Its narrow strip windows held only opaque glass, so no hope of finding some vigilant night-watchman garrulous with clues. Yet what was I doing hanging about here when I should be hitting the road to Limerick?

There's nothing quite so messy as a drenched fire. Black ash clung to my shoes and crept stickily on to my socks. My trouser edges were damp and flecked, and the uneven rubble made me wobble uncertainly. This odd restlessness, as if Joxer himself had returned to warn, had me jiggling nervously on the same corrugated iron where Ledger had uttered his ridiculous threats. I stepped off and the same bent piece of iron lifted out of the ash just as it had last night. It felt rough when I picked it up, not even warm. Maybe seven inches or so, it had been spindle-shaped, but now it was twisted along its length and curved into a crescent. Or, I wondered with quick interest, had old Joxer actually cast it in that shape? Holding it up, I turned for better light — and saw Sinead Morrison not ten feet away, standing watching me.

She was lovely, a picture. The sun falls through the great arches of the fawn-red ruins and pools the grass into green brilliance. Sinead was above me on the slope, a broad arrow of sunlight colouring her pale face and hair. The whole composition was breathtaking. I wanted to love her then, because she was lovable in her long swingback coat.

'Loot, Lovejoy?'

'Eh? Oh.' I dropped Joxer's old iron in the ash and climbed the slope. 'Look, love. Sorry about your Joxer.'

'Sorrow, Lovejoy?' Her pale eyes blazed into me. 'You don't know the meaning of the word.'

'Eh? Look, love, I did try—'

Her relentless voice was quiet but still shut me up. 'Last night in the tavern you realized that there'd be a chance of some loot, so you said nothing when that lady brought the news of the fire. Your evil brain just filed the information away, so you could come picking over the ashes like the carrion crow you are—even though Joe's hardly cold.'

I listened, aghast. 'No, love. Look, I honestly—'

'Honestly?' She stepped away to laser me with those radiant eyes. 'You, Lovejoy? Honest? I really fell for your flannelling at the hospital.'

This couldn't be happening, not to me. Not from her. 'But you don't understand—'

'Correct, Lovejoy. I don't understand you at all. But everybody else does. The point is, they're right about you and I was wrong.'

She left then, walking with grace along the slope's contour between two lichen-covered stones, her coat moving softly and her lifting heels shining among the grasses. It nearly broke my heart. I tried to call after her and couldn't.

It's really lucky for me that I'm used to bad luck, or I would have been too cut up to do anything at all the rest of that day. Anyhow, with my record I'm used to heartbreak, so within an hour I'd been to the bank and talked them into letting the cheque through. Ten minutes later I'd found Tinker. He was waiting forlornly for opening time on the step of the Three Cups near the old

Saxon church. I gave him a couple of notes and told him to get some tins of ale and meet me outside the Castle.

I went then to a travel agent's in Cross Wyre Street and booked a ticket to Ireland.

CHAPTER 11

Janet's car is a blue Morris, fairly easy to spot even in the usual tangle near our market. Tinker had cleared the contents of his tins by the time she came. She saw me, aloofly driving past and drumming her fingers on the steering-wheel, mad at something. I sighed at this hint of more trouble and gave Tinker one last reminder.

'Anybody asking after buying my cottage, you send them to Lyn and David's, okay? Down the lane.'

His rheumy eyes looked up quizzically from the bench. 'Here, Lovejoy. We really clearing out?'

'Are we hell, silly fool.' I ticked off on my fingers. 'Antiques: Liz over at Dragonsdale has a late Regency ostrich fan. Get her to hold it for me.'

'Christ,' he moaned. 'She'll want the Crown Jewels, Lovejoy. Where'll we get that kind of gelt?'

That is horribly true nowadays. You can buy a new car with less money. Still. 'And Margaret Dainty's got a collection of antique barbering instruments, combs, scissors, razors. Tell her I've a buyer—'

'Have we?'

Sometimes Tinker's thick. 'No. Try to find one before I get back. I should only be a day or two. And tell Big Frank from Suffolk I need a couple of George IV period stitch samplers, framed, dated and named if possible.'

'But we've a half-share in that pair of samplers Leggy Baldock's trying to sell.'

'Quite,' I said patiently, inwardly pleading God-give-me-strength. Tinker never learns. 'But Big Frank doesn't know that. So he'll go to Leggy's stall next Saturday and—'

Tinker's gnarled old face lit up. 'Hey, Lovejoy! That's great! But what happens when Big Frank buys them and fetches them to us?'

'We tell him we've already done the deal elsewhere, see?' Janet tooted her horn impatiently.

'He'll do his nut. Here. What you going to Limerick for, Lovejoy?'

'Holiday,' I said laconically. 'Ta-ra.'

'Go safe, mate.'

My train was at four, so I had time to invite Janet in for a cup of tea, as women euphemistically call it. I was glad about her willingness, because although she's quite a bit older than me I find more gratification in older women, and anyway they're better. It isn't just staying power, it's having more style or something. When she left at one o'clock to get some shopping done I had a sleep and was packing my small — actually my one-and-only — cardboard suitcase by two, and feeling fine. I remembered to put a three-foot length of hosepipe conspicuously in the centre of my garden. Cats think it's a snake and go elsewhere, so I'd find no dead birds about when I got back. Lyn and the twins would scatter bird cheese morning and afternoon for me.

There turned out to be only one snag when it came time to catch the train, and it was Jason at the station. I'd made Janet go, after borrowing some change for the phone, because I hate these farewells. I waved her off, then rang Helen, and Margaret Dainty, and Liz at Dragonsdale. Finally, thinking I was laying a false trail, I dialled Patricia Harvest, a money-mad investor who with her husband Pete ran a fruit farm down the Goldhanger estuary. Patricia's one of those rich women who dress like a scrapyard. She's always crying poverty, but then so do her three gardeners. I asked her what museum exhibitions were on at the moment. She can afford the posh antiques journals where they're advertised.

'Nobody else would know, not like you, Pat.' I awarded myself ten points on the creep chart for grovelling.

'Patricia,' she corrected mechanically. 'Where? National museums? Oh, Turner watercolours in the Brit Muzz—they're doing that sublime bit. Then there's Manchester . . .' She prattled on, visions of tax-free capital obviously warming her marble heart.

'And Dublin?'

'Yes. The Derrynaflan finds, with early exhibits from Armagh. And the Dublin Antiques Fair's on next week.' Her voice broke momentarily under the stress of listing so much wealth owned by somebody else. 'Ooooh, Lovejoy,' she moaned. 'Are you doing a sweep? Take me, and I'll see you right, darling. *Please*.' The thought made her frantic.

Weakness struck, but I remembered that lives were at stake—mainly mine. So I lied, 'See you in Dublin, sweetheart. That big hotel, the poshest one, right in the centre near that park.' I was smiling, because in any city there's always a big posh hotel in the centre near a park. 'I'll divvie for you. Next week, okay? You can pay me—in kind.'

Her voice went husky. 'You will, darling? I'll be there. You'll not regret it.' She's always trying to get me to divvie for her, and has heap big methods of persuasion.

Cheerfully I put the phone down and damned near scalped myself emerging from the idiotically-designed perspex hood—to realize a thin spread of waiting travellers had listened to every word. Of course they were carefully pretending, in the very best English manner, to be preoccupied with books and the middle distance. Even that crook in the ticket office was all agog. That would not have mattered much, but Jason mattered very much indeed after the warning Sinead had given me about him the other night.

He was buying a paper so very casually from the girl on the box stall. The local mental hospital sets it up to give the patients pin money. People mostly give more money than the newspapers cost. Like I say, folk are a rum lot. No good trying to work their motives out.

Jason saw me with a theatrical start of astonishment and took in my battered cardboard case.

'Hello, Lovejoy. Off on holiday?'

'No. Taking stuff up to Maggs on the Belly.' Even as I spoke I knew I'd made a mistake. It was too early in the week to be making deliveries to the Portobello Road antique market. And he could phone Maggs to check.

'Big dealer, eh?' He grinned, all even teeth and perfumed talc. 'Think you could wait a day or two and take a couple of things for me?'

'Due in today. There's this painting . . .'

'Ah.' He nodded wisely. 'I understand. Nothing I can say to persuade you to postpone your journey, Lovejoy?'

'Not really.' I grinned but without much conviction. What with Jason in his cavalry twills and his army-officer efficiency, the Heindricks and their murderous driver, and trouble with Ledger and his merrie men, I was really in the gunge now.

'You wouldn't be crossing to Ireland?'

'That *Paradise Lost* you got me to buy? No, Jason. Forgotten all about that.' That was the bookseller-printer I'd told Sinead about, who owed me.

'A natural mistake, Lovejoy.'

'Sure it was. See you, Jason.'

He said evenly, 'Soon, eh?'

Recognizing me, the ticket collector did not hold out his hand for my ticket, having once had his thumb clipped with his own clipper by a certain antique dealer to whom he had shown ferocious rudeness. I paused. He recoiled into his red booth, wincing at the memory, hands behind his back.

'Go straight through,' he said in a shaky falsetto.

'Go straight through . . . ?' I prompted.

'Go straight through . . . sir.'

The train was on time. Janet had made me some cheese and tomato butties, which lasted me almost till the station was out of sight. All I could think of was Pat Harvest, with annoyance. The British Museum Turner exhibition 'doing the sublime bit', indeed. That innocent exhibition of watercolours had suddenly informed everybody how important some ideas are — and promptly sent the price of first editions of Edmund Burke's book on the *Origin of our Ideas on the Sublime and the Beautiful* soaring five hundred per cent in three days among dealers and provincial antiquarians. A mint copy cost a few bob in 1757. It makes you sick.

Still, a few things stay the same in this murderous antiques game. Dear Patricia's idea of the sublime and the beautiful hadn't changed since she was born. Money. And at least I'd tried to lay a false trail by repeating those different locations to anyone who cared to listen. Like Jason.

On the plane they gave us those plastic dinners. I always get confused by so many little pots and get fed up halfway through. The hostess was bonny but their uniforms look so sterile they put me off. I dozed, worried about the mess I was in.

My mind goes funny when I'm sleeping yet not sleeping. Joxer had done some quiet jobs for the Heindricks, so quiet indeed he had been compelled to work in the night hours. Night, when there would be none of Marcia's amateur actors rehearsing on the greensward among the Priory ruins. Which meant stuff could be carried into Joxer's workshed and worked on without the chance of some stray actor witnessing Joxer's secret labours. I knew that Jimmy Day and Marcia and some of the others used Joxer's little loo, and occasionally persuaded him to brew up for them on his bunsen burner. He was usually pretty tolerant and pleased with company, though dramatics folk can't talk about anything else except drama.

As the plane banked, Joxer's last words came to me: *Can't you watch a minute with me?* Whether people ask for you to watch a minute or an hour with them, the answer's always no from goons the likes of me. Aren't people pathetic, I thought in my miserably fitful doze. And whatever I found in Kilfinney there'd be hell to pay when I zoomed home—Patrick would go berserk about being tricked out of my cottage, Lily would be demented about the money, the Heindricks would be decidedly upset when they found out I'd scarpered, and Kurak at having murdered Joxer for possibly nothing. But Jason was thick as thieves with Lena Heindrick, so Sinead said, and the bastard might have sussed me out at the station when I phoned Patricia Harvest. And Ledger distrusted everybody. I groaned inwardly, remembering I'd signed his bloody form the other night. Had its typescript included a promise not to leave the area without letting him know? What a mess.

The trouble is, I always feel like a chicken in a Western—under the pony's hooves, desperately at risk from stray bullets, unpaid, and never getting the girl. It's not much of a part.

The air hostess was shaking me then.

'Dublin,' she said, smiling nearly like Sinead. My heart turned over.

'Do we get off now?'

'Yes. Unless you want to go back.'

I thought a bit, then did what she said. Once a chicken, always a chicken.

CHAPTER 12

When you go to a new place I always find you have to adjust, but the adjustment isn't a matter of simple surprise or pleasure. You need a positive effort to rid yourself of preconceptions. Where the hell we get them from Heaven alone knows. If you're like me, you spend a time being astonished that it isn't at all like you'd somehow tricked yourself into thinking it would be. For a start, Dublin has no Tube. Why I'd ever assumed it would have, I've no idea. See what I mean? And Dublin's trains are noisy little diesels pulling orange-and-black coaches, another mind-blower. And their lads and lassies seem to smoke continually, everywhere. Like everywhere else, Dublin was showing signs of making living impossible in the interests of greater efficiency. And the traffic was at least as dangerous as everywhere. But I liked the way cars halting at traffic lights waited airily in the very middle of the crossing.

That evening I plodded round the darkening city looking for a place to lay my weary head, finding still more astonishments. Why no dots on the letter 'i' in names of streets and stations? And Dublin seems to do without those great office blocks most cities find indispensible, which is pleasing. The day was falling into its ember sky by the time I found a nosh bar near the Abbey Theatre and slammed a couple of pasties down in a sludge of tea. Time was getting on then, so I started blundering about a bit faster, trudging my cardboard suitcase along likely streets.

The River Liffey when I found it turned out to be as black as your hat, again a new fantastic fact. Guidebooks say Dubliners call it 'Anna', but I suspect they use the nickname as often as cockneys call their river Old Father Thames. Anyhow, I crossed by the Halfpenny Bridge feeling a bit lost and downhearted, wondering what on earth did I think I was doing here, miles from home, in search of more trouble than I had even back in East Anglia. But at least I was among people, though the city centre didn't have as many of those around as I'd have liked.

Dublin chimneypots are really great, genuine collectors' items. It's a wonder the whole lot haven't been whipped years ago. Believe it or not, but in one narrow street behind that big bookshop on the Liffey side I saw a good set of clay coloured Blashfield Hexagons, which are rare enough for those who collect London chimneypots, and a delectable group of eight Fareham Reds. Don't laugh. I honestly do believe the Fareham Red's pie-crust edging and its pretty white-painted rim band to be a work of art design. Anyway, why scorn a lovely piece of genuine eighteenth-century sculpture just because it's been stuck on a roof and become a bit sooty? You don't laugh at the Venetian crucifix on Giorgio Massari's reconstructed Church of the Pietà, same age. And across the road there was a triplet of tulip-shaped serrated crowntops, though mostly you see these 'Wee Macs' round Burton-on-Trent.

A fine drizzle started then. In despair, and not having pockets big enough to carry nicked chimneypots, I walked on and settled for a small terrace house with steps and nice but rusting Victorian iron railings, scrapers and door furniture. It advertised *Vacancies* and was not too far from the well-lit centre where the cinemas and pubs were still booming and buses tried to run you down at least as fast as I was used to. Inside, the house was a bit faded and peeling. Mrs Johnson the landlady was homely and chatty, gave me a room for an advance and promised to wait up to let me back in. 'You'll be off for a drink, I expect,' she said wisely. As I went forlornly off towards O'Connell Street I consoled myself that at least I was untraceable by practically everybody, friend or foe. Nobody knew I was here in Dublin, and tomorrow I could hire a car at first light and bomb off to Kilfinney. I'd still be ahead of the Heindricks' game.

Next morning the car hire looked quite a grand firm. It turned out to be the most complicated one on earth, what with phone calls to check my licence, a bloody test drive if you please, and a long wait while they did something to the mileometer. And I'd never seen so many forms in my life. Finally they said it was ready. I thanked them, and walked out to where the car stood at the kerb. I had this odd feeling as I went to open the driver's side door, telling myself not to get spooked in broad daylight.

' 'Morning, Lovejoy.'

Lena Heindrick was sitting in the passenger seat, giving me one of those non-smiling hilarities women emit when they see men squirm. She was as elegant and stylish as ever, diamond-stud earrings, a tight scroll hairdo, and a smart Donegal tweed suit. I didn't dare glance at her legs. The Edwardian silver-set sapphire brooch unnerved me enough as it was. She leaned across and gently pushed the door ajar. Her eyes were absurdly big.

I shrugged and sat. 'So that's why they took so long to hire me the car.'

'I had Kurak contact every firm, Lovejoy.' She smiled, her hand on my thigh.

'Then you just waited by the phone?'

'I did so want to . . . talk.' She traced with her fingers. 'It will be a great deal easier here, since Kurt has urgent manufacturing business to attend to in London.'

Finding somebody else, now Joxer was too dead to work for him? I swallowed. 'Where to?'

'That's better, Lovejoy. Drive out towards Sandymount. Don't be nervous. I'll direct.'

I always notice Daimlers, because they remind me of Daimler himself, who once prophesied that motor-cars hadn't much of a future—because there were only 1,000 chauffeurs in the whole of Europe. A large black Daimler pulled out behind us as I drove away. Lena hadn't come alone, it seemed.

The place at Sandymount was near a rugby ground. Over the flat sealands into which the duck-riddled river ran you could see the incongruous twin slender chimneys of the power station. It didn't look much like a pigeon-house to me—another nickname gone wrong. The area was largely terrace houses with oddly pleasant wide-arched doorways, and narrow, shaggily unkempt gardens.

'Left here, but park outside.'

The place was a walled garden surrounding a large house set back from the road. Nearby was a school noisy with playground squeals, and a little bridge over the river opposite. A couple of chatting women stirred their prams the way they do. Calm, quite nice really. Yet the feeling was tight in my throat. I switched off and met her eyes. I'd never known a woman smile as much as her.

'I needn't have come.' My defiant reminder only made her luscious red mouth smile wider.

'Of course you needn't, darling,' she said. 'Tell your conscience you were kidnapped.'

Women get me really narked. They always assume you have no bloody will of your own. Furiously I started up, 'Listen, you—'

She raised her hands to heaven in exasperation and broke in. 'Lovejoy,' she said wearily, 'for heaven's sake get me out of this car and up to Flat Five. Whatever you're going to do to me's not allowed in parked cars.'

There are some things you can be really proud of, like the times you help a person for nothing, or when you pull off

a coup you never really expected. The trouble is, those
events don't come along so often, and if they do it's
accidental as far as I'm concerned. The rest of life is filled
with occurrences you try to avoid remembering. Like
Lena.

Lena's one of those women like Helen, who want a
smoke after. And oddly it's then that they talk, when the
man is dozing after that minor death which finally washes
out the orgasmic rut of love. Women nark me like this.
Sometimes they're thick. Not everybody has to be
talkative the way women are. I'm not. When I was a kid I
went silent days at a time, sometimes for devilment, as my
old gran used to call it, but often because I just felt like
some useful silence.

'Darling?' Lena must have asked me God-knows-what.
The ceiling was a bit cracked. Her head of hair was lovely
on the pillow. She's got that sheen into it which Margaret
Dainty has. 'I said are you all right?'

'Ta.' Why are women's breasts always cold?

She half rolled and leant over me. 'What do you think
of, Lovejoy? You are always miles away. A woman doesn't
like to feel her man has slipped off into a world she
doesn't know.'

'Brew up, chuckie.'

She stared in astonishment, then laughed and laughed.
Her eyelashes were long and dark, her breasts full and
smooth. Puzzled, I asked her what was up.

'You're impossible, Lovejoy!' Shaking her head
disbelievingly, she rose and went through the corridor,
draping a bath towel round her waist. She had to step
over our clothes which were scattered over the floor. It
had been a right scramble into bed.

I shouted after her, 'How did you know I'd gone to
Dublin? Jason?'

'Yes.' She must have sensed me wondering about her
and Jason. 'He does try so, poor boy, but he's hardly your

rival, darling.'

There was a nasty sound of womanly permanence about all this. Better to keep it safely into matters of business, keep on playing dim. 'Lena. Why Dublin?'

A pause, a rattle of cups. 'You tell me.'

'You said that about not needing a passport but foreign. And Joxer is — was — Irish.'

If ever a mature living woman stepped straight out of one of those voluptuous Victorian engravings, it was Lena Heindrick when she came to the bedroom door and stood looking.

'The last time I waited on a man was ten years ago, Lovejoy.'

'Then you've been bloody idle. Get a move on.'

The kettle shrilled. She went out, laughing. I suppose Lena Heindrick seethed with breeding, because I'd never known a woman so sure of herself, so unbelievably positive. Oh, I admit every woman has this knack of somehow turning sexual supplication into a royal command, but never before had I encountered a woman who best-guessed like her.

'You brought your Slav gorilla over?' I called through, wondering if it wasn't overdoing the idiot bit.

'Have I?' she answered mischievously.

'The Daimler.'

'Well spotted. He was necessary — till now.'

Oho. I rose and padded about, looking for my trousers and my jacket. I could have sworn I'd shed them in the corridor between the living-room and the bedroom, but maybe Lena, in an epidemic of homeliness, had tidied. Women do that.

'Where are my clothes, love?'

'You don't need them yet, darling.' Her voice was smiling.

The window overlooked a stone-rimmed courtyard. Kurak, all million tons of him, was sitting on a decorative

stone. He was in a bad humour, and staring malevolently
up at our net curtains. He was cracking his knuckles,
straight out of a bad supporting feature. My soul chilled.
I'd seen that horrid habit before, in . . . in a bloke exactly
like Kurak, three years ago. In . . . in Northampton? At
an antiques function, where . . . where . . .

Lena returned carrying a tray with cups and all the
gear, pleased with heself. There's nothing prettier than a
well-loved woman just that little dishevelled. By then I
was in bed, trying not to look worried sick but restless as a
cat on hot bricks. She came in beside me without shaking
the house down or spilling everything, another female
knack.

'There! Well? Aren't you proud of me? Tea in bed?'

'I'll arrange the knighthood. Where's Kurt?'

She turned and put a finger on my mouth. 'Shhh.
Kurt's a man whose only interest is antiques and art. He's
not here, which suits me fine.'

Well, pretence is everything nowadays. 'Does he know?'

'Know, darling?' She stopped pouring, the spout
dripping.

'About you and Kurak.'

For a split second her nostrils flared, almost too quick
to notice, but it happened and should have warned me.
My only excuse for what eventually occurred is that a
woman in bed is a terrible distraction to common sense.
She poured the tea, stirred and carefully passed mine.

'There's such a thing as change, Lovejoy. Kurak's
served his purpose, now that . . .'

'Now I'm here?'

She lit a cigarette and jerked her head to show supreme
irritation the way they do. 'Too pure, Lovejoy? Well, are
you? I read your life story. Kurt had three agencies on you
for weeks. Every tart, every shady deal, every forgery,
those silly bored sluts of housewives pretending to be
Sweet Little Alice in exchange for a good rut. It was all

there, every detail.'

My life isn't the way she made it sound, really sordid. Anyway, Lyn's not a slut.

'Kurak had his uses, Lovejoy, just as Kurt had his.'

'Past tense?'

'Certainly.' Her brown eyes enveloped me. 'It's you now. Or are you too stupid to realize?' And, honestly, she smiled as she said the words, her lips widening and her cheeks dimpling. I swallowed tea to wet my throat, suddenly dry.

'Me for what?'

'Two things, darling. One, we find a fortune.'

'And two?'

She slid down, covering her shoulders with the sheet, and gave my belly a lick. 'Finish your tea, darling.'

I can't drink tea hot like women do, so I put it on the bedside table. The Duc de Charost actually read a book in the Terror's tumbril, and, when it came his turn for the scaffold, calmly turned down the page to mark his place. I wish I had panache like that. It would give you some control. Anyway, he'd still got the chop, poor sod, and I was trying not to.

A click fetched me conscious.

Lena was sleeping hunched, her back to me. We lay sideways across the disarranged bed. My leg was over her waist. In sleep my right hand had reached round to hold her breast. The pillows were anywhere. It was still daylight. I kept still and listened. No further sound. Kurak. It *had* been Northampton, that auction. Only he was no Slav then. I'd seen him across the crowd of bidders and dealers.

Without moving I estimated Lena's breathing. Regular. I stirred, moved my leg, freed my hand and rolled on my back. Lena didn't shift. Flat out. The click didn't come again. There was no movement in the other rooms that I could tell.

Her skin was flawless, full and smooth. It took an iron will slowly to reach the other way, and gently find the teacup. My finger touched the wet tea. Barely warm. Maybe an hour at the outside.

The edge of one sheet lay across my chest, but Lena had pulled a blanket over our legs and somehow got herself mostly burrowed under. Women do this in half-sleep, being naturally petrified of coldth.

One thing I'm a world expert in is leaving bed with great stealth. I've trained a lifetime. You don't do it inch by inch. You sigh, yawn, flop a bit, because those are the natural movements a woman's senses expect of a sleeping companion. Getting yourself vertical's the main problem. The best way is to sigh, then, making sure your limbs are free of all encumbrances, in one movement you smoothly swing your legs over the side, simultaneously bringing your torso erect. You stay sitting there, breathing regularly so the vibes of kipping lull any alerted senses back into oblivion. Then you slowly stand up, and you're off. Check first that your escape's not left her more uncovered than when you were *in situ*, so to speak, or chill will bring her to.

That should have been the end of it, except my jacket and trousers lay too neatly on the carpet of the living-room. Practically folded, as if the trouser crease was still traceable. Now, I didn't like this at all because I don't fold things. I liked it less when finding my wadge of money was gone. My gear had been cleaned out, down to the last Irish florin. No sign, though, of anybody—such as Kurak—in the flat.

Underpants, singlet, shirt (sleeves rolled up to conceal its button-free cuffs), trousers and jacket. A man feels better when dressed, probably because blokes look so daft in the nuddie. Socks were difficult, till I remembered I'd slung them off in the bedroom. Worse, Lena's handbag was missing. And I knew it should have been by the telly where she'd carelessly laid it as she lit a cigarette. I padded over to the window. Kurak was still down in the courtyard, now smoking a cigar and much less edgy. Just as sullen, but no knuckle-cracking. Exactly like a bloke who had just obeyed his mistress's command: nick Lovejoy's gelt, don't let him get away, and wait outside until you're told different. Well, I now knew how persuasive Lena could be. I was hooked on her myself, daft sod. Silently I floated into the bedroom, and found my tatty socks near the dressing-table.

Lena had turned over. She now faced the corridor door, and I was sure she was still sleeping . . . I think. Suspiciously, I waited a few moments but there wasn't a quiver from her eyelids. Her handbag wasn't in the bedroom either. That took a minute, which was fatal. The bed sounded, too sharply.

'Lovejoy? What are you . . . ?'

I'd clocked her one before I could think. She exhaled and slumped on the bed, moving slowly, in a daze from my blow. The recollection still makes me embarrassed, but what else is new? Anyway what can you do when it's courtesy or survival? Instinct takes over then. Nothing actually to do with thinking or behaviour or conscience. Another choice was on me now—keep on searching for the odd groat, or scarper. I settled for escape in poverty and hit the road.

The door had a simple lock. Kurak was a nerk to have let it click—you pass any modern lock with a comb or a few celluloid toothpicks. He ought to have known that.

The kitchen clock said two o'clock. There was part of the day left, but it was now much less promising. I left by the back door, climbed a wall and in an hour walked into Dublin town.

CHAPTER 13

Not a farthing, no help, no car. I sat on a bench in draughty old Pheonix Park, thinking, unable to go home or reach Kilfinney two hundred miles away. Hunted by vengeful Heindricks, trapped into immobility by poverty. And you need money to finance the kind of war I was in.

The quickest way of course is roulette, though it's a mug's game. Mind you, there's an infallible system — or, rather, there used to be. Clever Victorian Joe Jagger spotted it in the Monte Carlo casino by hiring clerks to sit at each wheel and list the numbers, but then Joe was a meticulous engineer raised on a lifetime of Lancashire cotton-mill spindles, and he knew all about eccentricities of balance mechanisms. His relentless winning streak is the reason that the roulette wheels of the world are now perfectly balanced by gimlet-eyed serfs at half past seven every dawn. Reminiscing, I grimaced to myself. The famous Joseph had more sense than most. Evenually rumbled by the panic-stricken croupiers, the world's only infallible — and sensible — gambler simply packed his bags with his fortune and scarpered. The trouble is, gambling isn't like antiques. It's guessing. Look at that con artist Charlie Wells, the original Man Who Broke The Bank At Monte Carlo. Kept on gambling, finished broke. Well, I was broke to start with.

A sparrow came to my feet full of hope, and went on its way. Not daft. It was going to where it had prospects.

Prospects! Like being *owed* money? I remembered Jason's promise of a genuine first edition from, where was it, that printer's shop . . . near here. Fenner and something. I was owed! Therefore I too had prospects! At an antiquarian bookseller's, not far from the park.

Eagerly I rose and headed towards my own salvation.

The place when I found it was off the main road near Phoenix Park. I was glad about that. The nearest bus stop was quite a few hundred yards away and nobody waiting. A tatty printing shop front leading directly off the pavement, but with a grand new Rover parked outside and a smaller white Ford further along. Surprised at its dinginess, I went in. An old shop doorbell clunked above. There was a long counter and two blokes chatting away behind it. An aroma of fag smoke mingled with the bland bite of printer's ink. Untidy rows of books threatened a few desperate shelves. Founts of type were casually racked on trays all the way along the shop interior.

'Fenner and Storr? Antiquarian booksellers?'

'I'm one. He's the other. And you'll be . . . ?' The stockier, shabbier bloke broke off and came to lean across the counter as if it was a taproom bar. He seemed pleasant and bright. I was glad about that for his sake, because I find people like being happy, even if it's only for a short time.

'Lovejoy.'

'And from the sound of you you'll be a book dealer from over the water,' he chirrupped. 'Now, what's your speciality?'

'*Paradise Lost*,' I said. The other bloke was nattier, county set in tweeds and twill with an elegant walking cane. He met my eye, nodded affably. I nodded back. No argument with him, only with this robber trying to flannel me across his flaky-paint counter.

'Ah. Blessed Milton, of the sweet tongue! Well, you're in luck there, sor!'

I let him rummage among the shelves a full minute before speaking. 'Two hundred and ten quid. Please.'

That caught him. He was in the act of turning towards me, blowing dust off a small ancient-looking volume, when the words arrived home.

'What's that you say?'

'Two ten. Please.'

The penny dropped with the other bloke first. 'Lovejoy,' he said softly. 'That name, Michael.'

'You're Lovejoy?' Michael the robber came slowly back, trying to judge my mood. 'East Anglia?' At my nod his jauntiness returned. 'Some mistake happened. You ordered *Paradise Lost*, first edition. We posted it, registered. Why, this is the very book.' He smiled and put it down between us. 'The parcel was returned-to-sender, wasn't it, Johno?'

'I returned it.'

'It hadn't even been opened.'

'But it had been paid for,' I said gently. 'Through Jason.'

'So now you've called for it in person,' Michael crooned. His stubble glinted in the sick light. 'And right welcome y'are—'

His voice choked off because my hand had his throat. I wedged the phoney book in his mouth and turned it till blood came.

'You sent me a shammer. I'd paid the price you asked, for a genuine first edition.'

'Hold your horses, Lovejoy.' The smartish geezer called Johno was tapping me with a sword. Honest to God, a sword in this day and age. I heard the cane sheath fall. A swordstick. Michael rasped breath in as I let him go.

'Glory be to God!' he croaked.

'Stand still, Lovejoy.' Johno Storr was calm, watchful. Risking his swordstick was too much of a chance. 'How do you know it was a shammer if you didn't undo the parcel?' His gaze cleared suddenly. 'Only divvies can do that. Well, well, well. We've a real find here, Michael.'

I said evenly, 'No, thanks,' slammed off out and went for a stroll.

A few minutes later I was back and placing two bricks into position in the gutter outside the bookshop. A Rover's a pretty wide motor so I had to measure it out with my feet. The car door wasn't locked, which pleased me because it saved quite fifteen seconds, and I was busily wiring the starter up and revving the engine before Johno Storr and his grubbier sidekick came to see what the hell was going on. Johno lost his cool then. He came banging on the motor's windows but I'd had the sense to lock all the doors and windows. Anyway, I was already moving, reversing across the street in the first bit of a three-point turn. Calmly I fastened the seat-belt while Johno yelled at Michael to phone the Gardai. He kept yanking at the handle my side. Michael Fenner had just gone in as I lined the big nose up with my two bricks and slipped the stick into first gear. Johno's expression changed from fury to incredulity as he realized my intention.

He screamed. 'Stop him! Stop him! For Christ's sake stop—!'

The run-up was hardly thirty feet, but the motor boomed into speed across the road, and I kept my foot down. My mouth was scared dry as the wheels bounced up on to the kerb.

The shop front abruptly filled the windscreen with a resounding slam. Glass shivered. Something thumped into my chest and the car burrowed into the shop in a hurtling nose-dive.

I suppose the impact dazed me a minute or two before I recovered my senses enough to look around. Through the dust I could see the front bumper was level with the top of the counter, and Johno was yelling blue murder while trying to unwedge his mate from the far corner. He was trapped by a printing press that had been crushed across the floor as my—well, Johno's—Rover stove the shop front in. I damned near sprained my ankle climbing out of a rear window, not realizing it would be so high off the floor. We were all three choking and spluttering in dust.

Fenner was whimpering, 'Help, for God's sweet sake —'

'Two hunded and ten, please.'

Rubble and glass seemed everywhere. Like being in a war movie. A couple of faces peered in, but I was past caring. I lobbed a brick fairly gently at Johno because Michael was in no fit state for more shocks. He was ashen and bleeding a bit. For the first time Johno looked scared. 'You're out of your mind, Lovejoy.'

Just in case, I broke his sword by swiping it on the edge of a press guillotine. Crummy modern crap. A genuine Georgian or William IV would have laughed at such treatment. Johno panicked then and fumbled out a wadge of notes a foot thick.

'Remember the rate of exchange.' That made him check and shakily restart his counting, but eventually the blissful feel of money warmed my digits.

Michael Fenner was fainting away when I left. Climbing across the shambles, I picked up a small booklet of gold leaf, as a kind of Lovejoy-tax on the two rogues, though what I could do with it I had no idea, and these booklets cost surprisingly little on account of the gold's thinness. A couple of elderly bystanders were outside admiring the unusual sight of a big Rover's bum sticking out of a shopfront window, its wheels a clear yard off the pavement. I hadn't realized till then how ugly cars are underneath. You'd think these car designers would at least try.

Somebody up the street was shouting so I broke into a trot, still coughing. I couldn't afford to get into trouble with the Gardai. The main road was fairly busy with cars. It was easy to slow to a brisk walk among the pedestrians — easy, that is, until Sinead stepped in front of me.

'Er, hello, Shinny,' I said brightly. 'Fancy seeing —'

'My car's here.' She had it parked by the kerb. For a

second I dithered, but here was suddenly a free way out. A lift from Sinead, and as long as she got me away from the district pretty fast, I could ditch her and be on my own.

'Why, thanks, mavourneen.'

'And you can stop that.' She was giving me the critical once-over as she slid into the driving seat. I must have looked as though I'd been in an accident, covered in dust with my knuckle skinned. 'Where to, Lovejoy?'

'Oh, anywhere. I'm in a hurry.'

We drove past the street where folk were beginning to congregate to goggle at those grotesque rear wheels. Shinny slowed, but I ahemed in annoyance and she accelerated past. I drew breath to make some cheerful crack about parking being such hell in Dublin, but thought better of it.

'We can't just drive anywhere, Lovejoy.'

'The National Museum, then.' That would be as good a place to ditch her as any. To show I honestly had no such intention in mind I said, 'If we get separated, meet at the Book of Kells, right? And I'll pay your entrance fee,' I finished grandly, remembering I owed her from the pub the night Joxer got done.

She shot me a mistrustful glance. 'Are you all right for money?'

'Thank you,' I replied gravely. 'Just been to the bank.'

CHAPTER 14

The museum didn't look much, but its displays were out of this world. A uniformed bloke sold me catalogues and let us in. 'Here, Shinny,' I whispered, 'did he get the prices right?' Some of the costlier-looking booklets were priced absurdly low. Sinead told me to keep quiet or the

civil servants would put them up double. 'Got them here
too, eh?' I was commiserating, when we hit the
Derrynaflan display. It occupied almost the whole of the
central recessed floor, case after case of the fabulous
treasure with comparison pieces from earlier finds. I
should have said it hit me, because my chest banged and
quivered at the sudden impact and the floor sailed from
under.

'Lovejoy!' Sinead had hold of me, grunting with strain
under my weight. 'Thank you,' she was saying, 'thank
you,' to an attendant who came helping. My legs went
funny again as I tried to struggle away towards that
dazzling display but she hissed abuse in my ear and
obediently I sat on one of the benches. An arrangement
of Irish glass impeded my vision of the cases, but the
vibrations thrummed out into my whole being. I was
shivering like a newborn foal and sweating cobs. 'He's not
long from hospital,' Sinead was excusing to the
attendants. 'He only needs a minute or two.'

'And not a drop in the place,' the senior uniform
soulfully deplored, obviously burned up about a long-
standing issue. People all about nodded understandingly.

'He'll be fine. A quiet sit.'

Heads shaking at this proof of an unmet need, they
drifted and left us. While the museum resettled to torpor,
Sinead delivered me a furious lecture in a suppressed
hate-filled whisper. She called me callous, thoughtless,
stupid, hopeless, bone-headed, selfish and ignorant. All I
could do was sit there in the bliss-giving glow of that
miraculous treasure find set in the glass cases.

'And furthermore, Lovejoy,' Sinead hissed into my
poor old worn-out earhole, 'you haven't even asked how it
is I'm here.'

'How is it you are here, alannah? I thought you'd
written me off.'

'I'm sorry I called you all those things in the Priory

ruins. The night sister told me later you'd rung up asking for me and she had refused to give my location.'

'Then Tinker, I suppose?'

'Tinker sent me to Lyn. The twins told me.' She sounded close to tears.

'Gabby little sods.'

'And what's between you and Lyn, Lovejoy?'

'Help me up, love.'

She did, but crossly. 'You get five minutes gawping at this rubbish, then it's eating quietly you'll be for a while.'

Well, five minutes was better than none.

'It's thankful I am to you, mavourneen.'

'And you can just stop that.'

I said gravely, 'Would you be knowing where the other verbs are in Ireland?'

Sister Morrison at last revealed her true colours. 'Just shut up, Lovejoy,' she said.

Irish nosh bars are as grotty as ours any day. We found this side-street one full of guitar-laden posters and stained tables, just like home. Beans inedible, bread soaked to extinction. Lovely. Sinead had tried to insist on a posher place but I won by pleading queer legs so we slurped together in unison, trying for silence.

Then over a good cup of tea she asked me about the crowd in That Street, and wouldn't be deflected when I tried my beam of dumb innocence. 'That street with the car sticking out of the shop window,' she added pointedly.

'Really? Honestly, the sights these days.'

'Fenner and Storr,' she went quietly on. 'Printers and antiquarians, near the park. You mentioned they owed you.'

'I did? Ah well, I just dropped in.'

Her eyes were on her cup. 'You might have been killed.'

If she'd seen me do it, what the hell. I explained how I'd sent them the money for a genuine first edition of

Milton and been posted a shammer, a copy the two rogues had fake-printed themselves. The sheer absence of vibes had told me it was dud.

'And you didn't even need to *look*?'

'Right.'

She glanced out towards the museum and gave a shiver. 'So your performance in the museum . . . ?'

'Too many vibes all at once.'

'It's spooky.'

Angered, I grabbed her coat with my good hand. 'It's nothing of the kind, Shinny. It's detectable love, the love the craftsman had for his creation, the love instilled into an antique by its admirers over the centuries.'

Her hand reached up and held mine, locked on her lapel though it was. She seemed suddenly shy, not furious at all.

'Everybody else looks at antiques and sees only money, Lovejoy.'

'That's only their excuse. Money's respectable, love's embarrassing. So they say it's investment. Deep down, they all know it's love.'

She had my hand in hers now. 'Don't trust your belief too far, darling, will you?'

'Me? Trust? An antique dealer?' I was still laughing at her innocence when we rose to go. Honestly, the blind folly of women.

'I'll pay,' she said evenly. 'Then you can tell me all about the Derrynaflan hoard.'

Everybody must know of it by now. The real treasure, and the legends which have sprouted in so very short a time. Already there's a million versions of the story. Here's only one:

Once upon a time, this angler goes fishing in County Tipperary. His son has one of these metal detector things for his birthday and gets a bleep. Naturally he shouts his dad, who comes to look. They dig down to an inverted bronze dish, which covers an enormous decorated chalice, a strainer, a communion patten and a circular stand. Okay, maybe the clear stunning similarities with the great Ardagh find a century back escaped our intrepid angler, and maybe the shattering artistic evocations of the Tara Brooch did not spring instantly to his mind that day, but he clearly knew his duty. He rushed to report — and legend has him variously hawking his news about all Saturday and Sunday trying to find some authority to tell, or forlornly going back to the field to sit on guard till some bureaucrat sleepily came to.

Well, there's no stopping Irish storymakers with such a plum. You can imagine the hilarious accounts that have been invented or passed on — how at last the penny dropped, the message got through and teams of archeologists cavalcaded across Ireland to the monastic site of St Ruadhan of Lorrha and collared the lot. And how the Dublin papers grimly reminded everybody of recent notorious scandals where archeological treasures had been flogged to the highest (and in the antiques game that usually means the quickest) bidder.

Of course, the Derrynaflan hoard is almost beyond belief. Precious in its own right, it ranks high in the ranks of the discovered treasures anywhere.

'Look at Gallows Hill,' I enthused, my eyes misting at the thought of all thirty-three Roman silver spoons, the gold hinge-bow satyr buckle and the partially-completed eight-stone rings, the engraved gems and the precious-metal ring blanks, the emeralds, the silver strainers, the gold necklaces and bracelets, the garnets and amethysts. 'A Roman goldsmith's entire workstore.'

We were back in the museum by then, among the museum's crowd, me going on nineteen to the dozen about other finds even more weird and almost as wonderful. The little brass token in a box of rubbishy old buttons and scrap coins in North Yorkshire—which turned out to be a unique hammered gold Tudor Saint George noble of Henry VIII's reign, previously unknown except for a mention in a Flemish merchant's sixteenth-century handbook. Everybody finds the bloody things but me.

'You don't have to dig for Troy, love,' I said, husky from being in the vicinity of that breathtakingly lovely chalice, huge and embellished. 'I've seen a Gujerat medal from a button jar. A valuable group of *ojime*—a Japanese bead to hang on the end of a cord which suspends an *inro* carrying box for seals or medicines—sewn on a school kid's bean bag. And fortunes in old slung-out handbags on street barrows—a Saxon silver penny, a mint and valuable boxlet of ladies' cheek patches straight out of Beau Brummel's period, and gold buttons, gold necklets, gold toothpicks . . .'

A little girl tugged at my trouser leg, lifting her arms to be hiked. Still prattling to the amused Sinead—though why women laugh at me like they do I'll never know—I one-armed the infant up and let myself be steered through the press of crowds and cases. The little girl kicked her heels and imperiously pointed, one hand clutching my nape hair.

'. . . an ancient Egyptian votive scarab, and *not* a crummy plastic Brit Muzz repro . . .'

Actually, you have to smile. We wound up at one of the cases of Celtic gold torcs quite tastefully arranged, but they could have gone to a bit more trouble over the background.

I was going on, 'An Inca bead, two Benin dice—'

'There!' The little girl was triumphantly banging her tiny flat hand on the case glass. 'Like mine! See?'

'Like what, love?' I asked blankly. She tugged at her hair in exasperation and I saw she wore a hooped thing to keep her hair in place, like the twins. It was gilt plastic.

'You mean your headband?'

'Alice band,' she said with scorn.

'Beautiful, love. Really great.' I handed her over to her breathless mother, while Sinead was being all amused nearby. '. . . and a piece of an abacus, only seventeenth-century but not to be sneezed at, and . . .'

'Go on,' Sinead was saying. 'I'm loving all this.'

'. . . and . . .' I looked after the little girl. Then at the torc case. Then after the little girl. Then back.

'What is it, Lovejoy?'

'Nothing,' I said, third go, after a lot of throat clearing.

But it was very definitely something. It's called knowledge. I knew why we were all here in Ireland, why Joxer had been crisped. And about that phoney Slav they called Kurak—no more Slav than me. And why the Heindricks wanted—*needed*—me. Nobody else would do. No wonder Lena Heindrick had pulled out all the stops. No wonder. The hooped Alice band. The hoop of iron in the ash of Joxer's shed. And the hoops of gold torcs in the cases around us.

'No bloody wonder what, Lovejoy?' Sinead was asking.

'Eh?' I must have spoken aloud. 'Oh, nothing, love. Look. Can you give me a lift?'

'Where to?'

'You drive. I'll direct,' I said, pushing through towards the exit and leaving her to hurry after.

But I meant Kilfinney.

CHAPTER 15

Sinead's car was gone. Nicked. I ask you.

Broad daylight, peaceful old Dublin town, people everywhere, and Sinead's car lifted by some drunken nerk. While Sinead rang the Gardai I perched on the wall outside and looked amiably about. Nobody I recognized, no big black Daimlers, and no sexy over-perfumed ladies with slightly foreign accents.

While Sinead marched out to confront the Garda who motored up and resignedly let himself be harangued repeatedly—women love saying the same thing; they think it's proof—I let my own mind drift back to the central problem of Kilfinney, poor dead Joxer, and now this business of Sinead's stolen car. We were stuck, stymied. With the car-hire firms under the eagle eye of Kurak the phoney Slav, and possibly with Jason's military brain ticking menacingly this side of the Irish Sea, a quick unperceived dash to Kilfinney was out of the question. The only good thing was that Lena and her strong-arm squad couldn't simply zoom on ahead and hang about till I came, because Lena had no way of guessing I knew that Kilfinney was the place she had rigged the scam. My main aim, now I'd rumbled her, was not to let on. Uneasily I wondered if it might be my one card.

Sinead was heatedly winding up her statement to the weary bobby. I felt sorry for him, but telling the truth would have made him wearier still so I said nothing. Sinead did a big finish, bleating about ruffians and Making Streets Safe For Ordinary Folk. Sundry aged birds nodded and tutted indignantly. One even joined in—exactly the same thing had happened three years ago to her sister's boy's motor over in Sligo, and what were the Gardai doing about *that* she wanted to know.

I just sat and thought about Kurak cracking his fingers down in that courtyard.

If I hadn't been so slow I'd have sussed him long before. What was it he'd answered, driving me home from hospital? 'Yooorr serffint fur life, modom.' Yes, Kurak was your actual dyed-in-the-wool grovelling serf—but he'd said lo-iff. Only Cockneys can make two syllables out

of a miserable titch of a word like life. I'd even thought of
Keats misspelling that sea-spray bit. The smile started on
my face, gradually creeping into the corners of me, then
splitting into a wide hundred-per-cent grin. And sweat
started, trickling down my neck, but it was only relief. My
whole body sagged. Suddenly I was on holiday, chirpy,
restful and happy all at one go. Because I knew Kurak.
He was that big knuckle-cracking Cockney bloke who now
lived in the Midlands. And it *was* Northampton, that
auction where he'd pulled the sleeper trick time after
time. I remembered now.

More than that, I even remembered who he really was.
Maybe not his name, but I knew him right enough. They
call him the Sleeper Man. Let me explain about sleepers
for a second.

Antiques are everywhere, bliss-giving and beautiful.
Right? But like I was telling Sinead in the museum, not
all see the light of day. Some do, like the poet John
Donne's painting by Titian now in the undeserving
Louvre, but some don't ever turn up. Others, such as the
vast antique wealth of the *Mary Rose* warship and Jawa
the lost city of Jordan's Black Desert, are still being
discovered piecemeal. Still more get themselves mislaid,
buried, hidden, nicked, pillaged, melted down, dismantled, lent, deposited in vaults, pawned, worn away,
lost, horridly vandalized, horribly mended by bungling
amateurs (or, worse, restored by alleged experts),
purchased by city museums to lie in storerooms so nobody
can enjoy them ever again, simply forgotten about, or
sold to anonymous purchasers (such as our railways
pension fund who secretly bought all that Regency
English silver in 1979 as an inflation-proof investment,
the callous sods). Or they get bank-vaulted as
appreciating tax-free nest-eggs by stony-hearted cynics
utterly incapable of love of any kind.

Or they 'go to sleep'. In the trade we call these antiques 'sleepers'.

Basically, a sleeper is an antique, usually of considerable value, which is not in general circulation among collectors and dealers. Oho, you say, immediately thinking of your Auntie Elsie's valuable George III commode which is about to shatter all Christie's records, oho. Your commode's a sleeper, and it's arrival will rock the London antiques world to its foundations. Well, not really. Your piece of furniture is really great, I'm sure, but it doesn't merit the appellation of 'sleeper'. There's one important characteristic which a sleeper has above all others: *it's existence is deliberately concealed*. In short, it is hidden from the cruel gazes and the jingling coins of the antique dealer fraternity. And your Auntie Elsie's commode is up for sale, remember? In fact, I'll bet you are screaming about it from the rooftops, pleading with the auctioneer to advertise it for all he is worth. No, it's no sleeper.

A sleeper is the treasure of the twilight zone. It is a legend in its lifetime, an ephemeral antique which slips out of sight and vanishes from public attention like Cinders at the Ball. One minute listed in the cold light of somebody's catalogue, and the next sinking into obscurity with only the odd rumour to mark its passing. Vague legends abound everywhere in the antiques game, of sleepers rare and priceless beyond measure. They exist in every country. A sleeper can be anything—coins, brooches, jewels, earrings, a valuable book, a miniature portrait. And there have been some notable near-priceless sleepers. But this hardly matters a damn unless you know where the sleeper is among the world's collections of ordinary run-of-the-mill antiques, junk copies, rubbish, forgeries, and laid-aside heaps of dross. And if you don't, then you're the same as the poor rest of us, living in hopes, right?

Yet one flaw remains in all this enduring ignorance. If you only *pretend* you know where a sleeper is, you have a very, very special kind of situation.

You have what people call the con trick.

I rose, mingled absently with the mob for a second, saw Shinny was still laying the law down, and slid across the road into a side street.

Then I ran like hell.

CHAPTER 16

She was a long time coming, but I didn't care. Women, basically unreliable, have one enduring characteristic: their conduct narks you endlessly, year after year. Irritating a bloke's their natural pastime. Yet a woman's a sort of necessary gout, especially if you're an itinerant antique dealer, temporarily broke in a strange country, and on the run from one—or was it two?—teams of rich homicidal fraudulent con-merchants. I had a headache.

The hall turned out to be a grand old place, everything I'd hoped. And a bonus, it was plonk in the middle of safe old Trinity College's grassy swards. The library was so worn and real that the coldest heart would have responded to the loving warmth of those emanations. Not just the walls and the books, but the flooring and the ceiling—and the Book of Kells.

One reason there's so much crap about nowadays masquerading as 'good' antiques is that most folk are too silly for words, too greedy, and bone idle. I mean, go and look at the blindingly clever artistry of the Book of Kells (it's actually in four 'books', but they put two on show usually) and you begin to appreciate the scale of the manuscript geniuses who created such illumination. Do the same with the British Museum's Lindisfarne Gospels.

Then try to copy a single inch of a single page of the complex decoration of either, and your education's under way. (If you can't afford the trip to see the real things, a postcard repro teaches you the same lesson.) That little try-out will only take ten minutes, but after it you will be ten—twenty—times harder to fool when some dealer offers you a 'genuine mediæval French page manuscript from a devotional Missal . . .' It's a very gratifying feeling to be able to look a fraud in the eye and say sweetly, 'Thank you. It's lovely. But do you have any *genuine* antiques, please . . . ?' See what I mean about being bone idle? A little effort, and you get the true feeling of an antique. That feeling is love, true love.

Apart from a couple of students reading on a central bench, an elderly geezer creaking among high shelves on a library ladder, and a pair of ladies blinking at such accumulated learning, the place was empty. I stood humbly before the open Book in its glass case, bathing in the unseen radiance of such a treasure.

You've seen some oafs pretending they're antique porcelain experts, by running a lead pencil round the rims of cups and saucers? Well, ask them why they do it and they'll have no idea. Oh, they'll say something like: 'If it leaves a pencil mark, it's genuine,' which sounds okay and deeply knowledgeable until you demand, 'Genuine what?' and they're stuck. As I say, too silly for words. The pencil-on-the-rim legend actually arose from the writings of a wise old Victorian character called Litchfield, who advocated this as a test for spotting Old Worcester porcelain, because its glaze often (*not* always!) shrank inside such rims leaving a faint crack. (Tip: let other people play at being experts. You just remember that a positive pencil test means only maybe; a negative pencil test does not necessarily mean no. It's only one poor test, after all.) Yet even genuine Old Worcester doesn't mean you should fumble for your cheque-book and pay through the nose. Much beautifully sparse Old Worcester was elaborately repainted and refired in Victorian days. The best scoundrel — and I therefore mean the worst — was Cavello, Italian chef to the Marquis d'Azeglio, Italy's London Minister. Nowadays dealers and collectors get taken in and pay highest prices, but don't you dare do anything so daft. Cavello's Worcester pieces give themselves away by thicker, clumsier decoration, and his colours are more opaque. All it takes is one careful look at one virgin piece and a suspicious mind. The price should be about a third of the un-repainted porcelain . . . Somebody touched my arm and I leapt a mile.

'What were you smiling at, Lovejoy?'

'Er, hello.' I clutched on to the glass casing to recover. My one and only helper had arrived, breathless, bonny and a bloody nuisance. 'Just thinking,' I croaked. 'Where the hell have you been?'

'You saw me, darling. That stupid Garda.' She linked my arm. 'Then I hunted for you high and low till I remembered you saying to meet here if we got separated. Why did you vanish?'

'They nicked your car so we'd be stuck, easier to follow. At least we've shaken them off now.'

She was pulling me briskly towards the exit. I tried to drag back. 'It's closing time, Lovejoy,' she pointed out. 'We have to go.'

Sure enough, the usher was edging people along the library. I hate women who're logical. Things are bad enough normally.

'Anyway,' she said, smiling. 'I got Gerald.'

'Erm, look, Shinny.' More help was the last thing I wanted. I still hadn't adjusted to her tagging along. She gave me a lovely beaming blast from her pale grey-blues.

'Gerald's different, Lovejoy.' Her voice had that quality.

I thought bitterly, oho, so we love this Gerald

character, do we? Great. That's what I needed. One more complication.

Gerald was different all right. I'd never seen anything like him. Thin as a lath, bespectacled, bad teeth, and the longest bloke you could imagine. Long as opposed to tall because he had all these unexpected joints. Even as we approached along the pavement he was folding and bending in odd places for nothing. He seemed all hinges. I couldn't help staring. He was my own age, and twice as shopworn as I felt.

'Ah, you'll be Sinead's feller,' he exclaimed, extending an arm like unfolding trelliswork.

'Lovejoy. Er, hello, Gerald.' We shook.

A bus honked, its way blocked. Somebody had dumped a derelict van outside the college's main gateway. Completely unconcerned, Gerald led the way to this decrepit horror and climbed into the driving seat, which was a wicker work laundry basket nailed in place. There was nowhere for me or Shinny except a small mound of wood and some sacks. Gerald folded behind the wheel like some fantastic stick insect, all limbs and angles.

'Will you be moving this wreck now?' The bus driver descended and yelled in at us through where our rear doors should have been. An interested crowd was assembling. Cars were queuing.

'Sure, how could I till I get the thing moving?' Gerald bawled over his shoulder. We pulled away, me and Shinny jerking and rattling like peas in a drum. The bus driver shouted something after us, probably as logical as Gerald.

'Don't look so worried, darling,' Shinny called into my ear above the din. 'Everything will be fine now Gerald's with us.'

I managed a weak grin. I'd been hoping to flit silently out of Dublin like a night-stealing Arab. Instead I was leaving the city with all the stealth of a carnival, in the loudest, most open-air, least unnoticeable and most police-prone vehicle on the bloody island. Still, Shinny always seemed to know what to do. Hopefully, I wondered if Gerald was some secret Bond-type agent, but the wretched man dashed my hopes. He bawled questions to me over the van's incredible din, wanting to know all about me, which was fair enough. The one that got me was what I did for a living.

'Antique dealer,' I yelled, clinging to Sinead.

'Are you now! I'm a poet.' He swerved us illegally along a one-way street, tutting irritably when two cars tried to make it in the legitimate direction. One car panicked and hit a wrought-iron railing on the pavement. 'Ah,' Gerald enthused, unabashed, 'isn't haste the terrible modern disease! Where to, Lovejoy?'

'North, please.' Great. We need the SAS and get a lunatic bloody poet.

'Anywhere particular you'll be wantin'?'

'Not too far north, please.' Quickly reverting to my earlier plan, I realized I'd need to be near a sizeable town to ditch Gerald and Shinny. Until nightfall I was lumbered.

'Ah. The old backtrack, is it!' He flailed the van in a clumsy arc and bumped us across a traffic island while tyres screeched all around.

Shinny cupped her hands and yelled, 'Gerald. Somewhere nearby. Lovejoy's all in.'

'Caitlin's,' he called back. 'Yes, Drogheda's the place right enough!'

My mouth into Shinny's hair for secrecy, I asked, 'What good's a poet?'

'You'll see, Lovejoy.' She turned and held me steady. It seemed natural for my head to fall on her shoulder.

'Will you be marrying me this year, Sinead?' Gerald bawled as the road straightened into the main N1.

'Oh, whist, you terrible man.'

'Poets pay no tax on the Auld Green Sod, Sinead.'

'Nor have two pennies to rub together!' Shinny gave back. My eyes had closed but I didn't care. It was all too complicated. With the rain coming on and trickling down the van's rusty interior, and Gerald's bald tyres slithering us uncertainly northward, there was no chance of us reaching anywhere so what the hell.

The world began to fade, taking that horrible cacophony of Gerald's van with it.

That night I slept a couple of hours with a strange lady called Eileen, after proper introduction of course. Or, rather, she slept with me. She was about eighteen months, and after nosh swarmed on to me as I dozed by the fire in Caitlin's little house. Her bare feet were perishing. Despite her lack of years, she had that female knack of winkling her coldest extremities on to your belly and murmuring gratification while you gasp at the shock. I should have expected it. I've had a lifetime of women and never met a warm one yet.

Caitlin was a vague relative of Gerald's and Sinead's and had that gorgeous Irish combination of gleaming jet hair and royal blue eyes. She looked me up and down candidly, saying to Sinead, 'Don't you feed the man, for God's sake?' but it was only women getting at each other and Sinead sharply told her chance'd be a fine thing. The two of them had a high old time while they got some grub, talking of families and exclaiming at who'd moved where. Caitlin's husband Donald, a pleasant grinning redheaded bloke who mended motors for a living, rigged up an outside lamp to have a crack at Gerald's uncontrollable van. Gerald spent a sad hour discovering I knew next to nothing about the Movement poets, but Shinny rescued my reputation.

'For heaven's sake say you like Milton,' she said sweetly,

'or Lovejoy throws a car in your window.'

'You did *that*?' Gerald said in awe. 'I saw it!' His face broke into smiles of delight. 'And no more than you'd deserve,' he cried, opening some bottles of that horrible black stout.

Caitlin and Shinny gave us one of those hyper-filling Irish meals with practically no veg, and tea strong enough to set. Then I joined the two old folk round the fire. Caitlin's dad was disappointed I'd not fought in his regiment at the Second El Alamein, though I wasn't, and Grandma was astonished I did not have the latest lowdown on our politicians' secret home lives. She made up for my ignorance by giving me intimate family details of the Taoiseach, their prime minister. Dozily, I kept asking how you spelled local words, but in the end gave it up. Ireland's the only place on earth with spelling worse than mine.

The whispering with my name in it woke me about nine that evening. Everybody was in the parlour, telly was on and little Eileen was snoring with her dewy head thrown back on my arm. Gerald and Donald were chatting competitively, Gerald about pararhyming techniques and Donald giving him a long tale of a dud carburettor. The old couple were reminiscing. Odd that a whisper in such family pandemonium can wake you. I suppose it's wavelength or something.

'Ask him,' Caitlin was urging.

'Not yet,' from Shinny.

'What?' I whispered, as if I didn't know.

'There! He's awake!' Caitlin ran upstairs to bring out the stuff.

Wherever a doctor goes, people automatically start hauling out their shirts or unhooking brassieres to show him their operation. Being an antique dealer's just the same—out come da Vincis and Gainsboroughs and the gunge. The big joke is that priceless antiques actually are there, sometimes and somewhere.

'Here!' Caitlin returned breathless, holding a small clipped leather case in the palm of her hand.

Grannie snorted. 'Them's old earrings.'

'Whist, Mam! Let him speak.'

Caitlin unclipped the case, only big as a Swan matchbox, and honestly it really gets to you. I'd never seen an original complete set before, though you come across singles. They lay in their velvet lining, two large thin gold rings and two genuine pearls on slender S-shaped stems with their stud loops. All four, perfect. Marvellous. I felt dizzy. Of course, women would never wear them nowadays.

'Breast rings. Those are breast jewels.'

'Glory be!' Caitlin cried. Grannie thought it was scandalous, though I expect the old devil had known all along.

Women of the 1890s had their nipples lacerated and perforated just like they have ears pierced nowadays. The gold rings were inserted through the nipple exactly like gold 'sleeper' rings for an earlobe. The jewels, most often diamonds, rubies or pearls (*never* baroque pearls, though, for obvious reasons) were mounted on either gold rings or on S-shaped gold stalks for passing through the nipple laceration site. The jewel either lies in the nipple's recessed tip, sits on the teat or is pendulated from the nipple's corona.

'But I've never come across any woman wearing them.'

'See, Mam! Told you they weren't earrings!'

If Caitlin and Shinny were fascinated, Donald was awed. 'Didn't it hurt, Lovejoy?' He prodded the gold rings with a large oily finger.

'Like hell, apparently, at first. The women's magazines of the last century are full of details—'

'Yes, well.' Shinny swept the case back into Caitlin's hands. 'There's such a thing as being too nosey.'

It's always like an outpatient clinic. They brought out a pewter dish next. You have to smile at some antiques. Pewter's a lovely metal, only now coming back into well-deserved popularity. If you were starting a collection of antique pewter, though, I'd go straight for 'pewter specials', as they're called in the trade, meaning pewter items a little different from the average. Caitlin's dish was essentially a plate, but nearly two inches thick. You can always tell these rare and highly-sought hotwater dishes because they are lightweight for their thickness, and they have two hinged pewter loops at the edge, the sort you pass straps through for carrying.

'For carrying,' I explained, 'though women used their apron ribbons often as not. The plate got hellish hot because . . .' I ran a finger slowly round the top edge, found the crack and flipped upwards. A tiny trapdoor popped up, revealing the dish's hollow interior. 'You pour scalding hot water in here.'

They hadn't realized about the hole. Caitlin asked about its value. I don't give valuations in money—however accurate you are, it's wrong tomorrow. Usually prices keep going on up and up, but you can go catastrophically wrong. Remember when the bottom fell out of the Old Master market in the London auction scene, July 1981? And the same happened to the mediæval silver coinage market all over the collecting world in the late 1970s following the discoveries of immense coin hoards on the Continent and in England? No, I give valuations in terms of time. The easiest way is to express an antique's money value as a proportion of the national average wage, because this tells whether your selling price gives a real or merely a numerical (and therefore false in inflation-riddled years) profit.

'Your cased nipple set's very rare. The pewter dish is about the same price actually at any local auction, but only because people don't recognize the nipple jewels for what they are.' I looked about for a point of reference for them. 'All your furniture could be bought new for what you should get from the two antiques.'

That set us all going for the rest of the evening. We talked into the early hours, the old folks bleating about things they'd used in youth which were now called 'antiques' and cost the earth in junkshops, and me waxing on household collectibles. It became quite a ceilidhe, a couple of neighbours joining us about midnight. They brought some bottled stout and two old pictures which had puzzled them for years. One was an English sandpainting done about 1837 or so, the heyday of that art (you arrange grains of sand of different colours into a picture, glueing them down to glass or fine-textured linen). The usual subjects are churches, landscapes and nature scenes. It's a vastly underrated art, highly skilled at best. An authentic picture, like Caitlin's neighbours', currently fetches only the average week's wage, or less. A gross underprice. The other picture was an aerophane— an early collage done by assembling fine silk-gauze colours into a scene, thread by painstaking thread. Nowadays, when embroidery and textile societies are all the rage, pictures such as these are at a peak price and a 'signed' one will buy you a good month's happy unemployment or even longer.

As the fire died and little Eileen snored, we nattered on. The rain pattered on the windows and the wind whistled, but we were cosy and safe and friendly. Everybody was smiling and talking. Nobody was daft enough to suggest banishing the little one, either. I was glad because it's always better for people to sleep on each other than on their lonesome, and that goes for infants too.

The reason I'm dwelling on this particular evening in Donald's house at Drogheda is that I began to feel I was trying to repay them in the only way I knew for poor

Joxer's loss. After all, he was from their family, distant relative or not. Also, it was peaceful.

The shambles and holocaust began the very next day.

CHAPTER 17

Next morning we really hit the road. North-west, away from the direction I wanted. The trouble with Ireland is the same as with England—for a townie like me there's just too much countryside. It's all green and boring and completely lacking in antique shops. I notched up another stray fact, though, under the stress of being torn from Donald's safe inglenook: Ireland's short on trees, really smoothish and bald. Weird fact, that.

I directed Gerald towards Ardee to make anybody following think we were hurtling for Ulster. Once through there, I'd simply nick the van, ditching Gerald and Shinny, and lam down the main N52 which transects Eire obliquely from Dundalk to the bottom of Lough Derg. A stone's throw to Limerick, and I'd be within an hour of my destination. Great. Better still, I'd be travelling light—by which I mean without help, which is always an advantage.

Caitlin had given Shinny two cushions and some blankets. 'Isn't it the world's worst deathtrap!' Caitlin exclaimed as we emerged that morning.

'It is,' I said, eyeing the van. 'Hey, Gerald. What's that glass thing on the roof?' There was this glass cockpit-like dome up there, partly concealed by lashed tarpaulins. I'd not noticed it before.

'That's my other motor-car, Lovejoy.'

Well, if he didn't want to tell me it was his own sarcastic business. I shrugged and entered the van. You don't kiss so-long in Eire like you do in England so I just said be seeing you and thanks and all that through the holes in the van wall. Caitlin said whist man and little Eileen clenched a hand in farewell. Donald strapped a long thin case to the van's roofing, probably Gerald's fishing tackle. Maybe it would lend the van some support, like a truss. Gerald folded a million or so joints in his anglepoise limbs, and we were off in a lessening drizzle.

'What was all that whirring, Lovejoy?' Shinny asked as the van trundled precariously down the slope towards the main road.

'Eh?'

'Early this morning.'

'Mind your own business,' I said sharpish, but suspected she knew all right from the way she was smiling in that irritating way.

I'd been up early. Donald had an outhouse-cum-workshop with a giant metalworker lathe, easy to somebody like me used to a homemade treadle. Unable to find any other wooden dowelling, I'd raided Caitlin's parlour curtains and nicked the curtain rod, replacing it with wool from Grannie's knitting to keep the curtain droopily in place. I'd slept downstairs on the couch so there was nobody to see as I slipped across to the outhouse and cut the dowel into four-inch sections. The electric lathe was unbelievably fast. My eight-foot length of dowel just made 24 lace bobbins of rather reduced Buckinghamshire style, with a three-quarter-inch recess for winding thread. Naturally, I'd have liked to make up the lot with a quartet of Devonshire dump bobbins, but they would have to wait. I like using walnut or proper fruitwood for these thicker ones and for doing the Midland ringed bobbins, but it wasn't my fault Caitlin's curtain rods were punk. As well, Eileen should have had a little apron of black sateen or velveteen (*never* white for lacework) and maybe an easel and lace-worker's cushion. Those too I would have to send over, once I made it safely home. Lace is definitely in since that hot 1981 August sun went to the bidders' heads and Sotheby's great lace auction started the stampede. The year before you couldn't give Honiton lace berthas away. Now, a tatty quartet of Victorian Bedfordshire lace cushion covers will bring a Troy ounce of pure gold. It's a mad world. I gave the set of lace bobbins to Grandad, swearing him on the honour of the regiment to give them to Caitlin for Eileen only when Gerald's lunatic van made it out of sight.

Caitlan had given us a good fat-riddled breakfast, a detail Sinead pointed out when I suggested we might stop for a look round Ardee. These places look grand cities on a map, but are hardly even towns.

'Coffee, then?'

'I've got a flask,' she said calmly.

'Ah,' Gerald sang out. 'If it's thinking to escape this terrible woman in the streets of Ardee y'are, Lovejoy, you're a terrible dreamer.'

'Nothing of the kind,' I lied, mad as hell that he'd spotted my plan. Where's all the trustfulness of the shores of Erin? Sinead was giving me one of her sweetest smiles, getting me madder still.

'Left, Gerald.'

Gerald swung us round a bewildered milkman's float on to the N52. 'But what can you expect when she's never once accepted my proposal, the heartless creature!'

Clinging on for dear life as we slid sideways into the thin traffic of the main road's south-westerly flow, I glanced at Sinead. She was still smiling and winked at me.

'We're sort of cousins, Lovejoy,' she yelled in the din. 'Proposal's his game.'

'She says we'll only have runts in our litter.' Gerald bawled the confidence, ignoring the road and turning completely round to enter the discussion.

'The road!' I screamed.

Horns sounded, tyres screeched. A white Ford saloon

rocked past on the outside, the driver fighting the wheel. I lost sight of it as we swung on a vaguely straighter course. More horns, a shout, then an ugly crunch of metal on stonework. We'd actually caused some poor sod to crash. Gerald, the bloody maniac, was expounding his virtues in a howled litany.

'I may not have many punts in the bank, Lovejoy,' he was going on, 'but I'm a born survivor. And once I get going, ah, what lovely poetry I'll be writing! I'll be on a pedestal like Billie Shakespeare, God rest the sainted man's sweet soul.'

I was trying to see back to where the white Ford was angled into somebody's wall but the road bent the ghastly scene from view.

Sinead reached across and patted my hand. 'It's perfectly safe,' she said. 'Gerald has his own way.'

'Never mind us. We might have just killed somebody.' My face felt prickly and drained.

'Is it the white saloon you're meaning, Lovejoy?' Gerald shouted. 'You mustn't be troubled about him, for heaven's sake. Sure now, he shouldn't have been hiding the night away down the hillside outside Donald's like a black-hearted heathen.'

I thought this over for a second or two while the van swayed hectically on down the main N52, drew breath to speak and thought better of it. Sinead leaned over.

'We're nearing Kells,' she yelled. 'Where your old picture-book comes from.'

'Ignore the silly bitch!' Gerald screeched over his shoulder. 'She's a vicious tongue in her head. Tell me, Lovejoy. Is it Milton's attitude to blank verse that grabs you, or his rationalized deism? I've been dying to ask.'

I thought, Christ, but Shinny saved me. 'Lovejoy doesn't subscribe to the notion of generative discourse, dear,' she pronounced.

'Ah, I quite understand!' Gerald howled. 'I'm a silent

man misself! Y'know I stand on Milton somewhere outside Professor Milner's sociological meritocracy ideas, though it's not at all a bad effort for a Yank from America.' He turned round and nodded seriously as though I'd disagreed. 'I know what you're thinking, Lovejoy: how does Goldmann's genetic structuralism fit in . . .'

I closed my eyes and ears to the racket and the yelling. Sinead said we would do a roadside stop for coffee beyond Delvin and work out the route. Gerald kept on bawling theories of Milton. The van bucketed on south-west down the road. Thinking back, the bloke fighting so desperately for control of the white Ford had looked very like that Johno Storr bloke, but I couldn't be sure.

'. . . And what of Hill's Third Culture theory?' Gerald was demanding of the world at the roadside. 'How far can you construct poetic analyses on a synthesis of that kind? Considering Saurat's repetitive Miltonic study in 1924 . . .'

We had stopped in a lay-by for Caitlin's coffee. Gerald had a couple of bottles of that black stout but I can't touch it to save my life. Shinny pored over the map with me. I kept trying to smile and nod politely at Gerald, who kept rabbitting on about poetry, but I'd have cheerfully throttled the noisy burke. At the back of my mind was that episode with the crashed white Ford. It *had* been an accident, due to Gerald's stupid carelessness . . . hadn't it?

'Excuse us, Gerald,' Shinny interrupted. 'Lovejoy's working out the route.'

'On the map!' He nodded like a pot Mandarin. 'That's a wise move, sure it is. I'd have brought my book of maps if I'd known we were going somewhere.' He unfolded himself and gazed at the clearing sky. 'First dry day since

St Patrick banished the snakes! I'll trot over the bog for an instant.'

I watched him stride out across the hillside. He travelled over the uneven rising round at a deceptively fast speed. He really did resemble an enormous malnourished scarecrow, his trousers flapping at half mast and his forearms protruding from his threadbare jacket. He was in a worse state than me.

Shinny was gazing fondly after him. 'Isn't he a darlin'! Always was the clever one of the family.'

'I can't make him out.' I nicked the dregs from the flask. 'Is he always like this?'

'Sure who'd want to change him?'

'Shinny.' I wanted to get a few things straight. 'Exactly what's he doing with us?'

'To help me protect you, Lovejoy,' she said evenly. 'Any other questions?'

Planning a trans-Ireland route isn't easy without revealing the destination, especially when a co-planner sits close to you and links your arm and doesn't pay much attention. We took some time. I must have become preoccupied because suddenly there was Gerald, theatrically distressed with hands spread on his chest.

'Ah, isn't it the bitter pill?' he exclaimed melodramatically.

'Eh?'

'Pay no attention, Lovejoy.' Shinny pointed at the yellow line of the N52 on the map. 'If it's Limerick you're wanting, we should keep on through Mullingar and Tullamore.'

'I turn me back and find you unfaithful! Marry me, Sinead. Get rid of Lovejoy! You'll have to sooner or later. The banns can be called—'

'Gerald!' Shinny tried her bandsaw voice but didn't quite make it. Gerald clearly had the knack of bringing out a bird's dimples.

'Very well!' He put on a show of inexpressible grief and collapsed his limbs behind the wheel. The engine wheezed into life. He bawled, 'Then, avaunt! I go!' The van jerked away, sending Shinny and me tumbling aside. We'd been sitting on the running-board.

'You silly—' I cursed after the goon.

Shinny was helpless with laughter as we got up. 'That Gerald!' she said.

I looked after Gerald's erratic hulk as it rocked on to the Dundalk road and headed back the way we had just come. An irritated saloon hooted at its sudden obstruction but Gerald's long thin arm only emerged to give it and the world a royal wave.

'I don't believe this. What the hell do we do now?' We had a dated map, now wet through from where it had fallen in a puddle, and an empty flask. I'd be surprised if that wasn't broken.

Shinny was still laughing. 'It's just his way, darling. He'll be wanting us to wait here.'

The recess was only thirty yards long. Another car swished by to Dundalk, and a container lorry pulled on southwards. It was a pretty lonely stretch of road. If we started walking we would be utterly exposed, caught in the open by any passing car. We were trapped.

'I'd strangle the lunatic. If I could reach his larynx.'

Shinny was astonished. 'Gerald? You *can't* be annoyed at *Gerald*!'

'He couldn't have left us in a worse place.'

'Can't you see? He's only looking after us!'

'Bring the flask and that map.'

The roadside was bare of cover, but the ground dipped from the road one side. I pulled Sinead's hand. We climbed over on to rather spongy ground. From there the slope undulated soggily up to a line of moderate hills. Walking across these fells would be murder, though Gerald had made it look easy somehow. Apart from a plastic bag or two, nothing. Another car hummed past heading for Mullingar. Another was coming from the south. Asking for a lift would be risky. What if it turned out to be Kurak?

'Here.' With some effort I dragged a longish stone astraddle two others. As long as we sat there we could not be seen from the road. Shinny came beside me, her arm through mine. She was still enjoying herself. I said sourly, 'Lunacy run in the family, does it?'

'Silly!'

'Is this bog?' I nodded at the damp brown-green countryside. We were leaning back. I'd never seen such a smooth fellside in all my life.

'Sure what else could it be, you stupid man!'

That surprised me. 'I thought it was a joke.'

'Some joke.' She told me there were several sorts of bog. 'I guess this is red bog. It came about 4000 years BC. Just grew, so they say, covering everything. People are always studying it for interesting plants and digging up bones.'

'Whose bones?'

'The Giant Deer. Lived here, poor things, before they died out. Red bog's ten yards deep.'

'Down to what?'

'Silly old stone, of course.' She snapped the words and savagely turned on me. 'Lovejoy. What *am* I doing here, wet through, talking about sphagnum moss when I could be warm and cosy miles away doing something useful? I must be off my head!'

Women get like this. I said helpfully, 'If you like, Gerald can drop me off at Mullingar—'

'*Lovejoy*.' She managed the bandsaw voice this time without effort. 'You think you can hide from everybody for ever. All your crazy tricks, all your pretending—'

There was more of this rubbish. On and on she went, yapping about my unnatural furtiveness and resentments of people's perfectly human willingness to become involved. I sat meekly by, nodding attentively as if I really was listening.

While she talked, though, my eyes were roaming the countryside and my mind was on the real surface of Ireland, ten yards down.

I'd imagined hearing that familiar clattering engine a dozen times and almost given up hope when Gerald returned, an hour later.

'Stay down, love,' I told Shinny. We listened as the van creaked to a halt.

'Repent, ye sinners!' Gerald's voice called. 'Do not think that you can hide your fornication—'

'It's him!' Shinny was delighted.

We climbed up sheepishly and got in. Gerald wagged a finger at us.

'Before we proceed onward,' he intoned, 'you'll be pleased to know I forgive you both!'

'For what?' I growled.

'Sinead for refusing to give me her wifely duty—'

'Whist, you terrible man!' Shinny was rolling in the aisles.

'And you, Lovejoy, for lack of trust.'

I wasn't having that. 'You left us stranded.'

'There's a petrol strike at the garages,' he announced inconsequentially. 'We're in terrible difficulty.'

The gauge had never moved off Empty since he had met us outside Trinity College. I was near to taking a swing at the silly burke. Sinead's hand fell restrainingly on my arm.

'Gerald,' she said, 'why did you go off like that?'

He looked suddenly shy and reamed an ear out with a little finger. Sinead reached for his hand.

'Please, Gerald. Say. Lovejoy's worried. He doesn't understand.'

Sheepishly he cleared his throat. 'While we were having

coffee and a chat, thirty-five motors passed us. One passed us twice, an old black Talbot. The second time, it was going back to Dundalk.' He jerked his head at the slope. 'Up there you can see quite far. The Talbot was parked a mile off. They followed me back into Kells. They're locked in a garage.' I drew breath to ask how come but thought better of it. 'To delay them,' he ended.

'There, Lovejoy!' Shinny's eyes were shining. She pulled herself forward and kissed him. 'Isn't he clever?'

'Then marry me, you stupid woman!' Instantly the old Gerald was back, and Shinny had to fight herself clear of his frantic leching.

'Get away with you!'

I was thinking, good old Lovejoy. Dim as a charity lamp. 'Look,' I said. 'Gerald, mate. Sorry. I'm just a bit thicker than usual these days . . .'

'Is apology needed between those who love the divinest poet — ?' He rolled the van out ahead of a demented two-tonner.

'Er,' I said, trying to make amends, 'er, what sort of poetry do you write, Gerald?'

'He hasn't done any yet,' Shinny explained.

'Ah! But what lovely words they'll be when they're spoken!' Gerald bawled, his limbs all on the go. 'I've thought of first using an overly-simplistic sonnet format . . .'

I subsided, Shinny holding my hand in consolation.

At Mullingar I told him to follow the N52 straight ahead to Tullamore and Birr. He cried out that sure it was a darlin' road, one to warm the cockles of your heart, and immediately swung us right on the N4 heading north-west for Longford. Shinny smiled at me. I swallowed, said not a word, smiled my best Sunday smile, and didn't raise a finger.

CHAPTER 18

That journey to Limerick was weird. It sticks in my mind. Partly of course because of Gerald's demented driving, his endless yap about poetry and thinking up daft schemes to get Sinead to marry him, and partly because of the route we took. On the map the N52 road does it all, running slap into the N7 Dublin-Limerick trunk only a few miles out of Limerick's safe haven. Instead, we travelled over 300 miles that lunatic day, all of it through bland, endless countryside. I never thought I'd long for the sight of a copse or a forest.

Gerald, spouting incomprehensible poetry, drove us all that day, through Longford and across the Shannon, to Roscommon where we might have turned safely south, on westward over the River Suck, then doubling back into Ballinasloe. There we had some fast grub and went to the loo, then clattering on south through Portumna and Scarriff into Limerick. It was getting dark by then, and we had to find a hotel with a restaurant. Even then Gerald couldn't stay still a minute, fidgeting and standing up and walking about while Sinead and I ate. She saw nothing odd in his behaviour. ('Oh, he's a born glassbum, Lovejoy. Take no notice.') Weirdest of all, nobody else in the hotel seemed to think him odd, either. They quite took to him, all prattling away over that black stout stuff.

'Does he never stop talking?' I asked.

'Gerald?' The question puzzled her. 'Sure why would he want to stay silent, a man like him?'

I gave up, still perished from that crazy journey. Shinny had been cold in the van's uncontrollable gales, but not spiritually like me. I felt like clinging to the stone walls of real houses, streets, shops. I knew from the map that luscious docks, post offices, libraries and churches abounded — an oasis of Mankind in all those miles of rivers, flat green-brown turf and low hills.

'Is it the chill in your soul you have, darling?' she said softly. We were in a hotel dining-room, me wading through the main course second time round.

'Just hungry.'

She smiled. 'Don't think about those horrible people if it frightens you—'

'Me? Scared?' I emitted a harsh laugh. The twins had thought the same. Women really nark you, forever reckoning they understand how you're feeling, the stupid burkes. 'Ice-cream was the third course at Henry the Fifth's coronation banquet,' I told her. 'Eat it up and be quiet.'

'Full, thanks. What happens tomorrow, Lovejoy?'

'We do the sights. Misericords in St Mary's Cathedral, antique shops.' Her eyes narrowed disbelievingly at this innocence. 'Is the Hunt collection still at that Education Institute? I've heard those Bronze Age gold torcs are local . . .'

I left Shinny and got through to Tinker in a phone booth a few minutes later. He was at the White Hart, and still only partly sloshed but delighted to hear me.

'Tinker,' I shouted into the hubbub of the taproom. 'That furniture auction, Northampton, three years back. Remember? You, me and Margaret?'

'Aye. That bloody escritoire.'

'Tinker, that big bloke on his own. Bid for a lot of Regency silver and got none—'

'You mean Big Joe Bassington? The sleeper man?' Tinker's emphysematous laugh ripped my eardrum. 'Never bought a thing at an auction in his life, thieving Cockney bastard.'

'Good lad, Tinker.'

'First met him pulling the old sleeper game down in

Bethnal Green with an early David Quare barometer—'

With a quick cheerio I hung up. Tinker's endless reminiscences were famous and intolerable. Besides, I had what I wanted. Big Joe Bassington was the sleeper man. So why all this Kurak-the-Slav business?

After supper Gerald was still flitting about somewhere like a talkative cranefly so we left him and went for a stroll. There's something about a town that no amount of picturesque rurality can convey, isn't there, bustle and contact and human endeavour. They say the Irish love a good gossip, and as far as I'd seen it's true, but Shinny told me that people living out in the remote countryside hardly ever spoke from one month's end to the next. Anyway, all that rusticity was past. In the safe confines of Newton Pery—the posh commercial bit—we wandered and looked at the shops and peered at the other hotels. We went to the bus terminus and the railway station. I began to feel quite warm again. Near there was an antique shop where I bought a dumb violin for the price of a box of fags. Shinny thought me off my head.

'What would we be wanting with that piece of rubbish?' she demanded. 'It's not even got proper strings.'

'We've just passed a music shop. Hurry, before they close.'

We made it with five minutes to spare, and I got a complete set of four new strings, including a good steel E.

I was delighted with it. 'It's a find, love. A really rare find.'

'Is it something for the stage?'

Dumb violins were made for practice, mostly in Victorian or late Georgian days. They are completely solid, not soundboxed like proper ones. This had rather faded sound holes painted on its table, and it's wooden bridge was tied round its fingerboard with a piece of old cord, thank God. The purfling was beautifully carved. Most exciting of all, the line between the bridge feet was a straight horizontal, not a modern curve. The bow had gone, but you can't have everything.

'No. Doesn't play at all — well, a sound like a trapped gnat. Only the player can hear, so you can practice to your heart's content. Even with other people living or sleeping in the same room.'

'Would you credit that!'

'When we've time I'll put the strings on and give you a silent tune —' I was quite serious, but she fell about.

'And you heathens think we are quaint! You'll serenade me with no tune at all?'

Her incredulity made me laugh and we returned slowly to the hotel calmer and happier than I'd felt for days. We looked in the bar but there was no sign of Gerald — or of Johno Storr, Jason, Kurak, the Heindricks, which was even better — so we settled down for a drink in the fug.

We laughed and chatted a good deal. Some time during that evening she took my hand to look at it for a minute and asked me to promise we would all stay together, Gerald, her and me.

'Promise,' I said, still in good humour. We'd got away from our pursuers, hadn't we?

'You'll keep your word, Lovejoy? It's important. Gerald's worried about something. I can tell. And I know you're on edge.'

'Hand on my heart,' I swore. 'Here. Keep my dumb violin as security.'

Pleased, she took the thing and put it on the seat between us, me ordering more drinks and thinking Lovejoy and my big mouth. That would probably be the last I'd see of it.

'Thank you, darling,' she said mistily. 'Now your money.'

'Eh?'

She said sweetly, 'I'll create a disturbance and get the Gardai called unless you do. As a token of your trust, darling.' I heard this in silence, was thinking, the mistrustful bitch. She leant over and bussed me, a cynical creature of no illusions. 'You can have it back at breakfast.' In silence I handed my gelt over. She bought the next round, which was big-hearted. That's women for you.

Gerald did not return before the bar shut.

The hotel gradually quietened, which meant Gerald must be miles off. I lay back and watched the ceiling.

Funny old place, Ireland. I mean, who'd guess that hotels organize the nation's babysitters? Or that the townships were all straight out of the old North Riding design of Yorkshire—a wide straight street of terraced stone houses? Or that obviously new graves were in evidence in practically every ruined abbey we'd seen, an indication of locals maintaining their familial right to monastic burial? Or that nobody much spoke Gaelic in everyday life? Or that you got money for actually living and working in the Gaelteacht, the Gaelic-speaking parts? Or that the museums and churches had such wealths of antiquities that set your breathing wrong even as you drove past? Or that there was so little noise?

Times like this, waiting for people to simply get out of the way, I wish I still smoked. Something to do. It was getting on for midnight. A few people used the stairs, one couple making me smile by talking loudly with the impervious good cheer of the tipsy. After that it got very quiet. I dozed a little, went over in my mind the possible antiques good old Tinker was hoovering up in East Anglia. I'd given him no money to slap deposits down on things, but locally they knew I was good for debts—useless with gelt, I thought wrily. If only I'd had a bit of credit. If I came this way again I'd bring every groat I could scrape up.

In a closed antique shop window Shinny and I had seen

a folding ivory fan. Closed, it was made exactly like a miniature 1780 musket, the unmistakable Short Land Pattern weapon. Only last year, such a mint treasure was an average weekly wage or less. Now it fetches half a year's salary in anybody's money. Look out for ivory fans in their original box if they're Cantonese, because that doubles the value, and remember that the fashion for Chinese stuff which followed MacCartney's embassy to the Court of the Imperial Dragon did much to stimulate copying Chinese art, but not much for imports. The almighty boom came around the time of the Opium Wars when Chinese (mainly Cantonese) bowls, carvings, screens, porcelains, statuettes, jewellery, clothes—much of it made in Kwantung mimicking Western fashions, to order—poured into England. I've yet to see an auction in any English town without a genuine piece of such date (1820-1850, give or take an hour) and origin.

Japanese influence, on the other hand, came . . .

My mind froze. 'Who is it?'

I could have sworn somebody scratched at the door of my room. Nervously I got off the bed and padded slowly across, wanting something handy to use as a truncheon. Nothing, of course, just when you want it. My throat felt funny.

The hotel corridor was empty when I managed to screw up courage to open the door and peer out. But that quiet sound had been very definite. An envelope lay on the carpet just inside the door.

Familiar scent and addressed to me in a woman's handwriting. Worse, the note was on hotel notepaper.

Dearest Lovejoy,

How very keen you are to get started! And wasn't that an absolutely lovely journey? *Such* pretty countryside! My husband has formed the strong belief that the fishing will be absolutely superb here this year, and is already talking of the salmon. He *so* hopes you will join him. We have a delightful place away from that dreadful new trading estate. Kurt would value your opinion on our recent acquisitions. They include a splendid sugar castor, Lamerie I am told. You'll love it. We will expect you in the morning for breakfast — say, nine o'clock? Our country house is on the old Ennis road, twenty minutes away. Kurak will call for you in good time. Please feel free to bring that scrawny female and her strange young man.

Love,
Lena.

My overworked sweat glands panicked into action.

That leaf-on-a-flood nervousness returned. Everybody else stirred up tides. Good old Lovejoy just drifted helpless. Lena's message was clear and manyfold: Limerick is home territory to us Heindricks; we are big in the land with many mansions and even our sugar sprinklers could buy and sell all the Lovejoys of this world put together. Not only that; the Heindricks' scam was so big that even zillionaires were keen on its successful execution. That last worried me. I dwelled wistfully on Paul de Lamerie, and knew that there had been one such 1719 piece of his up in a recent Dublin antiques fair for a mere 29,700 quid. Lena said I'd love it — as a bribe?

The phone rang.

Once I'd subsided and got my heart back I said, 'Yes?' A bloke said, 'Ah, just to check you're still there, sor. I'm to say if you want anything urgent the two of us will be down in reception.'

'Is this from Mr Heindrick?' I asked.

'His compliments.'

That did it. I slammed the receiver down. Enough's enough, even for pathetic creeps like me. I switched the light off, saw I had everything — in fact not a farthing, not a weapon — and looked out.

Nobody in the corridor. Terror lends wings to others,

but stealth to me. I floated towards the stairs past
Sinead's room—two along from mine. The passageway
lights were still on, and stair wall-lamps so artistic you
could hardly see a bloody thing. But in the well-lit lounge
two tweedy blokes were swilling that black foamy drink in
comfortable armchairs. The desk bloke was with them
and the talk was all horses. No way past them, that was
for sure, but I was past caring. The floor above had an
end window and a fire escape, which squeaked from
disuse when I trod on the fenestrated metal steps. Well if
they heard me all that could happen would be they'd send
me back to my room till 'Kurak' zoomed up.

Gerald's van was in the tiny carpark. A single neon
lamp gave shadows everywhere. Its light showed that
Gerald's weird glass bubble had gone from the van's roof.
As I climbed in and groped for the wiring I saw his long
thin case had vanished, too. The rope lashings and the
old tarpaulin had been chucked in a heap. The silly sod
had probably gone fishing, at this time of night. Or
maybe he and Sinead were, erm, upstairs and . . . A bloke
like him is really beyond me. I shrugged off the irritating
image of him and Sinead and got the engine going. In the
quiet night of Limerick City it sounded like a spaceprobe
blasting off. Naturally I couldn't guess reverse and had to
climb out and push the bloody crate myself to get room to
turn. As I did so I noticed a white Ford saloon, about
three cars off. Its front offside wing was badly damaged,
as though it had run into a wall somewhere. I went and
had a peer at it. Maybe it really was the one which had
been parked next to Michael Fenner's grand posh Rover
outside his bookseller's place. So it hadn't been Jason
driving after all. Well, birds of a feather and all that.

Mulgrave Street was the direction I wanted out of
town, parallel to the railway and heading for Tipperary.
Only one headlamp worked so I was fortunate to see the
turn-off. Within minutes the lovely safe city had ended,

and horrible countryside was all around. Rain made it more difficult, speckling the windscreen. The wipers didn't work, and I couldn't get top gear. The fuel gauge showed empty. The wind whistled in through the holes in the bodywork. Wrestling with the wheel, I bungled the lunatic vehicle through the worsening weather, peering blearily out for the signs I knew would be there.

The dawn came up on the lake shining right into my eyes and the surface glittering. An entire picture of innocence with blandness all around.

The rain had packed it up about three hours before dawn, thank God. It was quite picturesque, really, if you weren't drenched, shivering under a filthy old wet tarpaulin and hungry. A fish plopped somewhere and a bird chirped happily, bloody fool. Time to look around and see precisely where Lena's merry mob were going to hide the repro gold torcs and pull their miraculous 'find'. There couldn't be many places, not here in all this remoteness. So I thought, though a duckegg like me can be wrong without even trying.

Walking ploshily down to the lake from the roadside was not as easy as it sounds. For a start, you can hardly ever tell where these lakes begin and end. Not like lakes anywhere else, which have definite edges. This had a sort of longish brown grass fringe. You go towards the lake and the ground just gets wetter and this brackeny stuff more prolific, until finally you realize you are up to your calves in water and are actually awash. It's a rum business. From my position in the van reaching the crannog looked easy, but proved hopeless. A crannog's a small fortified island—sometimes artificially constructed as a kind of little waterbound citadel. They were made in the distant past and proved highly effective—after all, the powerful Republic of Venice began as nothing more than a kind of posh multiple crannog. I stared across, ankle-deep in water. The little crannog was out of reach on foot and there were no signs of any regular disturbances of the terrain between the road and the lakeshore nearest the crannog. It could have been the obvious place to plant a considerable number of gold torcs even if they had been manufactured by poor old Joxer in his workshed back in the grounds of St Botolph's Priory last month.

Squelching to drier ground, I went left and began to work round the lake. The size deceived me. From the road it had looked small, coming into the growing daylight from the amorphous slopes of brownish green. Now I realized it was over a mile across, and was indented on the opposite side into large smooth bays, to north and south-west of a fairly considerable hill. There was nothing for it but to go the whole way round.

Our library had pinpointed the known archaeology of the place quite well, though construction diagrams were not available. Still, I could tick off on my mental list the antiquities as I found them. The village of Kilfinney had been even smaller than I'd learned to expect, a mere thirty or so terraced houses asplay a single unlit street, with one shop, a couple of narrow tracks leading off to nearby crofts, and a diminutive chapel. The lake was a handful of miles off. Remoter farms were shown on the map far over the western side of the lake but nothing immediately in view. One stroke of luck was that the main Limerick-Cork road ran over to the east, and you wouldn't want to reach Mallow or Tipperary by this route. No car had passed once I'd found the lake in the small hours. I was clearly ahead, in a narrowing race.

It took two hours. Between road and lake were two stone circles, nothing like Stonehenge but still the real thing, and a ring fort. If you've never seen one of these, they are merely earthworks thrown up in a circle. Archaeologists and other wastrels burn air exchanging theories about ring forts (they were probably nothing more than cattlepens easily defended against pilferers from neighbouring tribes). They have always disappointed treasure seekers. Stone circles, whatever they were actually for, were certainly too sacrosanct for the ancients to go digging and burying many trinkets.

The ground outcropped stonily when I reached the north-west corner where the foundations of old dwellings stood, maybe nine or ten. Each was double, like spectacles, linked by a narrow strip—maybe cottages with adjacent storehouses. For me they'd be too recent by at least a thousand years. In any case, ruined houses were places people were always robbing in the Middle Ages and later for building material. Moral: too unbelievable that a whole hoard might have remained unviolated. I went on, south now on the sheltered side of the lake. I could see Gerald's tatty van waiting like a faithful friend in the weak sunshine.

A lane ran a couple of miles east, ducking round Kicknadun, the lake's hill. The remains here were far more likely candidates for Lena's sleeper trick. Ring ramparts were only to be expected on a hillside. What interested me more were the Stone Age house, and the lone burial tumulus. The self-effacing mounds are all over the British Isles. They are smooth, sometimes longbarrows, shaped like inverted boats. This one showed no signs of having been tinkered with. I walked a couple of furlongs towards the Stone Age house site, over the rough tussocky hillside, then paused. A horseman was moving along the distant lane, making as if to skirt the eastern side of Kicknadun Hill. He was riding casually, not looking.

The ground was undisturbed round the site. Genuine, though, from the strong inner vibes its lopsided stone mounds emitted. The question was whether Heindrick had the nerve to use a place like this—not quite in the right period, obviously partly excavated. I scanned to the south-west where the two stone fort ruins showed. Well, the hotel's guide book had explained they'd been occupied till the tenth century at least. No, Heindrick. The forts were out. There was no movement on the hillside. That horse had looked useful rather than racey. A crofter? A riding-school leader sussing out the day's route? The rider had been carrying a stick.

Going round the southern extremity, the lake's terrain included a castle ruin, pretty prominent on a small mound. It was infused by legends of the White Knights. It looked lovely, good enough to eat, but I was becoming edgy. A saloon car came along the road, slowed near the van, then droned on towards Kilmallock. Not quite Lena's style, however, and too far off for me to spot any occupants.

A horseman showed beyond the castle mound as I walked on. Now I was heading for the van, which came in sight in another few furlongs. Different horse, different bloke. He too held a stick-shaped thing, carrying it lance-like, the way Red Indians do in Westerns. He remained motionless, just facing the road.

That left only one archaeological site. The hotel's local guide marked as a wedge, calling it 'ancient grave'. These things are small, but as I came on to it I guessed it would be a gallery grave. Vibes began shivering through me as I approached. Gallery graves date from about 3000 BC for half a millennium. They consisted of a long wedge-shaped gallery made of big stones arranged to form compartments. At the mouth was a space indicated by standing stones. Of course it was now only revealed by mounds and the odd projecting stone, but you could easily guess where the grave's entrance might be. Big medicine, I decided, but which of all these places was the likely one? And still no sign of disturbance by busy little Heindrick-motivated diggers, except for a recent pile of dark brown peat a hundred yards off, probably drying and waiting collection for the fire.

Was the scam therefore going to be pulled somewhere in that tiny hamlet of Kilfinney, then? If so, how? It was bright day now. The horseman by the castle ruins was moving slowly parallel. In another few minutes he would reach the road a mile or so off. I stood on the nearest stone and looked back across the Lough. The first horseman was silhouetted on the skyline, moving along the crest by the ring rampart. Great. In the distance a shrill engine whined, maybe from that lane beyond Kicknadun Hill, too far off to be any help. Well, they were both behind me if I headed for the van. I hungered for streets and traffic, but keep to a steady walk, Lovejoy. In this state I'd never make it running. I struck out north, converging on the road along the western edge of the lake, hurrying and covering the uneven ground really well.

Apart from an ugly reedy patch near where I'd gazed at the crannog, I made fast if rather breathless time. The horsemen showed no intention to hurry, moving steadily behind me at a distance, one heading for the road, the other following me round the lough. I was almost past my first two stone circles and in hailing distance of Gerald's van when it dawned on me. They were merely herding me back. I was *supposed* to come this way.

Stumbling across the tussocks I kept an eye out northwards. Sure enough, there was another rider on that bend of the lake. He must have just watched from there all the time as I'd been shepherded nearer and nearer. The trap was closed.

Wearily I plodded slowly towards the van. Of course I could have sprinted to it and tried a dashing Brands Hatch start, but I'm not that daft. Nor were the Heindricks loony enough to send their cavalry to herd me into a getaway vehicle.

I made it and climbed in, utterly panned out. A big

hand clamped on my shoulder though I'd made no move to start the engine.

'Look,' I said over my shoulder. 'If you're trying to frighten me to death, yahboo doesn't work after puberty, okay?' And continued into the disappointed silence, 'Joe Bassington, isn't it? The sleeper king? Dropped off from that car, and hiding under the sacks as I got in, right?'

'Okay, mate,' Kurak said. He looked close to tears I'd not run screaming. 'Don't start yet.' We waited till the three riders clumped up. Their sticks were shotguns, only crummy modern gunge but still superior armament of a kind I did not possess. Two of the blokes were the boozers from the hotel reception area.

'Top of the morning,' I said.

'All right, is it, Mr Kurak?' one said, eyeing me with curiosity.

'Eeess agutt,' Joe Bassington said, narked off that I was there to witness his phoney Slav act.

I fell about laughing to get him madder. One of the riders held up a warning hand. We all listened obediently. The shrill whine of an engine came quite clearly to all five of us.

'Not a car,' the horseman from the castle mound said.

The second nodded, said something in Gaelic. All three riders looked over the lake.

'Sure, from the lane.'

'Lambretta?'

It actually did sound like one of those motorized scooters.

'Who'll be having one of them things?' the north horseman said. He stood up in his stirrups to see further. They were quite at home on their bloody great animals. One stuck its nose in the van and frisked me for sugar with its snuffler. I've always found horses real chisellers.

'Sod off, mate,' I told it. Now I'd been rumbled I wanted my own breakfast. Besides, the selfish creature had helped to catch me.

'That teacher down in Rath Luirc, and the O'Donnells in Croom.'

'Not them.'

We all listened as the tinny little sound buzzed into a fade-out. Fed up, I started the van's engine. One horse started but settled down at a word.

'Cheers,' I said.

'We'll be saying so-long to you,' the hillside rider said courteously. I felt I'd been knighted and gave them an arm-wag to show there were no hard feelings. They even waved back. I ask you. It's a frigging rum world right enough.

I trundled the van northwards.

'Don't tell me, Joe,' I said to Kurak. 'Through Limerick on to the old Ennis road, eh?'

'Eeess arite.' He shrugged with embarrassment when I turned to stare disbelievingly. 'Well, Lovejoy. Heindrick'll do his nut if you've sussed me out.'

'Okay, okay, mate,' I said. 'I'll keep pretending you're Kurak. Let's hope Lena's got the kettle on. Here, Joe. That sleeper job you pulled in Northampton that time, with those rectangular folding card tables. You remember, copied from Stalker and Parker in walnut? How did it go? I never did hear the finish of it . . .'

I drove on, into captivity.

CHAPTER 19

Coming down the wide staircase, I felt like Noel Coward, a right lemon. The dressing-gown was all I had on, dragon patterns and those flame-shaped clouds copied from Ming Period stuff. A maid—in this day and age—had knocked about the bedroom while I bathed.

She'd taken my clothes, leaving one penny and a coil of four violin strings on the dressing-table, all I possessed, thanks to Shinny's mistrust. The girl was pretty but wanted to do my nails with a sandpaper spatula. I said no thanks, and she opened the door indicating I was wanted downstairs. The point is, you can't escape attired in only a dressing-gown.

The house was magnificent, antique furniture and trappings everywhere. If it could be faulted at all, it was in the mixture of styles. The Heindricks had accumulated paintings of different character and periods and simply put them wherever they had the next bit of space. On the stair wall, for example. You've never seen such a jumble: a Rembrandt etching, a swirly modern Henry Moore drawing, a Dante Gabriel Rossetti watercolour of the wife of William Morris (DGR reckoned he loved her, but I think he only ever loved his own wife, Lizzie Siddall, who died so soon). This hotchpotch gallery went on through a modern John Nash, a Rowlandson (I hate those) and ended in a painting of a Shakespeare scene labelled 'H. Fuseli, 1741-1825,' which gave me a laugh. I moved on down the last three stairs because Joe's big fist grabbed me and pulled me across the marble-floored hall and into a vast plush room.

'Here, Joe,' I whispered, annoyed, 'stow it, mate.'

'Eessa Lovejoyee, modom,' Joe said.

'How pleased we are that you could come.' Lena Heindrick, Heindrick, and Jason. In that order, I think, though I'm still not certain.

'How do,' I said, making sure my dragon gown was arranged right. 'Hiyer, Jason.'

Lena rose, placed a hand on my arm and led the way smiling through double doors. We followed, dithering about who went first. Give Jason his due, he was not in the least put out when I gave him one of my special glances, just nodded back. Mixed oak panel-and-plush breakfast-room. We were helped to the grub — arranged buffet-style like in rep theatre — by another maid, as if the kidneys and bacon and eggs were heavy as lead.

That breakfast was really great, plenty of grub, and chat about antiques. Some chat is more innocent than ours was.

'Mind if I ask,' I started up, thinking no time like the present, 'if that *Christ Conversing With Law Doctors* is the one nicked from Lausanne?' The thieves had done a simple switch, with copies made from an art book. The curators said the stolen originals were so famous they would be unsaleable, which is a laugh. The antiques game is in a right state, but you still don't have to give Rembrandts away.

Heindrick was amused, sipping a minuscule glug of juice at the head of the table. 'The *Musée de L'Elysée* got them both back, did they not?' So he didn't mind if the maid heard about the odd antique rip. I'd hoped a quick seduction of an honest Limerick lassie would spring me from all this, and now quickly abandoned that impromptu plan.

'Oh.' I was a picture of innocence. 'Were there two?'

'*Touché!*'

'You admired our collection of paintings, Lovejoy.' Lena nodded for the toast to keep coming.

'Well, in a way. I like genuine paintings, one of the most satisfying artistic —'

'Genuine?' Heindrick's voice sharpened. 'Are you implying — ?'

'Your Fuseli's duff.'

'You mean . . . a fake?'

Jason was eating breakfast like the true ex-military officer he was, scrambled egg patted into squares and precise kidney slivers doing a flanker. His knife and fork paused.

I nodded. 'The goon who sold you it didn't get the

surname right, either.' I spelled it for them, having a high old time. 'Henry Füssli, though everybody else spelled it Fuseli. I've a soft spot for him because he too was a right robber.'

'In what way, Lovejoy?' I could have sworn Lena was enjoying the consternation my patter was creating.

'Füssli was Zürich Swiss. Not much imagination but great technique.' I cleared a mouthful to explain. 'And a real talent-spotter. Admitted that William Blake was the most superb source for the art copier.' I gave a benign grin. 'Though *he* used the word steal. Naturally, he made it into London society—wealth, position, status, the lot. Blake didn't.'

'That painting is genuine, Lovejoy.' Jason's edible army hadn't moved.

'Sure.' I gave him an ostentatious wink. Divide and conquer, somebody once said. Heindrick had gone quiet. Either Jason had charged them the earth for the Füssli or Heindrick was thinking of other possible fakes in his possession. Lena was smiling, full of hidden mirth, but then she'd learned how to divide and conquer many moons ago.

'Lovejoy might be joking,' she announced, patting her hubby's hand consolingly.

'Watch him, Mrs Heindrick,' Jason said quietly. 'I've seen him do worse than joke.'

'Got the torcs here?' I asked, to keep the serve. 'Or are they down near the—?'

Quickly Lena called to the serf, gazing distantly over my head, 'You can go now, Mary. Thank you.'

'—Because time's getting on and I've an appointment . . .'

The door closed. Lena was observing me. I was the only one noshing now. Heindrick was pale and uptight, Jason silent with his military mind on the go.

'Torcs, Lovejoy? What do you know about torcs?'

'That mean I can't have any more, please?'

'As much as you wish.' Lena gestured me over to the bureau where I refilled my plate. I really hate to see class furniture used wrong. The coffee tray was placed on a mahogany tripod table next the bureau. It was 1750-ish, with lovely 'piecrust' edging. Underneath, it was supported on a 'birdcage movement' through a single pillar of three carved clawfeet. The birdcage arrangement means its top can be folded down. Rotten luck to be used for a grotty coffee tray, especially as it antedated the bureau and silver by a century.

Lena ahemed. 'Lovejoy, please.' I returned, smouldering about the the antiques. 'Lovejoy. *What* torcs?'

Apologetically I edged the toast nearer and started on the grub. Eating alone in company's embarrassing, but it's their fault they stopped. I've noticed that self-starvation is becoming pretty common these days.

'The ones you had made.' I offered Jason the butter but he refused without moving a muscle. 'Joxer, remember? The one who died by accident, in a workshop fire. Once he'd made the repro torcs for you, that is.'

'Who revealed more than was advisable,' Heindrick added.

'How, Lovejoy?' Trust Lena to stay on course. 'You're not psychic too?'

'One of Joxer's rough casts in base metal was left in the ash. I stood on it by accident while the police searched.'

'Did you — ?' Jason began, but Heindrick silenced him.

'Lovejoy said nothing or none of us would have got this far.'

'Then I saw the museum exhibits in Dublin.' My continued story had blammed Jason's appetite. I wondered if he'd mind if I asked him if I could finish his grub for him. 'A lovely exhibition. Seen it?' Heindrick's head moved an inch in negation. 'You should,' I enthused with poisonous heartiness. 'It's in the same central display.'

'In the same central display as what?' Lena was worth ten of the rest of them.

I smiled. 'As the Derrynaflan Hoard.'

The silence was broken only by the sound of me finishing everything in reach. I went red because your mouth and jaws and teeth make a hell of a din when you're last to finish. Even a single swallow sounds like a sink emptying however hard you try.

'What's that particular treasure to us?' Lena again. Like I said, a real woman, boots and all.

'It's your blueprint.'

Jason rose abruptly and went to stand by the door. I nearly choked laughing. Big Joe, well, yes, especially if assisted by that cavalry. But Jason couldn't stop me in a million years.

Lena snapped, 'Sit *down*,' then turned to her hubby, smiling. 'Show them to Lovejoy, Kurt.'

Old Joxer, God rest him, had done a superb job, for all his habitual tipsiness. The weight of gold's difficult to judge—I mean, who'd think that a whole ton of the stuff makes a block only twenty-five inches long by ten by twelve? It's just so damned heavy.

Heindrick carried a case to a Pembroke table by the window and placed the torcs on a velvet cloth. There were fourteen, great twists of gold made into crescents to be worn by chieftans before the coming of Rome. Except they had been made over the last few months. They were exquisitely done, finished to a degree and gleaming with the love that the craftsman had put into them. My eyes blurred. That Joxer.

'One's genuine, Lovejoy.' Lena had approached.

'Balls—I mean they're all fakes, love.' There wasn't a vibe among the lot of them. I touched them to make sure.

'Well done. Show him now, darling.'

And Heindrick brought out a fifteenth. Well, I mean. If you've ever seen a diamond beside a burnt match—identical substance, but a world of difference. The ancient ages beat out of this pre-Roman Celtic torc with stunning impact. When my fingers lay reverently on its radiant surface all I could feel were the bell-like tremors in my chest. Genuine is genuine, and a real antique is nothing but pure solid love.

'What's the plan?' somebody said dully, and I thought with horror: *that's my voice saying that.* Whose side was I on for God's sake, theirs or mine?

'This way, darling.'

I don't know how, but the next thing Lena was walking me in the grounds, Heindrick and Jason presumably still mesmerized by all that gold.

The trouble is that women like Lena start life miles ahead of the rest. She was one of those birds who make your breathing funny soon as they're in reach. Attired in a loose high-collared knitted dress that could have given me security all year, and embellished with jewellery that made me moan, she was blindingly attractive. The fact that she pulled Heindrick's strings and therefore would effectively decide where the scam's profits went only weakened me further. Don't misunderstand: I really was honestly still bitter about Joxer's death, and being manoeuvred into joining the Heindricks was particularly shameful. In any case it should be obvious to anybody by now that in spite of not having much in a material sense I'm consistent and pretty honest. But I've always found that women tend to deflect you from the right course. I mean, I'd have been light years off by now but for Shinny, and if it wasn't for Lena I'd be hiding on Kicknadun watching her men plant the sleepers and readying myself to happen by with a spade in the dark hours . . . We held hands like lovers do. I thought she was carrying an apple till I looked: it was only the enormous velvety Muzo emerald (the world's best, if you've a spare fortune to spend) in her ring. She led me towards a summerhouse in the landscaped greenery.

'Time to be utterly frank, darling.'

'I always am.'

'You and I have a kind of duty, Lovejoy.'

'To . . . ?'

'Each other, no?'

'And the torcs?'

'Let's think of those as—' she hesitated, all girlish charm—'the ties that bind two hearts that beat as one, shall we?'

'That's a hell of a way to put it.'

A couple of gardeners grovelled and melted among shrubbery in a practised drill. Clearly other companions had strolled this way before me. By the tall garden wall was a low brick structure. I sniffed the air—somebody was running a paraffin-burning kiln without its door sealed.

I felt a right daffodil in my dragon-covered gown, very conscious of the fact that men's legs always look a scream.

'Do come in, darling.' She led ahead into the circular summerhouse. It consisted of one large room. I'd never seen so many curves, bed, furniture, rugs, the vast disc-shaped carpet, mirrors, the lot. The curtains began to hiss closed. Lena had touched a wall thing. 'Do you like it?' The curtains stopped, all but drawn to.

'Are we going round?' The sun was ducking slowly from one drape to another.

'Of course. The summerhouse can turn with the sunlight.'

'Oh. Right, then,' I said lamely and perched on the bed. 'You can't mean pull the old violin gig on your husband, Jason, Kurak—'

'Let me explain, darling.' Lena undid the belt of her

dress. 'Money of itself has very little attraction for me.'

'Mmmh?' I said politely.

'That's God's own truth, darling.' She sounded quite earnest, really convincing. Her arms lifted, the way they undo zips. 'I want more than changing numbers on a bank statement.'

'Everybody's a collector, Lena. Of money, sensations, porcelain, vintage cars, experiences. If money's not your thing, what is it you collect?'

'I collect people, darling.'

Her dress fell. She did not immediately step out of the heap like other women do, just stood there turning slightly and slipping her rings off, one by one and watching herself in one of the oval mirrors. A lesser woman would have crossed to the dressing-table and immediately done something to her hair. Lena simply continued undressing where she stood, smoothing her petticoat away from her hips. The faience necklace was Egyptian, as old as some pyramids, and its eighty or so pieces were splayed across her breast exactly as the pharaohs' wives had worn them. Faience jewellery is only glazed earthenware or early pottery done in small palmates, fruits, dates and figs thread-linked between tiny cylinders, but worn right it is breathtaking.

'Are people collectable?' I said.

'Certainly.' All her clothes were about her ankles. She turned and walked in one motion.

'In bottles of fluid, like the Royal College of Surgeons do?'

'Not quite.' She stood against me. My face pressed itself into her of its own accord. 'I collect them for what they do.'

She raised a knee to the bed and pushed my gown from my shoulders, slowly with introspective care.

'And what do they do?' I asked, muffled.

'Everything I say, darling. From being exquisite bores,

like your Jason, to those who will commit savage, awful things.' She was breathing quicker, but not as fast as me.

'You mean . . .'

'Even killing? Yes.'

'Like Kurak?'

'Yes, darling. Like Kurak killed Joxer. And like you.'

'Me? You're off your head. I've never killed anybody in my life.' Except when it was accidental or somebody else's fault.

'Including you, darling.' We were on the bed now, hands and breathing anywhere and any old how.

'Why collect us—me?'

'Because you'll respond against your will. To me, darling. For me. It's thrilling.' The luscious faience motifs from Ancient Egypt fell over my face as she murmured, 'Power, darling. I crave it like you crave me.'

'Am I for sale?'

'Everybody's for sale, Lovejoy.'

I had to ask what my price was for joining her collection of serfs, each one of us blindly obedient to her whims.

'You?' She leant up on an elbow, smiling down. 'Your payment is a choice of the torcs once the scam is pulled—plus a permanent salary. Plus me.'

I started to say I would consider her offer but didn't quite make it.

In that little death which follows after, I became aware that the curtains had somehow accidentally hissed apart all round, letting in sunlight upon us. Anybody could have seen us, even from the house. We were like tomatoes in a greenhouse. I should have been anxiously working out what bargain Lena and I had sealed, but sleep wouldn't let me go.

Dozing on some time later I heard a whining mini-engine start up in the distance and dwindle to silence. Lot of scooters about in Western Ireland, my mind registered. I rolled over into oblivion.

CHAPTER 20

The crime-briefing conference opened with Cockburn's white sherry and dry biscuits. Kurt was at his preening best. I was afraid Lena's mood of creamy elegance would give us away but need not have feared. Kurt was full of the forthcoming scam. Only Kurak smouldered. Maybe he had taken a forbidden peek into the summerhouse, an unpleasing thought. Jason had gone, presumably taking the gold torc sleepers with him. Lena wore a new dress with a low waist, almost 1920 flapper style. On any other woman her age it would have been called too young. She wore a single sapphire pendant on a gold S-linked chain. Your mouth waters of its own accord when you see something that delectable. I'd only ever seen one bigger — the 393-carat Blue Star sapphire from Ceylon at the Commonwealth place in London, and they'd guarded that with a four-foot Sinhalese monocled cobra. I caught Lena's look and smiled innocently into her dark eyes.

Believe it or not, we received the lecture in the library, Kurt enunciating with characteristic precision.

'The plan is simple,' Heindrick said. 'No fewer than fifteen gold torcs of genuine Celtic design are discovered in a well-known archaeological site on open land. A miraculous accidental find. They are authenticated by a divvie who happens to be visiting the finder.'

'Erm, the discoverer, erm, sir?' I said humbly.

'Ah. That will be myself.' Kurt gestured eloquently at Lena. 'Out walking tomorrow, we pause. A small cave-in, a prod of my walking-stick, and I glimpse gold. Before adequate witnesses. The authorities are summoned.'

'That fast, eh?'

He shrugged expansively. 'Naturally. I am obviously wealthy and will use all my resources to exhort them to speed.'

'And what is a society crowd doing wandering out in sloppy countryside?'

'Looking at a private exercise session of my horses.'

'Is that plausible?' It didn't sound so, to me.

'Several million punters will find it so. Especially if two of those horses are running in the big race six weeks hence.'

'Fair enough. But who examines this archaeological site?'

'A famous archaeological department, the coroner — and you.'

'What if they refuse to accept me?'

He tutted at such disbelief. 'I'm your host. I *know* your particular gift of detecting genuine antiques from fakes. I will encourage them to make any test of your knack. You will convince them, as always.'

'Exactly where's this site?' I asked, 'Please, sir? Kilfinney's riddled with a score of genuine archaeological remains. There are more Bronze Age places around than the parson preached about.'

'That needn't concern you, Lovejoy.' Lena's sharpness dispelled the calm. Lena getting edgy over something? Carefully I avoided staring in her direction.

'Which of the gold torcs will be first out?'

'You already know. It will be the genuine one, naturally. In fact, I will lift it from the ground. To—'

'—To establish your claim as legally binding.'

Kurt was smiling. 'Had you any other idea, Lovejoy?'

'With your armed outriders on the skyline? Hardly. But one thing's troubling me.'

'The archaeological site, I take it?'

'You've done your homework. As far as I can see there's no way round the fact that to get the torcs into an underground Bronze Age crypt, burial site, foundation, or cave, we've got to dig deep.'

'So?'

'So archaeologists are well aware that the commonest con trick is to fake an antique item and bury the bloody thing, then miraculously "discover" it *in situ*. The trouble is, you leave slight traces of penetration, such as great mounds of rubble, bulldozers and the cranes you need to lift the Old People's great stones. Some weigh many, many tons.'

'That problem's solved, Lovejoy,' he said smoothly, 'by Mrs Heindrick.'

Now I did turn and look. This was the biggest breakthrough since the wheel. 'You mean you've thought up a way of inserting a forged artefact into an ancient archaeological site without leaving evidence of a break-in?'

'Yes. Next problem?'

'It's impossible.'

Heindrick glanced at his watch. 'Wrong. Your ex-colleague Jason—under a considerable armed guard, I might add—has just gone on ahead to arrange matters.'

I insisted, 'But he's had to lift at least one of the stones, or simulate . . .'

'No.' He was enjoying himself. Even Joe-alias-Kurak was smiling. 'I do promise you, Lovejoy. From the old Celtic times until tomorrow when the archaeological team arrives hotfoot in response to my summons, not a grain of peat, soil or stone will have been disturbed.'

'But that can't be done.'

'And the authorities, archaeologists, and you will all be honest, independent witnesses to see me draw out the very first gold torc, and place it in the hands of the coroner himself. Indeed,' he smirked, really whooping it up, 'the archaeologists themselves will have to cut down through the layers to assist its being brought to light.'

I gave that one up. So Lena had attributes other than taste, wealth, beauty, personality, attraction, style, sexual skill. To them that hath shall be given.

'Okay. It can be done if you say. But how do you get the other fourteen?'

'By the time we get the genuine sleeper out, it will be nearly dark—'

'Kurt will claim to have seen the shine of other gold items,' Lena cut in. 'An armed guard will be found for the night.'

'Your men?' I guessed.

'Right.'

'—Who will look away while Jason and Kurak lift the others. You will then have "authenticated" gold torcs.'

'Don't miss the two main points, Lovejoy darling.' Lena sounded strangely bitter. 'There will be an outcry. The whole world will be informed next day that an unknown number of torcs were stolen from a proven Bronze Age site, which provides us with the most sensational—and free—advertising.'

'You said two points.'

'Authenticity. The more scientific tests they do on the one genuine piece they possess, the more they lend authenticity for our fourteen.'

'Why put them all in the site, then?'

'Soil analyses, radioactivity tracer counts, chromatography and spectrographic scans, mycological screening.' Kurt sighed heavily. 'Your undeniable gift, Lovejoy, blinds you to the scientific lengths to which cynical antique dealers will go in trying to establish authenticity.

'And forever there will be a reference standard.' Lena's bitterness was back again. Even Kurt peered doubtfully at her. 'Our buyers will naturally refer to the only known genuine item from the Kilfinney Hoard.'

'It does have a certain . . . ring to it, no?' Kurt was in dreamland.

'Will you get customers?' I asked innocently.

'As long as tomorrow's miraculous discovery goes perfectly.'

'I've seen your kiln. I trust your people have had the sense to take it easy with the temperatures. And get the soil samples right.'

'Of course, Lovejoy.'

You can't really tarnish gold easily. The trick is to heat it low and slow, then cool it in soil of identical composition with the site where you intend to plant it. If you do it right, the magical metal will look as aged as you can get it, and those cynical nasty-minded archaeologists will find no traces of 'wrong' dust.

'My last worry's fingerprints.'

Kurt's eyes clouded momentarily and I thought, got you, you bloody knowall. 'Whose?' he asked me.

'The Celts. Think scientists forget them, mate? We are probably bigger and fatter than the Old People, so our fingerprints are different. First you wipe off your own forger's prints with a shammy leather (don't use cloth for heaven's sake or they'll detect the fibres you leave behind on the tips of the torc). Then you find some old geezer about ninety—the smaller the better, jockey-sized if you can—and make him wash his tiny withered hands (no scents in the soap, please) and rinse them well to remove soap traces. Dry his hands in air until they look the same as usual (don't let him touch anything, fibres again) and give him the torc to fondle. Take it from him in your shammy leather, and bury in the allotted place.'

'Lovejoy,' Kurt enunciated crisply as I concluded my explanation, 'you have just earned your fee. We'll see to it. Otherwise, I do assure you we have organized it perfectly.'

'And Jason's already put the sleepers there? *In situ?*'

'No.' Kurt lit a cigar with tantalizing deliberation. 'I said that he had gone ahead to arrange matters.'

'But *some*body has to do it,' I pointed out. The ensuing pause lasted a decade or two. My smile died. 'Erm, any idea who'll do it?'

'Place them underground for us, you mean?' He did a smoke ring, really thick and absolutely circular. 'Oh. That's you, Lovejoy.'

'No deal.' My voice had thickened, though I wasn't really terrified of going underground into some ancient frigging burial mound or whatever it was they'd chosen.

'Yes it is. Definitely a deal. Isn't it, Kurak?'

Kurak looked at me. 'Eesa deal.'

'Why can't Kurak do it?'

He put on theatrical astonishment. 'Why, Lovejoy! How simple you are, under that brash exterior! Because only you will know which of the fifteen torcs is the genuine sleeper. And it is very, very important that it is placed with perfect precision.'

'On my own? I do it on my own?'

'Ah no.' He gazed at the tip of his cigar, smiling. 'Kurak will go with you, to see fair play as you might say.'

I cleared my throat. 'I could still do it wrong deliberately.'

Kurt laughed at that, really fell about, shaking his head ruefully at the continuing folly of Mankind.

'You'll do it right, Lovejoy. You'll see why, when we get there. Won't he, Lena dearest?'

'Oh yes,' Lena said, 'he'll do it. Against all his principles, wishes, inclinations. He'll do it for us. Perfectly.'

Each syllable fell on my eardrums like the clap of doom. I'd been collected. 'Then congrats again,' I managed at last.

We rose, and Kurt said we must all have a quiet,

peaceful day, because tomorrow we had work to do. All I could think of was how the hell you put a gold torc into a hole without excavating into the bloody thing.

Lena wanted to show me the library afterwards. I was almost sure one of those marital signal-glances was exchanged between Lena and Kurt but paid it no heed. Everything was beyond me by this stage. What was one more problem?

She kept her arm linked through mine as I admired the books. Both of us were a bit tired by now. She said very little to keep the conversation going and seemed more listless than she ever had.

'Who keeps your leather bindings intact?'

She shrugged. 'Kurt sees to that. The maids, I suppose.'

I ran a finger on a book's spine hard enough to squeak. 'Why do they use lanolin in neatsfoot oil? A lot of American book collectors don't like the British Museum formula because of its beeswax. Maybe Kurt thinks it blocks the penetration. The old London restorers often just use Propert's saddle soap. You'd be surprised how effective it is—'

'Lovejoy.'

'—on these ponderous Victorian half-calfs when the hinges weaken—'

'Lovejoy.' She turned me round. I thought for one frantic moment she was going to start undressing again but it was only warning time. She leant against the shelving, staring absently at my face, oddly like some child not wanting to start the next compulsory lesson. 'You won't do anything silly, will you?'

'Who, me?'

'Kurt has plenty of men, armed men. They have cars, boats, horses, guns. They know the whole district, inch by inch.'

'What *is* this, Lena?'

Her eyes lifted to mine. 'There's no choice, Lovejoy. Understand that, please. You'll go along with Kurt's plan, or you will be simply lost in the countryside. Everybody will assume you've simply gone home. The point is, I want you around after this is over.'

'I'll go along. I'm not daft, love.'

'Then you'll be mine. For ever.'

I nodded. 'Your people collection.'

'Don't make it sound Purgatory, darling.'

'What I've experienced so far has been . . . bliss, Lena.'

'And don't sound so worried. Kurt understands. He won't mind our meeting again in the summerhouse late tonight.'

I swallowed. 'That's all right, then.'

'Incidentally,' she said as we resumed our strolling inspection. 'About your friends.'

'Mmmh?'

'Your two friends.'

'Did you know your library ladder's a genuine Taylor Patent?' I stopped us to examine its smooth leather-and-brass-studded exterior, lovely mint condition. 'It adapts into a long shelf-ladder. They cost a fortune nowadays. If you unclip it, you'll see the patent date and stamp on its hinge—'

'That dowdy woman and her weird relative.'

'Eh? Oh, them. They just gave me a lift.'

She smiled a wintry smile. 'That's all right, then,' she quipped. 'They left the hotel an hour ago. On the Dublin road, in a hired car.'

'Really?' I said absently. 'Incidentally, is it true that the Hunt Collection out on the Dublin road has the world's best collection of Methers? Those two-and-four-handled wooden drinking mugs are not all that uncommon. Lots of places have some pretty fine examples, so the Hunt Collection must be really something worth seeing . . .'

She let me prattle, watching me carefully not watching her. My heart was in my boots, but I kept the chat going on and on and on . . .

CHAPTER 21

Before making my famous non-escape I lay on my bed, thinking of Shinny, of her lunatic suitor Gerald, of Lena, of Kurt, of poor old Joxer, of Jason. But most of all about antique dealers like good old Kurak/Joe. And money.

Way back in the days of yore, before priests got guitars and charities went bent, people actually *were* what they seemed. I mean, Caligula appeared somewhat antisocial, so naturally you wanted to keep out of his way. And, right up to comparatively recent times, town councils—apparently composed of respectable, trusty gentlemen—were respectable and trusty. And so on. Must have been an odd world.

Phase Two happened very few years ago. Money did it, going funny when politicians invented ever-dafter schemes guaranteeing themselves undying places in history. Well, they succeeded. Us poor goons got cyclic inflation in exchange. Which, you remember, sent everybody a little strange in the head. Blokes who were by nature Above Thoughts Of Sordid Gain practically killed in the hedgerows for inflation-index-linked pensions. Women, never creatures to quibble about inessentials, zoomed with unerring aim at anything possessing a guaranteed value.

The Great Antiques Boom was born.

Those twenty years from 1958 to 1978 were the heyday, and we are in its tail-off. The modern antiques scene is the spreading train of sparks behind Haley's Comet—apparently greater than the originating force but in fact full of rubbish which deservingly is destined for outer space. And let there be no mistake: your friendly neighbourhood antique dealers were in ecstasy during that G.A.B. They practically had a licence to print money — and some did even that. Mostly they laughed in their Jags and fluid-drive Rolls Royces and bought and bought, triple-priced any antiques as a matter of course, and howled with outrage if some elderly widow refused to part with her grandmother's heirloom Sheraton commode for less than a dud shekel.

But the end of the G.A.B. caught antique dealers on the hop. Their flat world went round overnight. No longer could you hire any old pantechnicon, load it to its panelled ceiling in Coggeshall, Norwich, Sudbury, Reading, and sell its load of 'old household furniture' in any lay-by on the Dover Road for cash. Gone were the days you could place a *Daily Mail* advert ('Wanted! Antiques For America! Will collect! Pre-1930 Clothes . . . !') and expect the owners of rare antiques to beat a path to your door. Suddenly, the supply of antiques dried up.

The public had learned.

They learned that anybody on earth is perfectly entitled to pop an heirloom into Christie's. That they could play off one dealer's offer against another. That they too could advertise. They learned how to use the reference library. How to hang on, stall, even (forgive me, please) lie a little or even a very great deal to 'authenticate' a shabby piece. The results were often ludicrous, frequently shambolic, occasionally disastrous. But mostly they paid off, in solid cash.

Antique dealers were appalled. Some went out of business. Some even got a job. Still others became more careful, and these survived. Oh, they did the usual — fake, cheat, fabricate, steal, forge, pull the auction-ring gig in every auction on earth, fiddle, pretend, lie, thieve, and all that jazz. But survive they did, despite monumental ignorance, in the maelstrom. It was in that turmoil that the 'sleeper' scam came right back into its own.

Of course, in antiques there's nothing new (Tinker's joke, this: in the antiques game there is probably more newness than anybody dares suspect). And in any case, they say old wine is best.

There are as many scams as there are antiques. A scam's a lucrative illegal exploit based on deception more far-reaching than the trusty old con trick. The sleeper is one of the best and oldest scams. Michaelangelo himself used it in his time. So did Hitler with his paintings — though with rather less success. And even famous museums have dabbled in this ancient (but far from extinct) trick, especially when trading items with other august and honourable institutions. Remember this: no museum in the world is blame-free when it comes to owning up where its treasures came from and giving honest-to-God accounts of provenance — and here I'm not specially knocking the Boston Museum of Fine Arts about its famous 137-piece gold breastpiece, or that weird business they indulged in during December 1969 with that Raphael attribute portrait, or the British Museum, or the Washington Dumbarton Oaks 1960s purchase of Byzantine religious silvers found in Asia Minor by the peasants of Kumluca village. No, honestly I'm not. Nor am I knocking collectors. I mean, it's great that people care enough to crave possession, I always say, and lustful possessors have always been great preservers. But a collector's craving is very, very big stuff. They've even been known to kill in order to possess.

What I am getting at is this: Your actual *dealers* don't often kill. They'll do anything else in furtherance of their latest purchase's career. But kill? No. And the most desperate dealers are the legits, those with posh addresses off Piccadilly and dinky offices in Rome, yet even these will not go about murdering. Terrible with reputations and bankruptcies, but they somehow never reach for the arsenic or the revolver.

I turned over, listening. Somebody was coming along the corridor, one of their regular heavy-footed patrols. The mansion was so well protected it was a rural Devil's Island. I listened them out of earshot and thought on. If antique dealers did not murder, and Kurak was really only a certain kind of antique dealer with a superdooper knack of pulling successful sleeper exploits, then Kurak did not crisp Joxer, no? And Jason, also a dealer, was therefore not above deception and a little honest thievery, but he too was excluded.

Ergo, Lovejoy, look among the fine upstanding collectors of this world for you real dyed-in-the-wool killer, not among the crummy load of inept nerks who constitute mankind's antique dealers. And that meant the Heindricks.

Well, I'd escaped from the hotel. It was time to do the same from Dotheboys Hall here. I swung off the bed, ready to go.

My plan—such as it was, I thought in disgust—was to steal down to the summerhouse at midnight to meet Lena, and take off if the opportunity arose. Lena's acquiescence had been full of pleasure, if somewhat guarded. I'd had to assume she still believed me to be in ignorance about those curtains in her circular rotating elegant wooden summerhouse.

To escape down, you climb.

Once in desperation from hunger I'd done a couple of jobs as a handyman's mate. Old Cedric was a jobbing builder, and I'm still convinced he only took me on because I was so useless. Still, Cedric and the world's worst handyman's mate (me) installed a series of thrystor switches, and automated a posh manor house down on the estuary. It had automatic everything down to cupboard doors and loo plugs. You could run that house by flicking an eyelash. Which particular eyelash Lena'd used while we loved in the summerhouse I wasn't sure, but I wasn't dumb enough to believe that a woman committing the ultimate indiscretion would fling open the curtains to the gaze of all and sundry. Therefore Kurt not only knew. The question was how far he walked the well-trodden thoroughfare to Lena's heart . . .

It was obvious the circular summerhouse could be openly seen from all top-floor windows, which was one floor up. Ten past midnight, and the mansion cooling into quiet the way these old places do. There was enough light coming up the staircase from the hallway to let me see. All I needed was to bungle my way into the staff quarters or Kurt's bedroom. In either case there'd be some painful explaining to do.

Double doors faced the top stair, which was a good indication of a drawing-room rather than a bedroom. Good panelled oak, maybe 1850, with the original handles. Reluctantly I opened one blade of the door. Even if you aren't really scared you can frighten yourself by imagining all sorts. I slipped inside, closing the door behind me and simply standing there, my chest thumping and sweat on my forehead.

It wasn't as dark as all that. A slender rib of light showed beneath a connecting door to the right. The three high grey rectangles directly ahead must be the windows. I felt my way towards the central one, hands slowly sweeping ahead of me in case I damaged a Chien Lung vase—more of a risk than getting caught in this place.

At first I thought it was a gun, mounted there on a swivel tripod with armrest and two chrome levers. The banked array of electronic gear, with its palpable arrays of knobs and sliders, gave it away as some kind of complex recording gear, maybe video-tape or the like. I stood as if to operate the gun thing, feeling along the barrel. Too thick for a gun, but like a . . . telescope? I put my eye to one end. Nothing. Yet it was directed at the summerhouse or very close to it. Apart from the flowers and the kiln there was nothing else to see down there.

Video-tapes are thicker than others. Feeling along the shelf, I naturally guessed the last one, fallen flat, would be the most recent. I inched my way across to the screen, thanking various electronic gods that screens pick up any old trace of luminescence to show intruders where they are. The only noise was the deep click when it slotted in and connected. I had the sense to turn down all knobs, and only rotate them slowly one at a time as the screen began to glow.

It was Lena all right. And me. By the time I got the picture right we were half way there, and in glorious colour. Odd experience, watching your own body behaving in complete disregard of anyone. And you learn things, too. Lena looked as dazzling as I knew she was, but I was a revelation. I'd always assumed I was a gentle, considerate bloke to my birds, kind of polite. The screen Lovejoy was an animal.

Great. For a second I stood there in a fury, then switched if off and turned to go and almost started the whole lot crashing down by falling over a wire. My pathetic luck held. I made the door on hands and knees, regretfully feeling the carpet's knottage — number of knots to the inch, measured along the fringe, though properly you compare oriental carpets by the *count*: knots per square inch. It felt as if it would count out at 250, maybe a Kashan. Somebody moved out in the adjacent room, probably Kurt the movie-maker getting ready, so I scarpered into the corridor.

Well, it seemed everybody in the vicinity was expecting a new performance of the Great Snogging Picture Show II, so what the hell. I strolled confidently downstairs, passed my own landing, and on out of the main door. Naturally I made it look coy there, eeling outside after switching off the hall light. Give Kurt another smirk or two, that surreptitious touch. Let them think I hadn't guessed.

Breathing a regret to Lena, I moved off the gravel among the beds of bushes and flowers. A particularly vicious cluster of heathers gave me a nasty moment, cracking and swishing like hell, but they were between me and the kiln so there was no way to avoid them. Nobody was around. I made the kiln—still warm it was—and clambered up to its roof, shelling my jacket. The flue chimney was metal of some sort. I held on to it to lean across the space between the kiln and the wall. A six-foot gap, and the wall topped with a crust of broken glass embedded in concrete. My rolled-up jacket lay across the glass, which was the best I could do. The trouble is, my hands cut easily on anything.

I was just about to risk the leap when something scraped over the wall and I practically infarcted, thinking, Sod it. One of Kurt's armed men. Caught good and proper. I might make it to the summerhouse if I got my jacket and denied everything . . .

A voice whispered, 'Would that be yourself, Lovejoy?'

'Eh?' I froze. The darkness thickened above the wall. Somebody's head. 'Who is it?'

'Shush your noise, man. Is it yourself?'

Gerald. It was Gerald. 'What the hell are you doing here? Have you got a ladder? Grab my arm—'

'No, Lovejoy. Wait. It's the planting of some old trinkets they'll be doing, isn't it?'

'Yes.' How the hell did he know that?'

'At Kilfinney?'

'Yes.'

'Sure, I knew it when I saw you wandering among those auld ruins.'

'You were there?' I'd have strangled the clown if I could have reached him. 'Then why the hell didn't you help when they nabbed me?'

'Ah, it's a terrible impatience you have on you, Lovejoy. Where's your interest in the scheme of your fellow men—?'

'Stuff that, you frigging lunatic.' My throat was raw from whispering. 'I'm imprisoned here. I want out. If you're not going to help, then shift, you burke.'

'What are the trinkets, Lovejoy? Those gold crusts the men were baking this morning?'

Oh hell. If he had seen the kiln fired on the gold torcs, he too must have seen me and Lena doing our stuff.

'Yes.'

'Then you play along with them. I've a plan.'

I hesitated fatally. 'You have? And leave us in the clear?'

He grew lyrical. 'As innocent as the snowflakes that, born in the high clouds of winter, descend to bless the earth with sweetness—'

I cursed him. 'What about me, though, you nerk? They want me to do the plant early tomorrow. Heindrick'll do the discovery bit.'

'Ah, there's a terrible temper you have, Lovejoy! But it's a grand scheme, right enough. Do it, Lovejoy.'

'Just as they say?'

'That's the thing.'

'But what about me being frigging safe?' I demanded.

'Ah, you mustn't let little things worry you, Lovejoy. I'll be there to see fair play, or Sinead'll give me a thick ear.'

'You sure?'

'On me auld mother's blessed—'

'Shut it. Is Shinny still here? They told me you'd gone to Dublin.'

'Sure where else would she be? Now you go back, Lovejoy, and leave it all to me.' The darkness where his head had been thinned.

'Gerald?' No answer, only that scraping. The swine had some sort of ladder there all the bloody time. He could have got me out. 'Gerald!'

The gravel scuffed on the drive near the house balustrade. That would be Lena. I reached over, grabbed my jacket and made it to the summerhouse steps just as she flitted along the path.

Kurt would be warming up his ciné-cameras now. I wondered which was my best side on infra-red.

CHAPTER 22

The lough made a soughing noise before dawn. Earlier, it had rained for a couple of hours, coming on while Lena and I, erm, met as planned.

That night we all must have had only about three hours' sleep, and while it was still dark were on the road in an ordinary rather oldish dark blue saloon. A nice careful touch that, including the fishing gear ostentatiously loaded up for us on the roof rack. Me, Kurak who drove, and Kurt full of himself as always. He was all tweeds and raglan, the country gentleman out for early fishing. There are people who really love the desolate country dawn bit.

'Where are the real anglers?'

Heindrick smiled at my question as we parked away from the vacant parking space and got out. 'Ah, we'll be spared those, Lovejoy.'

'Back in East Anglia there'd be a hundred fishermen here at this hour.' I'd been hoping to find enough innocent bystanders to mask Gerald's presence. As dawn lightened the lake sky it became obvious there was no witness, no help, and no bloody Gerald either.

'Light, Kurak.'

Kurt hooded the torch glass and flashed twice across the lough, twice again in the direction of the castle ruins.

'That for Jason?' I asked.

'Possibly.'

'We burying the sleepers in the castle ruins?'

Kurt waggled a finger. 'Curiosity killed the cat, Lovejoy.' He was holding this case, heavier than lead.

Depressed at all this military-style organization, I plodded after Kurt as he led the way to the right, Joe following, still doing his phoney Slav act.

A horse neighed once, the noise coming from near the crannog. Something clopped nearer, up ahead. There were other people in the countryside, all of them hostile. I dwelled on Gerald and Shinny with bitterness. Nobody lets you down quite as ruinously as friends, do they? Friends are famous for desertion and betrayal.

'Ready, sor?'

One minute there had been the grey-green dawn, then suddenly there was this quiet bloke standing close by the wedge-shaped grave.

'This it?' I asked. They ignored me.

'Yes. Ready.'

'You'll come then, and mind your feet.'

And he took us away from the lough, away from the grave, over to our right about a hundred uneven paces. We were at the turf digging.

'All's clear, sor.'

'Very well.' Heindrick dismissed the guide with courtesy. He nodded and faded into the hillside. The three of us were left alone.

'What happens now?'

I didn't much care for what little I could see of the turf digging. Narrow slabs of the stuff were slanted in rows, forming a barrier. Standing in the excavated hollow we could not be seen from the road. Even the hillside did not

overlook us. A darker patch was evident on the side
nearest the Bronze Age wedge grave. And it dawned on
me.

'I got it.'

'Spread the leather, Kurak.'

'Eees, m'sieu.'

Kurak unfolded a large chamois leather from its plastic
bag. Heindrick began lifting the torcs in their individual
chamois pouches from the case. Each was bagged in
stapled plastic. He began counting them out on the
spread.

I said, 'If you can't dig down or sideways into an
archaeological site, you dig upwards. Am I right? You
tunnel from below, starting some distance away. And
plant the sleepers through a tube, a drillhole.'

Heindrick finished it for me. 'Plugging the drillhole, of
course.'

'Having sucked the traces of drilling.'

'Vibration restores the dust to its even, pristine
condition, Lovejoy.'

'Who does that?'

'Eeesa mee.' Kurak had uncovered a small boxed
machine looking for all the world like a hurdy-gurdy
without its support stick. It seemed handle-cranked and
had a leather strap.

The sky was beginning to pale quite clearly now.
Spatters of rain tapped us. The wind had shifted to the
south. The dark oval in our hollow was now more distinct,
about four feet across.

'That the tunnel?'

'Yes.'

'Is it that wide all the way?'

'Not quite.' Trust the malicious sod to be smiling.

'Got a diagram?'

'As far as we've been able to visualize the burial
chamber.' Kurt brought out a paper and pencil torch.

'Done for us by a research archaeologist, for a fee.'

'Is he in on it?'

'There's that curiosity again, Lovejoy,' he reproved, indicating the diagram. 'The tunnel runs at the left side of the grave chamber's narrowest part. You will deposit the genuine torcs in the far right-hand recess.'

'My arms aren't that long.'

'You're provided with an extending arm. Kurak will carry that. The other torcs you will place beneath the adjacent compartment.'

'One more thing.'

'No, Lovejoy.' The swine patted my arm sympathetically. 'Just go.'

I needed to know. 'Who goes first?'

'You, Lovejoy.'

'Having Kurak between me and the exit? No, thanks.'

'Lovejoy.' Rain speckled Kurt's spectacles. He spoke with infinite patience. 'If this is done exactly to my order, we succeed. You get the price as we agreed, a torc. Plus other benefits. You come on the payroll, exactly like Kurak. This scam will make a fortune, for you and the rest. You join the wealthiest antique ring in the history of mankind. Or you proceed no further. Which?'

Good old Gerald, with his promise of help. Well, there were enough ancient graves about for people not to notice one extra.

Swallowing, I shelled my jacket, took the torch and stooped into the entrance. 'Let's go.' Kurak kept his hand partly raised in a chopping position. That was in case I made to flash the light anywhere else except into the tunnel.

From the level, the tunnel descended pretty sharply—too sharply for my liking, considering we were a million frigging miles from the grave. The aroma had a thick, curiously bittersweet character which made my throat clog up for a few moments. A tube ran along the

trodden peaty floor, of the kind you use for garden hoses.
Kurak gave me a push. I plopped on to all fours and
began to crawl as the tunnel narrowed into a cloy wetness.

'I'm going, I'm going for Chrissakes!'

'Eeesa time-a du goow, Lovejoy.'

'Shut your stupid teeth, Joe,' I grumbled. The tunnel's
closeness was bringing the sweat out on me. 'What's that
hissing?'

'Air. There's a battery pump back in the turf diggings.'
Kurak was Joe Bassington again, his corny accent gone.

'Here, Joe. Do they know who you are?'

'Sure.' But from the way he said it, I began to wonder.
Maybe Lena had procured his services by feeding him the
same sort of promises she'd given me. Women are famous
for that. It couldn't be that the duckegg actually believed
Lena and he were somehow to take over from Heindrick.
Nobody could be that thick, not even a bloke crazed by
Lena. I crawled on.

The tunnel narrowed further. I tried working out the
incline as we moved deeper underground. Why the hell
do they never teach you anything useful at school?
Teachers are idle swine. Maybe one in thirty or so? That
meant a depth of say ten feet after crawling a hundred
yards. In the damp brown-black pungency the torchlight
showed walls of rock and practically solid peat.
Remarkable how hard the rotten stuff was, compressed
into a fibrous woody texture. And wet, wet.

Carrying a torch when plodding on your hands and
knees is difficult. You need a hand to hold the thing, yet
you need that hand for your fourth corner, so to speak.
Alternating on my wrist and knuckles I moved lopsidedly
on. I could hear Joe pushing the gear ahead of himself,
the box and that tube thing slithering on the tunnel floor.

By counting the number of moves I'd made since I
crouched on hands and knees I reckoned we'd gone about
fifty yards, counting one foot per movement. That was

the point the tunnel suddenly compressed us further. To advance it meant a belly-crawl, elbows on the floor and wriggling like soldiers under fire. Grumbling at Joe — more of a whine now than a mutter — I led on, down into stickiness and mud, the roof such as it was showing more rock than peat. The hosepipe was still there, snaking ahead into the narrow black hole.

What I didn't care for was a sloppy dampness of the tunnel floor. As it narrowed it got wetter. I hesitated and pressed my weight on the torch rim. A moment later the bloody mark filled up with water. We were reaching the level of the lough. For an instant I panicked, moaning and quickly backing until my feet clonked on Joe.

'What is it for Chrissakes?'

'We're getting below water-level, Joe.'

'I'm not enjoying this either, Lovejoy. Get going. We're practically there.'

'Frigging hell. Can't we just leave them here and . . . and . . .'

'. . . And be buried in some bog?' He laughed, actually snorted a laugh, the nerk.

Ten paces further the tunnel angled up and to the right. At the dip it was about quarter filled with a stinking puddle of muddy soil. Everything Heindrick had given us was sealed, but I wasn't inclined to take chances and made Joe check the seals on every item after we'd sploshed through the dip. Only having one torch was a nuisance. Joe wanted me to pass it back for him to inspect the plastic wrappings, but I wasn't having any of that caper. The torch was mine and I was sticking to it, so I shone the light back between my legs until he said the covers were all still intact and we could go on.

It was no more than eight or nine yards, that short ascent. So steep was it that I actually slithered and had to pull along with a handhold. Then the tunnel stopped, and there I was mystified, staring at the end of a hole and wondering what to do.

'Above your nut, moron.'

'Eh?'

'It's obliquely angled, a four-inch stone plug.'

'I know, I *know*! Stands to reason it must be there.' I made to undo it but Joe's hand grabbed my leg.

'No! No! Turn off the air pipe first!'

'You stupid burke! We'll suffocate!'

'Not for a few minutes.'

'Why? Why?' I wasn't really panicking, but breath's important stuff.

'They might count the bacteria and fungi in the grave dust and on the remains. They circulate in the air. They're different species in the outside air than inside an old grave.'

'Who's going to think of *that*, you silly bugger?'

'Professionals,' he answered, cold. 'Switch that air pipe off.'

'So help me, Joe,' I swore, and turned the hose's end round. The hissing ceased. Straight away I felt myself gasping for breath even though I knew how daft I was being.

'Get on with it, Lovejoy, or we'll be here all day.' That did it.

The plug was supported by a latch like an old wooden gateway, except this latch was steel and slotted into sockets which were set in stone to either side. The space was about three feet by three. I lodged the torch against the wall. Joe had to rest his elbows just below me, his legs projecting down into the sloping tunnel, so merely passing the tube forward was a feat of skill. From it I took the expanding finger—only a crisscross of wood with a scissor grip at one end, and rubber tips at the other. Close the scissor grip and the crisscross extends, carrying whatever you've placed in its rubber-tipped 'fingers'.

'Hey, Joe. I'll have to do it blind.'

' 'Course you will, stupid. Have a shufti first, work out the length.'

Sensible. I began to realize how useful it was having a bloke as skilled as the Sleeper Man along.

'How?'

'From here to where you drop the sleeper's about nine feet. The finger's capable of twenty. So make a mark on the ratchet in that proportion. The angles are constant throughout, right?'

'Right,' I said blankly, thinking, Eh? In the end he did that while I unlatched the plug. I shone the torch, a good krypton beam.

The inside of any burial chamber's only pleasant in a museum. Seeing inside one for the first time since the Old People closed it is a frightener, really unnerving. We were near the apex of the triangular cavity. From there the ceiling—stone slabs laid crossways—widened. I could just see the edges of two of the compartments. These are kinds of booths which occupy the walls of the grave. The Old Peoples' mortal remains went in these recessed galleries until the place was sealed for ever. And ever. I found myself shaking.

'Lovejoy!' God knows why we were both whispering. There was no chance of being overheard even if we yelled our heads off.

'What?'

'Mind that plug! On to the chamois.'

Reverently I laid the stone plug on the spread leather, taking care not to rub the grave dust from its oval top surface, and whispered for Joe to pass up the sleepers. The fifth torc which he handed me from the case was the genuine one. It broke my heart to unwrap it and grasp it about its midriff by the expander. Joe tried to see my every movement but it was just not possible in such a confined space, in Indian file at that.

'Don't let it touch anything, Lovejoy.'

'You can trust me,' I said. Once I let myself think of Heindrick's threats I'd be finished, so I pretended confidence. I've always been good at lying, especially to myself.

It was surprisingly easy. I had to guess of course at the finish, as the luscious gold torc crept slowly out from the plughole and vanished from that eerie shadowy scene into the space of the grave. I hadn't allowed for the weight of the thing—you try holding a gold weight on the end of a nine-foot length with your fingers and you'll see how hard being a crook actually can be. Worse, I hadn't calculated for the extender's curve under the torc's weight. After cursing and struggling I thought what the hell and let the torc go. We heard a soft thud and Joe muttered an oath, but I was more concerned with bringing the extender back without reaming out the whole grave's interior. I told him it didn't matter, that I'd stuck it in the space Heindrick wanted.

After that the others were simple. I had a rest between each, exercising my hands to make sure I could do the others properly but it was only for show so Joe would bring back a good report to our master. It took longer to replace the plug than it had removing the wretched thing.

'That it?' I was close to panic and wanting to get out, but he insisted on passing me the mechanical vibrator on its flexible shaft. We had an ugly moment with Joe telling me it was absolutely safe and just to press the tapered end against the stone plug, and me whining for gawd's sake he'd electrocute both of us. In the end it functioned perfectly, juddering against the stone in a busy way until Joe reckoned the vibrations should have settled the grave's dust over any trace of our penetration.

'That's all, Lovejoy.'

Give Joe his due, he was a real pro. Though there we were underground and in the clear now our job was done, he would not budge until every piece of plastic, every trace of our presence, was carefully bagged in plastic—he'd even brought a pocket stapler to seal the bloody things. I was frantic to get out, whisper-yelling what if the frigging dip filled up with water and suchlike hysteria, all to no avail. He showed what a true pro he really was, calm and businesslike.

There was room for me to turn and crawl out head first. But he couldn't pass me, being simply stuck like a worm in its burrow. With a nod, he took hold of the tube in one hand, grabbed the case strap in his teeth, and began slithering backwards down the tunnel. Every yard he had to pause, pull down his jacket which kept rucking up his chest and impeding his elbow thrusts, but he kept calm and eeled along towards safety. I had a vested interest in his progress, but didn't feel like making humorous comments about the mess I was in.

That's how I remember Kurak, alias Joe Bassington: calm, mud-covered, strain showing on his face, but always edging on and on ahead of me in the torchlight. A real pro. Never once complained about the light in his eyes, knowing I would have worried about too much darkness. He even stuck his hands out to make sure my chin didn't risk going below the water-level at the dip. Great bloke, was Joe.

And when we got out, into the torrential downpour of a day hideously brilliant, bright and grey, Heindrick told us we'd been much faster than he had anticipated.

Joe only said, "Eeesa Lovejoy. Ee doo far well, m'sieu.'

'Good, good,' Heindrick said, all smiles. 'Shall we proceed homewards, Lovejoy? A late breakfast?'

'Right.' I scrambled from the turf workings and eyed the skyline. Still nobody to be seen, no Gerald, nobody. Great. My trusty helper had been rained off, the nerk.

'Oh, Lovejoy,' Heindrick called up. 'Your jacket's under the plastic. See you at the car. I'll just give Kurak his instructions. Tie up the loose ends, you understand.'

'You're the boss.'

Without another word I left them there in the turf diggings. I'd burrowed like a frigging earthworm, been scared stiff, practically buried, covered in mud, and left defenceless by my so-called friends. And now I was soaked through, exhausted and hungry. Great. I'd never felt so sorry for myself. We'd done it, though. Now all we had to do was act our way through our casual 'discovery' of the gold torcs, and it was done.

But it still gets to me that I never said thanks to Kurak, alias Joe Bassington.

CHAPTER 23

The last thing I expected was a house party. Two quartets of the Heindricks' friends were wading into a buffet when I cleaned up and rejoined Heindrick. Lena was in a shirtwaisted thing with bishop sleeves, fawns against white. On other older women it would have been a mile too young, but Lena carried it off. She brilliantly defeated two plump young Galway birds who thought they knew it all until she apologized for the Rumanian caviare and sweetly asked had they tried the metheglin. I liked them, but after Lena's broadside they only stood apart and muttered.

There wasn't an ounce of guile among the guests as far as you could tell. County set, wealthy and ruthlessly exclusive. I was introduced as Lovejoy the famous antiques expert, which is the only lie that ever makes me go red. Then I was treated like a refugee. When a smooth auntie-shaped woman discovered I hadn't seen the latest London Ayckbourn revival, the whole party realized I was simply contagious and drifted aside. I tried to nosh.

Eating posh grub is daunting: posh means microscopic, and everybody notices if you have more than one minuscule blob from a dish. We were given no time to eat properly — this also being diagnostic of a country set — but ample access to the hooch, a cunning move, considering our host's intentions. Some were already woozy when we lammed out in two big carloads. I drew four hairy blokes talking horses — and Jason as driver.

'Hey, Jase,' I said as we drove east among the traffic. 'See that Chelsea porcelain eel tureen Mrs Heindrick served the caviare from? Red anchor, original cover.' Worth a year's executive salary in 1967, its current value's mind-boggling. No response from Jason, and our companions were still on about nags. Bravely, I tried again. 'Mind you, Red Anchor fakes go big nowadays, eh? I hate animal shapes. Her Chelsea top-decorated strawberry-leaf teapot was definitely Raised Anchor Period. Worth twice the tureen. Don't you think Lena made a mistake?'

'Shurrup, Lovejoy. I'm driving.'

'Well, Jase, two different styles on one table and all that.' I shook my head regretfully. 'I'd have thought Lena might have avoided — '

'Gabby sod. I said I'm driving.'

Odd, horses having names just like people. These blokes in the back were nattering on as if nags were real individuals. Takes all sorts, I suppose. Jason negotiated a bend, allowing a car to overtake. We were three cars behind the Heindricks. More cars about now, early afternoon. One was a white Ford saloon. No dents, one bloke.

'If I'd been Lena,' I said, 'I'd have used that early Meissen Augsburg decorated gold-ground travelling service she has. Notice it in the hall case?' Ponderously I nudged him. 'Wouldn't you, Jase? The Indonesian mahogany table would have ballsed up the colour scheme, but there's a way round that—'

'I'm driving. Shut *up* or I'll—'

'Okay, okay,' I said, peeved.

He was puce by now, but it wasn't me that made him edgy in the first place. I'd only made him worse. I thought hard about that. The road forked and bent simultaneously. The white car was turning off on the branch marked 'Hospital'. Jason's left hand was on the wheel, but his little finger could have easily reached the flash lever. Anyway, something clicked and it wasn't Jason's sudden cough. I wondered if he'd read any good books lately, *Paradise Lost*, something like that. The bloke in the white car had. I was sure of that.

It went off exactly as planned.

The cars put us down by the lough. We were to walk to the top of Kicknadun Hill, from where the level exercise ground belonging to the stud farm could be seen on the western slope. I hung back, for a million reasons depressed and worried by it all. I was staring glumly at the crannog with the two Galway girls when the noise attracted our attention and we went to join in.

Heindrick's excited shouts, people yelling my name, and only me noticing that silent horseman standing so still on the skyline.

Then the plod across, and the whole charade. Spotting the gold torc's gleam by pencil flashlight shone down a tiny hole where Heindrick's stick had prodded between two great worn stones. Then Heindrick's dramatic race to the car to bring the authorities. Fortunately, about then Lena noticed two of her own estate workers riding on the hill. How lucky, we all agreed, and flagged them over to guard the find.

The classical sleeper scam: find, register, protect. All done.

It was at that point Jason asked me in a mutter where

did I think I was going.

'To have a look at the castle ruins.'

Jason was standing aside from the main excited mob, talking desultorily with Lena. She looked the part as always, the only woman I ever knew who became slender in Hebridean tweeds. He gave her a checking glance and she nodded imperceptibly. I was to be allowed to walk three hundred yards in open view. Only my chains were invisible.

'*Do* hurry back, Mr Lovejoy, if Kurt returns, won't you?' Lena said loudly, which was by way of announcing to her two men that she'd given permission.

'Not be long.'

But where *was* Joe? That's what was getting to me. I hadn't seen him since our escapade of today's rainy morning. Lena herself had driven the first car, Jason the second. No sign anywhere now of that relentlessly familiar Ford always on the outskirts of the action. No sign of Gerald or Shinny. I made a slight detour, taking in the turf diggings for old time's sake, hearing with bitterness the laughter and thrilled chattering of the Heindricks' guests gathered round the burial site. Everybody in friendly groups of self-interested grasping layabouts except me. Morosely I stared down into the excavated hollow of the turf diggings, and saw the idle nerk down there.

'Ah, 'tis a foine day, Lovejoy, sure enough!'

'You lazy bastard. Where the hell have you been?'

Gerald grinned up at me from his reclining position on an ex-army groundsheet. He even had that long thin canvas bag of fishing tackle with him.

'Ah, here and there.'

I climbed down. 'You promised you'd keep me safe. Do you know I was sent in there to . . . to . . . ?' I looked again. The mouth of the tunnel had gone, only a paler smudge where the drier peat had been replaced. Newly cut peat slabs covered the tunnel's position. Within hours the location would be practically untraceable. I felt ill. That's the trouble with being a coward. Courage gives everybody else a head start on you.

Gerald was quite unabashed. 'Did they let you go to see those auld castle stones, Lovejoy?'

'Yes.'

'You'd better be off then, unless it's those three riders over the hill you want chasing down to see what you're up to.'

I'd seen nothing new, and I thought I'd been watching the skyline now like a hawk.

'Christ.' I thought a second. 'Here, Gerald. Does one have a white car?'

'No.' The bum was settling down for a kip, shuffling his long endlessly-jointed limbs into a Chinese puzzle. 'That'll be auld Fenner the printer. Has a cousin in Connemara who plays a lovely fiddle. I remember one time—'

'What do I do?' I'd never felt so helpless. Everybody's plan was working out except mine. The whole thing had got away from me, without a cheep on my part.

'Ah, you go with them and tell your tale to the government people. Do as Heindrick says.'

'Then what?'

'Escape, o'course. Like a thief in the night. Or just walk out. Sinead will have a grand motor outside.' He grinned drowsily. 'Then we come back here, break into the grave—from the top like the honest men we are, and . . .'

Light dawned. 'Nick the torcs. Everybody assumes it's local layabouts. And we have torcs, complete with provenance?'

'You've hit it, Lovejoy. A darlin' idea. But we get the spoils of war. Ah,' he said lyrically, 'think of all the grand poetry I'll be writing with all that wealth!'

'With fifty per cent,' I corrected.

Gerald opened one eye. 'Ah, we all soldier on for poor

takings, Lovejoy, for the whilst. Anyway, it's the coroner's office you'll be talkin' to soon.'

'Here, Gerald. Seen Kurak?'

Both eyes open now. no smile. 'Isn't he back at the grand mansion?'

'No sign of him there when we left.' Anyway, no use worrying. It was one less rival, but I was no longer certain what the battle was about. If Lena's offer was genuine — and it was beginning to look like it — I'd soon be in clover. Maybe Joe had got the sack?

'I'll keep an eye out for him, Lovejoy,' said my trusty vigilante, his eyes closed in sleep. I shrugged and left him there.

The castle's ruins were still interesting me when they shouted for me from the grave mound down by the lake. The officials were arriving with Heindrick, two black cars in the distance. I went to swear the truth over my pack of lies.

Passing the turf diggings to join the others, there was no sign of Gerald. He'd vanished into thin air. I wished I could do that.

Official events seemed a lot more direct in the city than they'd be in good old shambolic East Anglia. For a start, the officials knew everybody by name and their bald-headed stout boss — their coroner, but God knows what powers he actually possesses — had to keep prising his way into small groups of spectators who seemed to want to talk about everything else. Horses were big in everybody's mind. The boring business of a zillion-year-old grave full of bones and trinkets was clearly a blot on the day. The official's only hope was to get a good natter going, to sabotage the dull proceedings.

We gave evidence against a fast-running verbal tide of gossip. My own heap of falsehoods was interrupted every second breath. Place names, I discovered. quite intrigued, would cause some shorthand lady to butt in ('Oh, Kilmallock's a lovely place! My cousin Sian's there . . .') which gave everybody else reason to say Croom was nicer still but sure wasn't it Mallow took the biscuit even if it was nearer Cork than the good Lord intended . . . How the boss geezer kept his rag I'll never know.

The Heindricks were in fine form, especially Lena. She killed all doubt about her status by casually mentioning that I'd been fetched over to decide which of her three Rembrandts were genuine. 'I am currently persuading him to stay longer.' She smiled, a thousand watts for each of us. 'His gift will be invaluable with my other Old Masters.' Everybody got the point. Heindrick was signed up as the actual finder, members of his posh house party excitedly taking turns to sign deposition forms saying exactly what they were doing when positively *tons* and tons of gold were actually *touched* by Kurt's walking stick honestly *miles* deep in that old burial mound . . .

I went for a pee, the way all suspects escape from courts these days. The trouble was Jason, standing patiently in the corridor with one of Heindrick's men.

'Leave the door open, Lovejoy.'

'Rude sod. Can't I just go to the loo?'

'The window's barred,' his assistant said. It was the turf-digging man, quiet and absolutely certain that Heindrick's will would be obeyed in all things. Jason wasn't having any and kept his eyes on me.

'Lovejoy's dangerous,' he said. 'You leave the door open or you wait.'

'Good, good,' Heindrick said from behind me in his sibilant voice. 'Well done, Jason. We can't be too careful, especially now.' He paused and smilingly reassured us that he wouldn't be much longer, for the sake of the girl clerk walking past carrying taped legal files. She shut the office door behind her. 'Once the torcs are out we'll need Lovejoy's presence even more. You two get him back to the house. He won't be needed here any more.'

'Here,' I began, but found myself propelled down the corridor and into the street. According to Gerald I was supposed to escape from here, leap into Shinny's waiting car, and —

They didn't quite put the elbow on me, seeing there was so many people about and the streets fairly active with traffic, but I was in the front passenger seat of Heindrick's Daimler with ugly speed. The turf man sat behind as Jason took the wheel. His eyes never left me.

'Mind that bus, Jason,' I yelped nervously.

'Mind your mouth, Lovejoy.'

The turf man pointed a finger at the windscreen, instructing me to look straight ahead.

'Okay, okay. Just go careful, mate, that's all.'

But I had seen what I wanted. Shinny's pale face, in a modest grey Austin parked across the road.

We left Sarsfield Bridge and the River Shannon behind and lammed off along the Ennis Road. I tried talking but Jason closed his ears and the turf man merely reached over to lock my door and leaned closer in case. I checked my safety-belt a hundred times or so, pulling it so tight I could hardly breathe. I got one reply from Jason, though, and it was that which made me decide he simply had to go.

It was while we were on the old north road to Ennis that it dawned on me that Jason was driving. *Jason* was driving. Not Joe. Relatively new and unproven Jason. Jason, who required to be accompanied by the silent watchful turf man to ensure his undying loyalty to the Heindricks. Not the trusty obedient doglike phoney Slav Joe Bassington. *Jason* was driving. No longer Kurak, the Sleeper Man, organizer of a thousand sleeper scams. Jason had displaced Kurak, Jason the ex-military officer. Who could be relied upon to organize, distribute, run an organization, now that the sleeper scam had been pulled.

I thought, Sod it, and asked my question.

'Here, Jase. Did Lena let on that she told me about Joe?'

He began his last minute on earth by saying nothing. Then he shrugged and said, 'Well, Joe was useless.' His last words.

Which made up my mind for me. Those words took it all out of my hands. 'Past tense, eh, Jase?' I said, and pressed the release of his safety-belt. He turned a puzzled expression on me as the belt's metal insertion flew across him and the belt snicked off. He managed to say, 'What—?' but by then I'd grabbed the wheel and turned us, and the car was going over and over.

Seat-belts are supposed to be great things, comfortable and safe. The trouble is they nearly break your neck saving your life. If you make it through the crash, you come round being strangled by the bloody thing.

The only way I could get out of the sickening petrol stench and that ominous grinding sound was by sliding from under the shoulder strap. I made it, shakily crawling out through the shattered windscreen and across the ground until I guessed I'd got clear. Funny, but only then did I realize the motor-horn was blaring.

Twenty yards, maybe. Unsteadily I moved another few yards and sat to focus on today's good deed. Jason was sounding the horn, his chest pressing forward into the steering-wheel for all the world as if he was rummaging for something under the dashboard. Except his face was a smear of blood and he was so still. That's the trouble with undying loyalty. It doesn't last.

The car was a crumpled write-off. Car designers these days say it's a good idea making them so they squash on impact, God knows why. Like saying sausages should have a standard dose of salmonella.

I felt nauseated so I turned to retch a bit and saw the

turf man. He was the reason there'd been no windscreen. A good thirty yards from where the car had slammed into the projecting rock, he lay awkwardly with hunched shoulders.

'Lovejoy? Lovejoy? Oh my *God*!'

'Aye, love.' I peered up. Shinny was above us on the roadside. I couldn't see her car but its thrumming engine was audible under that horrible constant horn. 'There's been an accident.'

She slithered down beside me. 'Dear God. I've no equipment with me. Are you hurt? Tell me, tell me. That dreadful noise. Oh my God . . .'

'See if you can help them, love,' I said nobly, doing my sinking act. 'I had my safety-belt on. Jason didn't. My poor old mate . . .'

'Stay absolutely still, darling. Oh my God!'

'Be careful, Shinny, love,' I called anxiously after her. 'There's petrol escaping. It might explode. The ignition, you see . . .'

I felt sore all over, but still made her car quite quickly. She gave a scream of alarm when she heard me pull away, but that's women every time. Always thinking of themselves. It was me in difficulties, not her.

CHAPTER 24

I drove like a maniac. For once I was ahead of the game. Everywhere you looked were advantages. One, Jason was out of the way—maybe only temporarily, because he might not have croaked, but for sure he'd not be chasing. Two, so was the turf man. Three, the Heindricks were still occupied with the lawyers and officials. Four, they didn't know I was free. Five, I had a car, and they wouldn't recognize it because it was Shinny's. Six, time was getting on . . .

Playing crafty, I stayed on the N24 Tipperary road heading east, leaving the more direct T57. It doesn't look far on a map but I was well in sight of the Galtee hills before I was able to cut back on the Hospital road, leaving the T36 Kilamllock fork on my left. All that took time, but it helped me to calm down and stop feeling ill from what I'd done. Like a fool, I explained aloud to the interior of Shinny's car that it had been forced on me. If only other people didn't drag me into their bloodsoaked wars I'd be able to stay holy and pure and unsullied as I normally was. Shinny's car, a little grey Austin saloon, was scented by her. The sweet woman's handbag lay on the passenger seat. She was a lovely creature. No binoculars or weapons in the glove compartment, though, which proved she was as thoughtless as ever.

I'd worked out that if I followed the road which ran a few miles to the west of the lough I could somehow reach the lane which curled round the west side of that low hill which overlooked the water and the clusters of archaeological sites. There would be the guards, of course. From there I could snake down . . .

There were two guards. One was the rider from the castle ruins, the other a stockier bloke with leather patches sewn to his jacket elbows. Two saddled horses were idling nearby the grave mound.

They were smoking, talking, occasionally looking around, but making the mistake of keeping an eye on the distant road rather than the terrain. That was just as well because I'd learned enough of these country blokes' ways to realize they could spot a flea on a ferret without even looking. Nobody near the turf diggings, thank God, and the castle ruins partly screened that shoulder of the hill.

Keeping to the blind side, I ran as fast as possible, actually a slow clumsy plod, over the uneven tussocky ground. Horse tracks showed me the way to go. That castle rider had used this way more than once lately. It was surprisingly easy but a bit knackering, moving at a low crouch and watching in case another of Heindrick's men showed up. Thick as always, I had never tried to discover how big Kurt's team actually was. I'd always assumed I was too much of a coward to take them on — and I was right. Hide, or run like hell, yes. But no to a dust-up, every single time. I made the turf diggings unseen, and was fairly certain no other riders were lurking about the landscape.

There could be no mistake about where the tunnel's mouth was, even though now turfs were stacked across it. The big question was, how far in had they arranged the roof fall, and whether they'd done it with explosives of some sort. Risking detection, I gave a long gaze from the edge of the dug recess towards the lough. Between me and the grave site where the horses and men waited a small area of roughening was visible, but I couldn't remember if it had been there before. The site of a fall-in? Or some unexcavated Bronze Age goings-on?

I pulled off my jacket and started lifting the peat turfs off. They were semi-dry. Clever move, that, showing they'd been dug up for quite a time and therefore unlikely to have been put there recently. It looks easy but isn't. Hurrying didn't help, and the tools which were stacked to one side proved too difficult to use. You had to have learned the knack. I even tried levering with one of the long straight steel poles which the diggers use for marking distances, but finished up swearing and cussing. My heart was thumping, not all from exertion. I went on, stacking the peat blocks slantwards on their narrow edges along other more weathered slabs. They were surprisingly lightweight, lighter even than wood.

Every twenty peats I paused to climb the few yards to the rim to suss out the riders. No cars still, no new battalions. Then back to the pungent aroma below, shifting the peats one by one to clear an opening. The idea was to make a crawlway into the top of the tunnel mouth. There'd be no sense in humping the whole lot. That would only mean more backbreak replacing them when I got out.

The fall just inside the mouth should not have amazed me, though it did. Loose rock mingled with soil and a crumbly peaty stuff had tumbled into the tunnel now. No tool marks on the rock. All in all a careful job, an infilling which would in time resemble the rest of the ground, giving no hint of the tunnel beyond. And just enough rock to make authentic peat-diggers move away from the tunnel line. Good military thinking.

A thin spade thing helped. It had a sort of useless sideways wooden finger at right angles from the haft, but I was past caring by then and had chucked up the idea of carefully sussing out the lie of the land. If the murderous sods found me, well, they found me. Presumably the city officials would send a Garda along to see fair play. I hoped.

The fall was about four feet thick. I got through the top end, working on the principle it was probably easiest and looser stuff there, less compression weight. The first gust of air from inside, when the turf spade penetrated without resistance, fetched out at me fœtid and stenching. It made me gag. I returned to don my jacket—no clues for the passers-by from clever old Lovejoy—took a breath of fresh rainsoaked smog and returned immediately to drag away more peaty earth and crawled inside. There had been no sign in the diggings of that life-giving air hose and its clever little battery-driven pump so I was up the traditional creek once I tumbled headfirst into the tunnel's gloom. What good is technology that's out of reach to those who need it?

'Joe?' I called. 'You there, Joe?'

My eyes were hardly adjusted to the brownblack gloaming before I started crawling forward. Every few yards I paused, wondering what the hell I was up to, and shouted Joe's name. Me being daft me as usual, I hadn't the sense to work out distances, so my progress was judged by the deepening darkness.

Shinny's car, besides lacking every possible amenity and utensil, had also lacked torch, rope, jemmy, crawlers, oxygen cylinders and pickaxes. Typical of a woman. They always crack on about their usefulness, God knows what for. Answers on a postcard. I was at the point where the tunnel narrowed and descended at an angle towards the wet bit, and grumbling under my breath at the stupidity of me and everyone else when I stopped crawling. I screamed then. A rock in my way had groaned, a long hoarse low moan of grief and loneliness and pain and desolation.

'Joe? Joe? That you, Joe?'

'Lovejoy?' the rock groaned.

'You frigging lunatic!' I yelled at his head. He was trapped somehow because he wasn't moving and other rocks and earth were piled on him, pressing his shoulders to the tunnel floor. 'You selfish fucking pig!' I went on screeching abuse at him till my breath gave out. 'You frightened me to frigging death, you stupid Cockney sod! Why didn't you let on you were in here? You silly goon!'

He whispered, 'It's my legs, my back, I think, Lovejoy.'

'Do you realize the festering mess I'm in?' I yelled at him. 'I could be safe out of here, you stupid burke—'

'Ta for coming back, mate.'

'Shut your stupid teeth. Where're you stuck?'

'Dunno. Me length, I think.'

I felt round him as far as I could. He was partly turned on his side, face prone. Supine, and his mouth would have filled with earth and suffocated him. Did I hear a rumble of earth along the tunnel?

'Where the hell are your arms?'

'Pinned.'

'Got anything, tools, ropes, light?'

'No.' His voice was a weak whisper. 'Mr Heindrick said it was best not to take anything.'

'What did he send you back for?'

'Disconnect the air hose. I should have remembered it myself, Lovejoy. He was really great about it, didn't lose his temper, just said to do it straight away.' His tone became anxious. 'You don't think he'll be mad because of the fall-in?'

I thought, I don't believe this. I don't *believe* he's frigging real. That pair of maniacal killers had got Joe to rig the best sleeper scam in antique history, then heaved a tunnel on him, breaking his back and walling him up, burying the poor gullible sod alive—and he still spoke reverently of them?

'Aye, Joe. Sure. Great pair,' I said. 'Look. No explosion or anything, just before the sky fell?'

'Explosion?' He honestly sounded puzzled. 'No. Just the noise of the rockslip.'

Thank God for that. 'I'll scoop beside your chest and top shoulder, Joe, right? Can you move your fingers?'

'Bit. Did Lena—Mrs Heindrick notice I wasn't back on time?'

'She was worried sick, Joe,' I lied, scrabbling the dross aside and shoving it behind me like a mole, thinking, Love is simply a kind of optic atrophy. The capacity for self-deception is infinite under the stress of love.

'I knew she would,' the cretin said, reassured.

There were definitely rumbles now from somewhere. Frantically I clawed the stuff away from him. That wasn't difficult. The problem was what to do with the mounds which kept accumulating between my legs and beside my thighs. The bloody stuff was everywhere. The stupid earth just stayed wherever you pushed it. What the hell did miners do, for heaven's sake? His arm came free a million years later. That meant between us we had enough muscle to prise his weight off his under arm.

Joe himself hit on the notion of trying to push the earth aside at the wall rather than shuffling it along towards the entrance, and him again who said the way to pull him free when the time came to try was for me to brace against the tunnel sides with my back arched and knees pressing against the opposite wall. He explained that his arms had more strength than mine, but then all Cockneys are arrogant swine. I'd be a plug against which he could pull. And he came free, sixth go, practically crippling me for life with the strain.

It was then I noticed I couldn't see at all.

'Joe?' I said, nervous and getting that damp fearish feel.

'Ta, Lovejoy,' Joe said. 'I can't move me back or me legs, mate. Sorry, but you'll have to—'

'Joe. Can you see anything?'

'No.'

I wondered about his eyes. Maybe pressure sends you temporarily blind. 'No pallor past me?'

A pause, grunt of exertion as he lifted his head. 'No.'

'Unless it's got dark since I came in here, something's blocked the entrance.'

We moved on, me feet first and Joe following head first using the strength of our two pairs of arms. Something stopped me, a pole or something. Breathlessly I halted, a leg either side of the damned thing.

'Hang on, Joe.' I felt with a hand over my back.

Steel, vertical. It came out of the tunnel roof and into the floor. It hadn't been there when I crawled in, couldn't have been. I tried pushing, pulling, lifting. Not a hint of movement. I scrunged up, put my feet against it, braced my hands on Joe's shoulders and pushed until Joe moaned with pain.

'Joe, mate,' I said at last, my teeth chattering, 'we're caged in. Somebody'd driven a frigging great bar through the tunnel.'

'Vertical?' He sounded so cool, the thick burke.

'Of course it's vertical, you loon! They drove it down so of *course* it's frigging vertical. It's half-inch steel. We're in a dungeon with one frigging bar!'

'The tunnel here is about a foot and a half diameter,' he mused. 'No way round it, eh, Lovejoy?'

'No.' It came out as a long moaning whine.

'No tools,' Joe mused. 'Nothing. Any chance of using a piece of stone to lever it out?'

I was hysterical. 'It's frigging rigid, you crass burke.'

'Hang on. You got anything, anything at all?'

'No.' I whimpered, practically screaming, babbling.

'You can't have nothing, Lovejoy,' he mumbled. 'I've got nothing because I planned to have nothing. You're so scatterbrained, Lovejoy, you must have something. Car keys, coins, anything. Can you reach your pockets?'

'I changed my trousers at the big house.' And I'd left Shinny's keys in the car. 'A violin string, for Christ's sake.' So we could play the violin, if we had a violin.

'Like that joke from the Depression, Lovejoy. If we had some bacon we could have eggs and bacon if we had some eggs.' He was doing his best.

'Wait.' The trouble was the air. If two men breathed at so many breaths per minute, how long before they croak in a tunnel say, eighty yards long by eighteen inches? 'Joe. Any loose earth against you?'

'We've brought a ton.' It had shovelled along in front of Joe as we'd manoeuvred him.

'I need a ton. Push it here.' I pushed it down under my belly, handful by handful, until a great wadge of soil was splayed against the metal bar.

'What're we doing, Lovejoy?'

'Getting out, you ignorant Cockney nerk. Close your

ears. I'm going to pee and make some mud.' I added politely, 'Excuse me, please.'

Five minutes later I'd made two vows. The first was to try to control my terror, keep cool and work on no matter what. The second was to donate a trillion quid to medical research so they find a way to let blokes pee in a horizontal position. It took me ages to squirt even a useful drop out. Grimacing, I ploshed my hand up and down in the loose earth bowl I'd fashioned, until the mess was thick and gruesomely squashy. Then I set to work, the E string looped round the metal bar, low down where the mud was.

'What's the noise, Lovejoy?'

'Sawing. Mud saw. It's how the ancient Han Chinese sawed jade.' I moved the metal string slowly, making certain there was mud where the E string moved across the bar. Hurry, and the metal string would break. Go too slow and we'd asphyxiate down here. Just right, and the wet soil would erode its way through anything. *Wheem*, the metal went.

'Mud saw? Are you kidding?'

'The mud's the saw, you burke. The Chinese cut opal, jade, stone, damned near anything, with a bent cane and string. But it takes time.'

A pause again. Maybe crumbs of reason were knocking about his thick skull. 'We got enough, Lovejoy?'

'Time?' *Wheem, wheem.*

'Air.'

'Fingers crossed. Keep me awake for God's sake. Don't let me nod off.'

'Lovejoy.' That reflective voice meant he was working things out, maybe for the first time. 'You don't trust Mr and Mrs Heindrick, do you?'

'Trust nobody. Save your breath, gabby sod.' *Wheem, wheem.*

'We're going to be partners,' Joe confessed, really quite

proudly. 'Them and me.'

'Oh, aye?' Such close partners that they decided to kill you, Joe, I thought, sawing away. Once Heindrick overheard me address loyal servant Kurak as Joe—as we entered the tunnel to lay the sleepers in the grave—Heindrick had decided to flop a landslip on to Joe, seal the tunnel and drive away. Oh, he wouldn't have done every little thing himself: orders to kill at a distance are so much less disquieting. So Lovejoy's carelessness had put Joe where he was. And, Joe, you may not realize it, but I'll bet you too are on a series of video films for Kurt's late-night viewing. *Wheem, wheem.*

'Lena and me are going to—' His voice was thick, drowsier. I felt a twinge—well, actually a wholesale cramp—of panic at the idea of being alone.

'Hey, Joe. Remember that sleeper gig somebody pulled in Worcester a few years back? Was that you?' More mud, and *wheem, wheem.* My forearm muscles were stiffer, worn out.

He roused, chuckled. 'Sheffield plate? Yeah. Josh Hancock, 1755, a saucepan.'

'Honest? You old devil! People my way said it was the Manchester men. They're pretty good—'

'Them?' Awake now, he delivered a few choice opinions on the merits of the Mancunian sleeper man. 'We cleaned up on that.'

'And who did that cinder job over Cambridge way last summer?'

'That was me too.'

'You? How many pictures was it? Somebody said it was half of them—' A plosh of mud, then pull the string across the metal. *Wheem, wheem.*

'Lovejoy,' he said solemnly, 'we had the whole bloody lot copied—best repros money could buy. Then we sleepered the lot. The whole collection!'

'Go on!' My fingers were sore as hell, and I had to rip

strips off my shirt and use them as finger loops before continuing. 'Didn't you burn the whole manor house?'

Joe chuckled. 'Scared ourselves to death. The old squire's lady — eighty-two if she was a day — was upstairs. The firemen got her out in time.'

'So all your fakes went up in smoke, and — '

' — And the whole collection's been sleepered. Next year they get discovered.'

'Congrats, Joe. Really great.'

We kept each other going, reminiscing over the great scams of the past and filling in for each other bits of news. We talked of the fake 'originals' in the antique postage stamp markets. We invented a guessing game, telling of the best fakers we knew and arguing over awarding points. Two for the best true story, one point for a draw and nil for losing. We covered the great Tompion clock scandal, the Tom Keating trial for his fake Samuel Palmers, the long, long story of the Louis XV giltwood console tables which those world-famous London auctioneers did over with such apparent transparent ignorance for a fortune. We cackled and joked about the phoney South London collections of Daguerreotypes. I revealed all about the set of Roman legion's surgical instruments, on display in a Midland museum, which I'd broken my little index finger making a twelvemonth ago. And the saga of Jason's scam with the phoney *Paradise Lost*. And the best way of semi-ageing pearls just so their radiance can just be rescued. And the perennial argument about how the new synthetics are doing down the trust in antique diamonds because nowadays anybody can fake an antique brooch if their fingers are nimble enough. And the stupidities of recycled glass forgeries. And how to age papers and new parchment. How the sapphire glaze can be copied on modern reproductions. How to age wood and simulate Cuban mahogany. How to . . . how to . . .

A hand on my shoulder. I'd nodded off and Joe was shaking me awake.

'Okay, Joe.' By now the air must be fœtid, horrible, and I couldn't tell it from fresh. I had to feel again to locate the groove in the metal bar. No good cutting at a new place when the bar was part way through in the centre.

'You were saying about the thumbprints, Lovejoy.'

'Aye.' *Wheem, wheem* my E string went. I seemed to have been doing this all my life, bent as far as the tunnel would allow and hauling on alternate ends of the string. Pack the groove with more muddy mess, fix the string carefully in the groove and *wheem, wheem*. 'Aye, Joe. After that Elizabeth Barrett Browning manuscript "Prometheus Bound" was sold for over eleven thousand quid — it had her thumbprints, remember? — every bloody crummy book on sale anywhere had bloody thumb- prints . . .'

I'd no idea how long it was, but Joe was suddenly shaking me and urging me to have a go and kick at the bar. I took a hell of a time explaining that the E string kept passing through the bar and I couldn't find the grove before it dawned on me that I'd cut through.

'You've been doing the top for donkey's years, Lovejoy. It might break with a kick. You did the bottom hours ago.'

That was news to me. We counted 'One, two, three' and I kicked. Something scraped all up my calf, right through the skin. I wept deliriously real awakening pain, but realized then that there was space where the bar should have been, and I was blubbering and slithering and dragging Joe after me and him saying, 'Great, Lovejoy, great, eh?'

And I felt air.

CHAPTER 25

Rain and cold, mud, chill wind. The lot. But beautiful air, rasping like lung ice in the chest. Fingers bleeding, leg stinging and shoeful of blood, but that air.

I'd dragged Joe out on his face. With my last erg, turned his face sideways so he now projected from the peat barrier as if he'd been fired from a cannon and come through the wall. And the peats that had seemed so light now weighed a ton. He looked unconscious.

A figure moved on the rim of the diggings, and looked down.

'Jaysus! Is there no killin' you two?'

My luck, to find the castle rider. I'd hoped for enough solitude to somehow drag Joe over the hillside to Shinny's car and escape him, to hospital maybe. Surely there'd be a hospital in the town called Hospital? I glanced at Joe for help, but he'd clearly switched off, the selfish sod. If only he weren't so big I'd have got him away by now. You'd think giants like him would naturally go on a diet as a matter of course, thoughtless burke.

'Give me a minute, mate.' I wanted it to sound terse but it came out a bleat of terror.

'Back in there, the both of yuz.'

'Please, mate. Do a deal? Them golds—'

He grinned down at me from the bleak skyline. 'Mr Heindrick's the boss. Kurak's too much muscle. Back into that tunnel.'

Where he'd give me both barrels this time, to make sure. I felt like it was the end of the world.

'Look, mate,' I wheedled. 'It's Joe they want dead. Not me.'

'Both of yuz.'

'Let me go,' I blubbered. 'Do Joe, but let me go. Lena said me and her were partners—'

He chuckled. 'You and Kitchener's army. Every boyo in the West's ridden that lane. We call them Lena's cowboy pictures on the estate.'

Get up and kick him, Joe, I prayed, but he slept on. Sleeper man in more ways than one. The castle rider shrugged, raised his shotgun with that ugly practised speed, hardly seeking aim.

'Have it here, then, me boy.'

I screeched, 'No!' and flung myself sideways hoping to shield myself with Joe, though there was nowhere to run. My arms folded themselves about my head as something thunked up above. Silencer? But nothing hit me. And no bang. I was only in the same old agony, no pain added for once.

Wincing, I peered out between my arms. He was up there looking puzzled, stockstill and legs apart, plucking at a stick near his collar. He turned to his left, moving the shotgun with him. Another thunk sounded. Another stick, black against the grey underclouded sky, joined the first. The shotgun fell, and the castle rider lay sideways into the air. I watched, stunned, as he flopped into the turf pit a yard away. Peat spattered my face. He was still. The two arrows projecting from his neck had broken in the fall. Their fractured ends were ever so clean, varnished a bright translucent acid-oaken yellow. They proved there was a bright safe world still in existence somewhere out of this drab wet brown-greenery.

'Glory be to God!' Gerald was up on the rim. 'Where did you come from?' He cast a look around, then climbed down with all those jointed limbs. He examined the castle rider's body.

'That's wasn't me screaming,' I explained. 'It was Joe just before he passed out.'

'Sure it was. I recognized the voice,' Gerald said

diplomatically. 'He looks done for.'

'Maybe a broken back. Anybody else about?'

'Just this blackguard, God rest his poor soul.'

'We'll have to hurry, eh?'

'Not so's you'd notice.' He winked and began to slot his bow and quiver of arrows into that long thin canvas case. 'Somebody lodged an appeal against the Heindricks.'

'Another cousin?' I guessed.

'Aren't you the amazin' one, Lovejoy! How'd you guess that? It's me cousin Sean's boy Liam. A terrible Wexford man, to be sure, God forgive him, but goin' for a lawyer and wantin' to take on every judge in Munster—'

'Got any tools, Gerald? Hammer, chisel.' His surprise didn't stop me asking. 'I've a little job to do before we get the torcs.'

'Long job? We haven't many hours.'

I saw again those small ledges of rock supporting the last wall slab of the burial chamber. 'No, not long.'

'I'll see what I can find.'

'You take Joe to hospital. I've Shinny's car over the hill.'

'I saw it.'

I wasn't surprised. He seemed to have seen everything since we started. I hadn't.

'You know,' I said. 'I thought that bag was for fishing stuff.'

'And hurt them little innocent watery souls?' He paused to look at the castle rider. 'We'll put him in the tunnel before we go. Two good arrows wasted. D'you know the price of them things? 'Tis a scandal, a scandal. You'll wait here?'

'Promise,' I said, and meant it.

I'd misjudged Gerald.

CHAPTER 26

That last hour changed me for life.

Gerald was indefatigable. His multi-hinged limbs all angles and his prattling tongue never silent two seconds together, he did countless journeys across the hillside, and made a stretcher from those horribly familiar steel marker-poles tied with twine so we could hump Joe's recumbent mass over the hill. The arrangement was for Gerald to drive Joe to hospital while I finished a small task that was on my mind.

I was near dropping and had to ask for a rest when finally we tottered within sight of Shinny's crate. Gerald was all for sprinting on, but I had the heavy end and insisted.

'Here,' I puffed. 'What the hell's that glass thing?'

A shining bubble was on the track next to the car.

'My bubble car.' He sounded really proud.

So he had spoken the truth when I'd asked about the glass bubble on the van roof at Caitlin and Donald's house in Drogheda. I remembered the shrill whine of an engine.

'I kept hearing scooters,' I said.

He was enraged. 'Scooters? You evil black-hearted Englishman! Don't you know that bubble cars are the engineering wonder of the age and scooters are nothing but cardboard cut-out Heath-Robinson toys that shame the purest principles of engineering poetry—'

I sighed. Resourceful he might be, but he was still a nut in my book.

'Lift,' I said.

He kept up his tirade all the way to the car.

I watched the car go and returned reluctantly to the

turf digging. Leaving the dead castle rider there like a dead guard at a tomb made me feel ill, but there was nothing for it. Everything was out of my hands now. Once I decided that, it went like clockwork, maybe twenty minutes or even less. I went the length of the tunnel. Gerald had somehow purloined all the equipment everybody else seemed to lack. He'd found a hammer from somewhere for me, and a chisel that weighed a ton, and one of those tiny disposable torches that last for ever.

Though I say it myself I did a marvellous job underneath the burial chamber. I chiselled away the underlip from one side of the last slab completely, packing the chippings into the space created to give it some slender support. Then I did the other side but going cautiously, inch by inch. The great cross-slab formed the last paving of the burial chamber, and in turn it supported the place where the two converging walls met to form that characteristic wedge shape.

Heindrick's original tunnellers had cut away a great deal to make enough tunnel space, so in a sense they'd done me a favour. There wasn't much to do to make the whole structure unsafe. I scrabbled out in a panic only when there came a slight grating sound above me as the great slabs shifted and settled, their first movement for millennia. Gerald talked a soft welcome in my earhole before I even knew the swine had returned. He fell about when I nearly infarcted in fright, a great joke of the kind only imbeciles like him appreciate. When I came down through the superstrata I explained we'd have to go canny breaking in to lift the gold torcs out.

'I've made it a bit unsafe,' I told him apologetically.

'Ah, it's terrible careless y'are,' he gave back without batting an eyelid. 'How've you done that?'

'Anybody standing on the apex slab'll go through.'

'Won't that bring down the sides and the top monolith? Them graves are nothing more than a card house.'

'Afraid it might. How much do you reckon they weigh?'

'Them stones? Ton, maybe ton and a half.'

'Good heavens,' I said evenly. 'I do hope there isn't an accident.'

We broke into the chamber from above as dusk fell. Oddly, I noticed the two saddled horses idling patiently in the distance. The other guard seemed to have gone. Gerald said nothing about them so I was inclined to keep mum too. He seemed boss, full of plans and way ahead of me. Just how full I'd yet to discover. I may be good at antiques, but I'm dud on people.

Gerald had not done too badly this far and me and Joe were alive to prove it. But that evening he did us proud, with a pulley-operated metal claw which fixed on connecting rods fetched from his bow case. We—he, rather—lifted the gold torcs one by one from the chamber. I was really proud of their placing, pointing the krypton beam time after time to show him exactly how perfectly I'd positioned them. The ignorant sod was too stupid to appreciate my skill.

'Ah, Lovejoy,' he said sadly, sprawled out across the gap we had made by simply pulling a stone from the entrance roofing. 'Ah, what's the matter now? The sleeper game's the sleeper game. Different, y'see. This is your honest-to-God grave robbery.'

'Yes, but—'

'It won't count,' he insisted sadly, bringing out another torc in the metal claw and holding the pulley's nylon rope taut as he did so. 'Not in the annals and records of the great sleeper tricks of criminal history.'

'But you must admit—'

'No, Lovejoy. We're undoing all your great work. Nil out of ten, boyo.'

We left one torc on the dangerous slab at the grave chamber's apex. By then I was worn out. Gerald was still lively as a cricket, and got a thrill out of pretending every five seconds that the other guard was creeping up on us, the goon, just to see me leap and panic. Despite his tomfoolery we did the final gory job pretty well, making quite a good finish.

We—mostly Gerald—put the castle rider into the tunnel, walled it up with debris, closed the tunnel mouth with layers of peat, the whilst singing some old Gaelic thing ('An auld peat-layer's song from the Dark Ages, Lovejoy!')

The final insult was that he hadn't returned in Shinny's motor and we had to drive off in his bubble car. The worst ride I've ever had. He thought he was giving me a real treat, and praised its speed.

'We need to get away fast,' I complained, my teeth rattling in my head from the vibration. I'd never been so near the ground without lying down. 'For when they find the tunnel. And the castle riders, erm . . .'

'Sure, Lovejoy, we're not to blame if wicked people go digging tunnels under the countryside!'

'They know I was in the Heindricks' group.'

'Ah, but you stayed in town all day, Lovejoy.' He nearly turned the bloody machine over, laughing like a drain. How he managed to crumple all those limbs in that driver's seat I'll never know.

'No, Gerald,' I explained to the moron. 'I came back to the lough. In the tunnel. At the turf diggings—'

'*No*, Lovejoy,' he corrected. 'Don't you remember? You stayed with the rest of us. We all went shopping.'

'Who's "us"?'

'Me cousin Brian. Our Terence's three. Auntie Mary and her husband's brother Donald . . .'

'Right,' I said lamely. 'I'll need a list, okay?'

CHAPTER 27

Funny thing about women. They have this knack of putting you on the defensive, as if you start out guilty when they're in the right over everything. They're born with it. Normally it always unsettles me, though I manage by ignoring any guilt I might possess. Sometimes it doesn't work. That last night with Shinny was one of them, even though it was celebration time.

Gerald and I had driven eastwards in his daft van through Tipperary as far as the Irish Sea and then doglegged up to Dublin. There, on a waste ground in the city's outskirts, we gazed at the fourteen torcs gleaming on the unfolded leather sheet in his van.

'Well, boyo,' he said softly, 'isn't that the poetic sight?'

'What now?'

'I take the genuine torc to be authenticated. The rest get valued.'

'Authenticated? Not by a trained archaeologist?' Police were in my thoughts.

He grinned. 'My cousin Sebastian's one. Wouldn't it be time he earned his keep, now?'

'Then we'll market the rest on the sly?'

'Sure it's a terrible criminal mind you have, Lovejoy,' but he was grinning. 'Which is it's the true torc?'

'That.' I pointed instantly and waited while he wrapped it with reverence in a separate leather. 'Wait, Gerald. What's the split?'

'Equal?'

'Agreed. But look. Kurt Heindrick promised me one repro torc as payment.'

I'm not a greedy bloke, but fair's fair. We argued a bit, really quite mildly but meaning it. Gerald said payment for what. I countered that without my divvie sense there could be no sleeper scam at all.

'Like just now,' I insisted. 'How would you have known which torc to show Sebastian if I hadn't pointed it out just now?'

We settled—some more reluctantly than the rest—on my taking one from the delectable row of gold crescents. 'Only until we all meet after Sebastian's given us the certificate of authenticity, after his tests,' Gerald warned. 'Then we argue it out, you, and me and Sinead.'

'All right.'

He made me turn my back, mistrustful sod, face the toffee shop across the road and pick one without looking, on account of their possible slight variation in size. Which only goes to show how people trust people. I uttered a few harsh expletives on his attitude, which delighted him.

'Sebastian's tests will take three days, Lovejoy,' he said, wrapping the rest carefully. 'Look after Shinny till then, you wicked Englishman.'

'See you, then.'

He drove off, me waving at the clattering smoking hulk. I crossed the road as he'd instructed to catch the bus, smiling at the weight in my jacket pocket.

He'd told me to be at this restaurant dead on eight. I wasn't fooled any more—or thought I wasn't. Gerald was really a ball of fire, just made of hinged bits of angle-iron.

Shinny and I reached the restaurant simultaneously. There were a few awkward minutes looking at one another through candle flames while she asked what had gone on and I made blundering explanations praising Gerald to the skies.

'He's got the torcs,' I explained. 'A valuation by weight.'

She smiled. 'Couldn't you have done that, Lovejoy?'

'To the last farthing, but you know. Partner's foibles.'

'Yes.' She seemed sadder than yesterday's bunting.

'Gerald got a message to me through Kathleen. She's—'

'A cousin?'

'Mmmh. Our Patrick's side of the family. Joe's in hospital.'

'He might make it?'

'Oh, he will, Lovejoy. Gerald will take care of the bills and everything. He already has a job for him when he comes out.'

'What if he's maimed for life?'

'Trust Gerald.'

'If you say.' Though I couldn't see Joe doing anything but the con trick. Once a sleeper man, always a sleeper man. 'Erm, were you all right, love?' I cleared my throat and watched the waiters for a bit. 'I had to, erm, borrow your car after . . . that accident.'

'Of course you had, darling.' She touched my hand sadly. 'I understand.'

I didn't think she did but let it pass.

'Erm, Jason and the other bloke. Were they both . . . ?'

'Both. I waved down a motor and they phoned the ambulance.'

Thoughts of what might have been sometimes make you go green, so I focused on grub and gelt. We ordered a mound of food then I asked the question uppermost in my mind.

'Will Gerald be okay with those torcs? They're worth a fortune.'

'Trust Gerald.' She held my hand and gazed at me with those eyes through the golden flames between us. 'You can't beat an Irishman in a shilling race.'

We drove to the strand to watch the Howth lights and walked the dark streets. She was in the mood for reminiscing and talked of her childhood abroad, the dresses she hated and how shivering cold she'd been at school. I made her laugh once by telling her to teach me that Gaelic turf-cutter's song Gerald had sung while at the turf diggings. She fell about, helpless. I had to hold her up.

'Gerald? Him? Oh, Lovejoy, darling! Gerald hasn't a word of the Gaelic. He makes everything up. Everything. All the time. Don't you understand anything at all?'

So Gerald was a non-Gaelic Gael as well as non-poetic poet.

I mused, for her sad soul's sake, 'What else is he not? Better tell me now before our partnership really gets under way.'

She laughed at that so much she cried.

We walked over the little river and into somebody's garden. She was on their steps while I dithered at the gate.

'Come in, Lovejoy.'

Keys clinked. The door opened and she was silhouetted there, looking down the steps at me as the hallway light came on.

'Er, is it all right, Shinny?'

'There's nobody here, darling. It's my cousin Maureen's. She's away for three days.'

I went up the steps. 'Caitlin's side of the family? Sean's? Patrick's?'

'Mary's. You know, Mrs Heindrick's head maid.'

And there was I assuming Gerald always knew where to be by a kind of instinct.

'Tell her not to mix the porcelain styles in future,' I said severely. 'I was saying to Jason only the other day that Meissen Augsburg would have been ideal —'

'*Lovejoy*!' the bandsaw said, but I was already putting my torc in the kitchen's sugar tin, shoving it deep in the sugar. I found some plaster to stick its lid on tight.

'Safety, mavourneen,' I said. 'In case we sleep heavy, alannah.'

She rounded on me and hauled me close. 'Lovejoy,' she

said fiercely. 'If you start your silly rubbish tonight I'll—'

She was pulling my jacket off, then my shirt, then handing me along the corridor.

'Mind my arm, mavourneen.'

'One more word out of you,' she said in fury. 'One word, that's all.'

She slammed me into a bedroom on the first floor where an electric fire already burned. She swung me round to face her and kicked the door shut with a thud that shook the whole house.

'Ready?' she said, arms akimbo.

'I think so,' I said doubtfully.

'Right,' she said, shelling her coat. 'Get 'em off.'

Once, during the night, I thought I heard a familiar whining scooter engine, but Shinny's lovely cool breast was in my hand still, so I wrapped my legs over her and went back to sleep.

She was gone.

You will have experienced those moments of disorientation when you wake up assuming you are at home or somewhere, and suddenly every single sense screams *different! different!* and for a sick moment you feel utterly scared and lost. It was like that, opening my eyes into bright ten o'clock daylight with strangeness all around and the big double bed crumpled and . . . and . . .

And Shinny gone.

I shot up, heart banging, dashed into every room thinking of the Gardai and the Fraud Squad and Interpol and Sherlock Holmes, but there was only this envelope.

I thought, This is bloody rubbish. She can't have left, just when we'd become lifelong partners. The note was on the back of a shopping list.

Darling Lovejoy,

I'm gone with Gerald. I can hear you saying as you

read this that women always settle for what they can get. Maybe we are really like that. I don't know. I do wish I could have got you for keeps, but you will never be the sort.

Gerald wishes you good luck and says to tell you we'll do the sleepers proud. Last night's paper is in the kitchen. Gerald said not to show it you till now.

All my love, darling,

Shinny.

The paper had a front page chunk about a gentleman and his wife being seriously injured while involved in an amateur archaeological excavation in the west. The wedge grave had fallen in, the floor crumbling under their weight. In fact, there was doubt whether they would even survive. Gardai were making extensive enquiries. Two local men were missing, with some of the torcs. The Heindricks were highly respected pillars of the community, and there were lessons for us all in the sad events surrounding the accident. Poor them. I didn't bother reading the rest, and thought of Shinny.

Of course I should have spotted it. Gerald was in partnership with Joe—maybe always had been. He, Joe and Joxer had been in collusion all the time. And of course Shinny. They had all gone along with the Heindricks as a team within a team, to con the conners. I should have known. An Irish poet in East Anglia would have been coals to Newcastle, but a Dublin-trained nurse could arrive, work at a hospital and serve as go-between for Joxer and Gerald. A plan cool enough for Jason, the Heindricks and me to have missed the truth completely. No wonder Gerald didn't much care how deep his arrows went. And Shinny had the strength to leave me high and dry. As I'd said, I couldn't imagine Joe doing anything else but antiques con tricks. Once a sleeper man always a sleeper man. They could manage without me. Of all, I was superfluous. Tears came to my eyes. Honestly. Tears.

Me. At my age.

And Shinny, lovely eyes sad across the gold candle flames, had said it too: You can't beat an Irishman in a shilling race.

I'd been had. I'd been done.

Shinny and her team had conned me, conned the Heindricks, and played us all off against each other. Last night's love had been farewell, a kiss before flying.

Worse, I was broke, Not a bean.

Except . . .

CHAPTER 28

You won't believe this, but all morning I mooned about the place touching the bed and looking for traces of her and suchlike daftness. Love is a hell of a thing. I felt I would never smile again. I went to find the sugar tin in the kitchen. Gone. Good old Shinny had snatched it as she ran.

The trouble is, I thought, watching the children cross the road towards the school, love has to be made or you've got none. Like antiques. And 'made' means *made*, formed, laboriously worked into being in that creative act that is the terrible and utter act of loving.

You can't do it alone. Try, and all you achieve is a longing, a feeling, desire, hope, fondness. Certainly, to love somebody she has to be there to be loved. I was heartbroken.

Well, almost.

I made some tepid tea, drank it as a kind of St Giles bowl, and watched the women go past with their prams towards the shops near the green where the buses turn at the top of the road.

There wasn't a crust in the house, not a penny. Shinny

had taken every groat. Not that I'd had much. And
Shinny had paid for last night's supper in the posh
restaurant by St Stephen's Green. Still, it showed she was
thinking of her present and future comfort, which is
practically every bird's fulltime occupation.

About midday I brewed up again, worse even than
before, thinking. I was a long way from Dublin's centre,
and me with not even the bus fare. The train from the
level crossing would cost a mint because fares always do.
Stay here and starve to death? Or move about in hope?

Nothing else for it.

I heaved a sigh, rose and went back into the bedroom.
The gold torc, glowing with its ancient splendour, was
still underneath the bed where I'd slipped it after lofting
it from the sugar tin during the night. Loving Shinny to
exhaustion had been a pleasurable duty to protect the
torc.

The rare eighteenth-century old flat iron which I'd
substituted for it in the sugar tin wasn't to be sneezed at.
The rarer ones—Abraham Darby of Coalbrookdale,
incidentally, as that one had been—are almost priceless
now, real collector's items. I was very, very narked that
Shinny had taken it, thieving bitch. Even if she'd thought
the tin contained a gold repro, it was still me she was
stealing from. Well, all right, it still belonged to the
householder Maureen, but I felt annoyed with Shinny. *I*
could have nicked the flat iron instead of her. That's
women for you.

I slipped the torc into my pocket. As long as I gave the
whole coat to the archaeologist, he'd be able to
spectrograph his way to the undeniable truth—that in my
hand was the original gold torc. It had been easy to pick it
out simply by its vibes, even while Gerald watched me and
I gaped innocently at the toffee shop. Of course, sad that
Gerald and Shinny had only umpteen reproductions, but
gold's worth its own weight. They wouldn't starve. Just get

a nasty shock when they found everybody laughed at the claim that at least one of their torcs was genuine. Still, people shouldn't go trying to defraud friends.

To equal things up, I decided to look round the house. There was a small Henry oil on the wall, faded from stupid placing on the wall facing the window where the sunlight would hit. It was suffering from craquelure because of coal fires in the same room. Careless old Maureen.

The painting came free of its frame quite well without a scratch. I borrowed a pillowcase and folded it over the painting. (Tip: never wrap a painted canvas up with string directly. Fingers are kindest and therefore best for carrying.) Then I borrowed a small white-metal 'bronze', 1911 or so when they were all the rage and everybody wanted one of those stalwart heroes leading a prancing nag for the mantelpiece.

Patricia Harvest, the plump lustful sexpot from Goldhanger, like all antique dealers, couldn't tell white-metal from dandruff, so I'd get at least half the fare home from her. She was sure to be in the main hotel where the antiques fair was being held. After all, I'd promised to meet her there without dreaming I would actually turn up. In fact, thinking of her winning ways made me feel quite warm inside again.

Finally, I borrowed a small carriage clock from the kitchen. No longer going, but walnut-cased clocks, especially those with typical Belgo-French corner pillars, are highly sought nowadays even though they aren't much before 1870. Funny how fashions go in collecting. It fitted neatly in my pocket.

I found the right hotel sixth go. Bloody telephones, never any use.

Mrs Patricia Harvest was in suite 108, bless her greedy little heart.

'Pat?' I said, all casual. 'Lovejoy here, darlin'. As promised.'

'Patricia,' she corrected. 'Lovejoy?' She was already breathing hard. 'Darling! At last! I've been waiting and *waiting*. Where are you?'

'That's me at the door now,' I said prophetically. 'Be prepared to (a) pay for a taxi at the hotel, (b) rape me in your circular bed, and (c) make a fortune with me at that antiques fair. Okay?'

'Oooh, darling,' she said, practically groaning.

Before departing with my loot, I totted up my expectations on a scrap of paper lying around. When I turned it over I realized it was Shinny's farewell letter. I hadn't meant to be so casual about it all, still busy being heartbroken for life, but the trouble with heartbreak is it's not much use. Yet that thieving swine Gerald had nicked all my gold torcs. I felt like strangling him, but hunting the bastard down might leave me full of arrows in some desolate bog. It was either revenge, or immediate solace in Pat Harvest's sexy wealth.

What was it I'd said? Sooner or later someone *has* to chuck in the sponge on vengeance and settle for forgiveness. Otherwise we're all at war for ever and life's nothing but a succession of holocausts.

But why should that somebody be me?

Then I thought of Sal, Joxer, the two duckeggs off the motorway bridge, Jason and his oppo, how close I'd come to it. And suddenly there were reasons it had to be me. Wait for all the other idle sods in the universe to walk away from revenge and you wait for ever. Besides, I remembered the ugly thunk of Gerald's arrows as they hit the castle rider. I might even win the torc back, but there's no pockets in shrouds.

And there were other antiques waiting, to get to know and to love.

Patricia would be delighted to see me. She always was,

being so clueless about antiques. And I'd let her see my latest purchases, a valuable Henry oil, and an original Celtic torc, for a consideration. She'd agree, of course. Patricia's considerations were famous and very, very considerate.

The trouble with Paul Henry as an artist was that he copied his own Irish paintings, which causes a bit of turmoil when connoisseurs glimpse one of his. There's always this row about provenance, too, though I'd have to play that one off the cuff. But nobody achieved that green like him, and those white cottages—always too stark when you look too closely at the brushwork—melt into the lovely landscape when you step back.

I wondered if anybody had tried to forge them yet. Maybe Pat—sorry, Patricia—was still friendly with that faker in Goldhanger and we could do a deal. I'd have to watch his technique, though. Him and his lunatic use of yellow ochre and umbers. In this game you can't be too careful . . .

I slammed the door and stepped out, whistling, heartbreak forgotten.

THE GONDOLA SCAM

For
A story for Lal, Jackie, Pam, Elizabeth, Roy, Ruth and
Al, and Susan as always

This book is dedicated to the ancient Chinese God of
Literature K'uei Hsing, whom the sea-monsters eternally
rescue from drowning in the rising waters of the ocean.

Lovejoy

scam (skam) *n. slang*. A fraudulent scheme, especially one for making money quickly.

Oxford American Dictionary, Oxford University Press, Oxford (1980)

CHAPTER 1

Usually people say women come first. Other times it's money, survival, anger, ambition. But deep down it's none of these delectables.

It's antiques.

Antiques are everything. First, last, every single thing. For ever and ever.

Fingers tapped on the table, regular as a metronome. *Dup, dup* they went. And the price rose in tens with each tap from the ring of dealers. *Dup*. Ten. *Dup*. Plus ten. *Dup*. Another ten. And another and another. My face felt white.

Ever been on tenterhooks for nothing? Think of an illegal auction in a seedy upstairs pub room. No public, only a ring of hard grubby antique dealers tapping on the table, watching through the fag smoke with crinkled eyes. Not an antique in sight. Ten blokes and two birds all bidding in utter silence for a painting, with the pub yard and the taproom below heaving like anglers' bait. And me, mouth dry and chest thumping, wishing the whole sordid mess would simply go away. I tell you, this antique game seems quiet and contented—from the outside. Inside, it's horrendous, utterly crazy. I was frightened and fuming.

The genuine auction had ended half an hour ago. The merry old public—that shoal of piranhas—were either celebrating hilariously in the boozer or crawling home in tears according to their degrees of success at today's bidding. Up here, the real business of the day was being done: the closed ring auction of dealers illegally re-auctioning among themselves the items they'd bought a few minutes before.

Dup. My player tapped again, the maniac, though I'd told him no. Five antique dealers had dropped out and now sat sulking. That left seven, including Linda from Tolleshunt. And that lovely ash blonde who seemed so determined. Then there was Sam Wiltshire, he of the merry jokes, supposedly bidding for himself. There was Big Frank from Suffolk, with wives and gelt to spare and antique silver always on his mind — he gets married like other blokes go to the races, meaning to say frequently and never quite sure of the outcome. Then a hoary old dealer from Salford I didn't know but who was taking all this silent bidding in his stride, kippering us all with a dustbin of a pipe. Instead of tapping, his finger nudged a little electronic print-out calculator, a neat way of anticipating the arguments which often happen after the dealers' ring 'knocks down' — stops at the highest bid. He had sense. Jasper Coke (his real name, incidentally) was also keeping in but gradually losing impetus. He's a cheerful square-shaped bloke with a shop somewhere down the sea estuary, supposedly expert in porcelain and Georgian household furniture. That only means he's thick as a plank, because antique dealers always are, though rumour has it Jasper can actually read and write.

That leaves only my player, the goon I was mad at. Mr Malleson was pretty well-known from his 'sweeps' through East Anglia in search of antiques for his London showroom. When he has any doubt, he simply hires somebody like me for a day or so. A sound rule, you might think.

'Call up,' he said at that point. I could have kicked him, almost groaned aloud. 'Five.'

The old Salford geezer thumbed his calculator to increase by fifteens now instead of tens. Malleson tapped the table, and round the morons went, *dup, dup*. Only this time Linda lifted a flat hand, the sign of dropping out. I was glad, because I've a soft spot for Linda. We once got up to no good together in Norwich after selling a Gantz watercolour of Madras, genuine early 1820s. (His paintings in the past three years have soared in value since the greetings-card people discovered them; if you pass one up, don't say you weren't warned.) She carefully avoided my eye (she often does) but must have caught a vibe of my impotent rage. That luscious blonde sitting directly opposite my idiotic player was still in there, tighter lips though and increasingly bitter about something. Pretty as the picture we were bidding for—a million times more authentic. I'd twice told my player, the duckegg, that the painting was a fake, but he knew best like all lunatics. Now he was well on the way to losing a fortune. Serve the silly sod right.

Sam Wiltshire folded, both palms flat, cracking, 'A Carpaccio oil sketch just can't be worth nine whole pence.' He got a wan smile from Jasper Coke, who was already out of his depth and dropped out next round. The blonde fingered her pearls (real, a risky baroque single string) and tapped. Three left.

Malleson, still knowing best, tapped.

The Salford dealer took some snuff, varoomed droplets over us all and tapped. I was practically screaming inside.

'Call up, five.' The blonde did a complicatedly casual ritual with powder compact and mirror. It entailed a lot of lip play, and was watched with fascination by almost all. Even the morose dealers huddled in the corner stopped grumbling and admired her. Linda sardonically lit a fag and walked to the window to show she thought the blonde was a scheming bitch. You now had to bid on in twenties. Old Salford disgustedly clicked his calculator off, raising a palm.

Two left.

'Call up to twenty-five,' Malleson said calmly. My name would be mud after this lark.

The picture they were after was a clear fraud. Some

mauler had tried to fake that complicated bit of gear from Carpaccio's *Knight In A Landscape* which they guard so carefully in Lugano, with enough grounding to suggest his authentic brushwork. Nice attempt, but done by some soulless cretin, doubtless with a string of diplomas to show how 'expert' he was. Pathetic.

'Call up, five,' the blonde said, which made even the hard drinkers freeze. Bids now in thirties. Disconcertingly, I found the bird's eyes on me. *Stop your man*, her lovely eyes signalled, stop him because he's a fool. I reddened. I don't need birds telling me that, but what could I do? Malleson was big money. I didn't have two pennies to rub together. As usual.

'Call up, five,' said my player, the world's expert know-all. The maniac had raised the bidding to steps of thirty-five quid. I almost fainted. He'd gone bid-happy, that weird state of compulsion in which you'll bid to any level, for any old piece of tat. It happens. I once saw two women go bid-happy, stunning a whole mob of dealers into a dazed silence while they duelled for a Woolworth chair off a junk-heap. It's a very dangerous state to get yourself into, because you just can't — *can't* — stop.

A hand on my shoulder pressed me down. I'd actually reached for Mr Malleson's neck in my blind rage.

'Want a drink, Lovejoy?'

'Eh?' My gaze cleared. Linda had come to stand close, and was smiling calming messages into my face. Some dealer snickered at my name. Some friend interested in his welfare quickly shushed him.

'A drink.' Linda held up her own glass to prove nourishment was available on the premises.

'Er, no, ta.' I jerked my shoulder away to see the blonde spread her palm. It was over. The bird had spotted that Mr Malleson had gone bid-happy, and ducked out.

He turned and glanced at me, proud as a peacock. The London dealer immediately got his tabs out — addressed

IOU blanks. There was a flurry as scribbled IOUs changed hands.

'Hurry up. Next item's Lot Seventy,' Sam Wiltshire said. 'Who got it?'

'I did.' Jasper Coke pulled a face as somebody muttered the price. 'That early monk's chair. Genuine.' Genuine all right, I thought, in a sulk. Only, a wooden armchair which has a rectangular back that hinges over to form a small table resting horizontally on the chair's arms is called a chair-table, or a 'table-chairwise'. We dealers call it a monk's chair (a fairly modern, invented name like 'grandfather clock') to put mediæval flavour into the price-tag. I caught Jasper's eye and he had the grace to give a wry smile.

'Okay,' Sam said, grinning. He always acts as auctioneer. 'Start at ten, up in twos.' He tapped the table and they were off again.

'Cheers,' I said, clearing out.

'Oh, Lovejoy,' warbled my erstwhile player, but I was heading for the bar downstairs. If he didn't want to listen to me, he was beyond hope.

I got my pint after a bayonet charge through the mob of dealers and paid for Tinker's pint to be sent into the taproom. The filthy old devil gave me a gappy grin through the bar hatch but it quickly changed to consternation when I gave him the bent eye. He eeled into the porch.

'What's up, Lovejoy? We in trouble?'

'The goon bought it.'

He goggled, wiped his stubble in a tattered sleeve. 'Christ. An' you let him?'

'What the hell could I do? He's in the ring, not me.'

There are two good things about Tinker. He's the world's best barker—slang for antiques finder—and he stinks to high heaven. The first is great because I'm Tinker's wally, the antique dealer he finds for. The second is great because his pong clears a space in any crowd, so I can pay for more beer. Like now.

'He must be off his friggin' nut, Lovejoy.' He hitched his frayed ex-army greatcoat and shook his head, mystified. 'He know you was a divvie?'

'That's why he hired me, you burke.'

'Here, Lovejoy.' Grinning, he plucked at my arm with his grease-stained mitten. 'I'd like to be there when them London buyers tell him it's a fake.' He fell about at the notion, cackling evilly.

'Everybody'll think I guessed wrong,' I grumbled.

'Nar,' Tinker said scornfully, grabbing another ale. 'Every dealer in East Anglia knows you.'

'Everybody but Malleson. Where is she, Tinker?'

'Your bint? By the fire.' He took the note I slipped him. 'I reckon she's makin' for 'flu, Lovejoy. She only has orange juice.'

Even fuming, I had to laugh at that. The thought of anybody drinking an orange's crushed innards makes him giddy. I told him, 'Be in the boozer eightish. Find out who vans off that Yankee silver salver, and if that Tadolini *Venus and Cupid* changes hands before tonight.'

'Right, mate.'

The rare Edward Winslow salver was a delight, made in Boston about 1695. The illicit ring upstairs would bid for it soon. I had to know who eventually owned it because that's where tomorrow's fakes would come from. It was worth a couple of new cars in anybody's shop window. The Tadolini figure was as beautiful, but only 1845 or so and about a quarter of the price. Rome always did nice stuff, with or without an empire.

Sure enough Connie was there, scrunged up over the pub's log fire. She's always perished, even in the hottest bed.

'Darling. At last.' She reached up to my hand. 'It's so

draughty here. Can we go?'

'Bring my bag.'

We sliced the fug and reached the great beyond where my zoomster waited hub-deep in its flaking rust.

'Why *do* we carry this stupid thing, darling?' Connie indicated the plastic bag. It carried Christie's insignia, 1766, South Kensington.

'To impress customers.'

If her teeth hadn't been chattering from the cold she would have screamed with laughter. She just muttered, 'In this ancient open boat?' and climbed in. Lovely legs.

'You can always walk,' I countered, flipping the switch and going round to crank the handle. It's an old Austin Ruby. People are always trying to nick its candle-powered headlamps and door handles. Connie gets mad because it has no top roof, and the cover doesn't work.

A young bloke nearby laughed, disconcertingly shrill. He was in one of those de Loreans and seemed all fawns and yellows. I shrugged, deciding not to take offence. His lemon leathers could have bought and sold me. I tend not to argue with wealthy dealers because they're the dumbest. Just to prove it, a familiar if irritating voice sounded in my earhole.

'A word, Lovejoy.' Good old knowledgeable wiseacre Mr Malleson had caught us up and stood there in his posh gaberdine. 'Good day, Mrs Lovejoy,' he added, eyeing Connie. I didn't mind that because you can't help looking long and hard at Connie.

'A friend,' I corrected quickly, in case she developed a craving.

'Excuse us, please,' he said with courtesy. I could tell he was frosty. 'Lovejoy. I wanted you for the Flemish marquetry cabinet the northern dealer was putting in the ring. The one with the metallic-paint effect.'

'It's genuine.' I'd told him this a hundred times, but London antique dealers are as thick as those from anywhere else. And, after today's performance, maybe thicker. 'Antwerp, say 1670, 1680. And while we're at it, that metallic paint is chip mother-of-pearl.'

'I failed,' he said, stone-faced. 'The bidding went quite extraordinary after you left —'

'Almost as if the others were ganging up?'

'That's right. I'm not blaming you, Lovejoy —'

'No, Mr Malleson. But *I'm* blaming *you*.' I gave the handle a savage crank and the engine spluttered obediently. If it hadn't I'd have kicked it to bits, the temper I was in.

'Me? Why?' The duckegg was honestly amazed. I ask you.

'You hired me to suss out genuine antiques, right?'

'Of course. You have the reputation of being a divvie. A very valuable gift.'

'Which means I can *feel* genuine antiques, right?'

My car door falls off if you pull the handle, so I stepped over the door and slid behind the wheel.

'Well, yes. That's the supposition, Lovejoy.'

'Not supposition. Truth. I tipped you that painting is modern phoney, and you still bought it.'

'That was your opinion, Lovejoy.'

'Wrong, Mr Malleson.' My frost was at least as cold as his. 'A divvie just *knows*. That's very, very different from a mere opinion.'

'I see. Offended pride.' He gave one of his wintry smiles, clearly the London zillionaire dealer coping with troublesome provincial riff-raff. 'Tell me, Lovejoy. Are you an expert on formalisms in Tiepolo's composition?'

'No.'

'Canvas microscopy? Spectrographic analysis of paint? Chemicals?' He went mercilessly down a formidable list, getting a denial every time. 'It may interest you to know, Lovejoy, that I am an expert on all those topics. And there's one other proof.' He eyed me and my zoomster.

'The fact is you are threadbare, frayed, generally ill-attired and clearly subnourished. Your obsolete car is falling apart. I, on the other hand, have the best from each year's motor show. Three London tailors work very hard to please me. Do I make my point?'

'You'll not be the first expert art dealer I've visited in clink, Mr Malleson,' I said evenly, and gunned my half-pint engine as a hint. 'Sell that fake, and Scotland Yard's fraud squad'll come peering in your window.'

He was examining me curiously. 'You're so sure?'

'There's no question. That gunge was painted this side of Easter.'

He smiled a disbelieving smile and pulled out a bolster-sized wallet. 'We can only agree to disagree, then. Here's half your fee.'

The sight of the notes he held out made my heart fill with longing but to my horror I felt my stupid head shake. My voice said, 'No, thanks, Mr Malleson. I won't help you defraud yourself.'

The engine wheezed and the little Ruby trundled off leaving him standing there. A couple of dealers cheered derisorily and Linda gave me a wave from the saloon bar's window. I saw the ash blonde by that elegant lemon-tinted customed de Lorean. She must have heard every word. As we clattered out on to the main Edmundsbury road Crampie tried flagging me down. His real name's Cramphorn, but with a name like Lovejoy you learn discrimination at an early age.

'Can't stop, Crampie,' I bawled over my engine's din. 'On my way to a deal.'

'Get stuffed, Lovejoy,' he yelled back. 'Thought you were in a Rolls-Royce, not a sewing-machine.'

'Lovejoy!' Connie was scandalized. 'He's your dealer friend! You can't leave him standing in the cold wind.'

Honestly. People are so innocent. Ben Cramphorn's a roadman — that is, he procures lifts pretending he's on his way to buy his poor dying friend's priceless antique. His 'poor dying friend' is fit as a flea because it's his partner Phil Watmore, made up to look ailing. The 'priceless' antique is any old chunk of dross they can't sell. The aim is to get the kindly motorist interested in buying the antique and driving to Phil's auntie's house in Wivenhoe, which is the place they usually work from, seeing she pays the rates, rent and all other costs. Sounds very dicey, doesn't it? Surprising how often it works.

'You're awful, Lovejoy!' Connie was fuming.

'I'll tell Ken you said that.' He's Connie's husband. They own this small chain of shops, shoes or something.

'Where's the heater on this thing, Lovejoy?' That's the best about Connie. Predictability. Her thoughts never leave temperature for long. 'Is there no way we can stop this terrible gale? Take your hand off my knee.'

'I'll stop for a hot-water bottle,' I said.

'Will you, darling?' she said eagerly. 'That's a good idea.'

I glared at her, marvelling. There she sat, hair streaming in the wind, slender throat deep in her mohair, eyes sparkling, luscious lips moist, eyes dazzling. As exciting a picture of beauty as ever a woman can be, and still she takes a sardonic crack as gospel.

She put her arm through mine. 'I hated Mr Malleson. He has no right to speak to you like that. Even if you do look a mess I love you, darling.'

'Er, thanks, love,' I said. Sometimes women baffle me. We pulled in this dark lay-by because I was getting desperate. Only a woman can rub out the toxic anger of a failure such as I'd endured, and Connie regarded sex on the move as vulgarity gone mad.

Which is how we came within a few seconds of seeing the whole terrible thing.

My old crate, wheezing and panting, was waiting to get back on the road—no mean feat, this, because it was uphill at the lay-by's re-entry point—when a limousine cruised out of the darkness behind its great headlights, and I recognized it as Mr Malleson's.

'How lovely!' Connie cried. 'He gave Mr Cramphorn a lift, Lovejoy.'

'Shut up.'

I too had glimpsed two figures in the car. Narked at being reminded yet again of my stupendous failure at the ring auction, I trundled us out clattering into the slipstream. So Crampie was working his antiques scam on Mr Malleson. I wished him luck. The rate my old Ruby trundles, it would be a good hour before I reached my cottage, where Connie would raise me to paradise and send the memory of this catastrophic day into an oblivion it richly deserved.

It was to be a lot longer.

CHAPTER 2

'Stop, Lovejoy! Please!'

'What for?'

'It's Mr Malleson's car! With the police!'

East Anglia becomes a desert of country darkness after dusk. Those roadside cafés are oases of light in the pitch night, because we lack those natty road lamps which make towns so wonderful.

'No.'

'Please! You *must*, Lovejoy! Your friends are in trouble.'

Nothing's so poisonous as a woman bent on Doing Good. These days nobody in their right mind stops at these lonely road noshbars. And you especially don't when those irritable blue lamps are blinking ghoulishly from ambulances and police cars. I tried explaining that yobbos had probably nicked some dealer's antiques from his car—par for the course, really—but Connie turned ugly.

'No love, then, Lovejoy.'

She didn't really mean it, couldn't in fact, and she knew it. But what she did know was that her threat would make me dispirited. I tend to lose heart easily. Teachers at school used to call me spineless but never taught me out of it. I applied the brake—note that singular—and my Ruby contemplated itself to a dawdling stop, drifting sideways as its one block persuasively caressed its feeble motive power into clattering idleness.

'Come *on!*' Connie was already out and trotting back towards the lights. Miserably I followed, cursing. My instincts were drive on with every erg my rusty old zoomster could generate.

Two ambulances hurtled out in tandem, nearly flattening Connie and me. Several bored police constables were hanging about. A few lorry-drivers chatted and exchanged cigarettes, eyeing Connie as we entered the ring of lights on the forecourt.

It was a typical roadside caff. Low hut, depleted neon sign, a few multicoloured bulbs on trailed flex, dark trees crowding in beyond. A few parked lorries, one or two ordinary cars. Mr Malleson's car was prominently agape nearby. Connie, with all the tact of a Stuka, rushed into the fray squealing questions. By the time I came up the whole world knew that Mr Malleson and Crampie had been rushed to hospital. Connie has a habit of repeating in a shrill cry any answers she gets.

'Before you start, Mr Ledger,' I said to the older of the two CID men, 'I must caution you that anything you say will be taken down and flatly contradicted by my alibi.'

'Lovejoy.' He's not a bad old nerk, as cretins go, but we've never got on. Not because he has this unshakable belief that I'm a villain, but because I have this unshakable belief that he's a bigger one. 'Where were you?'

I walked on past while Connie squealed yet more questions. The lorry-drivers, six or seven, were being questioned in turn by a constable with a tape-recorder. The space age. I selected a squat, canny little bloke who'd obviously got fed up and was sitting on his lorry's running-board.

'One of them was my mate,' I said, sitting by him.

'Oh, aye?' Rossendale accent, clean-shaven, tidy. A family man keen on simply polishing off his congealed egg-and-chips and roaring off northwards.

'See much?'

'Not really. There were four or so. Three heavies and a girlish bloke in a bright suit. Sports car, but I didn't see it. Only heard it go beyond the hedge. Stocking masks. A little van.' He spat expertly. 'They drove it across the frigging intersection.'

Smart, that. It was illegal, so nobody could legally give chase.

'Were they bad?'

'Sorry, mate.' He shook his head. 'They both looked poorly, especially the scruff who came in to phone.' He meant Crampie, doing his road trick. 'The city gent was waiting in the car. We heard the hullabaloo. Me and my mate come running and chucked stones, but the buggers were gone. Yon bobby says they pinched a picture.'

'A painting?'

'God knows.' He looked at me, offering a cigarette. I lit up as politeness, though I don't smoke them. I'm in enough trouble. 'Here, lad. If you're going after them I'd watch yon pansy bloke. He clobbered both your mates after his mob had emptied the car. A wrench.'

'Ta, mate.' I rose. 'Regards to the Duchy.'

His face lit in a smile. 'Go careful.'

More common sense in two minutes than you'd get in a

thousand years at university. If only I'd listened to the man.

'Come on, love,' I said to Connie, not pausing. ' 'Night, Ledger.'

'Lovejoy. Where were you when—?'

Connie trotted after, holding her coat round herself as tightly as she could in the night wind. 'That was very rude of you, Lovejoy.'

'Darlin',' I said. 'It's very rude of Ledger to let Crampie and Mr Malleson get done in a crash-wallop. So criticize me second, not first.'

'Some men stole all Mr Malleson's things! Did you hear? And Inspector Ledger's police cars are already searching for the culprits!' She was in raptures at how wonderful our police were.

'Cheapest way of getting antiques,' I said cruelly. 'And the safest. Get in.'

We got to the hospital in Black Notley a few minutes too late, though I don't suppose Crampie would have been able to tell us anything. He was unconscious for his last moments. When I came out after seeing the house surgeon Connie said the police cars had just pulled away.

Connie pulled her overcoat tight round her lovely knees. 'It's freezing. Did you see Crampie?'

'Crampie just died, love. Mr Malleson was dead when they got here.'

'Darling. I'm so sorry. That little man we didn't even give a lift . . . ?' Tears filled her and she wept.

It wasn't any use explaining that Crampie'd not even have accepted a lift from me even if I'd offered him one. Anyway, I was becoming exhausted explaining every little problem to hangers-on. I sat listening to her sniffing, watching the nurses and sisters move beyond the Casualty glass and the tired young house surgeon slumping over the desk writing up case-notes. All their training, all their labour over Mr Malleson and Crampie, had been a gigantic waste.

'Help me, Connie, love.'

My voice must have given something away. She blotted herself dry and nodded.

'Ready.'

Connie may have cold blood, but she sees things I don't. I drove us back to my cottage, talking all the while and explaining my slight problem. Why would certain dealers bid themselves almost into poverty for a fake, and antique thieves pull a raid for that same fake? Worse, at least one of them had found a sadistic glee in needlessly making murder.

Hours later we were still going over the lorry-driver's story, the pansified bloke in the lemon-tinted suit, the events at the auction.

Getting on for seven we were lying in bed at my cottage.

To feed us, Connie had knocked up a soup thing in my little kitchen alcove, and did something called goulash. It had been good, but I was narked with her for throwing my last pasty out. She claimed it wasn't fresh, bloody cheek. Apart from these visits from enthusiasts like Connie, pasties are my staple fare and seeing my last pasty get the sailor's elbow was disheartening. It was a sign that my days of wine and roses were over. Locusts would soon settle on the land of Lovejoy Antiques, Inc. I was about to be spring-cleaned.

'You should have taken Mr Malleson's money.' Connie was propped on one elbow, her lovely skin glowing and her smooth breast cool against my face. 'You earned it.'

'Accepting payment means I'd be responsible for him, the goon.'

'You shouldn't speak ill of the . . .' She shivered and caped the bedclothes round her shoulders. She hadn't understood the mysticism of the secret auction ring of the antique dealers, so I had to explain.

Auctions have been around a long time but have changed very little. Oh, we don't any longer do like in Ancient Rome — stick a spear, the famous *hasta publica*, upright in the market square to show one's about to begin — but we do more or less the same as in Pliny the Elder's day. But be careful. There are different kinds.

Everybody knows the common or 'English' auction where the bidders' prices start off low and simply go up a notch with each bid. However there's also a 'Dutch' auction, where the auctioneer starts at a high price, and then calls out ever-lower prices, until a bidder stutters out that he's willing to pay that much. And there's the so-called market auction, where you bid merrily, English-style, but for *one* representative sample of a particular lot, and where you needn't accept more than that one at the price you've successfully bid. Market-style auctions are pretty rare in antiques, except where there's a whole batch of stuff which the auctioneer's willing to split, say a load of old desks, plates, chairs, cutlery and so on. Then there's a 'time' auction, where you get a length of time to *complete* (not start, note) your bidding. The most famous example of this is that French wine auction business, where anybody can carry on bidding anything — for as long as the auctioneer's candle-stub stays lit. It's a real cliff-hanger, because the bidding ends the exact instant the guttering candle snuffs. And there's the famous 'paper' auction, where the auctioneer announces a price below which he won't go, and bidders have numbered or named cards. You simply write down your bid, and the slips are collected by minions. Antique dealers hate this, because it calls for frankness and honesty, probably why it's going out of fashion.

Yes, it pays to suss out the rules governing the particular auction you wish to attend. It might prevent you going broke. But auction risks don't end there. There's the new-fangled cheque trick (bid high, pay the 10% deposit immediately by cheque, try to sell the item for a fast profit that day—and, if you can't, just stop the cheque claiming all sorts of false catalogue description). There's the 'knock-out', where antique dealers resort to any trick to impede or con the public out of bids. There's even evil in some auctioneers themselves (Lord save us!), their assistants, vannies, valuers, clerks, experts and, last and most, the public. We don't have state-owned auction-rooms like the Dorotheum in Vienna, and I'm quite glad about that. 'At least in our system roguery is predictable and perennial,' I told Connie. 'I'd hate it to be legal too.'

Connie thought the ring auction a lot of pointless trouble. 'Why auction among yourselves if you've just already bought them?'

'The dealers all agree not to bid at the public auction. Only one dealer bids. So the price is lower, right? Then the dealers gather in a pub and have their private little auction. The difference in Gimbert's price and the ring's price is the profit, and is shared out. See?'

Connie was outraged. 'But that's not fair!' she cried.

I pulled her down and inevitably her perishing cold feet climbed inchwise up my legs.

'I know that. But the first-ever successful prosecution for an illicit auction ring was in 1981. It's hopeless.'

She forgot the draughts long enough to raise her head off my chest and peer at me. 'But why were you there, darling?'

'I was made to go,' I lied, putting on my noble face. 'Wanted to buy you a present.'

Her eyes filled with tears. 'Darling,' she said, all misty. 'And you risked being caught, put in prison for *life*, just for me?' Even I felt quite moved by my story, and I'd just made it up.

'Well, love,' I said brokenly. 'I don't give you much. And this cottage isn't much of a place to bring you . . .'

'It's absolutely beautiful!' she cried defiantly. 'I just love the village and your lovely little home!'

If she'd agreed it was crummy I'd have thumped her there and then. Hastily I told her how wonderful she was, with inevitable consequences. Also inevitably, she briefly halted the romance for meteorological reasons.

'Darling, couldn't we make love the other way round, then we can stay under the bedclothes?'

'For you, anything,' I said. She said I was so sweet, which is true, though when I came to afterwards I was still narked with her about my last pasty. A single pasty can keep you going a whole day sometimes, which is more than can be said for almost anything else you can think of.

I saw Connie off about ten to eight. She helped me to fold the bed away (it's really a divan thing) and lent me some money for tomorrow's grub. She also sprang a present on me, a pair of shoes obviously nicked from one of husband Ken's shops.

'They're expensive, darling,' she said. 'Real handmade leather.'

'Thanks, love.'

'They look marvellous.' She was thrilled because they fitted. Two days before she had measured me with a complicated sextant-looking gadget. I could tell she was worried in case she got the width wrong. 'Now *wear* them. Don't let me find them in a cupboard weeks from now. Cross your heart?'

'Let me cross yours instead.'

'Oh, you,' she said.

We went to the porch arm in arm. The porch light doesn't work. I'll mend it when I get a minute, but for the moment it was usefully dark. Still, nobody could see us because the people across the lane are always out sailing or racing motors round Silverstone and that, and our lane leads nowhere in particular.

'Got your car keys, love?'

'Yes, darling. See you soon. I'll come early.'

I groaned inwardly. A morning tryst meant she had designs on my dust. She usually brings a vacuum cleaner and blizzards through the cottage till I'm demented.

' 'Night, love.'

She clung shivering for a minute to show the cold night breeze that she knew it was out there, then ran with a squeal of hatred into the pitch dark. She leaves her grand coupé on my gravel path so customers won't spot her car parked in some leafy lay-by and go prattling gossip.

'Go in, darling!' she cried back. 'You'll catch your death!'

'Right, love.' I didn't move. It was quite mild, really, but I've noticed women talk themselves into a shiver. Connie's headlights washed over my garden, shrinking it and fetching the trees comfortably closer. They struck a gleam off something beyond the hedge. I wondered idly what it was. Maybe I'd have a look when I could get round to it.

Connie revved, ambitiously stirring the gears and frightening my garden voles by showering the countryside with flying gravel as she backed and veered. I counted her turns. Three, four, five, six. The horn pipped a triumphant pip and she was off, her rear reds flickering as she zoomed past the hawthorns. That was good, I thought approvingly. She usually takes seven goes to negotiate the gateway.

Nothing can gleam down in our lane except glow-worms and a parked car. I felt daft just standing there so I walked out. No engines roared, no yobbos bawled.

'Good evening, Lovejoy. Caterina Norman.' The ash-blonde bird showed faintly in the greenish dashboard illumination. 'Your phone is disconnected.'

'Er, a slight misunderstanding about the bill.'

'You're to come with me,' she said, dead cool. 'Tomorrow. My grandfather wants to speak to you.'

That's all I wanted, another bird giving me orders. 'I'm busy tomorrow.'

'Surely you can stop . . . *work* for a moment or two.' Her tone was dry. She'd obviously seen more than she wanted when Connie departed. 'It's not far.'

'Well, look. Can't we leave it?' I was knackered. What with the whole day in the auction aggro, the failure with Mr Malleson, and Connie, I needed a restful day reading about beautiful antiques.

'He's an antiques collector, Lovejoy. And he has a task for you.'

That did it. Maybe grandad was a potential buyer. Never mind that I hadn't a single antique in the place. Potential money's only heading one way, right? And that word: task. Not 'job', not 'some work'. Task. There's something indelibly mediæval about it, isn't there? Beowulf and the Arthurian knights did tasks. Profitable things, tasks—or so I thought.

CHAPTER 3

Next morning I was up as usual about seven, frying tomatoes. The robin came flicking along the hedge to the wall where it plays hell till I shut it up with diced cheese. Blue tits were tapping the side window and the sparrows and blackbirds were all in round my feet. A right lorryload of chisellers. And soon the bloody hedgehog would be awake and come snuffling its saucer for pobs, greedy little swine. How Snow White kept so bloody cheerful with this menagerie I'll never know. I tell you I'm the easiest touch in East Anglia.

It wasn't raining for once so I took my breakfast out — it's only bread-and-dip really — and sat on a low wall I've nearly finished. I set my trannie to a trillion decibels to frighten off scrounging wildlife, but the robin only came and nonchalantly cleaned its feet on it with such pointed indifference that I had to share the brown bread.

The robin cackled angrily and flew off, though I'd been stuffing it with grub. Somebody must be coming. Sure enough, Tinker came shuffling up the path, muttering and grumbling.

' 'Morning, Tinker. Get a ride on Jacko's wagon?'

'Aye, thieving old bleeder. Charged me a quid.'

Jacko's a senile villager who runs a van (summer) and a horse wagon (winter) between our village and the nearby town. The van's an elderly reject from the town market. The wagon's a superannuated coal cart pulled by Terence. Jacko sings to entertain his passengers, which is one way of lessening the load.

'You didn't pay him?' I asked, alarmed.

'Nar. Gave him your IOU.'

I sighed in relief. Great. One more debtor. Tinker absently took a chunk of bread in his filthy mittens and dipped in. Like I said, the easiest touch in East Anglia. Still, no good postponing the bad news.

'Crampie and Mr Malleson got done, Tinker.'

'Yeah. Rotten, eh?' I wasn't surprised that he knew. 'That's what I came about, Lovejoy. Patrick see'd last night's rumble.'

I knew better than to doubt his mental radar. 'Patrick? Actually witnessed it? Anybody else?'

'No. But some of the wallies was askin' at the hospital, like you.'

'Who?'

'Patrick. Helen. Margaret Dainty. Linda who was in the ring. That Manchester bloke who comes after antique lacework and Queen Anne clothes. Big Frank from Suffolk.'

He knew this was disturbing. Even if my old Ruby can hardly raise a gallop, I had happened along pretty smartish, and yet Crampie and Mr Malleson had died.

'Margaret's out,' I said. She's the only one of us who's respectable. Tell you about her if I get a minute. Helen's beautiful but hardly a gang leader. Linda was my old flame from the ring. The Manchester bloke was a regular and had his own turf. Big Frank was only interested in marriage, divorce, and antique silver—in reverse order. No suspects among that lot, but a witness is a witness. Jacko's wagon would be starting for town in half an hour.

'Tell Jacko to wait, Tinker. I'll catch you up.'

'The Three Cups opens in an hour, Lovejoy.' He ambled off—his idea of speed—cackling with enthusiasm.

We trundled into town just as the pubs opened, with me still thinking. Something's not quite right, my imbecilic mind guessed. If they gave a Nobel Prize for indecision I'd win it hands down.

I gave Jacko another scribbled IOU and told him the fare was scandalous.

'That why you never pay me, Lovejoy?' he bawled after but I pretended not to hear. I'm sick of scroungers.

We stopped at the corner of Lion Walk, The Three Cups obviously pulling at Tinker's heartstrings. 'Okay,' I surrendered, giving him his note. 'Where's Patrick?'

He thought hard. No mean feat this, when sober. His rheumy old eyes creaked open after a minute. 'Patrick's with Elsie. They're in the Arcade.'

My heart sank. 'Don't you mean Patrick and Lily? I thought—'

'Nar, Lovejoy. He gave Lily the push last night over him seeing that sailor.'

'Ah,' I said as if I understood.

He shot into the boozer with my last groat. I plodded down the town's expensive new shopping precinct—think of redbrick cubes filled with litter—into the Arcade. This is a glass-covered alley. To either side is a series of tiny antique shops, only alcoves really, with antique dealers moaning how grim life is and how broke they are. Tinker was right. Someone emitted a screech.

'Ooooh.'

I followed the shrill groans—the only known groans higher than top G. Today Patrick was in magenta, with purple wedge heels and an ultramarine sequined cape. As if that wasn't enough, he was being restored by Elsie who was frantically patting some pungent toilet water across his cheeks. Margaret Dainty was looking harassed because Patrick had carefully selected her little shop to swoon in, slumping elegantly across a 1765 Chippendale Gothic chair in mahogany. I didn't even know she had one of these rarities.

Awed shoppers were milling about. Understandable, really, because Patrick standing still's a ghastly enough spectacle. Doing Hamlet's death scene he's beyond belief.

I decided not to ask Elsie about Lily. I'm no fool.

'Ooooh,' Patrick moaned, false eyelashes fluttering.

I crouched down, avoiding Elsie's cascade of eau de Cologne. 'One thing worries me, Pat. Why is it you always get bad news before anybody else?'

His stare gimleted me in sudden recovery. 'Patrick!' he screamed, giving me a mouthful of invective. 'Pat's so . . . uncouth.' He instantly reverted to a swoon. 'Ooooh!'

Elsie wailed, 'Please don't upset him, Lovejoy!'

'Mr Malleson and Crampie,' I prompted the reclining figure. 'Who, when and why, mate?'

Patrick sobbed dramatically, beating his breast in anguish. 'Poor Mr Malleson! How many more catastrophes can I be expected to bear?' His voice went suddenly normal. 'Mind my handbag, dear. It's handmade crocodile.' And immediately went back to showbiz. 'Oh, woe! Oh, heartbreak! Oh—'

I looked across at the distraught Margaret. She's a lovable friend, if you can imagine such a thing, though she's a mite oldish and limps a bit. Still, you can't pass up someone who loves you and has looks and compassion. Saints get beatified for less. Look at Czar Nicholas. 'You tell me, love.'

'We haven't been able to get a word out of him—'

'Right.'

I tipped Patrick off the chair with a crash. He screamed, which is hard to understand because the Chippendale antique wasn't even scratched. 'You perfect *beast*, Lovejoy! And *you* can stop *drenching* me in *stink*, you silly cow!'

I'm sure Patrick only does all this to get an audience. God knows what he does when he's alone, probably just goes into suspended animation.

'Sorry, dearest,' Elsie sobbed. 'Now see what you've done, Lovejoy!'

A bobby was pausing outside in the High Street to inspect the swelling crowd in the Arcade. Things looked like getting distinctly out of hand. I put a knee on Patrick's chest.

'Tell, or I'll crumple your cravat. You were there, weren't you?'

He wheezed as I pressed harder. 'Yes. Three great *bruisers* out of a lorry did it. Wrenches and things. They hit poor Mr Malleson.' His eyes welled with tears as he sniffed out the rest of the story. 'Crampie positively *begged* for mercy. It was *ghastly*, Lovejoy. They *snatched* that perfectly delicious painting.'

'Where were you?'

'In my car with . . . a friend.'

'What were they like?' I know it was night, but there

had been some light.

'Oh, quite *plain*, really, though one could have *really* improved himself with the right suit. Quite young, rather light hair for a foreigner . . . ghastly primrose leather jacket . . .'

'Foreigner? How do you know that?'

The bobby had decided to move into the Arcade. Sensing a bigger audience, Patrick immediately shrieked his way into frank hysteria.

I knew enough about lay-by scuffles to realize it was hopeless getting anything more definite. I kissed Margaret so-long and said I'd honestly see her soon. She told me to be careful and to come for supper one evening. I promised to and managed to say honestly twice more as I shot out.

I'm not much on the police force. Its useful bits are mostly hooked on its own problems, and the rest is a monstrous anachronism. Ledger'd tell me nothing, so they were best forgotten.

Instead I got hold of Tinker and told him to drum up news of any antiques genuine or fake, resembling the painting. He was narked at that because the boozer was still open but I gave him the bent eye and said get going. The lazy old devil went shuffling off, a couple of brown ales clinking in his shabby overcoat.

Then from the phone-box by the war memorial I rang Connie and asked her to lend me a few more quid and could she please fill her motor up with petrol and let me borrow it. I had a secret notion to impress the blonde bird instead of being embarrassed in my old Ruby. She hesitated. I said, 'If you don't I'll make you do all the sky bits in my next jigsaw puzzle.'

'Sadist.' Then she sweetly added she'd come along too, because we didn't want Lovejoy using borrowed wealth to pick up some bone-headed young tart, did we? Bitterly I agreed that we didn't want that, and stood miserably by the traffic lights near the Castle Park entrance thinking of her bloody cheek. Women have no trust in their fellow man, that's what it is.

CHAPTER 4

'Suss this out, love,' I asked Connie in the torrid heat of her vast motor. We were parked among the trees by the football ground for secrecy. One other good thing about Connie is that she loves gossip. Attentively she sat in her pale apple costume, with pearl necklace and earrings revealing class. I gave her Patrick's account. As far as I knew it added nothing, but Connie with her devious woman's mind instantly saw a crack.

'Why didn't the police ask Patrick all this?'

'They did. He wouldn't tell them.'

'Why not, if he told you he'd actually seen those three brutes?'

'Well, er, he was, er, with some bloke . . . You see, love, erm, Patrick's, erm . . .'

'Another queer,' Connie said, nodding briskly. 'So now we must find his lady friend.'

I had my doubts. 'Elsie? No use, Connie. I heard she was in Ilford until late. And Patrick had some row with Lily last night.'

She got excited. 'Don't you see? Lily must have learned about Patrick going to meet his friend and followed.'

'So Lily maybe knows something extra?'

She gave me a sweet smile. 'You're learning, darling. Close that car window. There's a draught.'

Lily was part way through a bottle of gin by the look of things, and dark blue gondolas of sorrow hung fleshily beneath her eyes. Worse, she instantly took against Connie, even when I'd introduced them with my best Edwardian gallantry. Plainly she would reveal nothing while a strange woman was in the house so I had to ask Connie to wait outside. She left Lily's hallway, managing to slam three doors on her way to sulk in the car.

'Come through, Lovejoy. My husband's abroad again.' I breathed a sigh of relief and followed her in. The telly was on. Lily's living-room was a fug of fag smoke. 'Have you seen Patrick?' she asked wistfully. 'How is he?'

'Upset,' I said lamely. I'm not much good at this sort of thing.

'Is he?' she looked up hopefully. 'I suppose that crabby geriatric rat-bag Elsie Hayward's smarming round him.' When I said nothing she grew aggressive. 'Now you tell me the truth, Lovejoy.'

'Yes. In the Arcade.'

'Bitch. She's had more false starts with men than all the tarts in Soho. He'll come back to me, Lovejoy—won't he?'

'Erm, quite possibly.'

She subsided on to an armchair. 'Oh, Lovejoy. What a mess. Why can't he *see* that it's *me* he needs?'

'Last night, Lily. You followed Patrick.'

'Mmmmh. He'd got some man in his car.' She looked piteous. 'It's only a weakness, Lovejoy. This phase.'

'Sorry, love,' I said helplessly. 'But you saw?'

'Yes. It was that horrid sickly sailor man he usually—'

'I mean the goons, Lily. Patrick said one was foreign. What accent?'

'I didn't pay much attention. I was frightened. The van had been waiting for Mr Malleson and Crampie. They hit them, really *hit* them, Lovejoy. Then the young man shouted "Get the painting!" The men didn't care. They jumped in the van.'

'And you rang the police, Lily?'

She shook her head. 'No. I just sat there and watched.

The lorry-drivers came running, but the van went.'

'No other facts, Lily?'

'He was continental, Lovejoy. Maybe Austrian, that sort of accent. And flashy.' She shivered and pulled her dressing-gown tighter round her. 'Lovejoy,' she said, heartbroken. 'He was laughing. The young one, in bright colours. Once they had the painting he ran back and hit Mr Malleson and Crampie. While they were on the ground. Oh, they lay so still.'

I consoled her as much as I could, saying thanks and Patrick was sure to come back soon. She asked tearfully did I really think so and I said sure, just you see. I felt I'd been through the mangle when I escaped.

Connie was freezing but excited to know what Lily had seen. I told her all of it, hoping she might do her helpful guessing trick again.

'Didn't she tell Ledger any of this?'

'And get Patrick in trouble? Ledger would ask what she was doing herself, parked in the night hours near the scene of an antiques robbery. After all, she's an antique dealer herself — on good days.'

'Darling. Who *would* want the fake so badly? It doesn't make sense.'

'That bird.'

'In the auction?' Connie's mental radar blipped hatred into her mind. 'That one trying to attract everybody's attention in the car park with the wrong hairstyle?'

'She bid a fortune for the fake even though she knew it was duff. Mr Malleson went bid-happy so she ducked out.' Maybe she had decided to acquire the painting by the most decisive of all methods — armed robbery. Thugs are easy enough to hire anywhere these days, God knows. 'Drive me to the High Street.'

'Only if you take your hands off, darling. Your fingers are freezing.'

'How else can I get them warm?'

We argued all the way back to the cottage. The rest of the day was full of pleasure, and therefore uneventful.

CHAPTER 5

It was coming dusk when Connie finally left. I was in good time and ready when the bird called. I cranked my zoomster's engine and lit its lamps while she went on at me.

'You're not coming in that thing?' The blonde leaned from her perfumed cocoon and gazed down at me. 'We'll take all night.'

'Race you,' I said with dignity.

Her car rolled, sneering, up the lane. My crate clattered reproachfully in its wake. It hates being out after dark. The bird was waiting by the chapel, deep engine thrumming and her fingers doubtless tapping irritably. Pricey motor-cars like her are all very well for a year or two. After that they go wrong and decay in forgotten yards. It's filthy little heaps like mine that keep going. Grandeur tends to rapid obsolescence. Unaware I'd reasoned my way to a conclusion which ought to have warned me of impending danger, I drove through the dark village. Wheezing, backfiring, creaking at every joint, Lovejoy Antiques, Inc. was on the move and full of confidence.

Sometimes I'm just pathetic.

Fingringhoe's one of these straggly villages a stone's throw from the sea. You can scent the sealands. Many of the inlets are reserved for birds and mice and whatnot to do their respective thing, making a crashing bore of the whole soggy area. I mean, not an antique shop for miles, a few scatterings of houses along lost lanes, a field or two with yawning cows, and that's it. Our diligent conservationists are busy keeping it that way. They've a lot to answer for.

Following the blonde bird's car in my horseless carriage was like rowing a coracle behind a liner. I kept coming upon it, lights at every orifice, revving impatiently at dark crossroads, but I kept cool. I've been humiliated by experts in my time so degradation at her hands meant little. We turned left at the pub. She tore into the black countryside behind her monstrous beams and I puttered after.

We were close to the sea when she hurtled into a gateway set back from the lane. Apart from a distant low gleam of the sea horizon and the bright windows of the Georgian house beyond the beeches there was nothing to guide you. The drive was paved, if you please, not merely gravelled or tarred, proving that pride had not yet vanished among the country set. Nor had scorn. She gave me some derision free, airily walking through the porch and leaving me to park my knackered heap and hurry after.

The house inside was beautiful. The inner chimes from the antiques all around reverberated in my chest so strongly I had to pause and clutch at the doorway for support.

'This way.' The bird was narked by the delay. Impatiently she waved away a motherly-looking serf who was coming forward to process this stray nocturnal visitor. There was a world's wealth of antiques everywhere on walls and floors and furniture. Mesmerized, I advanced reverently over the Isfahan carpet which partly veiled the mosaic hall floor. It was hard work. A Turner watercolour radiated its dazzling brilliance on the wall, and you can't say fairer than that.

In contrast, the study was not well lit. Panels of original

oak (none of your modern imported Japanese stuff), shelves of books with delectable white parchment covers, a Gainsborough nude drawing, furniture mainly by Ince and Mayhew and a real Canaletto I failed to recognize but which finally fetched out of my anguished throat that moan I'd been hoarding.

The old man in the chair was pleased.

'You are impressed by my possessions, Lovejoy,' he piped. His voice was a pre-Boehm glass flute, sonorous yet high-pitched and miles off. 'I cannot convey how gratifying your response is.'

'*Are* there people who puke at fortunes?'

He tried to roar with laughter, actually falling about and swaying in the great leather chair. His roar was practically inaudible. I've heard infants breathe louder. Politely I waited while he choked and the bird resuscitated him with well-meaning pummels between his shoulders. She had to blot his eyes, blow his nose, find his specs and generally cobble the old geezer together. It took a hell of a time. I was drawn to a jewelled snuffbox set on an illuminated covered stand. It looked very like Frederick the Great's cartouche-shaped favourite which Christie's sold for nearly half a million quid. The Emperor was a great collector of them, but this thing was never one of his famous 300. It was a clear fake. Not a tremor of love in it.

Somebody gripped my arm, broke the spell.

'Sit down when you're told.' The bird, clearly an apprentice matriarch, shoved me at a chair. 'Grandfather shouldn't have to suffer your rudeness.'

'Caterina.' The gentle reproof was enough to shut her up and leave her seething with irritation. I sat and waited humbly.

Sometimes it's difficult not to grovel. If the old man's task for me was pricing the mixed antiques and fakes I'd seen so far, I was in for a windfall. Obviously this geriatric was the owner of a significant chunk of the antiques universe. The situation called for the classic whining Lovejoy fawn.

'I am astonished you are not older,' the old man said.

'I'm trying.'

'Mmmmh. Caterina recounted your behaviour at a village auction.' There was a pause. Good old Caterina had flopped across an armchair somewhere behind me. Her irritation beamed straight on to my nape. The pause lengthened.

I gave in. 'You want me to say anything in particular?'

'Mind your language,' Caterina snapped. 'Just remember the gentleman to whom you're speaking could buy you *and* your village.'

The old man winced at her bluntness and flagged her rage down with a tired gesture. Money was beneath mention, which meant the bird spoke the truth.

'Can you account for your perception, Lovejoy?'

'You mean about the painting?'

'Of course, dolt!' from the sweet maid behind.

'Is there,' the old man fluted, 'is there really such a person? A . . . a divvie? You can detect antiques unaided?'

Oho. Caterina had taken the trouble to suss me out pretty well.

'Yes. I'm one.'

He asked the girl to offer me sherry. She slammed about and glugged some. I was scared to touch it. Maybe it was polite to let it hang about an hour or so. Better wait till he'd slurped his, if he was strong enough to lift the bloody thing.

'How is it done?'

'I don't know.'

Caterina snorted more free scorn.

'Six out of six antique dealers with whom I have discussed the matter, Lovejoy, pronounce you to be an authentic . . . ah, divvie.'

'They're in league with him, Grandad!'

The old man smiled. 'Now, Caterina. Lovejoy hardly looks affluent. May I?' he added benignly to me.

'Yes,' I said, wondering what he was asking.

'Caterina. Lovejoy was given the freehold of his cottage by a lady now living abroad. Subsequently he has raised money on it by two mortgages, fraudulent. Both are now in default. The building society is suing for possession—'

'Here, dad,' I interrupted, annoyed. 'That's libel.'

'You mean slander,' he said absently. 'Furthermore, he has a police record. I was advised by all six dealers not to employ him. He owes money to nine dealers in Colchester, and approximately eleven others.'

I found my sherry had emptied itself into me of its own accord. This gentle old man was a deceptive old sod. Well, I had nothing to lose. I was unemployable after that heap of references.

'Which raises the question why you asked me here, dad.'

'Quite so, quite so.' Too much good literature makes these old characters talk Dickens, I suppose. He girded his loins for the plunge. 'I wish you to perform a task on my behalf, Lovejoy.'

A sweat of relief prickled me over. Maybe I was back in.

'A valuation? An auction deal?'

'Ah no.' The old man was suddenly apologetic, evading my eyes. And I remembered Caterina's determined bidding for a fake. And in a dealer's ring, that highly illegal enterprise. My throat went funny.

'Bent?' I asked. He gazed at me blankly, so I translated. 'Illegal?'

'Ah, well, you might say there *is* a rather, ah, clandestine aspect to the activities, ah, which . . .'

I stared. Dear God. Geriatrics were in on antiques scams these days. Still, a zillionaire with Turners and

Canalettos would not think in groats. Whatever it was, I'd soon be eating again. And the ill-tempered lass might revert in time . . .

'An antiques scam?' I struggled to suppress my exultation. Nicking antiques lifts the lowest spirits.

'No.' The old man's gnarled hand gestured to calm my alarm at his denial. 'Not *an*. The.' The scam of all time? I could only think of the British Museum and the National Gallery.

'How big?' I asked. Naturally I assumed the old geezer wouldn't want to reveal all, but I was wrong.

'It's Venice.'

'Venice, eh? Exactly what in Venice?'

'Venice itself. All. I am in process of, ah, borrowing everything Venetian.' His opaque eyes stared into me. God, he was wrinkled.

Well, lose some, win some, I thought bitterly. I managed to smile indulgently. You have to make allowances for idiocy. The daft old sod was rich, a possible future customer whom I couldn't afford to offend even if he was barmy. 'Look, Grandad,' I said kindly. 'You *can't* nick Venice. It's fastened to the floor in that lagoon. I've always wanted to nick the dome-dialled Castle Acre church clock, but I've more sense. The village bobby'd notice. Get the point? I'd give anything to possess its marvellous dead-beat escapement, but daren't risk trying it.'

'I'm serious, Lovejoy.'

I got up and said compassionately, heading for the door, 'Good luck getting Venice through the Customs, but don't say I didn't warn you.'

'Stop him, Caterina,' the old bloke quavered.

Some hopes, I thought. Short of undressing there wasn't a lot she could do, but women are wily. 'Money,' she said casually as I passed, not even bothering to look up.

'Eh?' My treacherous feet rooted.

She gazed calmly at me then, idly perched there on the chair arm, swinging her leg. 'How much will you earn in the next hour, Lovejoy?'

'Erm, well,' I lied bravely. 'I've a good deal on.'

'Unlikely. But we'll buy one hour.'

'To do what?'

'To sit and listen.'

I looked back at that walnut visage, then back to the bird. She too was serious. For a family of lunatics they seemed disturbingly sure of themselves. Well, money's nothing, not really. But without it the chance of acquiring any antiques at all very definitely recedes. I weakened.

'What's an hour between friends?'

The old man nodded approvingly at the luscious bird as I sat down.

'Lovejoy. You speak fluent Italian, I believe?'

How did he know that? 'Not really.'

'Oh, but you do. You learned the language to, er, rip the Vatican.' He leant forward earnestly, the elderly perfectionist. 'Rip. The word is correct?'

As a matter of fact he was right, but my past sins are personal property.

'You want to nick Rome as well?' I said cruelly.

'That'll do from you, Lovejoy?' Caterina spat.

'Shush, my dear. Lovejoy, you have never been to Venice.' The knowing old sod was reminding me, not asking. His gnat's-whine voice became flutier and dreamier. 'You poor man, never seen the Serenissima. It's the ultimate glory of Man.' His eyes were on me, but looking through to some distant image. 'I'll tell you a secret, Lovejoy.'

'Grandfather!' Caterina warned, but he shushed her.

'I've never experienced either contentment or ecstasy for thirty years.'

'Don't give me that crap,' I blurted, 'er, sir. With all these antiques?'

'True, Lovejoy.' He seemed near to tears. 'Thirty years ago I first saw the Serene Republic, a routine holiday. Within two days I'd bought the Palazzo and knew it was for life. Ah, the hours I have watched the *traghetto* men smoke and talk in the *campo* below my window on the Grand Canal!' He collected himself. 'I saw Venice, the greatest man-made structure the world has ever known. Paintings, architecture, sculpture, clothes, weapons, everything living and vital.'

'I know the feeling,' I said enviously.

'You do *not*, young man. You believe I am talking about greed. I am not.' Now he sipped his sherry, hardly wetting his lips. 'On that visit I learned of something so terrible, so near nightmare that I never recovered. I have never felt happiness since. Despair, too, is absolute.'

'You all right, mate?' His nightmare, whatever it was, had turned him grey.

'Yes. I thank you.' He replaced his glass and leant back, weary. 'To avert that nightmare I am prepared to give everything I own. You see, nightmares should vanish with the dawn, Lovejoy. Mine does not. It is descending upon that magical city with every minute that passes. In your lifetime you too will suffer it. And when you do, Lovejoy, you will never smile again.'

In spite of myself I had to clear my throat and look about to make sure we were all okay. 'My nightmares are pretty boring. What's yours?'

'Venice is sinking.'

That old thing. 'Aren't we all?'

'Silence!' cried the old bloke, enraged.

'That does it!' Caterina was rising, also enraged.

I'd had enough. Even hungry cowards get fed up. 'Shut your gums, you silly old sod. And as for you,' I said to the bird as I crossed and poured myself sherry entirely without assistance, 'dial nine-nine-nine for the Old Bill if you like. But just remember you invited me here to listen to your lunatic crap. I don't have to agree that it's gospel. Okay?'

After an ugly pause old Mr Pinder said unexpectedly, 'Okay, Lovejoy,' to Caterina's fury. I went and sat down.

The old bloke was simply watching. The bird was for Armageddon.

'Right, then,' I said. 'Venice.'

He smiled with a gleam in his eye. 'Venice. If you saw a lorry carrying a small parcel containing a Verzelini drinking glass accidentally slewed over the wall of the Chelmer canal, what would you do?'

I wanted to get the hypothesis absolutely clear. 'No danger to me?'

The sly old devil shrugged. 'Well, Lovejoy. Broad daylight. You can swim like a fish, I'm told. Canals are only a couple of feet from the towpath. Surely . . . ?'

I thought, sensing a trick. Verzelini was a Murano glassmaker from Venice who made it to Good Queen Bess's London and turned out richly valuable Venetian-style glass in his little City factory until late 1590s. A single glass nowadays would give you enough to retire on. Well, in for a penny . . . 'Okay, I'd try and save it.'

'Now. Supposing that Verzelini glass, in its precarious parcel, was multiplied a million times.'

'Still no danger to me?'

His distant-reed voice cut in. 'Yes or no, Lovejoy?'

'Well, yes. But there's less than a dozen Verzelini glasses knocking around. And Venice isn't a parcel on a lorry.'

Grandad smiled then, his face like crumpled kitchen foil. 'All Venice's art can be made into such parcels, Lovejoy. And it is certainly about to fall into water, Lovejoy.'

I thought about that. 'You mean . . . ?'

'Piecemeal.' There was a pause. He added, 'Bit by bit,' as if I didn't know what piecemeal meant. 'A UNESCO expert—'

'They're cretins.'

'—says that every year Venice loses six per cent of its marble treasures, a twentieth of its frescoes, three per cent of its paintings, and two per cent of its carvings.'

'That's not the sea, dad. It's collectors.'

'Which proves my scheme can be done.'

'This is insufferable!' Caterina said the words like aggressive teachers used to in school, only she didn't thump me on each syllable. She flung out, the door shaking my teeth.

In the newfound calm I gave the old fool a fresh appraisal. 'That's an awful lot of bits, dad. One parcel's fine. Two's not beyond belief. But three's just asking for trouble. And nobody on earth could nick four of Venice's precious antiques without all hell being let loose.'

'Ah,' he said, as if spotting some troublesome little flaw in my argument. 'You're apparently assuming, Lovejoy, that we don't replace each, ah, bit by the very best reproduction that money can buy. Paintings, stonework, carvings, statues. You'll no doubt remember your own escapade in the Vatican?'

I wished he would give over about that. I'd made my own repro to do the Vatican rip, so I'd known it was up to scratch. What this old duckegg was suggesting meant trusting a load of other forgers to be as perfectionist as me, and that was definitely not on. You can't trust just any faker.

'You'd need an army of superb forgers. I can only think of three.' What worried me was the Carpaccio fake that Crampie and Mr Malleson had been murdered for. As soon as I got a satisfactory explanation for that, I'd be off out of this looney-bin like a shot and he could do what the hell he liked with Venice or anywhere else.

'I see you're beginning to understand, Lovejoy,' Grandad said. 'There are many, many more than three. And I do assure you they are being produced at a Dunkirk rate, Lovejoy. Money no object.'

'But where and how?'

'Ah.' He pondered, grimaced, creakily raised a finger and said knowingly, 'Are you in or out?'

'In or out to do what?'

'You will check the authenticity of the items involved in our, ah, scam. We've lately had one or two unfortunate events.' A frown crinkled his face worse than ever. 'One point. I sought the derivation of that word *scam*: "scamble" is hardly convincing, yet it's modern currency . . .'

I waited for a bit. The old criminal had nodded off.

I cleared my throat. 'Dad?'

He partly roused, muttered, 'Ammiana . . . Ammiana . . .'

'Eh? You awake?'

No sound. The old man was snoring, a squeak of a distant bat. I poured another glass and had a think.

CHAPTER 6

Joyce the serf found me padding around the upstairs landing. The first I realized she'd caught me was her abrupt, 'Downstairs, Lovejoy!' Just shows how sly women are. She led me to the kitchen—takes a serf to spot a serf—and brewed up some repellent broth designed to 'warm a man's blood'. A learner grannie if ever I saw one. But her tea was good, and from the vestibule window I could see a gilt-framed George Webster seascape in oils hanging on the stairs so it wasn't all wasted time. The frame, a quite early plaster-gilt job, worried me. Maybe

I'd seen one rather like it recently, maybe in an auction . . . Joyce had an open kitchen fireplace and a lovely old cast-iron Mason's grate of about 1865.

'I was only looking,' I told the interfering old cow, in case she had the wrong idea.

'You put the map back?'

The question was off-hand, but I smarted inwardly. Women nark me, always suspecting the worst. The hand-coloured map, by the Dutchman Dirck Jansz van Santen, was dazzlingly illuminated in gold. The silver had oxidized a bit, but that's only to be expected for something done about 1690. (Tip: look for deep precise printing—showing the map was an early print from the engraved copper—and the more embellishment the better.) The thought of nicking it honestly never crossed my mind. No, I'm really being honest now.

'You're just like old Mr Pinder,' she told me. Praise indeed.

'Me? Like Grandad?'

'Mad about stupid old things.' She wet her wrists and started to attack the pastry. 'Of course, Mr Pinder's so taken with Venice these days he's useless for anything else. Him and Caterina's stepmother alike.' Her tone was disapproving. 'Things would have been different if her real mother were still here, God rest her. This house is like Piccadilly Circus some days. You wouldn't believe the sorts of folk get fetched here. Long-haired layabouts in fast cars, foreigners from boats, every language under the sun.'

'What does Caterina do?'

Joyce gave a sharp, inquisitive glance. 'Helps Mr Pinder to run the estate.'

'And Mrs Norman?'

'You'll need more tea, ducks.'

'Er, ta.' I knew a shut-out when I heard one. Caterina's stepmother was clearly not to be discussed. 'Does the old boy kip most of the time?'

She glanced at the hour, a highly-sought Lancashire Victorian wall-clock with the familiar keyhole stage and cased pendulum. Five years ago you couldn't give them away as ballast.

'He'll sleep till tea-time now. Are you going to help him with this foreign thing? Like Mr Malleson?'

Like Mr Malleson? Well, I thought. Let's see if her idea of 'this foreign thing' was the same as old Pinder's. 'Yes,' I lied.

'Then be careful. Mrs Norman has altogether too many hangers-on if you ask me. Though I must say Mr Pinder's pleased at how she copes with the big house there, Palazza whatsit.'

'How long do you think he'll want me to go for?'

'You'll have to ask him, dear.'

'Can't Caterina decide? She seems in charge.'

'Doubt it.' Joyce's lips thinned. 'That end's always left to Mrs Norman and her . . .' She petered out, maybe deliberately. The old shut-out again.

I said I'd better be off unless she had designs on my body, and got another smile. I like smiley women.

'Can I leave Mr Pinder a note?' Without letting Joyce see the words, I scribbled thanks, but the task wasn't quite up my street and some other time, and told Joyce it was private and she wasn't to look inside the minute I was gone, which made her cuff me amiably. 'My husband will run you down the road.'

She gave me an Eccles cake to be going on with, laughingly scorned my offer of thirty quid for her aspidistra — they're genuine antiques nowadays — and shouted her husband from the stables.

Mr Lusty drove me all the way into town, chatting laconically about the Pinders' benevolent support of poor artists. It seemed the old gentleman ran a sort of complicated trust, which was quite interesting, but not as interesting as the short cut we made as we left the Pinder estate. A cart-track ran down to the waters of the estuary. Mr Lusty was so proud of the new stone wharf that he stopped the car to show me. He explained that a sizeable ship could come up-river from the sea-reaches. I said I'd no idea it was such a responsible job, and was duly amazed at the size of the two boatsheds. There were two biggish yachts moored out in the tide-race, the bigger with two masts.

'Yes,' Mr Lusty said all modest. 'The *Eveline* came in two nights back. A young painter. Be gone tomorrow. Sometimes we're so busy we can't keep up with the routine estate work.'

'Is that so?' I walked on to the wharf.

'It's dredged,' he said, seeing me peer over into the river. 'The real thing, big dredgers up from the Blackwater.'

'It must cost a fortune.'

'All comes out of the trust, you see.'

'And these artists train here, I suppose, eh?' We walked back to the car. The wind was whipping at us from the sealands. Beyond the low banks and sedge lay the North Sea and the Low Countries.

'Heavens, no, Lovejoy. Most of them just pass through, except when Mrs Norman's home. Then maybe her, erm, erm . . .' He coughed, recommenced. 'A right motley mob they are, too. But Mr Pinder's a perfect gentleman. Always gets himself wheeled down to every boat that calls, even if he's not feeling so good.'

'Where do they come from?'

'Oh, all round the coast. You name it.'

He drove us beside a few acres of reforestation and we emerged on the Fingringhoe road, but as we'd pulled away I couldn't help looking downstream across the marshes. The Roman Empire had shipped its products up this very river. Somebody could ship things the other way, right?

I caught the bus after waiting with Mr Lusty in his car a few minutes. All the way back to town I kept wondering about Mrs Norman and her Erm-Erm who together seemed to be responsible for the Venice end of the whole scam — if it existed.

One thing was sure. Everybody trod very, very cautiously round Mrs Norman.

The next two days were hectic. I sent Connie to dig· out the Pinder family gossip. She's a cracker at collecting gossip — God knows how, because she never stops talking long enough to listen to anything anyone else says. Tinker's job was to ferret out local antiques which were possible fakes of anything Venetian. My own contribution was to think, read, and find why my private antiques world was spinning off its wobbly little orbit.

The best way to think about crime is to work, preferably at something slightly less than legal.

Connie was only able to stay with me the first afternoon, so I had a lot of solitude. We got up about tea-time and put the divan away, with still a sizeable chunk of the day left. At the moment I was making an 'antique' papier-mâché chair. Don't laugh. In its time, papier-mâché's been used to make bedsteads, tables, practically any sort of chair you can imagine, picture frames, boxes, vases, clock cases, even parts of coaches. Elderly French women came into mid-Georgian London to chew (literally: *chew*) cut-offs from stationers into a gooey mash for pressing on to a metal framework. Varnished, pumice-stoned and decorated, it can be beautiful and anything.

In this cruel lying game of antiques, you take all stories with a pinch of salt. Respectable history's a pack of lies. I mean, an eighteenth-century bloke called Clay reckoned his papier-mâché hot-mould stoving process was new, but it's only the same old system speeded up. And that carver-gilder Duffour, who worked from a Berwick Street pub in Soho, even claimed he'd invented papier-mâché. That's rubbish, too; the Persians were making it donkeys' years before he got into bad company in The Golden Head pub in 1760. You can forge anything from papier-mâché.

There I was, in my workshop—actually a grotty shed deep in garden overgrowth—honing down the chair with pumice. It was to be a cane-seated drawing-room chair with a spoon-shaped back splat. Oh, I know quite well that this sort of chair's the favourite of the modern faker, but I have two secrets up my sleeve which can make a three-day old fake look an original 1762 piece from Peter Babel's place down Long Acre.

The robin had followed me in because it knows I like silent company. It stabbed its cheese on the workbench, cackling angrily to warn possible intruders off its patch. Very like women. I wear these leather gloves or your hands wear off. You need *many* varnishings and honings. I intended to japan the whole thing because black lacquer's easiest to make antique-looking. You do it with an electric sander, but for God's sake remember to replace the emery paper with a rectangle of buffing cloth. Buff the lacquer *anywhere on the chair a human would normally touch* until the lacquer's worn thin. Then take a 2-kilowatt hairdrier and from a distance of two feet blow hot air at every part of the chair a human *wouldn't* normally touch—underneath, the legs, the lot. My favourite bit is a touch of class: a spoonful of house dust at all the intersections before your hot-air bit gives an unnervingly authentic appearance under a hand-lens. Then buff (shoeshine action) the seat edges and the splat's top until the undervarnish begins to hint through. All that's my first secret. The second's the way a fake's pearl-shell inlays are dulled from their brilliant newness to a century-old opalescence —

'Sceeeeech!'

'Sorry, mate.' I'd reached out for the red tin in which I keep my McArthur microscope and inadvertently got the robin. 'Well, you're both red. Same size. No need to carry on like that.' I put the disgruntled robin back on the bench. It stood dusting itself down, glowering. The red tin was almost exactly the same colour as the robin. Not far from a Carpaccio red, actually.

I stood looking. Red?

The robin was the same size as the miniature microscope's tin can, which had luckily been just right to hold the instrument. But so what?

'So the same holds good for picture frames, right?' I said to the robin. 'Sizes count as well as colours.'

It cheeped in a rage and flicked on to my shoulder so I got the message. Time for the idle little sod's biscuit. I sighed and turned to go in for one.

'What does a robin know about picture frames, Lovejoy?'

The light was draining fast from the day. Odd, though, that Caterina should be framed the way she was in the sun's last glim. Some women are enough to stop a man's breath without even trying. Things conspire. 'Eh?' I said, cool.

'What picture frame? You just told the bird.'

'That conversation was private.'

She came in and walked round the chair. 'You're restoring it. Nice. Late Regency?'

'Early Lovejoy.' That shook her, made her think a minute. 'Your killer's got a posh car, Caterina. I'll bet he earned it by doing fakes nearly as good, eh?'

The robin cackled and flew off in a sulk. No biscuit. I shouted after it, 'Give you two tomorrow,' and explained to her, 'He'll be in a hell of a temper all week now. That's your fault. Trouble is, he suspects blackbirds. One knows how to undo the catch on my breadbin, and the robin's not tall enough. Gets him mad.'

'Did you say my killer?' She'd gone all still.

'You know, the murderer you go about with.' I was all affable. 'The de Lorean. Old lemon-shirt.' I spoke quite conversationally and started tidying up. 'He owns the *Eveline*, doesn't he?'

Still and pale all of a sudden, so I'd struck oil. 'I knew you'd be trouble, Lovejoy. How did you guess?'

'The frame on that Webster seascape in your grandad's hallway. You tried to lend that Carpaccio fake some authenticity by putting it in an old frame before sending it to the auction. Then you realized your mistake— Grandad missed it, so you had to try to buy it back. Something like that?'

'Nearly. But go on.'

'Feet.' I began to sweep round the chair. She moved her feet obediently, watching, listening. 'Mr Malleson went bid-happy and got the fake against your bids. So you had him and Crampie killed by your tame murderer, naughty girl. You told him to make it look like a routine motorway café rumble.' I emptied the workshop dust into the plastic bin and looked round for her verdict.

'Almost, Lovejoy.'

'Only almost?' I was so bloody sure.

There was a trace of bitterness when she spoke, but it was Crampie and Mr Malleson got done, not her. 'You obviously think the worst of me.'

'Almost, Caterina,' I said evenly, and went past her to switch the outside light on.

'You won't go to the police, Lovejoy.' No question there, only the assured flat statement of a bird in charge of everything which intruded into her world. 'They already suspect you of every local antiques crime. They wouldn't listen to your wild suppositions.'

So she had changed my accurate logic into wild

suppositions. I held the shed door for her to walk out, and locked up. We stood in the darkening garden, each waiting for the other to speak.

'Your mistrust means you won't work for my grandfather, I suppose?'

'Correct.'

Oddly, she drooped as if accepting a still heavier burden. 'Then that's the end of it,' she said resignedly. 'Can you be trusted to take no further action?'

'Where my skin's concerned, yes. But just remember, if my robin goes off his grub, it's your fault. And I can be very narked.'

'Are you never serious, Lovejoy?'

'Lady,' I said wearily, 'I'm serious all the bloody time. It's everybody else that's jokers.'

Nowhere. I'd got nowhere. I knew more or less how, why and who. And still I'd got nowhere, stymied in every direction. I was getting narked.

CHAPTER 7

Speaking of sex, so many things puzzle me. Like a woman's all chat immediately afterwards, then she zonks out an hour later. But the man's off into a melancholy twilight doom-riddled world, a comatose grief from which he only slowly returns to remember the ecstasy and delight. In particular, the last thing he wants is his bird prattling gossip into his ear, like Connie was doing to mine. The fact that she was only reporting the gossip I'd told her to collect was no excuse.

'Darling! It's so interesting! Mr Pinder's daughter, Caterina's mother, passed away. Her stepmother Lavinia—'

'Who?' I reared blearily out of coma.

'Lavinia married Geoffrey Norman. He's hopeless and she's a tramp.'

Rear and blear. 'Who? Caterina?'

'No, silly. Lavinia. I keep *telling* you, darling. Eventually she got so bad the village shunned her. Scandal, the lot. *Lovely*, darling! People are sorry for Caterina . . . Old Mr Pinder runs some sort of arts foundation . . .' Her voice faded. My mind went into neutral, and the world went away.

That old man had been on my mind half—if not all—the night. Clearly he was a nutter. Even if he and his syndicate were worth a king's ransom, a nutter's still off his rocker any way you look. What with Caterina's hatred and Grandad's whispery voice, his scam seemed more unreal.

'The steps leading down to Venice's lovely canals were for a lady's descent from the gondolas,' he'd said, eyes glistening. 'But the bottom steps never emerge from the water now. And the Piazza San Marco itself is underwater in the great yearly tides from the Adriatic Sea. The ground floors are thirty *inches* above sea level. Oh, the tourists pour in and see the Queen of the Inland Seas resplendent there in all her ancient glory. But they go, and the sea again takes over. Only each year Venice is lowered and the sea more rampant. Politicians promise. Engineers measure. But the duckboards, the *passerelle*, are left out now, to disfigure the loveliest of cities.

'And do you know what is the most shameful thing of all, Lovejoy?' he concluded, his cracked-flute voice embittered. 'Our belief in our own permanence. We little know that what passes for permanence—' he paused a second, wondering whether to be pleased at a possible pun, waved it away—'is only the gift of constant endeavour. Man's priceless art treasures must be ceaselessly protected, or they vanish. Like Venice is emptying of treasures and people.'

'How can one man—?' I'd interjected, but he washed out my objection derisively.

'There are many of us in my syndicate, Lovejoy. Finance is no problem. Let me tell you a story. Vivaldi's church, the Pietà, stands on the Riva—the lagoon waterfront—and contains the most pathetic memento you could ever imagine. A marble rectangle set in the floor, inscribed that the church's Tiepolo painting was restored by American money.' He paused to allow the world time to prepare for his next utterance. 'Is that immortality? Lovejoy, the entire flooring, which records in immutable marble the generosity of the Samuel H. Kress Foundation of New York, USA, will soon have settled for ever beneath the waters of the Adriatic.'

'But it's a try,' I found myself protesting. 'Worthwhile.'

'Pointless patchwork, Lovejoy. Darning the cabin curtains on the *Lusitania*. Only success is worthwhile. Don't you see?'

Eventually I did see. The love, the old man's conviction had swept me along. I almost forgot he was bonkers.

Which was all very well. In the cold light of day.

That same noon, Connie, Tinker and me held a council in the White Hart.

'You first, Tinker.' I told him to be quick about it, because Connie was supposed to be on her way back from a shoe-buying trip to Northampton.

'Nowt, Lovejoy.' He took a note and got another pint for himself. Connie leaned away as he shuffled back. Some days he's worse than others.

'Eh? I told you anything Venetian, Tinker, you burke.'

'Don't blame me, Lovejoy. Worn my bleeding feet orf, I have.' He slurped his pint dry and spoke with feeling. 'There's not a single frigging Venetian antique, real, fake, nicked, bent or just passing through, in the whole frigging Eastern Hundreds.'

He rose to shamble off for another pint. 'Ted,' I called
to the barman wearily, 'keep one coming or we'll be here
all day.' I beamed a rather worried look at Connie,
because she'd have to pay and I owed her a fortune
already. By her reckoning I possibly owed very, very
much more. Quickly sensing she was one up, she
immediately asked Ted to stop the draughts which were
positively *whistling* through the pub, and to please turn
up the heating while he was at it and put more logs on the
fire—

I concentrated. 'None? That's impossible, Tinker.'

'I know, Lovejoy. It's bleeding true. I went down
Brad's, Ernie's, Jessica's, Mersea Island . . .'

With Ted rolling his eyes in exasperation and Connie
enjoying herself giving him anti-chill orders all over the
saloon bar, I closed my ears to Tinker's mumbled list of
negatives, and thought: one or two negatives, fine; but a
whole East Anglia of negatives is serious cause for
concern.

There and then, my mind made itself up.

Until hearing Tinker, I'd assumed that sooner or later
Ledger would find the three blokes who did Crampie and
Mr Malleson. Now, it was all too clear that things were
beyond reach. It was too big. Think of the resources to
clear out every special item from East Anglia. It took
expertise, men, time, knowledge and money, money, and
more money. Old Pinder and his syndicate were not so
daft after all, just wealthy and obsessed. I half-listened to
Tinker's boozy drone. '. . . then Liz at Dragonsdale, who
reckoned she'd seen an early Venetian black-letter book
eight weeks back, but . . .'

Which left the question of what the hell *I* was worrying
about. Caterina's warning was crystal clear: keep out of
it, and Lovejoy will not be troubled in the slightest.
Honestly, I wasn't feeling guilty. No, really honestly. It

was nothing at all to do with me. Admitted, Mr Malleson wouldn't be dead if I'd dissuaded him enough. And Crampie wouldn't be dead if I'd maybe stopped, insisted on giving him a lift. Or maybe I shouldn't have shouted all over the pub car park that the Carpaccio was a fake. I can shed guilt like snow off a duck. Anyway, I always find it belongs to somebody else. No, I was absolved.

'Then I went to Jim Morris at frigging Goldhanger . . .'

'Ooooh, you poor thing! It must have been freezing!' from good old hot-blooded Connie. By now she'd got us all hunched over the pub fire. My mind was busily doling out absolution, mostly to myself. 'I was, too, in the library.'

That reminded me, and I opened the book she'd brought. It was the wrong one.

'But darling, the library was freezing—'

'I distinctly said the History of Venice, you stupid—!'

'It's a book on Venice, isn't it? It's not my fault.'

Of course it never is with women. I tried to sulk driving all the way to the Colne estuary but got interested in the book in spite of myself. The index listed Ammiana, the name old Pinder had mentioned. It was an island, one of the many which made up the Most Serene Republic of Venice. A thriving centre of culture, of religious activity, eight gracious antique-filled churches—until it had sunk beneath the waters, never to be seen again. There were others. Reading in a car makes me unwell, but it wasn't just that that made me feel prickly.

'It's perishing in here, love,' I said. 'Put the heater on.'

She did so with delight. First time we'd ever seen eye to eye.

CHAPTER 8

'I'm so frightened, Lovejoy.'

'Don't worry, love. Just do it.'

'When do I put the money in?'

Connie and I were crammed in the phone-box. One of her stockings was tight over the mouthpiece. We'd had a hell of a time getting it off her lovely leg in the confined space pretending we were doing all sorts so people wouldn't stare. She was shaking from fear.

'You don't need money for an emergency call.'

I dialled, pressing close. Connie whispered, 'Darling, this is no time to—'

'I'm only trying to listen!' I whisper-yelled, thinking, swelp me. I'd do a million times better without help.

'Police, please,' Connie intoned. I'd tried training her to speak low and gruff for disguise but she was hopeless—thought that pursing her mouth into a succulent tube made her into a bass-baritone.

'Mr Ledger, please, Constable,' Connie boomed falsetto into the mouthpiece.

'And don't keep saying please! You're supposed to be a criminal!' I spread the crumpled paper for her to read from.

'Hello?' She turned a pale face to me, eyes like saucers. 'He's answered, darling!'

'Read it! Read it!'

'Erm . . . get this, Ledger, mate,' Connie read in her tubular voice. I closed my eyes. It was like a bad dream. 'I'll only say this once. Go down the estuary, please. Off the old Roman fort there's moored the sea-going yacht *Eveline*. She's full of fake antiques . . .' Her voice faded.

'What is it? Keep reading!'

She dropped the receiver in a panic. 'Darling. He said to put you on.'

'Eh?' We stared at each other.

'He said, Just put Lovejoy on the blower, lady.'

Slowly I unwound Connie's stocking and listened at the receiver.

'You there, Lovejoy?' Ledger asked wearily. 'Stop tarting about.'

'This is a recording,' I said, embarrassed.

'So's this. You seem to think we do bugger-all here. We've checked out everybody who was known to be at that auction, at the caff, on the trunk road—including your posh lady Caterina, especially as you've been seeing so much of her these days. You still there?'

'Aye.' I felt a right twerp.

'Then pay attention. I'll only say this once.' He sniggered at nicking one of our lines. 'You're meddling, lad. And I don't like it, because meddlers usually have a reason. And your reason is vengeance. Don't think I don't know. I can read you like a bloody book. Last warning. Understand?'

'You can't arrest me, Ledger,' I said weakly.

'There's such a thing as protective custody. Just remember that if you're on my patch I've signed for you. Oh, one more thing. The *Eveline* has sailed. She was clean as a whistle. We looked.'

My heart sank. What a flaming mess.

'I hear your lady is a cracker, Lovejoy,' Ledger said pleasantly. 'Funny voice, but I don't expect that worries you too much—as long as Ken Bridewell doesn't find out, eh? Cheers.'

Click. Burr.

We left the phone-box, me ashamed because the trick had failed and Connie still shaking. She looked worried sick. We were near the football ground in town.

'Darling,' she quavered. 'It's . . . it's become rather

serious, hasn't it? All this, I mean.'

She must have caught Ledger's final threat. I sensed an incipient farewell, the state she was in.

'No more serious than usual, love.'

She stood there drooping. 'The police, Crampie and the other man, the whole business. I'm frightened, darling.'

'Only temporary difficulties,' I said like a cheery weather-forecaster in an unexpected blizzard:

'You're going to Venice to find them, aren't you, darling.' Another lovely woman who could make a simple question into a flat accusation.

'Of *course* not,' I said, beaming. 'Honest.' And I looked into her eyes with all my innocence.

'Really honest, or Lovejoy honest?'

'Same thing, love.'

'Is it?' she shivered but only listlessly from habit and looked about. Her car was nearby. Women never trust a bloke when he's trying to be truthful.

I fumbled in my pocket to see what gelt I had left. Maybe enough.

'Come on, love,' I said, pulling her across the road to the shop. 'I'll buy you a replacement stocking. Can I put it on your lovely leg?'

'I've two legs, darling.' She managed a wan smile.

'A whole pair, then,' I said recklessly. 'Hang the cost.'

Any woman leaving is the end of an era. No two ways about it, Connie's absence was bad news. Lucky I was so busy, or I'd have suffered even more. The worst bit is realizing how sad she'd be too. I couldn't see the point of her going, but women are always boss in a relationship and, if that's what she felt was timely, I suppose it had to be. I mean, a man can't simply leave a woman, not off his own bat. Oh, of course birds complain about blokes 'leaving', but that's only punishment for failing to live up to her expectations. At least Connie had given me the sailor's elbow for a material—not emotional—reason, which is good going for Lovejoy Antiques, Inc.

I'd just put her stocking on her. It had taken three hours. She was overlying me the way she liked to afterwards.

'If I ask you not to go, Lovejoy . . . ?'

I gave her my million-watt stare of transparent honesty. 'Who said anything about going anywhere, love? Where's this daft idea come from?'

She sighed then, and dressed slowly because she knows I like to watch. I could tell she didn't believe a word, but women are notorious cynics. She came back to give me a kiss before she went, blotting her eyes. I waved her off from the bed. She was just in a funny mood.

A ten-point turn to negotiate the gateway, the engine sounding horribly final.

Gone.

I lay there thinking, money. I must get money. Venice is such a hell of a way. This called for one of my antiques orgasms.

By four o'clock I was going full steam. I'd sold my papier-mâché fake chair—as a genuine antique, of course—in a part-exchange high-mark deal to Elena on North Hill, coming away with a rough old oil panel of a long-haired bloke with lace cuffs and a cravat. Genuinely oldish—say late eighteenth century—but poor artistry. You can still get them for a song in any antique shop in East Anglia. I inscribed some famous-sounding name on the reverse, like 'Port^t. of Abraham Cowley' and an illegible signature, and decided to flog it for twice what Elena could, and before nightfall too. A high-mark deal is one where you part-exchange items and come away with money as well, because your item is worth more than the other bloke's. I did well out of Elena and my chair.

With the money I put a deposit down on a nineteenth-century wrought-iron church porch lantern, all bonny hexagonal panels intact, told Brad I'd pay him the balance by the weekend, and carted it to Patrick's (resplendent today in a vermilion poncho). There I sold it for a profit and used the gelt to buy a group of six French hand-shuttles, Georgian, from Margaret Dainty. These little things come in old engraved steel, ivory or wood, and are avidly sought by collectors nowadays. I borrowed John Cronan's phone in the Arcade to contact a Midland shuttle-collector from my book, priced them high and got him to promise to post off a money order within an hour. I told John I'd owe him for the phone call when the stingy swine moaned, and sent Tinker to the post office to wing the shuttles off northwards.

Ten minutes later I sold 'Abraham Cowley's' portrait for a good price to Markie and Beatrice in the Red Lion. I pretended to be broke — this comes easy — and desperate for money. 'I'd meant to restore it,' I said, hoping to God the marker-pen signature which I'd scribbled on the bottom corner wouldn't rub before they got it home. I'd thoughtfully pencilled a Christie's auction number on the frame angle beneath the canvas tacking, and pretended not to notice when Markie spotted it and nudged Beatrice surreptitiously. They claim to be Expert Antique Picture Restorers. They'd need to be, I thought fervently, pocketing the gelt.

Crossing the Arcade to Jessica's place, I took a deep breath and plunged into her incense-riddled alcove. Ten minutes later I staggered out stinking like a chemist's shop but happy with my loot (got on deposit, ten per cent) which consisted of a Waterford crystal comport dish, jug and decanter. I'd persuaded her they were 'new-factory' wares — post-1951 — instead of the 'old-factory' crystal which extends back from 1851 to the 1720s. Of course I'd lied in my teeth, and agreed to pop round her house tomorrow night and settle up what I owed.

Meanwhile, Tinker had a brass chandelier with a brass 'Bristol dove' finial at the top (no feathers, smooth wings closed). It was mixed-period because some know-all has always mucked about with them, but it looked fine. I bought it there and then, added a thirty per cent mark-up and told Tinker to phone Sandy and Mel (not got time to tell you about them, thank heavens). They agreed to buy it. Tinker would ferry the chandelier out, get the money, zoom it to the Arcade and there buy Margaret's small Japanese shouldered tea-jar outright. It had its original tiny ivory lid (think of a decorated draughtsman off a chequerboard). I told him to up the price by half, phone a London dealer in Museum Street, say I had 'flu but needed the cash by morning. It broke my heart. If I clapped eyes on it again I'd never let its dazzling little body out of my sight ever again. As it was, Tinker knew enough to hand it to one of the long-haulage drivers who run England's unofficial nocturnal antiques delivery services nationwide faster and safer than ordinary post. It would be in Museum Street by midnight. Then Big Frank from Suffolk bought the Waterford crystal at a good price . . .

I reeled on, hurtling Tinker about the town and cadging lifts while I borrowed like mad, spending like a civil servant. Oddly, sometimes when you go berserk things go for you. We found antiques which were unbelievably rare. Tinker even dug out a musical book—Victorian 1880, little projecting tabs trigger a cuckoo's call when you turn the cuckoo picture. I'd never even seen one before. Naturally, you also pick up the dross—two 1671 water clocks 'by Ed^d Larkins, Winchester', for example. People get really narked when you tell them that these are *all* repros by Pearson Page.

The day faded into dusk. In the Arcade, lights came on. People scurried among the closing shops. Traffic queued at intersections. Stores shuttered for the night. Night schools opened. Car parks filled for our one theatre.

I stormed on like a mad thing, dealing, buying, borrowing, selling—and above all promising, promising, promising. At the finish Tinker and I were knackered and swilling ale in the Three Cups. He's not daft, and got courage up to ask it after a couple.

'What do we do about all these frigging IOUs, Lovejoy? You wuz giving them out like autographs.'

'Do the best you can, Tinker.'

'Eh? Me?' He felt so faint he drank both our pints. 'Where'll you be?'

'Somewhere else for a few days.'

'Leaving me to cope with the whole mess . . . ? Jesus.' He stared at me, appalled. 'They'll have my balls, Lovejoy.' He slurped his new pint, and gave a sudden gummy chuckle. 'Hey, Lovejoy. I can't wait to see Jessica's face when she sees me turn up tomorrow night, instead of you. I knows you pays her in kind, randy sod.' He rolled in the aisles at the notion.

No real need to worry about Tinker. He's the sort who could scratch a living bottling fog. 'Hold them off payment till I come back.' I had the money to reach Venice. That was all that mattered.

'What about your woman Connie?'

I thought a minute. The beer seemed to have gone off. 'Forget her,' I said, and pushed him my glass.

Which only goes to show how useless I am at knowing women.

Early next morning, as I was putting together my spare clothes in my grotty battered suitcase, a special messenger arrived at the cottage with a big manilla envelope and an accountant's letter. It read,

I am informed by Mrs C. Bridewell, director, that you

have accepted responsibility for purchasing on commission ladies' Italian seasonal styles in pattern for the Bridewell shoe-shop chain. Please find accompanying this an open return air ticket to Venice, and funds calculated at average Continental daily rates, as permitted by HM Inland ˙Revenue. We estimate ten days.

They remained mine sincerely.

It was Connie's godspeed. My hand shook as I signed the receipt.

The lad proudly burned off on his motor-bike, with me standing there looking at the air ticket with vision suddenly gone blurred. She hadn't believed me one bit.

Bloody women, I thought, and locked up.

CHAPTER 9

Venice. If you've never seen it you can't believe it. And when you clap your eyes on it you still don't believe it.

I stood on the Riva waterfront utterly bemused. It really *is* waterborne, floating in the sunlit mist of the lagoon. I've never seen anything like it. Nor, incidentally, has anyone else.

Since meeting old Mr Pinder I'd read like a maniac. Even on the plane to the Marco Polo International airport—we'd left at an ungodly hour—I was scrabbling through a potted history without gaining much. Clearly, the little maritime republic founded on a mudbank on Friday, 25 March, in the Year of Our Lord 421, had done okay for itself. Venice had an eye for the old gelt. But when I got to the bit about the Venetian calendar starting on March 1 and Venetian days officially starting in the evening, I chucked it aside. I was confused enough. I even started on my old Italian course notes, but what can you do with a language where the words for 'need' and 'dream' are so disturbingly similar? I chucked those aside too. My usual Lovejoy method would have to do— osmosis, fingers crossed, and a penny map.

Like I said, pathetic.

The whole waterfront was on the go. Busy, busy. They were all there, massive black and white tugs, barges, the water-taxis, waterbuses, all nudging the Riva. I must say, the poles to which they were moored looked decidely wobbly to me, but there was a jaunty confidence to the scene, as if Venice had had that sort of useless criticism before and so what? Crowds ambled around the *vaporetto* terminus. Early-season tourists drifted, gazed at the souvenir stalls, peered into canals from bridges.

Across the lagoon the beautiful San Giorgio Maggiore rose from the vague afternoon mist, and, away beyond, a suggestion of the Lido's buildings showed where the Adriatic Sea was kept at bay. To the left, the Arsenal shipyard which had turned out a completed warship every day when the Serene Republic was doing over the Turks. To the right, across the water the gold gleams of the Salute church, still celebrating the end of that bubonic plague, 1681, and marking the start of the Grand Canal.

But where were the streets, the avenues, the cars? Odd, that. I'd heard of Venice's canals, of course. I just wasn't prepared for the fact that they were everywhere and completely displaced roads. I stood to watch a big liner shushing slowly past, turning in towards the long raised spine of the Giudecca island. Another odd thing—despite the bustle, no noise except for the occasional muffled roar of a water-taxi. I finally got the point of Joker Benchley's cable home: 'Streets full of water. Please advise.' You walk in tiny alleys between the canals, on bridges over the water, or in and out of tiny squares and that's about it. The *fondamenti*, places where an actual pavement exists, are practically major landmarks and rare enough to have special names. All right, I thought. Venice is simply one hell of a tangle, with hardly anywhere to put your feet.

But it was still the place where I would find that yacht-owning lemon-coloured smoothie and his two goons who did for Crampie and Mr Malleson. Ledger couldn't touch me here, and with luck some delectable antique might fall my way.

Right, now. Where to start? I looked about expectantly.

'You find a welcome, signore?'

The boatman was smoking nearby. I nodded, 'Yes, thank you.'

The water-taxi which had brought us from the mainland airport was idle at the wharf. From the way the driver was grinning he had spotted my deception. And I thought I'd been so slick, mingling discreetly with the Cosol tour mob who had flocked off our plane, getting a free sail into Venice. He offered me a fag. I declined with a head-shake.

'First time in Venice, signore?'

'Very first. It's beautiful.' No grass, no countryside, I suddenly realized with delight. Everything— *every single thing*— in sight was man-made. Boats, canals, houses, wharves, bridges, hotels, churches. Everything. It gave me a funny feeling, almost as if I'd come safe home.

'*Grazie.*' He read my glance with the keen skill of centuries. 'We have trees and fields, signore— out at Torcello island and places.'

'*Deo gratias*,' I said, thanking God with ambiguous politeness, which restored his approving grin. 'Your little signorina was uspet because I, ah, borrowed a ride?'

The Cosol courier was a pretty but distraught girl who had engaged in a ferocious whispered row with him at the airport. She was still inside the hotel seeing to complicated room allocations. He pulled a face.

'The other girl refused to come this week. Signorina Cosima will have to run all our tours.' He shrugged eloquently as if that was the ultimate calamity.

'Your boat wouldn't be free for a half-hour . . . ?' I said, a little too quickly. The penny had dropped at long last.

'Possibly,' he said in a way that left no doubt. 'Perhaps I show the signore the Grand Canal, the Rialto Bridge, the—'

'May I give directions?' I suggested politely.

He already had the painter in his hand. He nodded at my words, as if Venice constantly received complete strangers who knew their way about.

The weird familiarity of Venice is quite unnerving. Like coming across your own backyard in, say, darkest Abyssinia. Five minutes after leaving the hotel I was looking expectantly for landmarks which I *knew* would be there. 'Vivaldi's church of *la Pietà, non è vero?*' I said even before we cast off. It was only five or so buildings along the Riva wharf from the hotel. An instant later, the romantically misnamed Bridge of Sighs, the Doge's Palace, the great campanile and the Piazza of St Mark's. Every lovely thing exactly where you expected. We swept grandly past them, me rapturously thinking I was dreaming at the splendour of it all.

Thin crowds meandered between the long tethered line of nodding gondolas and the start of the slender Merceria shopping lane which runs off the Piazza. Harry's Bar was in action not far from the waterbus stop. We came abreast and ploughed into the Grand Canal. I asked if it was always this crowded.

'Worse, signore. *L'estate* . . . !' The boatman rolled his eyes at the problem of the summer. 'Even the Accademia Bridge groans then. The trouble is, everything in Venice is famous.'

'You must be glad—so many customers,' I said, 'though I suppose many bring their own boats?'

'Not many,' he replied, slowing to deflect his prow from a gondola crossing the canal up ahead. 'Visiting boats moor over the other side, facing the Giudecca.'

Important news, for when the *Eveline* arrived. 'I hadn't expected the Grand Canal to be so wide.'

All innocent, I asked him to let me watch the gondola. In it, four people stood solemnly upright while the gondola crossed the canal. Our boat idled by the little wooden jetties.

'Fixed fare from the *traghetto*, the gondola ferry.' He spoke with scorn. 'That's all they do—to and fro.'

My eyes were drawn to the adjacent buildings fronting the canal's splashy water.

'Do many foreigners have a palace here?'

'Palazzo,' he corrected politely. I'd used the English word by mistake. 'Merely means a grand house, in Venice. Yes, plenty come. Most stay in hotels such as that, in the campo there by the *traghetto* ferry.' His gaze idled across the campo to the tall pink-washed palazzo opposite. 'Others, the rich, buy their own palazzo.'

It was all I could do not to turn and stare at the building. What was it old Pinder had said so dreamily by his fireside when trying to persuade me to work for him? *The hours I have watched the traghetto men smoke and talk in the campo below my window in the Grand Canal* . . .

'No pavement,' I observed, my excitement barely under control. The houses just drop sheer into the water. Therefore no place to stroll casually past in the dark hours and test the strength of the palazzo's drainpipes, because there was simply nowhere to stroll.

'*Vero*,' the boatman said. 'Except one can walk in the campo, and even reach the Basilica on foot.'

The narrow space had once been a tiny field, hence its

name. One side, that hotel. The other side, the palazzo of Mrs Lavinia Norman—if I'd guessed right. I needed my map, where the palazzi were named.

'Are there many *traghetti* in Venice?'

'Very few.' He coughed to draw my attention. 'Signore. The waterbus is approaching. And the *traghetto* has crossed long since . . .'

'Ah. Sorry. Fine.' I nodded for him to go ahead, irritated at being too obvious.

The waterbus was creaming towards its stop, a wobbling T-shaped jetty with a cabin full of intending passengers.

'To the Rialto Bridge, signore? Or the Fenice Theatre? You'll know we Venetians invented opera.'

'You've a lot to answer for.' His face fell, but I honestly can't understand why every little opera takes a fortnight. I glanced forward. 'Show me the shape of Venice, please.'

'*Subito*,' he said, and we took off up the Grand Canal.

Everything is fantastic when you think about it long enough. But some things are just simply mind-blowers by nature. Venice is one of them.

It's a manmade universe of alleys, ancient houses, and great—*great*—churches crammed on to a maze of canals. And where? On 117 islets, in a lagoon of over 200 square miles, that's where, with the Adriatic Sea muttering sullenly just over a mile from the main island cluster of Venice proper. Like the water-bloke said, everything in Venice is famous. But to grow accustomed to Venice you'd need a lifetime. I was amazed at everything.

Venice is singing cage-birds at canal-side windows. Venice is exquisite shops and window-dressing. Venice is inverted-funnel chimneys, leaning campaniles, wrought-iron at doors and windows, grilles at every fenestration, little flower-sellers, droves of children and noisy youths. Venice is bridges every few yards, narrow alleys where you have to duck to get under the houses which have crammed so close they've merged to make a flat tunnel. Venice is patchy areas of din—from speedboats racing to deposit their owners in cafés to do nothing hour upon hour—and silence. It's uncanny, really, how it can be broad day and all is silent. The canals glass. Nothing moves. The *calli* empty. Bridges hang in permanent solitude of space and time, as if the world was concentrating. Then, somnolently ambling round a confined corner, you're suddenly wedged in a dense people-jam pandemonium between glittering shops. It's the abruptness of the transition gets me every time: tranquillity into hubbub. Venice is a million separate sound barriers. Venice even has its methods—police boats, waterbuses, grocery boats, even funeral gondolas and barges conveniently moored facing the Madonna dell' Orto church on the side of Venice nearest the cemetery island. And the whole set of islands and lagoon on the go.

The boatman put me down exactly on the Riva. He had a high old time arguing the price for my two-hour jaunt, but deep down I was badly shaken. From every side I had been slammed by emanations from antiques—the buildings and the treasures they contained. I could hardly see, let alone breathe or argue sensibly. Even so, I had a shrewd suspicion the boatman surrendered too easily to a price which was almost fair. Something was wrong. I made great play of standing on his wood jetty watching the tourists stroll among the café tables set out along the waterfront.

'Apologies to Signorina Cosima if I made you late.'

'Cesare,' the boatman said. 'Like Borgia.'

'*Grazie*, Cesare. Lovejoy,' I said. He didn't even guffaw.

He tried the name experimentally while folding the money away. 'Should you need to travel to the palazzo of

your friends, ask along the Riva anytime, *per piacere*.'
He'd used the singular, palazzo. So he meant one in particular.

I said carefully, 'Friends? I know no one in Venice, Cesare.'

'Of course not,' he said with gravity. 'I meant should you wish to.'

'You know all about Venice.'

He smiled deprecatingly. 'We Venetians know some, though not all. Much is rumour—especially about newcomers in rich houses.'

There it was. He had detected my interest in the palazzo. I smiled and nodded. 'It's a deal. Give me a day to find my feet. Oh.' I stopped on the stone wharf. 'Give me a tip about Venice. Anything.' I explained away his puzzlement, 'I collect facts.' All too often they mean survival.

'Ah, *capisco*.' He thought a second. 'How long have you got?'

'Ten days.'

'Then it will be useful for you to know that we Venetians buy wine by taking an empty bottle for a refill. Make sure it's a one-litre bottle.'

Bigger bottle, same price. 'Very useful. Thanks, Cesare.'

'Wait, signore. In Venice we too collect useful facts.'

After a quick think I said, 'Santa Claus is also patron saint of prostitutes.'

He nodded seriously, coiling the painter. 'You are a careful man, Lovejoy. My tip will be most useful to you. Yours is without value.'

'Not everything is money.'

His audible gasp at this heresy gave me a grin. On my way past that daft plumed statue of Victor Emmanuel on the Riva, the Cosol courier Cosima hurried out, pretty with exasperation. Almost before she reached Cesare's water-taxi she was blasting him for being late.

Ten days, minus one.

CHAPTER 10

Food is definitely funny stuff. Miles from home, it takes on a weirdness that either turns you into a gourmet or repels you for life.

To me, a plate of spaghetti is a full meal. To Venetians it's no more than a windbreak. After noshing enough to sink a fleet they just soldier on through a jungle salad, then wade into half a fried calf followed by a *gelato* ice-cream all the colours of the rainbow. It's nourishing just to watch. Mind you, it takes nerve. Seeing a Venetian whittle a mound of whitebait is like watching a seal cull.

Go away from the Riva down one of those little alleys where your shoulders practically touch both walls, turn right, and you'll find one of the best nosh places in Venice. It's tucked under the shoulder of a bridge before the San Zaccaria. Venetian boatmen use it, so I felt it was as near to Woody's caff as I was likely to find, and in I went for a slammer of a meal. Some kinds of strange grub you can guess at, like how they'll do their veal. Others — fried rings of squid for example — you don't know until you take your courage in both hands. Then there's *polenta*, which I tried because I'd never heard the word before, and got this yellow woolly maize breadcake, toasted hot as hell. It's the local equivalent of our pasty — filling, cheap, eaten anywhere anytime. Made me feel quite at home, especially when I began to get slightly pickled on the wine.

Only a couple of rooms, and a counter by the door, everybody was in earshot of everybody else. That was half my reason for choosing it, but the talk turned out to be money, family, money, trade, money, and money. Not a whisper of antiques or fakes, and nobody mentioned the big house by the *traghetto* gondola ferry—the Palazzo Malcontento on my guide map. Of course, somebody within earshot mentioned the scandalous theft of St Luce's remains and the mysterious ransom demand of 1981, which focused brief attention on money. And no sight of Cesare. A longshot, really. After an hour—to me a good meal should last five minutes at the outside—I went out to explore Venice on foot.

It's easier said than done. During the meal I studied the map. Venice seems nothing but landmarks. In the end I'd picked out a few. St Mark's Square was a natural, and the Ponte di Rialto is the world's most famous bridge, sure to be well signposted. Two. And Mrs Norman's palazzo near that gondola ferry lay somewhere between. It looked easy. After all, the whole place was only about three miles by one. The canals were sure to be named, and Cesare's circular tour had shown me Venice's shape. The position of the other islands would show you which bit of Venice you'd reached. Simple, no? Answer: no. Unless you've a superb sense of direction, you're bewildered after a hundred yards and find yourself going anywhere but where you want.

A mist had descended. This seems to be the pattern in late March, foggy mist till mid-morning, then hazy sun till dusk when the mist comes back for the night. A bell was clonking monotonously out in the lagoon beyond the Riva wharfside. Tugs, ferryboats, water-taxis, and the rows of covered gondolas nodding between Harry's Bar and the Doge's Palace were inactive now. Few people, the tables and chairs stacked, the ornamental tubbed trees cleared away, a handful of young wanderers with haversacks waiting dozily for a night boat. It was all very evocative, listlessly beautiful. I'm not a sensitive bloke, but the melancholy quickly seeped into my bones. I wasn't cold, not like Connie gets. It must have been the unrelenting vibrations emanating from ancient Venice and sounding on my recognition bell. I shook myself, plodded over the Rio del Vin bridge, and was off, weaving slightly.

Lights guide you at all 449 bridges, and the *calle* alleyways are fairly well lit so long as you are near the main centres where elegant shops and posh restaurants abound. Yet it's an odd feeling being able to touch both sides of the high street as you walk. You soon get so used to it you're astonished when you come out unexpectedly into an open square.

Away from the main Merceria shopping thoroughfare, though, the tangle worsens. The canals develop an annoying habit of looking familiar when you know for a fact you are seeing them for the first time. The *calli* become narrower and more convoluted as you walk on. Bridges become more frequent and acutely-angled. I gave up trying to follow door numbers as a bad job. They are supposed to be supremely logical—start at nil and simply progress consecutively until the district runs out, but I couldn't quite get the hang of where Venice's six *Sestieri* or districts actually were, or which way the bloody numbers went at the trillion intersections.

In Cesare's water-taxi I'd worked out that the Palazzo Malcontento was less than 800 yards from the Riva as the crow flies. On foot it took me an hour, and I'm a quick walker. When finally I emerged into a narrow *campo* beside a church, and saw at the end the Grand Canal with the *traghetto* jetties, I knew it was luck more than judgement.

The place was ill-lit. The hotel one side was barely into its tourist season. A few tatty trellis-works marked off stacks of café tables, but the tub plants were dead and the ornamental electric bulbs trailed forlornly on frayed wires. The hotel seemed stuporose. The gondola ferry seemed to have jacked it in for the night. I strolled down the *campo* to the Grand Canal. Obliquely across and left was Santa Maria della Salute. Right, if I dangled out far enough, would be the Accademia bridge but beyond there the backward S of the Grand Canal concealed everything else. Well, well. Casual as any actor from amateur rep, I gaped left. Carrying a camera has always embarrassed me but I badly felt the need of one now. Nothing would be easier from here than to pretend to photograph the string of lagoon lights near the island of San Giorgio, and accidentally include the canalside aspect of the Palazzo Malcontento, but it was too late for good ideas like that. Typical. Several lights were on in the house, but mostly the windows were shuttered. No surrounding garden, of course, though there might well be a tiny courtyard hidden somewhere behind those house walls. I'd seen enough stray tendrils here and there to suggest that little manufactured gardens lurked out of sight. The two doors had that terrible implacable continental finality about them—doors are there to be closed, not necessarily opened. The lowest windows were firmly shuttered. No finger holds. It was all bad news.

The hotel reception clerk glanced up as I passed the door. He must have caught the altered shadows. The *campo* was better lit than I'd appreciated. An outside wall lantern on the big house and the hotel hallway shed more light than a thief would want.

Depressed, I found a dog-leg *calle* and came out on a little bridge at the back of the palazzo. The canal below ran at right angles into the Grand Canal. A small but elderly barge thing was moored in it. One of those water doorways, heavily barred, tunnelled its way into the side of the house, presumably where groceries and whatnot were delivered from supply boats. Great, I thought bitterly. The one nooky way in, and bars a mile thick.

By the time I'd found the wider *calle larga* which ran towards St Mark's Square I was miserably sober. The big house was virtually impregnable. I knew nobody in Venice, so no chance of wheedling my way in as a friend of a friend. That fashion-conscious killer who had smirked in his fancy yellow de Lorean would be on his guard as soon as he showed up in his posh yacht and spotted me. It was hopeless.

Even St Mark's Square looked hardly alive. A few strolling night owls crossed in front of the great basilica, peering up at the bronze horses which stand in front of the upper façade's central window. Venice acquired them in the Fourth Crusade, but they were made a thousand years before that shambles. Only one place was open, a crowded coffee bar where distracted young blokes slogged to serve late customers along the counter's entire length.

'Coffee, please.'

'Two, please,' a bird's voice corrected at my elbow.

'Two,' I agreed, wondering what the hell. The crush was too great for me to turn, but I glimpsed Cosima's drained face in the mirror.

No place to sit. I made it to the stairs where people were clustered. Cosima helped. We squatted on the fourth step.

'Upstairs is closed this late,' she said, huddling the cup to her and breathing in the steam. 'Nobody'll push past.'

'Lucky for us.'

'You look like I feel.' Her dark eyes held me briefly, let me go.

'Eh?'

'Exhausted. Fed up.'

She was right. I suddenly realized I was all in. Time to chuck in the sponge for today. I didn't quite cheer up, but it was close.

'I'm glad you happened along, Cosima.' I meant it.

'You stole Cesare,' she accused. 'Made me later than ever.'

'Sorry. Your partner didn't show, eh?'

'No. The bitch never does. One phone call from that lout in Mestre and she's flat on her back. Leaves me to do it all.'

'Extra money, though?'

'That's a laugh. I've phoned nine agencies for a substitute but it's too early in the season, you see.'

Honestly, for the first time I really looked at her. I mean, really looked, to see the person she was. Of course I knew she was a bit of all right from having seen her at the airport and on the Riva. Black hair straying and bouncy, with her distraught air lending her youth an added charm. She dressed in bird's clothes, too, which is something of a novelty in these days of scrapyard-lumberjack fashion. Travel couriers can go practically anywhere they like, right?

'Are you really desperate?' I asked, all offhand.

She looked at me, also probably for the first time. 'Yes. I've not stopped. Been doing tomorrow's reservations since your lot arrived, not counting the afternoon flight.'

We went quiet for a minute, watching the crowd.

I said, 'I'm a registered travel courier.'

'You are?' Her eyes widened so suddenly at me I nearly fell into their darkness.

'Except . . .' I hesitated for form's sake. 'I've only ever done the Portugal runs . . .'

'That would be all right,' she said eagerly. 'Do you have your cards?'

'Well, no. I'm on holiday leave. But I know my registered number. It's X-2911894, London.'

With some excitement we got it written down in her notebook. I invented a travel firm called Leveridge and Kingston in Bury Street, near St James's, because snobbery is a con's greatest ally. Anyway, it would take them at least four days to check. By then I hoped to have sussed the Palazzo's secret and be independent of Cosima. Optimism's always a laugh.

'This is very kind of you.' She was having doubts as we finished our coffee. 'Why would you do this? It's a waste of your own holiday. And the pay isn't . . .'

I looked away, working as much embarrassment into my face as fatigue would allow.

'Erm, look, Cosima.' I tried to go red, but you never can when you want to. 'I've never done this before . . . Follow a girl, I mean. I only hired Cesare to find out who you were,' I went on, inwardly a tortured soul. I turned on my most transparently sincerely honest gaze and looked at her. 'I don't know quite why, but when I saw you standing there at the airport . . .'

She flushed, glancing away and back. 'You mean . . . you mean you were . . . ?'

My shrug wasn't as Latin as I wanted, but I did my best. 'I suddenly had to . . . well, find out where you went . . . Are you angry?'

'No,' she said, still uncertain but trying for emotional distance. 'Not really.'

'I'm trying to be honest with you, Cosima,' I said hesitantly.

'Oh, that's very important,' she agreed.

We agreed for a minute or two that honesty was vital in relationships and finished our cappucini among the café's throng.

'Positively no obligation,' I said as a weak lightener. 'But I'll help. And I'll not bother you. Word of honour.'

'Only if you're sure . . .'

Worrying I'd acted too well, I assured her I wouldn't mention my catastrophic love-smitten condition ever again. Gravely she accepted the promise. We made pedantic arrangements for next day. I was to come with her to organize the morning arrivals, then do the afternoon airport run to collect tourists on my own. Cesare apparently knew the ropes well enough to help if I got in a mess. Self-consciously she wrote a telephone number and an address on a torn page.

'That's me, Lovejoy. For business purposes.'

'For business purposes, Cosima.'

'I'll arrange pay on a daily basis.'

We rose to go and I risked a joke. 'You mean I also get paid?' but I was so clearly trying hard to be brave she gave a relieved smile.

She needed the No. 1 waterbus so I walked her past the great campanile to the San Zaccaria stop on the lagoon waterfront. I couldn't help asking as we crossed into the Piazzetta.

'*Two* horses?' She squinted up into the gloom. 'You mean four. See?'

'Four, yes, but only two genuine. The two on the right are fakes.'

'Who told you? It's practically a state secret. They are being replaced by official authentic copies. The originals will go into the Marciano Museum.'

'In the interests of conservation?' I'd blurted out the bitter remark before I could stop myself.

She glanced at me. 'Why, of course.'

We made only stilted chat after that until the waterbus came and we shook hands like folk leaving a party gone suddenly sour. For all that, I stood on the undulating jetty and watched her go. I waved once. She didn't wave back. I suppose she needed to think, same as me.

CHAPTER 11

It being so early in the year, the hotel was only able to provide half-board. Breakfast was tea and a wad, unless you went mad and ordered English breakfast of eggs, bacon, toast and the rest, then extras were written on your bill. It looked like being a hard day, so I stuffed with everything I could lay hands on. Maybe the hotel management wouldn't care for the idea of a guest transmuting into a courier. So long as I didn't actually starve, I could always sleep dangling in some belfry.

Airports are all madhouses. God knows what they're like in high season, but on my first full day I learned the hard way that Cosima's exasperation was completely justified. Our own band of tourists were insane. Before we'd been in action ten minutes I could have cheerfully shot the bloody lot. Cosima had me stand in the thin crowd of couriers, depressives to a man, and hold up a placard labelled Cosol in red. I felt a conspicuous twerp, and Cosima said that's what it's all about. 'Believe me, Lovejoy,' she warned anxiously. 'If they can fall into the lagoon, they will. Last week I lost a whole Ami family—they turned up in Belgrade.' She stuck three badges on me.

Cesare had taxied us across the lagoon before nine. Cosima was lovely in the morning haze, her hair blowing as our boat creamed between the lagoon marker posts. She looked really stylish, almost too well turned out for a travel courier. We avoided each other's eyes and did a great deal of agreeing. I wondered vaguely if she was dolled up because of some bloke coming on one of the flights. None of my business. Still, my improvised confession of instantaneous love had worked a treat.

Before long I would be in charge of a tourist band and able to trail them anywhere. What more natural than select a 'typical' Venetian palazzo—the Malcontento, for instance—and call to ask if the lady of the house would permit visitors to inspect the elegant interior of so classical a dwelling?

That was the last coherent thought I had for a couple of hours. The tourists came through the Customs like a football crowd. We couriers held up our placards and bleated our firms' names, me carolling 'Cosol Tours, folks.' The whole row of us was overrun within seconds. I was engulfed by a motley mob, all ages, that plucked at my clothes, explaining mistakes, complaining, waving documents, showing me passports and tickets. One woman had lost a child and expected me to find it. One bloke had acquired two infants and wanted to hand them to me. One senile old crone had left her hand-luggage in Zürich. A tiny psychopath nicked my clipboard to play with. It was a nightmare. 'Cosol,' I kept calling, holding my stick aloft to attract more of these psychotics.

Cosima had to rescue me finally because I couldn't match up the sea of expectant faces with the names.

'They're all foreigners,' I whispered frantically. 'They aren't English or Italian.'

'German, American, Danes,' she whispered back. 'Talk English slow.'

She made me stand by the door and tick them off. Apparently the greatest mistake of all is to take away tourists from some other courier's group because you can never completely undo the documentation. Cesare loaded their cases—my God, did they bring frigging cases—until his boat was heaped high with the damned luggage. Cosima hung back to settle a Customs officer's apoplexy over something a young couple were bringing in, while I tried to put the flock into the boat in some sort of order. We had two hotels to call at, eighteen people all told. I almost lost an elderly bloke with a bad leg; another boat looked easier to board and he nearly escaped. It was only when Cesare noticed some old bird's anxiety that we recounted, and I went running hectically among the other water-taxis yelling the old bloke's name to get him back. Silly old sod. My head was splitting as we made space for Cosima and set off south towards Venice.

Trying to be a typical courier, I assumed a boisterous Italian accent and pointed out landmarks, mostly wrong, giving out exotic snippets I'd picked up about Byron, so much a part of Venice. That started them all asking breathless questions. Odd how people go for extravagant behaviour. We're all a bit like that, deep down, wanting to hear about Byron's Venetian roistering, scandals, his wild affairs. People are weird. Like, it's exciting to hear of the great poet-hero's splendid triumph in the swimming race from the Lido all the way up the Grand Canal. It's somehow less pleasant to hear that he loved to display his superb grace in the water because his ungainly club-footed lameness was so obvious on land. Hence his love of the night hours—the superstitious Venetians of those days would not stand within thirty paces of the deformed. I had the sense only to mention the posh bits.

We passed the cemetery island of San Michele that Napoleon got organized, and penetrated Venice proper. From then on it was bedlam. We separated our mob into two groups, luggage and all. Distributing them into separate hotels took us over an hour. Two people had not arrived on the plane and we had hell's own job persuading the second hotel we hadn't sold them into slavery, or—worse—to another hotel.

That gave us fifty minutes before I re-zoomed to the airport for the next horde. Cosima sat with me at one of the Riva caffs and went over the procedure. We were still very proper with each other, but I didn't mind. She would look after this morning's lot. The Ami tourists now due would be my sole responsibility.

'I like Yanks. I'll guide them round Byron's haunts.'

'You can't do the guide's job, Lovejoy. They're two different roles in Venice. I suppose they're combined in Portugal?'

'Mmmmh? Oh, mmh.'

More bad news. She saw me off in Cesare's water-taxi, calling worried last-minute guidance till we left earshot. I gave her my most confident grin and waved. She wore fawn and cream. All the way, till Cesare gave a bad-tempered swing of the bow taking us behind the Arsenale, I could see her slender loveliness showing against the pastel-coloured buildings. Well.

Cesare said very little on that trouble-free run back to the mainland. Almost as if he was furious at something. Still, the guidebook said Venetians were secretive, so I tactfully didn't ask him what was up. Deep down I'm a pretty sensitive sort of bloke.

That afternoon everything went right. Unbelievably, I found myself ahead of schedule. By two o'clock my tourists were ensconced in the hotels, signed for, the desk registries satisfied, Cesare's books made up, the Cosol dockets filled in on Cosima's clipboard, and not a single family in Belgrade. I kept my phoney Italian accent to lend authenticity and it worked quite well as long as Cesare wasn't too near and giving me the bent eye.

Even better, they were a talkative friendly bunch, as Yanks tend to be, and wanted me to be in the downstairs bar at three to advise on restaurants and other aspects. A pleasant, shapely bird called Nancy, mid-thirties, caught my eye, with Doris and Agnes, two attractive blue-rinsed middle-aged women, all towing a mild-mannered tubby bloke called David and forming a separate mini-group 'being from California, y'see'. Nancy explained she was David's secretary from Sherman Oaks, saying it as if the rest of California was a suburb and getting a laugh.

We reassembled downstairs in such high spirits I was more than a little narked that Cosima wasn't there to see how well I was doing. I dished out Cosima's little pamphlets full of shopping and dining hints, and gave them all a brief account of the tourist map in that dulled voice couriers use when they've said it a million times before. Though I say it myself, I was very convincing. The one hassle was something to do with a bathroom plug, easily passed on to the desk clerks.

David Vidal, the tubby Californian, suggested we take a quick stroll 'to catch the light', whatever that meant. Doris and Agnes eagerly agreed, and I was coopted to lead a small schismatic group out there and then, even though I explained their guide would be along to give them their private countdown at breakfast tomorrow. I must say, they're keen in California, and nearly as hot in Florida — two elderly Miami couples wanted to come along too. So it was that, under Cesare's sardonic eye, I emerged on to the Riva leading a party of eight towards St Mark's with David turning around judging the sky and holding up three little camera-like gadgets he had hanging on him. Still, it takes all sorts.

They wanted to dash into the Doge's Palace. Going all debonair, I paid the pittance entrance fee, pretending it was my pleasure to treat them. Actually it broke my heart but I was desperate to wheedle my way into favour. Maybe they'd insist to Cosima that I be promoted to a guide . . .

In the mad dash round the Palazzo Ducale before it closed, I was a real ball of fire. The faster we went, the more pleased my minimob became. We saw the Great Council Chamber, the Lion's Mouth letter-box where you slipped denunciations of treason — in the days of the Doges, Venetians got a hundred pieces of gold for each accusation, so a lot of it went on — and the exquisite ceilings. I was practically in tears as we zipped in and out of the chambers, corridors, prisons, galleries. To me speed is the modern disease. Dashing past Veronese's *Juno offering gifts to Venice* is a crime. It's the only genuine one of that set, as I pointed out to Nancy—the French kept the rest after 1797, though you're not supposed to notice. We were lucky and got into the Room of the Three Inquisitors, but Tintoretto's ceiling paintings have been replaced. David Vidal sympathized with my abject disappointment when I told him what was the matter.

'Look okay to me,' he said, quizzically peering upwards. He simply hadn't stopped judging the sky. Even surrounded by these massed treasures he was still glancing at windows, the bum.

'What *are* these things?'

'These? Light meters.'

'You a photographer?'

Agnes laughed. 'David's a movie-maker, here on assignment. We—'

A quick glance from David cut her prattle. I pretended not to notice and carried on my distilled guidebook patter. I had a few successes—the Bridge of Sighs, the prisons from which Casanova escaped in 1775—but mostly missed out. David was mad at Agnes. Agnes was pale. I was still trying gamely as we emerged on the quayside of St Mark's Basin, pointing out which of the 36 palace capitals were real mediæval stone carvings. Nancy was up in arms at the idea that half were modern replacements.

'That's cheating, if the guidebooks say only three are reproduction!'

I had to smile. Trust a woman. 'Mostly a harmless trick, love.'

'Well, so long as somebody keeps records.'

'I'm sure somebody probably does.'

'Don't you *know?*'

'Of course,' I said smoothly, thinking: Oh hell. I'd forgotten for the minute I was a Venetian. 'Erm, in the, erm, Venetian Antiquities Section of the, erm, Buildings Ministry.'

'Well, *that's* a relief!"

David examined one of the phonies closely. 'How can you tell the difference?'

'They feel, erm . . .' I recovered quickly, and gave a convincing laugh. 'Well, actually we couriers are given Ministry notices.'

He looked doubtful. 'If you say so, Lovejoy.'

The Floridans wanted to tip me as I got them back to their hotel in the gathering mist. I refused, all noble, saying it was my pleasure. Tom, an elderly Miami boatbuilder, said how well I'd learned English for an Italian. Nancy was the only one who'd cooled appreciably during the brief walkabout.

'Almost too idiomatic,' she said sweetly. She was having a good laugh inside, the way women do when they've rumbled that you're up to something.

'I spenda two years inna London.' I did some hurried bowing and scraping, but she gave me a sideways look.

They thronged the bar. I escaped by pious pleading that it was too early for me to drink intoxicating fluids. I was knackered and tottered into the lift amid a chorus of bye-byes. My room was 214. It overlooked Ferrari's rotten garish statue of Victor Emmanuel, but you can't have everything.

I practically fell inside, looking forward to a hot soak, a brief kip, then a long read about Venice and a quiet nosh at the boatmen's caff near the San Zaccaria. The light in my room was on.

Cosima was sitting on my bed, reading my Venice book.

'Lovejoy. Where've you been?'

'Working,' I said. 'You?'

CHAPTER 12

The next two days I worked like a dog. We handled six planeloads of mixed tourists, two on charter flights, which necessitated taking on an extra two water-taxis for those. Cesare saw to them. He was great but ever more taciturn, not at all like the cheery bloke I'd met on my first day. The better our little trio functioned, the surlier he became. Odd. That earlier banter we had enjoyed was gone. Cosima on the other hand was blossoming, looking more radiant every day. Shrewd as always, I supposed her bloke had finally showed and that after working hours she was enjoying life to the full. Though I must say she wasn't getting much of his company the rate we were going. We hardly had time to snatch a bite in the waterfront caffs. We noshed like a Biggin Hill fighter squadron waiting for tannoys to shout the scramble.

For all that, I was oddly happy. It was as if I'd found a safe niche where the problem of Crampie and Mr Malleson, and the scam which old Pinder's grand-daughter and her killer boyfriend were supposedly helping the old fool to plan, could be comfortably forgotten. Maybe it was Cosima's accusation which had cleared the air, something like that.

That night I got back after showing Nancy and David and their pals the Ducal Palace, she had chucked the book aside but stayed on my bed, and demanded to know where I'd been. Women always have me stammering, as if I've really been up to no good. And honestly, hand on my heart, I honestly hadn't even thought of Nancy like that until Cosima said her name.

'I was only out walking,' I'd explained.

'With eight of the Americans,' she blazed. 'Including

that fat bespectacled Waterson woman who fancies herself—'

Nancy wasn't fat. 'They wanted to see San Marco. I thought I was helping you out.'

'Lovejoy.' She swung off the bed, furious but pretty as a picture. 'I've seen the way you look at these overdressed tourist bitches. Well, just let me tell you that if you step one single inch out of line I'll have your courier registration cancelled. On the spot! Do you hear?'

'But—'

'But nothing! Couriers and tourists are not allowed to . . . to . . .'

The trouble is, pretty women have the edge. They make you tongue-tied even when you're honest. It's bloody unfair.

'Look, Cosima, love,' I said brokenly, taking her arms. 'I didn't want to do this job. I was on holiday, remember? It's only that I, well, falling for you like I did makes me . . .'

'All *right*, Lovejoy!' She pushed away, not at all mollified. God, she was lovely. Her hair was sheer silk. I'd never seen any hair as lustrous as that. I bet it would be lovely spread out on a soft white pillow, just like Margaret's and Helen's and Liz's. 'All *right!* But you just remember.'

'I was only trying to do what you said, love.'

She spun round on her way to the door. 'What *I* said?'

'The tourist is always right.' Biting my lip, I subsided on the bed, clearly misunderstood and close to heartbreak.

She hesitated. 'Well, yes. I know I did say that . . .'

I shrugged, deeply hurt. 'You don't know how it feels . . .'

'Look,' Cosima said, but less firmly. 'I don't want you to take it too much to heart, Lovejoy. I just had to speak out before you got, well, *drawn in*. I've seen it happen.'

'I'll remember,' I said bravely, Gunga Din on the battlements.

'Very well. Then we need say no more about it.'

There was a brief pause. I didn't raise my eyes because we Gunga Dins are soulful creatures and don't particularly want our innermost feelings revealed.

She too was hesitant now. 'Lovejoy. Have you had time yet to find any more of those restaurants I listed for you?'

'No.' I heaved a sigh. 'I was going to have a bath, then go out with the map.'

She said seriously, 'As it happens, I was intending to, well, take a quick walk round the Cannareggio. Since neither of us has really eaten properly today, it might be convenient to take the opportunity . . .'

'So long as you're my guest,' I said. 'Please. It would give me such pleasure.'

'Very well. Eight o'clock at the Fondamenta di Santa Lucia? We needn't be too late.'

'Thank you, love.'

I waited until the lift doors clashed before recovering from my heartbreak. Already I knew enough to know that the Cannareggio Canal was not really a tourist area. If anything, it was somewhat out of the way. Still, another crisis was averted by the simple tactic of agreeing to spend the evening with such a beautiful bird as Cosima. Painless.

In the bath I bellowed some Gilbert and Sullivan, making myself laugh by trying to translate the words into Italian as I went.

What with the hectic state of our affairs I saw very little of my favourite group, that minimob of eight who had rushed and talked me off my feet in the Doge's Palace. Only after those two endless slogging days did I happen to bump into Nancy Waterson in the bar. Honestly, it really was accidental.

It was pretty late, going on midnight. As I entered the bar, worn out, a lovely but older woman beckoned me. Lovely perfume, bluish eyes, dressed to kill with that elegance middle-aged Italian women capture so perfectly. And tons and tons of make-up—always turns me on, that. She wore a seventeenth-century Florentine crucifix as a brooch pin, not quite her only mistake. A two-carat central stone of that rarest of gems Royal Lavulite, a translucent luscious purple, carried off its misplaced setting in the crucifix's centre with utter nonchalance.

She looked me over like they do horses. 'You the guide? Get me a Rusty Nail.'

'What for?'

She pulled me round. I'd been walking past. 'You're supposed to be a guide and you don't know the great Italian invention of the cocktail?'

The penny dropped. A rusty nail must be a drink. That wasn't quite as important as the fact that this high-class bird thought I was a serf. I shook her off. Venice was full of people she could order about without starting on me.

'French tradition, please. Amédée Peychaud was a Froggie pharmacist in New Orleans, love, and *he* invented the cocktail.' She still looked blank. ' 'Course, he did it mostly with absinthe and cognac in those natty little eggcups—*coquetiers*—now so highly prized as collectors' items—'

'Who are you?' she said, wondering.

'My grannie said not to talk to strange women in honky-tonks.'

I moved on, her chain-saw laughter following me as I pushed in. The barman tried. 'Lovejoy. A Rusty Nail's half-and-half Scotch—'

'Great news,' I said. 'Stick at it, Alessandro.'

The presence of Nancy in the far corner straightened my gaze. The older woman departing, that left nobody else about except the barman watching a telly screen, and Nancy. She flagged me over and gave me a glass of her wine. Her bar table was covered with notebooks. Too casually she shut them one by one. David, I learned happily, was out.

'Look,' I said. 'I didn't mean Agnes to get in trouble by asking—'

'Forget it. Movie people are like that. Touchy.'

'You too?'

She finally could not hold back and burst out laughing. And I do mean rolled in the aisles. She was helpless. The night barman smiled with the distant politeness of his kind but kept his eyes on the video-recorded football match.

'Your accent's slipping again, Lovejoy.'

Well, I was so tired I'd become confused. So many faces, nationalities, different hotels. I was bushed. And I'd told different stories to each lot. To the Danes in the Danieli—or was it the Londra?—I was a penniless music student working out my tuition fee. To the West Germans in the Firenze—or was it the Bisanzio?—I was an Australian spinning out the grand tour. To the Americans I was an Italian ex-waiter scratching a living . . .

Narked, I sat glowering while Nancy dried her eyes and made a gasping recovery, clutching her ribs. 'Oh, Lovejoy! That laugh did me good!' She touched my hand and refilled my glass. 'Don't be annoyed, honey. Only, it's so obvious. What exactly's going on, for heaven's sake?'

'Nothing.' Do Yanks really say 'honey', or was she mucking about?

'Come on. Don't sulk.' She was still laughing, silly bitch. 'We're all full of different theories about you. You know Tom and George are running a book? Dave Vidal's got six-to-four you're an antiquarian down on his luck.'

'Oh, he has, has he?' I said bitterly, thinking, I was

bloody well born that. 'What's favourite?'

'Agnes and Doris put ten dollars evens you're an actor practising different roles.'

'And you, Nancy?'

She quietened. Her smile vanished. 'Me, Lovejoy? I can't quite make up my mind between some sort of policeman—'

'They don't work this hard, love.'

'—or some sort of, well, criminal.'

'They don't work this hard, either.' I pinched the rest of her carafe and asked if her budget would run to a slab of nosh.

'Maybe,' she said, still grave. 'If you'll tell me what drives a man harder than hunters and hunted.'

It was bloody difficult, but I forced a buoyant smile. 'It's a deal.' I pulled her to her feet and helped her to sweep her books together. 'Come on. I'll introduce you to *polenta* in a boatman's nosh bar in a *calle* around the corner. Positively no obligation.'

She started smiling again and found her coat. 'Stop it, Lovejoy.'

I kept a weather eye out for Cosima all the way to the little bridge caff by the San Zaccaria. Not that I was worried. I just didn't want her getting ideas.

Then I nicked this gondola.

CHAPTER 13

Love's supposed to be the great pacifier. It is nothing of the sort. It's a torment, a stirrer, the ultimate hellraiser. Really great.

Oddly, Nancy and me were friendly, not at all like the usual carry-on with savage undertones, riotous misunderstandings, bitterness and suchlike. It only rarely happens. I found it very strange, almost weird, to be lying awake in Nancy's bed, hardly knowing who she was yet actually liking her. And not a scar on either of us. The mayhem was missing. A very disturbing sign, this. I was worried. It might be the way serfdom starts.

She was in the bathroom when I got dressed and slipped out. Luckily we were on different floors, so I was able to nip downstairs quite legitimately. Nobody was about. The phone in my room started ringing as I collected my map. That would be Nancy looking for me and ready to play hell. I didn't even pause. The reception-counter clock said three-thirty, almost too late to embark on a night prowl.

Turn right along the Riva degli Schiavoni in the mist under the line of waterfront lamps. Right at the Doge's Palace. Cross St Mark's Square obliquely left, avoiding the famous Clock Arch. Do a quick double dog-leg, and you are at a small canal basin between a hotel, a tiny pavement and a couple of side *calli*. A few bored gondoliers usually chat there in pre-season slackness, not really hoping for custom. Seven or eight gondolas are always aligned in the basin, the tarpaulin covers mostly left on.

Nobody on guard. No signs of life. No wonder, since there's nowhere you can go in a Venetian gondola except Venice. I took the end gondola with ease — no way of locking one, hence my brilliant choice of vehicle. Its cover was murder to shift and twice I nearly fell in. As a sign of good faith in case I got nabbed I took pains to fold the damned thing, and finally made a wobbly cast-off.

Living in the estuaries of East Anglia, I'm not too bad on a boat though they've minds of their own, but a gondola's the queerest craft I've ever tried to handle. For a start, it's deliberately built off balance. I mean it really is asymmetrical, with its bum leaning over more one side than the other. You propel it by this one stern oar. Easy enough, yet you have to keep guessing how much space you have over that toothy *ferro* thing at the front. Add to that the bridges which try to brain you every few yards, and you get the idea it's not plain sailing. It is so low down, especially in a night mist with the damp house walls rising into the night on either side.

There was only me afloat at this godforsaken hour. I poled out of the basin, turned a shaky left mostly by scrabbling along the canal's wet walls. Three bridges later, left again for two. Then three split fingernails, a few muttered oaths and two head thumps, and I dog-legged out of the Rio di Fenice to see the Grand Canal in the gloom straight ahead.

So far nobody on the bridges on in the *calli* as far as I could tell. I pushed wearily into the thinner *rio* at the back of the great theatre, and a waterbus swished across about a hundred yards away, frightening me to death. From the vantage point of a gondola it looked like the *Queen Mary*, all lights and motion. The best about these little side canals is they get no tidal wave to speak of, so I was able to shove the gondola across the *rio* and ride out the minuscule disturbance. I'd no idea the wretched things ran at night.

Which meant that leaving the safety of the narrow *rio* was out of the question. That worried me even more.

I shoved the lopsided craft nervously forward beneath the bridge from which I'd examined the side of the Palazzo Malcontento. A few more strokes and I would be alongside that tunnel-like archway I'd seen, so thoughtfully barred against furtive intruders like me.

A silent Renaissance building, tiers of rectangular shuttered windows. Seen close to and from the water level, Venice is alarmingly tattered and patched. Even by the poor *rio* lights I could see that the palazzo was in the same state as the rest. I gave my gondola one more push and glided along the wall.

The barred archway allowed a head space of about four feet. I had no torch—me being stupid again—but beyond the bars, which seemed to be sort of padlocked double-hinged doors, there was a stretch of water about fifteen feet long running underneath the house. I had the idea I could make out a couple of wet steps and a kind of cellar space. Of course, there'd be no other way to move furniture in or out, there being simply no streets. This kind of entrance must be the Venetian equivalent of driving up to the front door.

Assuming I could somehow get past the barred entrance without springing some alarm, it was a way in. It was possibly wired top to bottom. But it only needed one—*one*—late-night bridge-stroller to happen by, and there'd be a hue and cry at a stray gondola poised outside a respectable palazzo in a distinguished part of the city. Too chancy.

Depressed, I handwalked the gondola back up the *rio* to the bridge. A small *fondamenta* pavement makes it easy to land there. I tethered the gondola, left a note under the tarpaulin and strolled nonchalantly off in the direction of St Mark's. I'd never felt so utterly down.

Lesson: Venetian cat-burglary using a gondola is simply not on. I'd have to think of another way, and fairly soon. I was running out of options.

I sat on my balcony overlooking the lagoon lights. I'd tried dialling Nancy's number but the phone maintained a sulky silence, so I gave that up. Some convenient lie would spring to my rescue when I saw her in the morning.

A big cargo ship was coming in, slowly threshing the night westwards between us and the San Giorgio. Soon she would turn leftish to avoid the Grand Canal by passing between the long shallow curve of the Giudecca island and the Zattere. Who would think that some of the most efficient docks in Europe lay beyond those beautiful churches and elegant rooftops?

By the time the ship's lights passed into the darkness I was pondering the curious spin-off problem of David's little group. Talking with Nancy while, erm, resting in her bed, I'd learned nothing. But what was wrong with being in Venice 'on assignment'? Their business, not mine. I should forget this side problem and concentrate on my main hassle of Mr Pinder and his lunatic scheme to nick Venice. I fell asleep trying to work out how you could fold up Venice and stuff it into a single palazzo.

When I woke from my doze, stiff as a plank and damp from the dawn mist on the balcony, I had at least one answer. If you can't gain entry into a lady's house by dishonest means like good old reliable burglary, you just have to resort to honesty. That's really underhand. Hard, but there it is. Nothing for it.

Plan X.

Incredibly, next day was free of incoming flights. All Cosima and I had to do was see off one taxi-load. After that, nothing. I tried being my usual pleasant unassuming self to Cesare but he was more sullen than ever and hardly responded. Maybe I'd absent-mindedly said a wrong declension or something.

Cosima was standing beside me on the Riva as our boat slewed into the Canale dell' Arsenale with the departing toursits. Cesare would be at least an hour away.

'What now, love?'

'You handle the first flight arriving tomorrow, Lovejoy. The rest of today is yours.'

Neither of us moved. It was blowing gently. Cosima had on one of those plain headscarves which even the tiniest Venetian girls wear to match their little sober brown boots in March. I could have eaten her.

'I, er, look, Cosima—'

'Yes?'

'I'll understand if you say no, but are you doing anything, well, particular today?'

'Well, no. Not really.'

That might have been untrue. Every day she was becoming more stylish. Today she would outshine the most elegant bunch of tourists. In fact I was a bit embarrassed just being with her because I look a scruff at the best of times. Vaguely I wondered who the bloke was, though it didn't matter. If she had a couple of hours to spare she could help Plan X along its thorny road.

'Would you show me the bits of Venice you like?'

She hesitated at that and I hurried to reassure her. 'I've a clean shirt I can put on. I've no other shoes but—'

'No,' she said quickly. 'Don't. It wouldn't be you, dressed up.'

I didn't know how to take that. It narked me, really. Everybody has their own twists. I admit I'm not exactly Savile Row, but I'm clean underneath. In fact my old Gran had this perennial nightmare I'd get knocked down and be carried into the doctor's surgery where All Would Be Revealed, and she laboured for years to pass on this paranoiac delusion to me, so it's second nature by now to de-filth daily. But some people can look stylish in anything, like Cosima, and others like me just can't so it's no use us bothering.

She was looking at her foot. 'I must call at the office first. Then I'll be free.'

'You mean you'll come? With me?'

She took my arm. It made me tingle. 'With pleasure, Lovejoy.'

Our office—I didn't know we had one—was near the San Giorgio dei Greci church, its tower inevitably leaning at an alarming angle over the canal. I only hope the people living nearby got danger money, at least a rent rebate.

You get used to Venice's leaning campaniles, but at first you go about hoping you'll escape before they topple. They all look scarily out of true, and I do mean a terrible angle. Pisa's got one sloper. Venice has a forest of them. You could plonk Pisa's leaning tower in Venice and nobody would notice.

Cosima insisted I come in with her. Cosol Tours, Inc., seen close to, was less than munificent. One small office heaped with forms, a small computer thing with its flex unconnected, a couple of phones and Giuseppe Fusi. Our big wheel. He was homely, portly, comfortable, and proudly showed me photos of his numerous offspring while Cosima delved irritably among the dust.

'Any tourist problem, Lovejoy,' Signor Fusi announced grandly, 'I solve instantly!'

'Giuseppe, that charter special manifest,' Cosima said.

'Think of my office as the hub of the Cosol Tours empire!'

'Great,' I said uneasily, thinking, God Almighty.

'Giuseppe,' Cosima said, endless patience in her voice.

Giuseppe's shoulders slumped. Work called. 'Yes, Cosima?'

While Cosima gave him a drubbing over the tourist manifests I had a quiet smile. Giuseppe was obviously one of those blokes who love gossip and a glass. Everything else was death. He must look forward to Cosima's visits like the end of the tax year.

The canal below the window, wider than most, ran straight to enter the lagoon where Vivaldi's La Pietà church stands on the Riva. Lovely, strikingly unique Venice. It really does warm you. I looked round to find somewhere to perch and enjoy the view while I waited. Smiling to keep out of her firing line, I gently moved a pile of papers and sat on the desk edge to watch a small motorized minibarge amble up the *rio*. These craft carry everything from soft drinks to groceries, and are steered with skilled recklessness by young blokes in overalls . . . *Norman? One of the papers I'd just moved had Signora Norman's name on it.*

'Ready, Lovejoy!'

I nodded, eagerly watching the barge go below the window. 'A minute, love, please. I want to see how he shoots the *ponte*. He might go left.'

'Ah, Lovejoy!' Giuseppe swiftly sensed a chat. 'No. He will go straight ahead, because the angle is too acute. Now, let me explain. If he wanted to make deliveries near the Palazzo Priuli, he would always come up the Rio del Vin, to meet this *rio* at a point below the Rio dei Greci. And why? Because—'

'Giuseppe,' Cosima said, too practised to waste a minute, bless her heart. 'This Geneva flight . . .'

Giuseppe's only satisfaction was that the barge went straight on. Mine was that, turning to tell Giuseppe that he had been proved right, I accidentally knocked over some of the desk papers. It took us a full minute to restore the heap to its original shambles. I of course was very apologetic, and took particular care the papers were all in order.

We left with Cosima happily calling exhortations up the stairs and Giuseppe shouting endless devotion-to-duty down. Cosima and I were laughing about Giuseppe as we crossed the bridge, but all the way along the narrow Fondamenta dell' Osmarin all I could see was Signora Norman's name. It had been on an invoice, address the Malcontento house. Mr D. Vidal and Miss N. Waterson had flown at her expense. I came to with Cosima shaking my arm.

'You've not been listening, Lovejoy. I said where to?'

'Sorry, love.' I went all misty. 'I was just thinking how happy I was, being with you like this.' Her arm seemed so natural linked with mine. 'You're showing me what Venice is up to, remember? Lead on.'

*

We combed Venice, exhilarated. Of course, I was constantly looking for something different from what Cosima was showing me. As the bridges came and went in a confusion of buildings, elegant façades, canals and alleys, Cosima blossomed. Her rather guarded anxiety vanished and we walked with what can only be called merriment. She astonished me with a zillion odd facts.

'Galileo's house,' she'd say. 'He showed our Doge his new invention at the top of the Campanile,' and you would know she meant *the* Galileo, his new invention being the telescope and his demonstration that business in 1609. No accident that the Flanders spectacle-makers zipped to Venice with their improved magnifying lenses, spying practically being a Venetian patent. Galileo just happened to hear of these lenses there. 'That place was Napoleon's,' she'd say, not even bothering to look. 'Your Lord Byron lived over there; a lady threw herself into *that* canal for love of him.' And occasionally her dear little face would frown with intensity as she asked a question to check that she was not leaving me behind. 'Casanova was born in that *calle*. You know Casanova?'

'Yes,' I'd say gravely, as if he was still around.

'Good,' she'd say, all serious, and her animated smile would return. 'That palazzo is Cristoforo Moro's. Your Shakespeare changed his name to Othello—you know Othello?—but Shylock lived across there—you know Shylock . . . ?'

Soon she was eagerly urging me along, anxious to show me her favourite spots and prattling all the time.

'Hitler toured Venice on his own at night—at a fast trot,' was one of her gems, supposed to be encouragement. 'Didn't stay long, though.'

She had a collection of entertaining sights as well. One of her favourites was the rubbish collection. Household rubbish is collected at the lagoon-side entrance of each canal about half-nine each morning. The brown cardboard boxes and black plastic bags are lifted into a long barge-like boat of military grey and black by the steersman's two blue-overalled shore-based helpers. They actually sweep up after themselves. Incredible. I couldn't get over it.

As we walked, I realized there's this great trick Venetians have, of pretending people from antiquity are still knocking about. We have a similar knack in East Anglia, but don't take things quite so personally. She showed me Vivaldi's Pietà church, which old Mr Pinder had practically wept over. I thought it beautiful, clean, chill and excessively neat. 'So different from the Red Priest himself,' I mused, as we gaped at Piazzetta's *Visitation* painting. 'I wonder if that soprano Vivaldi shacked up with was as attractive as her sister, and which of them he really loved?' Cosima disapproved and quickly pulled me out of the side entrance.

'Father Vivaldi's troubles were of his own making,' she said sternly. 'If he'd paid more attention to his church and less to . . . to his music, he wouldn't be defrocked.'

'Falling for the lady was perfectly natural, Cosima.'

She drew away, appalled. "You're not advocating free love?'

'Is there any other kind?' I was a picture of innocence.

'It's Father Vivaldi's business, not ours.'

That's how I came to learn the Great Venetian Trick. Antonio Vivaldi: 1678-1741; you must speak and think as if he were still concert-master at the girls' school on the Riva degli Schiavoni. You give the same courtesy to other Venetians. You can mention Marco Polo, but not that he came from China to knock on his own door and got himself detained because nobody recognized him after a score of years. You can praise Veronese's masterpieces to the skies, but not his shameful trial before the Inquisition about his *Feast in the House of Levi*. The Great Venetian trick operates at all times: you can speak about Italians and all others any way you choose, but Venetians are respectable.

I wish now I'd thought about the implications, but it's no good crying over spilt milk. Especially when that spilled milk turned out to be Cosima.

The market near the Rialto Bridge was another of her favourites. ('Not the gaudy shops on the bridge itself, Lovejoy. They should never have been allowed there in the first place,' she said severely, criticizing the practice which began in 1592.) The Erberia vegetable market is everything women love to look at — raw grub in all its horrible pristine state of execution. Cosima dived in like a footballer, hauling me after her and yapping indignantly of the price of onions, greens, fruit, artichokes ('Look! A scandal! And Venice the fountain of all artichokes!') until she noticed I was pale about the gills and asked what was wrong.

'Those.' I indicated with a jerk of my head but didn't dare look. There was this stall selling dead seagulls and bald quail dangling on hooks.

'Poor dear! Is it the price? We might get one cheaper round the corner —'

'No, love. It's just . . .'

'Ah. *Simpatico!*' She hugged my arm as if enormously pleased, then remembered and dragged me among barrows to confront a granite statue, a little burdened bloke carrying steps which led up to the Egyptian granite rostrum.

'Our laws used to be proclaimed here. He's the Gobbo.'

The statue looked knackered, humping that enormous weight. She was smiling and reached out to pat him. We had to shove aside a heap of old vegetable boxes.

'When I was a little girl I felt so sorry for him.' She told me how in the old days wrong-doers had to run the gauntlet naked from St Mark's Basilica to touch the

Gobbo. 'He's a lovely old thing. If the bad men reached him all was forgotten. For a statue to do so much good!'

'And if they didn't?'

'Ah, well.' She was thinking of my faintness at the sight of the hanging seagulls and decided the fewer explanations the better. 'Now we go to our beautiful fish market!'

I didn't quite make that, and had to wait shakily at the San Giacomo for her after only a brief glance at the masses of stalls covered with eels, squids, every sort of glistening fish imaginable, crabs, shellfish. I know that grub turns a lot of people on. I mean, Cosima made a breathless return, hugely pleased with herself and carrying a parcel. 'What a pity you wouldn't come with me, Lovejoy! They're lovely fish today, but the *prices!* Scandalous!'

The single arch of the Ponte di Rialto has been severely criticized over the centuries, but as I paused to give it a last look I couldn't help thinking that Antonio da Ponte didn't do too bad a job. Cosima stood by me, looking.

'Is it true about Michaelangelo?' I asked her. I wasn't worried about her answer, but asking some daft question gave me time to glance casually at the motor-boat idling near the Riva del Ferro.

'Competing to design the *Ponte?* Yes. But he didn't get the contract.'

'Why not?'

She gave that lovely tilted Latin shrug I keep trying to imitate. 'He wasn't Venetian, of course.'

Of course. We had coffee in a *campo* near the Formosa church. Cosima told me how they used to have bullfights in the *campi* spaces between the canals. I don't know how much I took in of all she told me that day, but I wish now I'd burned every word into my brain. All I did was gaze at her lovely animated face, watch her delectable mouth move, and try to suppress the craving growing in me. The trouble is that hunger comes stealing into you when you least expect it. All I hoped was that her bloke wasn't an all-in wrestler, and that he wouldn't show.

She took us on a detour and paused at a *sottoportego*, a little alley going under a building. Politely she asked me to wait a moment please. I said of course, and watched her go through into a small courtyard beyond. She'd probably gone inside to make a discreet check that he hadn't arrived yet. Okay, so I was second fiddle. So what? Where was the harm? There was one of those disused well-heads in the *campo*'s centre so characteristic of Venice's tiny open spaces. While I waited I had a smile watching a pigeon bathe beneath a water tap. I wouldn't have smiled if I'd known what was coming.

The motor-boat idling up the Riva del Ferro was on my mind. It had been a weird pastel blue, with a thickset bloke at the wheel. And I was nearly certain that the affluent older woman seated in the centre was the rich cocktail bird who had argued with me in the hotel bar last night. The boat wasn't going anywhere, just idling. And again she had given me that incisive stare. Now, a bloke staring at a bird is merely being his usual magpie self. But a bird ogling a bloke is either on heat or the warpath. And us complete strangers.

Five minutes later Cosima appeared without her fish parcel. We solemnly linked arms and walked on like repleted lovers at peace with the world.

CHAPTER 14

At ten o'clock that night I ambled down the Riva degli Schiavoni, in absolute Paradise. It had been a magic day. Magic.

Cosima's bloke hadn't shown after all. Real luck, that.

A whole day going about with Cosima, and she had taken me back to her place — a cramped little third-floor flat, through the *sottoportego* as I'd guessed. I'd had her bloke's supper. Odd, but she'd enjoyed the whole bit, cooking shyly but with that determination women get. I didn't look, just read and watched her telly, occasionally calling out questions about things that caught my attention. She said the inky stuff she served the Seppie fish in was the right colour, and gave me polenta which she made herself. It was good stuff. I told her she was hired, and made her laugh. And she even promised to show me some of the lagoon's outer islands tomorrow. Magic.

Nothing happened much after that. No, honestly. I really didn't lay a finger on her, and she showed no sign of dragging me into the closed room beyond the tiny kitchen, stripping me naked and savagely wreaking her crazed lust on my poor defenceless unprotected body. And neither of us said it was a long walk back for me to the hotel. Or said how lonely beds are on your own. I have definitely nothing to report. Which is how I came to be ambling home along the Riva beneath its double rows of lamps in the night mist.

Two odd things, though. A boat started up suddenly as I neared the Victor Emmanuel statue. It sounded familiar, like Cesare's, but it tore off towards the Arsenale before I could see whose it was. That's the trouble with standing in a well-lit place, even if it is the mist-shrouded waterfront of the Venice lagoon: you can't see them, but they can see you. Daft as a brush, I thought nothing of it at the time. One boat in a nation of boats is nothing, right?

That night I fell asleep blissfully happy. Well, I would have done but for a silly game I used to play which sometimes comes back to me at the oddest times, like a daft jingle you can't get rid of. The game's called Edgar

Allan Poe. He once said the ingredients of a good con trick are minuteness, interest, perseverance, ingenuity, audacity, nonchalance, originality, impertinence—and grin! That's nine ingredients. In my game, you must assume that Poe was wrong. You are allowed only *three* of his nine, so which six ingredients do you chuck out? I always end up with minuteness, nonchalance, and the grin. Except I tossed and turned most of the night, ecstatically happy with memories of Cosima but playing my stupid game over and over in my head. It's usually a sign I'm worried, but what the hell could I possibly be worrying about? Cosima liked me. I was almost sure she did.

An hour before dawn it came to me: the worrying thing was that nobody was grinning at all, except me.

And when I woke and went down to breakfast at eight o'clock, Nancy, David, Agnes and Doris had booked out. Not a word. Sad, but no need to worry. It happens. And anyway nothing to do with my main problem. Right?

Cosima and I were down for the airport run for an incoming flight that day. There would be no afternoon arrival so I suggested she take the morning off but to my delight she said no, she'd come and we would do the run jointly with Cesare.

While I waited for her to arrive after breakfast I chatted with Cesare whose boat had been moored by then. Today he was at the Riva near where the big tugboats berth against those creaking, wobbling posts.

'Got a fact, Cesare?' I said to lessen his sourness.

'Yours are never worth any money, Lovejoy.'

That was a bit rough, but I trotted out a cracker. 'Turner the painter did a watercolour of the Rialto Bridge. It's lost.'

He nodded. 'Worth a fortune, eh?'

'Two fortunes. Your fact?'

He looked over the water. 'Every year, Lovejoy, people drown at night in the lagoon.'

I thought. 'That's not worth much.'

'It may be worth more than you know.'

Narked, I started to say something but chewed the sentence off. I shrugged and strolled over to watch the people embarking at the waterbus, nearly falling over that old geezer who sits there selling lottery tickets. White beard, tatty cap, his club foot thrust out to trip the unwary. I'd made him laugh the day before by nicknaming him Ivan the Terrible. He always looks asleep but he's not. Rustle a banknote within ten yards and his eyes are wide awake.

The Riva seemed to be filling early today. The San Zaccaria waterbus stop was thronged with people trying to get off. Cosima would arrive from the direction of St Mark's, so I walked past that daft statue as far as the bridge over the del Vin canal and stood watching.

My jubilation of the previous night had dissipated in the strange problem of Nancy. I had asked the reception clerk earlier if he had a message for me but no luck. That narked me. Nancy might at least have dropped me a line or two, even if it was only a 'See you again sometime.' I decided that was typical of women's callousness and leaned over the bridge parapet to see one of the pavement artists at work, a bearded lad with a small patient dog. Cosima couldn't miss me even in the crowd, stuck up here.

The bearded artist was really quite good and I became interested. He seemed to specialize in views of the Salute church and San Giorgio Maggiore, both easily visible from here—but he was not averse to dashing off the odd portrait masterpiece in charcoal. He was doing one now, of a coloured girl. She sat on the little camp-stool, aware of her attractiveness and the interest of the crowd.

Somebody made a remark, pointing at the sketch. The

artist was provoked by that. It's just the way artists are, but this one was especially vehement and gave the critical bystander a mouthful which made us all laugh. To prove a point he pulled out an unfinished sketch and held it up, gesticulating with his charcoal. There was a lot of good-natured backchat, but I didn't care about joining in. All I cared about was hurtling down the bridge steps, suddenly and breathless, getting hold of that unfinished sketch.

'The sketch almost finished and she runs off,' the artist was complaining. 'All my time and genius wasted! Leaving me unpaid! Because of thoughtless comments such as yours!'

'Finish it,' somebody suggested, amid chatter. 'Then sell it.'

'Who to? Who would buy—?'

'Me, signore,' I interrupted, winded but struggling to sound casual.

'Ah!' the crowd exclaimed, interest quickening. I grinned amiably.

The artist was delighted. 'You know the sitter, signore?'

'Afraid not.' I made a comedy out of the denial and people laughed because anybody could tell the sketch was of a lovely bird. 'But you have caught a certain light . . .'

'I'll finish it for you—'

'No. That would be a mistake. I prefer it as it is.' I had the sense to apologize to the coloured girl for interrupting. Amid the babble of conversation I paid the artist a full fee and went to sit on the bridge to examine the unfinished sketch. Old Ivan the Terrible cackled a laugh nearby. The old devil was watching.

'Such bad luck with the girls that you have to fall for a picture?'

'Shut your gums, silly old sod.'

It was definitely Nancy. I didn't want to ask the bearded artist when he sketched her because the presence of the girl now posing for him made me somehow uneasy.

I was worrying sick about possibilities. Suppose Nancy had waited on the Riva to be collected. It might have occurred to her to have herself drawn . . . perhaps intending it as a souvenir? Or as a present she could leave me at the hotel? That was like Nancy. Which raised the interesting question of why she had done neither, and had left it in the hands of a complaining and unpaid artist. So she must have left in a rush, under sudden compulsion. David's special 'assignment'?

'*Buon giorno*, Lovejoy.'

'Eh? Oh.'

Cosima was standing there, smiling, absolutely dazzling. Hastily I scrambled to my feet, trying to roll the sketch up so she wouldn't see. I didn't want her, of all people, thinking I was loose or immoral or anything. We descended the bridge steps and moved along the Riva to where Cesare's boat was moored.

'Thank you for yesterday, love,' I said. 'Cesare's ready.'

'Not at all, Lovejoy.' She eyed the scroll I was clutching. 'Souvenir?'

'Only a little sketch of the airport.' My eyes were downcast and soulful. 'Where I first saw you.'

She paused. 'Oh, Lovejoy.' She said my name as if I was nothing but trouble. 'What sort of man are you?'

'Erm, only ordinary. What do you mean, love?'

Her enormous eyes made me dizzy. It was like looking down two deep wells. 'I feel so foolish. Sometimes you're just absurd.'

'Absurd?' I was just about to give her a mouthful when we heard Cesare yelling angrily and saw him at the jetty pointing at his watch. We walked along and boarded, a bit guiltily I thought, though God knows why either of us should feel guilty for nothing. Cesare's attitude hadn't improved. Cosima's brilliant mood had dulled somewhat. I sat there seething.

Absurd? Me?

Bloody cheek. That's the trouble with women. No judgement of character.

Somebody once said that death and Venice go together. Soon I would learn the hard way that they were right. If I'd had half the sense I was born with I'd have stopped daydreaming about sex and the precious ancient glass of the ancient glass factories, because all the clues were there for the asking. But, me being me and having only the brains of a rocking-horse, I ignored all the portents and simply sat in Cesare's boat and was wafted graciously to the Marco Polo.

At the airport Cosima bustled about with her clipboard in the arrivals hall. I stood like a suspect while she checked my three badges and my Cosol Tours placard.

I said lightly, 'Here, Cosima. What's happened to Agnes? You know, David thing's elderly bird. The hotel said she'd booked out.'

Cosima pursed her lips, pushing me into a more favourable position along the row of tour operators' reception stalls opposite the Customs exit. 'They were recalled.'

I tut-tutted. 'Holiday cut short, eh?'

Cosima said absently, frowning with concentration at the flight indicator, 'They flew out during the night.'

'Shame,' I said.

'Film people,' with a pretty tilted shrug. 'Sudden people, *non è vero?*'

'Lives not their own,' I agreed sympathetically as the concourse filled with our arriving passengers. 'Cosol Tours,' I started up. 'Cosol this way, please.'

CHAPTER 15

The trouble with some people is their heads never switch off. I'm the same. Even kipping's a busy time with me, all manner of guesses and frighteners swarming through a grey matter that's basically angry that the rest of the body's dozing just when it wants to play. What with all this free activity you'd think I'd be marvellous at planning ahead, a veritable Sherlock Holmes.

Wrong.

I'm a duckegg. Absolutely pathetic. There's proof: that bad day at Torcello.

It was all my idea. I admit that. But having an idea doesn't mean everything that happens is my fault.

Like I said, Venice is a mass of islands and Torcello was practically the first of the Venetian islands ever to be colonized by the people fleeing from troubles on the fifth-century mainland. In those early days it was even boss island, with tens of thousands all doing their thing in the new maritime nation. They say it's dying away, but aren't we all? It's the speed that matters.

Everybody's heard of Torcello and its famous detached campanile (again leaning at a perilous angle) and the lovely wood-domed Santa Fosca church, so I was all agog to catch the *vaporetto* out and see it for myself. Heart-rending to tear myself away from Venice proper, but we needn't be too long about it. In my mind I suppose was the notion of a last fling before I tackled the Palazzo Malcontento. Of course, I was here because I'm always genuinely concerned with justice and truth, with preventing that yellow-suited nerk from committing murder again.

But everybody deserves a rest now and then. So to think

up a day in luscious old Torcello with the delectable Cosima was perfectly reasonable. A well-deserved rest.

Among the mob I'd handled the previous day were two Australian blokes, doing Europe on a shilling with Venice their launch-pad. I'd shared a bottle of vino with them in the bar. One was a flaxen-haired drifter called Gerry, a real dreamer. Farthing-clever-penny-daft, my old Gran would have called him. He claimed to paint butterflies, and lived this great vision where suddenly the whole world rushed at him demanding canvases covered with acrylic butterflies. I asked him if he ever painted anything else and he looked at me as if I was off my nut. It takes all sorts. His mate Keith was lankier, cooler, more on the make and poisonously practical, daft on engines. Opposite poles attract and all that. Synergism implies difference. So clever old Lovejoy in a drunken stupor put the big dig when the fourth bottle was easier to lift than its predecessors, but they knew nothing about David and Nancy.

'Never met them, sport,' Keith said. That was as far as I got, because Gerry wanted to talk about painting butterflies and Keith about engines.

'Engines,' Keith insisted tipsily. 'They're the future. What's missing in Venice, Lovejoy? Answer: engines! What's missing in the air, in Europe, in outer space? Answer: *engines!* Same in Australia, Africa, India, everywhere!'

Nodding, I got blearily sloshed. Nancy had gone without trace. I felt so kindly towards this weird pair I got the next bottle, carefully charging it up to Cosol Tours to show off, and bragged to them about Torcello. In a drunken humour I told Gerry I'd heard it was riddled with butterflies and Keith it had lots of old engines.

I was still part-sloshed when for the umpteenth time I fell over Ivan the Terrible near the second bridge along the Riva, scattering his unsold lottery tickets. He was nearly as pickled as me and we exchanged a mouthful of friendly abuse while I helped him to find them in the lamplight.

'Drunk because you couldn't find your lovely American lady?' he demanded, to rile me. He made a crude gesture.

'Shut up, you old fool.' I paused. 'Here, Ivan. How d'you know she was a Yank?'

'She spoke like one. I'm not yet deaf.'

So he'd seen the whole scenario: Nancy being drawn by the artist, somebody coming urgently for her, the artist shouting rape because his fee went missing.

'Was he a Yank, too?'

'The one who took her? One was. But the other.' Ivan the Terrible spat into the canal and closed his tatty old case. 'One of them pretty-pretty boys from the Malcontento. Suit of many colours. They should all stay in Naples.'

In a fit of misguided generosity I gave him a note for another bottle and went to watch the reflected lights out on the lagoon. If I hadn't been stewed I'd have tried to think. As it was, I did nothing but watch the lights until I nodded off and woke shivering.

That next morning Cosima and I caught the boat from the Fondamenta Nuove. I was a bit embarrassed seeing Keith and Gerry already on the boat among the crowd in the bows, but was pleased they saw me with a beautiful bird. I was proud of her. Some things are so beautiful you have to look at them piecemeal or they blind you. Cosima was like that. They both waved back, Keith especially smiling wide. Cosima, I observed, pinked up and gave them only the briefest nod.

'Glad they came,' I said conversationally.

The boat goes to Murano and Burano before reaching Torcello. Naturally I'd forgotten my map so Cosima had to point out the places we passed. A true Venetian, to her Murano was a sort of industrial slum island and she barely glanced at it as the *vaporetto* chugged nearer, past the posh bright brickwork which rims San Michele cemetery island.

'We had to put all the glassmakers in one place safely away from the rest of us,' she explained casually. 'Their furnaces kept setting Venice afire.'

'Recently?' I was only joking, but her pretty-serious face showed concentration reflected in the boat windows.

'Thirteenth century. Of course, it was as well they were moved out to Murano, Lovejoy. It became a little . . . depraved.'

I'd heard that too, but never in such tones of reproof. Moral indignation from a Venetian is a scream, seeing they invented Carnival and the cicisbeo, that cissy upper-class version of the gigolo. Still, depravity makes you even more interested so I looked with fascination as we stopped to let droves of folk on and off, then puttered past the line of glassmakers' slipways and wharves. Lovely to see higgledy-piggledy industry flourishing exactly as it did six centuries gone. The pleasure-gardens are now all vanished beneath hundreds of tiny crammed glass factories but I thought it looked lovely. My sort of scene. Especially the idea of all those lovely special glasses made by those old-generation glassmakers on every mantel-piece. She'd made the glassmakers' banishment sound somewhere near Mongolia. It's hardly a mile.

'Pity Cesare couldn't come,' I said as our prow turned towards Burano. 'We could have gone to see the church of San Donato if we'd had his boat.'

She did glance at the gliding islands then. Her hair was moving in the wind that breezed down the length of the boat's interior, silkier than on any telly advert. 'I am content,' she said quietly.

'Yes, er, great. Me too.' For the first time I realized she

looked even more like a million quid than usual. Were relatives lurking on Torcello? Were we going to drop in on a mob of uncles and crones for *colazione*? An ordeal loomed. God. I felt in a state, sloppy as always. 'San Donato,' I said lamely. 'Not every day you see a saint whose spit kills dragons. The Muranese say they've the dragon's bones behind the high altar . . .'

She shrugged dismissively. 'The Muranese!'

The boat moved slowly into the northern waters of the lagoon. Still a warming sun, still that lovely brittle daylight. But as the occasional island stops came and went and Venice's doomed city receded in the morning mists the beat and rush of the boat seemed lonelier than it had. The water seemed brackish, less blue. We could hardly see the long lines of the islands and banks to seaward, and the islands now seemed threadbare and even desolate. Cosima touched my knee.

'Are you well, dear?'

I grinned with every erg, determined to show I was on top of the world.

'The best day I ever had so far, love.'

She drew breath the way women do when checking they won't be overheard. About us the passengers had thinned, so out it came. 'Please do not jump to conclusions, Lovejoy,' she said. 'I am merely anxious to accompany you to Torcello, since you appear to have read of the Teocota Madonna.'

I hastily agreed to whatever it was she was blathering about, and dismissed her mood as one of these weirdities they often have, because Burano was in sight, its splash of blue, red, yellow houses a brilliant set of nursery bricks crammed any old how among the drab lagoon marshes. You can't help loving it. It is toytown. Its campanile leans like a Saturday drunk. Everything, from canals to doorways, is dinky. No wonder they're born lacemakers. Delighted as I was, though, Cosima stayed aloof.

'They made a lace collar of blonde hair for Louis XIV,' I babbled, delighted at the colourful island. 'They have a museum for Venetian point lace—'

'Torcello soon, dear,' Cosima said, her face lighting into a smile that dried me up.

'Er, good.'

Only love illuminates a woman's eyes with that kind of radiance. Love and all its works. My instant conclusion: lover-boy lives somewhere on Torcello, and we'd presumably bump, accidentally of course, into this rustic cretin which would give her the excuse to leave me stranded. Don't get me wrong. I wasn't narked. I mean, all's fair in love and all that. But even gigolos get paid. I'd somehow got myself into the position of unpaid stooge. For a few minutes, as the boat moved on serenely through the bright delicate mists of the morning, I maintained a pained silence so pointedly that Cosima shyly reached across and took my hand, her eyes avoiding mine. My frost didn't last long. It couldn't. Nobody's frost can last long when that ancient warmth beats out of the waters and the stones shriek at you of past human existence and love preserved in the works of Man.

'Torcello, dear,' Cosima was saying. 'I hope you'll—'

But I was already eager to be on the landing-stage and only later, when it was altogether too hopelessly late for both of us, did I piece together the conversation on the *vaporetto* with my lovely Cosima.

Like I said. Pathetic.

Torcello.

We'd gone a few hundred yards when I stopped.

'Where is it, love?'

She paused with me, holding my arm. 'This *is* Torcello, dear.'

'But the city. The great palaces.'

Her eyes moistened, gazing at me. 'You didn't read

quite enough. Torcello is . . . ending.'

'There's twenty great churches,' I bleated, standing on the overgrown path beside the canal.

'Two.'

'—and thirty thousand inhabitants.'

'Less than a hundred souls.' Her eyes were brimming now, hers or mine. 'I'm so sorry, darling.'

The canal runs straight from the landing-stage into the heart of what is left of Torcello's great square. Now it's not even a village green. The great stone arches of the fifteenth century bridges, the dazzling *fondamenta*, the might of empire literally fallen and overgrown. A wooden bridge crossed near a canal junction. A couple of cottages, a scruffy field or two, a few lanes of artichokes here and there in the dampish fields. A line of peach trees. Weeds and reeds. A tiny file of ducks. I sat on the canal edge.

'It . . . it sent a fleet of galleys to the Chioggia wars.' My voice hardly reached a whisper. 'It was a whole empire.' It had even sent two Torcello agents to steal St Mark's body from mighty Egypt.

'Gone, dear.' She was hugging me, kneeling beside me and rocking gently. 'Don't be sad. You live too much inside your head. You must come out, darling.'

Lucky there was nobody else about. We were the only ones to have disembarked at Torcello except for Keith and Gerry who had set up Gerry's easel by the landing-stage, so we were unseen. Cosima took my hand and led me then into the orchard, me trailing like a heartbroken schoolkid, and we lay beneath the spreading branches.

She hand-shushed me from calling out at the pinnacle, then murmuring and rocking my head on her breast while her fingers made sure we were decently clothed again so as not to give offence to any ghosts which happened by.

She talked to me, even though I was almost oblivious in

that small death which follows loving. We must have looked so incongruous, a delicious colourful bird with dazzling lustrous hair, sitting-kneeling in a lost orchard with her elegant new dress crumpled, nursing a slumbering dishevelled oaf who wasn't paying the slightest heed to a word she was saying. Odd, but women I actually love are the only ones who can switch off my nightmares. That hour in Torcello I dozed deeper and more restfully than I had for many a month. She did everything for me that magical time, with the reeds soughing and the stalks clashing softly all about the edges of the waterways. Once I half-woke to hear a couple of children shouting, but Cosima calmed me out of being startled. 'They're the little ones playing *al pangalo*, darling. Only a game of batting sticks. Shush.'

At the finish she had to wake me to get me moving. Our aim had always been to nosh at Cipriani's. Until Cosima explained how the famous restaurant had come to the rescue of poor old Torcello practically single-handed I hadn't realized that the famous *locanda* was the one remaining epicentre of life in Torcello. She had booked us in, and so we dined in sunshiny elegance looking out over the small vegetable gardens next the tiny central square of Torcello. Beneath us, around us, entirely covered and unseen, the ruins of one of the powerful mediæval empires of Europe. Around, an innocent spectacle of market gardening with a bloke hoeing vegetables, and a couple of buildings in view, with a farmhouse a little distance off.

I got up courage to ask her. 'What about your, erm, intended?'

'Intended?'

'Your bloke.'

'Cesare thinks too much of his own wishes.' Cosima reproved me at the impertinence by wagging her head so her hair swung.

'Cesare? The boatman?' I needed a minute to take that in. No big bruiser meeting us? No bloke back in Venice?

'Cesare. But only a little. Anyway, Lovejoy. He never has been so . . . close. Certainly not my intended.'

Hence the glowerings. Hence his growing surliness. Hence I'm as thick as usual, because Cesare saw me threatening his own ambitions for Cosima. That's what I needed all right, an enemy I'd picked unerringly to reveal my interest in the Palazzo Malcontento. He was also my one means of independent transport, apart from stolen gondolas. Which raised the question of what Cesare was doing back in Venice while Cosima and yours truly were whooping it up in Torcello.

'Listen, Cosima.' I'm always awkward saying thanks. 'Giving me, erm, love . . . My soul gets sort of damp when it feels antiques go wrong.'

'I know, darling. Learning about Torcello. I told you too suddenly.'

'My fault.' I got my money out to pay for our meal. 'But you have the right to know everything.' I meant almost everything. 'It's time for you to ask me about myself, love. I'll answer every question with complete honesty. Promise.' I meant almost complete.

'No.' Firmly she poured the last of the wine for us. 'It is time for *me* to tell *you* about myself. We shall exchange information while we examine the remaining pieces of Torcello. There are several hours of daylight left, darling.'

'It's a deal.'

'And I have arranged a surprise for you.'

I couldn't help wondering as we raised glasses. A deal of planning had gone into this day at Torcello. I only wished I'd been in on it, so I could work things out. I was beginning to think I'd been surprised enough.

The dusty little centre of Torcello pulled me up short.

The Piazza—its proper name—was once the great meeting-place for the all-powerful Tribune. I expected at least *some*thing, a sign, some spectacular ruins. Anything to ablate this terrible feeling of melancholy.

Instead, there's threadbare grass, dusty paths, and two or three little cottages. A building converted to a tiny museum. To one side is a low octagonal church, all fawns, and this taller cathedral with stone swing-shutters to protect its windows. A canal runs by. A lady in traditional dress had a stall selling unbelievably mediocre modern lace. A big stone chair stands improbably in the centre of the space, God knows why, just asking for a stray tourist to clown for a comical holiday snap.

And that's it. Get the point? That's it *all*. Exactly as if we'd gone to find a bustling Times Square or Piccadilly and found instead a derelict yard.

I felt ill.

'Come, darling.' Cosima hauled me to come into the cathedral. 'We'll sit for a while. I'm sorry about the tower, but lightning's taken its top off.' This temporary setback happened over three centuries gone. I watched her fold a headscarf to enter the cathedral. Most underrated of all woman's decorations, is the old headscarf. I touched her cool cheek to show I approved.

She said gravely, 'Dearest, I want to pray. Only to . . . explain. Not apologize. You can look at the Teocota while I do.'

I almost started a grin thinking, What is all this? But she wasn't joking, and moved towards a transept, her heels clicking echoes down the nave. Grumbling inwardly that there wasn't any need to put on airs or assume fetching little tableaux—she'd already hooked me in the most permanent way—I turned to move parallel, along the northern length of the nave, and saw it.

Maybe it was the sheer spectacle or its unusual form, though I'd been expecting something profound because everybody on earth's heard of the Teocota Madonna. Or maybe it was just having loved Cosima. Whatever the cause, I was blammed by it. The background's gold and faint, and the Madonna herself is somehow elongated like an El Greco, but those are just technical points. Ignore them. Technique is only the irreverent dogma of forgers and curators. Concentrate on technique too much and you miss love and feeling. The mosaic face weeps. The Madonna gazes above your head, not at you, but beyond as if at the things you've left undone and the cruelty you've enacted on the way to Torcello. Of course, I found myself reasoning, the Madonna didn't really mean me. She was reproaching the rest of the buggers, because I'm always reasonable and fair-minded and have a pretty good reputation for doing the right thing and never hurting people. Beautiful, stunning. I shivered, but only because it was colder in the cathedral than I thought.

Or it could be the lurking horror of realizing that the image of old Mr Pinder had suddenly shifted in my mind. He might not be a batty old lunatic. He could possibly be what he actually presented himself to be: an elderly man battling against neglect and ignorance with the only forces at his disposal to protect ancient brilliance like this Madonna.

Christ, I thought. The notion made me glance suspiciously at Cosima, but she was oblivious, contentedly crossing herself from having lit two candles. No artifice, no pretence, as she came across and whispered eagerly, 'Did you like the Madonna, Lovejoy?'

'Yes, thanks.'

'They say some Greeks made it.'

'They did a good job.'

'Darling! Your hand is freezing.'

'I'm cold.'

'Then it's time for sunshine, and my surprise. Come, darling.'

We left, the Madonna's tearful gaze burning down above the crown of my head.

CHAPTER 16

'We've come absolutely miles,' Cosima answered.

We lay on a reedy island no higher than a mud flat among a myriad small water channels. The day was still hot, but a steady breeze had sprung up causing the dense reeds to make a dry clattering sound. Here and there a duck splashed, businesslike, but that was it. Great for secret loving picnics, but nothing else.

'How far, love?' I hate countryside, and this remoteness was at least partly that.

She raised her head, finally kneeling up to see across the *pulude* flats. We'd seen Torcello's campanile when putting the *sandolo* boat ashore. 'About two kilometres, I suppose. Almost.'

'Good idea, your lady's engine.'

Cosima laughed and fell sprawling, embracing me. 'Is the signore tired, then?' This witticism made her roll in the aisles when she came to the punch line. 'May one ask why?'

I had to laugh with her. The surprise had been a *sandolo*, a small curved-looking boat. You row it standing up like a gondolier does, but mostly with two oars. The oldish lady from whom Cosima had hired the *sandolo* had mischievously explained that the object humped in the stern beneath a black plastic dustbin bag was an outboard motor. 'Wise to take precautions against the lagoon,' she'd said. 'And for exhaustion, on your return.' Cosima had given her a mock scolding at such suggestiveness but the old Torcellana had cackled all the more and pushed us off. She'd used the ancient greeting

'*Salve*', showing she was local.

Cosima wanted to row but so did I. I felt I'd rowed a race but had a high old time losing my way before Cosima said we should stop. We had a picnic and love on the blanket she happened to have brought along. I called her a scheming hussy and she said she didn't care.

'What's that noise?' The dozy afternoon kept being punctured. 'It's nearer.'

'Shooting, beyond Santa Cristina. The Doge of Venice used to give five ducks to the noble families every Christmas. Folk still shoot.'

'I hope we scared some off to safety.'

We'd made rather a racket the second time around, which was okay because apart from the occasional shrill outboard and lazy squawkings from the dense reeds there was almost total silence. I reached for her again but she pushed my hand away.

'There's a boat coming. Listen.'

'Stopping.'

At the canal back in Torcello we'd glimpsed Gerry and Keith puttering past the *locanda* intersection in a motor dinghy. Keith had waved. Gerry was too preoccupied consulting a paper, apparently giving directions as they'd headed out into the lagoon. Hardly anything to paint around here, that was for sure. Except me and Cosima. And ducks, but they were being decimated.

Another shot sounded, not quite so distant. No echoes like the others. Cosima drooped over me, our faces inches apart in the hair-filtered sunlight.

'Maybe somebody looking for the San Lorenzo. It was a great church. Now it's just a mound in the water. People dig at low water for rubble.'

'Saint Francis loved the ducks when he came here,' I accused.

'Dear Lovejoy. Always looking for somebody else to blame.'

'Bloody cheek.'

'It's true. You should look at yourself, darling, instead of the rest.'

She was smiling and rubbing noses but it's the sort of chitchat that gets you narked, especially when you know for a start that you're twice as reasonable as everybody else.

'It's this place, love.'

'Vanished splendour?'

'Maybe.' I was beginning to feel lost, remote, altogether too far from civilization and safety. All this silence, these miles of empty shallows and tangled channels with only the occasional distant campanile slanting to catch the late afternoon sun.

'Want to get back? There's a *vaporetto* from Torcello and Mazzorbo in an hour. We've plenty of time.'

There it was again, the spooky reminder. Mazzorbo's name means 'great city', and I knew for a fact it was nothing more than a few villas, a boatyard, one cypress tree and an ivy-covered campanile. Perhaps I was letting myself become nervous. Silly, really, because there was nothing to be worried about. Especially not out here.

'Know why I came?'

'Ulterior motive.' She was smiling, kneeling up doing her hair, mouth full of hairclips, head to one side.

'Several.'

'How many are female, Lovejoy?'

'One. You.'

A warning shake of the comb at me before she resumed her hair. 'That's all right, then.'

'Then I wanted to find out why you've cornered the world market in television people.'

'That's easy, darling. They're a rich signora's playthings.'

I sat up. 'Eh?'

'We did a group charter—unfortunately through those

Milanese agents, absolute gangsters with their endless moans about commission.'

'Signora Norman,' I said, relief washing over me so I prickled with sweat.

'*Si*. You'd think a rich woman wouldn't worry about a special price, wouldn't you, but she argued over every single lira . . .' She rapped me on my belly with the comb. It didn't half sting. '*Bruto!* You said *one* female, Lovejoy! How did you know her name?'

I reached, tried to pull her down while she elbowed me off, hands in her hair still. 'Never even seen the woman, love. I was only worried because it was you who approached me in the café that night.'

'Why are you so suspicious, Lovejoy? About what?' She nudged me with an elbow so I tumbled. There she was, kneeling up in the daylight above me, clipping her hair, head illuminated by the lowering sun, when they shot her and she fell with a cough on to me.

I was helpless laughing at her sudden slumping weight, not realizing. '*Now* you change your mind!' The hairpins rattled on her teeth. She was making a coughing noise, moving on me, pinning me down.

Another shot sounded. The dry reeds gave a concerted tap, loud.

'Cosima? Cut it out. Somebody's playing silly buggers.'

I'd stopped laughing. Her face was on my chest, eyes closed, and her breathing was a two-tone hiss between teeth where a hairpin clattered. There was a brown redness, wet and new, spoiling her white blouse above her right breast.

'Love?' I tried to get up under her weight. '*Love?*' Then I was scrambling, scrabbling erect and yelling for help and bawling abuse and fury at stupid careless pigs of duck-hunters who loosed off in any direction.

'Help, for Christ's sweet sake! Help!' Like a fool I stood up and waved both arms, any direction, anywhere over

the endless expanses of reeds. 'Somebody's been hurt!' I
even bawled for an ambulance. Hysterical, I turned
because I couldn't see anybody, not a boat, between us
and Torcello's distant campanile, and stood on Cosima's
ankle and fell aside as the reeds did their concerted snap.

'What?' I remember bleating as if somebody had asked
me a daft question. 'Eh?'

But I stayed down. Shooting. It was coming this way.
At us. Then I grabbed for Cosima, careful and low and
on my belly because she'd been shot and there was no
chance of help, not from anyone except ourselves. And
that meant me, because Cosima was lying in a strewn
attitude, still breathing but no thanks to me who'd
fetched her out here to get her beautiful lovely life shot to
oblivion. I was blubbering all sorts, holding her and
heartbroken because I hadn't realized and had been
laughing my silly bloody head off when she was getting
herself shot. She kept making that coughing noise,
endless and soft.

I fumbled in her handbag. My own hankie's always
months out of the wash, but hers was pristine. Gingerly I
blotted the blood. There was a circular wound, a little
swollen, no longer leaking blood. That was a good sign,
wasn't it, on the pictures when the cowboy's shot in the
shoulder and a single wadged bandage did miraculous
things for recovery? I looked about helplessly, frantic.
The reeds snapped again, once. Two shots. Two shots of
that lighter, businesslike cracking sound of the rifle. No
shotgun, that. If I'd not been so preoccupied with my own
thoughts and my own selfish bastard schemes I'd have
realized hours ago somebody out there had a rifle, not a
shotgun. We'd have been safely back in Torcello, tea at
the *locanda*, the crowded *vaporetto* on its tranquil
way . . .

Cosima moaned faintly as I lay down and pulled myself
and her along the ground through the reeds. It's damned

hard, especially when you're still sobbing incoherent remorse and you don't know what the hell you're supposed to be doing. And you've no idea what to do next and . . . and that noise. Outboard motor, but which direction? There hadn't been any engine sound before. And definitely no boat in sight when I'd goonishly stood upright to wave to our murderers to show exactly where I was and how very sensibly I was responding to the whole frigging mess.

Think. I tried, but it's difficult when you're frightened to death. We were within a few feet of the *sandolo*. I'd wedged it among the reeds ashore as far as I could. God alone knows how big the flat island was, or how much of it got covered by tides. I tried thinking. The rifleman—two of them if they were Gerry and Keith—was being careful. No need to rush up through the reeds. After all, I might have a knife or even a gun and lie in the tall reeds in ambush. Wiser to wait until I made a move into the open water between the island and the mudflats.

Yet stay too long and we'd be awash. Anyway, Cosima couldn't wait. Move, and we'd reveal our track of escape by the movement of the dense reeds.

The engine sound was shifting. It sounded like a low-powered outboard motor on a *sandolo*, going once round the island. A patrol, just making sure. Clever sod. The rifleman was in the boat. I knew that for absolute certain because I'd raised such a hullabaloo in my first panic that any innocent fisherman or duck-shooter must have heard and would already be calling out asking directions as they came closer. It had to be him. Them.

Sprawling, I cradled Cosima. I was almost screaming with the fury of impotence, at my own stupidity and helplessness. We couldn't stay much longer. He'd come closer each circuit, more and more sure of himself. Swim for it? But how far could I get pulling Cosima through the water before he caught us up? He might simply see us and shoot casually from where he was. Sitting ducks. No wonder some maniacs go hunting. Bloody ducks can't shoot back. No weapons. And Cosima's picnic was too neat, too prepared. One plastic spatula between us. Plates cardboard, little basket, nothing. Good for starting a fire but not for making into weapons to . . . Fire.

'Wait, love. I'll be a sec.'

I laid her down and edged back to where we'd lain. Her handbag was open where I'd fumbled for her hankie. No matches, but a small lighter, heart-shaped, red enamel. It could click, and fired a light damned near into my eyes. Gas, flame height adjustable with one of those small wheel things. I tried it on a blade of grass which flared, a reed which shrivelled vertically almost in a flash, but snuffed both immediately. Nothing must happen as long as that outboard engine kept whining and the hunter kept moving closer out there among the reeds.

Cosima was coughing less now, still comatose, still breathing. I tried cupping my hands round my ears and turning slowly to get some idea of where the bastard was, but couldn't for the life of me fix the direction. I'd have to stand up for that to work properly. Presumably he knew more or less where our *sandolo* lay, but for an accurate shot he'd actually need to see us clearly. He'd only hit Cosima second or third go, so far as I could recollect from thinking back on those noises the brackeny reeds had made, and even then he'd been trying for me. If we'd not been fooling about, up and down at the moment of shooting, he'd have got me and then it would have been anybody's guess what would have happened to Cosima.

It had to be done. 'I'm back, love,' I gasped, trying not to quake, and reached up a hand to haul on the *sandolo*. Obediently it moved down almost into the water, six hauls. These boats are all curves, pointed up at the front and having a funny wedge-shaped decking there. To get Cosima in without being seen I'd have to pull the *sandolo*

somehow on its side. I got the boat round after shoving it
out to the end of its rope, then pulling it hard round as I
crawled. The stupid thing nearly rolled on to me, and I
must have created quite a disturbance in the reeds, but at
least I had it slewed on a thick clump so it showed its
interior towards us.

That outboard was still whining away out there, and no
more shots. Sooner or later the swine would have to land
on one of the zillion creeks to loose off a reasonable shot.
Teeth chattering in fright, I stripped and lobbed my
clothes any old how near the front of the *sandolo*. I'd
carefully put Cosima's little red lighter on a mass of dry
sedge, some old nest built by exterminated ducks, I
suppose. With gasped apologies and endearments to my
lovely crumpled girl, I clasped her tight and shoved
myself along through the reeds.

Easy to criticize, and I know everybody else could have
done it better, but the only way I could think of getting
her in was to lift her legs in, then shove her bum on the
gunwale, then worm beneath her poor bloodstained
trunk and rise up so she more or less rolled in. Hardly a
fireman's lift, with me groaning in sympathy with every
murmur of pain from her. The effort left me wheezing
and in anguish at the needless hurt I'd caused her, but I
kept going and slowly manoeuvred the *sandolo* away from
the ground until it floated.

Three or four minutes of waiting, with me whimpering
at the slightest sound from the reeds and inwardly cursing
hate upwards to where a jet trace indicated a planeload of
selfish swine living it up while I was starkers down here
getting frigging murdered in the mud. Then the hunter's
boat cut its sound, then sounded louder and gave that
diminishing whine. He was turning somewhere. Not
closer, but definitely about to cut his engine and run
ashore and . . . He'd glimpsed our *sandolo*, or seen my
disturbance of the reeds. Even as I realized that this was

it, that he'd pinpointed us accurately enough, his engine coughed into silence and I was scrabbling like a mad thing, ripping at the reeds and twisting them into vertical clusters.

Surprisingly they hurt like hell, maybe because they were so dense, but I clutched and twisted until I'd cleared about a square yard of reeds and got them all doubled over in coils. I'd seen the men do it often enough along the sea marshes at home, while idling down the estuaries. The watermen always clear a space as wide as the reeds are tall. He must have left his boat, and now be crawling among the sedge grass towards us. A click, a spurt of flame, and the looped reeds caught, the sedge grass caught. The nest caught. The funny low tangles of grass caught. Every bloody thing caught, swooshing up flame and sprinkling the air with sparks and black fluff. The reeds caught up the flame, passing it across the island, I ran at a crouch, scrambled at the *sandolo* and floundered the stupid slow thing out among the thinner reeds into the channel, swimming like the clappers at the stern. Smoke spread everywhere, lying over the water.

None of these channels is very wide, and they're all completely irregular. That whole area of the lagoon is a jigsaw of islands, *barene* flats covered at high tide, with shallows and treacherous mudbanks everywhere. You can hide, but always only temporarily, because if you can take a boat anywhere down these labyrinthine little channels, so can the hunter. A shot sounded, clearly angry guesswork on his part. No buzzing and reeds cracking about us. The fire was spreading fast. I was going too slowly. Smoke billowed over us as I swam on, praying for a hidden creek where I could lay up a few minutes unseen and fix our outboard engine. With that thing mounted—if it went—I could make a run for it. And I'd not stop till I reached the Fondamenta Nuove in Venice where the hospital was.

Opposite where we'd beached the *sandolo* there was an inlet about twenty or thirty feet off, but it was too obvious. Instead, retching and spluttering, I kept to the smoke and shoved to the right following the channel, the silly boat's curved stern bumping on my head as I swam and pushed. It was then I made the most miraculous and ecstatic discovery. My knees — not my feet, even — touched something down in the water. I'd squealed and let go of the boat before I realized it wasn't a shark jawing my poor defenceless flailing limbs. It was mud, glorious mud. The lagoon here was shallow enough to stand up in.

It takes some doing if you're as terrified as me. But honestly I actually did drop my feet and start shoving, still hunched from cowardice yet thrusting that *sandolo* now at a hell of a lick. The hunter's engine still hadn't started up to show he was coming after us when I swung the *sandolo* to penetrate the thick reed-beds. We hadn't come this way, and heaven knows where we were heading, but I shoved on and on, moving always where the reeds were thinner but now never breaking out into any of the tempting open channels which sometimes showed to either side. Definitely I avoided the thick patches of reeds. Already my fire was proving as much a risk to us as to him. Sparks were carrying the fire across the reeds in jumps rather than a slow spread, and somewhere to the left a new fire had begun. Worse, the wind seemed erratic and once I practically choked in the smoke which seemed to stick to the water. Cosima was coughing again at the bastard smoke. I'd lost all direction, staggering on practically on my knees, shoving as hard as I could go and trying to guess which way to take by peering along the side of the *sandolo*.

How long it was before the sound of the outboard motor penetrated my consciousness I'll never know. By then I'd adopted this method of gaining momentum by using my weight. Head tucked down, left shoulder rammed hard against the stern and my hands raised to clutch the gunwale and take my weight partly on my arms, I could then kick my legs down into the muddy lagoon bed and keep the boat moving at a fair speed. Now, though, I let my legs trail me to a gurgling stop. No use giving our position away by unnecessary motion. I relinquished my hold and slumped my head against the curved wood, gasping and retching water. Smoke covered us once or twice, thinned, thickened again, thinned. Cosima coughed gently, moaned occasionally. I blurted out a whispered assurance, thinking, What a bloody mess.

The hunter's boat sounded no nearer. A few yards off, the reeds caught a floating spark and flared vertical fire and soot for a moment. Away in the distance I actually heard a man's voice call in one prolonged hail over the sound of his engine, but it was never repeated and there was no way of telling from which direction. Or whether he was a friend or foe, for that matter.

The engine sound was dwindling. Varying a bit, as he swung in and out of the inlets, but very definitely receding. Odd, that. No sense in rising to risk a look. One glimpse of us, and he'd come at us. We'd be lost. I let it go on for another minute, put my skinned shoulder at the stern again, took hold and got my aching legs going. Nine or ten shoves and we emerged into an open channel. I almost infarcted doing a frantic back-pedal but should have realized the only straight waterways in the Venetian lagoon are the manmade canals. All the rest are snaky shaggy thoroughfares, no two alike, and bending any way they want every few yards.

My brain managed to insert a reasoned logical thought among its waves of terror: So long as that droning engine didn't sound nearer, and so long as the channels didn't straighten out to give a clear long-distance view, it was better for us to move along the open water. That way, no reeds would waggle to reveal where Lovejoy was panicking his untidy shambolic passage through the water foliage, and no traces would be left of his movement.

Mentally I measured the intensity of the swine's outboard, then edged cautiously into the channel and rotated to move off along it. As I resumed my shoving, unbelievably I glimpsed a campanile in the distance. Only a glimpse, snatched between two coincident channels between slightly raised *barene*, but it was real and definite. I'd recognize those great stone shutters anywhere. Torcello. It was to the rear, back over my poor old knackered shoulder, now scraped raw and bloodied. We were moving away from it.

Still smoke everywhere. As I floundered on along the narrow channel, I was becoming certain the bastard was between us and where I'd glimpsed the great campanile. Difficult to judge, but the sound was constant. Maybe he thought we would head for Torcello and was patrolling between the burning area of the lagoon and the tall cathedral tower.

Sickened at the implication I kept on, ploughing my legs down into the soft mud, thrusting, dragging my weight on one hand or the other to keep to the channel. I wanted to avoid the wretched boat running aground and jarring Cosima, but was terrified of creating any more reed-shaking.

When you work at a particular horrid thing — like blindly sploshing a tiny boat through a muddy lagoon — your mind detaches and floats off somewhere, leaving your poor old hulk timelessly slogging away down there in the clag.

Eventually, though, two events filtered through to my basking brain. The first was gradual awareness of that engine sound. It had all but dwindled away. Whether we'd simply moved apart, or whether he'd stayed put as

I'd blundered further and further away, was impossible to say.

The second thing was this long white wall.

CHAPTER 17

The smoke had diminished by distance and eventually, I suppose, lack of reed fuel by the time the long white wall really made its mark. Of course I'd been dimly aware for aeons of a vague blur up there, but what's one blur a million miles away when you're being drowned, burned, smothered and shot, hour after bloody hour?

When I finally halted and groaned a few sloshed hunchback paces into the reeds the wall was there, across a wider spread of water than the narrow channels through which I'd slaved. I couldn't straighten up and stayed mud-covered and gasping, hands on my knees and waist-deep in lagoon water. Blearily I noticed with astonishment that, the further I looked away from the white wall which rimmed the island, the darker the world seemed. It took several re-thinks before the penny dropped. Daylight was leaving the lagoon. No bright sun, no brilliant blue. That ochre sediment was washing upwards making a dusted haze out of an azure sky. It was approaching dusk. All I'd done was knacker myself, and get Cosima no nearer to a hospital. What I needed was a stray *vaporetto* or a holiday cruiser to happen by. Instead, I thought bitterly, I find a long white wall sticking upright out of the frigging lagoon.

No engine sounds now. Nothing. Not even a duck's quack. The island seemed fairly tallish for this part of the lagoon, raised vegetation showing over the wall. It didn't look inhabited. Except for some low water-steps over to the right, where a solid gate interrupted the line of the wall, there was no indication that anybody had ever even lived there.

I had to chance it. A bit of solitude, with Cosima carefully concealed out of sight beyond the wall, and I might even get the chance of mounting the outboard motor and possibly making a run for it in the manner to which I was accustomed—namely, with a hell of a lot more speed than trogging across this reedy expanse like a stranded cod.

Weeping at the bloody futility of everything, I bent to the stern and strove my slow course out into the open water separating the reed channels from the island, making for the steps. To my alarm the mud vanished underneath my flailing feet and I was back to swimming, pushing the boat with my head or hands or wherever my dwindling strength made me meet the useless frigging *sandolo*.

The sudden stop had slammed the stern's long curved rib into my shoulder. I blubbered and wailed in agony. I was sorry for myself, quite justifiably, but Cosima moaned, thank Christ, and I looked to see what had stopped us. It was the water-steps of the white-walled island, hit straight in the middle.

Above me was a tall barred gate, padlocked, chained. The wall was continuous and quite tall, but over to one side was a bit dishevelled and lower where scrubby wild bushes and undergrowth showed. Admittedly a low-lying sort of place, but still high enough to be a better vantage-point than anything else in the lagoon except the campaniles.

By now I was utterly flaked. How I got Cosima out and over the wall I'll never know—that's untrue: I know only too well the way I handled her, finally just straddling the wall in the lessening light and letting her slide in an untidy heap on to the surprisingly white ground below. I hate to think of the pain she must have been in because I was too scared and shagged out to lower her properly.

From the foot of the wall the island sloped almost immediately into the water, only a few feet of rim at most. Even that was whitish stonework. Funny bloody place, I remember thinking, hauling myself along the pale slope back towards the steps. Why, even the ground inside the perimeter was whitish. Clever old trees to stay green in all this ghostly pallor. No signs of a house, though, from the one quick dazed glance I'd had.

An engine. An outboard engine. The sun was gone, and the sound was distant, but there hadn't been one a minute ago. Same sound. Presumably our same old faithful hunter.

'Oooooh.' That was me, scrabbling down to the *sandolo* and all but rupturing myself lifting the outboard in its plastic bag. The only place was over the wall, so clunk it went among the bushes any old how. Fine thing if I'd ruined it. My clothes too and the oars went over. Which left our swine of a boat.

The stones were loose, possibly dropped there by one of those dredgers to reinforce the base of the wall. I got a monster one, put it into the *sandolo* and tilted the boat by sitting astride the gunwale. She filled with maddening slowness, and even then hung about below the surface with her prow and stern tips showing. No good if she bobbed up just as our hunter came cruising past. I kicked her to one side of the water-steps, in case the bastard landed and saw it. Even in my state that *sandolo* astonished me. I'd thought that one puncture finished the average boat, but this wretched thing kept cheerfully floating up even when I'd actually sunk it. I hauled more dredged stones from the artificial shore. It took eight of the damned monsters to keep the *sandolo* convincingly down and I could scramble over the wall into the scruffy brush.

No signs of life here among all this perennial whiteness.

Not even a dilapidated palazzo or other building. Stiffened into a hunchback, I found it murderously hard getting to where I'd dropped Cosima. The white ground seemed to be made up entirely of these irregular pale stones. They gave a hollowish clatter as I stumbled along so I had to steady myself with a hand on the wall. A rum place, with its patchy mini-jungles of undergrowth. Odd that the Venetian authorities had taken so much trouble—dredging, the wall, the gate, that expensive littoral shoring with valuable masonry—especially since nobody lived here.

My teeth were chattering when I found Cosima and straightened her. It had become quite cold . . . but of course I was in my nip so I went and collected my clothes and tried arranging them round her. No good me hugging her till I dried because I was perished and I'd only wet her through. That horrible whining noise of the boat on the lagoon was coming closer. Queer how menacing a slow approaching threat can be.

Any movement on these white-mound stones might create a clatter I couldn't quieten so I froze. He was here. The engine droned, dropped a tone. Closer. To look at the gateway? Me and Cosima were about twenty yards from the gate, very close to the wall. I couldn't take the risk of looking because I suddenly might have had to duck back into cover, and set these hollow stones rattling.

He didn't stay, just cruised slowly past between the island and the reed channels from which we'd blundered. Once, he returned with his outboard deeper and slower. Not too close, I prayed, or you'll run into my sunken *sandolo* and get yourself sunk. Then he might climb out of the water and I'd have a scrap on my hands. I was in no shape to start hide-and-seek in this loony place.

The engine snapped into higher pitch. He was off. I listened as the note gradually dopplered off into the gathering dusk. Of course, he could be encircling the white island to come at us from the other side, but I was beyond working it all out any more. For the minute I was safe with Cosima, which was more than we'd been ever since we left Torcello.

Light was now surprisingly poor. I clambered to my feet and did some exercises. Once I got myself unperished and that outboard had dwindled to zero I'd chance a look out over the wall. Maybe then I could think about getting away.

Twenty minutes later I'd realized two things. One was that I was a million miles from Torcello. Vaguely, the slender line of Torcello's campanile showed against the sky glow which must be Venice itself. So that was south. I must have struggled northward all afternoon long. Not by reason of skilled knowledge of the lagoon, but only because the reed-beds and the channels and the smoke had given most chance of concealment. Well, the lagoon had to end somewhere even in that direction, but it might prove all too easy to waste away the night frantically careering among the marsh channels. And an outboard motor makes a telltale sound. No, getting the boat up and Cosima to a doctor was our priority. Since the killer had only to sit in Torcello and wait for us, which was presumably where the bastard had gone now, we had to go travel in the opposite direction.

The second thing I realized was what all these mounds of white stones were.

I was sitting mournfully by my lovely wounded Cosima when it dawned on me that I could maybe arrange some of these hollowish white stones into a pillow and make her breathing a bit easier. My trousers could be wadged on top for softness, and the movement would keep me from freezing to death because it was now becoming bitter. You can die from cold. Every muscle screeching, I listlessly fumbled for a rounded stone, got one, and felt it to see which of its aspects was most regular. My finger waggled. I felt some more. My thumb was on teeth. My index finger was in an eye-socket. It was a skull. I screamed and leapt, flinging the bloody skull away so it clacked and clattered among the foliage.

And I felt the ground. No soil. Only long bones, thin bones, round skull bones, spine bones, shoulder bones and hip bones and skull, skull, skull bones. The whole frigging island was one great charnel house. We were on Santa Ariana, the *osseria*. The bone island. A world of bones. Gibbering, I danced clumsily, trying to keep my feet off the bloody things before I found myself over the wall and dementedly floundering down into the water where I'd sunk the *sandolo* and lobbing those great stones out of her as though they weighed nothing.

It seemed years of shuddering feverish activity hauling the *sandolo* on its side up the sloping margin to get it empty, then screwing the outboard in place, all by feel and murky peering. Probably it was no more than half an hour or even less before I got the damp *sandolo* floating in soggy obedience. Going back for Cosima, my clothes and the oars was the hardest thing I've ever done. I didn't even wait to dress. The old woman's engine started first yank of its string, and I was off into the gloom any old where. My own noise, my own engine, choice surging back into me with all the power it brings.

CHAPTER 18

Choice is power. Some poor bloke enjoying a well-earned nosh in that roadside *trattoria* west of the village church of Altino found that out when I nicked his car in the time-honoured way (comb through the window rubber, join the starter wires under the dashboard) and recklessly drove it down the path as near to the water as I dared. It was quite fair, really. If the people of Altinum hadn't migrated into the lagoon fifteen centuries back to found Torcello and Venice, Cosima and me wouldn't have been in all this frigging mess. If anybody owed us, it was Altinum.

I'd chosen — well, guessed — landfall where shore lights showed and where the black-pointed hulk of a boathouse promised there was access for a car. Cosima hadn't coughed now for some time, maybe hours. Speed. I wanted — *had* to have — speed, but making a safe landfall wasn't easy. Once I almost ran full tilt into a marker post, and twice I tangled with those projecting tops which crisscross patches of the lagoon and mark the limits of the *valli* fish farms, and had double nightmares ripping myself free. Somehow in my mad scramble away from Santa Ariana I'd lost Cosima's lighter, my only source of light. I had to go by what glimpses of road lights showed to the north and west, and even then had to cut speed to a slow crawl in case I ran aground or entangled again. In the conditions I was lucky to reach the lagoon shore as I did, only having to shove the bows off a dozen or so times when clumping into the *barene*.

There was a clear reach of water and a channel running to the north-west from the boathouse. That structure was pretty derelict, maybe even unused. All the better, because I didn't want telltale clues like *sandoli* showing we'd got away.

'Come on, darlin',' I said to Cosima as I lifted her from the boat. 'We're nearly there.'

I swear she almost muttered something but there wasn't time to chat. I staggered up the truckle landing-stage and with only two rests made it to the car. No lights. She had to go in the passenger seat upright, head back, because like a nerk I'd stolen one of those small two-door things without a lift-up rear door. I'm pathetic when it comes to planning. The position she was in made her breathe funny and hissing. I rushed down to the *sandolo* and untied it. It was only a couple of hundred yards down-channel to open water.

That engine was great. I used the stern rope to fix the outboard handle to dead ahead and opened the throttle to half speed. Then I pointed the *sandolo* out into the mid-channel heading into the lagoon and let go.

Away she went, straight as an arrow. I found myself shouting, 'Thanks, mate,' as the little boat trundled off on its own into the darkness. For a few seconds she showed blackly against the pallor of the waterway, then only the faint scut of white water gave her position. Then that too was gone and only the engine sound remained, receding as she ran the channel. With luck she might even get an uncontrolled mile, or even further, before she struck and exhausted her fuel aground on one of the *barene*.

Utterly knackered now, I lurched up to the car. As the channel ran inland, it widened to include a couple of small reedy mid-river islands. A road crossed above there, showing bits of the terrain when motor headlights swept over. Probably the road from Altino village. Follow that coastwise, and you'd reach Mestre, Venice's oily landbased neighbour. It had to be that way.

No signs of agitation as we drove grandly past the *trattoria*. Altino is now no more than a village, maybe only a hamlet. Signposts told me it was a few miles to Mestre, to Treviso, to Padua.

'Hold on, love,' I told Cosima. 'We've a little way still to go.'

A little way meant twenty-five kilometres. I decided to aim for the hospital in Padua. The motor clock placidly showed it was ten past ten. Astonishingly, the Marco Polo airport lights showed to our left after we'd gone barely a couple of miles, and we were in Ca'Noghera. Unbelievable. The whole swinish world had been living normally while my poor Cosima got shot and I'd been terrified out of my skin. I swallowed my hate and concentrated.

We drove serenely towards Mestre as if we'd been out for a quiet supper. There was an overcoat in the car. Useful, for a born planner.

'Johanne Eich,' I explained, beaming, to the admission nurse. Going the whole hog, I gave that brilliant Regency gunsmith's Swiss home address as well. 'Though,' I added with a flourish of invention, 'I work in Geneva.'

'And you found the lady . . . ?'

'A short distance from Vicenza. There she was,' I said, graphic and eager, 'staggering along the road. She actually fell! I actually saw her! Naturally I thought she was drunk, until the headlights revealed her condition.'

'The doctor says she appears to have been shot.'

'Shot?' I was a picture of the flabbergasted Swiss businessman. 'Then how fortunate I urged you to contact the police! Who knows,' I speculated grandly, getting carried away with jubilation now Cosima was safe in hospital, 'what disorders have been perpetrated? You must order the police to investigate instantly!'

'Do you know her?'

'Certainly not,' I lied. 'Incidentally, shouldn't you ask for my car licence number? Identification. You must also ask for my detailed account of—'

'Of course.'

The lass was plump and fetching, and swiftly becoming irritable. I was sorry to rile her, but I had to portray the classical image of solidity or I'd never get away before the police came pouring in.

Heel of my left hand to steady the admission form, because fingerprints and characteristic skin impressions end at the wristline. Meticulously I recorded the number from the Swiss-registration saloon I'd memorized from among the cars in the street near Padua's railway station.

'It's a company car,' I solemnly informed her. 'Now, signorina, you must record that the injured young lady gave me her name. Maria Guardi, she said. Please write it down.'

'I am, signore.'

'But you must not simply take my word for it,' I preached maddeningly. 'You must demand to see the documents. They are in a special double-lock compartment in my automobile,' I announced affably, twinkling what I thought might look like a Swiss businessman's affable twinkle. 'I'll get them. The signorina will not mind if I leave one or two of my company's business cards . . . ?'

'There's no need for all that,' the poor nurse said wearily.

'No trouble, no trouble. All records must be *complete* at all times. It's practically my company motto. An incomplete record is no record at all. You agree, I'm sure . . . ?'

I strolled out, then ran to the car. I was on the main road as the police car zoomed in the hospital entrance.

Half a tank of petrol. Quite enough for what I wanted. Well, not *wanted* exactly. Had to do, more like. Compelled. Everything was out of my hands now. The others, whoever they were, had forced the issue. They'd tried to kill me and Cosima. After my trick with the *sandolo*, perhaps they even thought they'd succeeded.

The geography of Italy's a mystery to me, and the car's owner proved to have been an uncooperative blighter. Not a single roadmap. Sometimes you can't depend on anybody. Vaguely I had a notion that Padua lay between Verona and Venice, but exactly where was anybody's guess. I'd told the nurse Vicenza because I'd seen it on a sign pointing in the opposite direction to that indicating Mestre.

Trains would run from Verona towards Switzerland. If the police found this car and news got about, the hunter might assume I'd lit out for Geneva and safety—as long as it was found nearer the Swiss border than Padua, since he might learn of Cosima's presence in hospital sooner or later.

Before carrying Cosima so dramatically into the hospital's casualty area bawling for assistance with the exaggeratedly odd accent, I'd used a ballpoint to write in her palm *One. You.* That way she'd realize I was in the land of the living and probably still somewhere around.

The other bastards were going to discover that fact the hard way. I'd make sure of that.

For a steady thirty-six hours after I dumped the stolen car by the railway, I slept in the station at Verona, ate, rested in the museum, noshed, went to the pictures for another kip, noshed. And phoned the Padua hospital asking how Maria Guardi was coming along, please, and giving the name of the Verona newspaper when asked for my name by the diligent ward sister. I was a wreck, but with a vested interest in recovery of all kinds.

The day after the day after, I felt at last I'd returned from outer space, and caught the train to Mestre.

CHAPTER 19

A heartfelt love message before this next bit: Dear ugly town of Mestre, Lovejoy adores you.

Now, nobody likes Mestre. Worse, nobody even *pretends* to like it. Everybody who works there wants to work somewhere else. People who live there loathe it because it isn't beautiful. Tourists zoom on into Padua or Venice. Nobody likes it.

Except me. I thought, do think and will forever think that good old Mestre is great. Ten out of ten on the Lovejoy scale. One corrosive breath of its poisonous smog, and my heart warmed with love.

For a start, it's horribly industrial. Its traffic is a shambles, its buildings ridiculous. It is definitely shop-soiled. Its docks are full of oil and all the greasy activity which that undesirable substance brings. Love on sight.

Soon after arrival I stood watching traffic along the Ponte della Libertà, comparing. At one end of the long causeway sits sluttish old smog-riddled Mestre. At the other lies queenly Venice, glittering, spectacular. And make no mistake. Venice is a luscious sight, pulling and compelling.

The sky was a balmy blue. The lagoon shone the azure back into the air about the Serene Republic, imparting a fluorescence so bright it almost hurt your eyes to look.

It was over to the left, out there in the lagoon from where I was standing, that my little Cosima had nearly died. The hospital said she was now over the worst and was expected to make a steady return to health and who was speaking because the police . . . ? Don't get me wrong. I wasn't actually planning revenge. I'm not that sort of bloke. No, honestly. Ask anybody. All right, I admit that revenge is a pretty good way of getting even, but it's hardly my style to hold a grudge. Reasonable old me, always trying to be fair. The bad temper I'd felt, the hatred, the panic and sick fear were all gone now. I was my usual smiley self.

Standing there near the causeway in the sunshine, I thought of Venice.

These days we can't even begin to perceive what 'Venetian' meant to the ancients. Oh, the factual bit is clear: Venice was viewed as a strong maritime power simply because she was. And okay, Venice meant self-interest. Like when the thousands of knights and soldiers of the Fourth Crusade arrived at the Venetian Lido asking for help in the name of God, charity and compassion, the Doge of Venice actually demanded what was in it for him.

But beyond Venice's blunt greed there was something deeper and especially horrid. To the ancient people of the past centuries Venice simply meant fright, evil, everything sinister. Venice meant perverse secrecy of the most surreptitious and malevolent kind. Venice meant secret trials, silent stabbings, spies, clandestine murder and sudden vanishing without trace. Venice meant a slit throat while sleeping, and violent unfathomable assassination. Venice meant poison — it took a Venetian priest to murder a communicant by slipping poison into the very Host. Venice meant sly crime and refined treachery and skulduggery. Venice meant a reign of hidden terror, brutal but stealthily quiet imprisonments. Venice meant stark cold cruelty.

Throughout the long centuries of her prime, Venice was a permeating fear, a cloud of terror over Europe, a world of malevolent horror. Strong men quaked before her. Wise men shunned her. Rich men durstn't trust her. Poor men were simply out of Venice's reckoning, and thankfully praised God for being so. Even her glass industry was partly tainted by this weird fame: Venetian glass was reputed so delicate that it would shatter if poison touched it.

Her reputation was not undeserved. Venice's secret councils saw to that. Venetians learned to go about their business with a cool disregard for the abrupt absence of friends. One morning, the feet of three miscreants were observed sticking up out of the paving in St Mark's Square where they'd been buried alive — and all Venice passed by this fearsome execution blandly regardless: God was obviously in His heaven, and the dreaded Council of Ten was simply doing its usual Venetian stuff in the dark hours. Naturally, other nations were at it too. Like the time the Venetian ambassador was shocked to find his current secret correspondence, neatly labelled and bound into volumes, pointedly displayed on the shelves of a London library—possibly the all-time put-down for a spy. Despite these occasional setbacks, though, it was generally conceded that for dank dark deeds Venice took the biscuit. Nobody argued.

Well, with a reputation that formidable against me, I'd have to fight fire with fire. And forgery is the only skulduggery I know. Somebody had to knock on the door of the Palazzo Malcontento. Old Ivan the Terrible had given me a good enough clue: the fancy bloke from there had whisked Nancy away.

I thought, Right, you bastards. Here I come.

The money I had left wasn't a fortune. It'd have to do, though, because there wasn't all that much time. A sense of urgency was coming on me.

By evening, I'd got a part-time job as a kitchen help washing up afternoons and evenings in a biggish nosh bar near the docks, not far from a toolmaker's workshop I had my eye on. Day pay.

About a mile from the nosh bar I found Signora Lamberti. She was one of those massive affable ladies who understands every customer's need. To her, speech was a necessity, but only for purposes of agreement.

'Is it quiet here?' I asked, meaning were people of the district inclined to be nosey.

'*Certo*,' she bawled over the whistle of a passing train. 'You cannot even *hear* the station!'

'*Molto tranquillo*,' I yelled in agreement, paying her a day's advance for a tiny but clean room. She took down her 'Vacancy' sign as I howled promises to fetch my non-existent but voluminous luggage.

'At the signore's convenience!' she shouted understandingly as a goods train rattled by. We smiled at the fiction. Words are fine up to a point, her bustly attitude said, but don't let them get in the way of money.

That was the easy bit. It took me two whole days more to find the little piece of wood I needed. It was in a small lumber-yard, nothing more than a squat piece of sycamore with closer grain even than usual, taken from some nineteenth-century furniture. None of those distinct rays you sometimes see in sycamore wood, so I was happy. The driver in the yard said I could have it for nothing. I told him ta, my warmth showing him he'd done somebody a really good turn.

In case you don't know, sycamore's one of the Acer genus. Like Mestre, it's a real pal. For a start it is a strong, hard, pretty heavy wood. It can be artificially weathered by rotten crooks like antique dealers to look much older than it actually is, if you know how (tell you in a minute) and it stains up and polishes like an angel. The point of all this is you can work it quickly and accurately and expect very little trouble even if you're not expert. Its 'comparative workability' is 3.0 (white pine, that corny old stuff you can carve practically with a bent pin, is the basic 1.0).

You get the idea. Sycamore is faker's wood. The wood of the forger.

The bloke slogging away in the toolmaker's workshop looked up and saw me grinning at him on my fourth morning in gorgeous old Mestre, and he said good-morning. I'd passed by there and paused on the third day, but he'd tolerated my presence in his doorway without a word. He'd not once nodded or let his work be interrupted. Evidently he had no helpers. His wife, a hurrying tub of breathlessness, came out and gave him a coffee, glanced across at me with curiosity but said nothing.

I'd already decided this was my scene: a man

scratching a living, working a one-man show with no time to rest, crucial orders due for delivery and all that. Politely, that fourth morning I replied good-morning, still watching.

'Nice to have no work, eh?' he said. I liked the look of him, a short and beefy baldish bloke who worked without fuss and whose eyes were steady as his hands.

'I'm a hard worker, Signor Gambello.' The faded name was flaking off a plank nailed over the yard door.

'But not this morning, eh?' He had a ready if wry grin.

'My job is kitchen help. Over at the *trattoria*.'

'You, is it? I'd heard they got a stranger as kitchen skivvy.'

'But the mornings bore me.'

'Looking for another hour, eh?' He shook his head. He was lathe-turning short pieces of metal rod about eighteen thou. 'Not here, I'm afraid.'

'Tomorrow morning,' I suggested. 'Free work.'

'No pay?' That interrupted his work all right. He leant away, cut the machine. 'Why would anyone do that?'

'For an hour's use of your lathe. Private job.'

He wiped his hands on a cloth, gauging me. 'What's the catch? Key for your employer's safe? An illegal gun barrel?'

'Wood, signore. I want to make a present for my auntie's birthday. A surprise.'

'That's original.' The bloke was cynical too.

'You can watch me if you like. To check.'

He still eyed me. 'Maybe I will. What's the present?'

'Eh? Oh, only table mats.'

'Very well. Tomorrow, right?'

He watched me go, disbelieving. I left, smiling again. I'd turn up if I had to crawl.

Our agreement was that I'd slog in Gambello's yard from nine till eleven each morning. From then until noon I'd have free use of those tools not in use.

His actual job was lathing cylindrical metal rod into spindle-ended mini-shanks, and putting a screw-thread part way along it. God knows why. Something to do with engines. Signor Gambello had to make six thousand before the end of the week. I tried explaining how much more interesting the job would be if we rigged up a sapling gear like the Benedictines used for furniture, but he only stared, mystified. So we did it his way, on this shrill electric Woods lathe that turned his little metal sticks out like shelling peas. Great, but bloody boring.

The first morning I just helped and saved my own hour. Second morning I lathed for him while he did his books, and then got out my sycamore dead on eleven. It took me forty minutes to turn my piece to a perfect cylinder. First I needed a thin slice four inches across and three-eighths thick. Ten minutes flat. Then a flat cylindrical box, perfectly round, made to stand squat. That meant machining it in two bits so its lid settled easily inside — never an external-sliding lid for Elizabethan table-mat holders, remember.

There was an old tin in the yard. I half-filled it with pieces of bark I'd flaked off the elderly Quercus tree standing near the eastern crossroad traffic lights, on my way in. An old brown leather shoe I'd got from a dustbin, cut in slices, filled the tin; top up with water, and set it boiling in a corner of the yard. Signora Gambello touchingly brought me out a coffee and some *panini* breads and cheese. I explained I was only doing my own thing, that I'd really finished the proper yard work at eleven, but she said to have it all the same. I thought that was really kind.

Waiting for my stew to darken, I had the nosh and then fetched out my pound of black grapes. I only wanted the seeds and skins. It nearly killed me eating the pulp and sucking the skins clean, but I did it after an hour. Added to the stewing mess with as much Chinese green tea as it would take, and my tin ponged to high heaven. Twice I crossed the yard to apologize to Signora Gambello. Before going to work at the nosh bar I put the horrible mess to cool in the corner by the gate.

Next day my flat circular box and the thin disc went in and out of the dark mess about ten times while I worked the lathe between times. Gambello had a coke furnace for annealing wrought-iron, and he said it was all right if I dried my wood pieces on the flue between each soaking. Neither of the Gambellos asked anything, but their curiosity was more and more apparent as the phoney Elizabethan place-mat and its container became increasingly warped and stained. A split developed in the thin disc about noon — I worked on at the lathe unasked — and Signor Gambello was itching to point this out, but still I pressed on. He'd want to weld it. Every few minutes both pieces went into the tin of stain for a soak, then were warmed to dryness on the furnace flue.

That noon I postponed my nosh to impose coarser turning-marks on the surfaces, using a coarse bastard file and setting the Woods lathe to a laborious two hundred revs, then had my *colazione* while Gambello resumed the metal work in my place.

Next day at ten-thirty we knocked off the last of his mini-shanks and got them boxed and loaded on his truck. That gave me nearly three hours before I'd have to leave for my washing-up job.

The inscription I'd chosen was something vaguely remembered from school. Old Benkie, our literature teacher, once clipped my ear in a temper over forgetting a Chaucer quotation: *The answer to this lete I to divines.* Which divines, and answer to what, was anybody's guess, but the quotation was enough to fill the centre of the disc if I arranged a dot-and-vine-leaf pattern round the edge. At least it was the right period. Ordinary red ink, diluted, for the inscription, and a tube of artist's black acrylic paint for the pattern. The quill and steel with which the Elizabethans wrote was a difficulty. The way out is to take the cap of a ballpoint pen — use a Bic top for forging everything except parchment or paper manuscripts — and file the projecting bit down to a sixteenth of an inch tip. Cut a part-thickness groove all the way along, and perforate the top to hold a bit of dowelling rod. Epoxy resin to fasten, and there's your Elizabethan pen. I nearly spelled the inscription wrong like a fool, but at the finish held it up proudly. One more fast dry to fade the ink (remember phoney reds fade faster than phoney blacks) and . . . and . . .

Signor Gambello was watching me. Oho.

'Nice job,' he said, coming close to look. 'You know,' he went on, examining my piece, 'if I hadn't seen you make it, I'd swear it was really . . . old.'

'Good heavens,' I said evenly.

'*Certo*. It has that look.' There was a pause. 'I'm sure your auntie will be very pleased.'

'Eh?'

'Your auntie. It's her surprise present, *non è vero?*'

I remembered. 'Ah yes. Let's hope so, signore.'

There was a pause while we looked around the workshop and out into the yard. Signora Gambello was listening, arms folded, by the door.

'You will not work more, eh?'

'Just the *trattoria*. One more day.'

'Then, thank you.'

'Thank you, signore,' I said fervently. 'The debt is mine.'

Next morning I left Signora Lamberti's establishment — a bawled farewell over the racket from the shunting engines — and made my special purchase. With the money I'd saved from washing-up I had enough.

Mestre isn't exactly bulging with antiques. It had taken me a lot of searching to find something Venetian and genuinely antique. The book itself was ordinary, a third-edition Venetian dialect dictionary, falling to bits. It contained a few scraps of paper, though, on which people had doodled and drawn occasional shapes. This only goes to show how you can pick up a fortune. I bought the book, went around the corner and chucked it away. One doodled-on paper I cherished: only a figure study, pen with brown ink on a greyblue wash. Even with four elementary figures there was a lot of vigorous activity going on in swirly-clothed classical tableau round a sprawling babe.

Art has a million mysteries. Many of them occur in Venetian art, which was pre-eminent by a mile in the eighteenth century. To me, one of the most fascinating of all art mysteries is the great R.V.H. Mystery — R.V.H. for 'Reliable Venetian Hand'.

It must have been really miraculous in those days. Walk around the corner in Venice and you met artists like Canaletto, Tiepolo, Piazzetta, or Ricci, or bumped into musicians like the Red Priest, Antonio Vivaldi already on his way to getting himself defrocked. It was all happening in Venice then.

The tragedy is that artists die unrecognized, obscurely, in poverty. I mean, we don't know enough about Mozart or Constable, while the discovery that Shakespeare's dad sold a few condoms, 'Venus gloves', on the side — quite customary for all glove-makers those days — is treated as a major revelation. Not even collectors take enough notice of artists, until the artists pass on and it's all too late.

But once upon a time one collector *did*. Back there in that miraculous eighteenth century in Venice one collector bought the doodles, sketches, plans, any little drawing he could afford, from the original artists themselves. And he saved them, tidily, in complete safety until the day he died. By then he—she?—had scores of them, and of course they were dispersed to the four winds after that. But this collector did one last inestimable service for Art. In lovely copperplate handwriting, he labelled each tiny scrap with the name of the original artist. And he's always—*always!*—absolutely correct in his attributions. Museums the world over reflexly search every old stray paper for the names of Venetian artists in that precise elegant give-away handwriting. We don't know who that collector was, so we call him the Reliable Venetian Hand. Now, promise you'll never go browsing in old junk shops again without a fervent vow to remember old R.V.H. of blessed memory. And just occasionally light a candle for him/her. He did a greater job for civilization and art than the lot of us will probably ever do.

The dashed-off drawing I'd picked up had the name 'Sebastiano Ricci' evenly subscribed in that immortal copperplate. In my whole life I've seen three of R.V.H.'s items found, and the great museums of Europe abound with them, so you've no excuse for ignorance. Sebastiano Ricci, as far as I remembered on the spot, painted a chapel apse in Chelsea Hospital, but most of his stuff is in Windsor Castle or at Venice's Accademia.

Fully armed for battle, I got the train across the causeway. By eleven I was disembarking from the No. 2 waterbus at the Rialto on the Grand Canal, and cutting through the narrow *calle* that brings you out by the Goldoni Theatre. Ten minutes later I was ringing the brass push-bell of the Palazzo Malcontento, and smiling with fright, but in sure anticipation.

Looking back on it now, I think how reasonable I was to go berserk.

CHAPTER 20

The bloke who eventually opened the door was twice my size. All curly black hair and droopy moustache. Nothing to match Ivan the Terrible's description this time. He might actually be the man in the waiting motor-boat who watched me the day Cosima showed me round the Gobbo's market. We greeted each other politely, friendly politicians.

'Name of Lovejoy.' I offered the information into his longish silence. A waterbus rushed past. The *traghetto* man cursed in his rocking gondola.

'The *locande* are—'

Cheeky swine. I didn't want a place to doss down. 'I want to see the lady of the house, please. Signora Norman.'

'Not in.' Slam.

Ah well. I idled over to watch the *traghetto* come and go across the Grand Canal, keeping an eye on the Palazzo Malcontento. I'd never seen so much wrought-iron. Even the balconies of the great tall rectangular windows were covered with the damned stuff. Lovely and antique, but you'd need oxyacetylene and a Sheffield gang just to let in some fresh air. Clever Mrs Norman.

No sign of any motor-boat moored alongside the house, but then there might be all kinds of sneaky little private canals which we tourists never even see. No action by the time the *traghetto* gondola bumped into its pier on its eighth rocky trip, so I went and pressed the bell again.

He came out ready for a dust-up, moving with aggression written all over him. I begged with the speed only cowards achieve for him to accept a gift for the signora. He halted at that.

'A gift. Personal.'

'Where is it?' He stood vigilant and still while I drew out the flat cylindrical box. I rattled the sycamore disc inside, tempting.

'It's a genuine Elizabethan coaster, signore.' I opened it and showed him, passing the box but keeping the inscribed coaster. 'Hang on, though.'

Signor Gambello had let me have—well, I'd nicked it, actually—a ten-inch piece of his metal rod to sharpen on the lathe. While this goon looked on in amazement I put the coaster flat on the palazzo wall and slammed the pointed metal through the wood. Quick as that, I chucked it to him to keep both his hands occupied.

'What—?'

'*Grazie*.' I smiled, swiftly backing off to where the two *traghetto* men were now still, looking at our little scene. No arguments, not even with aggressive goons, until I knew whose side I was on. Or better, who was on mine. The nerk went in slowly, staring at me with malevolence. He'd remember my face now, but then I'd remember his.

Ten minutes later he came for me. I was sitting perched on the *traghetto* pier railing reading notices about long-gone gondola regattas, and let myself be invited in.

'The Signora's assistant will see you now,' he announced at the air over my head.

'Ta,' I said, slipping round him and into the palazzo's doorway at a rapid trot, slamming the door behind me so he was left outside. Assistant, indeed.

These Venetian palazzi have an aroma all their own. Some find it claustrophobic, even musty. To me it's beautiful. It's antiques, antiquity projecting from the lovely ancient past into this crappy modern world, and still going strong. Still lived with, despite the folly and stupidity of our modern-day daftness. It's love, hallowed and enshrined—

'I don't *believe* it!' A staccato laugh ripped down the stairs at me. Ugly, shrill. 'It really is the tramp with that ridiculous car!'

A young bloke wearing a pink cotton suit and a cravat was staring down into the hall over a luscious oak balcony. The wall lights were subdued greens, yellows, rose colours in ghastly Murano glass, but I recognized the laugh from the day Mr Malleson had outbid the ring dealers and Connie and me were in the Ruby at the pub. I'd found the Norman family's hatchet man. The one who'd done in Crampie and Mr Malleson.

'Good day, signore.' I spoke up the staircase, swallowing my hatred and smiling. 'Lovejoy.'

'What have you done with dear Placido?'

'Locked him out, I'm afraid. Sorry.' Placido was a laughable name for a ten-ton mauler.

'You have?' the pink apparition said with awe. 'He'll be in such a temper!'

'What *is* it, Tonio?' a woman's voice called.

'Some scruff, dear. No need to come. I'm getting rid of him.'

The door was being pounded. Excited people outside were asking what was going on. It was all getting rather out of hand.

I yelled, 'Signora? Don't come out if you're ugly.'

'*What?*' the voice demanded.

'You heard.'

The enemy was coming down the stairs, practically quivering with anticipation at the excitement of taking me apart, when she appeared on the landing above us.

'*Wait.*'

Tonio halted his pigeon-toed descent. 'Don't spoil it now, dear.'

'You're the cocktail man,' she observed to me.

'Eh? Oh.' That middle-aged aggro over the cocktail in the hotel bar the night me and Nancy made smiles. I went up, ignoring the burning hatred in Tonio as I passed. 'You're the lady with more money than sense. I remember. I'm Lovejoy.'

She was being amused at it all when I finally stood beside her. She was holding my skewered coaster. 'Explain your insults.'

'You've got to be rich to buy a two-carat Royal Lavulite stone. You've got to be senseless to plonk it in the middle of a Florentine-set gold crucifix like you did.'

We processed, me first, into a grand chandeliered room of rectangular windows, darkened paintings and heavy furniture. A telly was showing muddy red lines across peoples' faces. The clue to her amusement was in her screaming boredom. Well, if the script called for me to be a diversion, I'd divert all right.

'It was done by a great craftsman, Lovejoy. Are you a jeweller?'

'I'm an expert forger, love. That's a million things a jeweller isn't.'

In the room's light she was lovely. No, gorgeous, rather. Her hair could only be called rich, obviously shaped daily by dedicated salon slaves. Her clothes had that casual fawn style only wealth brings. She'd not been expecting visitors but her make-up didn't war with her earrings and her opal nail-varnish didn't drain the colours reflected from a single one of her three rings.

'Or an expert lunatic who impales a genuine Elizabethan posset coaster?'

Her eyes never left me — God, her black eyelashes were a mile long — as she failed to take a cigarette from a carved box of Bengal ivory. Failed because my fingers were there first, crushing the cigarettes into an unsmokable mess. She recoiled slightly.

'You're insane.'

'No smoking where there's these lovely oil paintings, missus. Even the rich shouldn't be that dim. *Especially* them.' I looked sadly at my ruined handiwork. 'And *I* made the coaster. Finished yesterday.'

'You?' Tonio came sulking beside her as she spoke. 'I suppose you've witnesses?'

'Two in Mestre. One here—me. I'd never do that to a genuine antique.'

'You're always stopping me, *cara*,' Tonio grumbled. I was beginning to hate the way he kept his opaque stare fixed on me. It's the way folk look at the salad in a restaurant—dull stuff, eating a chore, something to be got on with, then forgotten.

She sat to show how beautiful her shape was. 'Hush, Tonio. Bring us a drink. What else can you make, Lovejoy?'

'Not for me, thanks,' I said quickly. The sudden pallor round Tonio's mouth meant he was determined to keep Venice's mediæval reputation alive even if it meant poisoning my sherry. 'What else? I can fake anything.'

Tonio pigeon-toed out of the room, a lot of paces before he looked away to see which way he was going. I'd made a real friend there. Shallow eyes unnerve me. I get to imagining there's nobody behind the corneas.

'Prove it.'

I fetched out my little Ricci sketch for her.

'*You* did this?'

'*Certo*, signora.'

'How?'

'Mind your own business.'

Tonio returned, with Placido carrying a salver. She reached unlooking for her glass. The nerks guided it into her hand. I'd found the boss all right. I presume the brownish fluid was her famous Rusty Nail cocktail, but the glass was a perfect glowing example of Venetian eighteenth-century ware. I almost wept with longing. The two goons stood about in hope of an order to exterminate.

'*Cara*,' Tonio said as she placed her lips loosely about

the rim. 'This man's a dealer. I saw him with your daughter.'

His putting the relationship so spitefully into words shocked me, but I did my innocence bit, glancing about with quizzing curiosity before letting my brow clear and recognition show. '*You're* Mrs Norman?'

'Yes.'

I sat, unasked, nodding slowly as if realizing. 'I see.'

'You see what exactly?' She hated me for knowing Caterina. Notions of aging thickened the atmosphere. We all ignored them, but I wouldn't like to be in Tonio's lemon-leather shoes when she got him alone. Odd how older women don't realize they're twenty times better than young popsies.

'If I'd known you were the lady in charge here, it would have been a lot easier for me, signora.'

'You have one minute,' she said. 'Time him, Tonio.'

I spoke from a dry throat. 'I'm a dealer, true. And I've forged a few antiques in my time. The woman in the dealer's ring took me to see old Mr Pinder. He told me about some scam in Venice, a lot of forgeries and fakes. Wanted me to work for him.'

'Why didn't you agree?'

'I'm no glue-and-saw hack, love. I'm superb.' Tonio snickered and nudged Placido but I kept on. 'The old man seemed nice enough, and the girl said the wages would be high. But that's not enough. I've given you proof I'm a great forger. So I want a percentage. No flat rates for me, love, if it's a really big scam.'

'To which Mr Pinder replied . . . ?'

I shrugged. 'No offence, but it was obvious that the boss was here in Venice, not him.'

'The address!' Tonio spat, putting a hand on her shoulder. There was a lot of possessiveness in the air, and none of it anything to do with me, worse luck.

'Daddy and Caterina would never tell you, Lovejoy.'

'Mr Pinder got reminiscing. I pieced it together.'

'He's lying, *cara!* He's some sort of agent—'

'No. Babbo does, all the time.' She held out her glass as if in disdain. They leapt to collect it. 'I want this sketch examined. Bring Luciano.'

'He's on the island.'

Tonio bent and whispered into her ear. She smiled, gleeful, like a little girl given a pleasant surprise.

'Yes. Give Lovejoy the cigarette lighter.'

Placido passed me a gold cube. 'Ta. But I don't smoke, missus.'

'And pass him the sketch, Tonio.'

Lighter. Ricci's sketch. I held them both. There was no danger to anyone, but I felt my chest chill with that awful cold which true terror brings.

'Let me look!' She came across, knelt in front of me. 'Now burn it, Lovejoy.'

'Eh?'

'You heard the lady, tramp.' Tonio toesied over to enjoy the fun. 'Light the lighter. Burn the—your— sketch.'

He clicked the thing in my hand. The flame was blood red, some fancy gimmick. She had her forearms on my knees. Her eyes were enormous, dark, made into deep tunnels by the reflected fire. Excitement was making her breathe quicker. Our faces were inches apart, her lovely arms on my knees.

'Well?'

Neat. A true forger would burn it uncaring. He could dash off another fake in a trice on the back of an envelope. A phoney—especially one with some vested interest—couldn't or wouldn't, or would risk his neck with some hesitation . . .

The sketch hurt my fingers. It was already charred, fell on to her carpet. I'd lit it practically without thinking. I watched the flame move casually along to the corner, eating away Ricci's name in that painfully meticulous copperplate. Gone.

Her hand lifted my chin, exposing my mind to those luscious, fevered eyes. I gave her a delighted grin which felt from the very depths of my soul. I knew I'd kill her now. It was out of my hands. Tonio and this lady had not only done for Malleson and Crampie. They'd just foully murdered a precious antique from the hand of Ricci himself. My own laborious crap could be crisped or slung out, for all I cared. But people who murder antiques shouldn't be allowed. Everybody knows that.

I pulled a face, almost laughing now the responsibility had passed from me.

'Sorry about your carpet, missus, but you told me.'

For one instant she seemed a little puzzled. Then she shrugged and rose.

'What's your preference, Lovejoy?'

'Faking? Oh, furniture, jewellery, sculpture, if I'm on my own. Tapestries and oil painting, with the right help.'

'Stone work?'

My grin was wider and more heartfelt than ever. I even felt happy. '*Anybody* can fake stonework.'

'Take him on, Tonio.'

'Don't, *cara*. There's something wrong.'

'Nothing that a new suit wouldn't cure, Tonio.'

She snapped her fingers and they fetched her another cigarette box. I drew breath, glanced at her oil paintings. Her eyebrows rose inquiringly. I answered with an apologetic shrug. 'Light, Lovejoy.'

The same red fire, miles inside her exquisite pupils. She blew the smoke into the air with an upward jerk of her chin, and gave me an amused glance of understanding. I was one of her serfs now. I cleared my throat.

'Any time you want your oil paintings cleaned, lady.'

'Clean yourself up first, tramp,' from Tonio.

'Do you always dress like that?' Her interest stung me.

'Geniuses are allowed. And if I'm to work anyway.'

'Working clothes are different, tramp.'

I looked Tonio up and down. 'Apparently. Mrs Norman, that percentage.'

'Two things, Lovejoy. First: the money from our scheme is so vast that your pathetic little requirements are insignificant. You'll see in good time. Take him out there in a few days, Tonio.'

'Better be tonight *cara*. There's an *acqua alta* due soon.'

'Tiresome. Tonight then.'

'Out where?' I asked.

Nobody spoke until she said coldly, 'And the second is speak when you're spoken to. Understand?'

Everybody paused while I assimilated her last instruction. 'You mean like them?'

'Well.' She flicked ash on the carpet just too quickly for them to streak for ashtrays. They'd both twitched. I hadn't moved. 'Well, almost.'

Placido gave me a handful of money at the door. Tonio told me to make myself presentable, bloody cheek, by fitting myself out at a tailor's near the Calle delle Bande, to be on the Zattere, tramp, by eight tonight. He shut the door without waiting for my reply.

The San Moisè's hardly the prettiest church in Venice, but even ugly churches do for lighting candles. As I lit the four—Mr Malleson, Crampie, Cosima and a just-in-case for Nancy—I saw again those huge wells of eyes with their distant reflected scarlet flames. A second later, thinking, I put more money in the slot and lit a fifth candle for her.

On the way out I thought, Oh what the hell, returned and did a sixth though Tonio didn't deserve it. He was just lucky that generosity is my strong suit.

Pleased, I went shopping among the crowds, looking for Goldoni's shop where they sell the big navigation maps of the lagoon.

CHAPTER 21

Resplendent in a new off-the-peg, I tasted the coffee and sank a couple of giant *margherita* pizzas in the corner nosh bar on the delle Bande. Not that I was pleased about being well-dressed. As my usual grubby self I could fade among the mob. Immaculate as any wedding guest, I'd stand out like a daffodil in a goalmouth. The lady brought over my omelette and some of those thick *torta* slices that make Italy a green and pleasant land, so I was in good nick to wrestle the problem of the vast nautical chart I'd tried to spread on the world's narrowest counter while perched on the world's most pointed stool. One thing's sure, I thought fervently, in the nosh bar din, it's a hell of a lagoon. When I saw where I'd been, pushing Cosima to safety, I had to order some more cakes to stop myself throwing up from sheer fright. It's those deep blue channels and pale green sedgy *barene* that scare me.

The big problem was how an ultra-nervy supercoward weakling like me could make headway in this game. It had all escalated in a way I couldn't understand. Easy, though, to see why old man Pinder was eager to employ a divvie—best to be careful even if a bird as aggressive as the luscious Signora Norman was here at the business end of so much syndicated money. Clearly Caterina didn't trust dearest Mama. Her mistrust had reached Grandad Pinder—perhaps the penny only dropped when he realized that his lovely quiet scam was going awry after the savage assault of Mr Malleson and Crampie. Hence he suddenly needed a divvie that bad, to seek exactly which fakes had gone where.

Another big curved-horn *dolce* with cream, and I could look my own enormous ineptitude in the face.

What the hell did I do now? Not just the ultimate in cowardice, but an incompetent one at that.

My one bonus was that Cosima was fine, so they told me on the blower. From their guarded inquiries they taped incoming calls but I was past caring. Anyway, I changed my voice each time, talking through combs, tissue paper, doing it in funny accents and being different relatives and whatnot. No worry there.

Ranged against me was my monumental ignorance, my thoroughly chicken-hearted nature and innate incompetence. I didn't know practically everything. For example, what Mrs. Norman was up to. Tonio's role anybody could guess but was he Mrs Norman's bloke or Caterina's? Both? Playing one against the other, with Mama's money as encouragement?

There were some meagre bits of knowledge. The scam was painfully real. Cosima had nearly died, and gunshots were proof of the most absolute kind. And now I knew some of the participants. Mrs Norman was boss, with gelt *and* power. They'd mentioned Luciano, presumably an expert faker. And an island. And if Luciano the faker was there, with Lovejoy the newly-recruited forger being taken there, the island was the centre of the scam, right?

'Another two of those cakes, signora, please,' I asked, to keep out the cold, and settled down to memorize the islands of the lagoon from my chart.

As long as I got the direction and distance of tonight's boat journey, I'd be able to identify the island, then find my own way there whenever I wanted, right?

Answer: no. Because there's such a thing as a blindfold, and such a thing as suspicion. They turned out to possess both.

Curiosity made me peer from the St Theodore's column in the direction of the Riva. Curiosity drove me among the crowds past the dozing Ivan the Terrible, past my artist—still grumbling to all spectators about money—to the second bridge where I sat to watch for Cesare.

His boat was there. He was there, too, with a harassed new girl courier I'd never seen before, clipboard and all. Maybe Cosima's ex-partner, now relieved of her boyfriend, and holding the fort?

Cesare's boat left with a load of tourists about five, probably to the Marco Polo for the departing Alitalia 294, which meant a good hour even if little boats like his don't have to go all the way round through Murano like the big ones do. Reluctant to risk being accidentally spotted from the hotel or by the boatmen, I ducked down past the San Zaccaria, long way round, and popped into Vivaldi's Pietà church, the one which old Pinder got so burned up about.

I should have gone round to the Cosol office and steamed Giuseppe's garrulous mouth open, demanding all he had on Mrs Norman's private planeloads of moviemakers, but I was tired and dozed off in one of the pews. Dozing is a mistake in Venice. The vibes of ancient life come out of the walls at you. Bound to, in a place like that. I dreamt of wading and drowning, woke in a cold sweat when a drove of chattering children came pouring in to draw the orange, white and black mosaics in their school exercise books. Then I realized my dream was true, except it wasn't me drowning. It was children. The lovely church which harvested Vivaldi's music and Tiepolo's magnificent artistry belonged to the foundation which reputedly harvested the newborn illegitimate babes thrown alive into the canals, to drown in the filth and darkness. What with the men of Venice away on the war-galleys for so long, the Pietà did a roaring rescue service.

The little bar on the Garibaldi was open. It's the only one in Venice without a big glass of coloured water for you to drop tips in. Six o'clock and dark when finally I left. Seven-thirty I was outside of another three pizzas and waiting for action at a table on the Zattere waterfront, watching the big ships thrash by. Never know why, but a ship entering harbour always looks reluctant, and one setting out looks eager. With me it's the other way about.

This boat taxi picked me up exactly at eight.

The water-taxi man didn't have to ask my name. He simply walked up among the tables, tapped my shoulder and led me to his boat. Shoddier than Cesare's, the boatman wore the air of a part-timer, not an authentic Venetian taxi.

'Where are we going?' I asked chattily.

'Talking not allowed.' No information, but no secrecy either. I sat inside the cabin, able to see us head noisily away from the Zattere waterfront cafés.

His crummy boat just about made it to the Giudecca, a long thin island which curves round Venice's bottom forming a wide natural harbour. He dumped me quite illegally on an *Azienda* waterbus jetty where the No. 8 stops near the Santa Eufemia church and chugged off without waiting to be paid. An all-time Venetian first. It unnerved me more than any rip-off.

Ten minutes later, wandering and wondering if Tonio and Placido had forgotten, I was collected by an equally decrepit but open boat steered by the hairiest boatman on earth, a real Cromagnon. He transferred me in the darkness to a more respectable cabin craft, an unnerving experience which left me shaking. They could have drowned me. A cheerful geezer hooded me with a bag thing. There were no lights. He tied my hands and sat me on a bunk in the cabin.

'Look,' I said in an appalled muffled falsetto. 'What if we sink?'

'We drown, signore,' he said pleasantly. 'I can't swim either. We Venetians have this superstition: learn to swim and the lagoon thinks you distrust her.'

'She does?' I bleated, scared out of my wits.

'And takes revenge. Especially at the time of the *acqua alta*.'

'High water?' That's what Tonio had warned Signora Norman about.

'Signore, *acqua alta* is one hundred and ten centimetres above sea level. When the sirocco meets the north bora winds, it will rise twice that.

'But Venice is only thirty inches above sea level as it is. You mean she could go *four feet under?*'

I gave a bleat. He fell about at that, so much that the boat swung and I lost my sense of direction. I'd never met such poisonous hilarity before. Before that, I'd been sure we were heading in towards the Fusina channel. Portia had set out from there to defend her lover's friend from the wrath of Shylock.

I listened. For anything. That clonking lagoon bell. The long cacophony of bells San Giorgio Maggiore sometimes stuns you with, warning women to keep away. Well, hormones and monasteries don't mix.

'What's up?' I croaked inside my hood. The engine had cut. 'Are we okay?'

'*I* am.' A guffaw, the sadistic pig.

Then it dawned on me. You can detect the way a small boat is turning sometimes by its engine sound, depending where you are. The swimmer's trick in the water. Cut power, and a boat can bob in any direction. Bitterly I sat cursing the time I'd wasted memorizing that bloody massive map. We did the engine-cutting trick four times in the next hour. At the finish I didn't even care where we were, much less know, and nodded off in my hood.

And screamed. The boat had touched something solid, immovable. Feet clumped, hands pulled me and blokes talked quite casually. I tried kicking and holding on to the cabin door but was prised loose by a simple nudge. They shoved me, wailing inside my hood, on to the gunwale step and over the boat's side. Legs together in a panicky attempt to hit the water feet first, the jarring concrete nearly popped my head off. Land. I was on land. I'd nearly peed myself from fright, tumbling over and lying shivering while everybody had a good laugh and a boat bumped small vibrations into the stone. Then I was tugged to my feet and hustled up some steps, me holding back and trying to foot-feel my way while they hauled me along, telling me, 'You're all right,' as I stumbled behind my captors. My elbows kept being brushed, first this side, then that, and now and again my hood was scratched.

'Duck,' my merry boatman advised every few yards. I did, slow to realize it was another joke to make my blind antics all the more comical. I blundered on, pushed and pulled by anybody that felt like an ego trip. A born duckegg, I decided the joke had gone too far and kept going without crouching—and brained myself on some low arch. You can imagine the jollity and all-round merriment as I was lifted and elbow-walked down two flights, eighteen steps each. Twenty-seven paces one direction, a right turn. Thirty paces, a door. Twenty more paces, another door.

Hood off, and somebody untying my hands. Light so blinding my head felt lasered. Vision returned with some pain. The first person I saw was Tonio. The second was my boatman, still making everybody laugh but this time acting out for Tonio's benefit my blind falls on the way from the boat.

It was a massively wide bricklined room, strip-lit. Huge. A ventilator hummed but the place's scent was dankish, cool. A score or so men worked silently at easels, on wall-benches, at desks. One chipped at a piece of masonry in a screened corner. Hardly a glance from the lot of them. Clearly a dedicated bunch. From a tall monastic-looking lecterned desk at the far end an old grey-haired bloke peered down at us. It was a factory.

'Another scratcher, Luciano.' Tonio gave me a bored jerk of his head to report. Luciano the expert, presumably foreman of all this faking industry. 'And you can go, Carlo.'

My friendly boatman and his two goons were actually at the door when I said casually, 'Oh, Carlo. Sorry about your chart,' and I headed for Luciano's desk.

'*Wait!*' I paused agreeably at Tonio's command. 'Chart? What chart!'

'Eh? Oh, Carlo's.' Tonio's pale stare worried Carlo. You could tell that from the way his smile had frozen.

'I keep no chart, signore,' Carlo said, his voice an echo of my own terror-stricken croaking.

'It was an accient,' I explained, ever so anxious to avoid misunderstanding. 'I nudged him. Carlo said I'd spoil this chart he was keeping, if I wasn't careful.' The two goons took a quiet step away from Carlo. Nobody was laughing now. I was really pleased at that. 'But it wasn't my fault, you see. I couldn't see a damned thing, for that hood.'

'Shut it, Lovejoy. You keep interesting secret charts, Carlo?'

Carlo went grey. 'He's lying. There are no charts . . .'

'I never actually saw it,' I put in, so anxious. 'Does it matter?'

'Carlo.' Tonio's reproachful voice was a sickly purr. I went cold. Carlo began to sweat.

'Signore. I swear before God . . .'

'Find it, you two.'

The goons whisked him out of the door before I could grin and tell Carlo to mind his head. It would have been my little quip, but my throat had clogged. I still feel rotten about Carlo, God rest his soul. Not wanting to face Tonio's gaze, I ambled down the factory towards Luciano, who had my skewered Elizabethan coaster on his high desk. He looked straight out of Dickens: tidy dark suit, if you please, neat dark tie and white cuffs showing, even pebble specs. His voice was the quavering of a lamb in the next county.

'What was all that about?'

'Dunno. Some chart or other.'

'Crummy piece of work, this, Lovejoy.' His eyes bubbled at me through the thick lenses.

'Never said it wasn't.'

That tickled him into twinkly humour. 'Not had time to put the word round to see if you're any good as a faker, Lovejoy.' The unyielding complaint of the disciplined serf.

'Faker? Me? I'm an authetic antique dealer.'

An artist painting nearby overheard and snickered, a sound I heard with a glow of pleasure. So long as we were all being sensible.

'You did a perfect sketch, I'm told,' old Luciano said. 'And burnt it.'

'Hardly perfect.' I cleared my throat. 'Yes. The signora was playing games.'

He harumphed, nodding, indicated the nearby artist. 'Take a look. Tell me what you think.'

I went over, asking, 'Where'd you get the photo?' The artist, a skeletal bearded geezer shoddied in smeared denim, took no notice, working steadily on at his canvas. It was laid horizontal on a trestle, first time I'd actually seen that trick used. As long as your paint's consistency is exactly right, once the canvas is dry enough you can lift it erect and judge the craquelure as it actually develops. This is great for artificial aging. I'd have to try that when I got a minute. A huge photograph was mounted on the wall, skilfully lit. 'I thought cameras aren't allowed in the Correr.'

'They're not,' Luciano said.

'Well done.' The Correr museum forbids cameras and handbags. It makes you deposit them in the ticket office anteroom at the head of the stairs, and that's the only permitted entrance. So a marvellous colour print of Carpaccio's *La Visitatione* spoke volumes about Tonio's powers of organization. 'Isn't your photo a bit small, though?' The canvas looked about right, four feet by four ten or so.

'It's the way I work,' the artist said.

'Mmmmh.' Fakers sometimes do this, copy from smaller photographs because it prevents that telltale woodenness from creeping into the fake, the bane of all art forgers since the beginning of time. Don't try it when forging watercolours, incidentally. Doesn't work.

He was 'squaring'. This means dividing the photo of the original into squares, and painting his repro square by square. Makes faking easier, but is a dead give-away to seasoned connoisseurs—especially if they have an X-ray machine handy. Almost anybody can create a fake which will pass for original at a quick glance. It takes somebody like Keating or On to do class jobs. Or me, on a good day. This bloke was using a *camera lucida* to cast reflected lines on to his canvas. It saves drawing them and leaving telltale marks, and seems like a good idea. I raised my eyebrows. Luciano gave me a rueful shrug as I strolled back.

'Is he careful enough, Luciano?'

'He's not bad.'

'I can't see his reference lines.' Forgers using squares from a *camera lucida* must have a standard measured square, because you have to adjust the damned thing when you switch it on at the start of every session. Most of us—er, I meant those nasty illegal fakers—nail a piece of card to the top rear of the canvas frame and focus in on it for accuracy.

'Domenico does it by eye.'

'Two cheers for Domenico.' A steady but faint thump-thump-thump came from behind the brick wall.

Somebody must be forging the Great Pyramid with a steam-hammer. As I listened it faded into silence.

'Decided, Luciano?' Tonio called.

The old man quavered instantly, '*Si* Tonio. Lovejoy can start helping Giovanni on the Doge's Palace stonework. We're behind with those.'

'Eh?'

'Over there.' Luciano pointed to the far corner with his quill, a real quill.

'Me?' I said indignantly. 'I'm only here to advise, you ignorant old sod.'

He shook with inaudible laughter. 'I work too, Lovejoy. Look.' He showed me what he was doing, a large Missa Solemnis on his high bench, faking away at a hell of a lick. He had black and red inks. It's a saying among forgers that a fake must be even better than the original. Well, grudgingly I had to admit his massive pages looked superb. The cunning old devil was even annotating the margins in a diluted ochreous brown as he went. Lovely work. 'Get to it, Lovejoy,' he scolded amiably. 'Remember. Idleness was a capital offence among the Incas.'

'They're extinct, right?' I groused back, and ambled over towards the screen in the corner.

Tonio saw and nodded. 'You do exactly as Giovanni says, Lovejoy,' he ordered. 'We want our money's worth.'

'Cheek. What money?' I peered behind the screen. The corner space was rigged out exactly like a mediaeval stonemason's workshop. This thinnish bald bloke, presumably Giovanni, was chipping away at a supported capital.

'The signore will explain.' Tonio wasn't smiling so presumably he meant it. 'Get to work.'

'I already told him that,' Luciano piped querulously.

'Yes. Get to work,' the stonemason said, not even bothering to look.

'Coming, bazz,' I greeted Giovanni cheerfully. 'Call that carving? Shift over and give me a go.' I'd made it. A worker in old Pinder's factory of forgers and fakers.

CHAPTER 22

'Cocky bastard.'

That was Giovanni's greeting, almost all he said during that long working night.

'Ducal Palace, eh?' I said chirpily, coming in and shedding my jacket while I gave his stone carving the once-over. 'Name's Lovejoy. Why'd you choose the Judgement of Solomon, Giovanni? You should have started with that lovely stuff by Bon.'

'Get to work.'

'It's from the capital next to the Basilica, isn't it?' I fondled the stone, checking its progress against the plaster-cast mould he had ledged on a chair. 'Look, Giovanni, old pal. D'you really believe it's old Jacopo della Quercia's work? I mean to say, 1410 AD's a hell of a—'

'Get to work.'

'Your Archangel Gabriel's head's too protruberant.'

I reached for the sander. Giovanni moved aside and called, 'Ventilator's on, lads.' I looked about inquiringly. The others all down the factory called fine, okay. Giovanni nodded, pushed down a boxed switch, and a hood above us hummed into action. The lazy blighter sat while I smoothed part of the angel's form. He also had his lunch from his sandwich box, offering me none. Lucky I'd stocked up with that bellyful of pizzas. He didn't offer to lend me his goggles, either.

I slammed into the task of copying the plaster cast. Go to the corner of the Doge's Palace and look at the capital nearest the actual Basilica. These capitals are grand stuff as sculpture, but they're too grim for my liking. All with the same despondent message of mortality, and what a horrendous business life is. Not a smile anywhere.

Still, I was happy, doing what comes naturally. Don't misunderstand. Forgery's not as bad as it's painted. Not even factory-sized.

I mean, generations of collectors have enjoyed their 'Canaletto' paintings sublimely unaware that the young William Henry Hunt actually painted many of them as copies in Doctor Monro's so-called academy, (for 'one shilling and six pence the hour,' Hunt's little fellow-slogger John Linnell said bitterly). Some were sold as originals, as Linnell knew, but that doesn't really worry me. Why should it? The 'Canaletto Secret' was to paint a series of colour glazes over a monochrome painting. That extraordinary light effect he achieved in his natural-history pictures has given a zillion people pleasure. So if little William and John painted just as brilliantly, what the hell. And I don't mind that El Greco by 1585 had a cellarful of minions turning out titchy copies of his own efforts while he dined grandly upstairs—to the scrapings of a private orchestra in the 24-roomed pad he'd hired from the Marqués de Villena. The morals of fakery are the same by the ounce as by the ton. Make a note of that.

As I worked I tried merry chat as a way of collecting some news. Giovanni was impervious. He chomped, swilled his vino. Then he sat, dozily coming to every few minutes to see how I was getting on.

'How many of us are there, pal?' I tried, and, 'How long you been at this game, eh?' And, 'What's the going rate, Giani? Paid piece by piece, from the way you stick at it, I'll bet!'

Not a word. A Venetian's silence when the subject's money spoke volumes. Gossip was therefore forbidden, the penalties very, very heavy. I began to worry about that ashen look on Carlo's face. Worried sick about being worried—now about the flaming enemy, I ask you—I gave the somnolent Giovanni a friendly kick and told him to start roughing out the next stone capital.

Luciano put his head through the screens at this point, smiled and nodded and moved on. Doing his rounds of the forgery factory to see we were all doing our stuff, I supposed. Whatever the rest were like, I was determined Lovejoy would be exemplary. I'd see I would do twice as well as these fakers. If they worked fast, I'd work faster. And I'd make their natural forgers' versatility look like the ploddings of pedestrian hacks. I told Luciano not to interrupt the workers.

All that long night we worked, and I learned nothing useful. A couple of odd details, though. One was that thump-thump-thump, which recurred occasionally. Another was that Tonio disappeared once I'd got settled in and working. He was replaced by the two goons.

And there were other oddities. For instance, I'd never seen a forger worth his salt simply stand aside and let another bloke take over his handiwork, because forgers consider themselves artists of a high order. Yet Giovanni, the slob, had let me take charge of his sculpture. And, at least as strange, nobody talked. Three times I went past the other busy forgers on my way to the loo, and paused to make a friendly comment. No avail. Even Domenico gave me the bent eye.

The loo was a chemical can. No chance of flushing into the lagoon a message in a bottle, or a marker dye to trace. And no watches. No clocks. No radios. No apparent ventilation except the hood which hung suspended over Giovanni's masonry corner.

The goons knocked off after about four hours, and were replaced by a bloke who whistled through his teeth and read a kid's colour comic. Occasionally he chuckled, and sometimes read a difficult passage, moving his lips, with his forehead frowning in concentration.

They took us away one by one about an hour after this Neanderthal was replaced by our two originals. Home time. I was last to go apart from Luciano.

'Why the ten-minute intervals, Luciano?'

'It's the arrangement here.'

'Who makes the arrangements?'

Silence. Luciano polished his specs and had a good look at my carving. 'Not bad. Good and fast.'

'Better than your crummy plaster cast of the original. Careless.'

He murmured apologies. 'Done officially while they restored it a couple of years ago. We weren't really organized and used all sorts of rubbishy labour.'

'At least tell me about my pay, Luciano.'

'They'll tell you.'

I gave up and wandered about looking at the others' progress. For all my criticism of Domenico, he'd fairly shifted. A youngish bloke across the other side was faking one of the monumental arched Tiepolo paintings from the Madonna dell' Orto apse, but I noticed he'd had the sense not to use the *camera lucida* trick for that majestic piece. As the goons called me I felt a gentle bong of recognition in my chest and went past Luciano's high desk. An illuminated page lay fully exposed on it among his forged pages. The forgetful old lunatic had carelessly left a priceless original, beautiful and redolent with age, glowing in all its serene tempera brilliance for any careless nerk to scrape its wonderful surface with a ruinous elbow. Luciano must be past it. I tutted and manoeuvered it gently under the protection of a new sheet of parchment. Then I cursed myself. Luciano was regarding me quizzically. The sly old sod had done it deliberately, been watching all the time.

I said pleasantly, 'You're not a bad advert for senility, Luciano. Keep it up.'

'Don't talk so much, son,' he said. Not a smile. 'Go home and rest.'

I went up to the goons and obediently bent my head to be hooded.

'Be at the same place, same time, tonight,' the nerks said. 'Understood?'

'Carlo's day off, eh?' I asked jokingly into my hood, but nobody answered.

A stranger in a stranger's boat dropped me off at the Zattere waterfront after four blundering and scarey switches of craft out in the darkness of the lagoon. It was getting on for five-thirty.

When you think of it, having no place to sleep's no hardship for an hour or two. Or three. Or five. After that it gets to you. Gradually as the hours pass a kind of restlessness seeps into your soul. You don't *need* a place to rest, but the idea that you haven't got one to go to eventually becomes pretty horrible. You become desperate.

Maybe that's what made me burgle Giuseppe's Cosol office.

It's less than a twenty-minute walk from the Zattere across the Accademia Bridge, even going a long way round to avoid my old pals of the Riva wharf. True to the style of the Venetian early worker, I whistled, kicked the occasional carton and generally made myself part of the local scene.

Giuseppe's precautions consisted of a chain with a padlock, and the old double-lock. Two keys are supposed to make it difficult. As if two hands and two bits of bent wire were rarities.

Half past six o'clock in the morning when I found the lists. The garrulous chatterbox hadn't even filed the damned things. Cosima would go berserk at all this untidiness. I risked the light after shutting the door to the staircase. The lists were almost complete. Giuseppe was hardly in for Venice's Dedicated Worker award, so he'd probably bowl up no earlier than nine a.m. Plenty of time. I made myself some instant coffee on his office's mini-boiler, and settled down comfortably to read.

Signora Norman had truly forked out. First class for David, Nancy and the older pair. Which raised a lorry-load of new questions. Why exactly did a lady pulling an antique scam so huge that it needed a whole factory full of forgers need a movie mogul? And why had he vanished so suddenly that his secretary Nancy wasn't even allowed time for the entirely harmless purpose of leaving her erstwhile lover a thoughtful little souvenir?

Nearly seven o'clock when I'd finished searching, and the dawn showing and the mists clearing. Nothing, except more suspicions. Grumbling, I nicked the paltry sum of ready cash scattered around in the drawers, and left.

I didn't shut the door. Let somebody else worry for a change. Even if it was only Guiseppe.

My first two goes on the phone were hopeless. Something to do with time zones. Third go I got a secretary after spending a fortune in these *gettoni* you have to buy in order to use the Venetian blowers. My accent was phoney as anything.

'Iz zatt joo, David?

'Mr Vidal's at a signing conference today, sir.'

'I particularly want speaking wiz eem. Eez ee reeturned from Venice, ja? Ee said me ring most urgent. Zee financial contract—'

Uncertainty crept in, thank God. 'Hold, please.' I was down to my last three tokens when the girl said breathlessly, 'You're through, sir.'

And David's voice said, 'Hello. Vidal here.'

Lips pursed, I gave a crackly electronic splutter and

downed the receiver gently.

Message: David vanished fast, but made it home. And it probably was the same for the other three. I'd have to think some more when I wasn't so knackered.

Happier now the possibilities were narrowing, I went down the Lista di Spagna looking for lodgings.

Not far from Harry's Bar is the Giardinetti near where poor distended tourists queue for a million years to go for a pee. Always there are the relieved halves of couples hanging about while the other half, still bulbous with agony, wait in agonized lines clutching their 200-lire tickets, praying for an empty loo. Sitting by the trees, I decided it might be my last chance to see Cosima so, knackered as I was, I'd have to take it. I went among the mobs to the boat terminus at the San Marco.

Maybe it was because I was so exhausted that I accidentally made an astounding discovery. A Lido steamer was pulling out as I plodded towards my waterbus stop. What with the droves of children and the engines I put my fingers in my ears. There was an odd beating sensation. I stopped, removed my fingers. Stuck them in again.

Block your ears, and the big boat's engines went thump-thump-thump. Remove them and the engines whine and growl amid the pandemonium of the crowd, the rush of water. I did it so often, just to check, that two little children on the concourse started laughing and imitating. With a sheepish grin I moved away, then went into a café for some wine and a quick change of mind.

The walk to the railway station took me thirty minutes and half a litre of bianco. The train journey to Padua was about the same.

CHAPTER 23

For the purposes of visiting Cosima I became the excitable relative of a patient in the women's surgical ward. My mythical sister was suffering from some unspeakable — not to say unpronounceable — malady, and my anxieties knew no bounds. I explained this to everyone I met in the hospital corridor. The most baffled country cousin in Padua that day, I managed to blunder into the outpatients' entrance and got myself redirected. God, but they're patient in Padua. If I'd been that nurse in Outpatients I'd have flung me out.

Cosima was up! I mean it. Really sitting up and having a drink. No tubes, no drips. And bonny as a bird, in a new nightie with her hair done and her face shining. Her face lit to see me. And I too was all of a do, until she asked me where Cesare was today.

'Cesare?' I hadn't mentally cleared him of shooting Cosima, so her mentioning his name with such expectation pulled me up short.

She searched my eyes. 'Didn't he find you? I've had him searching all Venice for you.'

'Lazy old Cesare.' When I'd glimpsed Cesare he hadn't looked at all like a boatman doing a desperate private eye. And there are ways of putting the word out which only boatmen know. Cesare hadn't searched very hard.

'Then how did you know to come today? I go to convalescence in an hour.'

We talked of our day out on the lagoon. The police had maintained a bedside vigil until she'd given her story. Mercifully, she'd told them I was just a casual acquaintance, that we'd met somewhere at a party . . . She actually remembered very little of our escape, except being lifted ashore and the *sandolo* rocking, and having this dreadful cough which pained.

'And hearing you blaspheme, Lovejoy.'

'Me?'

'In a car. Everything was dark. Your face was lit by the dashboard's glow. You were threatening fire and slaughter against everybody on earth. Even Cesare.'

'*Me?*' I was appropriately amazed. 'I'm not like that. Delusions, love. Common in gunshot wounds.'

She shook her lovely hair. 'I tried to ask you to stop shouting, Lovejoy. But you looked . . . possessed. A fiend.'

'When did Cesare show?'

'Giuseppe and Cesare come almost every day. And the two Australians. They've all been so marvellous.'

I was so busy crossing suspects off my mental list that I had no response. My silence was her big moment.

'Where did *you* go, Lovejoy?'

'Go? Me? Well, I was so exhausted—'

'You vanished.' She looked aside along the ward, colouring slightly. 'I read your message on my hand. The police said a Swiss businessman found me and fetched me in. They thought you'd drowned.'

'They're always red-hot.' I'd made the bitter crack before I could prevent myself. The comprehension in her gaze was unnerving.

'So you were simply keeping on running. I knew it. Why?'

'I had to, love. What did the police tell you?'

'Nothing. They thought some madman had shot me, or a stray bullet from an illicit marsh hunter.'

'Accidental, eh?' Good old police. Same everywhere, desperate not to get too involved in troublesome mischief.

'Lovejoy. If Cesare didn't find you to bring you here today, why did you not keep on running?'

Honestly. Women are always after motives.

'That was me phoning,' I said indignantly. 'Didn't you get messages?'

She smiled, my downfall. 'Practically every two hours. However did you manage to dash around to all those different places so fast?'

'I was in Mestre all the . . .' Caught.

'All the time?' she completed for me. 'So you only pretended to run.' No smile now. Just a terrible sadness and eyes slowly filling. 'Darling. What is it that you're doing? Even before this . . . accident, I wondered about you. So many things unexplained. And your mind's always miles away.'

See what I mean? Women are really sly. Even when there's nothing wrong their busy little minds are working out different angles. It's no wonder most of the world's bent with all this suspicion going on.

After that it wasn't a lot of use. I tried hard being happy and friendly and she tried hard to match my poisonous chirpiness, but we parted a few minutes later, me with the address of her convalescent home written out and her with my bunch of chrysanthemums. She'd be gone a few days.

'I'll phone, love,' I promised.

'Where will you be, Lovejoy? In Venice?'

'Certainly,' I said heartily. 'Where else?'

'At the same hotel? Honestly, now.'

'Of course! I'll keep in touch, through Cesare.'

'And you'll look after yourself? Promise?'

'Hand on my heart,' I said fervently. That was how we parted, truth and lies approximately half and half. I was heartbroken, because I sincerely really honestly loved Cosima, and now she'd as good as told me it was goodbye. That's always heartbreaking. But at least things were a lot clearer.

From Padua railway station I phoned my lodgings along the Lista di Spagna in Venice and explained that

Lovejoy, who'd taken a room there today, had just died in a plane crash over the Aegean and wouldn't be needing it any more, thank you.

Another two half-litres later I broke into Cosima's little apartment, locked the door after me and went fast asleep.

Watching Cesare and that thin lass going over their clipboards in the dying sunshine made me quite envious. It's the humdrum blokes of this world that get on. The meek really do inherit — if not the earth, at least the leavings. Cesare'd kept a low profile. Then, when the Lovejoys and other scatterbrains have blundered on their lunatic way, idle sods like Cesare inherit the birds.

When he was on my list of suspects it was simple to hate him. Now he was proving a real stalwart trusty loyal pal for Cosima in her adversity I hated him even more. The smarmy creep.

Because of the coming night's labour I'd had a couple of tons of pizza along the Garibaldi. As I walked towards Cesare's boat a bottle of wine clinked in my pocket and I carried three spare pizzas for the late hours working on Giovanni's stone capitals.

'Wotcher Cesare. Got me a tip?'

He jumped at that, recovered enough to keep calm and finish his list. The thin girl eyed me speculatively, tit for tat, and asked what time Cesare should report tomorrow. He simply said, 'Later,' so it was him and me in the late afternoon on the Riva jetties with crowds all about having a last *capuccino* before getting sloshed for the night.

'Lovejoy. You're back, then.'

'Never left, did I,' I said, quite pleasant. 'As you well know. I went to see her today.'

He shrugged, unworried. In a scrap with him I'd last half a minute. 'You're no good for her, Lovejoy. You know it. Now Cosima does, also. You went through four of those tourists in as many days. Randy sod. Leave Cosima alone.'

'Three,' I said indignantly.

'Three plus Nancy. Four.'

'Tell me who shot Cosima, mate.' I leaned crossed forearms on the wobbling handrail to show my pacific intentions.

'She was shot,' he said thoughtfully, gauging my motives. 'The police said so. And somebody took her to safety. I've that to thank you for, Lovejoy—'

Bloody cheek. *Him* thank *me* for Cosima? 'Get on with it.'

'—But without you, she'd not have been shot in the first place.'

'Does all this paranoia mean you don't know?'

'If I did . . .' He let me guess what the silence meant.

I wondered for a second how useful another falsehood might be. Could do no harm, so I said, 'She sent you a message, Cesare. Before she left.'

'She has gone?' The alarm of a thwarted lover leapt to his eyes.

'Yes. Sorry about it. She's going to convalescence and she wanted me to see you got the address.' I scribbled a fictitious name of any old mythical sanatorium.

'In Palermo?' he said, suspicious sod. 'Sicily?'

I nodded. 'There's a special team of doctors there, for the, erm, thoracic oesophagus. Wise to go far afield. That shooting was an attempt on her life, no?'

'Very wise.' He folded the paper and put it away carefully. 'Thank you.'

I didn't altogether like the way he said that, but didn't realize exactly why until much later.

We parted, scarcely the best of friends. He saw me as the arch-villain. I saw him as a non-ally, that most unpredictable species of friend. I should have remembered that.

For an hour I sat in a pew in the Gesuati church,

poring over a replacement map of the lagoon and laboriously working out possibilities by the light of the candles on the second altar.

When the boatman came for me at eight o'clock I was mapless and dozing fitfully at one of the café tables on the waterfront, and pretending not to notice the lovely white yacht *Eveline* moored two hundred yards away, which I'd last seen rocking in the cold wind of an East Anglian estuary.

The drill was frighteningly familiar: searched, hooded and exchange boats here and there. Drift. Turn, drift again. Motor on a short while, cut engines, move on. Finally, bump and ashore with more than one pair of hands pushing me along and the same old inertness of those taps on my elbows. No funny ducking jokes, though, ending with me brained on some low overhang. And no Carlo. Well. Maybe it was his night off, I thought as they took me down the steps and doors clanged shut behind.

Third in, this time. Luciano was already hard at it up there on his high desk, giving me a friendly specky twinkle. Giovanni wasn't there yet, but Domenico was slogging away. A new bloke was painting across in the opposite corner, on panel as far as I could tell at a distance. No Tonio, either. Placido, motioning me to the stonemason's screens.

'Start immediately, Lovejoy,' Luciano called.

'Got my wages sorted out?' I shed my jacket and waded in with the ventilator on above the stone block.

Now I was more or less used to the place and didn't have Giovanni breathing down my neck I had the chance to suss the workshop out as I worked.

Definite thump-thump-thump noises passed close to the brickwork three times during the first four hours or so. Very near a lagoon channel for biggish boats?

'Most of these things,' I observed to old Luciano when I stopped for a bite after a good couple of hours, 'are paintings. Why's that, pal?' We were now up to twenty, others having arrived one at a time under escort.

'Decisions, Lovejoy.' A shrug which accidentally displaced a mound of his manuscripts. I let them fall. His quill work was good on the Gregorian chant, but the forged paper wouldn't pass as original in a Finsbury pub. He climbed down, grunting, to retrieve them.

'Same old tale, eh? When're we going to do Venice's bronze horses?'

He smiled at that. Not pleasantly, sadly and almost wistfully. I couldn't understand it. Upset, I wandered about, having a bite of pizza and a swig from my bottle. I became more than interested at our team of slaving troglodytes. You could put us into two main groups, stone fakers and painting fakers. I was doing another capital from the Ducal Palace, that heart-rending cycle of love, life and death in tiny scenarios, while a surly unesponsive bloke under another extractor hood was doing a copy of that altar bas-relief from the church of San Trovaso. They simply call the anonymous Renaissance genius Il Maestro di San Trovaso, and a lovely piece of marble work the original is, too. A metal faker was putting the finishing touches to a bronze candelabrum — God knows where he'd slogged over the initial stages; hell of a dust and heat. It had more than a look of the Santa Maria della Salute's piece by Bresciano, though when you think of it, their conditions in 1570 were probably much worse than ours.

The others were painters. There was a rather shifty geezer doing Jac Tintoretto's *Last Supper*, another San Trovaso piece, and I saw Titian's *Descent of the Holy Ghost* in its early stages of fakedom being done at frightening speed by the pimpliest bloke I'd ever clapped eyes on. Long-haired and young, but bloody good. I was delighted, because Titian's original in the Salute has been all but massacred by lunatic restoration. Yes, I definitely approved of Pimple's labours.

It was enjoyable, like having your very own mediæval artist's shop. I was annoyed when one of the overseeing goons came over and warned me I'd idled long enough.

'I know,' I said wearily. 'Get to work.'

The ships which thumped so very close to that brick wall weren't tiny *vaporetti*. They were big double-deckers. And 'island', they'd said. A third clue was the freedom with which they moved and talked between our landing-point and the steps leading down into our underground factory. Which meant uninhabited. Fourth: those taps and scrapes on my elbows, as I was marched to my night work, spoke of an overgrown place, perhaps some once cultivated island which was now abandoned.

As I slogged on the capital, copying from the plaster cast, I mentally cancelled out the far northern part of the lagoon and the more westerly bits. Big ships avoid shallows, and I'd discovered the hard way that those areas were covered in *valli* fishfarms and crisscrossed by perimeter nets.

That left the Lido runs, the island channels like to Burano and Torcello, and the southern bit to Chioggia. I'd never been south, but it must be a longish trip. Now, you don't need to stop and feint to conceal direction on a long boat trip, because you can turn ever so casually over a distance. Therefore delete Chioggia and the south. The Lido is always thronged with beach-hunting sun-grilled skin-peelers. So it was among the islands.

Delete the cemetery island of San Michele—too near, too visited, too much underground to leave room for this vast factory. And cross out the island where Bryon (with a little bit of help from his friends) dashed off his Armenian dictionary, because the resident Armenian priests wouldn't appreciate our particular brand of artistry. Delete, too, Saint Francis of the Desert. The legendary friendliness of the eleven resident priests would convert us load of crooks by sheer dogged holiness. No quiet deserted overgrown paths in Murano, because of their obsessional glassmaking taking every inch of space. Ditto for Burano, that incredibly pretty 'island of the rainbow barque', where each house is a brilliant spectacle of colour and its leaning campanile shows that gravity's all balls. Torcello? Well, maybe, but tourists and fishermen and its few inhabitants and that posh *locanda* where inquisitive visitors can stay . . . No to Torcello.

There were undisguised recesses in our brickwork wall. Seats, where monks could perch and read their office for the day. Adding two and two, as I ground out the maiden's dress in stone, it came down to one island in one exact spot. I began whistling, to everybody's annoyance. They all shouted to shut up and get to work. I did, remembering what the deserted island of San Giacomo in the Marshes looked like from the boat. I'd seen it with Cosima as we'd sailed past on the steamer, of course, but in Venice appearances are entirely for concealment. Cosima's Law.

Now I had everything, or so I thought. Explanation of the scam. Knowledge. I even knew who was on whose side. Now the fur could fly. I worked on more carelessly than usual, because there were only a few hours left to a showdown. My showdown, with Signora Norman. As long as I winkled her away from that viperous Tonio for a few minutes . . .

'What're you doing?' Giovanni asked me.

'What do you think?' I said rudely, wielding the electric drill. 'Stone's too soft. It has to be hoisted.' The wretch called Luciano across just the same. I greeted him with scorn. 'Please, teacher. May I erect a ribbed hoist, to double the speed of this idle burke? There's a strong crosspiece among the heaps of waste materials over there. It'll take an hour, and save us days rolling these bloody stones all over the factory floor. If we've over two dozen to make . . .'

The old man looked at me, then at Giovanni. 'Do you really need one?'

'Answers on a postcard,' I prompted, not pausing, doing a couple of shallow holes in the mortar. 'Get up off your bum and fetch me some of that chain.'

'It would be easier,' my mate said reluctantly to Luciano. 'I'd have put one up before, but I've not really had time.'

That made several of us give a derisory snort. Old Luciano plodded off back to his court-hand script. The guards relaxed. The painters painted. And I went inside my head: now if a wall measures four bricks wide, plus mortar of one inch between bricks, then . . .

'Shut up whistling, Lovejoy,' Luciano called.

'Sorry, sorry,' I called back to everybody. 'Won't happen again, lads.'

That was a dead certainty, for the lot of us.

CHAPTER 24

'Luciano.' I stepped out of the alley.

The old man halted in the patchy darkness which Venice has patented. 'Lovejoy? Is that you?'

The Calle dei Frati leads off the Zattere waterfront. There's always a lot going on at the Maritime Station end. The advantage is that the Zattere is straight. You can see all down the fondamenta paving. Precious few boats at that ungodly hour, though. Twice I'd been disappointed waiting for Luciano, and once I'd startled a lady who was sneaking ashore from a muted water-taxi near the great

Gesuati church. We'd both recoiled in alarm, then snuck on our respective ways. Live and let live. I was pleased that somebody at least was keeping the exotic carnival days alive.

I asked Luciano, 'Are they watching us?'

'At this hour?' That amused him. 'You overestimate their dedication. Once they hand over to the day shift . . .' He stopped and tutted at his carelessness.

So each transfer between boats was a two-way swap. One forger going on duty, one off, the factory continuous.

'And compulsory silence to make sure nobody slips up, eh? What's the punishment, Luciano?'

'For indiscretion?' The old man glanced apprehensively across the Giudecca Canal. An early thousand-tonner was shuffling eastwards towards the Adriatic. 'Nobody knows.'

'Except Carlo, eh?' I restrained him with a hand. 'Where is Carlo, Luciano?'

For the first time he actually seemed tired. His old body sagged. 'Don't do it, Lovejoy. You're young and silly. I'm older, wiser. Money's too powerful. It has given us our orders. It will wreak a terrible vengeance on those who oppose its wishes.'

'Don't be a bloody fool. Money's nothing except its own myth.' There must be something in the air of Venice that makes everybody talk like reading Shakespeare. 'The forgery factory's a send-up, *non è vero?*'

'Lovejoy.' The poor old bloke sounded knackered, standing in the waterfront gloom. '*Do as you're ordered.* Work. Take the money. Do like the rest.'

'I came to warn you, old man. Get out. It's a matter of hours.'

'What can one man do, especially a stupid one like you?' He patted my arm, dabbed his rheumy eyes with a hankie. 'Go home. Sleep. Come to work. That's the way to live.'

'Like you do?' Look.' I snatched his hand and turned it palm up. 'The best manuscript hand I've ever seen. And you work for a nutter like Tonio? You let people get executed and still do nothing?'

Gently he took his gnarled hand back. 'We can only do nothing. Not even run.'

'But it's evil, absurd.'

He actually chuckled. 'It was evil and absurd that a whoring alcoholic horse-thief could rule Russia. But Rasputin happened.'

He walked away, stooping with the grounded gaze of the elderly.

I called after him, 'You've got till ten o'clock, Luciano,' but received no answer. To think, I had my breakfast in a nosh bar. Day was up and boats were really on the move as I reappeared about an hour later feeling quite good. Sad that Luciano hadn't heeded my warning, but at least I'd tried.

The *Eveline* had been moored nearby the previous night. Gone now, but she hadn't been an illusion, though I sensed she represented some sort of threat I hadn't yet reasoned out. At 9.15 a.m. I was inquiring at the *Magistrato alle Acque*, local ruler of the waves since 1501. Carlo was right about the high water, and so was Mr Pinder. Two such flood tides happened annually in the 1880s; there were seven a year by 1930; sixteen frighteners by 1955, and now forty annual dunkings. Long ago the *acqua alta* barely wet the pavement. Now, it could waterlog your belly-button however tall you stood. I learned too of Venice's six round-the-clock water-watchers, and the emergency phone number for tide forecasts: 706-344. I would use it.

I thanked them, and went out memorizing the number and feeling ill.

*

'Signora got the kettle on, Placido?' I halted obediently because he had his vast mitt on my chest. 'She told me ten o'clock, Placido, so don't blame me if you get your cards.'

He hesitated at that, and I walked into the palazzo and on up the stairs. It's odd how convictions alter things. I don't just mean attitudes, or the way people respond. Once you're committed, a curious order takes over as if all is suddenly well once a battle's begun. No indecisions, doubts. Berserk conflict is tranquillity, utter peace of mind and soul. And if the body suffers it's cheap at the price.

It was coffee time in the grand salon. Signora Norman in startling orange, with silver jewellery and a brilliant lipstick. She had me gaping. You have to hand it to these older women. Tonio was unbelievable in clumsy-looking satin gear that was probably the height of fashion. I had the odd idea they were waiting for guests.

'Have I spoiled things? I won't take long.'

Tonio moved his face, smiling his opaque smile. '*Cara*, we simply can't let this peasant continue—'

'The white yacht means Caterina's hit town, I suppose?' I went to the window and looked down at the gondola ferry, already busy across the Grand Canal.

Tonio rose. His expression was exactly that of those newspaper cartoons which have empty circles drawn for eyes. I quickly went and sat by Signora Norman. I'd have to stick fairly close to the truth to survive.

I said kindly, 'There's something wrong with your forgeries, chuckie.'

'Isn't there always?' She was being unexpectedly entertained, so was all smiles.

'He wants Luciano's job,' Tonio interrupted. 'A chiseller. On the make.'

'Luciano said he's good,' the signora reprimanded. 'Continue, Lovejoy.'

I said to her, ignoring him, 'Name any forgery your factory's doing this minute, missus.'

'Paintings.'

'Right.' I drew breath, ready to judge the effect of all this on Tonio. 'Most are doing them wrong, love. Wrong canvas, wrong paints. Wrong brushwork. A kid could spot they're duff.'

'Are *you* so expert, Lovejoy?' Tonio was in his pigeon-toed stance now. His expression became almost human with delighted anticipation. 'Better than all our fakers?'

'You know how long it took us to recruit the teams?' The signora's smile was gone. She got her cigarette in action. I edged away from her smoke and her fury as she surged on. 'Two whole years! And a fortune. The best artists, goldsmiths. The world's greatest woodcarvers, manuscript fakers, stonemasons. From every country in Europe—'

'There's only one worth a groat, from what I've seen,' I interrupted. 'Your scam's clever, love. But it's cack-handed.' I had to turn away from her blinding face. 'Look. You age a canvas *before* you paint it. With a high-intensity ultraviolet light and a thermostatically controlled inspissator you can do wonders to a modern canvas. Yet not one canvas out there has been aged. That Domenico has no idea of brushwork. And he's using some acrylic paints, for God's sake.' In outrage I began ticking off the faults. 'Nobody's even got a smoke-gun for age-colouring new varnish on your fake oils. The woodcarving's done in American pine, a clear give-away—'

'You've not seen any pine carvers,' Placido put in.

'It stinks the frigging place out,' I said contemptuously. 'And that San Trovaso altar bas-relief's supposed to be marble, not light-weight crap made up of laterite dust, Polyfilla powder and polyurethane varnish. Fakers gave that trick up decades ago. And why no watermarks on the paper? It takes a skilled antique paper faker about ten minutes to knock up a class watermark.' I nudged the signora offensively. 'You're so proud of inventing Italian traditions about cocktails, Signora. Watermarks really *are* a local tradition. Right from the thirteenth century Italy was streets ahead. The Arabs, Japanese, Chinese, none of them could do a class watermark till modern times. And they gave me York stone, far too light, to fake the Ducal Palace's carved capitals. Want me to go on?'

'But we proved it, Tonio. Our reproductions are faultless.' She sounded puzzled. In a minute she'd move to worse anger as my news sank in. I rose apologetically, ready with my explanation.

'I know we did, *cara*. That's why Lovejoy's a fraud.' Tonio was practically quivering with eagerness. Placido carefully put the door to and turned to face me. War.

'You mean that auction? Your Carpaccio painting?' I smiled, but my knees were beginning to wobble so I rose and walked to the window. Tonio nearly fell about at that, thinking I was sussing out an escape route by a Douglas Fairbanks leap. How wrong he was. Even the thought of all that risk and energy made me palpitate.

'Why, yes.'

'Didn't Tonio or Caterina tell you? That the wooden stretchers weren't properly plugged?' I lied. Actually, they'd been reasonable. 'That the canvas was obviously modern?' It had actually been well aged. 'And the varnish could have done with a little more nicotine discolouration, especially over the—'

'Lies!'

The doorbell rang, halting Tonio. It rang, rang, rang. A furious knocking on the door accompanied it, non-stop. My relief-sweat broke out. I almost fell down. For a million panic-stricken heartbeats I thought the *traghetto* ferry men had simply taken my money and welshed. She could learn the horrible details now.

'Is it lies about the murders, Tonio?'

'What murders?' The signora's cigarette smoke was vertical.

'Two antique dealers. They also spotted the flaws. Malleson, Cramphorn.' In the din from the door I kept my eyes on Tonio but was speaking to the signora. By a lucky fluke I found myself standing behind the settee. A born coward.

'He's making it all up, Lavinia,' Tonio said.

'Am I? Signora. Phone any East Anglia newspaper.'

She put a hand to her temple, trying to concentrate. 'That *noise* . . .'

'It's the fire, police and canal ambulance out there,' I explained cheerfully. 'I bribed the gondoliers to phone and give this address.'

'Get rid of them. Both of you.' The signora rose and crossed to the window. The palazzo's door into the *campo* was not visible from inside the room. I'd checked. 'Explain that it was some stupid tourist's hoax.'

Sadism reluctantly postponed, Tonio and Placido left me with the signora. I let them get half way downstairs before I spoke.

'Actually it's only the *traghetto* blokes. I bribed them to make a hullabaloo.'

She had to smile despite the new worries I'd given her. 'You're a pest, Lovejoy. You know that?'

'Not without trying, Lavinia.'

'And all this about the two murdered dealers and the fakes. Yet more annoying tales?'

'Come to my apartment at noon, Lavinia. I'll tell you what's really happening to your scam. And who's out to ruin you.' I gave her Cosima's address.

Her eyes were shining. 'I may not trust you.'

'Don't bring Tonio or Placido. Nor anybody else. I don't trust you either.'

The downstairs racket was lessening. Time to go. I

crossed the room, shutting her in behind me and turning away from the landing which overlooked the noisy hallway. It had to be left turn, and down past the dumb-waiter. That had given me the clue to where the kitchen was, directly below somewhere, and inevitably the back staircase which accompanied it. Which meant access to the low arches of the palazzo's canal exit I'd inspected from the nicked gondola that other night.

Incredibly, a stout oldish bird was amiably cutting stuff in the kitchen as if the world was normal, when I passed. She was caterwauling a song accompanying a radio. One more floor down, and I was through a dampish doorway into the sleaziest, longest and wettest cellar you ever saw. Talk about damp. I looked through a grille which emitted a feeble yellow.

He was sitting on a small camp stool beside a bed, his face averted from the grille set in the door. It was bolted on the corridor side. A patrician's dungeon, practically inaccessible and frighteningly private.

'Luciano? It's me. Lovejoy.'

He didn't even move. There was a small table lamp. He didn't look as if he'd been knocked about, but I was peering in at an abject picture of utter defeat.

'I'm undoing the bolts, mate.'

There were three. I tried the door and it opened, but by then I was so frightened at the vague thuds transmitting themselves through the palazzo's structure that I scarpered quickly along the passage and unbolted the end door. It had an old tumble lock. No key, but anybody with a wire in his turn-up can unlock it as fast as with the right key.

Beyond, that narrow set of steps and broad daylight on the canal. The barred portcullis-type gateway between me and freedom was still down, only inches from the surface of the water. It meant swimming, ducking under the portcullis and emerging into the open canal in full sight of anybody on the nearby bridge.

I waded down the steps until the grotty water was up to my middle. I drew a deep breath and plunged.

CHAPTER 25

It was predictable. Within two hours I was dry, free and anonymous as ever. Looking at it now, my public re-emergence from the canal's dark grot was a scream. Of course, anything's hilarious as long as it isn't yourself slipping on that comical banana peel, but on this occasion I needed to play the clown. I clambered out of the canal into an assembly of a few tourists and the stray Venetian, talking nineteen to the dozen. Two laughing Germans even took my photo. In the pandemonium I gave different versions — fell in photographing the bridge, tumbled in after a few drinks, etc. Rueful and grinning, I sloshed my way to the Giardinetti where I sat in the garden and watched folk queue for their loo tickets. Lots of cats and bonny trees — and me, drying out. Odd, but once you're seated you tend to vanish even if you're extraordinary. Stand up, and people are all attention.

At a different tailor's I bought a T-shirt and had them bag my stuff for carrying. Because I now had no need to hide from Cesare and the other water-taxi men, I walked quite openly to the Zaccaria and caught a waterbus.

The Australian butterfly painter, dreamer Gerry, was on board in the standing-room-only middle bit.

'Wotcher. Still at it, eh?' He looked rather heavily daubed and was carrying his gear, to everybody else's discomfort.

'Lovejoy! Where did you get to? Poor Cosima! We searched for you, you know.'

'Oh, all over with now. Cosima's great, off to

convalescence,' I reassured him, at which he showed great relief. No questions after my health, mean sod.

'Keith's playing with one of those dredger engines near Murano. He'll be sorry he missed you. Are you free for supper?'

We chatted all the way. They had shacked up somewhere near the station; after returning from Padua ('Queer light for painting in Padua, and no engines'). Gerry gave me their address. We said so-long and swore undying determination to meet for a drink, the way folk do. Honestly, I was pleased at having met a confirmed neutral for once, and kept thinking of Keith's fascination for engines. An artist is a poor sort of ally, but a bloke with a dredger is a different matter.

At Cosima's tiny apartment I had a bath, generally defilthed, and was flitting anxiously about the narrow *calli* when midday struck.

Ten minutes later, with me all but demented from depressing convictions, a gondola tapped its hollow tap on the nearby canal and a woman's heel-clicks echoed through the *sottoportego* archway. Alone, I watched her silhouette take colour as Signora Norman emerged from the shadow. The gondolier pushed away, calling his warning 'Ioooo' at the sharp corner. The gondola had looked genuinely fresh from its three-weekly tarring, so it was probably innocent, not some cunning private craft ballasted out with an armoured division. I stood forward, in the little *campo*.

'Hello, Signora. This way.'

She was amused because I peered in every direction. 'You're like a little boy playing Indians. Were you frightened I'd bring Tonio?'

Derision's a woman's chief weapon, probably because it always works. 'Deep locked cellars are fine for Casanova and Luciano. Not for me.'

'Tonio was furious with me for letting you go, Lovejoy.'

'I'll bet. Erm, excuse me, please.' Red-faced, I fumbled with my wire and let us both in. 'Sorry about the shambles, but I haven't had a minute lately.'

'Night work, I suppose,' she said evenly. Women entering somebody else's home look about with peculiar intensity. 'Is this *it?*'

'It's nice,' I shot back, irritated. 'No dungeons.'

'You mean Luciano?' She walked about, swishing her finger along surfaces and distastefully rubbing the dust away. They always make you feel to blame for everything. 'Tonio explained that Luciano came with some tale of you making trouble. Placido had him wait downstairs—'

'Like they did Carlo?'

'Who on earth's Carlo?'

'Never mind.' She was probably not in on Tonio's detailed arrangements—like life and death. 'Erm, would you care for a drink, signora?' I had this little tray with two glasses and a bottle of cheap wine. It was decked out with a few small carnations in a cup, though I'm normally on the flowers' side.

'How kind.' She sat in a wicker chair, clearly still slumming. Suspicious she was taking the mickey, I waited for the guffaw at my floral poshness but it never came. I was glad of that, and poured the wine with only the odd shred of floating cork.

'Who is she, Lovejoy?'

'Eh?'

'The woman so conveniently absent.'

You have to admire a woman like that. Never been here before, and instantly she spots that its a woman's flat. Clever. It's a female knack.

'Oh. A friend. She's not here now.'

'She forgot to leave you her key.'

'Careless,' I agreed, working out how to start. 'But you've been a bit careless too, lately.'

Actually her presence was worrying. There was none of

that naturalness which Cosima brought, that inner shining. Older, with a brittle quality which somehow overlay her wealth. She knew she was beautiful, which intensified her as if her movements announced: I have power, you peasant—bring me more. Uneasily I remembered that it was in a nearby palazzo that poor old philosopher Bruno was betrayed to the Inquisition—by his patron, of course, in true Venetian tradition. You have to watch friends.

My remark had touched some nerve. 'I'm never careless.'

'Indiscriminate's careless.' I gave her a filled glass. 'Your scam must have seemed as foolproof as Mr Pinder's.'

She looked into wine. 'There's only *one* plan, Lovejoy.'

'No, love. On the one hand there's your dad's plan—forgeries galore, replace Venice's fabulous stuff as you go along. All,' and I couldn't help smiling, 'for the very best motives, preserving the treasures for when Venice sinks. Then there's *your* plan. Very different. Your plan requires teams of expert movie people to make advertising videos of the fakes and the nicked antiques, right? In a score of different languages for marketing in different countries.'

'I'm simply carrying out Babbo's orders—'

'Not you, love. Not once you'd shacked up with Tonio. Was it his idea to defraud your dad's syndicate, and keep the originals? Or yours?'

She smiled beatifically. 'Mine. I have a safe house in Tuscany.' She did that breast-tilting shrug I was coming to know and love. 'They're morons in Tuscany, but what choice has one?'

'And instead of taking them to the refuge Mr Pinder's syndicate had organized you'll send the counterfeits? Naughty girl.'

She took a swing at me, blazing. 'Don't you lay that

tone on me, Lovejoy.' I only just escaped another clout as she spat out, 'Or your word *counterfeit*. Everything's counterfeit, or didn't you know? Belgium exports counterfeit heart pacemakers, for Christ's sake. France counterfeits wine. Italy exports counterfeit car brakes, even counterfeit medical drugs. Britain exports counterfeit jeans. America's mass-produced counterfeit African tribal designs for ages—the Yoruba, Kuba and Senufo have never got a bent cent in royalties. Taiwan counterfeits spares for Boeing jets, Cartier watches, every damned thing.' She was breathless, heaving with fury. 'Want me to go on?'

'And you'll have hundreds and hundreds of originals?'

'Only some originals, Lovejoy,' she pouted. 'The best ones.'

She sounded so indignant I had to laugh. After a startled second she laughed with me. That really set me off. We sat there like fools, falling about, wine spilling so much she squawked and held her glass away to save her skirt, and that made us howl all the more.

I roared till my ribs hurt and I lay spreadeagled at the sight of the lovely bird, helpless with her eyes streaming and her luscious shape skewiff in the chair. Just when we'd start subsiding, one or other of us would gasp, 'Only *some* originals,' to set us off wheezing and choking with laughter.

Gawd knows what Cosima's neighbours thought.

As it turned out, Cosima's neighbours kept their thoughts to themselves. If they heard anything at all they showed no sign, not even later when the little bed thumped the wall under the stress we inflicted on it, Lavinia desperately shushing us by shoving her hand, still erotically gloved, between the headboard and the wall but to no avail. Her ungainly attempt set us laughing again so much it nearly made us ill. Sooner or later I'd have to make a list of the enemy, complete with reasons, but for the moment Lavinia's softness was all over me and I'd other things on my mind.

Eventually after love we slept, Lavinia giving occasional moans as the laughter's ache returned now and then. Just before I fell into oblivion, I tried hard to work out why the hell she didn't know the real truth, but with my head warping her soft belly and my sweat drenching our sticky slumber I hadn't a chance. It's an odd fact that oblivion is better shared. I remember thinking how this truth in itself was a problem. What I wanted for the next two days was no friends and no lovers, and with luck I'd manage to pull off my own private scam. Instead, I leap into bed with the naked—you can't count gloves—boss enemy and develop this weird feeling that she and I are on the same side after all. Typical.

'I thought real Venetians didn't use gondolas.'

'Only in extreme necessity. They're a diminishing breed.'

We were at the canal by the arch. The approaching gondolier couldn't believe his luck at getting a fare. I tried not to remember that Lavinia held Tonio's arm exactly like she was holding mine.

'Do I report for work tonight?'

'Certainly not, darling. It's suspended for two days.'

'Any reason?' I tried to sound thick, but I knew the *acqua alta* was coming.

'Don't bother your head, darling. I'll be here with you tomorrow, after breakfast. You'll receive further orders then.' She descended grandly and took her place. 'Your flower is artificial,' she reproved the man severely. Gondolas have a little gilded vase fixed near the prow. Its carnation was plastic.

'Apologies, signora,' the gondolier bleated.

'Genuine is infinitely preferable,' she said primly. The gondolier gave a puzzled glance at my snort of incredulity, and even Lavinia looked round in surprise. She caught sight of my expression and got the joke.

Her laughter echoed along the chasm of the narrow canal and reverberated under the pretty bridge until the gondola was out of sight. I remained there, smiling reflectively, in case she had second thoughts. When I was dead certain she'd gone I streaked off over the bridge and down the narrow *calle* in a hell of a hurry. I needed Cesare urgently. And Keith. And Caterina. And I was due at my own private funeral by midnight.

When you need friends, where are they? Or even enemies. Cesare was nowhere, the bum. Two solid hours it took me, zooming exhausted around the Riva, searching. I asked Ivan the Terrible, who only laughed. I spent a fortune on water-taxis and gondolas. I even crossed hopefully to the Giudecca, and funds were becoming dangerously low.

Eventually, would you believe, I found him half-sloshed in that same bar down the Garibaldi laying down the law about a football match to two old geezers doing mental battle about who'd buy the next round. He was practically pickled and glared blearily up at me when I accosted him.

'Cesare!' I made sure I looked elated and breathless. 'Congratulations. Come quickly, mate—'

'Eh?' He peered, and chuckled. 'Oh, Lovejoy.'

'Help me!' Pulling him to his feet wasn't easy. The old blokes blinked while I tapped Cesare's face. 'You drunken sod. We've got tenth prize in the Irish Lottery! Come *now!* Where's your boat? The money—' At the magic word, the Venetian catalyst, three elderly blokes and the young barman had Cesare up and out in a trice.

'It's down the Garibaldi, signore. This way.'

Another geriatric propelled me along at a sprint. Everybody fired questions about the money, the lottery, the money, as we tore through the market to where Cesare's water-taxi rocked in a small *bacino*. I told my eager helpers Cesare and I had equal shares.

'Lucky I caught sight of our names on the board,' I gasped, flopping into the boat. 'Don't know how much, but . . .' Willing hands cast us off amid shouts. Cesare's drunken attempts at the controls were too much for the spectators who were frantic at the thought of escaping gelt. Two of the bar blokes got us going and reversed fast to the intersection so I could turn.

I yelled thanks above the roar and was off, with Cesare giving a boxer's triumphant handclasp and falling over. The crowd babbled satisfyingly on the *rio*.

'Lovejoy,' Cesare cried in a drunk's thick voice. 'Where's my ticket? I've not lost it, have I?'

'There is no ticket, stupid burke.' Boats go faster than they seem. It was hell to control, trying to rear up out of the water. I had to put her down to walking pace. A hand clamped on my shoulder.

'*You* got my ticket, Lovejoy?'

'No,' I said wearily. I'd have to go along with him until he sobered. 'A lady's keeping it for you.'

'Where? Where?'

'I'm not exactly sure. In the *Eveline*, a big white yacht. It *was* on the Zattere . . .'

Drunk as a newt, he determinedly took the controls then. I was glad and sat back. I didn't want time to be too much of a problem. After we found Caterina I'd need every second.

Boat people are funny. Drunk or sober, they can manage very well thank you. Like antique dealers, really, though on the whole we're ignorant of our pursuit whereas boatmen know all about fathoms and other nauticals.

Exactly two hours later, after umpteen shouted discussions with other boats and a long run down the lagoon, we found the *Eveline* wharved among smaller leisure fry in Chioggia.

Beginning of the end, you might say, I thought as we stood off and looked at the great two-masted yacht from the lagoon. For whom I wasn't quite sure, but it was coming, almost within reach.

CHAPTER 26

'Chioggia's the *enemy* port,' I once heard a Venetian explain, nastily referring to some long-vanished barney at the bottom end of Venice's lagoon. It's very different. Venice is as unplanned as tangled wool. Chioggia by comparison is mathematical, its canals practically straight and the bridges predictable. The mediæval Chioggians knew their trigonometry.

Cesare had sobered by the time we hauled into port. He of the bloodshot eye and bleary gaze no longer believed the tale of my invented lottery. During our dash southwards he'd sussed that I was still labouring in some criminal vineyard. That put him in a foul mood. I was really pleased about that. It meant Cosima was being as distant with him as she'd been with me. Served him right, surly sod. Cosima had judged him to a nicety, even if it was odd how little she trusted me. He hovered us off the wharf while I gazed at the lovely vessel and schemed.

'Park down the canal, okay? Be in that café.'

'Moor,' he groused. 'Cars park. Boats moor. Any more orders, Lovejoy?'

'It's all in Cosima's interests,' I explained sharply.

'It had better be, Lovejoy. What *are* you up to?'

'Look, mate. If you won't help . . .' I stamped ashore and marched along the narrow *fondamenta*. Why the hell people aren't more trusting I'll never know. Just because I'd nicked his girl, ruined his happiness, tricked him about a lottery, wasted his day and conned him into assisting my criminal enterprise was no reason to get narked. I ask you. Where's trust gone?

Here in Chioggia the *Eveline* assumed a wholly disproportionate grandeur, a cathedral visiting a shanty town. Stooping with reverence, I walked its ridged gangway and knocked politely. Ship doors always look misshapen to me but I suppose shipbuilders know what they're doing.

The cabin was hangar-sized after Cesare's titchy boat. I'd never seen such floating opulence. Modern gunge, apart from an expensive small Malayan dancer carved riskily from stained meroh wood, but all of it costly and therefore full of messages to the world's poor. Malaysian meroh wood's usually reserved for the planks from which those Red Sea dhows are still built, so it took a particularly skilled ancient carver to tackle that length of grain—

'Tonio! Darling!' Feet clattered and Caterina practically tumbled into the cabin. She'd been washing her hair and was wet and turbanned. And astonished, and then furious. Her female mind instantly blamed me, because she was the one who'd misunderstood.

'Well, not quite darling. Only me.' Even messy she was beautiful.

She hated me, as usual. 'What are *you* doing here?'

I had to make something up, now I suddenly knew everything. 'Erm, is Mr Pinder with you, please?'

Her lip didn't quite curl. 'He stayed home, like the little piggy in the nursery rhyme.' She towelled her hair, thus casually stating that appearances didn't matter for the likes of Lovejoy. 'Grandad's too old to come out much any more. I want to know why you're here, Lovejoy.'

'I came with a message for anybody who . . . represents Mr Pinder's interests.'

That spun her, stopped the towelling. It put naked alarm into her eyes. The fear was clearly for Tonio.

I thought, Well, see if I care; and said, 'I've been working for Mr Pinder's scam, night shift. I called round at . . . Signora Norman's palazzo.' To hide my near-mistake—I'd nearly said Lavinia—I crossed the cabin and peered at the wharf. 'You see, Caterina, I think your grandad's being fobbed off with inferior stuff. Deliberately. I told your mother that.'

'What did she say?' Still frightened. The picture was becoming clearer. Hard-hearted vicious nympho Lavinia was looking purer by the minute.

'She didn't believe me. Slung me out.'

She smiled then without fear, resumed towelling her head. 'So you came to tell me.'

'Naturally,' I lied, now just wanting to get the hell out. 'I can give you proof.'

'You would.' She stood before a mirror, fluffing her wet rats-tail hair off her nape. 'Has it ever occurred to you, Lovejoy, that you're an arrogant pig? You always right, everybody else always wrong?'

'Be at the island about midnight,' I said through a throat suddenly gone thick. First time I'd told any enemy I knew where it was. 'It'll be empty then. Tonight's our night off. I can show you what I mean about the antiques.'

'Why me?'

'Nobody else I can trust, is there? But come alone.' Dangerous to look into her mirrored eyes, in case she spotted that I'd guessed her sudden new plan, so I moved towards the cabin steps. 'It wouldn't be any use telephoning Mr Pinder. He wouldn't believe me. And I've not enough money to stay here any longer. Your mum's lot hasn't paid me yet.' I spoke the last bit with honest bitterness, which pitched everything safely at a proper level.

'I might come.' Her mind was going like a racing pigeon. Tonio had a real ally.

'Want me to call here for you?'

'No,' she said quickly. 'Somebody can boat me over—if I do come.'

'Right. I'll have everything ready. You'll see.' I made the steps to the outside world.

After a quick check to confirm that Cesare's boat was really and honestly moored outside the canal café where I'd said I'd meet. him, I trotted off in the opposite direction. Now back to Venice, leaving him stranded and completely out of the picture. About time Cesare'd done something right for once.

Gerry and Keith were in a fine old sulk when I got to their place. They'd rented a garret straight out of *La Bohème*, not quite as tidy. It was only then, seeing them arguing, that the penny dropped, and Cosima's faint blush whenever they came up in conversation tipped off my stupid mind. I looked at the two fuming Aussies thinking, Well, well. The row was something about painting.

'It was a perfectly *innocent* remark, Gerry.' Keith pushed me to a chair while Gerry broke out the wine. Neither said hello. I said wotcher, and sat there feeling an interloper.

'No remark's innocent! Is it, Lovejoy?' Gerry demanded, white as a sheet and glaring at his mate.

'Erm,' I quavered. I was in crossfires of my own.

'That's right! Side with *him*.' Gerry fetched a glass, pointedly leaving Keith's on the tatty sideboard.

'I wasn't,' I said quickly. 'Honest.'

Keith's turn to go all frosty. 'Oh? So *I'm* in the wrong! Is that it?'

I began to get a headache. 'Honestly. I don't even know what it's all about—'

Gerry went all dramatic. '*He* said I should paint

engines instead of butterflies. Would you stand for *that* poisonous remark, Lovejoy?'

'I said nothing of the *kind*, dear—'

'You *did!* I distinctly *heard* you.'

Christ. People say they're worse than women, don't they?

'Keith can't have meant it like that, Gerry,' I said in an inspired moment.

'Then how *did* he mean it?'

'Erm, probably, erm, that your talent should, well, conquer new fields . . .'

'Lovejoy's right, Gerry. You *know* you're better than you think.'

Gerry was mollified. 'Am I?'

' 'Course you are,' Keith said. 'Plain as silly old day.'

'Really? Honestly?'

Keith rushed the bottle over to us, and it was end of World War III, thank God. We drank to Gerry's new career as engine artist and chatted amiably about the merits of oils and egg-tempera. Gerry was impressed, once we got talking, because I knew how to transfer Old Master oil paintings to new canvases. We all finished up slightly merry, which suited me because I was keeping a frantic eye on the wine and the time and working out how to get round to the all-important question of doom.

'I'm so glad we met up again,' I confessed eventually. 'Cosima's glad, too.'

They were pleased. 'She is?' Keith popped another bottle. 'Nice little thing. Wrong clothes, of course, and scandalously thin feet for wearing cage heels. Be sure to tell her that having no dress sense isn't her fault.'

'I like her, too,' Gerry added. 'You've made an absolutely marvelloso choice, Lovejoy. Remember, you don't actually have to *look* at her dreadful blouses. Somebody said she cooks, though women can't. Can she do kibbeh?'

'Think so,' I guessed hopefully. Sounded like swimming.

'We *must* try them.' Gerry gave a beatific smile. I'd have to warn Cosima to be on her best culinary form that night. Nobody gets criticized like the cook at the best of times.

'It's a date,' I said. 'Not too soon, though. I've an engine problem.' So much for tact.

'Engine?' Keith unglazed. 'What engine?'

'Somebody I know wants to, erm, borrow a powerful boat.' I scraped together a little circumspection. 'Any idea where I, er, he could get one?'

'Of *course!*' Gerry nudged Keith into a reply.

'How fast does it have to go, Lovejoy?'

'Not speed. Strength. Like those stone-lifters.'

'A working dredger?' Keith really lit up. His subject.

'Something like that, I suppose.'

'Funny. I've just been giving two of those a good going-over,' Keith said.

'Astonishing coincidence,' I agreed gravely.

Gerry refilled Keith's glass, giggling. 'Know what I think? I think naughty old Lovejoy didn't come just to see us. He was only after our dredgers.'

Keith was looking wary, mistrustful swine. 'Hire, Lovejoy? Borrow? Or . . . ?'

I cleared my throat and peered into my empty glass but Gerry stood there holding the bottle. Both were watching me, exchanging glances. No good mucking about.

'This friend of mine was wondering where he could, well, get on to one that's, well, moored. Just interest. No, er, need for anybody to spot him. Like the two near the Sacca Serenella, in Murano.'

'See what I mean, Keith?' Gerry relented with the plonk. 'Watch him.'

Keith nodded, still suspicious. 'They're blocking the wall near the Canal of the Angels. Istrian limestone.'

'Look, Keith. How strong are they? Pulling.'

'Depends what you—your friend, I mean—wants to pull. Suppose this glass here is a pile of pine, like they use . . .'

He was off, frowning with concentration, moving crockery and matches about the coffee table and muttering lunatic technology. I settled back with relief. These amateur enthusiasts are great. No, really. I mean it. Daft as brushes, every single one, and boring as algebra, but great. All I wanted to know was if there was a night watchman and how to work the damned thing.

'Paying attention, Lovejoy dear?'

I looked up into Gerry's sardonic gaze. 'Of course,' I said, at my most innocent. 'I'm really quite interested in engines.'

'Don't you mean your *friend* is?'

'Erm, sure. My friend.'

Gerry tapped Keith's wrist. 'If you lend Lovejoy one of those filthy machines, dear, make him promise to put it back, won't you?' He smiled roguishly. 'We don't want the police calling here spoiling our breakfast.' Keith fell about at that. Some private joke.

Yet it was an important point. Keith must be well known as the keen amateur who had been dissecting the bloody dredgers, and police jump to nasty conclusions.

Keith abandoned his gear ratios. 'Would tomorrow do, Lovejoy? Your, ah, friend could come over with me. The foreman's a sweet bloke.'

'My friend hasn't much time,' I said. 'It'd have to be tonight.'

Keith ended the long pause by saying, 'You—he—can't see much of the engine in the dark, Lovejoy.'

'He'll manage.'

'There's an *acqua alta*.'

Suddenly apprehensive, Gerry sat beside Keith. 'The sirens will go soon, during the night. The radio said.'

'Dredgers don't work on, in a high water.' Keith was asking a question.

'But one could, right? And nobody'd see.'

Gerry suddenly said, 'Don't ask Keith to go with you, Lovejoy.'

'Go where?' I demanded indignantly. 'Look, Gerry. Have I said anything about Keith going anywhere? Well? Have I?'

Gerry had a hand on Keith's arm. He'd gone white. 'Send Lovejoy away, hen. For his own sake. He's a bad dig.'

I said disgustedly, 'Keith. Just tell me how to move one of the damned things, and I'll do the best I can.'

Keith tried, 'Don't get upset, Lovejoy. Gerry only meant—'

Hamming away, I kept it up, all brave and quiet and hurt. 'Honestly, there's just no trust anywhere nowadays. I didn't come here to drag you into my troubles. Tell me quick. Is there a guard, and how do I switch the bloody thing on?'

Over Gerry's protestations Keith began to explain, gradually submerging in his subject. Gerry glared all sorts of despair at me but I ignored the silly nerk. I wish I'd been cerebrating, because things might have turned out different, but all I could think was, If Keith won't nick a dredger and bring it to the island dead on time then I'd have to do it myself. None of it was my fault. God alone knows why people keep blaming me.

Listening to Keith, I took notes.

CHAPTER 27

The No. 5 vaporetto emitted its departing roar and left me standing on the rocking boat-stage in the night. God, I felt forlorn. I had a stupid urge to shout after it, try a flying leap as it churned away. Daft for a grown man, but those vague Venetian mists can give anybody the spooks. The canals and bridges have a weak bulb or two bragging haloes but they don't seem to deliver the light where it's actually needed, and the occasional distant chug of an engine and the warning 'Ioooo' of the gondolier make it spookier.

The Madonna dell' Orto church square was empty. I made sure by strolling round, pretending the aimlessness of the tourist to an old lady who creaked into the gold-glowing church doorway for a quick spiritual high. Venice was retiring for the night. The canal was a street of black oil, what I could see of it. Above, scudding clouds soaked in moon kept me rain-guessing. It wasn't my scene, especially when I got near the funeral place.

I needed to steal a funeral barge, and they were placidly moored facing the church. The trouble is, there's no real school for thieves, is there? How do you suss out a canal in a night mist? Twice I walked across the bridge which marked the end of the canal, and peered hopelessly out into the dark blanket covering the lagoon, imagining I saw the distant lights of the cemetery island of San Michele. The Sacca della Misericordia turned out to be a big rectangular stretch of water facing north-west, the way I wanted to travel. It was as handy an exit as ever I was to find now I was having to do every bloody thing alone as usual. I walked back towards the church, keeping close to the wall of the doorways and touching drainpipes, not wanting to vanish with a splash.

Nowadays even posh antique dealers, like most other criminals, use those little disposable Keeler pen-torches, and I carried two. The light just about made it to the wall. I climbed over and dangled cautiously from the church bridge. The bridge's own single bulb was practically useless. A good stabbing night, when you came to think of it. Uneasily trying not to think at all, I replaced my pen and swung to and fro from my hands till I was sure of the momentum, and let go. I hit the foredeck of the funeral gondola with a hell of a loud thump, nearly braining myself on one of its little gold decorative lions. But I'd made it. I clung and looked about.

From canal level the bridge looked impossibly far out of reach. Visibility was pretty bad, worse than on the canal bank. I could see the wall of the funeral building, of course, the winch, the double doorway. The bridge's feeble bulb. The narrow pavement opposite, and vaguely the oblique gold blur of the church's doorway. A single lit window in one of the terraced houses across the canal. That was that. Above, the moon showed but too irregularly to be much help.

I clambered along the gondola. Behind it, a larger boat was moored, and beyond that the indistinct darker mass of a third. It looked as if I'd collected a funeral gondola and two funeral barges. A fleet.

A funeral gondola is rowed by sad gondoliers, but a funeral barge is a wide motorized thing, maybe thirty or so feet long. It has a kind of well where you stand to drive between two glass-enclosed cabins. There are tidy little white lacey curtains lending elegance to these cabins. Uneasier still, I shone my torch to see I wasn't accompanied by any terrestrial beings before making sure the starter motor could easily be fired by slitting the insulation in the same old way. I'd have to trust it was fuelled up. The Volvo-Penta service station, about a hundred yards down and on the right, would presumably have its own night-watchman to guard petrol supplies. I undid the ropes, swearing because they'd got wet somehow, and pushed off.

It was only then that I noticed how high the water was. I barely scraped under the bridge, poling away with the nicked pole. The water had risen. Not only that. It was moving. Mostly canal water just hangs about. One push on a pole and your craft careers along until something stops it. Not now. I was struggling just to gain headway. I even heard a gurgle as water eddied past, coming in from the lagoon to lift the canal even higher. The barge moved with sedate grandeur bumping into the wall of the Palazzo Mastelli with a nasty hollow sound which frightened me to death and re-echoed for a million noisy years.

It's only about a hundred yards from the church to the Sacca, but it felt like a circumnavigation. I was reduced to giving two desperate long pushes, shipping the pole and trying to keep the barge going forward by manhandling her along the canal wall. That worked once or twice, but I was scared of rousing people. Even the most tranquil Venetian would be alarmed at the sight of a stranger's claws emerging from a mist-bound funeral barge to scrabble at his shuttered windows.

I knew the stone bridge had arrived when I bonked my forehead and got a mouthful. The barge just made it beneath, at the expense of a cracked glass pane or two as it scraped under the arch, but by then I was too worked up to care. I was late, and I still had to start the wretched boat and get across to the island.

Visibility across the Sacca was worse, if anything. The Volvo-Penta fuel depot's light was barely visible. No lights showed out in the opaque blackness of the lagoon. Christ, but it felt spooky. I'd assumed lights, direction easily found, maybe that ironic moon being some use. Me in control. Instead, I was floating blind and becoming terrified of letting go of nice˜solid stone. Once out there it'd be hit or miss. I tied the barge to the bridge's balustrade and had a crack at the starter motor. You won't believe this, but the engine was going a full minute before I realized it. The boat was shuddering slightly and gently butting the bridge's arch while I like a fool kept on trying to start it. Unbelievably quiet. It was a wonder I hadn't electrocuted myself.

For a split second I dithered. Then Caterina and her tame psychopath came to mind. And the fortune in fakes they were going to double-steal. Plus some originals. All those desirables going to undeserving nerks was a tragedy. I discovered I'd cast off without thinking.

Okay, I thought. Sod it. In for a penny, in for a pound. I turned the tiny wheel. My great one-speed barge trundled out into the void. I hoped there was water out there.

Caterina kept coming into my mind. She had everything — looks, youth, wealth, intelligence, that commanding manner which proved true breeding. Normally I'd have been grovelling near her ankles. But here I was, risking life and limb in a pathetic attempt to do her down. Surely it wasn't because of Cosima? Or was I subconsciously so hooked on Lavinia after today's carrying-on that I was talking myself into saving her skin at the expense of Tonio's? It was all too much for my addled brain. I concentrated on not knowing where I was instead.

The moon stayed where it was, thank God. Even when it was cloud-obscured I could get an idea of its direction by the glow. That mist was really odd, dense patches which suddenly thinned or ended, leaving my silent runner quivering its nose towards a thick blob of the stuff.

It made the lagoon surface change, too, into a pasty kind of translucent oil. Until then I'd assumed I knew everything about fog.

This was rotten stuff all right. Worse, a siren went, almost frightening me out of my skin. Presumably the high water was on its way, and here was me still a million miles — well, nearly four — peering anxiously at the bright fog-glow which indicated the Fondamenta Nuove where the big Lido steamers lay. Counting to a quick hundred to allow for getting past the monastery (it's a barracks now, sign of these ugly times) I swung left and knew myself heading for San Michele.

Venice's marine engineers aren't daft. It would be cheaper and simpler to put these lights on floating buoys or shorter posts, but you'd lose them in this dense lagoon mist. They've worked it all out. As long as you know where the last one was, and the next one should be, you can keep going fairly accurately by staring upwards and slightly wall-eyed until the mist begins to glow on your retina. That's how you follow the chain of lighted blobs across the dark water. It's quite an art.

The channel forks past Murano where the St James Marshes start. Right, a baffling course to the sea through stretches of marshy islets. Left, more or less direct between two lines of marker lights towards Mazzorbo and Torcello. I knew from my terrified checks of the marker lamps that, in the vast open expanse between Murano and the islets, the lanes of double lights ended. They became single. and finally the smaller channels had none at all. Where they continued, though, they would show to the right. That gave me a file to move along.

The island didn't actually surprise me much, though even an unsurprising island can scare you a bit when it moves swiftly out of a pitch-dark fog. I remember yelping, flinging the barge into a dangerous turn and cutting the engine. Speed lost, sweat wiped from my streaming face, and I was shakily in control again, able to take a mental line from the moonshine and the one mark-light still visible. Somehow I must have come up on the channel side of the island rather than the western aspect because I thought—or imagined, in my fear—I'd glimpsed a less dark rectangle set in brick. Possibly the relief of the Madonna which tourists competed to photograph as the steamers pounded past. The pale stone patch had looked disturbingly near the water.

Apprehensive, now with more to worry about than merely getting lost on a foggy night of the dreaded monster tides, I put the barge at a silent glide along the southern approach.

San Giacomo's a low island. Soldiers occupied part of it until 1964. The nearby Madonna del Monte had a munitions factory, but I'd guessed from what I could recall of seeing the gaunt derelict building that it was just too obvious for old Pinder's scheme. From some parts of the lagoon you can practically see nothing else. The San Giacomo's a different thing altogether, and I could remember the rough vegetation overgrowing the few low red-tiled buildings, as seen from the boat to Torcello. The island's unused landing-point was the stepway beneath the Madonna relief. Round the side might be a grottier but often-used landing-stage which my feet might just recognize.

Once you leave the main channel, you're lost. No lights. Heart in my mouth, I set the funeral barge creeping at right-angles to my original direction. Bravery shouldn't feel like terror, yet in my experience it always does. I was so sure I was being heroic. The island is more or less rectangular, so I knew the barge was nosing through the fog a matter of mere yards off the shore. Scared as always, I fancied just then that I heard a soft thud from out there in the misty blackness, but froze until I was certain no boat was approaching. The question was when to turn inwards and meet the island to find the landing-stage. Seven times my prow, with its golden two-winged ball and little lions, nuzzled to a stop against a solid dark island. Seven times I slipped her in neutral and crawled forward to push her off before resuming the journey. The eighth time I found nothing but a level step all awash, and a low brick-supported archway with tendrils and small clattering pods dangling in the opening.

That was a measure of the appalling height the tide had risen. As far as I could recall, they had made me climb steps. Now they were all awash. All height is relative. Everybody knows that. But any increase is bad news when you're looking for some underground factory.

Some things were on my side: my barge was black and quiet, and Tonio wouldn't come with lights blazing. He'd come with stealth like me, the smarmy bastard, determined to rely on unfairness in a fight. That meant my boat might remain undetected if I tied her close inshore further along. This I did, moving by grope till I found a rickety post about fifty feet from the submerged landing-stage. Caterina might come alone, in which case it was a waste—only partial, but still waste. But like all women, she could have done the natural feminine thing and lied in her teeth.

The island was silent. The path felt right. I risked the Keeler torch, crouching to peer at the ground and trying to guess directions. Even the vegetation felt right. It was great. The watch I'd borrowed from Gerry—at least they'd lent me that, I thought bitterly—showed one hour to Caterina's arrival. For Caterina read Tonio.

Being alone on a derelict island isn't good for one's nerves. For a lily-livered no-good like me it's terrifying. The place through which I was creeping was obviously some kind of derelict vegetable garden, with stupid shoots trailing about and the path crumbling. A couple of times

I came close to brick walling, one with broken or shuttered windows. Either monks or military. Originally, when blindfolded, I'd counted my paces. I wasn't to know there'd be no need. The path led only to one place.

The doorway was steel, rivets driven in at its sides and its two padlocks reinforced by a welded steel plate. The purist would have been disappointed at these feeble precautions. I was relieved and delighted. Of course, there was normally our full-time night shift of industrious fakers busy in the subterranean forgery factory, and two or more murderous men watching over all. It was only on such a night as this that guards would seem superfluous.

Nothing looks more daunting than a padlock, and nothing's easier. If you've got one on your garden shed, try picking it with a thick hairpin. Some come simple, like this first one. Five seconds. The second had some combination rollers I'd never seen before, so I sawed it through with my hacksaw—always carry the smallest and cheapest, incidentally. The door gave, beautifully oiled.

Funny feeling, seeing a familiar corridor for the first time. We'd all been blindfolded, of course, but I wasn't prepared for how narrow the corridors were. I put the door to, and followed my little torch. Finding a handrail just where I knew it always was, by the steps, was somehow astonishing. There were no other obstacles, no alarms, no angry shouts. Two careful minutes, and I entered the subterranean factory. I was in possession. Exactly as I'd planned.

A quick look round. Everything just as left, fakes in various stages of completion, each faker's position showing his own particular level of tidiness. All predictable and well. My wall-plate had not been disturbed, thank God. I slung my jacket and started work.

CHAPTER 28

A couple of tallow lanterns did for light. Domenico, hamfisted as ever, aged his handiwork by tallow smoke. Only the Cantonese still try that kid's trick nowadays, which shows you the level of my fellow fakers' expertise. Duckeggs.

In our stonemasonry corner I'd drilled a steel plate, head-height and as wide as a man can stretch, nothing more than some old shoring batten left by the military. Now it was pinned into the thick wall by four long steel bolts. From its face projected three metal pegs. Ostensibly it was a simple reinforced lifting device. To me it was one gigantic cork. If anything pulled at it from outside, a hell of a gap would appear in the cellar wall, and maybe the wall would go with it.

Nothing like fear to make you crack on speed. I used a cold chisel to bang out the bricks, levering with a crowbar and flinging the debris anywhere like someone demented. One brick to either side, top and bottom. Then another between. And another. When I could reach my arm round behind the big steel batten, I was satisfied. Then I set to weakening the wall still further, slamming the chisel into mortar, peppering my face with brick fragments.

There came that ugly moment when the mortar in one of my new recesses grew damp and started seeping water. I drew off with a terrified yelp. Like a fool, I even began cramming bricks back to stop it before I realized my stupidity and made myself pause to think straight.

Every faker of Old Masters carries packets of childrens' balloons, to hold his pigments. They're a godsend. They can be tied at the neck. They're waterproof, airproof. They're cheap, lightweight. They don't crack or shatter, so buy a bumper pack and you can match the balloons with the pigment each contains. The cleverer the forger, the neater he is. I easily blew up a whole bag of Domenico's to about a quarter of their capacity so quick I went dizzy. By now I was going like the clappers and reeled a bit as I tied the balloons to a string, a long multicoloured chain. The string I fastened to a strong cord, and the cord to the metal chain. I fixed its free end to a metal peg on my plate.

Now for the nasty bit. I'd no idea where the water level normally came to on the outside. All I knew was it would be hellish high out there now. Shaking scared at the possibilities, I procured one of the polythene tubes from Luciano's rolls of painting canvas. They're about four feet long, and wide enough to take the chain. The balloon string went into it easily, trailing the rope and chain. There'd be a hell of a squirt from the water out there, so I collected great bags of clay from the sculptors' enclave across the factory floor, and made sure it was handy. Then, all ready, I slammed my chisel into the seeping mortar and tore the half brick out.

The water shot me off my perch like a popgun going off. The horrid filthy stuff cascaded into the cellar with such force I was slithering screaming across the floor, scrabbling for a hold to stop myself. I was lucky not to have been brained. Panicking at the near-destruction I'd cause, I avoided the violent rush and climbed up underneath it to see what I'd done.

My hole into the lagoon was about as big as my palm. Enough for the tube. The water which had clouted me so savagely was merely a thin spout, as if from a hose. Not much, but it leapt over my shoulder and hit the cellar floor about half way across. I lifted the tube and got drenched shoving the damned thing into the waterspout, driving it in. Naturally the chain and my balloon rope was washed out so I had to do the whole thing again.

That's where my time went. It must have taken all of half an hour to fix it in place, the seeps sealed with clay and the edges of the tube held with nailed battens. I was a wreck. The clay packed the tube, so no seepage from that.

Out there on the surface of the lagoon, beyond the cellar wall, there now bobbed a string of multicoloured balloons. Easy enough for anybody to find. I could have done with a kip, but drove myself to make certain my chain was securely fixed to the steel plate. Once that went it'd need more than Lovejoy with a handful of clay to stop the water flooding and sweeping in, rising . . .

'Agh.' I'd yelped, scaring myself even worse, but only for a split second—it took me just that long to grab my jacket, blow out the tallows and dash out of that now-vulnerable cellar, with its puddles of water and mini-workshops crowded along its walls like huddles of untidy market stalls. Even so, leaving that mass of fakes and forgeries there, some hopeless, others not really too bad, was a pang, but I've always found that terror's a better prime mover than petrol ever was.

Odd, but I felt clean in my funeral boat as I did the rest of the job. Even though I knew that time had gone faster than my plans wanted, I was somehow content. Almost confident. I found the balloon string by creeping the barge along the building's lagoon wall and dangling over the side with my Keeler torch practically on the water.

Still in that extraordinary mood of euphoric contentment when it seems nothing can possibly go wrong and everything's going right, I cut the engine and gently hauled the balloon string aboard. The chain came into my hand. I hauled as much aboard as would come. About eight feet, until the chain stopped with a jerk and I knew it was holding taut on my steel plate in my weakened wall. I cut the balloon string and rope and airily chucked them overboard. Let some seaborne sleuth work that one out when they were found bobbing mysteriously on the briny. More cavalier still, I let the little stern anchor go overboard and used its shackle to fasten the chain to the barge's stern. Now my barge would stay there for sure. No worrying nautical complexities to worry about.

But where was Keith? And the dredger?

Phase X of my plan had depended almost entirely on Keith nicking a dredger and bringing it over to the island. Fix chain to dredger, drive off and out comes the steel plate bringing half the cellar wall with it. Cellar flooded, and the subterranean factory would be submerged forever in a torrent of lagoon. That was the idea. Do Tonio in the eye and leave old Mr Pinder's scam untouched, if not vastly improved. If it wasn't for Keith, the idle sod. He was probably paralytic drunk back in Venice by now. I'd have to nick the dredger myself now, once I found some way of fixing the chain in some prominent way. Then I'd use the dredger's engine to pull the plug, and home to report to old Pinder and reap a richly earned reward. Pity about my stone carving, but I didn't mind too much because I'd signed *Lovejoy fecit* with the date to entertain any future archæologist who came diving through the nuclear fallout in years to come . . .

A dull boom sounded. Long, long pause while I waited and tried not to worry about it. An echo from one of those wailing sirens which sounded so mournfully out in the black night? That boom. *It was in the building*. I thought, Christ! Just when I'd been feeling all confident.

Cut and run? Every neurone snapped into action sending tingling messages of escape. I even found myself fiddling with the controls. Then I thought. Caterina. Okay, so she hated me and loved Tonio. So she was double-crossing stepmother Lavinia who made me laugh and promised me much. And so she possibly knew that

Tonio was a psychopath, possibly even knew he had done for Mr Malleson and old Crampie. But the cellar was a deathtrap. And what if she honestly had turned up, on her own in good faith, like I'd said? I thought, Oh hell. Just my luck. From perfect confidence I was plunged back into my usual dither, all because of some stupid noise. I'm pathetic, I told myself, pulling on the chain so the barge bumped against the brickwork and I could climb into the entrance above the plaque. My brain felt back-combed. I was completely befuddled, all reasoning gone. Don't think I'd fallen for Caterina. I hadn't. I'm not that daft. Just because a bird has everything and can't stand the sight of a bloke doesn't mean he can't take a hint. And so what, if she has a boyfriend who did for Mr Malleson?

The trouble was I hadn't come in this way. I'd sneaked in on the other side of the island. The steps were deeply awash and my feet sloshed nastily in my shoes, making silence difficult. The wretched lagoon was slurping greedily ever higher, bloody thing. As if I'd not enough to worry about.

Cursing everything, I fumbled round the wall, inching as if on a ledge. I actually might have been, for all I knew or could see. There was comfort in the notion that I could always find my way back to my funeral barge by simply following the wall until I hit.

A vague golden glow showed brightly to my right and I squelched a pace back. A light. It moved an instant, then was gone. I'd been in the entrance to the factory, not realizing I'd got that far, and the light had been flicked on briefly, as if from a torch. *Somebody was in there*. And that somebody was being damned quiet. I'd used the same trick myself with my Keeler, partly covering its light with the fingers and putting light ahead for an instant at a time.

I was almost on the point of deciding to scarper when I heard a low murmur. A man's voice. And a low laugh.

Another murmur, receding. They were moving along the corridor and down into my—their—cellar. Still I hesitated, scared, but the logic was inescapable. I knew they were in there. They didn't know I was outside. And I knew for certain there was no other exit except the corridor and this external door. *I had them*.

Exulting, I slipped my shoes and socks off, felt round me, and put them beside the door. No need to risk my mini-torch now. The glow down the corridor leading to the underground factory came more frequently, now they felt more certain they were unobserved. *Was* it plural still? I slid after them, palpating surfaces for stairs, handrails, any landmark at all as I went. They were in the cellar now with no attempt at concealment.

'He's tried to make a lifter. See? On the wall.' Placido? Or . . .

'What for?' Now that *was* Caterina's voice.

They were inspecting my handiwork.

A laugh. 'Hoping to lift all this to the floor above. Poor fool. The high water has defeated more than him.' Another laugh. At me, of course. Not Tonio's voice, though.

'Where is he?'

'On his way. No need to worry.'

'Come here.'

Then silence. The torch came on, stilled. No movement. Had they sensed me?

Out in the corridor near the metal door I listened in a fever. Caterina and a bloke, that's for sure. But why the stillness? And they'd gone very, very quiet. Maybe I should just cut my losses and get the hell out, leaving them to it. A faint regular sound, like a distant tapping, struck my ear. Worried, I glanced back along the corridor but it seemed to be coming from inside the cellar where Caterina was. And a—what?—a distant but steady beat of noise. As if of a rhythmic exhalation, even a grunting.

I peered round the door like a kid in a comic.

Cesare and Caterina were together down there, oblivious. In the torchlight their copulating shadows moved metachronally, explaining the rhythmic beats. Caterina's legs were splayed to take a grip of Cesare. Her arms clasped him. Her mouth was on his as he beat into her on the long central table where the artists and sculptors argued continuously over space to put their materials. Cesare. And—in—Caterina. Not Placido. Not Tonio. Or all the lot of them?

For an instant a voyeur's curiosity delayed me, almost fatally. I'd no idea clothes looked so ridiculous when couples were taken by storm, in the act as it were. I'd assumed they only got into a mess afterwards somehow. But there was a gun on the table near Cesare's hand and I saw sense.

'Sorry,' I said, as the door slammed and I dropped the great metal stave to lock it. I meant the sudden noise.

'It's Lovejoy!' came audibly from Caterina a moment later. I moved a few steps away up the corridor in case he shot that damned thing.

'Yeah, me!' I called. 'I see why you were so glad to know where Cosima's convalescing, Cesare.

He laughed, actually laughed. 'Placido's on a little Sicilian trip, Lovejoy. Don't think she'll make a complete recovery.'

'When did you take Caterina's shilling, you pig?' I blazed. 'Right from the start or only recently?'

'What you'd sneer at as patrimony we know as duty, Lovejoy.' He wasn't at all discomfited. 'You'll learn soon enough that others have the same honour.'

'Caterina!' I yelled, to shut the bum up. 'Did you know Tonio was going to do Malleson and Crampie?'

'Oh dear no!' she trilled, all little-girl.

Even as Cesare roared with laughter I thought: Surely she can't be joking? Not about people getting killed.

'Are you sure?'

'I'd never have let him go back and keep on hitting him that way, Lovejoy!' And she too laughed.

I turned and left them to get on with it, sickened.

'Thank you for locking me in with a lovely lady, Lovejoy!' Cesare's shout was just audible as I reached the gloom, fog and obscurity. My natural habitat.

Maybe my distress made me careless. Maybe I walked straight ahead for a few dazed steps. I honestly thought I turned the correct way coming from the exit door, but after a few steps I stopped and tried to backtrack. It was hopeless. I finished up crouched down feeling for the edges of the path. No good. I was lost.

Stupidity's an art. It seemed best to me, at that daft moment, to crouch down and pad round in small circles feeling as I went. Logically, move in increasing-sized circles, and you sooner or later touch on the place you've lost, right? Well, it's logical if you go in precise circles. Do an oval or a spiral and you're more lost.

The last thing I wanted to do now was use my Keeler torch, in case Tonio was already here. Cesare had sounded too confident. And all that shouting. I fell down, over a mound of soft earth among the vegetation.

Feeling more carefully, I tried to work it out. Somebody had been digging. Recently. A patch maybe big enough to bury a sizeable load of antiques? My hand touched an instrument. I lifted it. A hand-hoe. Something left by a monk, or the recent digger? It would be at least one way of getting back at them all, if I were to nick whatever it was they'd hidden. Possibly their most precious fake or antique. I decided to risk it and scrabbled at one end of the mound. Maybe six feet by three feet, possibly a good-sized original statue that wouldn't hurt from the water now ploshing about my ankles and seeping into the hole I was scuffing. An obstacle. I'd found something. Grinning evilly and whispering to myself, I put out my hand and felt. Definitely features. A face. Definitely configurations of . . . a face. Pliable. Soft. Waxen softness of eyelids. A fucking *face*. Whiskers . . . I screamed, screamed, and clawed babbling and screaming away from Carlo's face and ran crashing into every bloody thing and anything, flinging myself demented and still screaming through bushes with the aid of the hand-hoe and splashing through the encroaching water, leaving that ghoulish grave behind me in its solitary nightmare. Shivering and retching, I ran blind, the wavering blur of my Keeler light which I'd somehow got out doing more to make the fog opaque than show me the way.

A pane of glass cracked underfoot. A tendril lapped round my neck and I howled, terror-stricken. A building hit me. I reeled away, tried to find those precious bricks again, couldn't, and ran and ran. A tree, its roots awash in rising waters, shot out of the fog and dazed me as we collided. I screamed and wailed, reeling. Somebody told me to stand still and put my hands up. I screamed in terror and tried to run.

A hand grabbed my shoulder. I saw this figure. He looked immense, looming out of the fog like a Disney giant. I struck out with both hands, felt my hoe send a shock up my arm and struck again and again in the darkness because my light had gone. I ran, flinging the hoe into the space where the figure had stood. And ran until the water was up to my knees, and there was only stillness and the water. There was no direction, nowhere else to go. I was a ruin, breathing and coughing like a spent horse and weeping and whining at the whole frigging mess, hands on my knees and the black water rising.

God knows how long I stood there before I did the only

sensible thing I'd done since I came to Venice. I put my head back and bawled, '*Help!*'

And blessedly, out of the wet night, quite close, came Keith's voice delightedly yelling, 'Lovejoy! That you, blue? Keep shouting, mate! We're on you!'

And lights began to glow as I bawled and bawled.

CHAPTER 29

We worms of this world can't look heroes. I tried my best to seem noble while Tonio died on the dredger where Keith and his two burly mates had finally managed to carry him.

I could hardly look. He was covered in blood where my hoe had dug into his neck, his cheek, his temple. It was Gerry, astonishingly along, who did what could be done for him. In the brilliant light of the great dredger's cabin everything was ghastly. Blood and mud everywhere. But even in all this, Caterina had to get away.

'Caterina knew about you killing Mr Malleson and Crampie,' I said. 'She told me.' It came out like an accusation. I'd meant to sound kind. 'You had to do Malleson. Mr Pinder had hired him to recover that Carpaccio fake. He'd guessed about you and Caterina, hadn't he? And your plan to cheat Lavinia as well as his syndicate.'

He smiled, oddly friendly for the first time. 'She was there, Lovejoy,' he explained. His voice seemed oddly chatty, no hard feelings.

'Where?' I said blankly.

'She's left-handed. Ask the witnesses.' His neck ran brown blood. Gerry thrust me aside and did something with a folded white square that instantly bloomed bright scarlet.

'What's he saying?' one of Keith's burly dredger pals said irritably.

'I'm not,' Tonio informed us all in quite a conversational tone, and died in silence.

'Not what?' the dredger bloke demanded. He was annoyed with practically everything. I wondered what it all had to do with him.

'Not left-handed. He was telling us.'

'What the hell!' the man said. 'He died?'

'Poor, poor thing!' Gerry was in tears, kneeling beside Tonio on the cabin floor. 'If he hadn't been so hacked about . . .'

Christ, I thought, faint. It would have been *me* otherwise. Tonio had a frigging gun with him. No wonder Cesare and Caterina had laughed. Chains rattled outside.

Keith consoled, 'Don't cry, Gerry dear. Please.' A call sounded from the outside man and his mate yanked a lever and put the wheel over, probably turning us or something. Tonio's body rocked a bit.

Hopeless. Me nearly demented, frightened out of my senses on an island being flooded by the highest tide ever recorded, blinded in a fog, stumbling on buried corpses all over the frigging universe, attacked by an armed psychopath, and Keith tells Gerry please don't sob. I felt sick.

'Listen, you burke,' I said to Keith. 'Why the hell were you so late?'

'The fog. We were watching the island, but—'

'Watching?' I said, furious. The chains rattled. The outside bloke shouted in a slow shout. 'In *this*? I said eleven o'clock.'

The dredger's motor gunned. The cabin gave one shake as we began to move, and a sudden jerk. The driver swore.

'We couldn't come any earlier,' Keith said, apologetic. 'We had to call at the Rio dei Greci for permission.'

'Eh?' I began wondering if Keith was off his nut. There's nothing down there except the water police depot.

'Oh, Lovejoy!' Gerry sobbed. 'I *said* don't come out here tonight!'

'I'm so sorry, dear,' Keith consoled Gerry. I looked at the steersman for enlightenment, but he was preoccupied with something outside in his fog-blind searchlights. The big dredger lifted an inch, maybe the tide turning.

'What's he on about?' I asked Keith, suddenly uneasy.

Keith gazed fondly at his mate and explained, 'He's so tender-hearted. He feels things so, Lovejoy. And you're under arrest.'

'Eh? Me?'

'You.'

'Here,' I said queasily. 'You can't do that. Can he?' I added to the steersman.

He finally took notice of me, as he swung the wheel frantically. '*Si*, signore,' he said bluntly. 'And so can I.'

'Oh, Lovejoy,' Gerry wailed. 'I *said*.'

And he had. Don't go, he'd said to Keith. All the time he was pleading with his pal not to betray me.

'And your interest in these dredgers . . . ?'

'We kept the island under surveillance from the dredgers. They're the only vessels always left out on the lagoon. Come hell or *acqua alta*.'

'You a cop too?'

'Art squad. We both are.'

'We knew something's been going on, Lovejoy,' Keith explained, his arm consolingly round his pal. 'A bit amateur, really. None of the regular art thieves would be so careless. We never even find a trace of the London-Amsterdam teams. They're still the greatest thieves.'

'So you've been watching us all?'

'Fakes were appearing all over Venice. Stumbled on them by chance. We had an idea it was Tonio and maybe his grand signora—'

Tonio. Caterina. I tore out of the cabin to stand helplessly in the grotty fog-bound air. And saw the funeral barge trundling along astern from a towing chain.

'What's that?' I yelled to the burly man at the rail.

'Only the funeral barge you stole,' he said reprovingly. 'We were lucky to find it. It had fetched up against the wall—'

'Did you untie it?' I could hardly speak the words. 'I chained it to . . . to . . .'

'Thought there was a bit of a pull.' He shrugged. 'But what's an anchor worth on a night like this?' No wonder the wheelman had been struggling to control the dredger. He was wondering what had made it temporarily difficult to get moving. Oh Jesus.

They turned the dredger back when I managed to convince them. All we found was a caved-in building just submerged by a tide that had laid almost the whole island awash. No trace of a living soul. Caterina and Cesare were buried, under the ruins, and under the tide.

My idea had been to release them in daylight, select the best fakes, and exit laughing as I pulled the plug, destroying all trace of my filching. All I'd done was do for everybody else.

CHAPTER 30

The villa was set off the road a hundred yards or more. It looked pretty, absolutely colourful and charming. A tennis court, a swimming pool. A splendid orangery in true Victorian style. A delectable little enclave of vines climbing up ornate trees. And a walled kitchen garden.

'This it?' I actually felt pale. The car journey from

Mestre hadn't made it any more pleasant, sandwiched between Keith and Gerry, those two eccentric expatriate members of the Antiques Fraud Squad.

'This is it, Lovejoy,' Keith confirmed, poisonously cheerful.

'*Bellissima, non è vero?*' The police sergeant who had accompanied us was delighted it looked so fetching, as if he was trying to sell me the damned place.

'*Si, signore,*' I said courteously.

'So many amenities!'

'All securely netted, wired, walled.' It was a prison.

The sergeant looked despondent. 'So much money in antiques.'

'It's that rose-coloured wallpaper,' Gerry whispered to Keith. 'I'm just not sure.'

We walked in. The gate was wrought-iron, head tall, and gave a telling double click to shut.

'Before you case the joint, Lovejoy,' Keith informed me in proudly dated slang, 'your duties are to be available at eight-thirty each morning.'

'Where's the trial?'

'No trial, Lovejoy.'

I presumed he meant to give evidence. 'See the lawyers?'

'Not that either. You're going to do an honest day's work, Lovejoy. Every single day.'

That shook me badly. 'Look, Keith, mate. If you can pull a few strings . . .'

'No way, old sport.'

'It's to do with antiques, Lovejoy.' Gerry ushered us all into the living-room and waited hopefully for praise. I gave his decor a surly nod. His face brightened as if I'd exulted. 'Keith's done a deal with the police.'

The villa seemed full of crummy modern gunge. 'Signora Norman's villa is just over the hill,' Keith explained.

'A very beautiful, attractive lady,' the police sergeant put in huskily.

'You go there every day to examine the four caches of assorted antiques and fakes which the signora had distributed all over North Italy. They will be brought under escort . . .'

Scheming bitch. She'd told me one houseful. Still, Lavinia wasn't bad company, even after all this.

'And I will divvie them?'

'Too right, Lovejoy. The signora also came to agreement with us.'

'Come and see the kitchen!' Gerry cried excitedly. I trailed dejectedly after.

'How do you know I won't cheat?'

'A video film record will be made of every single antique. By a special film unit. We arranged it with Miss Nancy Waterson.'

'She too is a very beautiful, attractive lady.' The police sergeant's voice was huskier.

'True,' Keith said, staring into the distance while I tried to look ecstatic at Gerry's kitchen design. 'We chose her because Signora Norman once engaged them for making her private advertising movies showing what stolen antiques she expected to have on sale.'

'And, erm, where'll Nancy be, erm, based?'

'Oh, around,' Keith said.

'And I want no criticism from her about the bathroom tiles,' Gerry warned. 'I sweated *blood* over those. Come and see.'

We trooped after him. He extolled the hallway and the special windows on the way.

'Great,' I echoed morosely into the bathroom.

'*Not* avocado, note,' Gerry said proudly. 'I *hate* that colour.'

'And how long's this arrangement to last?'

'Six months in the first instance, Lovejoy. Renewable.'

'That's a sentence.' I was sussing out the grounds. I

was trapped in a bloody fortress.

'True.' Keith nodded to Gerry, pleased. 'I think he likes it, Gerry.'

'Do you think so, dear?'

'And Signorina Cosima,' Keith added as he plodded after Gerry who had squeakily decided we were to inspect the bedrooms next. 'She'll be here.'

'Eh?'

'A very beautiful, attractive lady,' from the sergeant in a husky moan.

'Well—' Keith shrugged—'we have to keep an eye on you both. Why not together? After all, you were . . .'

'And we do approve of her,' Gerry reminded us all. 'Not like that bossy cow who's just arrived.'

I was getting a headache. 'Erm. Look, lads. That makes, er, four.'

'You asked us to cable her,' Gerry said through pursed lips. 'When you wanted all those lawyers and thought you were going to gaol.'

'Connie? Here?'

'In Venice. She can visit you each evening.'

'A very beautiful, attractive . . .' the sergeant moaned.

Forty miles. Bloody hell. Lavinia over the hill, thinking me hers alone. Nancy nearby with a camera she would doubtless brain me with. And Cosima here in the villa frying up spaghetti pasties. With Connie who'd strangle me for just glancing at any of the others.

'Now the garden!' Gerry trilled, eyeing me keenly. 'This way! You're falling for it, aren't you, Lovejoy?'

Dear God. I'd not survive a day. How the hell do I *get* in these bloody messes? My heart was banging at the battles to come.

'What a good idea!' I cried, following Gerry. 'Yes. Let's see what sort of plants you selected!'

Gerry went ahead, anxiously watching my face as he listed the wretched fronds in the ground. I alternately frowned and beamed to keep Gerry on edge, and we walked along the perimeter path.

Between fleeting changes of expression my eyes roamed the surrounding countryside. A road ran along the nearby slope, and a path led up from the edge about two furlongs from the villa's tennis court.

'And these fuchsias, Lovejoy.'

'Lovely, Gerry.'

'I *knew* you *would* love them!' Gerry cried, calling the splendid news to Keith, who was watching me with narrowed eyes. The sergeant was lost in secret raptures.

'And over by the pool?' I prompted.

'Yes, well, lace-cap hydrangeas have such a riot of blues I almost went out of my tiny little mind . . .'

'A beautiful blue,' I said, pausing. 'Chrysanthemums?' If I could nick an antique piecemeal, and conceal it bit by bit near this perimeter fence, I might be able to get over the wire one dark night, and lam up that path—but there was a police patrolman having a smoke on his motor-bike up there. Hell fire.

'Pansies, Lovejoy,' Keith explained sardonically, suspicious swine.

I smiled. 'I just had to stop. My favourites.'

'*Are* they, Lovejoy?' Gerry gushed. 'Oh, thank *heavens* we decided to put some in that border!'

'They grow well, don't they, Lovejoy?' Keith was still watching me.

'Great.'

'Especially since the wire fence carries an electric current.'

Gerry saw my face. 'Positively *no* harm to your flowers, Lovejoy dear. We've been into all that.' Gerry gave Keith a sharp glance. 'Don't you start worrying Lovejoy, Keithie, there's a dear.'

'A car!' The police sergeant brightened. A red Acclaim was bowling over the hill, the way we'd come.

'Two.' A second car hove in sight.

'Your friends, Lovejoy,' Keith said. 'Here they come. All your little helpers.'

'Er, great,' I said in panic, thinking, Now if I could nick a tin-opener from the kitchen, I could maybe use it to fuse that frigging wire fence while the cop is mesmerized by the birds . . .

'We'll be off, then.' Keith and Gerry moved.

'Erm, look, erm,' I tried. 'Any chance of a deal . . . ?'

'Aren't you going to go down and say hello?' Keith said innocently.

'Not yet. I'll stay here a minute.' Maybe Earth would collide with Saturn or something.

Gerry's eyes filled. 'With his pansies! Oh, how sweet!'

I could have trampled the bloody things. In a desperate sweat I was working out: Now if I got Cosima or maybe Connie to sunbathe one day, then while the cops were mesmerized I could nick one of the antiques and cut the current and steal out . . .

'And the patrol police are on four sides, Lovejoy,' Keith called from the gate. 'Give them a wave now and then. To show you're still here. 'Byeee.'

I could almost swear the bastard was still suspicious of me. Why is there no trust in the world any more? Why is it that we trustworthy honest folk always come a cropper and everybody else gets away scot free? There's something wrong somewhere.

A car pulled up and a motor cut.

'Lovejoy! Darling!'

'Hello, love.' Smiling, I quickly developed a limp and went to embrace Cosima while the second car came nearer and nearer. She looked well and beautiful. 'Look,' I whispered to her. 'Can I go and lie down, sweetheart? And be left strictly alone? Only, I've had an absolutely terrible time since I saved your life in that lagoon . . .'

THE END